Ginna [...] *with her sen*[...]*ing heroes. F*[...] *here are* [...] *irresistible attraction turned into undeniable love....*

He knew that Joanna had been right: a casual affair between them would never work.

But straight talk and common sense helped little. Desire still clawed at Sean's gut. Not for just any woman, but for a willowy, young, hazel-eyed beauty he knew he had no business wanting.

—*Sweet Promise*

❤ ❤ ❤

"There's no law that says a man and a woman can't share the same roof without being intimate."

A slow smile spread over Ryan's face. "I swear to you, Cristen, that whatever happens between us will be only what you want to happen...."

—*Cristen's Choice*

❤ ❤ ❤

"My needs include more than just someone to do the cooking, Duchess."

Hank's voice dropped to a husky pitch. "Getting the job depends on how well you...satisfy those needs."

—*If There Be Love*

GINNA GRAY

Motive for Marriage

Published by Silhouette Books
America's Publisher of Contemporary Romance

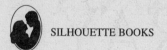 SILHOUETTE BOOKS

ISBN 0-373-20176-1

by Request

MOTIVE FOR MARRIAGE

Copyright © 2000 by Harlequin Books S.A.

The publisher acknowledges the copyright holder
of the individual works as follows:

SWEET PROMISE
Copyright © 1986 by Virginia Gray

CRISTEN'S CHOICE
Copyright © 1987 by Virginia Gray

IF THERE BE LOVE
Copyright © 1989 by Virginia Gray

Visit Silhouette at www.eHarlequin.com

Printed in U.S.A.

CONTENTS

Dear Reader,

People often ask me why I write romance. The answer to that is easy: I don't think there is anything more important than love.

Love is a driving force in all our lives. It is something for which we all yearn, something that our very souls need, and, whether we are conscious of it or not, something that we all spend a great deal of time and energy seeking. When you truly love and are loved in return you can weather any storm life sends. Love makes our tragedies and losses more bearable, our efforts and struggles more worthwhile, our triumphs more glorious. There is nothing that can top that wonderful feeling that comes from the security of knowing that your happiness and well-being matter to your beloved as much, and sometimes even more, than his or her own.

As a writer of romance fiction I have tried to analyze what love is, and I've come to the conclusion that true love is made up of many elements—physical attraction, emotional and intellectual compatibility, trust, tolerance, empathy, to name a few. To my way of thinking, one of the most important elements of love is trust. For true love to exist, so must trust.

The stories you are about to read reveal, each in its own way, the importance of trust in a relationship between a man and a woman.

Enjoy!

Ginna Gray

SWEET PROMISE

To Carol Brelish
No matter where she finally puts down roots,
she will always be my dear friend.

Chapter One

Wealth. Comfort. Warmth. The room exuded all three. Fine paintings, an exquisite cut crystal vase and a signed Paul Revere bowl shared pride of place with a bottle collection, a battered old hand forged copper scuttle and other items of whimsy. The furniture was of the highest quality and in excellent taste, but each piece proudly bore the marks of daily living, and each invited you to relax, to kick off your shoes and forget your cares. A cheery fire crackled in the stone fireplace and plush easy chairs cozied up to the hearth on either side. A pillow-strewn sofa, long enough for a tall man to stretch out on, stood foursquare before it. On the floor beside the sofa sat a basket of yarn, and draped across one arm was a half-finished afghan with a crochet hook sticking out of it. Underfoot, a thick oriental rug spread its faded beauty over the oak planked floor that had known over two hundred years of footsteps. This was a haven, a home, a refuge for the soul—not a showplace.

Two men occupied the fireside chairs. At first glance they appeared much alike. Both were big men: tall, broad shouldered, muscular. And both were dark and utterly masculine, with a commanding presence that immediately drew the eye. Yet there were differences. Matt Drummond's ebony hair was frosted silver at the temples; Sean Fleming's had the blue-black sheen of a raven's wing. Matt's face was rugged, with a weathered, lived-in look that was harshly appealing; Sean's was classically handsome. Matt's eyes were vivid blue; Sean's the deepest black.

The younger man sat slouched down on his spine, his long legs stretched out in front of him and crossed at the ankles. His head rested against the chair back, his hands across his abdomen, fingers laced loosely together. He looked almost boneless, nerveless. Only those who knew Sean well could detect the keen glitter in those seemingly drowsy black eyes, or see that behind that laid-back, easygoing façade was a taut restlessness, held rigidly in check.

And Matt Drummond knew him well.

Through half-closed eyes, Sean watched his friend leave his chair and walk to the old armoire that had been converted into a bar. He poured a generous amount of the finest Kentucky bourbon into two squat glasses, studied them, shrugged and added another splash to each for good measure. As he turned and started back across the room, Sean idly wondered what it was about these people, this place, that drew him.

Matt and Claire. Whenever he felt restless, troubled, unsure, he sought them out, preferably here in this huge old barn of a farmhouse that they called home. Somehow, just being around them calmed and soothed him, let him put things into perspective. It was strange, he thought with a wry smile. Strange...but damned comforting.

"Here you go." Matt handed him a drink. When he had settled into the chair on the other side of the hearth he gave Sean a long, steady look. "You know, ole buddy," he said finally. "Even though it's a cliché, there's a lot of truth in that old saw about opportunity only knocking once. You've always said you wanted to run for office some day. Well, if you're ever going to do it, now's the time, while you have strong backing. Turn Newcomb and his group down and they probably won't ask you to run again. And what with the incumbent retiring, the race for that Virginia Senate seat is going to be wide open."

"I know."

"When do they want an answer?"

"I told them I'd let them know in three weeks." Sean raised his drink and took a sip, exhaling a slow, raspy breath as the mellow bourbon slid down his throat. Holding the glass loosely between his hands, he rested it on his board-flat abdomen and stared at the dancing flames in the fireplace.

The fire hissed and popped. In the hall, the ancient grandfather clock ticked ponderously. The big room was lit by only two dim lamps and the fire, whose wavering glow was reflected in the polished oak floor and wainscoting. For a few minutes the two men sat in companionable silence.

Then Sean levered himself out of the chair and ambled over to the window. He twitched aside the green velvet curtain and looked out at the gathering darkness. A light snow was falling, their first of the season—fat flakes that looked like feathers floating in the air.

What the devil is the matter with me? he wondered impatiently. *For months I've been feeling this…this vague… What? Discontent? Depression? Hell, you jerk. You don't even know what it is you feel. Or why. You ought to be turning cartwheels. Everything you've ever wanted, everything you've worked for, is within reach.*

So why wasn't he happy?

With a sigh, Sean walked back to the hearth and stared

broodingly at the licking tongues of fire once again. "Before Newcomb approached me about running for the Senate, I'd been giving some thought to opening my own public relations firm, but I'm not sure I want to do that either." Grimacing, he sighed and raked an agitated hand through his blue-black hair. "Hell. The trouble is…I'm not sure what I want anymore. I feel at loose ends. Restless. Antsy." Sean gave a disgusted snort and shook his head. "I don't know. Maybe I'm going through a mid-life crisis or something?"

"At thirty-six?"

The dry amusement in Matt's tone pulled Sean's gaze away from the fire and his mouth twitched up in a self-conscious, half smile. "Well, something. I'm just not content with my life or my future anymore."

"So what are you going to do?"

"I'm—"

The peal of the doorbell halted Sean's words. He looked at Matt, a question in his eyes, but the older man merely shrugged.

Excusing himself, Matt went to answer the summons. A few seconds later Sean heard the murmur of voices and a soft ripple of feminine laughter and frowned. Sean liked women. Sean *loved* women. But tonight he wasn't in the mood for that kind of distraction.

Matt returned, bringing a young woman with him, and Sean's black eyes ran over her in automatic assessment. Nice looking, he thought idly. Great legs, too. A bit classy for my blood, but nice. Definitely nice.

"You remember Sean don't you, Joanna?" Matt said as he steered her toward the fireplace, and Sean felt a little dart of surprise.

This is Joanna? Claire's daughter? He eyed the softly feminine, poised young woman and expelled his breath in a long silent whistle. The Joanna he remembered had been a haughtily aggressive, rather obnoxious eighteen-year-old.

There have definitely been some changes here, Sean thought as he noted the friendly sparkle in her hazel eyes.

The dark mole just above the left corner of her mouth drew his eye. It was a tiny imperfection that added fascination to her face, drawing attention to the otherwise flawless skin, the lovely curve of her cheek. The beauty mark was one of the few things about her that had remained the same. That, and the elegant bone structure of her face. It was that, Sean decided, which gave her that look of patrician aloofness he remembered so well. But it was softened by a mouth that was a tad too wide and curved now in a friendly smile. Her brown hair, which she used to wear in that god-awful frizzy style, now swung loosely around her shoulders in a shining cloud. It was, Sean thought a bit uneasily, the kind of hair a man wanted to thread his fingers through, bury his face in.

"Yes, of course," Joanna said. "You were Mother's press secretary when she ran for the Senate."

Smiling, she extended her hand and Sean took it between both of his. It was small and soft, and to his surprise, trembled ever so slightly. Even her voice has changed, he noted. It was gentler, softer, without that hard edge that had made everything she said sound like a command or a challenge.

"That's right. Hello, Joanna. It's good to see you again. It's been a while."

"Almost four years. I haven't seen you since Mother and Matt's wedding." Joanna cast a curious glance at her stepfather. "Speaking of Mother, where is she?"

"She's in the kitchen getting dinner. She'll be out in a minute."

Withdrawing her hand from Sean's grasp, Joanna smiled politely and edged toward the door. "If you'll excuse me, I think I'll go see if I can help."

When she had disappeared into the hall Sean's stunned

gaze sought Matt. "*Joanna* is going to help in the kitchen?"

In the hall, Joanna heard the remark and stopped momentarily, her mouth compressing. It hurt to hear that incredulous tone in Sean's voice. Not that she blamed him. Four years ago she had been a brat. A spoiled, selfish brat.

As she continued toward the kitchen Joanna pressed her hand against her fluttering stomach, mildly surprised to realize that she was nervous. Which is just plain silly, she thought with a scornful chuckle. She'd once had a bit of a crush on Sean but that, thankfully, had died a natural death.

Joanna didn't think that Sean, or anyone else, had even been aware of her childish infatuation. At the time Sean had had his hands full with her mother's Senate campaign and had barely even noticed that she was alive. And she, to her everlasting shame, had been too busy trying to prevent her mother from marrying Matt to actively pursue him. In the end, when Claire had withdrawn from the primary race, her staff had disbanded. "And that had been the end of that, thank heaven," Joanna muttered under her breath. "Given enough time, I probably would have made a complete fool of myself over the man."

Actually though, finding Sean there was a stroke of luck, considering the reason she'd come.

Joanna pushed through the door and walked into the huge, old-fashioned kitchen, and Claire looked up from the sauce she was stirring, a smile lighting up her face. "Hello, darling. I was beginning to wonder if you were going to make it in time for dinner."

As always these days, at the sight of her mother Joanna felt a little jolt. She supposed it was natural, under the circumstances. For no matter how often she thought about it, no matter how pleased and happy she was, it was something of a shock to see her mother—her forty-three-year-old, beautiful, elegant mother—nearly seven months pregnant.

Smiling, Joanna crossed the room and gave Claire a kiss on the cheek. "Sorry I'm late. Usually on Fridays we knock off early, but tonight Senator Hartwell kept the entire staff working till five." Joanna tipped her head toward the living room. "You didn't tell me that Sean would be here this weekend too."

"Oh, Sean can't stay for the weekend." Claire looked at Joanna, her soft gray eyes filled with wicked laughter, and added drolly, "He has a date tomorrow night."

"Ah, I see." Joanna's smile was knowing. "Still giving his little black book a workout, is he?" She washed her hands at the sink, then began to set four places at one end of the long trestle table, chuckling to herself as she recalled how she had been eaten up with jealousy every time she'd seen Sean riffling through that book. How she'd sworn that someday she would rip it to shreds.

"I think it's now a two-volume set," Claire said, rolling her eyes. "Sean's as sharp as a tack and a dear, sweet man, but he is a devil with the ladies."

Joanna chuckled and began helping her mother dish up the food, enormously pleased that now she could laugh at Sean's romantic escapades. She poured the lemon and butter sauce over the broccoli and picked up the dish to take it to the table, turning just in time to see Claire lifting a roasting pan from the oven.

"Mother! For heaven's sake! You shouldn't be lifting that," she cried, rushing over to take it from her.

Claire looked disgusted and made an exasperated sound. "I swear, you're as bad as Matt. I'm not an invalid, you know. I'm just pregnant. Besides, I like to cook, and it's about the only thing I get to do anymore."

Poor Matt, Joanna thought, smothering a grin as she set the pan on the counter and transferred the roast to a platter. Becoming a father for the first time at age forty-five was hard on him. He was both thrilled and terrified over the prospect and tended to fuss over his wife like a mother hen. The day after Claire had told him she was pregnant he had hired a woman to do all the work around the house. If Claire hadn't put her foot down, he would have hired someone to do the cooking, too.

It was amazing, Joanna thought, as she had done countless times during the past few years, how drastically her mother's life-style had changed. Though Matt was equally as wealthy as Joanna's father and grandfather had been, his family had always lived a simpler life, and Claire had embraced it wholeheartedly. She had settled in this big old rustic house and adapted to country living with astounding ease. Claire had learned to cook and keep house, even to garden. And, Joanna admitted with a smile, casting a covert glance at her mother's glowing face, she seemed to thrive on it.

When the meal was ready, the men joined them in the kitchen, and Matt sat at his customary place at the head of the table. Instinctively Joanna shied away from sitting beside Sean and chose the place on the opposite side, facing him and Claire. It was a choice she soon regretted, for every time she looked up her eyes were drawn to him like a magnet.

During dinner, conversation was general, but for the most part Joanna said little. Her reaction to Sean surprised and disturbed her. She was acutely, uncomfortably aware of him. She found herself staring, as though mesmerized, at his finely chiseled, incredibly sexy mouth. And that voice. Its deep rumble did the strangest things to her insides.

Sean was a wildly handsome man, with an appealing air of devil-may-care rakishness. Joanna told herself it was perfectly normal to be attracted to him.

But she still didn't like it.

* * *

After dinner Matt and Sean returned to the living room and resumed their discussion while Joanna and Claire dealt with the dishes. When the women rejoined them, Sean had to bite back a smile.

Claire Drummond is probably the only woman in the world who can make a pregnant waddle look graceful, he thought wryly as he watched his hostess make her way to the sofa. But then, he doubted that anything could make Claire look awkward or unattractive. Her poise was an inherent part of her, like her beauty or intelligence. It was no wonder that Matt loved her to distraction.

Four years ago he'd come close to falling in love with her himself, Sean remembered, and his soft sigh held just the barest touch of regret. But it simply wasn't meant to be. From almost the very beginning, even before they had realized it themselves, he had known that Matt and Claire belonged together.

As Claire began to gingerly lower her bulky girth onto the cushions Matt jumped up to assist her, and the smile that Sean had been so valiantly holding in check broke through. When she was settled Matt picked up her legs and slid a hassock under them. Squatting on his haunches, he slipped off her shoes and began to massage her feet.

"How are you feeling, sweetheart?" he asked solicitously.

"I'm fine, darling," Claire replied in the softest of voices, her eyes warm as she gazed down at him.

The look that passed between them brought a tightness to Sean's chest, and his amused smile faded. Suddenly, inexplicably, he was swamped with a curious mixture of gladness and envy.

Jeez! What the hell's the matter with me? Sean shifted restlessly and battled down the uncomfortable surge of emotions. It was stupid to be envious of their marriage. He was *not* the marrying kind, for Chrissake.

But then...neither had Matt been.

And Sean had to admit, he'd never known two people more in love, or more content with each other than Claire and Matt. Watching them, it was difficult to recall that they had once come very close to not making it.

The thought drew Sean's gaze to Joanna. He had never known what had caused the breakup between Claire and Matt four years ago, but he'd always had a sneaking suspicion that Joanna had been behind it.

Looking at her now, though, it was difficult to believe. There was a softness about Joanna, a vulnerability that hadn't been there four years ago. And the look of affectionate tenderness on her face as she watched Matt fuss over her mother clearly revealed her feelings about the marriage and the coming child.

She really is a lovely young woman, Sean mused. She'll never be the elegant beauty her mother is, but she is striking...in a well-bred, reserved sort of way.

"Did Sean tell you that he is being urged to run for the Senate?" Matt asked as he settled onto the sofa beside Claire and draped his arm around her shoulders. "Bob Rastin is retiring after this term and the Virginia seat will be up for grabs."

"Why, Sean! That's marvelous," Claire declared. "You'll make a terrific senator."

Abandoning his study of Joanna, Sean turned to his friends with a lazy grin. "You mean *if* I decide to run, and *if* I get elected."

"What do you mean, 'if'? You've told me for years that you want to run for office."

"Yeah, well...now I'm not so sure. I've been thinking lately of opening up my own public relations firm."

Claire gave him a long, shrewd look. "Well, whatever you decide, you know that Matt and I will back you. But I'm sure, once you've given it some thought, you'll decide to run," she said confidently.

"Actually, think about it is exactly what I'm *not* going

to do. At least, not for a while. I've thought about it until my head is spinning, and I still don't know what I want. So I've decided to put the whole thing out of my mind for a while and concentrate on fulfilling one of my fantasies.''

''I'm almost afraid to ask what that might be,'' Matt drawled.

Sean smiled smugly and relaxed back against the chair in his habitual indolent pose. ''I've been working my tail off for the past few years and I've decided I deserve a break. I'm going to treat myself to a Caribbean cruise. Beginning next Saturday, I'm going to lie in the sun for two weeks and relax and unwind and watch pretty girls.'' The smile grew slowly into a wicked grin. ''I may even catch a few.''

Matt groaned and rolled his eyes, and Claire laughed.

No one noticed the dismayed look on Joanna's face.

The next morning Joanna hesitated before the closed door of Matt's study. Chewing at her lower lip, she wiped her damp palms down over her slender, jean-encased hips and tried to still the flutter in the pit of her stomach.

''Oh, good grief,'' she muttered under her breath, suddenly impatient with her own dithering. ''It's no big deal. The worst he can do is say no.'' Joanna drew a deep breath, and with a toss of her head, flipped her long brown hair back over her shoulder and raised a hand to knock.

A deep baritone carried through the oak door. Opening it partway, Joanna poked her head around the edge. ''May I speak with you for a moment?''

Surprise flickered across Matt's rugged face, but it was followed quickly by a pleased smile. ''Sure. Come on in.'' Tossing aside his pencil, he leaned back in his chair and motioned toward the rust suede sofa opposite his desk. ''Have a seat.''

When she had complied Matt smiled again and raised his dark brows. ''Is there something I can do for you?''

Trust Matt to get straight to the point, Joanna thought with faint amusement. He was a "take the bull by the horns" type, as different from her own father as night and day. Senator Joseph Andrews had been a born politician: diplomatic, smooth talking, clever, evasive when need be, a master at convoluted maneuvering and manipulation. Matt was direct, bold and decisive.

Which, Joanna freely admitted, was why he was such a force to be reckoned with in Washington. He knew the rules, written and unwritten, and when the occasion called for finesse, Matt could employ it with exquisite delicacy. But basically he was a mover and shaker, a man who was known for getting things done by going right to the heart of the matter.

"Yes. At least, I hope so. I have a favor to ask."

Matt's keen blue eyes sharpened ever so slightly. "Oh? What's that?"

"Well…uh, how do you feel about Sean running for the Senate?"

If Matt was surprised by her question he didn't let it show. Pinching his lower lip between his thumb and forefinger he tugged on it meditatively. "Actually, I think he's an excellent choice. Probably the best Newcomb and his group could have made. Sean's a good man, and he's had plenty of experience. He's a little weak when it comes to public exposure but that shouldn't be a problem. When he puts his mind to it, that Irish devil can charm the birds right out of the trees." Matt pinned Joanna with his penetrating stare. "Why do you ask?"

"Because Senator Hartwell and several others agree with Harry Newcomb. They all think that Sean should seek the nomination. The consensus is that he can easily beat the opposition's candidate. But, as you saw last night, for some strange reason Sean is being—" Joanna lifted both hands, palms up, then let them drop back into her lap "—noncommittal. Which is why I'm here. You see, Senator Hartwell thought that since you and Sean are such good friends, maybe you could persuade him to run.''

"Ah, I see." The thoughtful expression on Matt's face did not alter one whit, but inside he was filled with reluctant amusement. Subtle pressure. That was the way the game was played. Though she didn't know it, he had pulled a few strings to get Joanna her job on Senator Hartwell's staff. Normally he didn't resort to such tactics, but Claire had been worried about Joanna, and to ease her mind he had used his influence. And now the Senator was pulling a few strings of his own and using Joanna to do it.

But Matt didn't give in to pressure easily.

"I don't think that's a good idea. After all, it's Sean's decision, and he's perfectly capable of making it on his own."

"Yes, of course he is," Joanna agreed quickly. "And the Senator says he is seriously considering it. But it's such a big step, I thought...that is, Senator Hartwell thought that it wouldn't hurt if he got some encouragement from you. Oh, Matt, please talk to him," Joanna pleaded. She sat forward on the sofa, leaning toward him, her face animated and full of hope. "A nudge from you is probably all he needs."

"I don't know..." Frowning, Matt braced his elbows on the arms of the chair and pressed his spread fingertips together, gazing over them out the window at the crisp winter day. The flurries of the night before had stopped, and now a thin layer of patchy snow lay like tattered fleece over the rolling Virginia hills. As Matt idly watched, one of his thoroughbred mares trotted across the near paddock, her breath coming out in puffs of white mist that trailed away in the wind and vanished.

But Matt's mind wasn't on the mare or the scenery, or even the classified papers he had been studying, but on his stepdaughter's request. Sean was well suited for politics.

Matt had no doubts on that score. But he knew that it was useless to pressure him. Many people were fooled by that laid-back easygoing veneer. Few realized that behind it was a razor sharp mind and a fierce determination. Or that those slumberous black eyes could snap with temper. No, Sean Fleming was not a malleable pawn. If that was what Senator Hartwell and the others thought they would be getting they were in for a shock. Sean was his own man. When he wanted advice, he asked for it. He would listen to your opinion, weigh it carefully, but in the end he always made up his own mind. He was not a man you could prod.

Besides, even if he had been, Matt didn't believe in pressuring a man on a career decision.

Still, he hated to turn Joanna down flat. Claire was worried about her. With good cause, Matt felt. In the past three and a half years Joanna had changed drastically. Before, she had been a spoiled, self-centered brat, but at least she had been full of spirit, a vibrant, sparkling girl, filled with the zest and eagerness of youth.

Matt's eyes narrowed on his stepdaughter. They had once been enemies. Unconsciously, his jaw clenched as he remembered that time. Even now, when he thought about how close he had come to losing Claire, he felt a cold trickle of fear race down his spine. Dear Lord! Life without her would be unbearable.

But he had won, Matt reminded himself. Now he could afford to be compassionate.

Joanna's scheme to come between him and Claire had backfired on her. In the end she'd had to face a lot of unpleasant truths, perhaps the hardest being that the father she had idolized had not been the golden god she had thought him to be. Since then she had been subdued and serious—too much so for her mother's liking. His too, for that matter, Matt admitted. After that fiasco, Joanna had done an abrupt about-face. She had worked hard in college and had graduated with honors, and during the past six months, had buried herself in her job to the exclusion of everything else.

Matt cast a curious glance at Joanna's anxious face, his eyes narrowing once again. This was the first time in almost four years that she had shown even a trace of her old enthusiasm.

"Why is it so important to you that Sean run for Congress?" he asked quietly.

"Well...because I think he'd make a terrific senator, of course," she said in a voice that was just a shade too assertive, a shade too high. Not quite meeting Matt's eye, Joanna waved her hand vaguely. "He's bright and young and honest. Likeable. And as you said, he has that charismatic charm. He shouldn't have any trouble pulling in votes, and our party needs another seat in Congress."

"Mmm." Resting his chin in his palm, Matt studied her flustered face and waited for her to continue.

Joanna shifted restlessly on the plush sofa. After a while, she looked up and met Matt's steady gaze guiltily. "All right. I admit my motives aren't totally altruistic," she said with a rueful twist of her mouth. "If Sean does decide to run, I'm hoping I can get a job on his campaign staff."

Amusement tugged at the corners of Matt's mouth. "Things too dull for you in Hartwell's camp?"

"Something like that. Oh, Matt, he doesn't even come up for reelection for years yet. And anyway, he's held that office for so long he's practically an institution in his state. I'd like to be involved in something...I don't know...something with a little more challenge to it I guess."

Yes, Joanna was a campaigner, Matt recalled. She thrived on the excitement and challenge, the constant thrust and parry of a hard fought political race. Four years ago, during Claire's bid for her late husband's Senate seat, Joanna had worked tirelessly and had loved every minute of it. Claire's ultimate withdrawal from the race had been one of the biggest disappointments of Joanna's life.

Disillusionment. Disappointment. It had been a difficult time for the girl, Matt mused. Joanna was a mature, responsible, even loving young woman now, but sadly, she had had to gain her maturity the hard way.

Matt drummed a pencil against the desk top. If Sean did decide to seek the office, she would be an asset. There was no denying that. But still, even if it were possible, he couldn't in good conscience talk a man into making that kind of decision just to give Joanna's life a boost.

He was about to tell her so when Claire tapped on the door and poked her head into the room. "Is this a private party, or can anyone join in?"

The smile that wreathed Matt's features was warm and loving and heartstoppingly tender, transforming his rugged face into gentleness. "Come in, sweetheart," he said in that soft voice that was reserved just for Claire, holding out his hand to her.

An indulgent smile curved Joanna's mouth as she watched Claire give her husband a kiss, then perch rather precariously on the arm of his chair. She looped one arm across his broad shoulders. The other she placed on the turgid roundness of her protruding belly, in an unconscious protective gesture.

"So, what's going on?"

Matt reached up and tweaked one of Claire's short blond curls. "Joanna thinks I ought to persuade Sean to run for Congress. I was just about to explain to her I can't do that. I've already pointed out to Sean all the reasons why he should seriously consider running. I'm afraid that's all I can do. It's his decision to make."

"Oh, but—"

"Matt's right, Joanna," Claire said quickly, cutting off her daughter's protest. "It's his life and his future. And Sean wouldn't appreciate our interference."

Disappointment poured through Joanna. She had been hoping to get her mother's support. She knew that it was almost impossible for Matt to deny Claire anything, especially now. But it was obvious from their expressions that she was wasting her time.

Still, she wasn't going to give up. Rising to her feet, Joanna squared her shoulders determinedly. "Maybe. But someone has to talk some sense into that hardheaded Irishman. I can't just let him throw away a chance like this."

Without another word, she walked out, and Claire looked at Matt, her expression a mixture of bemusement and worry.

Matt grinned. "She wants a job on Sean's staff," he explained. "And you know Joanna. Once she's got the bit between her teeth there's no stopping her."

"Yes, I know," Claire murmured, nibbling worriedly on her lower lip. "Oh, Matt, maybe we should try. Joanna can be so headstrong. She has a tendency to just rush into things without thinking. If she angers Sean—"

"I know, I know. But, darling, you can't have it both ways. You've been wanting her to show some of her old spunk and enthusiasm. Well, now she has." A speculative gleam entered Matt's eyes as he stared at the doorway through which Joanna had just sailed, and slowly an amused smile curved his mouth. "It should be interesting, though. I've always wondered what happened when an irresistible force met an immovable object."

Chapter Two

The moment Joanna stepped on board someone called out "Smile," and a flashbulb went off. She stiffened and glared at the photographer, but in the next instant realized that they were taking pictures of everyone as they came on the ship.

Feeling foolish, Joanna handed the purser her boarding pass. Good grief, you're getting paranoid, she chastised silently. But she knew her reaction was a conditioned reflex, the result of a lifetime of having flashbulbs go off in her face. It was part of the price she had paid for having a famous mother whom the public idolized...the part that Joanna hated.

"Ah, Miss Andrews. We're honored to have you with us," the purser said as he checked the slip she'd handed him against the list on his clipboard. Glancing back over his shoulder, he motioned for the young man just behind him to step forward. "This is Riley, Miss Andrews. He'll

see you to your suite. Please let us know if there is anything you need.''

With a smile and a quick thank-you, Joanna turned to
follow the white-jacketed young man.

They passed through what seemed like miles of carpeted
passageways with literally hundreds of doors opening off
them and climbed several flights of stairs. Within minutes
Joanna was thoroughly lost...and thoroughly intrigued.
There was an air of excitement and anticipation among the
other passengers and crew members that was infectious,
and with every step she felt a growing eagerness, a sense
of adventure. Joanna had come on this trip for a purpose,
but now, for the first time, it occurred to her that there was
no reason why she couldn't enjoy herself while she was
about it.

Her guide kept up a steady chatter, pointing out the main
dining room and the shopping arcade, the gym and the
various clubs. They passed dozens of people, all anxiously
peering at the numbers on the cabin doors and checking
them against the keys they held in their hands. A wry
grimace curled Joanna's mouth as she noticed that she
seemed to be the only one with a personal escort. She
couldn't help but wonder if she was receiving this pref-
erential treatment because she had been recognized.

Her mother had grown up in the spotlight, the daughter
of one of the country's most powerful senators, and later,
the wife of another. Joanna had always detested the lack
of privacy that went with her mother's fame, and knowing
that, Claire had done her best to shield her from the constant publicity. Still, there had been enough over the years
that Joanna was often recognized. And the result was
nearly always gaping stares or fawning attention.

''Here we are,'' her guide announced when he finally
stopped before a cabin door and opened it with a flourish.

The moment Joanna stepped inside and looked around
at her plush accommodations, her uneasy suspicion faded,

and she chided herself for her conceit. No doubt anyone who booked one of these luxury suites received the royal treatment.

It was gorgeous. And huge. She hadn't expected that, even knowing that there were only two of these deluxe suites on board.

She had expected round portholes. Instead, there were two large rectangular windows. Between them a tufted brown leather sofa sat along the outer wall. Flanking it were Queen Anne end tables, which held exquisite lamps made of brass and polished walnut. At right angles to the sofa were two matching brown leather easy chairs and in the center of the grouping stood an oval, marble-topped coffee table. A copper bowl in the center of the table contained an arrangement of dried flowers in autumn colors that blended with the rust carpet and draperies and the soft rust, green-and-yellow stripes in the wall covering.

Through the large windows, Joanna could see the sunlight sparkling on the waters of Miami harbor. As the steward bustled, pointing out the small refrigerator and bar and rattling off information about the temperature controls, Joanna walked to one of the windows and watched another cruise ship glide gracefully by, heading out to sea.

"And through here is your bedroom," the young man announced.

Joanna turned in time to see him throw open the double doors set in one of the side walls. Bemused, she wandered over and peeked in, her eyes widening at the sight of the king-size bed and the long vanity console. The color scheme was ivory and pale green, but this room, too, was flooded with light from two large windows.

"It's lovely," Joanna said, and the young man beamed proudly.

They heard a noise in the passageway, and he turned and headed for the door. "That's the porter with your luggage. I'll get it for you."

When he had carried her bags into the bedroom he told her there would be a lifeboat drill shortly before they got under way. "Just follow the instructions here on the back of the door," he said as he turned to leave. "They tell where your lifeboat station is and how to reach it. When you hear the announcement over the intercom just grab a life jacket out of the closet and take the forward stairs to the deck above."

As the door closed behind him Joanna stood in the middle of the sitting room, her eyes growing wide with panic. A lifeboat drill? Oh, Lord. She hadn't counted on that. She had planned to remain in her suite until they were well out at sea.

Joanna chewed worriedly at her lower lip. It was entirely possible that she might run into Sean. With a bit of discreet probing, she had discovered when she booked the cruise that his cabin was just down the passageway from hers. It stood to reason that his lifeboat station would be close by also.

Maybe I could just ignore the announcement and stay here.

"Oh, don't be ridiculous, Joanna," she muttered impatiently the moment the thought flickered through her mind. "They would just come looking for you if you didn't show up." She walked into the bedroom and snapped open the case that lay on the luggage rack. Scooping up a stack of frothy lingerie, she began to move methodically back and forth between the open case and the built-in dresser. "Besides," she said stoutly as her normal self-confidence reasserted itself. "With hundreds of passengers on board, surely you can lose yourself in the crowd for a few minutes."

As she hung her clothes in the roomy closet behind the mirror-covered sliding doors, Joanna glanced around at her opulent surroundings and grimaced. She hadn't planned on booking the most expensive suite on the ship, but it had been the only thing available when she'd made her reservation.

Joanna stopped in the act of hanging up a cotton sundress and giggled as she recalled her conversation with Senator Hartwell five days ago. He'd been enthusiastic about her plan, so much so that in a fit of generosity he had offered to pay for her cruise.

"It's a good thing I didn't take him up on his offer," Joanna thought, chuckling. "He'd have had a fit when he found out how much this suite costs."

She wasn't too thrilled about it herself. She could afford it easily, of course, thanks to the generous trust funds both her father and grandfather had set up for her, but under normal circumstances, she would not have booked anything so grand just for herself.

Fifteen minutes later a repetitive three-gong signal came over the ship's intercom followed by a calm voice instructing everyone to go to their lifeboat stations. Joanna's heart skipped a beat and she hesitated for an instant. Then, abandoning her half-empty suitcase, she snatched the garish orange vest from the closet and hurried out the door.

By the time she reached the stairwell the companionway was filled with people, all wearing the bulky Mae West life preservers. Most were laughing and joking as they trouped up to the next deck. Joanna joined the throng, confident that her presence would go undetected in the crush.

That confidence slipped a notch, however, when she reached her lifeboat station. For there at the next station, not ten yards away, stood Sean.

With a start, Joanna ducked behind a large man whose girth almost equaled his height. She stood very still, her heart pounding wildly against her chest. After a moment, she very cautiously leaned to one side and peeked around him.

Surprise, a flicker of annoyance, then wry amusement

chased one after the other across Joanna's face as she
stared at Sean. She had been frightened for nothing. He
wasn't even aware of her. In fact, she told herself with a
twisted, self-mocking smile, she could probably strip naked and run up and down the deck screaming, and he still
wouldn't notice her.

Dressed in navy slacks and a short sleeved pale blue
shirt, Sean stood leaning over a voluptuous redhead, one
arm braced against the bulkhead above her shoulder. A
rakish smile curved his mouth. His handsome face wore a
look of undisguised male interest: predatory, and sensual,
his drowsy black eyes hot and sexy.

Joanna looked at the redhead and sighed. Typically, the
woman was gazing up at him with a besotted look on her
face, hanging on his every word.

A surge of irritation rippled through Joanna as she
watched Sean throw his head back and roar with laughter
over something the woman had said, but she quickly
squashed it. It wasn't the redhead's fault, she reminded
herself. Sean always had that effect on women. It was
those cleanly chiseled features, that lazy, heart-stopping
smile. And, of course, that devastating aura of sheer maleness.

Plus, Sean had a secret weapon: he liked women. Genuinely liked them. And he made no secret of it. Old,
young, short, tall, silly, serious. He found them all delightful and utterly fascinating. What woman could resist that?
Certainly none that she knew of, Joanna admitted grudgingly. Sean managed to make every woman he met feel
special, and they adored him for it.

And, as astonishing as it was, if what Joanna had heard
was true, he even managed to remain friends with his former lovers.

Ship personnel at each lifeboat station began to call off
the names on their rosters, and when her own was called
Joanna jumped and darted another apprehensive glance at

Sean before answering. But she needn't have worried. He was oblivious to everything but the curvaceous redhead.

Throughout the entire spiel on safety and emergency procedures Joanna kept her gaze trained on Sean and listened with only half an ear, torn between disgust and amusement as she watched him flirt.

At last the drill was over, and the groups around the lifeboats began to break up. Sean raised his head and glanced distractedly in her direction. Joanna doubted that he could pick her out in the crowd, but when his gaze rested briefly on her, she smiled and turned back toward the stairs.

No sense tempting fate, she told herself as she melted into the throng. A blast from the ship's whistle and a slight movement underfoot told her that they were about to get under way. Joanna was tempted to stay topside and watch, but immediately dismissed the idea. Not that it really mattered now if Sean did spot her, except that she preferred to pick the time and place of their first meeting.

Joanna? Is that Joanna Andrews? Sean stared at the brown-haired woman's retreating form and frowned. *No. No, it can't be. I must be seeing things.*

But even after the slender figure in the yellow sundress had disappeared from view he continued to search the crowds.

"Do you see the purser anywhere?"

Gloria Osborne's question finally penetrated, and Sean looked down, chagrined to realize that he'd gotten sidetracked. *For Pete's sake, Fleming! Why are you letting your imagination run away with you when there's someone like Gloria around?*

"Uh, no. Anyway, he's probably got his hands full right now. Why don't I just go find the maître d' and see what I can do?"

"Do you think he'll be agreeable to changing seating arrangements?"

"Sure. Why not? The cruise is just starting. It won't inconvenience anyone. I'll just tell him that we'd like to be seated at the same table."

Sean smiled at the hopeful expression on Gloria's face. *She really is a luscious creature,* he mused. A knockout figure, a full mouth that begged to be kissed, slanting green eyes. And she was a redhead to boot. His gaze lifted to the bright hair, and he wondered idly if it were natural. Probably not. But then, who the hell cared? Gloria Osborne was just what he needed. A worldly, uncomplicated, sensual woman, one who could indulge in a light-hearted shipboard romance with no illusions or expectations.

Reassured, Gloria toyed with a button on his shirt and gave him a sultry look from beneath her lashes. "Well, while you take care of that, I think I'll go unpack." She winked and stepped away, trailing her long crimson nails across his chest. "See you at dinner."

Sean watched her go, his smile turning decidedly wicked as he admired the provocative sway of her hips. It had been a pure stroke of luck, meeting her as they had stood in line to get their boarding passes, he decided with satisfaction. For the next two weeks he wanted to clear his mind of everything and concentrate on relaxing and having a good time. With a woman like Gloria around, that shouldn't be too difficult.

But suddenly Sean's smile faded, and he looked back in the direction the brown-haired woman had taken. Strangely, one of the things that had been on his mind lately had been Joanna. The changes in her had intrigued him and he'd thought of her often since that dinner last weekend at Claire and Matt's. Which, he told himself, is probably why you imagined you saw her.

Of course, it couldn't have been Joanna.

Hands in his pockets, Sean strolled slowly toward the purser's office.

But it had sure as hell looked like her.

Joanna entered the dining room behind two couples who were obviously together. While they identified themselves to the maître d' she adjusted the long full sleeves of her amber silk dress and casually scanned the room for Sean's dark head.

The tight feeling in the pit of her stomach was a curious mixture of anticipation and dread. How would Sean react when he saw her? Funny. She hadn't really considered that aspect until now. He would be surprised, of course. That was to be expected. But when his surprise faded, would he be angry? Pleased? Indifferent?

Joanna frowned. *Maybe I should have gone about this differently. Perhaps it would have been better if—*

"Good evening, miss. My name is Henri," the maître d' said, giving her a suave smile and a formal little bow, and with a start, Joanna realized that it was too late for second thoughts.

The urge to turn around and scurry back to her suite was strong, but she squashed it and gave him her name. You can't spend two weeks holed up in that suite, so just stay calm and stick to your original plan, she told herself, squaring her shoulders and falling in step behind the man as he turned to lead her to her assigned table.

Joanna felt a prickle of annoyance when she spotted the redhead sitting beside Sean. He was so absorbed in the woman he didn't even look up until the maître d' pulled out her chair. And then Joanna had to stifle a laugh. She had never seen Sean lose his blasé composure before, but the casual glance he gave her was followed instantly by a comical double take that had his jaw dropping and his black eyes bulging out as though they were on stalks.

"Joanna!"

"Hello, Sean." Joanna smiled pleasantly and took the seat across from him at the round table.

"It *was* you I saw earlier!" Astonishment and accusation blended in Sean's voice. He gaped at her as though he couldn't believe his eyes.

"Yes, I suppose it was."

"Oh, how nice," the elderly woman on Joanna's right exclaimed. "You two know each other."

Joanna turned to the woman gratefully. "Yes. Sean is an old family friend." Carefully avoiding his eyes, she pinned a bright smile on her face and introduced herself to the others at the table.

They were a good mix, Joanna noted as names were exchanged. Besides herself, Sean, and Gloria Osborne, there was another attractive single man and two married couples, one elderly, and the other so young Joanna guessed them to be on their honeymoon.

By the time the introductions were finished Sean had overcome his shock and was leaning casually back in his chair, his easy nonchalance firmly in place once again. His expression was bland and pleasant. There was even a hint of a smile curving his lips, though it didn't reach those probing black eyes. They were boring into hers like lasers.

The waiter appeared at that moment, and Sean's attention was diverted briefly as they all made their selections from the menus. But the moment the man retreated to the kitchen he focused on her again.

"I'm surprised to see you here, Joanna," he said in a drawling voice. "When I saw you last weekend you didn't mention that you were going to be on this cruise."

"Oh, it was a last minute decision. You made it sound like so much fun I decided to try it myself." Giving him a bright smile, Joanna mentally crossed her fingers that he would accept the white lie. She couldn't very well say that she was here to do a little arm-twisting. For all his easy-going charm, she had a gut feeling that Sean was not a person who would take kindly to pressure. In any case, she had learned from both her father and grandfather that the art of persuasion required subtlety and patience.

"I see. And that's the only reason?"

"Of course," she said, feigning innocence. "What else?"

Sean gave her a long, thoughtful stare, his chiseled lips pursed slightly, but he didn't comment.

"Well I think it's marvelous that you have a friend on board, my dear," Mary Wright said, patting Joanna's hand. "I imagine traveling all alone can be a bit awkward for an attractive single girl like you. And I'm sure Mr. Fleming is delighted to have your company."

Looking at those steady black eyes, Joanna doubted that. And she was quite positive that Gloria Osborne didn't share the sentiment. The redhead's face was tight with annoyance, her full lips folded inward in a thin straight line.

"You know, my dear, there is something about you that is very familiar," Mary said, gazing at Joanna intently. "I feel like I should know you."

"No, I don't think we've met," Joanna replied quickly. She looked at Sean and held her breath, expecting him to give her away, but he merely narrowed his eyes and watched her.

Turning back to the elderly woman, Joanna deftly steered the conversation onto safer ground. Within minutes she was sitting back with a smile listening to Mary explain that her husband, Charles, had just retired and that their children and grandchildren had pitched in to send them on the cruise.

Somewhere in her sixties, Mary Wright was a charming, utterly feminine little woman, slightly plump, with a cap of silver curls and faded blue eyes that still twinkled flirtatiously. Her delicate, age-spotted hands fluttered like graceful birds when she talked, and her voice was a soft, liquid drawl that conjured up visions of magnolias and mint juleps. It came as no surprise at all when Mary announced that she and her husband were from Atlanta.

Charles Wright was tall and distinguished looking, the epitome of the southern gentleman, and as quiet as Mary was outgoing. Joanna noted the fondness in his eyes whenever he looked at his wife, and she liked him instantly.

Which just shows how much your values have shifted, Joanna thought wryly, the admission stirring within her a mixture of chagrin and satisfaction. Four years of observing the love and caring that was so much a part of her mother's marriage had made Joanna sensitive to the subtle undercurrents between men and women and altered her perceptions and priorities. Now she found herself assessing a man, not by wealth or family background, or the amount of power he wielded, but by his capacity for tenderness and commitment.

The waiter returned with their food, and as they ate they gradually began to exchange background information.

Gloria Osborne was a divorcée from Dallas who worked as a buyer for a department store, and Tony Farrell was a junior partner in a New York law firm. To Joanna's surprise, Susan and Bill Adamson, neither of whom looked old enough to vote, were celebrating their sixth anniversary. Instead of appearing happy, however, they both wore a rather harried look, and Joanna couldn't help but notice the way Susan kept glancing at her watch every few minutes. They lived in Minneapolis, where Bill worked as an insurance salesman and Susan, until six months ago when she quit to have their first child, had been an elementary school teacher.

Sean was glibly evasive about his work, managing to give the impression that he was between jobs, which in a way was true, Joanna supposed, since he had recently resigned his post on the Vice President's staff.

Joanna merely said that she lived in Washington, and silently prayed that no one would make the obvious connection. She wasn't sure whether or not Sean knew about her job with Senator Hartwell, but in case he didn't, she decided to keep quiet about it, at least for the moment.

All during the meal Gloria flirted outrageously with Sean, and he responded with his usual devilish charm. He hardly paid any attention to Joanna, and by the time the meal was over she had begun to relax.

When they had finished their after dinner coffee Gloria put her hand on Sean's arm and in a sultry voice, said, "Why don't we go dancing in the Zodiac Lounge? One of the crew told me that they have a fabulous band in there."

Sean smiled regretfully and shook his head. "I'm sorry. Not tonight. There's something I need to discuss with Joanna."

Joanna wasn't sure who was more surprised, herself or Gloria. The other woman's eyes widened for an instant in outrage, but she recovered quickly and her expression grew cool and rigid. "Of course. If that's what you want," she said in a clipped voice. "Perhaps, if I'm not too busy, I'll see you tomorrow."

It was clearly a threat, but Sean chose to ignore it, giving Gloria a warm look and a wink as he rose to come around to Joanna's side of the table.

His hand closed firmly around her upper arm, and urged her, none too gently, to her feet. With a polite nod and a charming, encompassing smile for the others, he said, "You will excuse us, won't you?" Without giving any of their startled fellow diners a chance to reply, he turned and propelled Joanna toward the door.

His hand remained clamped around her arm. Joanna didn't have a chance to say a word as he hustled her up two flights of steps and out on deck. She risked a glance at him only once, when he paused to look around before marching her over to a secluded spot by the rail. His face wore its perpetual look of unshakable insouciance, but she could feel the tightly controlled tension in him.

"Now, I want an explanation, Joanna," he snapped without preamble the moment they came to a halt. "And you'd better make it good. Just what the devil are you doing here?"

Joanna swallowed hard. She had never seen Sean angry before. It had always seemed to her that he viewed life as a sort of ridiculous comedy put on for his entertainment. During her mother's campaign the strongest reaction he'd shown when things went wrong, as they invariably did, was a mild exasperation. Nothing had ruffled him. Even in the most trying situations, when others all around him had been flying off the handle, Sean had watched with ironic amusement in his dark eyes, and calmly gone about his business. But he was definitely angry now.

She widened her eyes, feigning innocence. "Why, I told you. You made the cruise sound like so much fun I decided to try it myself," she said brightly, waving her hand in a vague little gesture.

Sean spit out a searing expletive that made her suck in her breath. "Oh, come off it. Who the hell do you think you're kidding?"

Grim faced, he turned his head and stared out at the gently undulating ocean. Moonlight spilled like liquid silver over the bobbing waves and a salt-tainted breeze caressed Joanna's skin and toyed playfully with her long hair, but she didn't notice. She eyed Sean's harsh profile with trepidation and waited nervously, too stunned to even think.

Finally he looked back at her and expelled his breath in a long exasperated sigh. "We both know why you followed me on this cruise, Joanna," he said angrily.

Her heart gave a little skip. *Oh, no. He knows. And he's going to refuse.* Joanna looked at him unhappily, her shoulders slumping as her spirits sank like a rock in the ocean. But then his next words caused her to stiffen with shock.

"You're not here to have fun. You followed me because you're infatuated. You've developed a silly, schoolgirl crush."

Chapter Three

"Whaaat!"

It was all Joanna could get out for a moment. She just gaped at him, her eyes growing steadily rounder.

"Infatuated! *Infatuated!* Why that's— You— You're— I'm not—"

"It doesn't take a genius to figure out why you followed me," Sean continued, ignoring her incoherent sputtering. "After not seeing each other for years, we spend one evening together, and suddenly here you are, not only on the same cruise, but sitting at the same table. It wouldn't surprise me to find out that you have the cabin next to mine. What did you do, bribe the purser?"

Heat suffused Joanna's face and neck. Against her flushed skin the ocean breeze suddenly felt icy cold, and she silently blessed the darkness. He had completely misread her motive, yet was so close to the mark otherwise that she felt absurdly guilty. Flustered, Joanna groped for a plausible excuse other than the truth. Somehow, she didn't think he'd find that anymore palatable at the moment. "I...I..."

"Look, Joanna." Though Sean's expression was still stern, his voice softened somewhat. "I don't want to hurt you. You're the daughter of one of my dearest friends. But I came on this cruise to relax and enjoy myself, and I sure as hell don't intend to spend it dodging a love-struck young girl."

Joanna gasped. Stiffening, she drew her slender body up to its full height and gave him a cool look. She was angry now. Angry and humiliated. And, recalling the crush she'd had on him four years ago, more than a little uncomfortable.

"You won't have to worry about that, I assure you. Because you're mistaken." She tried to maintain a frigid hauteur, but with every word her anger grew and her words became more heated. "I am not in the least interested in you, except perhaps as a friend, and now I'm not even certain I want to be that. Just because you think you're God's gift to women, don't expect everyone to agree with you. You...you arrogant, egotistical, insufferable—" Joanna sputtered to a halt, almost choking on her rage "—jerk! I wouldn't have you as a precious gift!"

Her hazel eyes flashed fire at him. She started to say more, sputtered again, then clasped her jaws together and stomped off.

Sean stared after her. Had he been wrong? He frowned and shook his head. It didn't seem likely. If she'd only wanted to enjoy the cruise, then why seek him out? Why choose this particular cruise?

Stuffing his hands in his pockets, Sean began to stroll toward the bow of the ship, his expression pensive. *A jerk? And egotistical? Is that how she really thinks of me?* He didn't know whether to be angry, relieved or insulted. A reluctant smile tugged at the corners of his mouth as he realized that he felt a bit of all three.

Or had her tirade just been a face-saving tactic? Then again, maybe Joanna had been right, Sean admitted with a self-deprecating chuckle. Maybe he was simply jumping to conclusions because he was an arrogant, egotistical, insufferable bastard. Maybe...but he didn't think so.

What other possible reason could she have for following me?

Sean wandered aimlessly around the ship, a jumble of thoughts running through his mind: Joanna, the uncertainty of his future, his wants, the decision he was going to have to make soon. They taunted him, bedeviled him, and no matter how hard he tried, he couldn't tune them out.

When Sean had made a circuit of the deck he was on, he climbed the stairs to the one above. As he neared the bow, the heavy, pulsating rock music pouring from the Zodiac Lounge drew him, and he went in, pausing just inside the door to look around.

The walls vibrated with the pounding explosion of sound produced by the band, and on the dance floor couples gyrated wildly. The floor looked as though it were made of thick glass. Beneath it, colored lights flashed at random in time to the primitive beat, eerily illuminating the dancers.

It could be an ''in'' spot anywhere, Sean thought with a touch of bored cynicism. Dimly lit. Frenetic. Crowded with people who were working hard at having a good time.

Short-skirted waitresses bustled between the closely spaced tables. Laughter, raised voices, the clink of glassware, all blended into a dull roar that competed with the blaring music.

Across the room Sean spotted Gloria, sitting at a table with Tony Farrell and several other people. He considered joining them, but after only a few seconds turned and left. For some reason he just wasn't in the mood for partying.

Pausing by the rail, Sean looked at the peaceful movements of the moon-drenched ocean and felt inexplicably sad. Inexplicably lonely. Which is stupid, he told himself, considering the hundreds of people on this ship. One in particular who'd be more than willing to keep you company.

But the strange discontent that he'd felt for months settled around him like a lead cape, causing a queer ache in his chest, and Sean continued to stare out at the spill of liquid silver on the heaving water. Finally, he pushed away from the rail, went inside and loped down two flights of stairs.

With his gaze fixed on the multicolored carpet, his hands stuffed in his pockets, he sauntered down the long companionway toward his cabin. "Helluva way to start a vacation," he muttered under his breath.

Joanna paced the floor of her sitting room with jerky, agitated steps.

"I don't want to spend my time dodging a love-struck young girl." Sean's words ran tauntingly through her mind. Her jaw clenched tighter and an angry sound, very much like a growl, vibrated in her throat.

"I don't believe it. I just don't believe this is happening," she muttered to the ceiling, throwing her arms wide. "He actually thinks that I'm infatuated with him. That... that conceited, vain...Romeo!"

But even as the words came out of her mouth, Joanna knew they weren't true. Though females were drawn to Sean like flies to honey, he was no womanizer. Sean admired and respected women, enjoyed them—some intimately, true—but he didn't use them. And if ever a man had a right to be conceited about his looks, it was Sean. Yet he seemed supremely unaware, or at least uncaring, that he was every woman's idea of a Greek god.

Joanna stopped by one of the windows and gazed out at the moonlight dancing on the water. She took several slow, deep breaths, and after a moment began to calm, her anger draining away. In any case, she admitted reluctantly, it wasn't really Sean's masculine beauty that made feminine hearts flutter. It was that wicked grin and those damned bedroom eyes. That faintly reckless, devil-may-care aura about him. Joanna suspected that even if Sean were ugly as sin, he could still have his pick of women.

Abandoning the view, Joanna sank down on the sofa, slipped out of her shoes and propped her feet on the marble-topped coffee table. The soft leather crackled as she leaned her head back and gazed up at the ceiling. How ironic that four years ago when she'd fancied herself madly in love with Sean he hadn't even guessed, and now that she was over all that foolishness, he was accusing her of falling for him. The ridiculousness of it made her chuckle.

When she had made her plans it had never once occurred to her that he would think she was interested in him. But in all fairness, she admitted reluctantly, looking at it from Sean's point of view, she could understand how he could have misconstrued her actions.

Somehow she was going to have to convince him otherwise. Not only was it embarrassing, it was a sure bet that as long as he thought she was chasing him she'd never convince him to run for office.

As she had done countless times in the past few weeks, Joanna wondered at Sean's reluctance to commit himself. It wasn't like him at all. In his easygoing way, he was a decisive, determined man, and according to Matt, ever since coming to D.C. ten years ago, Sean had set his sights on eventually attaining a political office. Everything he'd done, everything he'd worked for, had been with that goal in mind.

The time was ripe. Sean knew as well as she that you didn't just blithely say one day, "I think I'll run for office." You had to have backers with influence who could drop a few words in the right ears, do a little civilized arm-twisting, who had enough clout in both the public and private sectors to sway opinions and drum up the enormous amount of financial support it took to run a campaign. Newcomb and his group were offering that backing.

So why was Sean hesitating?

Impatiently, Joanna pushed aside the fruitless speculation. Unless she could convince Sean that she wasn't attracted to him romantically she didn't have a hope of finding out the answer to that question.

Joanna searched for an explanation to give Sean for being on the trip, but after wrestling with the problem for several minutes she jerked to her feet and headed for the bedroom. *The devil with subtlety. The first thing tomorrow morning I'm going to tell him the truth. Then maybe we can talk seriously about his political future.*

But to Joanna's disappointment, Sean did not put in an appearance in the dining room the next morning. The only company she had at the table for most of the meal was Mary and Charles Wright. The entire time she was eating Joanna kept one eye on the entrance and at the same time pretended to listen to Mary's friendly chatter. But there was no sign of Sean.

As she sipped her after breakfast coffee, Tony Farrell slid into the chair next to Joanna, looking the worse for wear. Behind his fashionable glasses his eyes were bleary and bloodshot, and there was a decidedly sickly cast to his skin. Even his carefully styled hair was mussed at the sides, as though he'd been massaging his temples.

"Sorry I'm late," he murmured, reaching eagerly for the cup of coffee the instant the waiter had filled it. "Gloria and I stayed at the Zodiac until almost two this morning and it was a bit difficult to get the old bod in motion."

A curious feeling of relief flickered through Joanna. She had halfway suspected that after they had parted the night before Sean might have sought out Gloria. The chance that the woman might still be with him had been the only thing that prevented Joanna from knocking on his cabin door that morning.

When Tony had drained his cup of coffee he noted the vacant chairs at their table and glanced around the elegant empty dining room. "It looks like I'm not the only one who slept late. Either that, or everyone else chose the breakfast buffet on deck."

Joanna immediately gave herself a swift mental kick. She had forgotten all about the buffet.

As quickly as good manners would allow, she finished her coffee, excused herself and headed outside.

Stepping out into a brilliant world of blinding sunshine and vivid colors, Joanna squinted and shaded her eyes with her hand. The sky was a canopy of blue: perfect, flawless, so bright you could barely stand to look at it. The undulating ocean was several shades darker, touched here and there with frothy whitecaps. At the horizon, sea and sky blended together in a softly smudged line that made it difficult to tell where one ended and the other began. The white ship plowed sedately through the blue waters, creating more foaming waves at its bow and a wake that trailed behind like the lacy train on a bridal gown. Only the polished brass and wooden deck and the gay garb of the passengers added a dash of contrast to the great expanse of blue and white.

Smiling, Joanna breathed deeply of sun and salt air and fished in the deep pocket on her wraparound skirt for her sunglasses. There was still a line of people at the buffet table, but Sean wasn't among them. Most of the tables scattered along the deck were filled with people enjoying their alfresco breakfast, and as she strolled toward the stern of the ship Joanna discreetly glanced at each of them.

About halfway down the deck she spotted Susan and Bill Adamson, and to Joanna's surprise, Susan was holding in her lap a baby who looked to be about six months old.

"Well, good morning, you two," Joanna greeted, stop-

ping beside their table. "When you didn't show up in the
dining room I thought maybe you had made the rounds
with Tony and Gloria last night."

At the sound of Joanna's voice the baby looked up and
stared at her, her big blue eyes wide and unblinking. Her
intent gaze did not waver even when Susan stuffed another
spoonful of what looked like mashed banana into her
mouth. Smiling, Joanna reached out and touched the wispy
blond curl above the baby's ear. "And who is this little
charmer?"

"This is our daughter, Lori," Susan said distractedly,
using the side of the spoon to rake the globs of food from
around the rosebud mouth and stuff it back in. "Bill's
mother was going to keep her while we took this cruise,
but just a few hours before we were supposed to leave she
slipped on the stairs and broke her leg, so we had to bring
Lori along."

"It was either that, or miss it. It was too late to get a
refund on our tickets," Bill added dejectedly.

Susan looked up at Joanna with a wan smile. "Don't
misunderstand. We love Lori dearly. It's just that this was
supposed to be sort of a second honeymoon. Now we'll
have to take turns sitting with her in the evening while the
other one eats and sees the shows. We're going to try to
take her with us when we go on the island tours, but if
she gets too fussy one of us will have to stay on board
and keep her."

"Some honeymoon," Bill muttered morosely.

"Couldn't you hire one of the crew to baby-sit for
you?"

"Oh, yes. That's what we did last night." Susan wiped
the baby's mouth with a napkin and handed her a bottle
of milk. Lori lay back in her mother's arms and sucked
greedily, her unblinking stare still fixed on Joanna. "The
trouble is, we can't afford to do that very often. We had

to save for this trip for years, and I'm afraid we're on a very tight budget that just doesn't allow for baby-sitting.''

"That's too bad," Joanna said with genuine sympathy. "If there's anything I can do—"

"No, no," Susan cut in quickly. "We wouldn't want to impose on anyone. And don't let us spoil your trip with our problems," she added with a bright smile. "We'll work something out."

They talked desultorily for a few minutes more, but when Joanna spotted Sean leaving a table a few yards away, she excused herself and hurried after him.

"Sean! Sean, may I speak with you a moment?"

Sean turned, then groaned and looked disgusted when he saw who was calling him. "For Pete's sake, Joanna! Do we have to go through this again?"

"But you don't understand. I didn't come on this cruise to try to attract you. I—"

"Oh, Joanna, please," Sean pleaded wearily. "You aren't going to try again to make me believe that you're here just to enjoy yourself, are you? People in your set don't take cruises. They own their own yachts. Or if they don't, they have friends who do. We both know that if you got a sudden yen to cruise the Caribbean, all you would have to do is pick up the phone and call one of your jet-setting pals."

"Oh, but—"

"Joanna, I don't want to hear it. Okay? Just back off and leave me alone."

"Sean, if you'll only listen for a minute—" Joanna began again, but before she could utter another word Gloria glided up to Sean and linked her arm through his.

"There, you are. I've been searching all over for you. The calypso band is setting up by the forward pool, and one of the cruise directors is going to give lessons in island dancing. I thought maybe I could talk you into joining me." Smiling persuasively, the redhead leaned against him, pressing the side of her breast against his arm, her eyes flashing an invitation of another sort. Sean responded with a lazy grin.

"Lead the way, sweetheart," he drawled. "It sounds like fun." He turned his head and gave Joanna a pointed look. "Joanna and I were through talking anyway. I'm sure she'll excuse us."

Numbly, Joanna watched them walk away, arm in arm. Without warning a strange, aching tightness gripped her chest, and to her horror, she felt tears sting her eyes. She turned away quickly and walked to the rail. Resting her forearms along the top, she leaned against it and lifted her face to the wind, blinking rapidly. She pressed her lips together and drew a deep breath, struggling to control the wayward wobble of her chin.

This is silly, she told herself severely. For Pete's sake, there's no reason to get all teary and bent out of shape just because Sean won't talk to you? And so what if he's making time with that redhead? There's nothing new in that. Joanna stared at the smudged horizon and swallowed against the painful constriction in her throat. The stiff ocean breeze threaded through her hair, lifting and waving it like streamers of brown silk, and plastered her skirt against the front of her body. The thin cotton suggestively outlined the slender curves of hips and long shapely legs and flapped wildly behind her, snapping and cracking like a flag in the gusting wind.

Joanna held herself stiffly, her chin tilted at a proud angle, but after a moment her shoulders sagged. It was pointless to deny it: Sean's attitude did bother her. But more than his refusal to speak to her, more than his obvious preference for Gloria, what really disturbed her were his remarks about her background.

Not because they were unfair, but because at one time they would have been right on target. As recently as four years ago, Joanna admitted with lingering self-disgust, she would have looked upon this cruise as entirely too plebe-ian, beneath even her consideration.

Summers in the south of France or in Greece with her friend Irena or sailing the Mediterranean. Winters skiing in the Alps, and in between, flying trips to London or Rome or Madrid. That had been the pattern of her life. Her father had spoiled her outrageously. She had grown up so accustomed to having her own way she had not given a thought to the wants and needs of anyone else.

Looking back on that time, Joanna was appalled. Her selfishness had nearly cost her mother the only love and true happiness she had ever known and had driven a wedge between them. Even so, it had taken a series of shocks and disillusionments before she'd finally accepted the truth: about her father, about her parents' marriage, but most of all, about herself.

Joanna shook her head disbelievingly, her eyes full of regret. It all seemed so long ago. Sean, of course, really couldn't be faulted for his remarks. He had no way of knowing that she had turned her back on that life, that she had worked hard in school and now worked hard at a job, not because she had to but because she wanted to, that she rarely saw anyone from her old crowd.

But Joanna wanted desperately for him to know. For some reason she didn't fully understand, Sean's good opinion was important to her. If she could just talk to him, convince him to accept Newcomb's offer and then give her a job, he'd see for himself that she had changed. Some-how, she had to make him listen.

The ringing sounds of steel drums filled the air sud-denly, their lilting rhythm at once soothing and stimulat-ing. Joanna turned her head and looked toward the bow. As though drawn by a magnet, she began to stroll in that direction.

Many people were swimming or just lounging around the pool, but an equal number were standing in a semicir-

cle around the cruise director, who was moving to the calypso beat demonstrating the steps and body movements
of the dance. There was a good deal of laughter and joking
as the audience tried to mimic her.

Joanna started to join the group, but thought better of
it. Instead, she walked to one of the poolside lounges,
stepped out of her sandals and removed her skirt. But as
Joanna turned from hanging it over the back of the lounge,
she found that Sean was watching her, and her stomach
tightened into a knot.

It wasn't the look of annoyance on his face that disturbed her. She had expected that. It was the way his dark
gaze roamed slowly over her body, taking in the brief
strapless playsuit. A feathery tingle raced over Joanna's
skin as his eyes narrowed and lingered on her breasts,
which were clearly outlined by the elasticized top, then
slid downward over her narrow waist, the gentle flare of
her hips and the long, curving length of her bare legs.

Feigning indifference, Joanna stretched out on the
lounge, oblivious to the admiring looks she was receiving
from several other men around the pool. For the next half
hour she sunbathed and pretended to doze, while watching
Sean covertly through slitted eyes.

It was her intention to corner Sean when the class broke
up, but she never had a chance. The moment the band
stopped playing he marched over to her. Before Joanna
could even struggle to a sitting position Sean bent over,
braced his arms on either side of the webbed lounge and
brought his face down to within an inch of hers. His beautiful mouth was stretched into a dazzling smile, but his
black eyes were snapping with anger as he said in a
strained but soft voice, "Knock it off, Joanna. Because I'm
warning you, if you don't, I just may turn you over my
knee and give you the spanking you should have had years
ago. Now be a good girl and stay out of my hair."

Then he was gone. Joanna sat up just in time to see him

loop his arm around Gloria's waist and lead her away. Anger and indignation welled up inside Joanna as she glared at their retreating backs. Spanking! *Spanking!* In a pig's eye!

Her eyes narrowed, and a mulish expression that her mother would have recognized settled over her face. *Damn you, Sean. I'll make you listen to me if it's the last thing I do,* she vowed.

Bristling, Joanna stood up, stuffed her feet back into her sandals, snatched up her skirt and stalked after the pair. What she had to say no longer mattered. Getting a chance to actually say it had become a point of honor.

But trying to corner Sean, Joanna soon discovered, was like trying to capture a slippery eel with your bare hands. After scouring the ship for almost an hour, Joanna finally spotted him playing volleyball, but the minute she stepped onto the court, Sean stepped off. At lunch he once again opted for the buffet on deck. When she found him, he and Gloria were sharing a table with the Adamsons, but no sooner had Joanna joined them than Sean excused himself, leaving his lunch half-finished. Later she tracked him down in the casino, but when she tried to talk to him the dealer shushed her with a black look. She retreated to the slot machines on the other side of the room to wait, but somehow Sean vanished when she wasn't looking.

It was the same story all day. Whenever Joanna got anywhere near Sean he always managed to give her the slip. But the more he evaded her, the more determined Joanna became. That evening after dinner she followed him and Gloria and waited for her chance.

They went to the Club International and watched singing idol Doug Longworth perform. After the show they moved on to the Zodiac Lounge for dancing. Finally, around midnight Sean walked Gloria to her cabin.

Feeling utterly foolish, Joanna hovered around the corner, hoping against hope that Sean would not disappear into Gloria's room for the night. To her relief, after a steamy good-night kiss, they parted and Sean came sauntering back down the companionway, whistling softly under his breath.

Joanna flew up the stairs before he could spot her and hurried straight to her suite. Leaving the door open a crack, she stood just inside and peered out, and when Sean drew close she stepped out into his path. "Sean, I must talk to you. This is important, believe me."

"Oh, for the love of..." Sean stopped, his face hardening. "All right. All right, that's it!" He looked around, then grabbed her arm and propelled her into her suite. He kicked the door shut with his foot and at the same time thrust Joanna into the center of the room. "I've tried to be patient with you, Joanna," he began grimly, advancing on her, "but you just won't take no for an answer, will you? I guess I should have known better than to expect anything else from a spoiled, self-centered brat like you."

"I am not a spoiled brat!"

"Oh yeah? You sure could of fooled me." A quick look around brought a scornful twist to his mouth. "Just look at this setup. You couldn't just book a cabin like us ordinary mortals, could you? Oh no, nothing but the luxury suite is good enough for Princess Joanna," he sneered.

"That's not the reason I booked this suite," Joanna denied heatedly, her own anger beginning to simmer.

"The point is, you're an overindulged, self-centered little girl. You're so accustomed to having whatever your heart desires that when you decide you want something you think all you have to do is reach out and grab it. Well life doesn't work that way, sweetheart, and it's about time you learned that."

Anger flared in Joanna's eyes, but before she could speak Sean continued in a warning tone. "I'm not going to become involved with you, Joanna. First of all, I'm too old for you. Secondly, you're the daughter and stepdaughter of my two dearest friends, and I'm not about to jeopardize that relationship for a roll in the hay with an immature little snit.''

Joanna gasped, and Sean's expression changed to one of cynical amusement.

''Not that you're not attractive and appealing, mind you. You are, in a classy, well-bred sort of way.'' He stepped closer and ran his forefinger down her cheek to lightly graze the mole at the corner of her mouth. Joanna went perfectly still, her eyes widening. She couldn't have moved if her life had depended on it. ''But it simply wouldn't work because, honey, I guarantee you, I'm way out of your league.'' At her strangled sound of protest, Sean slipped his arms around her and pulled her close. His lids dropped partway, and his eyes glinted down at her, hard and steely with purpose. Slowly, he bent his head. ''And just so there's no doubt about it in your mind...''

The softly whispered words floated into her mouth as his lips claimed hers in a long, searing kiss.

Shock reverberated through Joanna. It was all sensation—sizzling fire and shivering ecstasy. There was no force, no gentle enticement: just pure seduction, bold and sure and devastating.

As his mouth rocked against hers he pulled her closer and one hand slid down her spine to press her hips tightly against his. Joanna gasped, and he thrust his tongue into her mouth, plunging deep to plunder with slow, evocative strokes that set off a throbbing heat in Joanna's feminine core.

Her heart was racing, sending blood pounding through her veins, and her chest was so tight she could barely breathe. In some remote corner of her brain, Joanna knew she should resist, protest, but her quivering body was enslaved. Years ago she had daydreamed endlessly of Sean holding her like this, kissing her like this. But those dreams faded into nothingness beside reality. This was a thousand times more potent—a shattering delight that robbed her of both strength and will.

Sean was experienced with women, and he used his vast knowledge to advantage. He knew where to touch, how to touch, and his roving hands drove her wild. When he held her close and rocked his hips suggestively she whimpered softly into his mouth and melted against him. Of their own accord, her arms lifted and her spread fingers buried themselves in his hair, the ebony strands sliding against her skin like warm silk as she clutched his head and urged him closer.

She clung to him, dizzy with the need he was so deliberately arousing, her mouth soft and fervent under his, her body aflame with sweet, hot desire. She lost all sense of time and place and purpose. At that moment nothing else in the world existed but Sean. Just Sean.

And then, suddenly, it was over. Joanna felt cold and bereft when his lips left hers. Colder still when he gripped her shoulders and held her away from him. Dazed, she stood like a rag doll between his hands, unable to respond for a moment. When at last she opened her eyes, she found Sean watching her strangely.

He stared at her in silence, his dark eyes narrowed and glittering. Then, abruptly, he released her and without a word, turned and stalked out.

Chapter Four

Joanna stared at the closed door. Slowly she raised her hand and pressed trembling fingers against her mouth. *Dear God, how could I have been so stupid?*

A sick sensation quivered through her, and she closed her eyes and let her breath out in a deep, shuddering sigh. Sean had been right all along; she was infatuated with him. She always had been. That one searing kiss had proved that.

A low moan escaped her, and she turned and walked listlessly into the bedroom. Dazed, she sank down onto the bed and stared out the window at nothing. *What a fool you are. What a complete and utter fool.*

The past few years had taught Joanna a lot about her weaknesses and her strengths. She knew that she was good at self-deception, seeing things as she wanted them to be. Typically, she had managed to rationalize her reasons for wanting Sean to run for office, and for following him on this cruise, but she knew now that the basic reason, the *real* reason, was this crazy attraction she felt for him. Firming her mouth, Joanna sighed deeply once again. No doubt, the only person she'd fooled with the weak excuse was herself. She certainly hadn't fooled Sean.

The attraction was crazy. And hopeless. Sean had made it obvious how he thought of her—a child, a spoiled brat.

And he's right, Joanna conceded unhappily. At least partially.

Flopping back on the bed, her hands balling into fists, Joanna squinted at the ceiling. "But I'm working on it," she muttered with grim determination.

Since causing so much havoc in her mother's life she had tried very hard to change. There were lapses now and then, Joanna admitted with brutal honesty. It was difficult to break the habits and attitudes of a lifetime. But she would...eventually.

Actually, viewing the situation rationally, Joanna knew she should be grateful that Sean did not share her feelings. Because the attraction was not only stupid, it was dangerous. Recalling the raw passion Sean's kiss had evoked, Joanna closed her eyes and shivered. It had caught her completely off guard and rocked her to her very soul. Even now, just thinking about it, she felt a tingling heat surge through her body.

Gritting her teeth against the disturbing sensation, Joanna rolled her head from side to side on the mattress. No, Sean was not for her. At eighteen she had been brashly confident that she could make him fall in love with her. Now she knew better. Sean was a confirmed bachelor, a man of the world. Even if they were to have a romantic relationship, the odds were that she would end up with a broken heart.

Sean had been right, she admitted with a wistful sigh. He was way out of her league.

For a few minutes she lay on the bed reviewing her foolish behavior, angry and utterly disgusted. The mental dressing down she gave herself was sharp, scathing and merciless.

But Joanna was not one to flay herself for long. She had tried that four years ago, until her mother had made her see that endless self-castigation was foolish and did no one any good. Now when she made a mistake, she admitted it, ranted a bit, then forgave herself and set about doing whatever she could to correct it.

Decisively, Joanna lunged up off the bed. Twisting her arm behind her, she lowered the zipper on her gown. The only thing to do was to make the best of a bad situation and get through the rest of the trip with as much dignity as possible, she told herself as the peach silk sheath slithered down her body and pooled around her feet. She would put the stupid infatuation out of her mind and simply relax and enjoy the cruise…and do her best to stay out of Sean's hair.

"Good morning, Mr. Fleming." The waiter poured coffee into Sean's cup as he slid into his seat at the table. "Looks like you're the only one eating indoors this morning."

Sean gave the man a lazy grin. "I'm not quite up to all that sparkling sea and sun just yet."

Aromatic steam wafted up to tantalize his nose, and Sean reached for the cup of coffee, taking a quick sip of the scalding liquid. It was the truth, up to a point, but the main reason he'd chosen the dining room over the buffet was to avoid Gloria. After the night he'd just had he wasn't in the mood for lighthearted flirting.

When the waiter had taken his order Sean settled back to wait. Broodingly, he stared at the shining surface of the coffee, a frown creasing between his brows.

Joanna. It annoyed him that he couldn't dismiss her from his mind. And, to his disgust, now just the thought of her made his chest tighten and sent a throbbing heat to his loins.

Sean shifted uncomfortably and took another sip from the cup. What the devil happened?

For half the night he had lain awake staring at the ceiling, asking the same question over and over, but he still had no answer. He had intended to teach Joanna a lesson with that kiss. Sean exhaled a rueful snort and grimaced. What a laugh! The moment their lips had touched rational thought had deserted him. It had been an explosion of pure passion, hot and raw and overwhelming. If he hadn't found the strength to end it, in another minute he'd have taken her right there.

Lord, Fleming! What the hell's the matter with you? She's just a girl, for Pete's sake. If you're not careful, you're going to turn into a dirty old man.

Yet he couldn't deny his response. She had felt exactly right in his arms, as though she'd been made for him alone. And that was what scared him. He had known many women, but never in his life had he wanted one as desperately as he had wanted Joanna.

The waiter topped up his coffee cup. Without thinking, Sean snatched it up, downed half the contents in one long swallow and gasped as the scalding brew seared his throat. Cursing under his breath, he returned the cup to its saucer just as Joanna took her seat on the opposite side of the table.

Anger, resentment and another emotion he didn't care to put a name to, gripped Sean at the sight of her. Her skin glowed and her hazel eyes were clear and direct. There were no dark circles under them, no drawn look. Dressed in a yellow sundress that left her tanned shoulders bare, her glossy hair pulled back at the sides and secured with white and yellow combs, she looked annoyingly fresh and lovely. It was obvious that Joanna hadn't spent a sleepless night.

"Good morning, Sean," she said politely.

Sean's mouth firmed, but before he could reply the waiter materialized beside her and filled her cup with coffee. When he had taken her order and disappeared Joanna folded her hands on the table and looked directly into Sean's eyes.

"Before you get angry all over again, I just want to say one thing. I'm sorry."

Surprise darted through Sean, but the only sign he gave was the infinitesimal narrowing of his eyes.

"I shouldn't have followed you on this trip. I realize that now," Joanna continued in a soft, serious voice. "But I promise you, for the rest of the cruise I'll do my best to stay out of your way."

Her discomfort was obvious, but there was determination there, too. A part of Sean admired the courage and strength of character it took to make the apology. But, dammit! He'd just spent the better part of the night agonizing over her and that damned kiss, and her freshness and composure were galling. For once, his lazy insouciance deserted him.

"Oh, sure." Sean's look was as deliberately skeptical as his tone, but Joanna met it squarely, one brow lifting.

"I'm sorry. That's the best I can do. I can't very well get off the ship in the middle of the ocean. I don't walk on water, you know."

Sean's admiration deepened, but he hid it well. "I don't suppose you'd consider getting off at St. Thomas and flying home?"

Hurt flickered in Joanna's eyes, but her steady gaze never wavered. "No, I wouldn't. But I promise I won't pester you anymore." Her chin tilted a bit higher at Sean's derisive snort, and she added with the barest trace of annoyance, "I've already asked the purser if I could change to another table, but he said it was too late. So, I'm afraid at meals we'll just have to make the best of the situation."

Sean just looked at her, his expression unyielding. After a moment she lowered her eyes. He watched her pick up her cup and take a sip of coffee. Then she folded her hands in her lap and gazed off into the distance. Only the pulse throbbing at the base of her throat betrayed her nervousness.

Her pride was evident in the tilt of her chin, in her stiff posture, yet she still looked like a defenseless waif. Even though he knew she'd brought the situation on herself, after a moment Sean began to feel churlish. Exhaling heavily, he raked a hand through his hair and let it slide down the back of his head to massage the taut muscles in his neck.

"Look, Joanna," he began, frowning, "About last ni—"

But the statement was never finished, for at that moment the Wrights and Tony Farrell arrived.

"Good morning, you two," Mary said, slipping into the seat beside Joanna. "Looks like you're the early birds."

Joanna looked up eagerly, a smile of pure relief lighting her face. "Good morning."

Battling his frustration, Sean greeted them cordially, then settled back in his chair and watched in brooding silence.

As Charles took the chair beside his wife, Tony Farrell chose the seat on Joanna's other side. "Hi." His gray eyes glowed warmly behind his glasses as they skimmed over her upturned face and bare shoulders. "You look terrific this morning."

"Thank you. You don't look bad yourself."

Tony flashed her a white smile that was an orthodontist's dream. "I looked for you yesterday. I was hoping that we could spend some time together, get to know one another. But I didn't catch so much as a glimpse of you until dinner. And afterward you disappeared again."

"Oh, Joanna had a very busy day yesterday," Sean interjected in an insinuating drawl.

When Joanna darted him a wary look he propped his chin on his fist and smiled tauntingly. Reminding her of the way she'd pursued him wasn't the gentlemanly thing to do, especially after her apology. Normally Sean wouldn't have dreamed of needling a woman—any woman—but Joanna had gotten under his skin, and for some reason he could not quite curb his irritation. Besides, there was something about Tony Farrell that set his teeth on edge.

Joanna turned back to Tony with a placating smile and placed her hand on his arm. "But I won't be busy today. If you'd like we could go up to the sports deck after breakfast and check out the activities."

"Great."

Sean studied them, his eyes narrowing.

The waiter brought Mary a cup of tea and poured coffee for everyone else. Gloria arrived as he was handing out the menus.

"Good morning, all," she greeted lightly as she settled in next to Sean. "I'm surprised to find you all inside on such a terrific morning." She shook out her napkin and put it on her lap, and slanted Sean a sultry, heavy-lidded look. "I looked for you on deck. For a while there I began to think you were avoiding me."

Sean looked at the red nails that were lightly scoring his forearm, then, slowly, his gaze lifted, and he studied the invitation in Gloria's slanting green eyes. After a moment he thought, *Why not? This is what you came for, isn't it?* Covering her hand with his, he leaned closer. A slow, wicked grin curved his mouth. "Now why on earth would I do that?"

It was all the invitation Gloria needed. For the remainder of the meal she flirted with Sean outrageously, and he flirted right back. He turned on the charm, his rakish smile and teasing black eyes underscoring the purring warmth in his voice, the teasing sensuality that colored their conversation.

But for all the effort he put into it, Sean was, to his disgust and annoyance, not totally engrossed in the flirtation. He was too aware of the fact that Joanna was ignoring him. Whenever he glanced across the table she was chatting with either Mary or Tony. Usually Tony. The few times Joanna's gaze met his she looked away as though he didn't exist, and when he asked her a direct question she answered him with a polite indifference that made him grit his teeth.

Joanna's low laugh drifted across the table and Sean glanced at her again. His eyes narrowed as he watched her wrinkle her nose at something Tony said. Surely she's not going to go off the deep end over that New York slick? he thought, frowning. He eyed the man's neatly styled hair, fashionable glasses, and immaculate, just right clothes sourly. He was too smooth. Too perfect. Hell, couldn't she see that? Sean's gaze dropped to Tony's well tended hands and one corner of his mouth curled disdainfully. He didn't trust a man who wore nail polish, even if it was clear.

Becoming aware of the trend of his thoughts, Sean shifted uneasily in his chair. Good grief, Fleming! What the devil do you care if the girl wants to indulge in a shipboard fling? You're not her keeper. And besides, you ought to be happy to have her off your back. Determinedly, he pulled his gaze away from the pair and turned back to Gloria with a lazy smile.

"Ready?" Tony asked a moment later.

Joanna took one last sip of coffee, then patted her mouth with her napkin. "Yes, I'm ready." With a murmured, "Excuse us," and a parting smile for the others, she rose and linked her arm through Tony's.

Broodingly, his eyes glittering slits of obsidian, Sean watched them walk away.

He was oblivious to the chatter going on around him until Gloria drew his attention with a playful rake of her long nails across the back of his hand. Stifling the unaccountable irritation that roiled through him, Sean turned his head and met her coy smile.

"Personally, I think they have an excellent idea." Gloria purred in response to his questioning look. "Why don't you and I pair off and go for a swim? I have a new bikini I'm just dying to try."

Sean stared at her, absorbing her ripe beauty, and wondered why the idea didn't hold more appeal. After a moment he impatiently thrust the thought aside and with one of his lazy smiles, drawled, "Sure. Why not?"

Suntan lotion, towel, sunglasses, paperback novel. Satisfied she had everything, Joanna added her room key to the contents of the canvas bag, pulled the door shut behind her and headed for the pool.

Her thong sandals slapped against her heels as she ran up the stairs. Rounding the landing on the next deck, she nearly bumped into Susan and Bill.

"Hi." Susan hitched Lori higher on her hip and eyed Joanna's white lace beach robe. It barely reached the tops of her thighs, and the fragile lace gave tantalizing glimpses of the cinnamon maillot beneath. "Going swimming, huh? We were just heading for the pool ourselves."

"Yeah," Bill chimed in. "It's one of the few activities that we can take Lori to. She's been swimming since she was five months old." He smiled proudly and tweaked his daughter's tiny nose. "She's a regular little water baby."

"Really?" Joanna smiled at the staring infant. "I'd really like to see that. Mind if I join you?"

"Of course not. Come on."

As they climbed the final flight of stairs together Susan slanted her a curious look. "I saw you playing shuffleboard with Tony this morning. He seemed…well…very interested. I'm surprised he's not with you."

"He's playing in a backgammon tournament," Joanna replied, biting back a smile at Susan's gentle probing. "He said he'd meet me at the pool when it was over."

"You didn't want to watch?"

"No. I'm afraid I find the game extremely boring."

Actually, Joanna had thought it wise to spend some time away from Tony. He was a nice man and pleasant company, but she didn't want to encourage him too much. There was no explaining it: he was attractive, in a smooth sophisticated way, eligible, and so far, had behaved as a perfect gentleman. But there was no spark between them— at least, not from her side.

The moment they came in sight of the pool Lori let loose with a string of ecstatic jabber, her arms outstretched toward the water, opening and closing her chubby little fists in a classic "gimmee" gesture as she bounced up and down in her mother's arms. Laughing and watching the baby's uninhibited excitement, Joanna didn't see Sean at first. When she did she stopped short.

He was sitting on a poolside lounge beside Gloria, who was stretched out on her stomach with her head pillowed on her crossed arms. The top of her bikini was unfastened, and Sean was methodically applying tanning lotion to her bare back. And if the expression on his face was any indication, he was enjoying the task immensely.

Joanna was appalled by her reaction. Pain sliced through her like a sharp knife at the sight of those tanned fingers smoothing over the woman's skin. For an instant she almost gave into the urge to turn and run back to her room. But then, as she studied the look of male satisfaction on Sean's face, her jaw tightened and she stiffened her spine. No. She wasn't going anywhere. She had told Tony she'd meet him here, and here was where she was going to stay.

* * *

Gloria's back glistened in the sun. The mingled scents of heavy perfume, coconut oil and heated flesh drifted upward from her supine body, making Sean's nostrils twitch and flare. This wasn't such a bad idea after all, he mused as he watched his palms glide languidly over her slick shoulder blades, then trail downward to her waist. The strange anger he had felt at breakfast had slowly dissipated. Smiling, he gently kneaded the soft flesh beneath his hands. This was what he needed to get his mind off things. A little sun and fun, a beautiful woman to add spice. And, he thought with pleasurable anticipation, he had a hunch that with very little encouragement, Gloria could add a great deal of spice to this vacation.

His dreamy complacency didn't last long. At that moment Sean looked up, straight into Joanna's eyes, and his hands stilled. Briefly, her cool gaze flickered over him, then she turned away and dumped her canvas bag onto a lounge. Sean clenched his jaw and cursed fluently under his breath.

Suddenly self-conscious, he finished applying the lotion to Gloria's back with a quick, impersonal touch. "There, I think that's got you covered."

"Mmm," Gloria mumbled sleepily.

Sean capped the bottle and tossed it onto the towel beside her, then moved away and stretched out on the next lounge with his fingers laced together behind his head.

Through barely slitted eyes he watched Joanna shuck her frothy little beach coat and drop it beside her bag. His eyes roamed over her, and he cursed silently once again as he felt an unwelcome surge of heat rush to his loins. The shimmering cinnamon material of her one-piece suit molded Joanna's high breasts and boldly defined every hollow and curve of her slender body. Cut daringly low both front and back, and high at the thighs, the suit revealed a great deal of creamy skin and emphasized the long length of her shapely legs.

"Come on in, Joanna," Susan called from the pool.

Without so much as a glance in Sean's direction, Joanna stepped to the edge and dove neatly into the water.

For the next half hour Sean watched as Joanna played with the Adamson's baby, who paddled with amazing agility between the three adults. After a while they each took turns caring for the child while the other two swam. Sean was just toying with the idea of joining them when Tony appeared.

"Hi. Aren't you going to swim?" Joanna asked, eyeing his cream slacks and bronze silk shirt.

"Not today. My back's still a little red from yesterday." Tony nodded toward the umbrella covered table at the end of the pool. "Why don't you take a break and join me for a drink?"

"Okay." Grinning mischievously, Joanna turned to Susan and Bill. "Come on, gang, Tony's buying."

"Great!" Bill plucked the baby from the water and urged the two women toward the side. When they had heaved themselves out he handed Lori to her mother and clambered out after them, and they laughingly dripped their way around to where Tony sat waiting.

Feeling unaccountably irritated, Sean stood up and plunged into the water. Submerged, he swam the length of the pool three times before surfacing for air.

He was resting at the side, breathing heavily, when Gloria jumped in beside him, feet first. She surfaced laughing and looped her arms around his neck, pressing her body intimately close to his. "Gotcha!" she cried gaily. "And now you have to pay a forfeit."

Gloria tightened her arms and lifted herself higher against his body. Closing her eyes, she tilted her head back and pursed her lips invitingly.

Unable to resist, Sean glanced toward the table at the end of the pool, then looked back at the lush red mouth. Joanna wasn't watching, and it wasn't any of her business who he kissed anyway, yet he felt absurdly guilty. Determinedly Sean leaned forward, then hesitated. After a moment his mouth twisted in a rueful half smile, and he reached up and detached Gloria's arms from around his neck.

"Behave yourself," he said, smiling to take the sting out of his words. He turned the pouting woman around and gave her a little push and a playful slap on the rump. "Come on. I'll race you to the other end. I'll even give you a three-second head start."

"You're on!"

Sean watched her thrash away and shook his head. How in hell was he supposed to carry on a seduction with his best friends' daughter watching?

Chapter Five

Barefoot and makeup-free, Joanna entered the gym smiling. She wore a rose-pink leotard and lavender tights with stirrup straps that hooked under her insteps. A pair of deep purple leg warmers were slung casually over her shoulder, the ends swaying against her back with every jaunty step she took. Anticipation sparkled in her hazel eyes. Movement. Activity. It was what she needed, and she was eager to get started.

Spotting the athletic instructor across the room, Joanna altered her course. A bare six feet away, her steps faltered, and she came to a halt. In front of her, lying back on a bench with his feet braced on the floor on either side, Sean was working out with a set of hand weights.

Indecision gripped Joanna. Gnawing at her bottom lip, she eyed him warily. Should she brazen it out and ignore him, or leave? She cast a longing glance toward the instructor and the other women who were already gathering around her and sighed. It was tempting, but remembering the past few days, Joanna decided that retreat was the wisest choice.

She poised to turn, but before she could move Sean sat up and their eyes met. Anger darkened his face. With a muttered oath, he shot up off the bench and stalked to her.

"What are you doing here, Joanna?" He stood with his feet spread aggressively, hands on his hips, and growled the words in a low undertone through lips so stiff they barely moved.

Joanna was both intimidated by his anger and fascinated by his body. He wore only a brief pair of athletic shorts and tennis shoes and his bronze skin glistened with a fine sheen of moisture. Without shoes, Joanna barely reached his chin, and she found herself staring at the damp black hair that lightly furred his chest. The heat from his body hit her like a furnace, bringing with it the smell of sweat and a dizzying, tantalizing musky maleness. Helplessly, her eyes focused on a bead of sweat trickling through the band of hair that arrowed downward from his chest. At his navel it halted, then swirled around the small cavity and streaked lower, disappearing when it touched the already damp top edge of his low-slung shorts. Joanna swallowed hard.

"I...I—"

"I'm getting a little sick of this, you know," Sean went on, ignoring her stammered attempt at a reply. "Everywhere I go I run into you. If this is your attempt at staying out of my hair, I'd hate to see you when you're in hot pursuit."

The sarcastic comment snapped Joanna out of her sensual trance instantly. Her eyes went wide and she sucked in her breath. "Are you accusing me of following you around?"

"All I know is I can't make a move without practically stepping on you. It's only been twenty-four hours since you so sweetly promised to leave me alone, and already

I've run into you by the pool twice, bumped into you in the library, the card room, the casino. Every time I go to one of the clubs or the theater you're within earshot. I'm beginning to think the only place on the ship where I can be assured of not seeing you is the men's room.''

That did it. Joanna's anger soared right along with her blood pressure. She stiffened and planted her fists on her hips, unconsciously mimicking his stance. ''Now just a darned minute!'' she flared, glaring right back at him. ''I promised to leave you alone, which I've tried my best to do, but I didn't promise to lock myself in my cabin for the duration of the cruise. I paid for my ticket, and I'm entitled to enjoy myself and to make use of all the facilities the same as you.''

They stood nose to nose, their bodies stiff and vibrating with anger, unflinching hazel eyes glaring defiantly into smoldering black ones.

Across the room, the athletics instructor clapped her hands loudly and called out, ''All right, ladies! Line up, it's time to get going.''

With a toss of her head, Joanna broke eye contact and moved to step around Sean. ''I came here to take the aerobics class,'' she informed him haughtily. ''Now, if you'll excuse me, that's exactly what I intend to do.''

Rock music exploded from the speakers on the walls as the instructor turned away from the stereo. Moving in time to the heavy beat, she faced the group of women who had spread out on the mat. ''Okay, here we go. We'll start with the hustle jog. Lift those knees! Lift! Lift! Three. Four. Five. Lift! Lift!''

Joanna scrambled to pull on her leg warmers, skipping and hopping on first one foot; then the other in her rush to join the class. When she had finally tugged them into place she found a position at the front of the group, stepped into the rhythm and threw herself into the routine with a vengeance.

"Now spread your feet, hands on hips and bend to the side! Bend! Bend! Get those elbows down! Come on ladies, reach! Reach!"

Joanna bounced downward, straining to make her elbow touch the side of her knee. Already she was breathing hard, and she could feel perspiration popping out all over her body. She glanced at Sean and found him standing where she'd left him, fists still propped on his hips, watching her. Joanna gritted her teeth and bounced harder.

Who does he think he is, glowering at me like that? Automatically following instructions, Joanna straightened, extended her arms to the sides and swiveled her shoulders in time to the beat.

Resentment bubbled up inside her as she thought of his accusations. She'd tried to avoid him. She really had. But it was impossible on a ship of this size. But did he take that into account? Oh, no. He preferred to see her as a man-chasing spoiled brat.

Joanna shot Sean a dagger-sharp glare. Up until now, every time they'd met she had either tried to make herself as inconspicuous as possible, or made an excuse and left. But no more, she decided pugnaciously. From now on, Sean or no Sean, she was going to enjoy herself. And if he didn't like it, *he* could leave.

"All right, ladies, move those buns! Get a little action in it! Shake it! Shake it! That's it!"

The music throbbed. Wild. Pulsating and primitive. Joanna's lithe body was an extension of it, moving to the heavy beat, translating it into a sinuous flow of fluid rhythm.

Her face was flushed, her hair flying. Sweat drenched her. It gathered between her breasts and streamed down the narrow trench that marked her spine, making dark blotches on her rose-colored leotard. Beneath the formfitting garment, supple flesh and firm, feminine muscles rippled with each undulating movement, and her small, up-tilted breasts swayed and bounced in unfettered abandon.

God! Sean thought a little frantically. *I've seen less erotic dances in X rated films.* He stared, unable to tear his gaze away. When the unconscious enticement of Joanna's gyrations had their inevitable effect on his body he cursed and snatched up his towel from the bench and held it in front of him, dabbing absently at his chest and arms, but his eyes remained trained on her.

Who would have thought that a leotard and leg warmers could be so damned sexy?

The neckline of the formfitting garment plunged in deep V's both front and back, but even so, it covered a great deal more flesh than even a one-piece bathing suit. Yet, somehow, its high, French cut and the bunched folds of wool that covered Joanna from ankle to knee managed to draw attention to her legs, especially the long, luscious curves of her thighs. That, in turn, led the eye irresistibly to those gently rounded hips and that tight, delectable derriere.

"Okay, ladies! Shake it out! Shake it out!" the instructor chanted. "Now bend and touch the floor! Bend! Bend! Bend!"

Legs spread and straight, her rump stuck up in the air, Joanna bent over, and with her palms flat on the floor, bounced her torso in time to the music and the instructor's chant.

Sean groaned and tightened his grip on the towel. *Christ, Fleming, don't stand here gawking like a sixteen year old in heat. Leave, for Pete's sake!*

But he didn't. He couldn't. The music pounded hotly and so did the blood in his veins. With each passing second both his excitement and anger grew. He didn't want to be attracted to Joanna, dammit!

He gave a snort of laughter at that. *Want it or not, you sap, you are,* he told himself in utter disgust.

Guiltily, he realized that his recent behavior was the direct result of the unwanted attraction. He'd never been deliberately rude to a woman in his life before, yet for days now he'd been glowering and snapping at Joanna every time she came near him. He'd told himself he was doing it for her own good, that sometimes you had to be cruel to be kind, but that had been pure self-defense. Just as the flimsy excuses he'd used for not becoming Gloria's lover had been pure self-deception.

Lord! This was crazy! Two weeks ago if anyone had told him that he would prefer a willowy, aristocratic girl to an earthy, sensual creature like Gloria he'd have told them they were nuts. But as he watched Joanna's sleek body move to the evocative music it didn't seem strange at all. Like a thoroughbred, she was all subtle curves and elegant lines. In comparison, Gloria's voluptuous figure seemed blowsy and overblown.

"Okay, straighten up! Kick and swing! That's it. Six. Seven. Eight. Good, ladies! Very good! Now we're really gonna move. It's time for a *Tom Jones*!"

The music throbbed on. Following the woman's lead, without missing a beat Joanna spread her legs, stretched her clasped hands above her head and rotated her hips in time to the sensuous rhythm.

Sean's breath hissed in sharply. *Dammit to hell!*

Clenching his jaw, he turned on his heel and stomped out.

From the corner of her eye, Joanna watched him go. Good riddance! she told herself firmly. She was glad he was gone. Sean Fleming could go butt a stump for all she cared.

But deep down Joanna knew that she was just using anger as a shield. Sean's attitude hurt. She hadn't expected him to fall madly in love with her, but neither had she expected him to treat her with such obvious dislike.

A surge of self-pity tightened Joanna's throat. Determinedly, she swallowed hard against the unwanted emotion and threw herself into the dance with renewed zeal.

An hour later, Joanna stood at the rail, watching as the ship glided into the harbor. Color. Serenity. She had always felt they were the two words that best described St. Thomas. The island rose gracefully from the sapphire sea in rolling green mountains. Ringing it like lace trim on the edge of a lady's full skirt were curving white sand beaches. At that distance Joanna couldn't see them, but from previous visits she knew that flowers of infinite variety and hue abounded on those verdant slopes. Ahead, the town of Charlotte Amalie spilled over the foothills and nudged the harbor, its red-roofed white buildings sparkling in the morning sun.

As the ship edged in close to the pier Joanna leaned her elbows on the railing and peered over the side and watched as the men on the dock hustled to secure the lines the seamen tossed out. She had never arrived at the island by ship before, and she was fascinated by the docking procedure.

Her grandfather had had a house on St. John. Occasionally, when she had been much younger, she and her parents had used it as a weekend getaway. Although mostly, Joanna recalled with a touch of sadness, it had been just she and her mother. On those times, though, they had always flown into St. Thomas and taken a boat across to St. John.

While they were lowering the gangway Mary and Charles Wright joined Joanna by the rail. "Isn't it simply beautiful?" the older women declared excitedly. "Oh my, I can hardly wait to get started."

Joanna smiled. "On what? Sightseeing or shopping?"

"Both. We're going to take one of the island tours and when it's over the driver will drop us off in the shopping district."

"Since this is a duty free port Mary feels honor bound to take advantage of the bargains," Charles said in a long suffering tone. "And I'm going along to make sure she doesn't 'save' me too much money."

"Oh, you." Mary gave him a poke in the ribs, but the affectionate sparkle in her eyes belied her reproachful expression. Turning back to Joanna with a smile, she said, "If you're going ashore, we'd be happy to have you join us, my dear."

As little as an hour ago, Joanna would have politely refused Mary's invitation. She had seen the island many times, and since she was fairly certain that Sean would be going ashore, she had thought it best that she stay on board, out of his way. But not now. After their run-in at the gym she'd be darned if she would curtail her movements on his account. Besides, after that strenuous early morning workout and a hot shower, she felt invigorated, eager to be doing something.

"Thank you very much. I'd like that."

Their tour bus turned out to be a stretch limo, which they shared with five other cruise passengers, one of whom was Tony. The driver, a gregarious young man in his midtwenties named Hugo, could easily have earned his living as a comedian. As he took them around the island he kept up a running commentary, an intermingling of history, folklore and local gossip that had everyone laughing.

Bluebeard's Castle was their first stop.

"It's a hotel now," Hugo explained as Joanna and the Wrights stepped out onto the terrace beneath the old stone tower. "But in the old days it was the stronghold of Bluebeard, one of the pirates that operated in the Caribbean. This is also where he brought his wives. No one is certain just how many he had, but it's said he murdered all of them." Hugo flashed a toothy grin. "Now the Castle is a favorite place for honeymooners."

Joanna looked up at the round stone tower and shivered.

Much of its rough surface was covered with ancient vines whose stems were as thick and woody as small trees. Among them scurried huge lizards, anywhere from nine to eighteen inches long. The feel of age and history about the place was intriguing, but it definitely was not her idea of a romantic honeymoon retreat.

"Brrrrr. How gruesome. Can you imagine?" Mary shuddered delicately and urged Joanna away from the tower. When they reached the low wall at the edge of the terrace her face brightened. "Well now, I'll say one thing for the old pirate. He may have been hell on women, but he sure knew how to pick a view."

Joanna laughed. "Somehow I doubt that was his prime reason for building on this particular spot."

"You're right," Tony concurred, as he and Charles joined them. "It wasn't the aesthetic appeal so much as military strategy that prompted Bluebeard to choose this spot. From here he could see any ship long before it entered the bay and blast it out of the water once it did."

The majestic three-hundred-year-old structure overlooked the harbor and the red rooftops of Charlotte Amalie. From where they stood they could see two white cruise ships docked at the pier, and another one, too large to enter the harbor, anchored just beyond the bay.

Joanna ran her fingertips over the cool surface of the ancient cannon embedded in the wall and gazed down at the blue waters. The island was peaceful and serene now, but she had no trouble imagining it as it had been all those centuries ago when pirates had ruled that part of the world.

"Say, isn't that Sean over there?" Charles said, craning his neck to see around a group of people.

Stiffening, Joanna turned slowly, but it took her a few minutes to spot Sean in the milling crowd that filled the terrace. He was with a group of people making their way toward the exit. Clinging possessively to his arm was Gloria.

When he didn't even glance in her direction, Joanna told herself that he hadn't seen her, but just before disappearing from view, Sean turned his head and looked straight into her eyes. Tilting her chin, Joanna stared right back.

The contact lasted only a second, then Sean stepped into the shadowed archway and disappeared from sight. Joanna looked back at the sapphire ocean. A mixed feeling of triumph and sadness gripped her, causing a tight ache just beneath her breastbone.

From Bluebeard's Castle Hugo took them to Drake's Seat. The lookout point high in the mountains offered a panoramic view of Magen's Bay, and as Joanna and her group climbed from the limo to view it, Sean and Gloria returned to their cab and drove away. It was then that Joanna realized they were following the same route.

Well, it could have been worse, she told herself philosophically. We could have been in the same tour group.

It was the same story at Coral World. The moment Joanna reached the bottom of the circular stairway she spotted Sean and Gloria on the other side of the undersea observation tower.

With Tony, Joanna wandered slowly from window to window and gazed out at the fantastic view of the ocean's floor. Sunlight streamed down from above, illuminating the crystal waters with a green glow. Starfish lay on the sandy bottom among the waving vegetation and goggled-eyed fish swam lazily by. At one window Joanna's heart leaped when she spotted the ghostly flutter of a stingray's wings. Even though several inches of glass separated them, she shuddered when the menacing looking creature came within inches of the window, gliding silently through the water, a restless predator in search of a victim.

A part of Joanna was fascinated and amazed by the clarity of the ocean, the myriad shapes and colors and types of underwater creatures, the grace and beauty of the plant life. But another part of her, the part she kept tucked away behind a façade of determined cheerfulness, was still smarting from her run-in with Sean.

Joanna told herself that jealousy had nothing to do with the way she felt. And for a while she almost convinced herself that it was true. But later that afternoon, when she walked into a jewelry store in the shopping district, she knew she'd been kidding herself.

Sean was just pocketing his wallet, and beside him, Gloria was admiring the gold bracelet on her raised arm.

"Oh, darling, it's beautiful," she gushed. Lifting up on tiptoes, she kissed his cheek. "Thank you so much for buying it for me."

Pain twisted in Joanna's chest. It's none of your business, she told herself. Sean is free to do whatever he wants, with whomever he wants.

Yet that knowledge did nothing to banish the feelings that were ripping away at her. Logical or not, the plain truth was—it hurt to see him with another woman. But hell would freeze over before she'd let Sean know that, and when he looked up and saw her watching them Joanna managed to hide her anguish behind a look of scorn.

To her surprise, for an instant Sean looked embarrassed, but then that easy nonchalance slipped back in place and his heavy-lidded black eyes met hers impassively.

Turning aside, Joanna gave Tony a bright smile and looped her arm through his. "Come on. Let's browse. I want to get something for my mother before we go back to the ship."

Tony grinned down at her, delighted by her sudden show of friendliness. "Blow in my ear, and I'll follow you anywhere, gorgeous," he murmured. "The North Pole. Darkest Africa. The moon." He paused a beat, then added hopefully, "Your cabin. Mine."

Joanna gave him a droll look. "The earring counter will do for now," she said repressively.

"And later?"

"Not a chance."

"Heck! I was afraid you'd say that."

Laughing at his woebegone expression, Joanna led him toward the back of the store.

Why do you still let it bother you? she thought despairingly. *You should have been over Sean long ago. By now you should be able to laugh at his little entanglements.* Joanna smiled woodenly at something Tony said and pretended to study the tray of opal earrings. *It's not fair. It's simply not fair. Infatuations aren't supposed to last this long.*

Three hours later, Joanna watched from her suite as the ship pulled away from the harbor. Slowly, inexorably, the lush green island receded, becoming smaller and smaller. When it was nothing more than a tiny dot on the horizon, Joanna sighed and turned away from the window. She dropped down onto the sofa and picked up the novel that lay open on the coffee table, but after scanning only half a page she put it down. With a sigh, Joanna stood and walked aimlessly around the room. She felt tired, but strangely restless. She needed to be doing something.

Of course, you could join the Wrights and Tony for a drink in the lounge, she reminded herself. They had invited her when they returned to the ship a half hour ago, but, pleading tiredness, Joanna had retreated to her suite.

After buying the opal and diamond earrings for her mother and a bottle of fine brandy for Matt, she had spent several hours with the three of them, browsing among the shops along the main street and those tucked away in the lush, gardenlike alleys in Charlotte Amalie's shopping district. They were nice people and Joanna liked them, but she'd had enough of their company for a while.

But still, she had to do something. Something physical. Something that required concentration. *Something that would take her mind off Sean and his redhead.*

Joanna walked back to the coffee table and picked up the printed sheet that listed the day's activities. After checking her watch, she ran a fingernail down the time column to four o'clock, and read through the choices available. "Bridge lessons, silk flower making, shuffleboard, astrology lessons, trapshooting, bingo..." Joanna's eyes backtracked. *Trapshooting!*

Her face brightened. "Perfect."

Joanna dropped the list back onto the coffee table and started eagerly for the door.

Trapshooting was done off the starboard side of the sun deck, near the stern. When Joanna arrived the ship's second mate, Mr. Ricci, and one of the crewmen were setting up the target thrower.

Joanna looked around, surprised to find she was the only passenger there. "Do you have to sign up for this in advance," she asked the officer, "or may I shoot now?"

"You may start just as soon as we get set up," he replied politely. "So far, you're the only one interested. I think everyone is tired from spending the day ashore."

When the crewman had the thrower ready Joanna paid her money and took her position by the rail.

"Have you ever fired a shotgun before?" Mr. Ricci asked, slipping two shells into the gun's magazine.

"Yes." Joanna bit back a smile. He was trying to be polite, but she could sense his uncertainty.

"Very well. You'll have eight shots altogether, two per gun. When you're ready you call 'pull' and crewman Belso will fire the thrower. While you're firing I'll load another gun for you, and after the second shot we'll trade. Are there any questions?"

"No, I understand."

Mr. Ricci worked the pump to feed a shell into the chamber and handed the shotgun to Joanna. She hefted it experimentally. Shouldering the gun, she sighted down the vent rib, testing for balance and fit. It was a plain-Jane model, but it wasn't at all barrel heavy, and it pointed perfectly. Satisfied, Joanna lowered the gun and turned to tell the officer she was ready—and froze when she saw Sean standing beside him, watching her.

"What are you doing here?" she blurted out angrily before she could stop herself.

"I came to shoot trap, the same as you."

"Since you and Mr. Fleming seem to be the only ones interested this afternoon, I suggest that you alternate shooting," Mr. Ricci put in. "A bit of friendly competition usually sharpens skills, I find."

Leaning a hip against the rail, Sean folded his arms over his chest and looked amused. "Suits me."

It had been on the tip of Joanna's tongue to refuse, but one look at Sean's face changed that. She tilted her chin defiantly and studied his complacent expression through narrowed eyes. "I'm game if Mr. Fleming is," she said finally.

"By all means." His smile deepening, Sean gestured for her to start. "Ladies first."

Joanna adjusted her stance and shouldered the shotgun. "Pull!"

The clay target sailed out from the ship, rising toward the bow. Sighting down the vent rib, Joanna swung the muzzle of the gun in a sweeping arc along the same path and pulled the trigger as the bead on the end of the barrel passed over the target. It exploded into dust at the same instant the gun recoiled against Joanna's shoulder. She pumped the gun and the empty shell ejected to the side. "Pull!"

This time the clay disc flew out at an angle to the stern, caught a down draft and began to drop rapidly, but Joanna powdered it just before it hit the foaming wake.

She exchanged the empty gun for a full one, and without hesitation, shouldered it and called for another bird. In rapid succession, Joanna demolished the remaining six targets, clipping two and powdering the rest.

As the eighth disintegrated, she turned and calmly handed the shotgun to Mr. Ricci. Then she looked at Sean.

The smug amusement was gone from his expression. He stared at her, one brow cocked in faint surprise. Finally he dipped his head in acknowledgement and smiled wryly. ''Good shooting.''

''I'll say!'' Mr. Ricci chimed in. ''That was great!'' He turned and grinned at Sean. ''Looks like you've got your work cut out for you, Mr. Fleming.''

Trying not to smile, Joanna stepped back and relinquished her place to Sean. As Joanna had done, for a moment he tested the gun for balance and fit, then shouldered it and called out, ''Pull!''

With deadly accuracy, Sean proceeded to blast target after target, and with each hit Joanna's spirits dropped. By the time the eighth clay pigeon disappeared in a pool of smoke, she had gone from euphoric to grimly determined.

Handing the shotgun to the officer, Sean turned to her with a maddeningly polite smile and said, ''Your turn, I think.''

It was a direct challenge, one Joanna was more than willing to accept. Bruised feelings and a day of emotional turmoil had her nerves strung fine, and she was spoiling for a fight of some kind. For the moment, a contest of skill would do. Returning his smile with cool assurance, she stepped back into the firing position. As she accepted the shotgun she said offhandedly, ''Let's make this round doubles, shall we? Just to make it interesting.''

Crewman Belso emitted a low whistle as Mr. Ricci shot Sean an inquiring glance. ''Very well. Doubles it is,'' he said when Sean nodded his agreement.

Concentrate, Joanna instructed herself, fitting the gun's recoil pad against her shoulder. *Just keep your eye on the target and stay calm. Don't rush.*

"Pull!"

Two birds sailed out over the water, one high and toward the bow, the other straight out from the side in a
steady rise. Joanna swung the gun toward the first, fired,
and a split second after it shattered, she pumped the action,
and in a continuous motion, swung back to the right and
picked off the second.

"Terrific!" Both the second mate and crewman called
out in unison. Joanna let out her breath and felt some of
the tension drain out of her. She traded guns and forced
herself to concentrate.

Her soft voice, the shotgun blast, the metallic click and
glide of the gun's precision action—for a while they were
the only sounds. Steadily, repeatedly, Joanna called the
terse, one-word command, fired, pumped the shotgun and
fired again. When finished, she had hit fifteen of the sixteen targets.

It was not as good as she had hoped for and certainly
not the best round she had ever shot, but it wasn't bad.
When she turned to Sean her eyes issued a silent challenge.
Top that, if you can.

Very quickly, it began to appear that he could. Joanna
stood gripping the rail, her face calm as she watched Sean
hit the first six targets without a bobble, but inside she was
mentally kicking herself. *Oh, Joanna, you fool. You
shouldn't have missed that last bird. And you wouldn't
have if you hadn't gotten overconfident.*

The next two birds sailed out over the water in opposite
directions, low and dropping fast. Sean got one, but the
other splashed into the ocean just as he fired the second
shot. Joanna had to bite her bottom lip to keep from cheering aloud.

The momentary exhilaration faded quickly though as he
proceeded to powder the next six. Joanna didn't question
why winning was so important to her. She only knew that

it was. Tightening her fingers around the rail, she held her breath when Sean called for the last two birds.

He fired twice. The first clay disc shattered; the other whirled away and dropped into the ocean.

Stunned, for a moment Joanna couldn't believe it. Then a feeling of fierce satisfaction exploded inside her. She managed, just barely, to resist the urge to kick up her heels and whoop, but there was no hiding the triumph in her eyes when she turned to face Sean.

She had expected anger. Instead Sean flashed his devilish smile and looked her over in that lazily curious way of his. "Congratulations. Where the hell did you learn to shoot like that?"

"My father used to love to shoot trap and skeet. He taught me." She gave him a saccharine smile. "One of the advantages of being a spoiled rich brat."

Sean stared at her thoughtfully, but if he detected the wounded pride behind the challenging little barb, he said nothing. "How about a rematch?"

"Sorry. It's getting late, and I promised Tony I'd meet him for a drink before dinner." She started to leave, but Sean stopped her.

"Joanna…about this Tony character. What do you really know about him?"

"What do you mean?"

"Well…you seem to be spending a lot of time with him."

"No more than you are with Gloria," Joanna countered, beginning to feel the first stirrings of anger.

"Maybe. But the difference is, I'm old enough to handle a shipboard romance."

"Oh, I see. And I'm not, is that what you're saying?" Joanna was furious now. She couldn't believe his gall. "Well let me tell you something, Sean Fleming. I'm twenty-two years old, almost twenty-three, and well past the age of consent. So just mind your own business."

Sean watched her stomp away, his brows shooting upward. Bemused, his eyes traveled down her stiff back to the angry sway of her very womanly hips. Almost twenty-three. It wasn't a great age, true, but Joanna was right: she wasn't a child.

Which was exactly how he'd been thinking of her—as Claire's little girl. But Joanna was a young woman. A very attractive, very desirable young woman. Recalling the way her hazel eyes flashed with anger, the determined way she tilted her chin, Sean's mouth quirked up in a lopsided grin. She had her mother's pride and spunk, and that unbending, ladylike dignity he'd always admired.

But she's also mule stubborn and competitive as hell.

Sean discovered, to his surprise, that he found the combination very appealing.

Chapter Six

Sunrise at sea, Joanna decided, was an experience not to be missed. She leaned against the rail and watched the sky lighten from dusky blue, to mauve, to pink pearlescence. She watched the shafts of sunlight shoot out from the horizon, streaking the dark turquoise sea with gold. The world seemed to explode with color and light: silver edged clouds of lavender and crimson, dancing waves spangled with glittering sequins, an orange ball of flame rising against the deepening azure heavens. In the distance, the island of Antigua was a dark speck that grew steadily larger and greener as the ship plowed majestically through the heaving water. Enthralled, Joanna took it all in, mindless of the cool breeze or the salt spray that dewed her skin and gathered in tiny droplets in her hair.

"It's lovely, isn't it?"

Blinking, Joanna turned her head to find Susan leaning on the rail beside her. She smiled and returned her gaze to the sea. "Yes. Yes, it is."

They stood in comfortable silence for a moment, soaking in the beauty of the morning. "I didn't expect to see you up so early," Susan said finally. "When you didn't show up for dinner last night I was worried that maybe you weren't feeling well."

"No, I'm fine. I just decided to have an early night, so I ordered a light dinner in my suite." Actually, it had been the prospect of facing Sean again that had kept Joanna in her cabin, but she wasn't about to admit that to Susan. "How about you? What are you doing up so early?"

"I wanted to get a look at Antigua while Lori was still asleep," Susan sighed. "Since I won't be going ashore, that's about all I can do."

"Oh, but you shouldn't miss Antigua. It has some of the most beautiful beaches in the world."

"I know. But we really can't take Lori. We tried it yesterday in St. Thomas, and she got so fussy after a few hours we were all miserable." Susan gave a fatalistic little shrug and grimaced forlornly. "Bill and I decided to take turns going ashore."

Joanna hesitated a moment, then placed her hand on Susan's arm. "Look, I have a better idea. Why don't I keep Lori while both of you go ashore?"

"Oh, Joanna! We couldn't do that—"

"Of course you can," Joanna insisted, cutting off Susan's flustered protest. "I was planning to stay on board today anyway. Besides, I've seen Antigua. So there's no reason why you shouldn't go. Unless, of course, you're worried about leaving Lori with me."

"Oh, no! I'm sure—"

"Good. Then that settles it. I'll have a quick breakfast on deck, then I'll go find a steward and have a crib set up in my suite. When you're ready to leave just bring Lori to me there." Before Susan could object further, Joanna hurried away.

* * *

An hour and a half later Bill and Susan arrived at Joanna's suite loaded down with two diaper bags full of supplies and babbling their thanks. Interspersed among them was a list of last minute instructions.

Lori whimpered when she realized that her parents were about to leave her, which set off another round of doubts and protestations, but Joanna finally managed to shoo the grateful couple out, with orders that they weren't to return until it was time for the ship to sail.

When the door closed behind them Lori really started to howl. Dismayed, Joanna watched the tiny bottom lip curl pathetically and tears spill from the big blue eyes, and for the first time she began to wonder if maybe she hadn't been just a bit hasty.

"Now, now sweetheart, don't cry," she crooned. "Your mommy and daddy will be back. And you and I are going to have a wonderful day together, you'll see."

Lori's cries rose two decibels. Joanna paced the floor and bounced the child on her arm. "Come on, sweetheart. Don't cry. Please don't cry. Look! Here's one of your play pretties." She grabbed a stuffed toy from the top of one of the bags and shook it in front of Lori's face. "See, Lori? See? Isn't this nice?" Joanna squeezed the terry cloth rabbit, and it made a shrill little squeak. Lori looked away and shrieked.

The child's nose ran profusely, and her cheeks were slick with tears. As her cries took on a hysterical note her face turned a brilliant shade, somewhere between red and purple.

"Oh, baby, please, don't do that. Please don't cry."

Joanna may as well have been talking to the wall, for all the good her pleas did. She made a desperate sound in her throat and bounced harder.

Could she hurt herself, crying like that? Joanna wondered frantically. It seemed likely. At the very least she was going to make herself sick if she kept it up. *Oh, you idiot! Why on earth did you offer to baby-sit? What you know about babies would fit into a thimble, for Pete's sake.* Lori screamed harder, right in Joanna's ear. She winced and sent up a silent prayer and continued to pace.

It took a moment for the sound to penetrate Lori's shrieks but finally Joanna realized that someone was knocking on the door. She rushed to open it, reacting to the summons like a drowning man who had been thrown a lifeline. To her it meant only one thing: help had arrived.

Her hopeful expression turned to dismay when she threw open the door. "What are you doing here?" she demanded.

Ignoring her question, Sean plucked Lori from her arms, stepped inside, forcing Joanna to take a hasty step backward, and closed the door behind him. "Hey, cutie. What's all the noise about, huh? If you don't knock it off they're gonna put us off the ship, did you know that?" He hoisted the baby in the crook of his arm and tickled her tummy with his other hand. Lori's cries quietened to sharp little snubs, and she stared at him solemnly with wide, tear-drenched eyes.

"That's my girl. You don't really want to be making all that racket, do you, sweetheart?" Very gently, Sean brushed the tears from her cheeks, and to Joanna's astonishment, Lori let out a shuddering sigh, stuck her thumb in her mouth, and laid her head on his shoulder, as docile as a lamb.

"How did you do that?" Joanna demanded, wide-eyed.

Sean absently massaged the baby's back, his big hand covering her from shoulder to waist. He fixed his intent gaze on Joanna, and once more ignored her question. "The Adamsons told us at breakfast that you'd volunteered to keep Lori today. I thought maybe I'd better give you a hand."

She bristled instantly, forgetting her desperation of only

a moment ago. "And just what makes you think I need help?"

"Have you had any experience with babies?"

Joanna hesitated, some of the fire going out of her. "Well, no," she admitted reluctantly. The look she gave him was part disparaging, part hopeful. "And you have, I suppose."

"I have four brothers and three sisters, all of whom are married and have large and growing families. At last count I have twenty-one nieces and nephews between the ages of two months and eighteen years," he stated calmly as he moved past her to investigate the contents of one of the bags. "I learned to pin on a diaper before I was seven."

Joanna watched him with something akin to awe as he held the limp baby on his shoulder and plucked a disposable diaper and a canister of premoistened wipes from the bag. Eight? He was one of eight children? The very thought was mind-boggling. As an only child, she couldn't even conceive of growing up in a family that size.

"Which, I'd say, is the first order of business now," Sean continued. "Part of Lori's problem is she's uncomfortable." Sitting sideways on the sofa, he laid the baby on the cushion next to him. He gave her tummy another tickle, and Lori kicked her legs and gurgled. "All that crying turned on the waterworks in more ways than one, didn't it cutie?"

With a nonchalance and expertise Joanna couldn't help but admire, within a matter of minutes, Sean had the baby stripped of the sodden diaper, cleaned and swaddled in a fresh one, and her ruffled sunsuit resnapped.

"There now, how does that feel, little one?" he said as he picked up the docile child and turned to Joanna.

Amusement twinkled in his eyes when he met her astonished stare and the corners of his mouth twitched suspiciously. "There are three things you've got to remember when taking care of babies," he drawled with just the slightest hint of superiority in his voice. "Keep 'em dry, keep 'em fed and keep 'em entertained."

Joanna sighed. "The first two I can manage. I think. But how do I do the third?"

"Go get your swimsuit on. We'll take her to the pool. Afterward we'll give her a bath and feed her. By the time we're through she should be ready for a nap."

Joanna hesitated. Accepting the plan meant accepting Sean's help, which would mean spending the day in his company. It was an appealing idea, and very tempting, but every self-protective instinct she possessed warned against it. It would be far better if she could stay angry with him, keep him at a distance. This attraction she felt for Sean was hopeless and idiotic, and the only way she was ever going to get over it was to stay away from him. It was foolish and self-destructive to even consider his offer.

Still, she reminded herself, the alternative was to cope on her own. The memory of Lori's inconsolable crying jag flashed through her mind and sent panic skittering up her spine.

Within minutes Joanna was in her bedroom, rummaging through the dresser for a swimsuit.

When she walked back into the sitting room a short while later wearing a yellow maillot and her white lace cover-up Sean's black eyes narrowed and flickered slowly over her. Joanna shifted restlessly under the silent scrutiny. "I, uh...I'm ready," she said needlessly.

Sean didn't hurry his inspection. The lacy top did little to obstruct his view, and his gaze slid down over her breasts and hips and the long curving length of her legs to her sandaled feet. Just as slowly, just as intently, he retraced the path. When their eyes met he smiled and tipped his head, rolling slowly to his feet.

"Why don't you gather the towels we'll need and slap a coat of sunscreen on Lori while I go change into my suit."

Lori was sitting on the floor, playing contentedly with a ring of plastic keys, but when Sean stood she looked up and grinned, flashing four tiny white teeth and crinkling her button nose. He bent and chucked her under her chin. "Behave yourself while I'm gone, princess."

Lori gurgled and shook the keys violently, whacking the floor and her chubby legs.

When he left she gave a little whine of protest. Joanna's troubled gaze went from the closed door to the wide-eyed infant, and she smiled sadly. "I know, sweetheart. He's devastating, isn't he. Even to females of your tender age."

Joanna was tense and jumpy when Sean returned, a condition that wasn't helped by the fact that he wore only a pair of rubber thongs and a tiny wine-red bathing suit that left little doubt of his masculinity. To Joanna's acute embarrassment and horror, she had difficulty keeping her eyes off his broad chest and lean, muscle-ridged belly.

With a short, "Here, you carry her," she thrust Lori into his arms, snatched up her beach bag and hustled them out the door. All the way to the pool she gritted her teeth and kept her gaze determinedly averted. Even so, from the corner of her eye, she could see his long muscular legs striding along beside her, feel the warmth that radiated from him, and she silently cursed and ground her teeth.

As soon as they arrived at the pool Joanna sat down on the end of a lounge to smooth on sunscreen. When she had finished with her legs and arms and reached around to apply the lotion to her back, Sean plopped Lori in her lap and took the bottle out of her hand.

"Here, I'll do that," he said, sitting down behind her.

The feel of his hands on her back was so shockingly pleasurable Joanna caught her breath. His palms were slightly rough and very warm. They moved over her skin in a slow, smooth glide, his fingers massaging lightly, sending shivers of delight skittering through her, making her heart race crazily. Joanna was drowning in sensations, awash with sheer bliss.

Closing her eyes, Joanna tilted her head forward until her chin rested against the wisp of blond curls at Lori's crown. She felt as though every bone in her body were dissolving. The coconut scent of the tanning lotion swirled around her, mixing with the smells of sweet baby and healthy, virile male. Vaguely, she heard the lap of the water, the hum of voices and occasional bursts of laughter, the vibrating tones of the steel drum band playing in the distance. The gentle heat of the Caribbean sun poured over her, but it was the tender abrasion of those hands on her back that made her burn.

How many times had she dreamed of Sean touching her like this? Dreamed of being with him, being the recipient of those warm looks and murmured endearments? With only a word, a glance from those dark drowsy eyes, a simple touch, Sean could make a woman feel special, cherished. It was heaven to relax and savor the feel of his hands smoothing over her back.

But the dreamy pleasure lasted only a moment before she remembered that he had performed the same service for Gloria, and with just as much care. And that the woman's face had reflected the exact emotions Joanna was feeling now.

Pain, jealousy and anger ripped through her, and she jerked away from his hands and stood up. ''Thank you, but that wasn't really necessary. I'm perfectly capable of applying tanning lotion myself,'' she said in a sharp voice.

As she walked to the edge of the pool she felt Sean's eyes on her back but she didn't turn around. Holding the child against her chest, Joanna stepped off into the shallow end.

After a moment Sean joined them, and soon, thanks to Lori's boisterous antics, the awkwardness passed.

They splashed and laughed and cavorted with the baby

for a couple of hours. Now and then they bumped into each other, or Sean would casually touch her shoulder or the small of her back as they stood close together playing with Lori. Every time, the casual contact stole Joanna's breath away, but Sean didn't seem at all affected. Disgusted, she told herself to stop acting like an idiot and kept up a determinedly blasé front. Once, when he took the baby from her, his hand accidentally brushed her breast, and Joanna felt briefly as though her whole body had burst into flame. She was appalled by the reaction but helpless to do anything about it.

Ambivalent feelings tore at Joanna. A part of her treasured this rare time of closeness with Sean and wanted it to go on and on, while another part of her longed for the sensual torment to end. That it could get worse didn't occur to her until Sean announced that it was time to get Lori out of the sun, and they headed back to Joanna's suite.

"While you bathe our gal I'll get her lunch ready," Sean said the moment they stepped through the door. He went straight to the two diaper bags and began to rummage through them. "It'll probably be easiest and quickest if you just take her into the shower with you," he added over his shoulder, pulling out a warming dish and two small jars of food.

Joanna stared at the rippling muscles in Sean's back as he leaned over the small dining table and used the curved baby spoon to scoop the contents of the jars into the dish. "A shower?" she said in a small, strained voice. She hadn't planned on that. The very idea of taking a shower while Sean occupied her sitting room, wearing nothing but a tiny strip of cloth, conjured up unsettling, wildly erotic— and admittedly exciting—images in her mind, which in turn brought a tide of color surging into her face.

But what choice did she have? It hadn't occurred to her before, but she doubted that she could bathe the baby in that tiny sink. Joanna cleared her throat and, holding Lori tightly against her chest, picked up one of the bags and began to back toward the bedroom. "Uh...yes. Okay, I, uh...I'll go do that."

The next half hour proved to be so difficult and so frantic Joanna found she didn't have time for erotic thoughts. Holding a slick, squirming little body while struggling to get both of them scrubbed, shampooed and rinsed, with only the use of one hand, was an almost impossible feat, and several times Joanna wondered suspiciously if Sean had known that when he'd made the suggestion. Holding onto Lori was like trying to hold a watermelon seed with greased fingers; Joanna was terrified that any moment the baby would squirt right out of her grasp. But finally, after much gnashing of teeth and contorting, the job was done. When Joanna emerged from the bedroom carrying her small charge on her hip, they were both dressed in loose sun shifts and smelling of baby powder.

Joanna stepped into the sitting room and looked cautiously around, only to discover that it was empty. She stood in the middle of the room, her face registering surprise, feeling both relieved and absurdly disappointed. "Obviously, he's decided he's helped enough," she muttered under her breath as she stalked over to the dining table.

The nauseating mess in Lori's dish was warm. Beside it was a bib, a wet washcloth and a baby bottle filled with milk. At the sight of the food Lori set up a demanding babble and began to bounce excitedly in Joanna's arms. "Well, sweetie, it looks like lunch is ready to be served," Joanna murmured as she set the baby in a chair and struggled to snap the bib around her neck.

Joanna felt guilty feeding such awful looking stuff to the child, but Lori ate it hungrily, at least, that portion that didn't end up on the bib or smeared all over her face. Every so often she would turn her head away and refuse the bite Joanna offered, then stretch her chubby arms out toward the bottle and demand a drink.

They were almost through with the meal when there was a light tap on the door. Before Joanna could respond, it was pushed open and Sean stepped inside. "Hi. I see you're managing all right."

At the sound of his voice Lori jerked her head around, and the bite Joanna was giving her smeared from the corner of her mouth to her ear. "Oh, just terrific," Joanna said in an aggrieved tone as she grabbed for the washcloth. "It would have helped though if you had waited until we were through to make your entrance."

Sean wore faded jeans, a red short sleeved cotton shirt and sneakers. His black hair was slicked into place, but it was still wet from his shower, and a heavy curl tumbled across his forehead as he sauntered toward them. His darkly tanned skin bore just a touch of color from its recent exposure to the sun, and as he drew near, Joanna caught a whiff of soap and woodsy cologne, and clean male. Suddenly it was difficult to breathe.

Sean hunkered down beside Lori's chair. "Hey, cutie, you're supposed to eat your food, not wear it," he said, tickling the sole of her bare foot. With a squeal, Lori curled her toes and gave his face an enthusiastic pat.

It was a struggle, but Joanna managed to shovel the last few bites into the child's mouth. Lori polished off the rest of the milk, and when Joanna had wiped her face clean Sean reached for her. "I'll go put her down for her nap while you take care of the dishes."

She wanted to tell him that he needn't bother, that she'd put Lori to bed. And if she'd had any idea how to manage it, she would have.

Joanna stared after him as he crossed the room and disappeared into the bedroom, feeling her heart pound and her chest tighten. This was crazy. Sean excited her without even trying. Being around him like this was definitely not a good idea. If he didn't leave soon she was going to wind up making a complete and utter fool of herself.

Wearily, Joanna picked up the dish and bottle and carried them into the bathroom. When she emerged a few minutes later Sean was bending over the crib, gently patting Lori's back and, foolishly, the sight made her heart contract. She tiptoed out to the sitting room, sat down on the sofa and wondered what in the world she was going to do.

A few minutes later Sean crept out of the bedroom and eased the door closed behind him. He plopped down beside Joanna, and with a sigh, leaned his head against the sofa back and stretched his long legs out in front of him. Joanna's insides began to quiver wildly.

After a while Sean rolled his head to the side and smiled that heart stopping smile of his. "I never realized before what an impulsive creature you are. What on earth possessed you to volunteer to keep the Adamsons' daughter?"

Joanna shrugged her shoulders. "It seemed like the thing to do at the time. It's only for a few hours, and Bill and Susan really need the time alone together."

"So what happens tomorrow? You can't baby-sit everyday. Even if you were willing, I'm sure they wouldn't allow it."

"I know. But I've made arrangements that will solve the problem."

"What kind of arrangements?"

"Well…I talked to the Captain this morning. His family is sailing with him this summer, and his sixteen-year-old daughter has volunteered to sit with Lori for the remainder of the cruise. In fact, she's anxious to."

"Volunteered?" Sean cocked a skeptical brow, then narrowed his eyes. "You're paying her, aren't you?"

A guilty flush crept up Joanna's neck. "Well…yes, I am," she admitted reluctantly. "But that's just between Maria and me. The Adamsons need never know. Maria's going to come by our table tonight and beg them to let her keep Lori while they visit the islands.'' At Sean's admonishing look Joanna tilted her chin. ''I know I'm interfering, but where's the harm? Susan and Bill can enjoy their second honeymoon, and Maria is delighted to be earning some extra money. And I can certainly afford to pay for a few hours of baby-sitting.''

After a moment Sean's stern look faded and his eyes grew warm. ''That was a very nice thing to do, Joanna.'' His voice was deep and soft, caressing her like warm velvet, making her skin tingle deliciously. ''And it was very nice of you to keep Lori today.''

''No, actually I was being selfish.'' Joanna glanced at Sean and her mouth twisted wryly. ''I needed the practice, since I'm going to have a new baby brother or sister in about six weeks or so.''

Sean studied her intently, then sat up straight and turned sideways on the sofa. Stretching his arm out along the back, he played idly with the spaghetti strap on her white terry cloth sun shift. ''You're really pleased over this baby, aren't you?''

''Yes. Yes, I am.'' The smile that tilted Joanna's mouth was soft and dreamy, full of pleasure. ''Matt adores my mother, and she him. It seems only right that a love like that should produce a child. And besides, it's what they both want.''

''And what do you want, Joanna?'' Sean asked softly, running his forefinger up the gentle slope of her shoulder to her neck.

A shiver rippled along Joanna's skin. She swallowed hard. Turning her head, she looked at him with wide, dazed eyes. ''Wh—what do you mean?''

''I mean you've changed. The Joanna I knew four years ago never had a thought for anyone but herself. It would never have occurred to her to help out a young couple, to saddle herself with a rambunctious child just so they could enjoy themselves for a few hours. Or to be gracious and attentive to a sweet old couple like the Wrights.'' His fingers trailed fire over her skin and caused goose bumps to spring up all over her as they moved up the side of her neck and tugged gently at her lobe. Joanna could barely concentrate on his words. ''And my guess is,'' he continued in an even softer voice, ''that Joanna would have been resentful, possibly even outraged by her middle-aged mother having a baby.''

Joanna tilted her head, trying to evade those tormenting fingers. Lord! Didn't he know what his touch did to her? ''We...we all grow up eventually.''

''True. But you've done it so beautifully.'' His fingers slipped from her ear into the thick, still damp hair at the back of her head. With his other hand he cupped her chin and drew her face around. She found herself staring into his dark eyes, and her heart began to flutter wildly at what she saw there. ''So very beautifully,'' he murmured huskily as his gaze dropped to her mouth, and his head began its slow, purposeful descent.

Joanna thought she was going to faint. Her heart was chugging like a runaway train. When his lips settled softly over hers its speed almost doubled. Her eyes fluttered shut and her breathing stopped completely. Every cell, every molecule in her body tingled with vibrant awareness, almost unbearable excitement. She was afraid that at any second her whole system would go on overload.

The kiss was warm, tender, tentative. His lips caressed hers with a gentleness that was devastating. Rocking slowly back and forth. Nibbling. Rubbing. Joanna sat there motionless, her insides aquiver, her chest tightening with a sweet, sweet ache.

He nipped her lower lip with gentle savagery, and her inner quakes became an ecstatic shudder she couldn't hide. Immediately the kiss grew bolder.

Seeking became hungry demand as his lips grew firmer

and his tongue probed the soft barrier of her lips. Without thought of denial, Joanna opened her mouth to grant him entrance and sighed helplessly as he tasted the honeyed sweetness with deep, evocative thrusts.

The hand that cradled the back of her head tightened. Grasping her hip with his other hand, Sean rolled her toward him, bringing her closer. The heat of their bodies combined, and the mingled scents of woodsy cologne and baby talc rose between them.

Joanna was almost afraid that she was dreaming. Only this was so much more wonderful than any of her dreams. Years ago she had spent hours trying to imagine Sean kissing her with tenderness and passion, how it would feel to be held in his arms, but now all those foolish fantasies faded into nothingness. They had been paltry, insubstantial things that had not even come close to the exquisite pleasure of reality.

As Sean's mouth rocked hungrily over hers the hand at her hip slid around and cupped her buttocks, squeezing the firm flesh while pressing her even closer. One of Joanna's hands clutched at his shirt front, the other crept up over his chest to his neck, and her fingertips tentatively stroked the side of his jaw.

Sean's mouth left hers, and Joanna's head tilted back as he trailed a line of kisses along her jaw and down the side of her neck. "Oh, Joanna. Joanna. You're so sweet. So very sweet." His warm breath dewed her skin as he murmured the words in a voice that was husky with passion. He nipped her lobe, then his tongue bathed away the tiny pleasurable pain and moved on to trace the graceful swirls of her ear.

Joanna shuddered, then drew in a deep breath. With it came a measure of reality and caution. This was wonderful, sheer heaven, but the tiny kernel of fear deep inside her would not let her ignore the danger. Very gently, she pushed at his chest. "Wh—what are you doing, Sean?" she finally managed breathlessly.

She felt him smile against her neck. "I would think that's obvious."

"Don't toy with me, Sean. Please."

He grew still, and slowly, he pulled back far enough to look at her. Her lips were slightly puffy and rosy, her face flushed, but the glaze of passion was fading from her troubled eyes. He remained silent, but Joanna knew by his expression that he understood.

"I...I'm very attracted to you, Sean. But...well...you could hurt me very badly. You must know that."

Sean released her completely, and Joanna sat up straight and stared at her hands, twisting them together in her lap. Feeling like a fool, she chewed at her inner lip, but after a moment she looked back at him. "Things could never be just casual between us, we both know that. There's your friendship with my parents. And your career. Plus I'm not...that is...I don't..."

Sean put his hand over hers, stopping their frantic writhing. "I understand, Joanna," he said with a tender smile that somehow made her spirits sink even lower. "And you're right. I shouldn't have kissed you. I, uh...I guess I just got carried away for a moment there."

He gave her hands a squeeze, then stood up and wandered aimlessly around the room, his fingertips stuck in the back pockets of his jeans. Feeling wretched, Joanna watched him, and when he paused and gave her a determinedly friendly smile she tensed, knowing what was coming but dreading it all the same.

"Look, I'm sure you can manage fine now on your own. Lori will probably sleep for two or three hours, and by then her folks will be back. So I think I'll go up on deck. I may even go ashore for a while."

Joanna stood up and mustered a smile. "Of course. Go right ahead. I shouldn't have any problems." When he reached the door she added in a stiff little voice, "And thank you, Sean, for all your help. I really appreciate it."

With his hand grasping the door handle, he paused and looked back at her. "Are you all right?" he asked with soft concern.

"Of course. I'm fine."

Her determinedly bright smile faded with the click of the door. She stared at it for several long seconds, and fought against the urge to cry. Why had she been so damned honest? Why couldn't she have just taken what he'd offered? At least she would have had something. A few memories.

But even as her mind voiced the protest, Joanna knew, despite the pain, that she had done the right thing, the only thing for her. She simply wasn't the kind who could survive on memories.

Grim faced, Sean strode down the companionway, silently cursing himself. *Of all the stupid, reckless things to do! God, Fleming! All right! So she's lovely and you're attracted. That's no reason to lose your head. Hell, you're a thirty-six-year-old man who ought to know better, not some randy teenager. What the hell's the matter with you, you stupid ass?*

With angry motions, Sean unlocked his cabin door, stepped inside and slammed it behind him. He paced the confines of the small room like a caged tiger and called himself ten kinds of fool. But what really bothered him, what made him feel like a thorough bastard, was the fact that it had been Joanna who had had the sense to call a halt. "You were too aroused to even realize you were about to step off a cliff," he spat out in a scathing voice.

What he felt for Joanna was more than just lust, and deep down, Sean knew it, but instinctively he shied away from the thought.

He knew that Joanna had been right: a casual affair between them would never work. And he certainly didn't want to hurt her. Even if he were ready for a permanent relationship—and that was something he wasn't at all sure about—he was too old for Joanna.

But straight talk and common sense helped little. Desire still clawed at his gut. Not for just any woman, but for a willowy, hazel-eyed beauty, a young girl he knew he had no business wanting.

Chapter Seven

Joanna entered the dining room with her head held high and a sick sensation in the pit of her stomach. She paused just inside the door to look across the room at her table, and the feeling grew worse. The others were already there, including Sean.

The temptation to return to her suite was strong, but she gritted her teeth and battled it down. She refused, absolutely refused, to play the coward two nights in a row.

Clutching her small evening bag in a death grip, Joanna drew a deep breath and started across the room.

As she approached the table the others were busy either talking or studying their menus, and Joanna slipped into her chair almost before anyone spotted her. "Good evening, everyone. Sorry I'm late." Smiling, she glanced around the table, being careful to avoid Sean's gaze.

"Joanna, my dear, there you are," Mary greeted warmly. "We were beginning to wonder if you were going to join us tonight."

"Yes, we certainly were," Susan chimed in. "In fact, Bill and I were beginning to worry that maybe Lori had worn you out."

"Oh, no. Lori was no trouble at all." Involuntarily Joanna's glance found Sean, and her pulse fluttered when she discovered him watching her steadily. Quickly, she turned back to Susan. "And anyway, I...uh...I had help. Sean stayed on board and gave me a hand."

"I wondered what happened to you," Gloria said, giving him an arch look. "I searched all over for you this morning. I even went by your room, but you weren't there." Sean frowned, and immediately her voice softened. "I was hoping that we could see Antigua together."

"Sorry." Sean's flat tone dismissed the woman's complaint, and without further explanation he turned his attention back to Joanna.

The Adamsons looked stricken. "Oh, Sean, I'm sorry," Susan wailed. "We didn't mean for you to give up your vacation time to baby-sit our daughter. I feel just terrible."

"Nonsense. I enjoyed it. We both did. Like Joanna said, Lori was an angel." He flashed her his most devastating smile, and Joanna watched Susan melt under its persuasive power.

Quickly, Joanna turned to Mary and asked how she and Charles had liked Antigua, and as hoped, the older woman launched into a detailed description of the tour they had taken, effectively changing the subject.

Though Joanna was tense and uncomfortable, the meal passed without incident. Several times she caught Sean staring at her, but he never spoke to her. Except for a few remarks directed to everyone in general, he talked mostly with Gloria. When she heard him agree to the woman's suggestion that they go dancing after dinner, Joanna kept her eyes on her plate and stoically battled against the ache in her chest, telling herself it didn't matter.

They had reached the after dinner coffee stage and

Joanna was trying to think up an excuse to leave when Tony surprised her by saying, "You know, Joanna, while I was at the beach today one of the passengers said the strangest thing. She wanted to know what you were like, and how it felt, having the daughter of such a famous woman at our table. Before I could ask what she meant her husband told her to mind her own business and dragged her off."

"Of course! That's it!" Mary exclaimed excitedly, clapping her hands together. "I knew your face was familiar. You're Claire Andrews' daughter!"

There was stunned silence, and Joanna cringed inwardly as everyone at the table stared at her. Instinctively, she glanced at Sean for support, but he merely grimaced and gave a fatalistic shrug, his look telling her that she should have expected it.

"Are you? Are you really?" Tony asked, at first with something akin to awe, then with growing excitement.

Joanna hesitated, but after a moment exhaled a small sigh of resignation. "Yes, I am. Only mother is Claire Drummond now."

The admission brought gasps and exclamations, which were quickly followed by a babble of questions. What was it like, having such a beautiful, famous mother? Were she and her mother close? Did Claire miss being actively involved in politics? Was she happy in her new marriage? Pleased about having another child at forty-three? They were the kind of prying questions Joanna had been asked all of her life and she was used to them, but she still found them amazing, and irritating.

Her maternal grandfather had been a powerful U.S. senator. So had her father. Yet it had always been Claire who had fascinated the press and public and been the object of their insatiable curiosity. Never more so than in the past five years since both her husband and father had perished in the crash of their private plane.

It wasn't her mother's fault. Joanna knew that. Early on, her grandfather had recognized what a political asset he had in his only child, and he had deliberately enhanced and promoted that special appeal she seemed to hold for the American people. Claire had grown up in the spotlight, admired, envied, often idolized, and always the object of curiosity and speculation. Sometimes people acted as though she were public property. Claire didn't like it any more than Joanna did, but a lifetime of coping and a more patient personality allowed her to accept the situation with good grace.

With the possible exception of Gloria, Joanna liked her table companions, but as she listened to their barrage of questions she wanted to tell them all to mind their own business. Instead she forced herself to do what her mother would under the circumstances. Smiling stiffly, she answered them as noncommittally and with as much charm and brevity as she could manage.

Sean finally took pity on her and diverted their attention by casually mentioning that he had been Claire's campaign manager during her aborted bid for the Senate.

Relieved, Joanna sent him a grateful look and settled back in her chair, content to let him field their questions. With his glib Irish tongue and easygoing charm, Sean was a master at handling awkward situations and inquisitive crowds. Many times during her mother's campaign Joanna had seen him hold his own with a whole room full of aggressive reporters.

"Well, I think this is just marvelous," Mary gushed. "I can hardly wait to tell my friends back home. Imagine! All this time we've been rubbing elbows with a celebrity and didn't know it."

"I'm hardly that, Mary," Joanna began, but a squeal from Susan cut off her self-conscious protest.

"Oh, my gosh!" Susan put her hand over her mouth and looked appalled, her eyes huge. "It just hit me! Joanna

Andrews, Claire Andrews' daughter, baby-sat with *our* daughter! No one's ever going to believe it. Unless—" she looked at Joanna hopefully "—maybe you could…that is…would you let me take your picture holding Lori?"

"Yes, of course," Joanna agreed pleasantly, but inside she was saddened by the difference in Susan's attitude. Only that morning they had been friends, equals.

Tony caught her eye and gave her an ingratiating smile. "Joanna, I just want you to know that I've always admired your family. Your father and grandfather were true statesmen, the kind this country needs more of. And your mother, well, everyone admires Claire Andrews. She's not only beautiful, she's a great lady."

The others were quick to voice their agreement, even Gloria. Gritting her teeth, Joanna thanked them, hating the fawning and the insincerity.

"I'm delighted, that we met," Tony added, leaning closer. "And I'm hoping that we can stay in touch after this trip is over, maybe even get to know each other better. It's not all that far between New York and Washington. You could come up for a weekend and we could take in a play, or I could come to Washington and you could show me the sights."

"Perhaps," Joanna replied noncommittally.

She had been wondering how she could escape without appearing rude, but now she didn't care what they thought. She had to get out of there. "If you'll excuse me, I'll say good-night," Joanna announced quickly, pushing back her chair. Before anyone could move or protest she stood and headed for the door.

Instinctively, Joanna sought the uppermost deck and fresh air. As she climbed the outside stairs the wind whipped her dress, plastering it against her body like a second skin. When she reached the top its full force hit her, and she had to lean forward and strain for every step.

The sea was growing rougher. Dark clouds scudded like

tattered banners across the sky, occasionally blocking out the moon. The threatening squalls had discouraged the fainthearted, and as she struggled forward Joanna found that she had the unsheltered deck all to herself.

When Joanna reached the bow she grasped the rail with both hands and stood with her head high, face to the wind. It clawed at her upswept hairdo with rough, maniacal fingers, tearing several silken tresses from their moorings until they trailed out behind her and whipped the air in a frenzied dance. Joanna raised one hand and removed the useless hairpins and, one by one, tossed them into the ocean. With her hair flying wild and free, her white silk Grecian style gown molded to her slender curves, she stood motionless and stared moodily at the storm-tossed sea.

That was how Sean found her. Small, proud, defiantly lovely—facing the elements and the night in brooding silence, like a ship's figurehead from days long past.

Joanna started when he came up beside her and leaned against the rail, but she didn't move except to slant him a sideways glance. "What are you doing up here? I thought you were going dancing with Gloria."

"I changed my mind." Joanna returned her gaze to the turbulent sea, and for a moment Sean studied her elegant profile in silence. "The question is, what are you doing up here?"

"I wanted to be alone."

"I can understand that, but you picked a bad spot. It's about to rain and these decks are slick when they're wet. It's not safe. Come on, I'll take you back down."

As he spoke the first drops began to fall, fat globules that splattered against their skin with an icy sting. Not waiting for her assent, Sean grasped Joanna's arm and hustled her back to the stairs. The wind at their backs pushed them along, aiding their retreat, and before the downpour began in earnest they had clattered down the two flights to the shelter of the covered Promenade deck.

Farther down the dimly lit deck there were a few other people, but most of those were going indoors. Heedless of the fine mist that blew in under the shelter, Joanna moved over to the rail and watched the fierce deluge lash and merge with the surging waves.

"What's wrong, Joanna?" Sean asked as he came to stand beside her. "Does it bother you that they found out who you are?" At her nod he frowned. "Why? I've never known you to be publicity shy. You campaigned for both your father and mother."

"That's different. I don't mind working for a goal or a cause. That's not on a one-to-one basis. But being well-known can ruin your personal life."

"How so?"

"Oh, Sean. Didn't you notice how they changed? How the minute they realized who I was, or rather, who my mother was, they started to gush and fawn? I've always hated that. Thank God all that adulation from mother's public only spills over me occasionally. But just imagine how she must have felt all those years. You never know whether someone likes you for yourself, or because of who you are."

"Mmm. I see what you mean. That's rough." He paused, then added, "But all this does prove my point."

"What point?"

"Don't you see? That's just all the more reason for you to keep away from guys like Tony. Involvement with Claire Drummond's daughter would give his career a boost, and you can damn well bet that he knows it."

The words hit her like a slap in the face. She gasped and stared at him with wide wounded eyes, hurt pouring through her. The only defense against it was anger, and that came surging to the surface quickly. "Oh, thank you very much! First I'm a spoiled brat who's pursuing you, and now you as much as say that the only reason a man would be interested in me is because I happen to be Claire Drummond's daughter!''

Sean winced, his expression chagrined. ''Aw, Joanna, I didn't mean it like th—''

''Don't touch me!'' Joanna snapped, slapping his hands away when he reached out to grasp her shoulders. ''Just stay away from me.'' Shaking her head, she backed away a step. ''All right! All right! Maybe I am spoiled and head-strong and…and all the other things you've accused me of being. And I realized a long time ago that I'm far from being your ideal woman. But, believe it or not, Sean Flem-ing, there are some men who like me just the way I am.''

Her voice broke on the last word and she had to fight hard against the emotions that clogged her throat and threatened her composure. *I will not cry,* she vowed si-lently. *I will not!* Joanna glared at him, her chest heaving, unaware of the revealing pain that swam in her eyes.

''Joanna, listen to me, please. I—''

But she'd had enough. Ignoring his entreaty, Joanna turned on her heel and stalked away, calling back over her shoulder, ''From now on you can keep your opinions and your advice to yourself. I don't need them.''

''Joanna! Joanna, wait! Let me explain! Oh, hell!'' Sean hurried after her.

Farther down the deck Joanna jerked open the door and rushed inside. Five seconds later, he did the same, and immediately barreled into an elderly, overweight woman, sending her staggering backward, arms flailing. Her purse hit the floor with a thud and a lipstick and several coins flew out of it and went rolling across the floor.

''Oh, I'm sorry. Are you all right?'' Sean asked distract-edly, taking hold of the woman's upper arms. Over her shoulder Sean caught a glimpse of a slender figure in a white silk dress scooting around a small clutch of people in the passageway. Silently cursing, Sean ground his teeth.

"Oh, my. Really, young man, you should be more careful," the flustered matron admonished. "You almost knocked me down!"

"I'm sorry. I really am. But I'm in a bit of a hurry." Sean steadied her quickly, then retrieved her purse from the floor, scooped up her things and crammed them back inside, and stuffed it back into her hand. "Please excuse me, ma'am." Ignoring the woman's outraged gasp, he rushed off in the direction Joanna had taken.

She was nowhere in sight. Sean sprinted along the passageway, hastily apologizing as he darted around people. When he reached the first stairway he came to a halt and grabbed the rail, his chest heaving. He looked down, and cursed vividly when he spotted a flash of white silk on the deck below. He'd never catch her before she made it to her suite.

Grimly, Sean loped down the stairs after her anyway. Though he knew it was useless, when he reached Joanna's suite he stopped and knocked on the door. "Joanna? Joanna, I know you're in there," he said as loudly as he dared. He paused and waited, but still there was no answer. "Joanna, we have to talk. You're taking this all wrong."

A woman emerged from her cabin farther down the passageway and gave him a strange look. With a muttered oath, Sean turned away and stalked the few yards to his own cabin. He stormed inside, slammed the door behind him and marched straight to the phone. When he'd punched out Joanna's extension he stood glaring at the ceiling, his jaw growing tighter as he counted off the monotonous rings at the other end of the line. On the tenth one he slammed the receiver down on its cradle. "Damn pigheaded female!"

Sean shucked out of his dinner jacket and flung it onto the chair. He flopped down onto the bed, shoes and all, and stretched out on his back with his hands clasped beneath his head. He stared stonily at the ceiling, his expression growing even grimmer as he recalled the hurt look on Joanna's face just before she had bolted. *Hell, I tried to explain, didn't I? But she wouldn't even give me a chance. What more can I do?*

Nothing. Not a damned thing, he decided angrily. If she wouldn't listen, he'd just let her nurse her hurt feelings.

Sean tried to maintain his righteous anger, but his conscience continued to prick him, and after a moment he exhaled a deep sigh. He sat up and swung his legs to the floor, propping his elbows on his spread knees as he bent his head and wearily rubbed the back of his neck. "No, you won't," he muttered to himself. "You hurt her with your clumsy meddling, you idiot, and you owe her an apology. And the first thing tomorrow morning you're going to give it to her."

It was a vow that was easier to make than to keep, Sean discovered.

Joanna didn't show up for breakfast. When a quick search of the ship failed to locate her he went to her suite. He found the room steward there cleaning, and the man told Sean that Joanna had gone ashore as soon as they had docked in Barbados that morning. "With Mr. Longworth," he added with a sly grin that stopped Sean in his tracks.

"You mean Doug Longworth? The singer? The one who's starring in the show in the International Lounge?"

"Yes sir."

Without another word, Sean turned and started slowly down the passageway toward his own cabin, a distracted frown drawing his brows together. Joanna with Doug Longworth? Lord! The very thought set his teeth on edge.

Didn't she know the man was the worst kind of skunk when it came to women? Of course she did. Everyone, both inside and outside show business, knew that Longworth used and discarded women like Kleenex.

Sean let himself into his cabin, and stood in the middle

of the floor, pulling thoughtfully at his bottom lip as he stared out the porthole at the Barbados dock. *Maybe I ought to go find her.*

Don't be an ass, Fleming. It's none of your business what she does. And like the lady said, she is past the age of consent.

Still, Claire and Matt wouldn't want to see her hurt. As their friend, the least I can do is watch out for her. Absently, Sean stripped out of his clothes, put on bathing trunks, then pulled his jeans and shirt back on over them.

No. No, I can't do that. No matter how you rationalize it, it's still butting in. Slinging a towel over his shoulder, he left the room. *Joanna has the right to do whatever she pleases. Even if it is a mistake.*

But it wouldn't hurt just to keep an eye on her. Make sure that Longworth doesn't get out of line.

No, dammit! I'm not her keeper. Besides, that's not my style.

All the way down the gangway the silent battle waged, but an hour later, after scouting three beaches, Sean found himself sitting on the sand, grimly watching Joanna.

"All right! Way to go, baby!" Doug Longworth shouted when she dropped to her knees and brought both fists up under the volleyball just before it hit the sand, sending it skimming back over the net.

Sean watched Doug reach down and help Joanna up, his jaw tightening when the singer's hands lingered at her waist. Joanna responded to his whispered comment in her ear with a chuckle and a saucy look and stepped away.

Eyeing Doug Longworth darkly, Sean tried to figure out just what it was about the man that women found so fascinating. As far as he could see he was just another flashy punk with blue eyes, a perpetually surly expression and bleached blond hair that was about four inches too long. With a minimal amount of talent he'd managed to turn out a few hit records, but as far as Sean was concerned he was purely second-rate, as a man and as an entertainer.

Joanna threw herself into the spirited game with the same zeal and determination she gave to aerobic dancing and trapshooting. Sean suspected it was how she approached everything. She lunged and leaped and put her all into every effort. And the whole time she flirted madly, not just with Longworth, but with Tony Farrell and several others. Sean, she ignored, though he knew perfectly well she was aware of him watching her.

Despite Joanna's efforts, her side was losing. Mainly, Sean decided sourly, because her teammates couldn't take their eyes off her. Not that he could blame them. In that tiny white bikini she was a sight to tempt any man. Even him, Sean admitted grimly, cursing under his breath as he felt the stirring warmth in his loins. Her lithe body was firm and supple, her flesh tanned a delicate apricot, and she moved with a natural, unself-conscious grace that mesmerized, drawing the eye to those slender curves, those lovely, endless legs.

Most of the men were content to just look, but Doug Longworth never missed a chance to put his hands on her. Watching him through narrowed eyes, Sean felt a savage urge to ram his fist through the jerk's face.

Sean stood up and edged closer to the field of play, but Joanna studiously pretended he wasn't there. Finally, when one of the men on her team dropped out, Sean stepped in and took his place. He subtly maneuvered around the other players until he was standing just behind Joanna and Doug. A moment later the ball came sailing over the net in their direction and Sean called out "I've got it," and stepped between them, spiking it back.

"Hey, watch it, fella," Doug sputtered when he bumped into him.

For a few seconds, they slammed the ball back and forth across the net, and during the fast and furious play Sean ignored the other man's glare. Finally Sean smashed the ball with such power it hit the sand before anyone could touch it. While their side prepared to serve he turned to Doug, his black eyes as hard as stone, and said in a soft, strangely threatening voice, "I intend to."

He turned and met Joanna's indignant glare and murmured, "I want to talk to you."

For just an instant Sean glimpsed uncertainty and vulnerability in Joanna's eyes, but almost at once the coolness returned. Without a word, she stepped around him, and grabbing Doug's hand, began to drag him toward the water. "Come on, Doug, I'm tired of playing. Let's go cool off with a swim."

He complied with alacrity, pausing only long enough to send Sean a smirking look over his shoulder before racing hand in hand with Joanna toward the water.

Oblivious to the scrambling efforts of the others to keep the volleyball in play, Sean stood stock-still and watched the pair splash into the surf, his narrowed eyes a glittering obsidian.

The mood in the Zodiac Lounge was gay, convivial. The dreamy music the band played blended pleasingly with the murmur of conversation, the occasional bursts of laughter.

Outwardly Sean appeared his usual carefree self. He sat relaxed in his chair with a forearm braced against the edge of the table, the tips of his fingers lightly touching the rim of his glass, rotating it slowly. A languid smile of anticipation curved his mouth as Bill Adamson drew out his humorous tale. When he delivered the punch line Sean laughed along with everyone else at the table, but inside he was seething.

As conversation flowed between the Adamsons and the Wrights, Sean lifted the squat glass of bourbon and took a sip. Over its rim his eyes once again sought the couple on the dance floor.

Hell, you'd think they'd be tired by now, Sean thought as he watched the blond singer sway to the dreamy music with Joanna locked tightly in his arms. *They've been out there for the past half hour. And he's holding her so close they look like they're glued together.*

Beneath the table Sean's hand closed into a tight fist as he watched Joanna lean back in Doug's embrace and smile seductively. All day he had watched her flirt with Longworth and Farrell and several others. Whenever he had tried to approach her she always managed to slip away. This was the closest he'd been to her since she'd left the volleyball game that morning.

Watching Longworth grin at something Joanna said, Sean's eyes narrowed ominously. When the little creep's hand slid down her spine and brazenly cupped her bottom, something inside Sean snapped. He made a harsh sound and slammed his glass down on the table with a thud. The others jumped and stared in astonishment as he lunged out of his chair and headed for the dance floor with long purposeful strides.

Reaching around, Joanna grasped Doug's hand and returned it to its former position at her waist. "Uh-uh, none of that," she scolded lightly. Her tone was teasing, but her hazel eyes flashed a steely warning.

The corners of Doug's mouth twitched upward in cynical amusement. "Sure, baby, sure." He pulled her closer and whispered in his sexiest voice, "I can wait."

Joanna sighed. It was her own fault. She shouldn't have agreed to accompany him to the beach, much less flirt with him the way she'd done. Doug Longworth was accustomed to having his pick of women. That the evening would end any way other than the two of them going to bed together would simply never occur to him. And why should it? She certainly hadn't done anything to make him think otherwise.

Joanna knew her behavior had been reckless and totally

out of character, but darn it! She had *felt* reckless. Reckless and angry and insulted. Sean couldn't have made it clearer; he didn't want her, nor could he imagine that anyone else would. Did he have any idea how much that had hurt? It had been foolish, perhaps even childish, to encourage Doug, but she had needed to feel desired, to feel that someone found her attractive, no matter how fleeting or shallow that attraction.

Joanna sighed again and gazed sadly over Doug's shoulder. Lord, it was awful to be attracted to someone who didn't want you. Unrequited feelings made you do the dumbest things.

Worrying over how she was going to handle the scene that was sure to take place later, she didn't see Sean until the instant before he tapped Doug on the shoulder. The expression on his face caused her heart to give a little leap, but there was no time to head off the confrontation.

"I'm cutting in, Longworth," he announced flatly.

Doug looked at him as if he had lost his mind, then grinned nastily. "Not a chance."

"Let her go, Longworth, or in three seconds you're going to be eating those pretty capped teeth."

Surprise, then anger flashed across Doug's face. For an instant it appeared as though he were about to argue, but a closer look at Sean's smoldering eyes changed his mind.

"Now, look here. Who do you think you are?" Joanna protested as Sean pulled her from Doug's slackened embrace.

"Shut up, Joanna." Placing both her hands on his chest, he wrapped his arms around her and brought her tightly against him. When she tried to wedge some space between them he gave her a painful squeeze and commanded sharply, "Stop that!"

Joanna was so astounded by his harsh tone she stopped struggling and lapsed into silence, automatically moving with him to the romantic music. This time she had pushed him beyond mere anger. He was incensed. Absolutely furious. She could feel it in the coiled spring tension of his body, the thunderous beat of his heart against her palm. Though he held her in a loverlike embrace she had the disquieting feeling that what he really wanted to do was throttle her.

She could hardly believe it. Sean, laid-back, devil-may-care Sean, was so enraged he was about to blow apart. It was frightening...and thrilling. Joanna stared over his shoulder, intensely aware of his freshly shaved jaw against her temple, the strength of the arms that surrounded her, the scent and the heat and the feel of his body, pressed so intimately to hers. Her insides were quivering wildly, and she didn't know if it was due to fear or his nearness.

They danced in strained silence, and when the music ended Sean clamped his hand around her upper arm and marched her toward the exit. Joanna started to protest, but one glance at his set face and those burning black eyes changed her mind. Out on deck he led her to a secluded spot by the rail and turned her to face him. Joanna braced herself and raised wary eyes.

"Just what the devil is the matter with you?" he demanded. "Don't you have any better sense than to get involved with a creep like Longworth? Lord, I'm beginning to think you need a keeper."

Joanna sucked in her breath. Trepidation gave way to shock, then anger. "Now wait just a min—"

"And as if that weren't bad enough, you were flirting with half the men on the beach. They were following you around with their tongues practically dragging in the sand."

"So what?" she shot back. "It's none of your business."

Sean's eyes narrowed dangerously, and Joanna's angry defiance fizzled as a shiver rippled its way down her spine. She took a step backward. "Now, Sean," she cautioned nervously when he matched it, and backed away another step.

"Then I guess I have to make it my business," he said in a low, purring voice that made the fine hairs on her arms stand on end.

"Sean, please, this is—"

He hooked an arm around her waist and pulled her up against him. With his other hand he cupped her jaw and tilted her face up. Beneath half-lowered lids, fire smoldered in the dark depths of his eyes as they fastened on her mouth.

"Shut up, Joanna."

Chapter Eight

His mouth closed over hers with the firm demand and possessiveness of a man staking his claim. This time there was no tentative seeking. It was a bold kiss, an explosive release of frustrated desire, an admission of needs too long denied. His lips were warm and devouring, almost brutal.

For a moment Joanna was too stunned to react, or even move. She just stood there with her heart booming, her hands clutching his shirt, while her knees threatened to give way beneath her. But soon exquisite sensations began to penetrate the barrier of shock, and she responded to the rough embrace with a matching hunger. She felt as though her body was suffused with heat, glowing like a molten ingot. Pressed against the hard wall of his chest, her breasts were achingly tight and tender.

In some remote corner of her mind Joanna knew that this was foolish, futile, that she should end it before she was hurt more, but it was no use. The feelings she had tried so hard to deny burst free, and her yearning heart

overflowed with love—a love that craved this moment of
bliss at all cost, that recklessly welcomed the passion that
flamed between them.

She was aquiver with longing, greedy in her need.
Straining closer, she ran her palms up over his chest and
shoulders and buried her hands in the thick ebony strands
above his collar, her spread fingers learning the shape of
his head, urging him even closer. Her mouth opened to
eagerly accept the deep bold thrusts of his tongue as her
own darted and entwined, luring him to taste his fill.

A growl rumbled from Sean's throat. He wrapped both
arms around her, tightening his hold. Shifting his stance,
he thrust one of his legs between hers. Joanna caught her
breath.

He was hard. And warm. So very warm. His heat seared
her, melted her, made her burn. As his tongue embedded
itself in her mouth once more, his hands cupped her buttocks and held her tightly to him. Joanna felt his hard
virility pressing against her, felt her body flower and throb,
and a soft moan sighed from her mouth into his. The desperate little sound brought an answering groan from Sean.

The last thing Joanna expected was for him to stop, but
suddenly he thrust her from him and turned away. Dazed,
she found herself swaying unsteadily on legs that felt like
rubber, shaking uncontrollably, and she groped for the rail.
The cool breeze off the ocean felt icy against her aroused
body. She stared at Sean's stiff back, confused…
frightened…hurting.

"Wh—why did you stop?"

"I'm sorry, Joanna. That shouldn't have happened."

"What is this, Sean?" she demanded in a voice raw
with hurt. "Some kind of game you're playing? Are you
trying to teach me a lesson? Punish me? What?"

Sean spun around, his face a tight mask of anguish.
"No! I'm trying my best to see that you don't get hurt."
Raking a hand through his hair, he sighed heavily. A look

of self-disgust made his expression grim. "And not doing a very good job of it, I'm afraid."

"But…but I don't understand. If you…" Joanna paused and swallowed around the painful constriction in her throat. "…if you aren't…attracted to me, then why…why did you kiss me?"

"Not attracted!" Sean snorted, his mouth twisting in a bitter little grimace. "Good Lord, Joanna! How could you think I'm not attracted to you? Oh, I've tried to deny it. I even had myself halfway convinced that I was merely looking out for a friend's daughter…until today." His face hardened as he remembered the sheer torment of the past twelve hours. "I've been eaten alive with jealousy, watching you with that creep, Longworth," he admitted with angry resentment. "Every time he touched you I wanted to smash his face in."

A great uprush of joy and hope filled Joanna's chest. *Sean cares. He really cares.* She wanted to throw herself into his arms but an inner voice urged caution. Something was wrong. She could see it in the grim look on his face. "If…if you feel that way, then what's the problem," she asked shakily.

"Isn't it obvious? I'm too old for you, Joanna."

"Too *old?*" Joanna gave an astonished little laugh. "You call thirty-six too old?"

"For you, yes."

"Oh, Sean, please. Be reasonable. So there's almost fourteen years between us? So what? It's not that big a gap. And it's not as though you're old enough to be my father."

"No. I'm not," he agreed. Watching her, he added softly, "Nor do I intend to be a father substitute."

"What's that supposed to mean?"

"Look, Joanna, everyone knows that you were the apple of your father's eye. He doted on you, spoiled you rotten, and you adored him. And now he's gone, and you miss him. It doesn't take a genius to figure out that you're unconsciously seeking an older man to take his place." Reaching out, Sean ran the backs of his knuckles down her jaw. His voice lowered and softened. "It's understandable, honey, but that's not a role I want to play."

Hurt and wounded pride shone from Joanna's eyes. She tilted her head back, freeing herself from his touch. Turning away, she grasped the rail and stared out at the phosphorescent glow of the white-capped waves. Her chin was high, her expression closed. "You don't have to worry about that, I assure you," she informed him coolly, though not quite able to control the quaver in her voice. "I've been through that once already. I admit that I usually have to learn life's lessons the hard way, but once they're learned, I never make the same mistake twice."

Sensing the distress behind her words, Sean stared at her proud profile, and after a moment asked softly, "Would it help to talk about it?"

Joanna sent him a sidelong glance, then looked back at the sea. For a moment he thought she wasn't going to answer.

"It...was while I was in college," she began finally in a diffident little voice. "Shortly after Mother married Matt. I had just found out some things about my father. Not...very complimentary things." She bit her lower lip and glanced at him again. "I guess...I guess I was feeling cheated. I wanted what I had lost; someone to idolize, to look up to. Someone to whom I would be...I don't know...special, I guess. Of course, I didn't realize that at the time." Her self-derisive chuckle floated out over the ocean. "I thought I was madly in love."

"Who was he?"

"Arthur Spelling, one of my college professors. He was in his forties—sophisticated, intelligent, distinguished. All the females on campus, students *and* faculty, were wild about him. When he singled me out I thought I was the luckiest girl in the world. I gave him my innocence and my heart, and for six months I lived in a daze of sheer happiness.'' A bitter little smile tilted Joanna's mouth, and she looked at Sean with sad, world-weary eyes. ''You know what they say: ignorance is bliss. One day I caught him with another girl and I thought I would die. Later I found out that he was known as the campus Don Juan. While he was having an affair with me he was also seeing two other girls.''

Sean spat out a vivid curse and gripped the rail tightly. All the while her tale had been unfolding he had felt a growing sense of outrage. Now he was filled with anger and an aching sympathy for the disillusioned, vulnerable girl she had been. But most of all, he was filled with a searing jealousy. *Damn that bastard to hell,* Sean thought venomously. *If I could get my hands on him I'd break him in two.*

''Oh, don't be upset on my behalf,'' Joanna said. ''Actually, I got over it all very quickly. That's when I realized that it wasn't so much heartbreak that I had felt, but disillusionment that once again my idol had turned out to have feet of clay. I knew then that I had just been looking for someone to take my father's place.''

''That doesn't excuse him,'' Sean argued. ''The bastard still took advantage of a young girl. He ought to be horse-whipped.''

''I think we took advantage of each other, really. Anyway, it's over, and I learned from it, so I guess it wasn't a complete waste.''

Looking into her sad hazel eyes, Sean fought a silent battle with the fury that burned in him. More than anything in the world he wanted to shield her, protect her, cherish her. If it were in his power he'd wipe out her past hurts, erase from her mind all memory of other men.

The thought brought back the clawing jealousy, and before Sean could stop himself he reached out a hand and cupped her face. "Joanna, it's none of my business, and you don't have to answer if you don't want to, but...since then...has there been anyone else?"

He hated himself for asking. He knew it did not deserve an answer, and no matter what it was it wouldn't change the way he felt. Yet he held his breath and waited for her reply.

Staring solemnly into his eyes, Joanna shook her head slowly, and a fierce gladness exploded in Sean's chest. "No, no one," she murmured. "No one else interested me...until now."

Sean's breath caught once again, and the joyous ache beneath his breastbone became so intense it was almost pain. He tried to subdue it. He told himself that it didn't change anything. Even if Joanna was truly attracted to him, he was still too old for her.

It didn't work. All the common sense and self-chastisement in the world couldn't banish the feeling of elation, nor stop the tender smile that slowly curved his mouth. Emotion shimmered warmly in Sean's dark eyes, and a fine tremor shook his other hand when, as if compelled, he lifted it to her face.

For several moments he just stood there with her lovely face cupped between his broad palms. She was a delight to his senses. With every breath he inhaled her sweet womanly fragrance, mingled with just a hint of floral perfume. The tips of his fingers were buried in the silken hair at her temples, and against his palms he could feel the downy softness of her cheeks, warm and satin smooth. Through the scant inches that separated them he could feel the heat of her body, sense its slight quivering.

He searched her features one by one, taking in the lush mouth, the elegantly sculpted nose and cheekbones, the gracefully winged brows and wide smooth forehead. With his thumb, he touched the enticing little mole at the corner of her mouth. *She's so lovely,* he thought wistfully. *So*

young. And so very vulnerable. You can hurt her badly,
and you know it. If you have any decency in you, Fleming,
you'll let her go, end it now.

But as their gazes met and held he knew both joy and
despair, for the hope and longing in her wide hazel eyes
struck an answering chord in his heart and made dust of
his good intentions.

"Oh, Joanna." He sighed her name in helpless surrender. The husky tone held uncertainty and a lingering touch
of resistance, but the current of emotions that pulled them
together was too strong. "Joanna," he whispered again,
and as his head slowly lowered her eyelids fluttered shut
in anticipation.

It began as the tenderest of kisses, soft, adoring, a warm
melding of mouths that made hearts pound and knees tremble. But the feelings between them were too intense to be
held in check for long. Passion flared, hot and intense, and
with a groan Sean wrapped his arms around her and pulled
her close.

Joanna responded eagerly, all the pent up longing of
years surging to the surface. She melted against him and
looped her arms around his neck, meeting the demanding
kiss with an ardent hunger that matched his own.

The heated kiss went on and on until finally, the need
for air tore them apart. Joanna cried his name weakly and
clung to him. When she attempted to recapture his lips he
cupped the back of her head and pressed her face against
his chest. Eyes closed, his chin resting against the top of
her head, he held her tightly and rocked her back and forth,
and struggled to bring his raging desire under control.

"Easy. Easy, sweetheart," he crooned softly when she
made an agitated move. He ran his hands soothingly up
and down her back and rubbed his chin against her hair,
feeling the silky strands catch on his faint beard stubble.
Gradually their labored breathing quieted, the thunderous
beating of their hearts slowed, but for several moments

they remained as they were, each giving and drawing comfort from the embrace. The only sounds were the splash of the waves against the ship's hull and the soft sighing of the wind.

"All my chivalrous instincts and common sense tell me to call a halt to this now, before it's too late," Sean murmured after a while. Joanna stiffened and grew very still, not saying a word, and he knew she was waiting for him to continue. Sean hesitated. He stared out at the dark ocean, his face filled with pained indecision, but finally he exhaled a long sigh. "Oh, hell. We both may live to regret this, but will you spend the day ashore in St. Croix with me tomorrow?"

Joy exploded inside Joanna like a starburst, and she closed her eyes against the sweet pain. She wanted desperately to say yes, but like Sean, she was leery of allowing things to go further. Despite the longing that tugged at her heart, Joanna could not forget that scores of beautiful women had come and gone in Sean's life. The thought that she might end up like they had, just another name and phone number in his little black book, made her feel sick.

She pressed her lips tightly together as the emotional tug-of-war raged within her, but in the end need won over fear. With her cheek still pressed against his chest, she whispered unsteadily, "Yes. Yes, I'd like that."

He grasped her shoulders and held her away from him. Her face was flushed with passion, her lips slightly puffed, and all that she was feeling was there in her luminous eyes for him to see. Sean felt his heart turn over. At that moment he wanted, more than anything, to carry her to his cabin and make love to her until neither of them could move, but he stubbornly refused to listen to his body's urgings.

He brushed her mouth with a feathery kiss and tucked her against his side. "Come on, sweetheart. I'll take you to your suite."

Neither spoke until they reached her door. When Sean unlocked it and handed her the key Joanna licked her dry lips and looked at him with a hesitant smile. "Would... would you like to come in?"

He sighed, his wry grin tinged with regret. "Oh, I'd like to. But I'm not going to."

His smile turned tender when he saw the mingled relief and disappointment in her eyes. "I don't want to rush into anything, Joanna. Not with you."

This time when his lips met hers it was with the merest touch. Softly, almost reverently, he skimmed her mouth with a warm moist caress that made her tremble, and she clutched at the sides of his lean waist for support. Her lips parted in sweet invitation and their breaths mingled, but he made no effort to deepen the kiss. Gently, with exquisite sensuality, he rubbed his mouth against hers, until Joanna thought she would faint from the tender torment.

Finally he lifted his head and smiled into her bemused eyes. "Good night, Joanna," he whispered.

Feeling as though she were walking on air, Joanna entered the suite and drifted toward the bedroom. Halfway there she stopped and hugged herself, then twirled around, arms outstretched, and sent a beaming smile toward the ceiling. She was so happy she was tempted to pinch herself to see if she was dreaming.

Yet, strangely, when Joanna did get to sleep her dreams were disturbing and disjointed, a phantasmagoria of blondes, brunettes and redheads with blank faces, all laughing tauntingly; thousands of little black books swirling through the air, trapping her in an ever narrowing vortex; Sean's face, looming eerily, floating and wavering like fog, his sexy eyes and wicked smile alternately soft and beckoning, or filled with amused scorn.

When Joanna awoke her euphoric mood was shattered. "What have you let yourself in for?" she fretted as she dressed for the day ashore. "You're just asking for trouble.

You know perfectly well that Sean doesn't expect or want permanence in a relationship.''

Joanna paused in the act of adjusting the spaghetti straps on her pink sundress, her eyes going slightly out of focus as she thought about her mother and Matt, about the love and tenderness that flowed between them, their total commitment to each other. She sighed wistfully. It was what she wanted. What she needed. Joanna knew she couldn't settle for anything less.

But Matt had been a confirmed bachelor too, before he fell in love with Claire.

Her heart gave a little leap at the stunning thought, but Joanna quickly tamped down the flare of elation. She shoved her feet into a pair of flat white sandals and stomped to the mirror. "Sean isn't Matt," she told her reflection severely. "And you'd do well to remember that."

The whole time she dressed, and later, while toying with the croissant she had ordered for breakfast, Joanna vacillated between despair and an almost desperate hope. By the time Sean arrived she was so worked up she was certain that the day could only be a disaster.

Even so, when his knock sounded she rushed to the door, opened it and went perfectly still.

They stared at each other in breathless silence, feeling the strong pull of attraction, the nervous uncertainty its newness caused.

Everything about Sean assaulted her senses. He was freshly showered and shaved, and she could smell soap and woodsy cologne, the faint hint of starch in his crisp blue cotton shirt. Tiny droplets of moisture still clung to the errant black curls that fell over his forehead, and to the sparser thatch visible in the V opening of his shirt. Joanna stared at his bronze throat and remembered the warm resilience of his skin beneath her lips, the slightly salty taste of it.

Slowly, Sean's gaze skimmed over her, taking in her bare shoulders, the enticing curves beneath the soft material of the pink sundress, then traveled down over her long legs to the white sandals on her feet. When at last his eyes returned to hers they glittered warmly.

"Good morning," he murmured with husky intimacy, and dropped a soft kiss on her mouth that sent shivers down her spine. "Ready to go?"

Joanna nodded and stepped out the door. Her heart drummed with excitement while her stomach churned with doubt. *We'll probably end up in another fight before an hour passes,* she thought miserably as they started down the passageway.

She couldn't have been more wrong. It turned out to be a perfectly glorious day, the best Joanna had ever known.

Hand in hand, Joanna and Sean poked through the quaint shops facing the Christiansted harbor, looking at everything from jewelry to T-shirts. After an hour of wandering through the tiny town they traveled across the island to Fredriksted in one of the van taxis, which they shared with three other couples.

Like St. Thomas, there was a lushness about St. Croix, a soft-edged beauty that Joanna found entrancing, almost too perfect to be real. The verdant, sloping mountains at the north end of the island gave way to a wide sweeping vista of cultivated meadows and white sand beaches. A profusion of tropical flowers abounded, dotting the island with splashes of brilliant color, while overhead pristine white clouds floated in the cobalt sky. The pace was relaxed, easy, the mood serene. It was quietly lovely, paradise on earth.

Or maybe I just think so because I'm here with Sean, Joanna admitted to herself wryly. Taking the path of least resistance, the road followed the dips and rises of the rolling plain past sorghum fields, banana plantations and sheep farms. Sean sat with his arm draped across the back of

Joanna's seat, and when the taxi driver pointed out things and places of interest he leaned across her to peer out the window. The feel of his chest pressing against her side, the heady aroma of clean, healthy male that surrounded her, sent delicious tremors quaking through Joanna, and she found herself wishing that the trip never had to end.

In Fredriksted they spent the first hour wandering through the old fort that overlooked the harbor. Afterward, opting for lunch, they bought sandwiches and soft drinks and carried them down to the pier where several sailboats were tied up.

Tiny waves lapped at the pilings, making slapping, sucking noises. The water level was only about a foot lower than the dock, and so clear Joanna could see the sandy bottom, littered with shells and pieces of coral and an occasional starfish.

The moment they sat down on the wooden dock Sean took off his shoes and rolled up the legs of his jeans. As he dipped his feet into the cool water he leaned back on his hands and sighed with pleasure.

"Ah, this is great. Sun, sea, tropical breezes. I think, with half a chance, I could easily become a beach bum."

"You?" Joanna smiled skeptically and handed him a roast beef sandwich. "Somehow I doubt it." For all Sean's deceptive, laid-back air she knew he was ambitious and hard working.

Sean grinned and took a healthy bite out of his sandwich. He stared thoughtfully at the horizon while he chewed and swished his feet in the water. "Naw, I guess you're right," he conceded. "The work ethic is too deeply ingrained."

He delved into the sack that contained their lunch, pulled out two soft drinks and popped the tops off before handing one to Joanna. Tipping his up, he swilled half the contents in one long swallow, then wiped his mouth with the back of his hand and flashed her a rueful grin. "Anyway, my old man would never stand for it. He may be seventy, but if one of his offspring so much as thought about dropping out he'd kick their tail from here to Canada."

"Really?"

"You'd better believe it. Thorne Padriag Fleming doesn't tolerate slackers." Sean took another bite of sandwich and washed it down with more cola. "Dad came to the States from Ireland when he was seventeen," he continued reminiscently. "He had twenty dollars in his pocket. It was tough, but he worked at any job he could find, and even managed to take a few night classes. When he was old enough he joined the police force and became one of New York's finest. He retired a few years back as a captain."

"He raised eight children on a policeman's salary?" Joanna asked in astonishment and awe.

Sean looked at her intently. "We didn't have much money, but we kids didn't know that. We were happy, well-fed and loved. Anyway, everything is relative. Compared to what he had in the old country, Dad feels well-to-do. He's proud of what he's achieved and the fact that he's raised eight kids to be solid citizens. To his way of thinking, he's a living example of the American dream."

The censorious note in Sean's voice brought a vivid flush to Joanna's face and neck. *Oh, Lord. When will I ever learn?* "Sean, I'm sorry. I know how snooty that must have sounded, but I didn't mean to insult you," she insisted anxiously. "Honestly, I just—"

"That's okay. I guess, considering the life you've had, it must be hard for you to understand."

Feeling miserable and horribly embarrassed, and unable to think of a thing to say, Joanna watched Sean polish off the last of his sandwich and drink, then toss the wrapper and can into the sack.

When done, he leaned back on one palm, propped a wet

foot on the pier and draped his arm across his knee, squinting his eyes against the light reflecting off the water. Joanna half expected him to suggest that they return to the ship, but after a moment he picked up the conversation again.

"I guess the point is, Dad believes that with hard work and determination you can be whatever you want to be. He encouraged all his children to set their goals high and reach for them." Sean shrugged and smiled crookedly. "In addition to loving his adopted country he's fascinated by the way the system works, and I suppose some of that rubbed off on me, which is why I got involved in politics."

"How about your brothers and sisters? What do they do?" Joanna asked hesitantly.

"Mike—he's the oldest—followed in Dad's footsteps and became a policeman. Kathleen is an attorney, and Dennis will be, just as soon as he passes the bar exam. Bridget is a social worker, Ryan's in med school, and, let's see…Colin just graduated from college and is starting out in sales, and Meghan…" Sean's face softened and his eyes grew tender. "Meghan's the baby of the family. It's hard to believe that she now has a baby of her own."

Sean looked at Joanna, and she could see in his face the deep affection he felt for his youngest sibling, plus a trace of sadness that she had left the innocence of childhood behind.

"She's the mother of the two-month-old nephew I told you about. Both Meghan and her husband work and go to school part-time. They're as poor as church mice, and it's a constant struggle for them to make ends meet, especially now with the baby, but they refuse to take help from anyone," he said with a frown, both irritation and pride evident in his voice.

"My goodness. No wonder your father is proud of his children. I'm sure your mother is, too."

"Oh sure," Sean said with a chuckle. "Although I think

the fact that seven of her eight offspring are happily married and producing grandchildren means more to her than anything else. Mom's never happier than when she's got her whole brood gathered around.'' He rolled his eyes eloquently. ''Lord, you ought to see us during holidays and family gatherings. It's pure bedlam. There's thirty-eight of us, for Pete's sake.''

''I can—'' Joanna stopped and laughed, shaking her head wryly. ''I almost said, 'I can imagine,' but I really can't. It certainly sounds interesting, though.''

''Oh, it is. It is.''

Enthralled, as only an only child can be, Joanna listened as Sean related several anecdotes about his family. Some were hilarious, some poignant. To Joanna they were all fascinating. She was well aware that Sean, with his Irish gift of gab, had probably embroidered and embellished the tales, but she didn't care. It thrilled her that he was sharing them with her, giving her a glimpse of that private part of his life. Somehow, she knew instinctively that it was a privilege he didn't afford many people.

Joanna laughed so hard after one particularly funny tale that she had to dig into the trash sack for a napkin to dab the tears from her eyes. ''Oh, Sean, that was pr-priceless,'' she choked weakly, mopping at her wet cheeks. ''Your nephew actually shaved off all the other kids' eyebrows?''

After a moment, when Sean didn't reply, she peered over the napkin and found that he was watching her, his face serious, intent.

''You really are a lovely woman,'' he said quietly. Leaning closer, he caressed her cheek with his fingertips, and Joanna felt her heart begin to pound. ''I wonder why I didn't notice that years ago?''

''Probably because I was a pushy, arrogant brat,'' Joanna said on a weak laugh.

Sean grinned. ''Yeah, you're probably right. But you've changed,'' he murmured, growing serious again. ''And I find that I like the new Joanna very much." Slowly, he trailed his fingers down the side of her neck, across the gentle slope of her shoulder and down her arm to her elbow, then back up. Joanna closed her eyes and shivered delicately. "Very much," he repeated in a husky whisper.

His breath feathered across her skin, and Joanna lifted her heavy lids to find that he had moved closer still, and that his gaze was locked on her mouth. The meandering hand slid back over her shoulder and cupped around her nape. With gentle but firm pressure he urged her forward until their lips met.

It was the softest of kisses. With the merest pressure, his lips rocked against hers in a slow seductive motion. The tip of his tongue slid enticingly back and forth between her barely parted lips, tasting, tempting. But for all its gentleness the kiss was filled with heat and power. Joanna trembled beneath its sweet hot touch as a shimmering flame raced through her and her skin prickled deliciously.

Their lips clung, then parted. His black eyes glittering with leashed passion, Sean pulled back just inches and studied Joanna's glazed look and flushed face. He drew his hand from her nape and cupped her jaw, smiling tenderly as his thumb swept over her trembling lips and touched the tiny beauty mark at one corner.

"I think we'd better go back to shopping or sightseeing, before I forget we're in a public place and do something to embarrass us," he whispered roughly, half teasing, half serious.

The lambent flame in his eyes filled Joanna with sheer joy. How many times had she dreamed of him looking at her in just that way? Of hearing that husky, intimate tone? It was a fantasy come true.

So was the rest of the day. Flushed with happiness, Joanna strolled with Sean through the Fredriksted's narrow, picturesque streets. In an interesting, tucked away alley paved with cobblestones and lined with unusual shops, they discovered a sidewalk cafe, where they enjoyed piña coladas beneath a huge poinciana tree and talked endlessly of nonsensical, inconsequential things. But with every look exchanged, every touch, they communicated on a far deeper, more basic level.

They returned to Christiansted and the ship late that afternoon. It was almost sailing time, and they decided to watch the ship get under way from the sun deck. When they reached the bow, however, they both stopped short at the sight of Gloria and Tony standing in the shallow end of the pool, locked in a passionate kiss.

Cautiously, Joanna looked at Sean. "Does that, uh... upset you?"

"No, not a bit," Sean said with casual indifference. Then his eyes narrowed. "Why? Does it bother you?"

"Me? Why should it bother me? Tony and I aren't romantically involved." Joanna shot him an accusing glance, then tilted her chin disdainfully and sniffed, "Certainly not to the point where I would allow him to buy me a gold bracelet."

A dawning light appeared in Sean's eyes and he grinned slowly. "Ah, so that's it. Well this may be hard for you to believe, but I bought that gold bracelet for Gloria because I felt guilty for *not* having an affair with her."

"Oh, please. You don't really expect me to believe that, do you?"

"It's true. Oh, I intended to. But somehow I just couldn't work up any enthusiasm." Sean picked up a handful of her hair, rubbed it experimentally between his fingers and thumb and gave her a look that caused her insides to flutter wildly. "Someone else kept occupying my thoughts."

"Oh." Delight percolated through Joanna, and she beamed up at him foolishly.

"Yes, oh." There was a hint of teasing in his voice, but

his eyes were very serious. "So you see, I'm not in the least upset about those two. I'm perfectly happy with the status quo. How about you?"

"Oh, yes," Joanna agreed softly. "I'm very happy."

Chapter Nine

Excitement and anticipation tingled through Joanna like the fluttering, whispering wings of a thousand butterflies.

On stage the dancers were performing a strenuous, precision tap routine to the band's rousing rendition of "Yankee-Doodle Dandy." It was an excellent show. Every member of the troupe was talented and professional, and Joanna watched them with every outward sign of enjoyment. But for all that her mind was on the performance they might just as well have been left-footed hippos in tutus.

Sitting beside Sean in the dim theater, their clasped hands resting on his thigh, Joanna could think of nothing but him—the day that had just passed, the night that was to come.

The theater seats were actually love seats, arranged in curving rows around the stage, and sharing one with Sean, Joanna could feel his heat, the tensile strength of him, all along her side from her shoulder to her knee. Against her bare arm his coat sleeve felt rough, slightly scratchy, wonderful. Her gaze dropped to their clasped hands and a smile played about her lips. The contrasts were marked: large to small, strength to fragility, dark to pale, rough to smooth. Yet, somehow, they looked so right together. And it felt so natural to be touching him.

The dance number came to an end, and all around Joanna the audience broke into enthusiastic clapping, snapping her out of her sensuous study. The Wrights were seated in the row in front of them, and when Joanna's gaze fell on Mary's silver head the hovering smile grew. Other than exchanging knowing glances, no one had seemed surprised earlier when she and Sean had arrived for dinner together. Shrewdly noting the warm look in Sean's eyes and the way his hands had lingered on Joanna's shoulders after he had pushed in her chair, Mary had merely leaned close and whispered in her ear, "It's about time," and then had laughed delightedly at Joanna's startled look.

Gloria had allowed herself one hostile glare before resuming her flirtation with Tony, who had seemed delighted with the situation.

Apparently everyone else was aware of our feelings before we were, Joanna thought wryly. At least...before Sean was.

"Ready?" Sean asked, and Joanna looked at him in surprise, blinking as the lights came on, only then realizing that the show had ended.

As they inched their way up the aisle in the midst of the crowd Sean walked just behind Joanna with his hands resting lightly on either side of her waist. Smiling, Joanna savored the feel of his body brushing against her back and hips, the blatant possessiveness of his touch.

"How about a walk in the moonlight?"

Sean's warm breath filling her ear sent a tingle racing over Joanna's skin. He nipped her lobe gently, and against her neck she felt him smile as a shudder rippled through her. Joanna could only nod.

They eased out of the crowd at the first exit and stepped out onto the Promenade deck. By silent mutual consent, they took the outside stairs up to the next deck, which was open to the star-sprinkled sky. Hands clasped, fingers laced together, they strolled toward the stern, their footsteps making soft measured thuds on the teak decking.

The warm night air flowed against their skin like a lover's breath, caressing, arousing. Resembling a misshapen silver disc, an almost full moon hung in the dark sky, bathing everything in its gentle glow.

Joanna felt as light as a feather, as though she would float away were it not for Sean's anchoring hand. She was drunk on happiness and the romantic atmosphere, the sheer magic of the night. Unlike the effects of alcohol, the emotional high did not dull her awareness, but made it sharper. As though her sensory perception had been fine tuned, she was acutely conscious of every nuance of feeling, every tiny detail around her: the slight salt tang of the air, the surprising calluses that ridged Sean's palm, and the wonderful warmth of it against hers, faint sounds of music and laughter floating up from the lounges on the deck below, silk drifting against her legs as the softest of breezes toyed with the handkerchief hem of her gown, lovers lurking in the shadows, whispering, embracing, the trembly feeling in her lower belly, resulting from the sure knowledge that they were about to reach a new turning point, one that would alter their relationship forever.

The hint of a smile hovering around Sean's mouth told her he was aware of her anticipation and shared it. His pulse throbbed beneath her fingertips, its rhythm exactly matching the heavy thud of her heart, and the occasional burning looks he cast her way made it beat even stronger and flooded her body with heat.

They walked in silence, their deceptively lazy steps

marking off the sluggardly passing of time. A heady tension crackled in the air around them like invisible heat lightning.

The shadows at the stern enveloped them, and they stopped by the rail to look out at the sea. With no wind stirring it was calm as glass, except for the phosphorescent froth of the wake that trailed behind the ship. Joanna stared at it, waiting, the trembling expectancy growing to a tormenting, delicious agony.

Beside her Sean turned, and she sensed his gaze drifting over her profile.

"Joanna." He uttered her name in a low voice that wasn't much more than a whisper, a sigh, yet the sound was filled with longing and entreaty.

With her heart kicking against her ribs, Joanna turned slowly and looked up at him. In the shadows Sean's face was barely discernible, but she could sense the intense emotion that gripped him. It mirrored her own.

Never taking his eyes from her, Sean lifted the hand he still held and pressed her palm to his mouth. With the tip of his tongue he traced a wet circle on the tender flesh. The contact sent a bolt of fire zinging through her, straight to the heart of her femininity, making it pulse and liquefy. "Oh, Joanna, what have you done to me?" he asked in a rasping whisper, moistening her skin even more with the dew of his warm breath.

"I... What do you mean?"

"I've never felt this way before. Never been this obsessed with a woman before." Back and forth, he rubbed his lips against her palm. "I haven't been able to think of anything but you since we left Florida."

"I have the same problem," she said throatily, shivering.

"Do you? Do you have any idea how much I want to hold you? Love you? It was all I could think about all day while we were ashore. And tonight during dinner." He grimaced, his face twisting in remembered frustration. "And that show. Lord! I thought it would never end."

Beyond speech, Joanna could only nod her understanding, then close her eyes helplessly as his teeth nipped the soft pads at the base of her fingers.

Sean's gaze roamed over her rapt face. The most delicate lids he had ever seen shuttered her hazel eyes, sweeping the lavish fringe of lashes across her cheeks like dark fans. Unable to resist, he laid her hand against his chest and bent forward, placing a feathery kiss on each one.

As though weighted with lead, Joanna's lids lifted slumberously. She gazed up at him with all that she was feeling plainly visible in her face, in her eyes. Even in the shadows Sean could see the emotion swimming in their hazel depths. Lord, he thought a bit desperately. She looks so fragile, so vulnerable, so very lovely.

Once again Sean experienced a pang of guilt, but he pushed it aside. It was far too late to be noble; he no longer had the strength to walk away. He wanted to kiss her senseless, to pull her to the deck and ravage that sweet mouth and body, but even more, he didn't want to frighten her. Controlling his raging impulses, Sean brought her other hand to his chest, slipped his arms around her and tenderly gathered her to him.

With an urgent little sigh, Joanna pressed closer and slid her hands up over his shoulders, burying her fingers in the silky hair at his nape. The tiny evening bag that hung from her wrist bumped gently against his back. As the soft globes of her breasts flattened against Sean's chest a moan of animal pleasure rumbled from him, and his head descended.

"Dear Lord, you're lovely," he whispered achingly against her lips. "So very lovely."

Sean kissed her with a depth of emotion that surprised even him. Hungrily, a bit desperately, he rocked his lips over hers. He wanted to devour her, absorb her, until they were one in mind, body and soul.

Joanna's instant, ardent response made his heart leap. Any lingering doubts Sean had about her maturity vanished as she kissed him back with a woman's passion, a woman's needs.

Desire flamed between them, and the kiss became hotter, more intense. Sean's tongue plumbed the sweet depths of her mouth. His hands roamed her slender curves. Joanna groaned and burrowed closer, her fingers clutching his hair in a desperate grip.

With an effort of will, Sean tore his mouth from hers and buried his face in the fragrant hair at the side of her neck. "Oh, God, Joanna. If we don't stop now I'm not going to be able to," he gasped.

Joanna made a strangled little sound, and he straightened and clutched her tightly against his chest. Tilting his head, Sean rested his cheek against her crown and rocked her back and forth. He was afire. Burning. He wanted Joanna more than he had ever wanted any woman in his life, but he knew it wasn't just physical. He hungered desperately for something more. It was a deep, gut-wrenching need he'd never experienced before. It clawed at his soul and made him tremble.

Shakily, he held Joanna away from him and stared down at her with feverish eyes. He knew, just as surely as he knew that tomorrow would come, this would not be a casual fling he could enjoy for a while, and then walk away from. And, to his surprise, he found that he was glad. "I want you, Joanna," he said in a voice roughened by passion. "I need you." His fingers tightened on her shoulders and he looked at her intently. "Will you come back to my room with me?"

Joanna's heart stopped for a millisecond before it took off at a gallop. Joy exploded inside her, creating such pressure in her chest she could barely breathe. Her body yearned for his touch, and her heart urged her to say yes, but even so, she could not shut out the niggling doubts. He could hurt her badly. The pain she had suffered after that ill-considered little affair in college would be nothing in comparison. And yet...

Joanna hesitated, hope and fear, longing and wariness warring within her as her emotions told her one thing, her common sense another. But it took only a moment for her to realize that there was really no choice to make. She loved Sean. It was as simple as that.

Looking up at him with her heart in her eyes, she drew a deep breath and smiled tremulously. "Yes. Yes, I'll go with you."

Something hot and wild flared in Sean's eyes. "You won't be sorry. I promise," he vowed in a rough whisper. He bent and kissed her hard, then tucked her against his side and started back the way they had come.

Every nerve in Joanna's body quivered like a plucked string. Sedately, their arms around each other, they strolled across the deck, down the stairs and along the passageway, all without speaking. They stopped at Sean's door, and he smiled warmly into her eyes while fishing in his pocket for the key without relinquishing his hold on her. As he fumbled to fit it into the lock with his left hand Joanna stared at his intent profile, her heart thumping as doubts of a different kind assailed her.

She was so inexperienced. What if she didn't please him? Sean had known many women. Beautiful, glamorous women. Women like Gloria. Joanna thought about her own plain brown hair, her slender, girlish body, her small breasts. Would he be disappointed? What if...

The door opened and Sean's encircling arm urged her into the cabin. When he turned to hang out the Do Not Disturb sign she stepped away and stood in the middle of the floor, her body rigid with apprehension.

It was a small cabin, not even as big as the bedroom in

her suite. The room steward had already removed the
spread and turned down the covers on the double bed that
sat flush with one wall. As she stared at it, Joanna felt a
quivering in the pit of her stomach and quickly looked
away.

Next to the bed a low chest of drawers sat beneath the
porthole. On the opposite wall were two doors, which she
presumed led to the bathroom and closet. The only other
furnishings were an upholstered chair, a tiny table and a
TV.

Sean moved away from the door, and she turned to him
with a determined smile. But some of her anxiety must
have shown on her face, for when he stopped just inches
from her, his expression was infinitely tender. His hands
settled lightly on her forearms and glided upward to cup
the rounded curves of her shoulders, the feathery touch
leaving a trail of goose bumps on her skin.

"Oh, love," he whispered, pulling her closer. "There's
no reason to be nervous. It's going to be wonderful. You'll
see." His dark eyes glowed with sensual promise, and his
slow smile made her heart thrum. His gaze roamed her
face, lingering lovingly on each feature. When it stopped
at her mouth, his lids dropped halfway and his voice became even huskier. "I've never felt this way about a
woman in my life, Joanna. Never. Something this special
just has to be right."

Joanna drew in her breath as, like magic, his words
swept away all her misgivings, all her fears. She had
needed so desperately to know that she was more than just
another in the long list of women who had fleetingly held
Sean's interest. She stared at him with wide, luminous
eyes, hope unfurling inside her with all the fragile tenacity
of a flower blooming in the desert. He hadn't said he loved
her, and maybe he didn't yet, but surely, surely, given
time, he would. Emotion clogged her throat and her shin-

ing eyes brimmed with tears. As they trickled over and streamed down her cheeks, she smiled tremulously.

"Oh, Sean." His name came out in a broken whisper, a soft sigh of adoration that told him all he needed to know.

Lovingly, Sean enfolded her in his arms and covered her mouth with his. The kiss was a tender ravishment that set her soul aflame. She quivered within the embrace, her heart overflowing with love as his lips moved against hers with a slow, heated fervency. Giving. Savoring. Sweetly devouring.

Joanna's mouth flowered open, and Sean's tongue dipped into it repeatedly, drinking from her sweetness like a man dying of thirst. "Lord, you taste heavenly," he said, as he rubbed his mouth back and forth over hers. "I'll never get enough of you. Never."

Joanna's tiny purse dropped to the floor with a soft plop. She clung to him, her hands clutching at the lapels of his dinner jacket while his worked their drugging magic, smoothing over her bare shoulders, her waist, the rounded curves of her bottom. When he lowered the zipper at the back of her dress and brushed the thin spaghetti straps from her shoulders she obediently lowered her arms. The garment slid down her body and fluttered to the floor in a billowing cloud of silk chiffon.

The fully lined dress required no slip, and when he eased her away she stood before him in only a wispy triangle of lilac silk and a wickedly sinful ecru lace garter belt and stockings. Sean looked at her, his black eyes glittering hotly, his chest heaving. His handsome face, distorted by desire, was rigid and flushed.

His gaze drifted hungrily down over her belly and silk covered legs, then returned to stare at her pert, uptilted breasts. As though mesmerized, he slowly circled one dusky pink nipple with his index finger, and something flared in his eyes as it tightened into a hard bud. He cupped the soft globe in his palm. "Your skin is like satin," he murmured hoarsely. "So smooth and warm." He raised his eyes to hers. "I can feel your heart beating."

Joanna quivered under that hot look. Her breasts felt heavy and feverish, and when he bent and touched his tongue to the aching tips she gasped and clutched at his shoulders. "Oh, Sean! Sean!"

Just as her knees started to buckle he groaned and snatched her back into his arms, burying his face in the silky curls at the side of her neck. "Oh, God, sweetheart! You're so beautiful. Just the sight of you drives me wild."

"I...I..." Coherent speech was beyond Joanna.

The scrape of cloth against her sensitized nipples was almost painfully erotic. When Joanna began to fumble with the buttons on his shirt Sean went perfectly still, then eased back a fraction to allow her better access. In her haste, her movements were jerky and awkward, but she finally managed the task, then snatched the shirt free of his trousers. Frantically, she pushed wide the gaping front sections of the garment and burrowed close, making a soft sound, somewhere between a moan and a sigh, as her breast flattened against his furred chest.

A violent shudder rippled through Sean, and his arms tightened around her convulsively. He held her close for a moment, but when her soft hands tunneled beneath his dinner jacket and the loose shirt to move searchingly over the taut muscles in his back, his control snapped. With decisive quickness, he swept her into his arms and carried her the few steps to the bed. He placed her on the soft, fragrant linens, and Joanna's breath caught as his fiery gaze blazed over her.

Then, methodically, he set about removing her few remaining articles of clothing.

Two soft plops sounded, one after the other, as he slipped the high heeled sandals from her feet and dropped them to the floor. With shaking fingers, he unhooked her garters and peeled the sheer silk stockings from her legs. As though unable to help himself, he bent and kissed the strip of flesh between the top of her bikini panties and the lacy garter belt. His teeth nipped her satiny belly. His nimble tongue swirled a wet circle around her navel, then speared into the tiny cavity, withdrew, and plunged again. Her hands helplessly clutching the sheet on either side of her, Joanna moaned and writhed beneath the delicious torment.

Sean raised his head and smiled. ''I'm going to love all of you. Every beautiful inch of you,'' he vowed in a raspy whisper.

He hooked his thumbs beneath the top of her panties, drew the lilac silk slowly down over her legs and tossed it to the floor. The wisp of ecru lace followed. His dark gaze sizzled over her again. ''Oh, babe, I burn just looking at you.''

Straightening, Sean stripped off his shirt and dinner jacket at one time, tossed them into the chair, and went to work on his trousers. Within moments he was naked, his discarded clothes strewn haphazardly over the chair and floor, and he was stretching out beside her, pulling her urgently against his heated flesh.

The kiss was a hungry outpouring of unleashed passion. His tongue delved into her mouth, stroking, probing, plundering sweetly.

With barely restrained urgency, his hand smoothed over her body, exploring the long, exquisite line of thigh and hip, the inward curve of waist, the gentle flare of ribcage. In a feather-light touch, the back of Sean's knuckles grazed the underside of her breast. Then his large hand cupped around the warm fullness, and Joanna shuddered as his thumb swept back and forth over the rosy crest.

Sean rained kisses down Joanna's neck and shoulder, the underside of her jaw, her collarbone, down into the scented valley between her breasts. As his hand moved downward over her quivering belly, he drew the engorged nipple into the wet warmth of his mouth and drew on her with slow, rhythmic suction.

"Oh, God, Sean!" Joanna cried out in surprise, tangling her fingers in his hair and urging him closer as the tugging pressure set off little incendiary explosions within her body that sent liquid fire racing to the core of her femininity, making it tighten and throb.

Sean lavished the same loving attention on the other breast, and the delicious agony became almost unbearable. Joanna whimpered and writhed in restless passion, her nails digging into the taut muscles in his back.

The whimper became a low, long moan of pure ecstasy when Sean's hand slipped between her thighs and probed the delicate petals of her womanhood.

Sean lifted his head and looked at her. His handsome face was flushed, his eyes a burning black. Silently, he questioned, and just as silently she answered. Obeying the tugging of her hands and the urgent plea in her eyes, he moved into position between her thighs. Braced on his palms, he remained poised above her for a second, his intent gaze locked with hers. Then with a slow, sure stroke, he made them one.

He thrust deep, sheathing himself completely in her velvety warmth, a slight smile curling his mouth as he watched Joanna's eyes grow smoky with passion. Watching her still, he began the smooth, rocking movements of love, and a look of fierce satisfaction tightened his face as her rapture grew.

"You feel wonderful. You are wonderful," he murmured.

Joanna gazed up at him languorously, her eyes swimming with love and sensuous pleasure. With a soft, beguiling smile, she ran her hands up his arms and linked her fingers at his nape. "Come to me, my love," she urged in a breathy whisper. "Come to me."

"Oh, God, yes!" Sean cried as he lowered his chest over the soft globes of her breast and felt her long limbs enfold him.

The pressure built. Their pleasure grew to breathtaking proportions. It swelled within them, around them. It pushed the breath out of their lungs and filled their hearts to bursting. Bodies grew taut, straining, movements rapid. The sweet agony built and built until it became too much for mere mortals to bear.

Then the explosion came—a fiery conflagration that consumed them.

Long minutes after their hoarse cries of completion died away, they lay without moving, clinging to each other, utterly replete. As their labored breathing gradually slowed, Joanna stroked her hands over Sean's damp body and drifted on a sea of languor, savoring his closeness, his pressing weight, the musky scent of satisfied male.

At last, Sean stirred. Raising himself up on his forearms, he toyed absently with her silky hair spread out on the pillow and looked down at her, his expression serious, a bit uncertain. "You okay?"

"Yes. Yes, I'm fine." Smiling, she lifted a hand and ran her finger over one heavy black brow, loving the wiry satin texture of it.

"No regrets?"

"No, none. That was wonderful, Sean. The most beautiful experience of my life." Her smile faded a fraction. "What about you? Are you sorry?"

"Hardly." The worry left his face as his slow smile grew. The sight of it made Joanna's insides flutter. "What we just shared happens to be the greatest experience I've ever had also. I've known a lot of women intimately, Joanna," he added when she frowned doubtfully. "And I enjoyed making love with every one of them. I won't lie to you about that. But it was never like this. I've never felt this…this…joy before."

"Oh, Sean." Tears filled Joanna's eyes, and she reached up and framed his face tenderly between her palms. It wasn't a declaration of love but it was very close, especially for Sean. It was more than she even dared to hope for this soon, and her heart felt as though it were about to burst with sheer happiness. It was all she could do to keep from blurting out her love for him. "I'm so glad," she whispered in an emotion-choked voice. "So very glad. I...I couldn't have stood it if you had regretted making love to me."

The sensuous smile that tugged at Sean's mouth held just a touch of devilment. "Does this feel like regret?" he asked lazily.

"Sean!" Joanna gasped, her eyes going wide as she felt his body stir within her. "So soon? How can you...I mean, I thought..."

He chuckled wickedly and nibbled at the tender skin just behind her ear. "Easy. I've been going out of my mind wanting you ever since this trip started. It may take all night to satisfy my hunger." His lips trailed moist kisses over her throat, across her cheek. His tongue flicked maddeningly at the corner of her mouth, and Joanna turned her head, blindly seeking. "In fact," he whispered huskily against her lips. "I don't think I'll ever get enough of you."

Joanna moaned a little sigh of ecstasy as his lips closed possessively over hers. Looping her arms around his neck, she returned his kiss with all the fervent love that swelled her heart and gave herself up to the spiraling passion he so easily aroused.

Much later, as she drifted off to sleep in Sean's arms, spent and satiated, Joanna's last drowsy thought was, *Who says dreams don't come true?*

Chapter Ten

The ethereal lavender light that heralds the coming of sunrise seeped in through the porthole. Joanna smiled and blinked languorously, watching the misty glow ease the shadows from the cabin. As sweet memories came creeping in with the dawn she sighed in utter contentment.

Sean lay beside her, his head on her pillow. She could feel his deep, even breathing against her shoulder, the heavy weight of his arm draped across her waist, the radiant heat from his body. Closing her eyes, she savored the tactile pleasure.

Sean stirred, mumbled something and hooked his leg over hers. Smiling, Joanna rubbed her silky smooth limb back and forth against his calf, delighting in its hairy roughness.

She rolled her head on the pillow and gazed at him, and felt her heart give a little bump against her ribs. His face was softened in sleep, his lips slightly parted and slack, making him look endearingly vulnerable. Overnight beard stubble created a bluish smudge along his jaw and upper lip, and his hair was mussed and untidy, lying across his forehead in tousled ebony curls. Pleasure came washing over Joanna at his nearness, at finding herself there, where she had never thought she'd be. He was so handsome and so male...and she loved him so.

Waking up in bed with a man was a new experience for Joanna. Because Arthur had insisted they keep their relationship secret, the time she had spent with him had been brief—furtive little meetings stolen now and then, that had lasted only an hour or two at most. Joanna had not liked the situation, but Arthur had claimed that it would jeopardize his position with the college if it got out that he was involved with one of his students. It wasn't until later that she'd realized it had merely been a clever means of keeping his various girlfriends from learning about one another.

That all seemed so long ago, Joanna thought with lazy contentment, feathering her fingertips over the silky hair on Sean's forearm. So unimportant now.

The circle of sky beyond the porthole changed to crimson and gold. Seconds later a splinter of sunshine beamed across the carpet like a tiny spotlight. As much as she hated to, Joanna knew she ought to return to her suite before the other passengers began to stir. It would be a bit awkward if anyone she knew saw her sneaking in at dawn, still dressed in her evening gown.

She lifted Sean's arm from her waist, eased her leg from beneath his and scooted gingerly over to the edge of the bed. Cautiously sitting up, she swung her legs to the floor, but the soles of her feet had barely touched the carpet when an arm hooked around her midriff and hauled her backward.

Joanna uttered a soft cry and slumped back against Sean's bare chest.

"Going somewhere?" he inquired in her ear. He nuzzled aside her hair and nipped at her neck with tender savagery.

"I...I... Back to my suite."

"Wanna bet?" His tongue bathed her flesh with loving strokes. "You're staying right here. Where you belong."

Joanna shivered as he trailed a line of nibbling kisses down her neck and over her shoulder, then back up to that sensitive spot behind her ear. Playfully, he drew a wet circle with his tongue and warmed it with his breath. "Ah...Sean...stop...I have to...have to..." Joanna's faltering thought processes shut down when Sean moved sensuously against her back. The feel of silky chest hair feathering across her skin set off a delicious tingle, and Sean chuckled wickedly when he felt her shiver.

"Have to what?"

"To...to..."

"Whatever it was, forget it." His free hand came around her and cupped her breast. He fondled it gently, testing its shape, its weight, its softness. "All you have to do is stay here with me. In bed."

"Oh, darling, I—" She gasped as he grazed his palm slowly over the tips of her breasts. "I can't...I have to go back to my suite to change clothes," she protested breathlessly.

His arms tightened around her midriff, and with a jerk, he rolled with her, bringing her over him and onto her back. Braced on his forearms, he grinned down into her startled face. "You don't need clothes for what I have in mind."

His tone was teasing, but his dark eyes smoldered with desire. Despite the night they had just spent together, the look kindled fires deep inside Joanna and brought hot color flooding into her cheeks. "And just what is it you have in mind?" she asked, striving for lightness.

"Oh...a good morning kiss, a room service breakfast—" he lowered his head and nuzzled the tender underside of her jaw ''—a leisurely shower, together if we can both fit into that cubicle...'' Joanna gasped as excitement shot through her, and she felt him smile against her neck, but he continued with his list of activities in the same casual tone. ''...a little talking, a lot of loving, maybe a nap later.'' He raised his head and gave her a slow, sexy smile. ''Not necessarily in that order, you understand.''

Simmering heat flooded Joanna's body and pulses throbbed. ''You have a one-track mind, Sean Fleming,'' she scolded with mock indignation, but her voice was low and husky, not quite steady.

''Uh-hmm,'' he admitted with such cheerful relish Joanna couldn't help but laugh.

But her laughter faded quickly as Sean's sensual gaze grew more intense. His night-black eyes roamed over her face, touching her lips, her flushed cheeks, the silky arch of her brows, before finally meeting hers. Joanna felt her bones melt beneath that hot, hungry stare.

''Don't go,'' he urged in a low, raspy voice. ''Spend the day with me, darling.''

Love welled up inside Joanna, swelling her chest with a sweet pressure. How had she ever gotten this lucky? she wondered. Placing her palms in a light caress along his cheeks, she rubbed her thumbs over his chin and the corners of his mouth and smiled tenderly when she felt the rasp of whiskers against her skin. ''There's nothing in this world that I want more,'' she vowed in the softest of voices. ''But first, I really must go back to my suite. I'll just be gone a few minutes.''

Sean looked as though he were about to argue, then his gaze dropped to her mouth. ''All right. But first I get my good-morning kiss.''

Joanna saw the determined glint in his eyes. ''Now, Sean, I don't think—''

He silenced her weak protest with his mouth. The kiss was warm and firm and deeply arousing. With exquisite, gentle insistence, Sean's lips moved back and forth over hers, stoking the fires, coaxing, expertly building her passion to a fever pitch. Soon Joanna was moving restlessly, breathing hard, her hands clutching at his shoulders.

All thought of leaving fled.

Sean's mouth left hers to trail a line of kisses downward. "Your breasts are so beautiful," he murmured against the pearly flesh. "So white and firm."

"They're...they're too small," Joanna gasped in weak denial and shuddered as his tongue lathed the rosy crest and left it beaded in desire.

"No, they're perfect. They just fit my hand," he insisted, curling his fingers around the satiny swell to prove his claim. His mouth closed around the rosy crest and he drew on her with a slow, sweet suction.

Clutching his hair, Joanna moaned and arched her back. She blushed hotly all over as he lavished attention on both her breasts, but his whispered accolades filled her with pride and joy.

The loving torment continued as his hand swept down over her abdomen and smooth, slightly concave stomach to the triangle of silky curls at the apex of her thighs. Without hesitation, he homed in on his target. "You're lovely here, too." His stroking fingers underscored his words. "So moist and warm and welcoming."

He made her feel beautiful. Womanly. Desired. Unselfishly, he adored her with his fingertips, his eyes glowing as he noted what pleased her, what made her eyes go soft and smoky. With exquisite care and tenderness, he stroked her feminine portal, giving her untold pleasure, sending her to the edge of mindless passion.

Joanna shuddered, her fingers digging into the taut muscles in the back of his neck and shoulders as he found the core of her womanhood and kneaded it gently with his thumb.

"Oh, Sean. Sean. Sean." His name was a breathless

chant on her lips. A plea. A command. A siren's song. Obeying its call, Sean moved over her, taking her mouth in an ardent kiss as he fitted his hips to hers, his firmness to her pliancy.

Joanna wrapped her long legs around him, her soft cries of love filling the room, as with long loving strokes, he took her to that glorious realm she had known only in his arms.

The end came quickly, an explosive burst of rapture that left them both spent and trembling. Eyes closed, Joanna held Sean close and ran her hands languidly over him, absently brushing away the sheen of moisture from his back. Their hearts thundered in unison. Their lungs labored for air.

After a moment Sean summoned the energy to move and rolled from her onto his side. Draping an arm possessively across her waist, he closed his eyes and kissed her shoulder. "Mmm, what a heavenly way to say good morning," he mumbled drowsily.

"Uh-huh. And a very effective method of getting your own way," Joanna scolded.

She tweaked the hair on Sean's chest, but he merely grunted and burrowed deeper into the pillow, neither admitting nor denying her accusation. Smiling, Joanna watched him, her eyes tracing lovingly over his handsome face, exulting in its nearness. She felt saturated with happiness, utterly content.

For a time Sean did not move or speak, and Joanna thought he had fallen asleep until suddenly he emitted a long, agonized sound.

"What is it? What's the matter?"

"I just thought of something."

"What?"

"Matt's going to kill me," he groaned.

"Matt?" Joanna's amused chuckle held surprise and skepticism. "Don't be silly. Why should Matt care?"

"Because you're part of his family now, and Matt Drummond takes care of his own." Sean opened his eyes and looked at her quizzically. "Didn't you know that?"

Joanna shook her head. "But...but I'm his stepdaughter, not his daughter."

"To a man like Matt, there's very little difference. And men tend to get a bit paranoid and protective where their daughters are concerned. Hell, if he'd known about that lecherous professor of yours he'd probably have given the man the beating he deserves."

Joanna raised up on one elbow and gazed at Sean with eyes as round as saucers. "Really?" It stunned her to think that Matt would be that fiercely protective of her. Would her own father have resorted to physical violence on her behalf? Joanna doubted it. Oh, he would have sought revenge by some covert method, but he would not have actually soiled his hands on the man.

"Yes, really," Sean assured her, smiling at her astonished expression. "Matt happens to be very fond of you. When you graduated from college with honors he was as proud as punch. He even cut short a meeting with the Secretary of State to make it to your graduation ceremony."

Dazed, Joanna fell back on her pillow and stared up at the ceiling. She and Matt had made their peace with each other years ago. Since that time she had come to admire and respect him, to like him as a person, but for some reason their relationship had never developed beyond a sort of cautious, polite friendship. Certainly she had never suspected that Matt harbored any paternal feelings for her.

But, as Joanna thought about it, a pleased smile began to grow on her face. She found that being regarded as a cherished daughter by a man like Matt Drummond was very pleasant indeed. It gave her a warm feeling she hadn't known since her father's death.

"Why are you so surprised?" Bracing on his elbow,

Sean propped his head in his hand. With deep absorption, he watched his other hand chart the long curve of her hip and thigh.

His intent gaze made Joanna suddenly aware of her nakedness. Though she knew it was ludicrous, all at once she felt painfully shy. Rising partway, she reached for the sheet to cover herself.

"Oh, no you don't." Sean chuckled wickedly and pushed her back down onto the pillow with gentle but firm pressure. "It's too late for modesty now, my sweet. Besides, there's not an inch of that beautiful body I haven't already seen. Or kissed." Holding her gaze, he smiled a slow, devilish smile and skimmed his hand up over her waist and the gentle flare of her ribs. "Now go ahead, answer my question."

"Matt...Matt and I got off to a bad start four years ago," Joanna replied unsteadily. She drew several deep breaths and struggled to ignore that marauding hand, the heel of which was now pressing rhythmically against the side of her breast. "We, uh, we worked it out, and we get along fine now, but, well...I, uh, I guess I just never expected him to care all that much about what happened to me."

"It's not really so surprising, when you consider how much he loves your mother. You're Claire's daughter, a part of her, and in Matt's book that makes you a very special person." Sean abandoned his sensual teasing and touched her chin with his fingertips, turning her head toward him. Smiling tenderly, he looked at her in a way that made Joanna's breath catch and said in a low, husky voice, "And I happen to agree."

He placed an infinitely soft, lingering kiss on her mouth, then pulled her close and settled her head on his shoulder. Joanna nestled against him with a happy sigh. Feeling utterly content, she absently threaded her fingers through the forest of black hairs on his chest, and after a moment a pleased smile began to build on her face. "Matt is crazy about Mother, isn't he?" she said, in dreamy satisfaction.

"Yeah, he is that," Sean agreed drowsily.

"It's amazing when you think about it. Matt knew Mother for over fifteen years and to tell you the truth, I don't think he even liked her. Then all at once they fell head over heels in love and got married." She chuckled at the memory. "That really knocked some people for a loop, especially the Washington social leaders. For years Matt had been D.C.'s most eligible, most elusive bachelor."

"Well, your mother is a special lady. She's beautiful, she's bright, she's nice and just about as classy as they come. It's easy to understand why Matt fell so hard." Sean's chest shook, and beneath her ear, Joanna heard the soft rumble of laughter before it left his throat. "Hell," he admitted with a little snort of rueful amusement, "I came very close to falling in love with Claire myself."

Joanna went perfectly still. Her heart began to pound with slow, painful thuds and a sick sensation curled in the pit of her stomach. Sean? In love with Claire? Oh, God!

A quivering hurt started deep in the center of Joanna's being and spread outward, encompassing every cell, every molecule. Suddenly she felt cold and achy and very fragile. She had to get out of there. Now! Before she shattered.

"Hey. Where are you going?" Sean asked in surprise when she firmly eased out of his embrace and sat up.

Joanna blushed when she saw her dress. The fluttery silk chiffon creation lay on the floor where she had stepped out of it the night before, like a circular puddle of pastel flowers. Beside it lay her bikini panties and her tiny gold mesh evening bag. The lacy garter belt and stockings were draped wantonly over the chair, just as they had landed when he stripped them from her and tossed them aside.

Keeping her back to Sean, Joanna picked up her panties and stepped into them, then hastily drew on the wrinkled chiffon gown. "I've got to go back to my suite," she said over her shoulder, struggling to keep her voice calm. "I told you that a while ago."

Sean exhaled a resigned sigh. "Okay, honey, if it'll make you feel better, go ahead. I'll take a shower and order breakfast while you're gone. What would you like?"

"Anything. It doesn't matter." After retrieving her purse from the floor, Joanna snatched up her garter belt and stockings and rolled them into a tight ball. With hurried, jerky movements, she stepped into her shoes and headed for the door. She was reaching for the knob when Sean's arms encircled her from behind.

"Hey, not so fast," he chided huskily in her ear. "You're not getting out of here without telling me good-bye." He kissed the sensitive spot he had discovered on her neck and playfully batted her lobe with his tongue. Moving closer, he settled his middle more firmly against her derriere.

Through the thin chiffon of her gown, Joanna could feel his manhood pressing against her. He had come to her naked, and his warmth and his male scent enveloped her. She closed her eyes briefly, swamped with conflicting feelings of despair and longing.

His splayed hands were gliding caressingly over her midriff and abdomen. Joanna grasped his forearms to stop the tantalizing motion. "Sean, please," she scolded with a feigned lightheartedness that required a great effort of will. "If you don't stop that I'll never get out of here."

"Promise?"

"*Sean!*"

"Oh, all right."

He reached up to turn her face to the side for his kiss. His muscular forearm fit snugly between her breasts, against her skin above the low cut gown. Their lips clung sweetly in the softest of kisses that served to increase her inner trembling. When he lifted his head Sean looked deep into her eyes and whispered, "I'll see you in a half hour. Now go, before I change my mind."

Unable to speak, Joanna nodded and fled.

Magnificently naked, Sean stood in the middle of the floor for several seconds after the door closed behind her, a bemused smile tugging at his mouth. Feet apart, hands on his hip bones, he threw his head back and chuckled at the ceiling, a soft masculine rumble of amused self-derision. Joanna. Joanna Andrews. If anyone had told him, even a week ago, that she would become the center of his world he would have said they were crazy. Yet, that was exactly what she was. She had gotten under his skin, become as necessary to him as food and drink, as breathing. Even now he had to stifle the urge to stomp out after her and drag her back.

God, Fleming. You've really got it bad if you can't bear to let her out of your sight for only a few minutes. Shaking his head, he turned and started for the shower.

All the arguments he had given her for not getting involved were still valid, he reminded himself as he adjusted the water and stepped beneath the spray. He was too old for her. Too experienced. Their backgrounds were totally different. Though not exactly poor, he certainly wasn't in her financial bracket. And Claire and Matt would probably have a walleyed fit when they discovered that he and Joanna were lovers. Sean rubbed the bar of soap over his chest and shoulders, creating mounds of creamy lather. His face wore a pensive smile. Hell, Matt would probably get out his shotgun.

It was a daunting list of negatives, but this morning they just didn't seem all that important. He squirted shampoo into his palm, closed his eyes and scrubbed his ebony curls until they squeaked. If he was going to have breakfast delivered before Joanna returned he would have to hurry. Sticking his head under the shower spray, he hummed happily as the bubbles streamed down over his face and sleek, wet body.

Damn, I feel terrific!

Joanna felt wretched. Confused, sick at heart, she paced the floor of her sitting room. Though she tried to banish it, Sean's casual comment played over and over in her mind. *"I came very close to falling in love with Claire myself."*

How close was close? A mild attraction? An infatuation? A burning passion? What?

Joanna stopped by the window and stared out at the ocean gliding by. They were cruising leisurely toward Jamaica. This was a day at sea, a day she should be enjoying with Sean, not hiding out in her room harboring these nasty suspicions. But she couldn't help it. They gnawed at her unmercifully.

Looking back, a lot of things were clearer now: the long, hard hours Sean had devoted to Claire's senatorial campaign four years ago—hours that had kept him in almost constant contact with her, the way he had been so protective of Claire when Matt had walked out on her, the fondness in his eyes whenever he looked at her mother. At the time Joanna had merely thought that he was an extremely good and conscientious press secretary, doing his job. Instead, it was unrequited love.

Recalling the crush she'd had on Sean then, Joanna gave a bitter little laugh. She crossed her arms over her middle and gazed, unseeingly, at the sky. Lord! No wonder Sean hadn't even noticed that she was alive. He'd only had eyes for Claire.

Not that she blamed him. Her mother was, then and now, a beautiful woman. She was also intelligent, articulate and very strong, yet she possessed that soft femininity that fascinated and charmed both men and women.

Joanna knew perfectly well that there had never been

anything between her mother and Sean, and that whatever Sean had felt, he had kept to himself. Claire was totally, passionately, irrevocably in love with Matt. Yet, every time Joanna thought of Sean loving her mother she felt a spurt of anger that terrified her.

Making a harsh sound, Joanna turned away from the window and raked both hands through her silky hair, slicking it back away from her face and pressing her palms flat against her temples. Lord, she didn't want to feel this way. Especially not about her mother. It had taken a long time and a lot of growing up on Joanna's part for her to appreciate Claire. In the past few years they had developed a close and loving relationship, and Joanna didn't want anything to jeopardize that.

She wanted very much to believe that Sean really cared for her, that what they had shared the night before had been special, but she couldn't help but wonder if she had just been a substitute for her mother. If the love that Matt felt for Claire could be extended to include her, then why couldn't Sean's?

Tormented by the thought, Joanna paced faster. With every circuit of the room her movements grew more and more agitated. "I will not run the risk of being used," she muttered forcefully, fighting back tears of despair. "Nor will I allow myself to be eaten up with jealousy. I *won't!*"

The vow had barely left her lips when the telephone rang, making Joanna jump. She swung around and stared at it as though it were a coiled snake about to strike. It shrilled repeatedly, but Joanna made no move to answer it. She knew who was calling.

When the insistent ringing finally stopped, Joanna walked to the sofa and sat down. As she had known he would, within seconds Sean knocked on the door.

"Joanna? Joanna are you in there?" She didn't reply, and after a few seconds he knocked again, harder this time. "Joanna?"

He tried several more times and though she could detect the growing note of concern in his voice, she remained still and quiet. When at last the pounding stopped Joanna leaned her head back against the leather sofa and closed her eyes. Tears squeezed from between her lids and her chin quivered. Her heart felt like a lead weight in her chest.

Joanna stayed in her room for the remainder of the day. Hiding. Hurting. Sean knocked on her door and called several more times, but she gritted her teeth and ignored him. She paced and cried. She lay on her bed and cried. She stared out at the sea and thought and cried. Over and over she told herself she was doing the right thing, but it didn't help.

Lunch time came and went and Joanna didn't notice, but by evening her empty stomach was beginning to protest. Briefly, she considered ordering dinner in her suite, but quickly dismissed the idea. They would be cruising for another week yet. Sooner or later she was going to have to face Sean.

Deciding that there was no point in prolonging the inevitable, she bathed her puffy eyes in cold water, applied her makeup carefully, donned a confidence-building strapless yellow voile dress and headed for the dining room.

Hoping that Sean would not make a scene in front of the others, she deliberately arrived late. It was a futile hope, for he bounded up out of his chair the moment he saw her. His expression held not even a trace of his usual nonchalance.

"Where the hell have you been?"

"In my room."

"In your room!" She couldn't have shocked him more if she had said she'd been on the moon.

"Yes." Joanna gave him a cool look and slipped into her chair, leaving him standing there simmering impotently. As she calmly shook out her napkin and draped it across her lap she could feel his incredulous gaze raking over her.

"I knocked on your door several times, and I called your room every half hour. Why the hell didn't you answer?"

"Sean, please, don't stand there shouting. People are beginning to stare."

"I don't give a good——" He bit off the profane curse he was about to utter and glanced around at the avid expressions on the faces of their table companions. A muscle rippled along his clenched jaw. With barely controlled violence, Sean flung himself back into his chair and leaned close to Joanna. "If you're worried about me making a scene, then you'd damn well better give me some answers, and fast. Why didn't you answer your door or your phone? For that matter, why the hell didn't you come back to my cabin like you were supposed to?"

"Sean!" Joanna turned a deep pink and cast an anxious glance at the others.

"Answer me."

"I had a headache. I didn't feel like talking."

"And you couldn't have picked up the phone and told me that? Dammit, Joanna, I spent the whole day searching this ship for you. I've been frantic. I was beginning to think you'd fallen overboard."

"I'm sorry, but I really don't feel that I have to explain myself to you or anyone. Now, if you don't mind, I'd like to order dinner. I'm starving. I haven't eaten all day."

Sean seethed. Joanna could feel the fury radiating off him in waves, and she held her breath, sure that he was going to explode at any moment. Apparently so did the others, for no one moved or spoke.

After what seemed like a small eternity, Sean said tightly between clenched teeth, "All right. We'll have dinner. But afterward you and I are going to have a talk."

The silence around the table was so tense it fairly hummed. At first Mary tried to make small talk but every-

one was so ill at ease, after a while she gave up. Despite
a day without food, Joanna's appetite was nonexistent, and
she did little more than move her food around on her plate.
Sean didn't even pretend to be interested in eating.
Throughout the meal he merely watched Joanna through
narrowed eyes and sipped from the glass of bourbon beside
his plate. The close scrutiny twanged her nerves like a
plucked string.

The others finished quickly and began to excuse themselves. When Mary announced that she and Charles were
going to the show in the Caribbean Lounge, Joanna made
a last-ditch attempt to avoid the confrontation that was
brewing between her and Sean.

"That sounds like fun. Do you mind if I join you?" she
asked ingenuously, rising to her feet as they did.

Mary and Charles exchanged dubious looks, but they
were spared the necessity of a reply when Sean said succinctly, "I mind."

Joanna sputtered, but before she could voice an objec-
tion he rose and clamped his hand firmly around her arm.
With a nod and a terse, "Excuse us" for the Wrights, he
turned and all but frog marched Joanna from the dining
room.

Without a word, he led her down the stairs to their deck.
She shot him a cool glare when he stopped outside the
door to her suite. "You surely don't expect me to invite
you in?"

"We need someplace private to talk. It's either this or
my cabin. The choice is yours."

Joanna gritted her teeth in silent frustration, but after a
moment, dug into her purse for her key.

"All right, now I want to know just what you think
you're doing," Sean demanded the moment they stepped
into the room, and the door clicked shut behind them.

"I don't know what you're talking about," Joanna replied haughtily.

"I'm talking about this little game of hide-and-seek we've been playing all day. What the hell was that all about?"

"I'm not playing a game."

"Then what do you call it?"

"I told you, I had a headache."

Sean's one word reply was blunt, to the point and crude.

Joanna sucked in her breath. "All right! That's it!" she huffed. "Just get out. This discussion is over."

Spinning around on her heel, she started to march toward the bedroom, but Sean grabbed her wrist and whirled her back. Momentum sent her stumbling forward until she collided with his chest. Sean's arms encircled her, and he thrust his furious face so close to hers their noses were almost touching.

"That's what you think," he growled. "You're not going anywhere, Joanna, until I have some answers. Last night we became lovers, and this morning you pull a disappearing act and now you're giving me the deep freeze treatment. I want to know why!"

Joanna braced her forearms against his chest and strained to break his hold, but she only succeeded in bringing their lower bodies into even closer contact. Though Sean's face remained stern the glint in his eye told her he was aware of the intimacy and enjoying it. After the miserable day she'd had, that was the final straw. Joanna's temper shot up like a Roman candle on July Fourth.

"All right! I'll tell you why," she all but shouted. "I decided that I don't want to be a substitute for another woman, that's why!"

"Another... Substi... What the hell are you ranting about? What other woman?"

"My mother, that's who."

Sean's arms fell away from her, and he took a couple

of staggering steps backward. Mouth agape, he stared at her in blank shock. Then, to Joanna's utter astonishment, he threw back his head and roared with laughter.

Chapter Eleven

"Don't you dare laugh at me, Sean Fleming!"

"I ca...I ca-can't...help it," Sean choked out between the deep, rumbling guffaws.

Joanna was torn between anger and hurt, but anger soon won out. She blinked furiously to keep the tears at bay, and stuck her chin out at a pugnacious angle, though it still quivered uncontrollably. "There's nothing funny about this situation."

Finally, either her irate tone or the wounded look on her face got through to Sean. With a struggle, he managed to control his mirth, but remnants of it were still visible in his twinkling eyes and twitching mouth. "*You* are what's funny, sweetheart. Good grief, Joanna, where on earth did you get the idea that I'm in love with Claire?"

"From you."

"*Me!*"

"Yes. You admitted as much this morning. When we were talking about how strange it was that Matt and

Mother fell in love, after knowing each other for years, you said that you had come very close to falling in love with her yourself.''

"So, because of that innocent comment, you think that I've been carrying a torch for Claire all this time?'' The amusement faded from Sean's face, and a tiny frown tugged between his brows. A hint of sadness touched his expression. "And because I couldn't have her, I settled for you, is that it? You actually think I'm the type of man who would do that?''

Joanna wilted and heaved a dispirited little sigh as some of the fight went out of her. "Oh, not consciously," she said, with a forlorn twitch of her mouth. "But unrequited love can drive us to do strange things. I ought to know. I followed you on this cruise on the flimsiest of excuses.''

Leaning back against one of the leather easy chairs, Sean crossed his arms over his chest and smiled crookedly. "So, you admit to that now, do you? And do you realize that you've as much as admitted that you're in love with me, and have been for a while?'' Sean tipped his head to the side and cocked one brow. "Did you have a crush on me four years ago, Joanna? Was I too blind to notice?''

"Sean, please, don't tease me," Joanna pleaded, giving him a desperate look and blinking against a fresh rush of tears. "Not now.''

"Ah, sweetheart, don't cry.'' Sean crossed the space between them and took her hands. As he searched her unhappy face his expression was a mixture of tenderness and exasperation. "Joanna listen to me. I am *not* in love with Claire. Almost falling in love is one heck of a long way from actually falling in love.''

"But you were attracted to her, weren't you?'' Joanna wanted to kick herself for asking. It was like probing a sore tooth with your tongue: you knew it was going to hurt but you couldn't resist doing it.

Sean sighed heavily. "Yes, I was. Claire is one heck of

a woman. And yes, I'll admit that *if* things had been different, *if* there hadn't been Matt, and *if* your mother had been attracted to me, it might have happened. But, darling, those are all very big if's. I haven't been pining away from unrequited love for the past four years. It never went that far. The truth is, I'm glad things turned out as they did. Matt is my best friend, and your mother runs a close second. I'm happy for them.''

Catching her bottom lip between her teeth, Joanna looked at him worriedly. A lingering trace of doubt mingled with the hope and longing in her hazel eyes. ''Are you sure?''

''Positive.''

Sean raised his hand and traced the elegant line of her cheek and jaw. Then he threaded his fingertips through the silky hair at her temple. His thumb skated lightly back and forth over the tiny mole at the corner of her mouth. ''Oh, Joanna, you goose. I can't believe you've put us through this miserable day over that one offhand remark. After what we shared last night, how could you possibly think that I was in love with another woman?''

Covering his hand with hers, Joanna pressed her cheek against his palm and closed her eyes wearily. ''I don't know. I…I guess I still can't quite believe that this is happening. Us, I mean. I suppose, deep down, it seems too good to be true, and I keep expecting something to go wrong.''

Sean felt his heart constrict. An overwhelming tenderness gripped him as he studied the fragile beauty of her face, the delicate sweep of dark lashes against pale skin. Lord, she was so sweet, so guileless. He couldn't remember ever feeling such a strong desire to protect a woman, to cherish, to claim her for his own.

Sean slipped his thumb beneath her chin and tipped her head up. ''Joanna, look at me,'' he commanded, and Joanna's lids drifted open. She gazed up at him with soft, luminous eyes filled with love, and he felt as though his insides were melting. "There is only you," he said in a soft, rough whisper. "There will be only you. Here, on this ship, and when we return home to Washington. You're the only woman I need. The only one I want."

It was more of a commitment than he had ever made before, but strangely, with this woman, it just wasn't enough. He wanted more. Wanted to give more. "Joanna, I..." He hesitated, his chest aching with a yearning pressure as he stared down at her. She was waiting, watching him with her heart in her eyes, and suddenly his own widened. "I love you." He said the words slowly, as though stunned by the discovery, his face blank with amazement. And then, softer, surer, in a voice deepened by awe, "I love you."

Joanna sucked in her breath. For a timeless moment she stared up at him, her eyes slowly filling with tears. "Oh, Sean," she choked out unsteadily through quivering lips. "Do you mean that? Please don't say it unless it's true. I—"

"Shhh. Shhh, sweetheart." He placed his fingers over her mouth to stop the anguished flow of words and looked at her tenderly. "I mean it. It took me by surprise, but I do love you, Joanna. Very much."

"Oh, Sean." She struggled valiantly to contain the tumultuous storm of emotion that buffeted her, but it was impossible. Her mouth and chin wobbled as tears spilled over and trickled down her cheeks, and with a joyous little cry she flung herself against him, burying her face against his chest and wrapping her arms tightly around his lean middle.

Sean held her close and rocked her gently. With a tender smile, he rubbed his chin against the top of her head as she laughed and cried at the same time. "I'm going to assume that you're crying for joy. Otherwise my ego is going to take a hell of a beating."

Joanna sniffed and hiccuped. Leaning back within his embrace, she laughed self-consciously and wiped at her cheeks with the back of her hands. "Of course I am. Oh, Sean," she said in an emotion-packed voice, looking up at him with melting eyes. "I've loved you for so long, but I never really believed that you would ever love me back. You never seemed interested in a serious relationship, even though there have been many beautiful, glamorous women in your life—"

"Hey." He stopped the flow of words with a quick, breath-stealing kiss. When it ended he smiled into her eyes. "That's all over now. I was never serious about any of them, because I didn't love them. I do love you, Joanna. Very much."

She cupped his face between her palms. "And I love you, darling," she whispered tremulously.

Their lips met in a slow, sweet kiss. Joanna twined her arms around his neck and held him close, her heart swelling with a pleasure so intense it was almost pain. Sean's arms enclosed her, binding her gently but firmly to him, flattening her breasts against his chest. His hand splayed over her buttocks, pressing her feminine cradle tight against the hard ridge of his arousal. Heat sizzled between them. Their aching bodies throbbed. Taut muscles quivered. And still the tender kiss went on and on.

When Sean's lips left hers to trail moistly over her cheek Joanna stroked her hands over his shoulders and neck and tunneled her fingers in the thick hair at his nape. A shudder rippled through her when his tongue wetly traced the delicate swirls in her ear, and she sighed. "Oh, darling, this seems too wonderful to be true. I'm terrified I'm going to wake up and find it was all a dream."

"This is no dream," he murmured, nibbling a wet path down the side of her neck. "This is real. I intend—" his lips pressed against the pulse at the base of her throat "—to show you just how real."

Sean's mobile mouth blazed a tormenting trail back up over the arch of her throat, lingering a moment to nuzzle the tender skin on the underside of her jaw. Then his lips claimed hers again in a slow, drugging kiss that made her senses swim, her knees go weak.

Breaking the thrilling contact suddenly, Sean scooped her up in his arms. He paused, holding her high against his chest, his dark, fiery gaze searing over her flushed face with a possessiveness that made Joanna's skin tingle. "It may take me all night," he said huskily.

Joanna looped her arms around his neck and smiled. "I hope so."

Sean growled, and his mouth came down hard on hers. Without breaking the thrilling contact, he headed for the bedroom with long, purposeful strides.

The next few days passed in a haze of sheer happiness. They were so perfect, Joanna still had trouble convincing herself she wasn't dreaming it all.

In the evenings after dinner they went dancing or saw a show in the main lounge, or just strolled the decks, arm in arm, before returning to either Joanna's suite or Sean's cabin. Their nights were filled with passionate loving so intensely beautiful it left them both shaken and awed, but their hunger for each other went beyond the physical. For hours, lying in each other's arms while the ship rocked gently beneath them, they talked quietly, sharing secrets, hopes, joys and disappointments.

The daytime hours were spent ashore on the islands. Together, Joanna and Sean explored Ochos Rios and toured Jamaica's heavily cultivated coastal lowlands and valleys and the inland limestone plateau. On Grand Cayman they visited a turtle farm and strolled hand in hand for hours down the beautiful seven-mile beach.

The ship's next port of call was Cozumel, where Joanna and Sean spent the morning strolling through the quaint shops before succumbing to the lure of the beach. With rented snorkeling equipment, they explored the turquoise water for over an hour. Then, like two children, they indulged themselves in a boisterous game of tag, splashing and dunking each other mercilessly. Finally, exhausted, they hauled themselves out of the water and collapsed on the large towels they had spread on the sand.

Sean flopped down on his back and flung his forearm over his eyes. "Whew! I may never move again. Keeping up with a sweet young thing like you is tough on an old man."

Joanna dropped onto her knees beside him and began to towel dry her hair. "Oh, come on, you're not that old. Don't tell me a little shopping and swimming has you tuckered."

Rolling his arm up a quarter turn, Sean gave her a long, sizzling look and drawled, "It's not so much the shopping and swimming, as all those strenuous nights."

"Complaining?" Joanna asked with a sultry smile.

Sean's face softened, and he reached out and lifted a drop of water from the end of her nose with his fingertip. "Hardly," he said huskily.

Joanna took his hand and brought it to her mouth. Holding his gaze, she kissed the end of his finger tenderly.

"Ouch!" Sean yelped when she nipped the pad, and Joanna laughed throatily, the sound full of delight and mischief and sensual promise.

"You little devil, you—"

"Oh, look," Joanna cried, cutting him off as she sprang to her feet. "There's someone selling ice-cream cones." She looked at him eagerly and began to search through her terry cloth beach bag for some money. "You want one?"

Sean's smile was indulgent. "I think I'll pass. But you go ahead."

"Okay. I'll be right back."

Rolling to his side, Sean propped his head against his palm and watched her trot away toward the vendor's stand. Subtly, his smile changed to one of masculine enjoyment as he admired her narrow, tapered back, the cute derriere, the firm lithe curves of her legs.

Sean was still amazed by the feelings that swamped him every time he looked at Joanna: love, pride, jealousy, a violent possessiveness. He'd never felt like that about a woman before. He'd liked many, been fond of several. A few he had even thought he loved, but it hadn't been like this. Never like this.

For the past few years a vague feeling of discontent had been slowly growing in him. As little as three weeks ago he had been besieged with doubts, and had felt restless and unsettled, unsure of what he wanted out of life, personally or professionally. No longer.

He knew now exactly what had been missing from his life: love, commitment, having that one special someone to share your triumphs and defeats, your joys and griefs. And there was no doubt in his mind or his heart that for him, that someone was Joanna.

Neither was there any longer doubt about which direction he wanted his professional life to take. The long-term goals he'd been working toward for years were still worthwhile. And now that he'd found what he'd unconsciously been searching for, he was eager to pursue them.

Joanna had her ice-cream cone and was strolling back at a leisurely pace. Sean smiled as he watched her pink tongue lick the fast melting sweet. His eyes ran down her slim, willowy body, deliciously revealed in the skimpy bikini, noting the way her hips swung with unconscious provocation, and he felt his body tighten, his heart flood with emotion. She was innocence and sensuality, youthful eagerness and gritty determination, girlish appeal and womanly allure.

And she was his.

At least, she would be soon if he had anything to say about it.

Joanna dropped down beside him and waved her cone under his nose. "Wanna bite?"

"Umm, but not of ice cream," Sean drawled, dropping his gaze to the soft swells of her breasts above the bikini bra. His black eyes glinted with drowsy sensuality, and as the flush spread up over Joanna's neck and shoulders his smile grew wicked.

"You're insatiable."

"Complaining?" he asked, in the same intimate tone she had used.

Joanna forgot all about her embarrassment as heat suffused her. When Sean looked at her that way she felt all tingly and weak. Her gaze went soft, and her voice dropped to a warm velvet pitch. "No. Not in the least." Holding her cone out to the side, she leaned close. "Since I can't do anything about that appetite of yours right now, maybe this will hold you until we get back to the ship."

Her mouth met his, open, sweet, soft. It was the gentlest of caresses, a mere touch, a delicate rubbing of flesh to flesh, yet its sensual impact was staggering. At the first touch Sean's heart slammed against his ribs and began to beat with a painful, heavy thud. Her tongue darted into his mouth, rubbed his and darted out again, and he shivered. She tasted of ice cream and salt water and woman. Of Joanna.

It was a taste he was becoming addicted to. Hungrily, he sought more. Over and over, without increasing the pressure of the kiss, he delved into the honeyed sweetness, plumbing the silken depths of her mouth thoroughly, slowly.

His hand slid up her braced arm to her shoulder, her neck. Lightly, he touched her jaw with the tips of his shaking fingers, then sank them into the damp hair behind her ear.

A squealing child ran by, followed by a yapping dog.
They didn't hear them, or the faint swish of waves tumbling gently against the shore or the dry rattle of tatter
palms overhead. Their lips nibbled softly, rocked back and
forth, clung. Their breaths mingled. The sun beat warmly
against their damp flesh, but they felt only the heat of
passion that surged so hotly between them. Tortuously, the
soft kiss went on and on as taut muscles quivered against
the tender restraint.

Joanna's fingers crushed the waffle cone, and the melting scoop of ice cream plopped to the sand.

Abruptly, Sean ended the kiss. Their gazes locked, and
for a moment they stared at each other in heated silence.
A few strands of Joanna's hair lifted in the gentle breeze.
Their chests rose and fell as they drew in long, shaky
draughts of air. With every breath they inhaled the smells
of sand and sea, of warm flesh, of coconut-scented tanning
lotion.

A muscle twitched along Sean's jaw. Without warning,
he grabbed Joanna's wrist and stood, dragging her up with
him. "Come on," he commanded in a tight, strained voice,
snatching up the towels and her beach bag. "We're going."

"Where?" Joanna cried. He marched across the sand
with long, ground-eating strides, and she stumbled along
beside him.

"Back to the ship. This beach is too damned public for
what I have in mind."

In the taxi that took them back to the harbor they sat on
opposite sides of the seat, stiff and silent, looking straight
ahead, only their clasped hands touching. The air between
them was thick with awareness. Their bodies throbbed with
anticipation.

When they boarded the ship there was almost no one
around. It was early afternoon, and most of the passengers
and crew were still ashore. As they walked down the long,

deserted passageway it seemed to Joanna that they would never reach her suite.

The moment the door clicked shut behind them they were in each other's arms.

"Oh, Lord, sweetheart, I can't get enough of you," Sean panted in between tumultuous kisses.

"I know. I know," Joanna agreed breathlessly.

Her clutching hands roamed frantically over his back, before they slipped beneath the waistband of his swimsuit and grasped his firm buttocks. Sean growled and grabbed the string tie of her bikini top.

In a frenzy of snatching and tugging, they worked to rid each other of their skimpy beachwear. Within seconds Joanna's bikini bra went sailing across the room. It landed on a lamp shade and dangled provocatively. As their lips met in a long hungry kiss Sean's fingers worried the string ties at Joanna's hips. When they wouldn't budge he growled in frustration and gave them a sharp yank, and with the sound of popping thread, the ties tore away and the tiny scrap of material dropped to the floor to join the pile of towels at their feet.

With her thumbs hooked under the top edge of Sean's brief trunks, Joanna bent her knees and pushed them downward. Dropping lower, she scattered frantic kisses over his chest, his abdomen, his lean belly. Her teeth nipped at his protruding hipbone, and a violent shudder rippled through Sean. "Oh, God, Joanna," he groaned and clutched her hair with both hands as her tongue traced a wet line down his thigh.

Desperately, he bent and lifted her to her feet. For a taut instant they looked at each other in silence. Then she melted into his arms, and their soft moans of pleasure blended together as warm flesh met warm flesh. Their mouths melded in a searing kiss. Joanna raised up on her tiptoes and coiled her arms around his neck, shuddering at the gentle rasp of his chest hair against her tight, aching nipples.

Sean's hands roamed freely over her slender curves while he kissed her with a hungry passion, his tongue thrusting slowly, ardently, into the sweet darkness of her mouth.

A few feet away the bedroom beckoned, but neither could wait. With their mouths still fused together, they sank to the carpeted floor. There was a wild hunger raging in both of them. We're like greedy children, Joanna thought, and briefly she wondered at her own wantonness. But it didn't matter. Nothing mattered but their love, and the delicious pleasure it brought them.

They touched and explored and stroked until they could not stand it a moment longer. "Dear heaven, you make me wild," Sean declared huskily, as tremors wracked his body.

Clutching at his shoulders, Joanna urged him to her and sobbed, "Now, darling. Oh, please, now." and Sean moved between her thighs and slid into her. He thrust deep, loving her with a ferocity that should have frightened her, but didn't. Instead she matched it, and the compelling rhythm built, faster, stronger, spinning out of control, until there was a vast, ecstatic explosion that sent them hurtling into space.

And then they were falling...falling...falling....

Joanna had no idea how long she floated in that delicious sea of languor, but all too soon Sean was nudging her. "Come on, sexy. That floor is okay in the throes of passion, but if you fall asleep there you'll be too sore to move later."

"But Sean," she groaned in protest as he hauled her to her feet. "I'm so sleepy."

"There's a perfectly good bed in the next room to nap on. But first we hit the shower."

Too lethargic to protest further, Joanna allowed him to

bundle her into the shower stall. She was thoroughly scrubbed and shampooed, and after she returned the favor Sean backed her against the tile wall, and there beneath the warm spray, they made love again. Slowly. Deliciously.

A half hour later, curled against Sean's side in the king-size bed, Joanna smiled drowsily and ran her fingers through the mat of hair on his chest. She felt content, sated, complete. Settling her head more comfortably on his shoulder, she sighed with sheer pleasure and wondered if anyone else had ever been as happy as she was at that moment. Sean loved her. After all this time it seemed a miracle, and she clutched the knowledge to her like a coveted treasure.

Sean's arm encircled her, holding her close, his hand absently massaging her hip. He stared at the ceiling as he nuzzled her forehead with his chin. Tipping her head up, Joanna gazed at his handsome face, pensive now in repose, and smiled. "What are you thinking?" she asked quietly.

He looked down at her and smiled with his eyes. "Oh, I was just wondering if you would be happy as the wife of a senator," he said, so casually it took a moment for his words to register. Even then she wasn't sure she'd heard him right.

Her eyes grew wide and her heart began to pound. "Wh-what do you mean?"

Sean's grin flashed at her confusion, and just as quickly his expression grew serious. "I've decided to run for that Senate seat, Joanna, and I want you by my side. As my wife."

Joanna's heart soared with joy. She looked at him in amazement, her eyes slowly filling with tears as emotion choked her. "Oh, Sean," she managed finally in a wobbling voice and reached up and touched his cheek with her fingertips.

Capturing the hand, Sean brought it to his lips. The teasing smile returned to his eyes as he lazily nipped her. "Does that mean yes?"

Laughing and crying at the same time, Joanna flung herself across his chest and covered his face with wet kisses. "Yes! Yes! Yes!"

Sean laughingly accepted the exuberant smacks, but after a moment he caught her head between his palms and brought her lips down to his for a hard, searing kiss. When it was over he eased her back and looked deep into her eyes. "I love you," he said with such depth of feeling that Joanna almost started crying again.

Love filled her heart and overflowed, spilling like a warm tide through her body. She blinked and gave him a melting look. "And I love you, my darling," she said with a tremulous smile. "Very much."

He wrapped his arms around her and pulled her against his chest. For a long, soul-satisfying time they held each other tight, absorbed in the wonder and beauty of the moment.

"You never answered my question about being a senator's wife," Sean said after a while, idly rubbing his hand up and down her back. "I want to make a bid for the nomination, Joanna, but not if it's going to make you unhappy."

Joanna's eyes popped open wide and she caught her breath. Good Lord! She had been so wrapped up in Sean, she hadn't even thought about the Senate race in days. Senator Hartwell would have a fit if he ever found out that she hadn't even brought up the subject.

She raised up on her forearms and looked at him. "Sean, I love politics. I'm delighted that you've decided to run. I don't mind campaigning. In fact, I love it. And I told you, I don't object to publicity, as long as it's for a good reason and isn't taken to an extreme, like it always has been with my mother."

"I was hoping you'd say that," Sean said, heaving a relieved sigh.

Tilting her head to one side Joanna looked at him quizzically. "When did you make up your mind about the race? And what caused you to accept? You seemed undecided a few weeks ago."

"Actually, I have you to thank for that."

"Me!"

Her astonished look drew a chuckle from Sean. "Yes, you. I came on this trip so I could put the whole thing out of my mind for a while, give it a rest, so that maybe I could put it into better perspective. With you on board, I was able to do just that." He lifted his head and planted a quick kiss on her mouth. "I haven't been able to think of anything but you since that first night."

Which, Joanna thought, thoroughly chagrined, *is exactly the opposite of what I was supposed to accomplish.*

"When I fell in love with you I realized that it was not my career, but the emptiness of my personal life that had been causing my dissatisfaction all along." His fingers stroked the side of her neck and played idly with the velvety rim of her ear. "Now that I have you, running for the Senate seems like a terrific idea. I'm itching to get back and get things rolling."

Joanna was deeply touched. And as she leaned down to kiss him she told herself that it was probably for the best that Sean had reached the decision on his own.

Chapter Twelve

Leaning close to the mirror, Joanna twirled the mascara wand over her lashes. When finished she brushed the merest touch of blusher across her cheeks, smoothed a deep bronze pink lipstick over her mouth, stepped back to survey the results and smiled. Without conceit, she knew that she looked better than she ever had in her life. Her eyes sparkled, and she glowed from within. Even her hair seemed to have taken on an extra shine. Love, Joanna decided, was the world's most fantastic beauty aid.

A glance at the travel clock beside her bed sent her scurrying to the closet. Sean would be back in a few minutes. A smile tilted Joanna's mouth as she riffled through the selection of evening wear. If she met him at the door in her robe they probably wouldn't make it to dinner at all. It was a tempting thought, but she resisted it and pulled out the bronze silk chiffon gown. Holding it in front of her, she twirled around to face the mirror.

The asymmetrical neckline draped low in the front and

still lower in the back, the soft folds gathering together at her right shoulder with a rhinestone clip. Below the nipped-in waist, a full, floating skirt swirled around her calves like a misty cloud. It was a deceptively simple dress that managed to be both elegant and alluring.

Still, it wasn't very colorful, and Sean had liked that blue crepe she had worn the other night. He seemed to have a preference for blue. Cocking her head to one side, Joanna frowned at her reflection.

She was still debating a few minutes later when a knock sounded on the door.

"Oh, Sean, why couldn't you be late for once," Joanna moaned, tossing the dress on the bed, but her face was alight with eagerness as she hurried through to the sitting room.

"Sean, you said—" she began as she pulled open the door, only to come to an abrupt halt when she saw the uniformed young man standing there. "Oh! I'm sorry." Joanna pulled the lapels of her robe together and tightened the sash. "I thought you were someone else."

"This just came for you, Miss Andrews." The young man smiled and handed her an envelope, then disappeared down the companionway before she could do more than offer a stammered thank you.

Shutting the door, Joanna stared curiously at the envelope, turning it over in her hand. As she opened the flap and drew out the folded sheet of paper she crossed to the sofa and sat down. It was a radiogram, and when her eyes darted down to the name at the bottom of the page Joanna winced. It was from Senator Hartwell.

EXPECTED REPORT BEFORE NOW stop PER-SUADED FLEMING YET stop DO WHATEVER NECESSARY stop MUST CONVINCE HIM TO ACCEPT BACKING stop TIME IS RIGHT stop CALL IN REPORT IMMEDIATELY stop

SEN HARTWELL

Joanna sighed heavily. She should have expected it. Her boss was not the most patient of men. She would have to call him. But not tonight. There would be plenty of time in the morning.

Reading through the message once more, Joanna felt a pang of guilt over the rash plan. She realized now that it had been incredibly arrogant and presumptuous of her to even try to influence Sean. Still, she couldn't regret coming on this trip.

Actually, everything turned out for the best all the way around, she assured herself. Senator Hartwell and the others were going to be pleased with Sean's decision, and it was one he had come to all by himself.

Three sharp raps on the door brought Joanna's head up, and her eyes began to sparkle. With a smile growing on her lips, she hurried to answer the summons, stuffing the radiogram into the side pocket of her robe on the way.

"Hello, darling. As you can see, I'm not quite ready, but it won't take but a minute to put on my dress."

"No problem." In a smooth, languid move, Sean stepped inside, closed the door and reached for her. "Mmm, you smell good," he murmured, nuzzling his face against the side of her neck. He mouthed the tender skin behind her ear. "And taste good." One hand slid down her back and cupped her buttocks, bringing her tightly against him. "And feel good."

The satin robe molding her curves was an erotic entice-ment, and his hands glided over her back and hips in a sensuous caress. His touch worked its magic, filling her with a quivering heat. Already Joanna could feel her body going weak and malleable.

"Oh, no you don't," Joanna chuckled weakly, pushing against his chest when his nibbling kisses edged toward her mouth. "If you don't stop, we'll never get out of here, and I'm starving. Now behave yourself, and let me get dressed.''

''Spoilsport,'' Sean growled, but when he lifted his head a devilish smile played around his mouth and his black eyes were gleaming.

It was a look that almost made her relent. Before she could succumb to its sensuous promise, Joanna pulled out of his arms and headed for the bedroom on shaky legs. ''I won't be but a minute,'' she tossed over her shoulder.

Smiling, Sean watched her until she disappeared into the bedroom. He took a step toward the sofa, noticed the crumpled sheet of paper on the floor and stooped to pick it up. He glanced at it, saw immediately from the standard form that it was a radiogram and started to toss it onto the coffee table, when suddenly his own name seemed to leap off the page at him.

He stopped, and very carefully smoothed out the sheet. By the time he finished reading the brief message his jaw was tight, his eyes flint hard. Except for the hand that slowly crumpled the paper into a tight ball, he stood rigidly still in the middle of the floor.

He was still there when Joanna returned a few minutes later.

''Will this do?'' Arms wide, she twirled around to give him a complete view, causing the bronze chiffon to flutter and float around her calves. He didn't reply. When she saw his face her smile faded, and she grew still. ''Darling, what's wrong?''

''I think this dropped out of your pocket,'' he said in a hard, flat voice.

Joanna's puzzled gaze dropped to his outstretched hand, and when she saw what it held she paled. She raised stricken eyes to his face. ''Sean, let me explain. I—''

''Oh, I think this is fairly self-explanatory. You're working for Senator Hartwell, aren't you?''

''Yes, I—''

"I seem to recall Matt telling me that he'd gotten you a job on some senator's staff, but I really didn't pay much attention. I figured you'd grow bored with it in a few months and quit." Sean gave her a hard, cold look, his hands bunching into tight fists at his sides. "It seems I was wrong. You must like your job one helluva lot to accept this kind of assignment."

"Sean, no! You don't understand. Yes, I came on this trip to try to talk you into running for office, but I didn't do it for Senator Hartwell. Actually, this whole thing was my idea. You see, I was hoping that you would give me a job on your staff if you won the nomination."

"Is that supposed to make me feel better?" Sean threw his head back and laughed mirthlessly at the ceiling. "Hell! I thought you had changed, but you haven't. You're still a scheming, manipulative spoiled brat. If there's something you want you just grab for it, with no thought for anyone else." He gave her a look of pure disgust and snarled bitterly, "You'll do anything to have your own way, won't you, Joanna? Including prostitute yourself." He threw the wadded up radiogram down on the coffee table so hard it bounced off and hit the wall, and Joanna jumped. "What was your plan? Seduce me? Soften me up with sex, then make your pitch? Well I saved you the trouble, didn't I?"

"No, Sean, please. It wasn't like that, I swear it."

She might as well not have spoken. Sean raked both hands through his hair and snorted. "Lord, and I thought you'd come on this cruise because you had a crush on me."

"I did!" Joanna cried. "All the other was just rationalization. Deep down, I just wanted to be with you. I love you."

"Oh, come off it, Joanna! I may be a fool, but I'm not that big a fool."

"Where are you going?" she cried when he stomped toward the door.

He paused with his hand on the knob and looked back at her with such fury that Joanna almost cringed. "Away from you," he spat. "Just as far as I can get on the confines of this ship. If we were back in the States I'd put miles between us."

Desolate, Joanna stared at the closed door for several seconds after it slammed behind him. Tears streamed down her face and sharp, wracking sobs began to shake her. She pressed her lips together and struggled to contain them, but it was no use. Bent from the waist, her arms wrapped tightly around her middle as though she were in mortal pain, Joanna staggered into the bedroom, flung herself across the bed and gave in to the emotional storm.

With her face buried against her crossed arms, she cried as though her heart would break. *Sean. Oh, Sean.* Harsh sobs shook her and hurt her throat, but she didn't try to fight them. The piteous, anguished sounds tore from her endlessly and reverberated in the quiet room. Tears flowed from her eyes in torrents, wetting her forearms until they were slick and forming a dark, spreading circle on the green silk bedspread. Her misery was soul deep. Fathomless.

The convulsive sobs went on and on until her chest ached and her throat was raw. At last, wrung dry, the wrenching cries gradually subsided to sniffles, then choppy sighs. Joanna rolled to her side and curled into the fetal position. She lay perfectly still and stared out the window through wet, spiky lashes, seeing nothing. Her eyes burned and her heart felt like a dead weight in her chest.

I've lost him. She closed her eyes and let the thought soak in, fighting back a renewed freshet of tears. She was going to have to get used to it. Accept it. *But, oh, God, it hurts so.*

It was her own fault, she knew, and the knowing merely

made the pain worse. Sean had been right. She was an immature, spoiled child, always trying to manipulate things to suit herself. Joanna knew she wasn't guilty of the charges he'd thrown at her, but she *had* set out on this trip intent on influencing Sean's decision, on having her own way. That it hadn't been her real reason for coming didn't matter. Even on a subconscious level she had been behaving true to form: she loved Sean and wanted him, so she grabbed at the first convenient excuse and chased after him. When was she ever going to learn?

Joanna sat up slowly and wiped her wet cheeks with the heel of her hand. Her gaze dropped to the bronze chiffon twisted about her thighs, a silent reminder of the boundless joy she had felt only an hour ago. Joanna drew in a shuddering breath and swallowed hard to ease the painful constriction in her throat.

The sound of voices in the companionway told her that it was getting late. Passengers were returning from their day ashore to get dressed for the evening meal. They would be sailing soon.

Listlessly, Joanna's gaze wandered around the luxurious suite. I can't stay cooped up on this ship with Sean, she thought in sudden panic. After what they had shared, the thought of being so close to him, and yet so very far, was more than she could bear.

Shedding her robe on the way, Joanna hurried to the closet and pulled out the warm suit she had worn on the trip from D.C. to Florida. Despite the seducing sunshine outside, it was still late November in Washington.

When dressed, Joanna called the purser's office and asked for assistance. She dragged out her cases and spread them open on the bed. Working as fast as she could, with no regard whatever for neatness, she snatched the designer clothes from their hangers, scooped frilly lingerie from the drawers and stuffed them and the rest of her belongings into the bags.

Twenty minutes later, leaving the ship behind the burdened steward, Joanna paused once on the gangway and looked back. The past four days had been intensely beautiful, the most wonderful in her life. And for a brief, sweet time it had seemed as though all her dreams were about to come true. Biting the inside of her lip to force back the threatening tears, Joanna tilted her chin and continued down the steps to the dock. *Grow up, Joanna. Only a child or a fool believes that dreams come true.*

Was I too hard on her? The answer came a split second after Sean's mind posed the question. *No, dammit! I was not!* Yet, once again he slanted a glance at the empty chair beside him.

With grim determination, Sean cut another bite of steak, forked it into his mouth and chewed. Around him the table conversation flowed freely. Tony, Gloria and the Adamsons had spent the day at the beach while the Wrights had browsed the shops, and they were all in good spirits. Sean was barely aware of their presence. On arriving, they had asked him where Joanna was, and after his clipped, "I have no idea" they had taken the hint and left him alone.

God, he hurt. He hadn't known it was possible to hurt so much...and live. He hacked off another chunk of choice steak and rammed it into his mouth. It could have been sawdust for all he was aware of its succulent flavor. He loved her, dammit! And she'd just been using him.

The thought tore at his gut like a rusty grappling hook. Sean didn't want to believe Joanna was capable of that type of deceit. For hours he had been trying to convince himself that he was wrong, that he had overreacted, but he couldn't quite manage it. The evidence was just too strong. Hell, she'd even admitted why she came on this trip. He took a long swallow of the scalding coffee the waiter had just poured and hissed as it seared his throat.

Joanna was used to getting her way, but did she really

want that damned job bad enough to sleep with him for it?

She did accept your proposal, remember, a niggling voice coaxed.

Yeah, but I had just told her that I was going to run for the Senate. She sure as hell wasn't going to turn me down at that point. As my fiancée, what would be more natural than for her to pitch in on my campaign?

But it's also possible that she really does love you.

Maybe. Against his will, Sean thought of the anguished expression on Joanna's face when he'd made those cutting remarks. *Maybe.*

A concern he didn't want to feel crept up on him when he shot another glance at her empty chair. Maybe he ought to check on her, just to be sure she was all right.

Oh, hell, Fleming, you've gone soft in the head over the woman. Sean tossed his napkin on the table, muttered a terse, "Excuse me" and strode from the dining room. *Joanna Andrews is a self-centered, grasping spoiled brat who will stop at nothing to get what she wants. She's probably just sulking.*

The thought brought his anger back full force. Jaw set, Sean loped down the stairs and headed for Joanna's suite. He'd be damned if he'd let her hide out in her room again. She'd created this mess, and she was going to face it.

Five minutes of banging on her door produced no results. Neither did a thorough search of the ship. For the next hour Sean checked out every shadowed corner on every deck, and poked his head into the theater, the casino and each of the nightclubs, but there was no sign of Joanna anywhere. By the time he had covered all the public areas twice he was growing concerned.

In desperation, he returned to her suite and banged on the door again. Just as he was about to give up, her room steward appeared.

"Are you looking for Miss Andrews, sir?" he inquired

tentatively, looking a bit uneasy when he spied Sean's fierce expression.

"Yes. Have you seen her?"

"Miss Andrews is gone, sir. She got off the ship in Cozumel, just before we sailed."

"What! Are you sure?"

"Yessir. I carried her bags off myself. She said she had to fly home because of an urgent family matter."

In a blinding flash, Sean's concern turned to impotent fury. As civilly as he could, he thanked the man and stalked to his cabin. Cursing fluently, he paced the narrow confines. He checked his watch and made a quick, mental calculation. She'd gotten off the ship three hours ago. Even if she'd managed to get a flight out, she wouldn't have arrived in D.C. yet. But maybe, just maybe...

Sean yanked up the phone, dialed the operator, and told him he wanted to make a ship to shore call. In a matter of minutes he was listening to the ringing tones at the other end of the line and cursing impatiently when Matt answered.

"Hello."

"Matt, this is Sean. Is Claire all right?"

"Sean? What the...I thought you were at sea. And why the devil wouldn't Claire be all right?"

"Then she hasn't had the baby?"

"No. It's not due for another six weeks."

"I see." Sean paused to grit his teeth, then asked, "Have you heard from Joanna today?"

"Joanna? No. Why do you ask?"

"Because she jumped ship in Cozumel three hours ago. I'm assuming she's on her way home. I thought maybe she'd called to let you and Claire know."

"Why would she leave the cruise?" Matt barked. "What the devil is going on between you two?"

"It's a long story, Matt. One I think you'd better ask Joanna. Look, I need her phone number in D.C."

"What do you—"

"Dammit, Matt. This isn't the time to go into it. Just give me the number, okay."

Grumbling, Matt complied, and a few minutes later when Sean hung up he stalked to the porthole and stared out at the night-dark ocean. "Urgent family matter, my ass."

Joanna entered her Georgetown home on a blast of frigid air. The wind had whipped color into her pale cheeks but there were dark circles beneath her eyes and a look of fragility about her that no amount of long solitary walks could cure. She pulled the knit cap from her head and shook out the snowflakes. She took off her coat and hung it and the cap on the brass coatrack to dry, before making her way to the kitchen at the back of the house.

Mechanically, Joanna turned the fire on under the kettle, got out a thick mug and emptied a packet of cocoa into it. Waiting for the water to boil, she leaned her hip against the counter and glanced around the room. It was not as immaculate as it had been when Mrs. Hall had worked there as housekeeper. There were a few dishes in the sink, a wadded towel on the counter, an apron slung carelessly over the back of a chair. But Joanna was fiercely glad that she had let the woman go. The last thing she needed to contend with at this point was Nora Hall's stiff formality. On her own, Joanna was free to weep or rage as she wanted.

Joanna had inherited the housekeeper along with the house. It had been her parents' home. Claire had signed it over to her when she married Matt, claiming she no longer had a use for it, but Joanna suspected that the place held unhappy memories for her mother.

Joanna understood. She was learning just how painful memories could be.

She poured the boiling water into the mug, and the scent

of chocolate rose with the curling wisps of steam. Cradling the mug in her hands, Joanna turned and was heading for the door when her gaze fell on the wall phone. She stopped and stared at it uncertainly. On arriving home two days ago she had unplugged it. She had needed the time and the solitude—craved it still—but Joanna knew she couldn't go on hiding forever. Her mother and Matt were expecting her back from the cruise today.

With a resigned sigh, Joanna walked to the phone and plugged it in. Before she could take a step away it rang, and she jumped, causing her cocoa to slosh over the side of the mug and splatter onto the tile floor.

Aggravated, Joanna snatched the receiver and snapped, "Hello."

"Joanna? Oh, thank God, you're home," Claire said with heartfelt relief. "Where in the world have you been? I've been calling for three days."

"You have? But why? I wasn't due back until today."

"Sean called us the night you left the ship," Claire said, and Joanna's heart jerked. "He's called every day since, and he's absolutely furious, Joanna."

Joanna was too stunned to reply. She hadn't expected that. She had thought, if he even noticed that she was gone, that he would be relieved.

"We assume that you two have had an argument," Claire said in a concerned voice, breaking into the taut silence.

"Yes, I guess you could say that." With a calm she was far from feeling, Joanna gave her mother an extremely watered-down version of what had happened.

When she had finished Claire murmured, "Oh, darling, I'm so sorry. But I can't say I'm surprised that Sean is angry. I was afraid something like this would happen. He's easygoing, but he's not a man who can be pushed or manipulated. And, though he doesn't lose his temper often, when he does it's explosive. What does surprise me, though, is that you let yourself get involved with him. I mean, darling, I like Sean very much. You know that. But...well...where women are concerned, he's not known for his constancy.''

Joanna blinked back tears and forced out a blasé laugh. ''Oh, well, you know how it is, Mother. You tend to get carried away with all that sun and surf and romantic, moonlit nights at sea. It was just a shipboard fling. No harm done.'' Joanna's heart felt as though it had split in two at the words, but they were necessary. The last thing she wanted was to cause Claire worry. Especially not now, with the baby due in just a few weeks.

''Well, maybe so. But as angry as he is, I doubt that Sean is going to pass it off that easily. If I were you I'd brace myself. I'm fairly certain he intends to pay you a visit.''

Joanna fervently hoped that her mother was wrong, but a short while later, just scant seconds after she had hung up the phone, her doorbell sounded. With a sinking feeling in the pit of her stomach, she went to answer it. Before she reached the entryway the bell sounded twice more, and then a hammering fist took up the summons. Drawing a deep breath, Joanna squared her shoulders and opened the door.

''It's about time.''

Sean stormed past her like an enraged bull and stalked into the living room. Shakily, Joanna closed the door and followed him. He was standing in the middle of the room, radiating anger, his back to her, but when Joanna entered he whirled around.

''I should have expected an irresponsible stunt like this from you,'' he snarled through clenched teeth. ''You connive and finagle to get what you want without a thought for anyone else, and then when things turn unpleasant, you turn tail and run like the spoiled, selfish brat you are.''

''I'm sorry.''

"Sorry! Sorry doesn't cut it, Joanna. What you did was inconsiderate at best. If I hadn't run into your room steward I would have thought the worst."

"Wh-what do you mean?"

"I *mean*, you just disappeared without a word after we'd had a serious argument. For all I knew you could have fallen overboard or been kidnapped or been seriously ill. And didn't it occur to you that your mother would be worried."

"If you hadn't called—"

"Was I just supposed to ignore the fact that you had disappeared in a foreign country without a word? The steward said you'd rushed off the ship because of an urgent family crisis. The first thing that came to my mind was that Claire had run into trouble with her pregnancy. So I called."

"I see," Joanna said weakly.

Sean gave her a disgusted look and turned away, then just as quickly turned right back, his eyes narrowed. "And while we're on the subject, just where the hell have you been since you walked off that ship in Cozumel? Claire has called a hundred times. She's been going out of her mind with worry."

"I…I've been here. I unplugged my phone."

The stream of expletives that shot from him were sharp and searing. Joanna flinched with each one.

He was angrier than she had ever seen him, and as she watched him pace back and forth across the oriental rug, Joanna felt wretched. She couldn't even work up any anger, because she knew that Sean was right. Once again she had thought only of herself and acted impulsively. Despite all her good intentions and the earnest attempt she'd made to change, the habits and conditioning of a lifetime were difficult to shake.

Joanna listened to Sean's scorching comments with the calm of utter hopelessness, and when he was through, said quietly, "You're right, Sean. And I'm sorry. I didn't mean to worry or upset anyone. I know that's inadequate, but it's the best I can offer."

Her calm agreement stopped Sean in his tracks, and he looked at her with a mixture of confusion and caution. Where was her anger? He'd come spoiling for a fight and had expected her to rage right back at him. After the frustration of the past three days he had relished the prospect of clearing the air. And now this.

He frowned as he watched her edge toward the door, leaving him with no option but to follow.

"I...I'm sorry things didn't work out between us, Sean, but I do thank you for your concern. I hope, despite everything, that you will run for the Senate." With her head held high, Joanna gave him a wobbly smile and opened the door, keeping one hand on the knob. "Goodbye, Sean."

Sean hesitated and looked at her closely, then nodded. "Goodbye, Joanna."

It was over. He told himself it was for the best. That he'd had a narrow escape. Joanna Andrews was all that he'd accused her of being: shallow, selfish, thoughtless. She was incapable of loving anyone.

Yet, as Sean walked past her and stepped out into the frigid afternoon all he felt was a terrible, consuming sense of loss.

Chapter Thirteen

Snow lay over the Virginia hillsides like a heavy layer of whipped cream, blown by a capricious wind into smooth, swirling patterns in some places, mounded into high drifts in others. Skeletal trees stood in sharp relief against the leaden sky, their branches piled high with snow and drooping forlornly beneath its weight. It was utterly quiet, except for the occasional loud crack of a limb breaking and the mournful soughing of the wind around the eaves of the farmhouse.

Over and over, Joanna's eyes strayed to the wintry scene while her fingers automatically carried out the task of breaking pecan halves into small pieces and dropping them into the measuring cup. It could be a painting, she thought as she gazed out the frosted panes of the kitchen window. The still, stark, haunting loveliness of it appealed to her somehow. In her present mood, blue skies and bright sunshine would be offensive.

"It looks like we're in for another snow before morning,'' Claire commented as she deftly fluted the edge on a fresh made pie crust.

"Mmm."

"On a day like this I'm always glad to stay inside where it's cozy and warm." Letting her gaze roam over the homey kitchen, Claire's soft gray eyes glowed with contentment as they took in brick patterned floors, pecan cabinets, massive beams and hanging copper pots, their polished surfaces reflecting the cheery fire crackling in the massive hearth. The large room was redolent with the tantalizing aromas of burning wood, spices, fresh-baked pies and warm, yeasty bread. "And it's a great time for baking."

Joanna gave her mother a faint smile. "Is that why we're having this marathon bake off? Because the weather is gloomy?"

"Well…kind of. Besides, with the Drummond clan coming for Christmas it's best to stock up on goodies."

But the real reason is you're trying to keep my mind occupied, and off Sean, Joanna thought fondly, her gaze sliding once more to the dismal beauty beyond the windows.

It wasn't working. She'd been home over three weeks, and during that time she'd thought of little else. And after last night, she was hurting worse than ever.

Oh, God, if only she hadn't let herself be talked into going to that embassy party. She hadn't wanted to, but her mother and Matt had been insistent, and because she had known they were worried about her, she had given in.

Bitter, silent amusement rippled through Joanna when she recalled the pep talk she'd given herself as they had entered the embassy. It's time to pick up your life again, she'd lectured. You can't pine away forever. And anyway, Washington is a big town. Just because you're going to a party doesn't mean you'll run into Sean.

Brave words. And totally inaccurate. She had practically bumped into him the moment they entered the ballroom.

He had been standing just a few feet inside the door, and at the sight of him she had come to an abrupt halt, her heart crashing against her ribs. Even now, Joanna could remember, with painful clarity, every tension fraught moment of that disastrous encounter.

"Sean."

She hadn't even known she had spoken, but as his name whispered past her lips he had looked up, straight into her eyes. For a small eternity they simply stared at each other. Then, at last, he said quietly, "Hello, Joanna."

"Hello," she managed to choke out. Her heart was booming in her chest like a kettledrum, and for a panicked second she feared she would pass out.

Sean's gaze switched to Claire and Matt, who were standing on either side of Joanna, alert and wary as they watched the tense tableau unfold. He nodded, and his mouth moved in a semblance of a smile. "Claire. Matt. Good to see you."

They returned the greeting, but Sean's gaze had already slid back to Joanna.

"How are you?"

"Fine. And you?"

"I'm doing okay."

"I…uh…want to wish you luck with your campaign. I read in the newspaper that you're making a bid for the nomination."

"Thanks."

"I…I was afraid you'd change your mind."

"I thought about it," Sean admitted, his eyes hardening a fraction. "But I decided it would be stupid not to, since it's what I want."

All through the banal conversation Joanna drank in the sight of him like someone dying of thirst who has just discovered a clear bubbling spring. She was so enthralled, it was several minutes before she even saw the blonde by his side, and still another before she realized that the woman's arm was linked with Sean's.

Seeming to become aware of the woman at the same time, Sean glanced down at her and looked back at Joanna sharply. "I'm sorry. I don't believe you've met Natalie Stone. Natalie, this is Joanna Andrews, and Claire and Matt Drummond."

"It's so nice to meet you. When Sean invited me to this party he said I'd probably meet some famous people but I certainly never expected to meet Claire Andrews," the woman gushed, eyeing Claire's protruding abdomen with avid interest.

"My name is Drummond now," Claire corrected with gentle firmness before glancing worriedly at Joanna's white face.

Helplessly, Joanna's stricken gaze went back and forth between Sean's face and the slender white arm resting on the dark sleeve of his tuxedo. In that moment, she thought she would surely die from the crushing pain that pressed in on her.

Joanna picked up another pecan and snapped it in two. During the past three weeks she had wondered if he was seeing other women. The uncertainty had been horrible, but knowing, she discovered, was worse. So much worse.

She wasn't sure how she had gotten through the rest of the evening. Now it was all a hazy blur of pain. She had thought that she'd concealed her feelings well though, until her mother had shown up on her doorstep bright and early that morning.

Joanna's gaze warmed when it lit on her mother. Over the past few years she had come to realize how lucky she was to have a mother like Claire, but never more than this morning. She hadn't pried or rendered judgment or offered advice, but had simply taken Joanna's hands in hers, and said, "You love him, don't you, darling?" And when Joanna had nodded and burst into tears, she had held her close until the storm had passed.

Then she had asked Joanna to move to the farm until after the baby arrived. "It will be good for you, and you can keep me company. And now that you've quit your job, there's no reason why you can't."

Joanna had tried to refuse, but where her loved ones were concerned, Claire wasn't above using a little emotional blackmail. "Please, darling. You'll be doing me a tremendous favor. With my due date so near Matt is absolutely terrified to leave me alone at the farm during the day. If you don't come I'm sure he'll end up hiring a nurse to stay with me."

Put that way, Joanna had really had little choice, but she didn't mind. There was some comfort in being with people who loved you.

A smile curved Joanna's mouth as she followed her mother's waddling progress around the kitchen. She wore plum-colored maternity slacks and a plum-and-lilac top that looked wonderful with her gray eyes. Short curls framed her face beguilingly and gleamed like spun gold in the warm light of the kitchen. Flour covered her hands and arms up to her elbows, and there was a smudge of it on her cheek, yet Joanna had never seen her look more appealing. Claire had always been beautiful, but now there was a Madonna-like quality to her loveliness that took your breath away. It was no wonder that Sean had almost lost his heart to her four years ago, Joanna mused with love and pride, and just a touch of envy.

As she watched her mother, Joanna wondered wistfully if she would ever attain that kind of serenity, the kind that comes with loving and being loved in return.

Sean's fingers drummed an impatient tattoo on the table. He darted another look across the dimly lit bar to the entrance and shifted restlessly. *Where the devil is Matt?* A glance at his watch told him that Matt wasn't even due for another ten minutes, but knowing that did nothing to curb his restiveness.

Cupping his hand around the back of his neck, Sean squeezed the knotted muscles and rolled his head from side to side. God, he was tired. Between strategy sessions, hiring a staff, setting up a headquarters and scaring up backers, he'd been run ragged these past few weeks. It had been years since he'd actively worked on a campaign; he had forgotten just how hectic it could be.

But not so hectic that you don't think of Joanna a hundred times a day, he thought with both resentment and longing. Sean glanced at the door again and took a sip of bourbon. *Hell, face it, man. Nothing is going to wipe her out of your mind...or your heart. Even if she is too young, even though she's reckless and willful and spoiled—you love her. Which is why you're here, and why you asked Matt to meet you for a drink.*

Had he been mistaken? No. No, he was almost certain that had been pain he'd seen in Joanna's eyes last night when she'd realized he was there with Natalie.

The memory of that wounded look brought a grimace to Sean's face. The last thing he wanted to do was hurt Joanna. Why the devil had he even asked Natalie to go with him to that party? He hadn't wanted to. But like a pigheaded idiot, he'd been determined to prove to himself that he didn't need Joanna, that he could still enjoy the company of other women. What a laugh.

Still, his date with Natalie may not have been a total washout. If that was pain he'd seen in Joanna's eyes, then that meant she did care. Didn't it? And if she cared, that changed everything.

What Joanna had done was pushy and presumptuous, but he could overlook that, as long as he could know for sure that she had gone to bed with him out of love, and not for what she could get from him.

While Sean was lost in his anxious thoughts Matt sat down in the chair opposite him.

"How's it going, buddy?"

"Matt! Hey, glad you could make it," Sean responded just a shade too jovially. "What'll you have, your usual?"

"No, nothing for me, thanks," Matt said when Sean started to signal for the waiter. "I can't stay long. I want to get home to Claire. And anyway, it looks like we're in for more snow. I need to head out before the roads get too bad." Leaning back in his chair, Matt eyed Sean speculatively. "So, how's the campaign coming along?"

"So far, great. Jerry Calder's managing it for me. Of course, he was my second choice." A lopsided grin crooked one side of Sean's mouth as his eyes met Matt's. "But I knew better than to ask you. I figured once that baby gets here you're going to want to stay close to home."

"You figured right."

Sean's expression grew serious, and he looked down at the squat glass he was absently rotating. "And then there's this…"

"This thing between you and Joanna," Matt finished for him when he hesitated.

Sean's head jerked up, and he found himself pinned by his friend's keen blue gaze. "Yeah, there's that," he admitted grimly. Sean tossed back the last of his bourbon and set the glass down. Black eyes met blue ones in a long, searching look. "How is Joanna?"

Matt's impassive expression did not so much as flicker, and at that moment Sean recalled why he never played poker with the man. He stared back at Sean for what seemed like minutes. "Do you really want to know, or is that a polite question?"

"I want to know."

"All right then...she's miserable."

The quick flare of hope Sean could not hide brought a hint of a smile to Matt's mouth. "Look, I don't know what happened between you two on that cruise. I don't think I even want to know, but it's about time you patched this thing up. Because to tell you the truth, old friend, you don't look too hot, either."

"Do you think it's possible?"

"You won't know until you try, will you?" When Sean didn't answer, Matt gave an impatient sigh. "Look, Joanna is staying with us until after the baby is born. Why don't you come home with me for dinner and talk to her?"

It was tempting. Very tempting. Sean looked at his friend searchingly, torn between doubt and longing. *What if I'm just kidding myself? Seeing something because it's what I want to see?*

Finally, a look of determination tightened his face. Pushing back his chair, Sean stood up and tossed some bills on the table. "Let's go."

"Matt's home," Claire announced as they saw the car headlights flash by and continue on to the barn.

Standing by the sink preparing a salad, Joanna looked up and had to suppress a grin when she saw the way her mother's face had lit up. Her amusement grew as she watched Claire quickly dry her hands, then fluff her curls and smooth imaginary wrinkles from her maternity smock before going to the back door to greet him. Shaking her head, Joanna returned her attention to the celery she was dicing. She'd never known two people that much in love.

Joanna heard the door open and felt the blast of frigid air against her back, but, discreetly, she didn't turn around.

Matt's "Hello, darling" was followed by a few seconds of heady silence that signaled a lingering kiss.

"Mmm. How's my favorite pregnant lady?" he asked finally in a caressing voice.

"Still pregnant."

"Good. Uh…as you can see, I brought company for dinner. You don't mind, do you?"

"I…why no. No, of course not." Claire rushed to assure him. "Uh…Joanna, darling, look who's here."

The note of uncertainty in her mother's voice, as much as the request, brought Joanna around to face them, but her smile of greeting froze and faded away when she spotted Sean.

He was standing beside Matt, watching her in that intent way of his, still and silent, waiting for her to say something. Joanna felt as though an iron fist had knocked all the wind from her body. Her eyes skittered to Matt. How could you? How *could* you, they asked silently. She had thought he cared about her. Didn't he know how much this would hurt?

Joanna felt panic welling up inside her like a geyser. She couldn't endure an evening of polite conversation with Sean, act like he was no more than an old family friend. She couldn't.

With a silent plea, her gaze went to Claire. In her eyes Joanna saw compassion, in the regal lift of her head an unspoken call for courage. Joanna's jaw clenched and her hands curled into tight fists. Every muscle in her body quivered with the urge to flee, but from somewhere she found the strength to battle it down. Tilting her own chin in a way that unconsciously mirrored Claire's elegant dignity, she stepped forward and said calmly, "Hello, Sean."

"Joanna," he replied with a nod, still watching her with that disconcerting intensity.

Even in the midst of shock and panic, Joanna's mind registered a myriad of irrelevant details about him: his upturned overcoat collar, the tiny pieces of sleet peppered across his shoulders and in his blue-black hair, the look of fatigue around his eyes and the deeper lines that bracketed his mouth, the faint shadow of beard, the scent of cold winter night that clung to him. He looked tired, worried and unhappy. Even so, to Joanna's aching, lovelorn heart he looked wonderful.

More than anything, she wanted to throw herself into his arms, but she couldn't. Sean was lost to her. She had to accept that, and she would. Someday she would be able to look at him without feeling as though her heart had just been ripped from her chest. But not now. Not yet. It was too soon.

"Here, let me take your coats," Claire said, breaking into the tense silence. "While Joanna sets another place at the table you two go wash up. Dinner will be ready by the time you're finished."

For Joanna, sitting across the table from Sean was exquisite, excruciating torture. While the others talked she kept her eyes on her plate and moved the food around with her fork. Her stomach felt as though it were tied in a hard knot, and throughout the meal she only managed to choke down a half-dozen bites.

Sean regaled Matt and Claire with stories about the cruise, telling them about the people they'd met, the places and things they'd seen. With his teasing, devilish charm, he managed to make incidents that had been only mildly amusing sound hilariously funny. The others laughed uproariously, but every word tore at Joanna's heart and scraped her nerves raw.

Several times Sean tried to draw her into the conversation, but she spoke only when he asked her a direct question, and then she kept her replies as brief as possible. She could feel his gaze burning into her, but she refused to look at him. All she wanted was for the interminable evening to end, for a chance to escape to her room and cry.

To Joanna's vast relief, after the meal the men retired to the den, leaving her and Claire to deal with the dishes. Knowing that they would join them as soon as they were through, Joanna worked with meticulous care, drawing out the task as long as possible. When at last everything was put away and the dishwasher was chugging monotonously, she started to sweep the kitchen, but after only two swipes Claire took the broom from her.

''I know what you're trying to do,'' she said, giving her a mildly reproving look. ''But, sweetheart, it's pointless. You can't hide in the kitchen forever.''

Panicked defiance flared in Joanna's eyes for an instant, then faded as her shoulders dropped. ''I don't want to go in there, Mother. I can't.''

''Yes, you can, Joanna. I know it's hard, but it's something you must face and accept, because the problem isn't going to go away. Sean is a dear friend of ours. He has always been welcome in this house, and he always will be. Unless there's something you're not telling me.'' Claire cocked her head to one side and gave Joanna a long, thoughtful look. ''Should we be angry with Sean? Has he done something unforgivable?''

''No, of course not.'' Pressing her lips together in a grim line, Joanna sighed her defeat. ''And you're right. It's time to stop running away.''

''That's my girl.'' Claire gave Joanna a quick hug, and with a hand at her back urged her toward the door. ''Now, come on, we'll— Oh, my God!''

With the startled exclamation, Claire stopped in her tracks, and Joanna turned to find her staring straight ahead, her eyes wide with shock. As one, they both looked down at Claire's drenched slacks and the spreading puddle at her feet. When their eyes met again both women had paled. ''My water,'' Claire said, in a faint, amazed tone. ''Joanna, my water has broken.''

At the words, Joanna's heart jerked. She looked around wildly for a second. Then she leaped forward to put a supporting arm around her mother and at the same time screamed for Matt at the top of her lungs.

Five seconds later he came barreling through the door with Sean at his heels. "What is it? What's the ma—"

He stopped abruptly, his eyes going wide with horror when they lit on Claire.

"My God! It's the baby!"

"Now, Matt, calm down," Claire cautioned as he rushed forward, but before she could get all the words out he was scooping her up in his arms.

He swung around and barked, "Sean, call Dr. Harris. His number is by every phone in the house. Joanna, you run upstairs and get her bag. It's right beside our bed. Move! Both of you!"

Sean's face was even whiter than Joanna's, but when she rushed out the door he swallowed hard and followed right behind her. He grabbed the phone in the hall, and as she sprinted up the stairs on legs that felt like rubber sticks she heard him demanding to be put through to Dr. Harris. When she raced back down with the overnight bag a few seconds later, he was just hanging up the phone, and Matt was striding toward the front door with Claire in his arms.

"Sean, go get my car and bring it around to the front. Joanna! Hurry with that bag!" he yelled without even looking around.

"Matt, I can't go out in this weather without a coat," Claire reminded him.

Swearing, Matt swung back toward the closet. Before he got there Joanna had already pulled Claire's coat from its hanger, but when she held it out to Matt he just stood there with his wife in his arms and scowled.

"Darling, you have to put me down so I can put it on."

Matt looked at Claire in sheer horror. "Do you think you can stand?"

"Of course. I'm fine, darling. Really."

With a great deal of reluctance, Matt very gingerly lowered her to her feet. Joanna helped her mother into her coat, but she had barely gotten the first button fastened when Claire gasped and bent over, clutching her distended abdomen.

"What is it?" Matt cried in alarm.

"It's...okay, it's...just...a labor pain," Claire gasped.

Matt's face turned ashen. His curse turned the air blue.

He started to snatch her up in his arms again, but Joanna stopped him. "Give it time to pass first. And in the meantime, here, put your coat on."

Cursing fluently under his breath, his eyes never leaving his wife, Matt snatched the coat from her outstretched hand as Joanna pulled her own from the closet. By the time they had scrambled into them the pain had eased and Claire had started to straighten. Before she could finish, Matt swept her up in his arms again.

"Dammit! What the hell is keeping Sean?" he roared as he headed for the door.

As if on cue, a car horn blasted outside. Carrying the overnight bag, Joanna rushed out the door after Matt, and gasped when she was hit full in the face by blowing snow.

"When did this happen?" Matt grumbled as he bundled Claire into the back seat, and Joanna scrambled in beside Sean. "The weatherman said we were in for a light snow, for Pete's sake!"

Sean sent the car shooting down the gravel drive toward the highway, a mile away. "He miscalculated," he said tersely, leaning forward to peer through the swirling flakes. "This has all the earmarks of a blizzard."

Matt muttered a curse and Claire murmured soothingly to him. Staring straight ahead Joanna held the overnight bag in her lap and gripped the handle with both hands.

Visibility grew worse by the minute. By the time they reached the highway it didn't extend the length of the headlight beams. Grimly, his jaw clenched, Sean eased the car onto the paved road, but they had barely gone ten feet when it began to fishtail. By the time he brought it to a stop they were almost in the ditch.

"It's no use, Matt. That sleet has formed a solid layer of ice over the road. We've got to go back."

"We can't!"

"Matt, we have to. If we don't we'll end up freezing to death in a ditch."

Matt opened his mouth to argue, but at that moment another pain hit Claire, and he clutched her to him, his panic-stricken eyes seeking out the other two over the top of her head.

Joanna checked her watch and swallowed around the knot of fear in her throat. Striving to keep her voice calm, she said, "It's only been six minutes since the last pain. Matt, we have no choice but to go back."

Without waiting for his reply, Sean put the car in reverse.

When Matt rushed back into the house with Claire in his arms she was in the grips of another wrenching contraction. With Joanna and Sean right behind him, he took the stairs two at a time and hurried to the master bedroom. Joanna darted around him and flipped back the covers, and Matt eased Claire onto the bed, then sat beside her and gripped her hands tightly.

"Hang on, sweetheart," he said with gruff tenderness when the pain had passed. He snatched up the phone on the bedside table and began punching out numbers. "We'll get you to the hospital, don't worry."

Two minutes later, Matt had Dr. Harris on the phone. Quickly, in a voice bordering on panic, he told him what had happened. "I want a helicopter out here, Bob, and I want it now," he ordered. "The damned pains are already less than six minutes apart."

There was a moment of silence, then, his face livid, Matt shouted, "What the hell do you mean, they can't fly in this weather? They have to!"

Chapter Fourteen

"Dammit, man! Don't you understand? Claire is in pain! She's going to have the baby! She needs help!"

Sitting on the opposite side of the bed, Joanna held her mother's hand and cast anxious glances at her stepfather. The knuckles on Matt's left hand were white where they gripped the phone. His face was a rigid mask of fear and rage, his eyes wild. He looked ready to commit mayhem. Joanna didn't have to be told that the news was not good. She had seen Matt angry before, but never this close to losing control.

"*What!* Are you crazy?" he roared into the receiver. "We can't deliver this baby! You've got to do something, dammit!"

As Matt listened to the doctor's reply Joanna watched his expression grow more desperate, and fear crawled up her spine. "Now listen to me, you sonofa—"

Claire cried out and clutched her abdomen, and the vitriolic curse cut off in mid-spate. The phone slid from

Matt's grasp and dropped to the floor unnoticed as he sank back down on the edge of the bed and grasped both her shoulders. "Easy, sweetheart. Easy," he crooned desperately as Claire writhed in the grip of a clawing pain.

Joanna looked at Sean, but he was standing at the foot of the bed, an expression of sheer horror on his face. Gathering her courage, she rose, circled around to the other side of the bed and picked up the receiver from the carpet. "Dr. Harris? This is Joanna Andrews, Mrs. Drummond's daughter."

"Ah, good," Dr. Harris said in a relieved tone. "I'm glad you're there, Miss Andrews. From the sound of Matt, he's not going to be of much use. I'm afraid it's going to be up to you to deliver that baby."

Terror washed over Joanna in an icy wave, sending a shudder rippling through her. She wanted to run and hide. Dear, Lord! She couldn't deliver a baby! But when her panicked glance fell on Claire's pale face Joanna drew in a deep breath and clamped down on the fear. "Tell me what we have to do."

Joanna listened intently to the doctor's instructions, and scribbled on the notepad by the phone the list of supplies she would need. "You will stay on the phone and guide me?" she asked shakily when he had finished.

"Yes, of course. Now you just stay calm and do what I say, and everything will be fine."

"All right, doctor. Hold on just a moment." Joanna put the phone down on the bedside table and started issuing orders as she headed for the master bathroom. "Sean, you man the phone and relay Dr. Harris's instructions. Matt, you stay right where you are and do what you can to help Mother."

Matt came up off the bed with a roared, *"No!"*

Joanna spun around and found him glaring at her, his rugged features distorted with anguish and stark fear.

Putting a bracing hand on his shoulder, Sean said,

"Matt, take it easy. Can't you see we don't have a choice?"

"He's right, Matt." Joanna walked back to him and gripped his upper arms, feeling the tense muscles ripple beneath her hands. "There is no way on earth we can get to the hospital, and like it or not, that baby is going to be born tonight. Probably within the hour, Dr. Harris says. We just have to do what we can to help Mother."

A shudder shook Matt's big frame, and he squeezed his eyes shut as though in agony.

"Darling, please don't worry," Claire called softly, and Matt spun around and dropped down on his knees beside the bed. He grasped one of her hands between both of his and brought it to his mouth, his blue eyes darting frantically over her face, wide with fear and concern. She looked at him tenderly and touched the silvered hair at his temple with her other hand. "It will be all right, my love. Women have been having babies since the beginning of time."

"Oh, God, Claire!"

Joanna left them and went to look for the things she needed. She returned a few minutes later carrying clean sheets and towels, scissors, a ball of string, a bottle of alcohol, newspaper, and a plastic dry cleaner's bag.

With Matt's help, she stripped Claire of her soiled clothes and dressed her in a warm gown. Joanna then spread several layers of newspaper over the plastic, covered both with a sheet and slid the makeshift pad under her mother's hips. As she covered Claire with a sheet another pain bore down on her.

Joanna checked her watch and looked at Sean. "Tell Dr. Harris the pains are now four and a half minutes apart."

Matt muttered a frantic "Oh, God" and gripped Claire's hand tighter as he dabbed the beads of perspiration from her forehead with a tissue.

Stepping to the side of the bed, Joanna touched her

mother's shoulder and studied her with concerned eyes.
"Are you okay?"

"I...I'm fine," Claire panted.

Swallowing down another rush of fear, Joanna hurried
away to finish her preparations. When Matt came storming
into the bathroom a few minutes later she had just finished
removing her nail polish and was hurriedly clipping her
nails.

"For God's sake, Joanna!" he yelled. "What the hell
are you doing? This is no time for a manicure!"

At any other time Joanna would have taken offense at
his tone, but she knew that Matt was distraught. "Matt,
I'm trying to make my hands as germfree as possible,"
she explained patiently. "As soon as I scrub I'll be there.
Now go back to your wife."

"Well hurry it up," he snapped, only partially mollified.
"Claire needs you."

As if on cue, they heard a stifled scream from the bedroom. Matt paled, cursed, and shot back through the door.
When Joanna followed him a couple of minutes later another hard contraction was building. Anxiously, her eyes
sought Sean, and he muttered, "Two minutes apart."

Fear clawed at Joanna. Claire was drenched in sweat,
her golden curls darkened and plastered to her head. Her
hands gripped two of the oak spindles in the headboard
above her head, and she was pulling and straining, writhing from side to side. Her lovely face was ravaged with
pain, her eyes and jaws clamped tightly shut, but little
sounds of distress came out with every breath.

Joanna climbed onto the foot of the bed and knelt between Claire's knees. She placed her hand on her stomach,
and her eyes widened as she felt the rippling movement
against her palm. Claire's moans built to a hoarse scream
that seemed to tear from her throat, and her back arched
off the bed as her abdomen tightened into a tortuous hard
ball.

"Dr. Harris says not to fight it, Claire," Sean advised in a strained voice a moment later as the agonized sound faded away. "Pant with the pains and relax in between."

When the next pain hit a minute later Claire tried, but toward the end her breathless pants dissolved into a high, keening wail. Two more spasms came before Joanna cried out, "I can see the head!"

Sean related the news to Dr. Harris and announced, "He says it won't be long now."

The undulating contractions were so close together now there were only scant seconds of respite in between.

"You're doing fine, Mother. Just fine. Okay, here comes another one. You're going to have to push now."

Claire gulped in air and strained with all her might as the wrenching pain twisted her insides. Her face turned an alarming purple-red with the effort. She dug her heels into the mattress and pushed, and her hands pulled at the oak spindles until her knuckles were bone-white and the tendons in her neck, shoulders and arms stood out like taut wires.

"That's it. That's it. You're doing great. Just a little harder," Joanna coaxed.

As Claire strove to comply the sharp crack of splintering wood sounded above the guttural moans that rasped from her throat.

Three pairs of eyes went to the split and bowed oak spindles still held in Claire's iron grasp.

"Oh, God. Oh, God. Oh, God," Matt chanted weakly.

Sean stared and swallowed hard. "Christ."

Gritting her teeth, Joanna forced her gaze back to the birth area, and her eyes widened in delight. "Oh, here it comes! The baby's coming! Oh, this is so beautiful!" she cried, laughing and sobbing as the head emerged. "You're doing terrific, Mother. Just a little more. There, that's it. That's it. Oh, my," she murmured in breathless awe as she caught the slippery newborn in her hands.

Joanna looked up, her eyes swimming with emotion. "Oh, Mother, you have a son. A beautiful little son."

The baby choked, then squalled lustily.

"One with a healthy set of lungs," Sean quipped, and everyone chuckled in relief. But a few seconds later, when Joanna had dealt with the cord and laid the infant on her mother's stomach they were all blinking back tears.

"Oh, Matt, look," Claire exclaimed. "Isn't he perfect."

Before he could answer, her features contorted as another pain hit her. Matt jerked in alarm. "What? What is it?"

"It's okay," Joanna assured him. "This is the last of it. There. That's it." She looked up at her mother and smiled. "Feel better now?"

"Yes, darling. Thank you." A look of deep understanding and love passed silently between mother and daughter, and Claire added softly, "For everything."

Sean talked quietly to the doctor while Joanna made her mother comfortable and removed the soiled linen. Claire, her face glowing, counted tiny fingers and toes, touched the rosebud mouth and quivering chin, the delicate soft spot in the top of the baby's head. Matt watched her with open adoration, tears running unashamedly down his face.

"Oh, Matt, we have a son," Claire said in wonder. She looked at him with eyes brimming with inexpressible happiness and love. "Isn't it wonderful?"

"Yes, love, it's wonderful. You're wonderful."

"Wouldn't it be perfect if next time we had a girl?"

"No!" Matt almost shouted the word. He shook his head, his expression growing bleak. "No, darling, I'll *never* put you through that again," he declared vehemently, in a voice gone rough with emotion.

"Matt—"

"No, I mean it." He bent and pressed his face against her breast. "Oh, God, Claire, it was awful. I was so scared. So scared..."

"It's over now, darling. Don't think about it." Claire stroked her fingers lovingly through his hair, and over the top of his head her eyes sought the other two with a silent plea.

Understanding, Joanna lifted the crying infant and carried him into the bathroom as Sean slipped quietly out the door.

As Joanna cleaned and dressed her protesting baby brother, her heart was filled with emotions so intense they formed an aching knot in her chest. The experience they had all just shared had been the most profoundly beautiful, exciting and frightening of her life. That she had had a part, no matter how small, in bringing this perfect little human into the world both touched and thrilled her beyond words.

When the baby was tucked into a warm knit gown and swaddled in a receiving blanket, he quieted. For a moment, Joanna cuddled him close, rubbing her cheek against his downy head and breathing in the delicious scent of baby.

Matt and Claire were holding hands and talking quietly when she returned to the bedroom. Joanna laid the baby in her mother's arms, murmured a few appropriate words, which she doubted either of them heard, gathered up the soiled linen and slipped out the door, leaving them engrossed in each other and their child.

In the hall, Joanna leaned weakly against the wall and closed her eyes as the enormity of it all hit her.

"Come on," Sean said beside her, and her eyes popped open in surprise as he slipped a supporting arm around her waist. "What you need is a good stiff drink. At the very least a cup of very sweet tea." Taking the bundle of linen from her, he led her down the hall toward the stairs.

Joanna leaned on him heavily, grateful for his assistance. "I feel so weak and shaky," she complained in a bewildered voice.

"I think it's called delayed shock. And after the evening you've had, I'm not at all surprised."

He guided her into the den and sat her down in a chair. "Take it easy for a minute. I'll be right back," he said, and disappeared through the door. When he returned he went to the bar and poured a glass of brandy. Squatting down on his haunches, Sean pressed the glass into her hand. "Drink this, sweetheart. It'll make you feel better."

The endearment brought Joanna's head up, and she looked at him sharply. At his urging, she took a tentative sip of the brandy and felt it burn its way down her throat. When she would have put the glass down Sean shook his head. She took several more sips, watching him cautiously over the top of the glass.

When at last she had finished he took the glass and placed it on the table beside her chair, but he didn't move. His dark eyes bore into her. "Joanna, we have to talk."

"About what?" she asked warily.

"About us."

"Sean, please. Not now. Not tonight."

"Yes, now. I came here with Matt to talk to you, and I'm not leaving until I do."

Joanna slumped back against the chair. "All right. Since I seem to have no choice, go ahead."

"First of all, I want to apologize." He smiled crookedly when her eyes widened with surprise. "I called you a lot of uncomplimentary things, and said that you were spoiled and immature, but I was wrong. Anyone who can do what you did tonight is certainly not a child."

"Just because I did what had to be done?" She gave him a sad smile and shook her head dejectedly. "No, you were right before."

Sean frowned. "By that, do you mean I was right about you looking for a father substitute?"

Fatigue and emotional turmoil had taken its toll and Joanna's laugh bordered on hysteria. "Hardly. If that was what I wanted, why on earth would I pick you? You're nothing at all like my father. Nor do you even remotely resemble the type of man I've always envisioned myself loving, but that doesn't seem to be something we can control.''

A look of hope flickered across Sean's face. "You do love me then? Even now? After all that's happened?"

Tears she could not control welled in Joanna's eyes, and she looked at him reproachfully. Why was he doing this to her?

When she didn't reply, Sean took hold of her hands and stood up, pulling her to her feet. He looked at her intently and smiled. "Do you, Joanna?"

"Yes. Yes I do. Does that make you happy?" she said peevishly as the tears spilled over her lower lashes.

"Yes, it makes me very happy. Because I love you too." Sean's expression was filled with tenderness, but when he went to pull her into his arms Joanna pushed his hands away.

"That doesn't change anything, Sean," she insisted tearfully. "I'm still headstrong and impulsive. I've been indulged and petted all of my life, and to some degree I will probably always be spoiled. Maybe...maybe someday—" She stopped and drew a shuddering breath, fighting against the urge to fling herself in his arms and bawl. "I'm trying very hard to be the kind of woman you want, the kind of woman my mother is—mature and giving and...and unselfish. But I'm not there yet," she admitted in a shaky, dispirited voice, her eyes swimming with sadness and longing.

Sean grinned and folded her into his embrace. His dark gaze skimmed over her woebegone face like a loving touch. Then his lids dropped partway and his head began a slow, inexorable descent. "Maybe not. But you do have promise, my love," he whispered tenderly against her lips. "Pure, sweet promise."

The kiss was shattering. Warm, tender, blatantly possessive, it set off explosions that shook Joanna to her very
soul. The strain of the past three weeks and an evening
fraught with emotional trauma had her drawn taut and fine,
and at the first touch of his mouth her precarious control
snapped.

She clung to him helplessly, quivering within his embrace. The sweet, searing kiss went on and on, throbbing
with the aching need of three lonely weeks apart, of love
too long denied. Lips rocked together hungrily. Tongues
teased, tasted, entwined. Passion built quickly and the kiss
became hotter, deeper, recklessly greedy, until their hearts
raced and their pulses pounded.

When at last the kiss ended Sean's eyes burned hotly
over Joanna's dazed face. "We've both made mistakes,
Joanna, but the biggest one would be if we parted. I love
you, darling, and I want you for my wife. I want to spend
the rest of my life loving you."

"Oh, Sean, are you sure? I—"

"Hush. Hush." A finger over her lips stopped the anguished flow. "None of us is perfect, Joanna. I'm certainly
not. But that doesn't matter." He touched the mole at the
corner of her mouth and gave her a lopsided grin. "Because, I love you just as you are, faults and all."

"I love you, too," Joanna whispered shakily, gazing at
him with dewy, emotion-filled eyes.

"So, will you marry me?"

Joanna blinked and strove for a stern expression. "On
one condition."

"And that is?"

"That you give me that little black book of yours so
that I can rip it to shreds."

Sean threw back his head and laughed, then kissed her
hard. "You've got a deal. In fact, we'll make a ceremony
of it, first thing tomorrow. But tonight—" the laughter in
his eyes was replaced by a hot, hungry look, and his smile

changed to sensuous anticipation ''—tonight I have something else in mind.''

He bent and scooped her up in his arms and started for the door.

''Sean! Where are you taking me?''

''To bed.'' He took the stairs with ease, grinning into her startled eyes. ''You'll have to show me which bedroom is yours.''

''Here! But Mother and Matt—''

''Are so wrapped up in each other and their son at the moment, I doubt they even remember we're here.'' He stopped at the top of the stairs and looked at her, his expression tender but unyielding. ''In the morning I'll tell them that we're going to be married. I think they'll understand. But if there's any flack, I'll deal with it. Now which way is your room?''

Wordlessly, her heart pounding in her chest, Joanna showed him.

He set her gently on her feet beside the bed and, cupping her face between his hands, he kissed her. Then he stepped back and gripped the bottom edge of her sweater in both hands. Holding her gaze, he slowly pulled the coral sweater up over her head and tossed it aside. Her bra came next, baring the smooth fragrant skin that he had dreamed about for weeks.

Joanna quivered beneath his hungry look, and when he reached out, almost reverently, and cupped her breasts she caught her breath. His hands were warm and calloused and exquisitely tender. Their gazes met and held for a long heady moment.

''What are you thinking?'' His voice was soft and velvety, his eyes caressing.

''That I love you,'' she whispered. ''More than life.''

''And when I do this?'' His thumbs skimmed the silken peaks and they beaded with desire.

Joanna's head tipped back and her breathing became

labored. "That I want you...so much." His thumbs swept again. "I...I...oh, Sean, I can't think when you do that."

"Good. Don't think. Just feel. Feel how much I love you. How much I want you." He lifted her breasts, pushed them together and buried his face in the tender mounds. With lips and tongue he worshiped her, dipping evocatively into the tight cleavage, stroking the pearly swells, suckling the rose velvet tips.

"Oh, Sean." Joanna bent over him and clutched his head, her silky brown hair spilling over his shoulders as she held him near.

His hands slid down her ribcage to the button on her slacks, and Sean dropped to his knees before her. When he had divested her of slacks, panties, stockings and shoes he worked his way back up, pausing to kiss her knee, her thigh, the silky nest of feminine curls, her belly, her breasts, the soft hollow at the base of her throat. Sliding his arms around her waist, he brought her close and kissed her trembling lips last.

His mouth was hot and demanding, the abrasive rub of his clothes against her bare skin oddly erotic. Joanna pressed close and clung, losing herself in sensation.

With his mouth still fastened to hers, Sean lifted her in his arms and placed her on the bed. His own clothes were dealt with swiftly, and then he was there beside her, pulling her into his arms again, his sigh echoing hers as warm flesh met warm flesh.

They held each other for a long, appreciative moment, savoring the closeness, the warmth, letting anticipation build. Joanna's breasts pressed achingly against his muscled chest, the nipples turgid buttons of desire. His masculine shaft throbbed against her soft belly, yearning, seeking.

Joanna's hands roamed over his back, then down his spine to cup his buttocks. Sean's knee lifted to separate her silken thighs, then pressed hard against her moist, pulsing flesh.

"I want you so much, Joanna. So very much," Sean rasped as her body arched in response to his touch.

"Oh, yes, Sean. Please!"

After the three lonely weeks apart their desire for each other had reached a fever pitch, and neither could wait any longer. Rolling her to her back, Sean rose above her. Gazing into her lambent eyes, he whispered tenderly, "I love you" as he made them one.

Epilogue

Soft strains of organ music filled the small chapel. The pleasing scents of flowers and burning candles wafted in the air. The pews were filled with close friends and family, waiting with hushed anticipation. It all reminded Claire poignantly of her own wedding, almost four years ago. It was the same chapel, the same minister, the same witnesses. The only difference was that then it had been spring, and now it was winter, and snow covered the ground.

"Are you ready, Mrs. Drummond?"

Smiling up at the young man beside her, Claire nodded and placed her hand on his sleeve, and with four-week-old Daniel Ethan Drummond tucked securely in the crook of her other arm, she allowed him to lead her up the aisle.

When Claire was seated in the first pew she looked across the aisle at Maggie Fleming and smiled. As Sean and his father entered the chapel through the side door, Claire's eyes were drawn to him, and her heart filled with thankfulness that this man, whom she and Matt loved so dearly, had chosen her daughter.

As though sensing her gaze on him, Sean's eyes met Claire's, and held, and after a moment of silent communication, he smiled and lowered one eyelid in a lazy wink. Then the stirring strains of the "Wedding March" rose from the organ, and his gaze sought the ivory clad figure at the back of the church. As Matt led Joanna toward the altar Sean had eyes only for her.

Tears pooled in Claire's eyes as she saw the look of love that passed between Sean and her lovely, radiant daughter. With a heart overflowing with happiness and a throat so tight it ached, she watched Matt place Joanna's hand in Sean's.

A short while later the minister asked who gave the bride in marriage, and at Matt's strong, "Her mother and I," Claire's tears spilled over.

She was crying unashamedly when Matt joined her on the bench. As Joanna and Sean repeated the solemn vows Matt picked up Claire's hand and squeezed it, and their eyes met in a long, poignant look, each remembering that day four years ago when they had spoken the same words.

The minister pronounced them man and wife, and Sean lifted Joanna's veil and drew her into his arms. The kiss was so loving and tender that Claire's tears began to flow again. One plopped on the baby's cheek and he awoke with a start and immediately began to wail his displeasure. Everyone laughed, including Joanna and Sean when they broke apart.

The recessional began and the swell of the organ music covered the baby's crying as the newlyweds started their walk down the aisle. When they drew even with the first pew, Joanna stopped and kissed her squalling, red-faced baby brother on the forehead, before doing the same to her mother and Matt.

Then, her eyes shining with love, she turned to Sean and held out her hand.

CRISTEN'S CHOICE

Dedicated to Harriett Chaney
In appreciation for her expertise,
as well as her friendship.

Chapter One

The clock on the dresser erupted, shattering the dawn silence with its strident buzz.

Sprawled beneath the tangled sheets, her head partially buried under the pillow, Cristen Moore attempted to cling to blissful sleep and ignore the rude noise. When the sound persisted, she gave a low moan and opened one eye a slit.

The small sign of life drew the attention of the gray Persian cat curled in the chair, who raised her head and stared at her mistress with an air of expectancy.

When Cristen saw the soft morning light filtering through the curtains, her eyelid dropped, and with another moan of protest, she burrowed deeper under the pillow.

For almost a full minute she didn't move, but finally it became impossible to ignore the clock's irritating, relentless blare.

Slipping a leg over the side of the bed, Cristen groped for the floor. When her foot encountered the plush carpet, she slowly struggled upright. For a moment she sat teetering on the edge of the bed, groggily tugging her wispy blue nightgown more closely about herself.

Finally, grumbling inarticulately, she hauled herself to her feet and, with her eyes still closed, staggered across the room. "All right! All right! I'm coming, for Pete's sake!" she muttered as the raucous jangle grew louder. Blindly, she slapped her hand across the dresser top until she located the clock. After several fumbling tries, she finally managed to shut off the alarm.

The cat yawned, lowered her head and curled into a tighter ball.

Zombielike, Cristen stumbled toward the bathroom.

Just inside the door she came to a halt, swaying on her feet, vaguely aware that something was not quite as it should be. Opening her slitted eyes a fraction wider, she spied a pair of big bare feet sunk into the thick nap of the blue and green bath mat.

Befuddled, she peered at them for several seconds, frowning. Big feet? Jennifer didn't have big feet.

Cristen lifted her heavy lids another fraction, and her bleary eyes tracked a slow path upward over hair-covered, muscular calves and thighs to a towel slung low around narrow hips. Above the moss-green terry cloth, her gaze followed the path of a narrow band of dark silky hair up over a board-flat abdomen to where it swirled around an "innie" navel, then up still farther to where it thickened and spread out over a brawny chest. A faint warning bell began to sound in the far regions of her sleep-fogged mind as her gaze skimmed upward to encounter vivid blue eyes twinkling down at her from a tanned, rugged face that still bore a few remaining dabs of shaving cream.

Cristen stared back. She blinked once, twice. It took a full five seconds for her brain to assimilate the information her eyes were relating. When it finally clicked she blurted out inanely, "You're a man!"

The sensuous mouth below the sable mustache curved

into an audacious grin, creating deep grooves in the man's freshly shaved lean cheeks. His mischievous gaze dropped to her breasts and lingered appreciatively on the rosy crests thrusting impudently against the filmy blue silk of her next-to-nothing nightgown. Then his gaze slid downward to leisurely enjoy the scantily veiled allure of her tiny waist and the delectable womanly roundness of her hips before tracing the curving line of impossibly long legs all the way down to her feet.

"And you, sweetheart, are very definitely a woman" came the smooth reply as those startling blue eyes slowly retraced their path.

The deep, velvety voice threaded with laughter and the man's blatantly sensual inspection set the alarm in Cristen's head to shrieking, snapping her out of her stupor.

In a panic, she let out a squawk, grabbed the shower curtain and hastily wrapped it around her.

Anger and indignation seared through her. She pulled herself up to her full five feet ten inches and fixed the man with a fierce glower, her eyes shooting sparks.

"Who are you? And what the devil are you doing in my bathroom?"

Grinning, the man leaned back against the sink and crossed his arms over his massive chest. Devilish blue eyes roamed with undisguised interest over her wild tumble of auburn hair before moving on to inspect her oval face. She knew her normally full lips were set in an angry line and her green eyes were snapping, but her ferocious expression seemed only to amuse the man as his gaze dropped once again to her breasts.

"Uh, if you're trying to protect your modesty, you'd better make some adjustments to that thing," he advised, flicking a finger toward the enveloping curtain. His lips twitched suspiciously.

Distracted, Cristen looked down…and gave a strangled cry.

A moan of distress issued from her throat as she grappled with the shower curtain. Made of clear plastic, with only a few water lilies splattered at random over its surface, it was almost useless as a shield.

Her face flaming, Cristen snatched frantically for three of the white flowers and, after a brief struggle, managed to maneuver them into strategic positions over her body.

Catching sight of herself in the mirror did nothing for her composure. She looked—and felt—like a complete idiot, standing there nearly nude, clutching three painted flowers to her body with both arms. And that big jerk's enjoyment of her predicament wasn't helping matters a bit!

Giving him a killing look, she hissed, "Before I scream the house down I'll ask you just once more. Who are you, and what are you doing here?"

With a casualness she found infuriating, he picked up a hand towel and calmly wiped the specks of shaving lather from his face, then cocked one brow and gave her a guileless look. "Jennifer invited me."

"Jennifer?"

Cristen stared at the man, slack jawed. Then anger surged through her, and her mouth snapped shut. If she could have gotten her hands on her roommate at that moment she would have gladly strangled her, even if it *did* mean she'd have to drop the stupid shower curtain. How *dare* that girl bring a man home with her to spend the night!

Rigid with anger, Cristen closed her eyes, threw her head back and screamed at the top of her lungs, "Jennifer O'Malley! Get in here this instant!"

The door at the opposite end of the bathroom connecting the condo's two bedrooms opened, and Jennifer's tousled black curls poked around its edge. "What's all the racket about? It's enough to wake—"

Jennifer's grumbled complaint halted abruptly when her gaze encountered the room's two occupants. To Cristen's utter astonishment, instead of being embarrassed or remorseful, her roommate slumped against the doorjamb and burst into peals of laughter.

"Oh, no! Oh, th-this is too…f-funny for words," Jennifer sputtered between spurts of hysterical giggling. "I t-told you…sleeping in those X-rated nighties would… g-get you into tr-trouble one of these days."

"Jennifer! This is not funny!"

"Oh, but it i-is! I-it is!" Jennifer choked.

Her boyfriend merely smiled and looked back and forth between them, his eyes dancing.

"No it is not!" Cristen insisted through clenched teeth. "I am shocked and disappointed and—and *furious* with you. How dare you bring one of your men friends home to spend the night!"

The reprimand merely set off another fit of laughter. Cristen watched in shock as her friend and roommate staggered across the room and threw her arms around the grinning, half-naked man. She collapsed against him, resting her forehead on his shoulder, and howled uproariously. Finally, still shaking with laughter, Jennifer turned, wiped the tears from her cheeks and shook her head at her friend's stiff expression.

"Cristen, you dolt! This isn't a boyfriend. This is my father!"

"That's no excuse. You—"

Cristen stopped abruptly. Horror-struck, she stared at her young roommate. Finally, realizing she was gaping, she snapped her mouth shut again and swallowed hard. "D-did you say your father?" she managed to croak in a voice not much more than a whisper.

At Jennifer's confirming nod, Cristen's heart sank. Her gaze slid helplessly to the man at Jennifer's side.

He smiled and winked.

Mortified, Cristen closed her eyes and groaned. If there

is any mercy in this world, she thought hysterically, the earth will open up and swallow me.

Jennifer's father! Good grief! I'd have been better off if he *had* been one of Jennifer's boyfriends. He's probably going to insist that she pack her bags and move out today! Jennifer was of age—barely—but Cristen knew that it was Ryan O'Malley who paid his daughter's share of the rent.

Gradually, in addition to shock and humiliation, Cristen began to feel distinctly irritated. Why the devil hadn't the man identified himself, instead of ogling her like some oversexed playboy? Probably because he *is* an oversexed playboy, she decided.

Of course, she had known he would show up eventually. He had written several times, expressing doubts about his eighteen-year-old daughter rooming with a thirty-year-old divorcée. In her answering letters Jennifer had extolled Cristen's virtues and character in the most glowing terms, but even so, she had warned Cristen that he would probably descend on them to check her out for himself.

Cristen hadn't minded. On the contrary, she had approved of his protective attitude. She had been confident that she could win his approval. Of course, at the time she had naively visualized a nice, middle-aged, fatherly man—a bit overweight, perhaps, with thinning hair and a noticeable paunch. She certainly hadn't expected Ryan O'Malley to be this…this…sexy, good-looking devil!

Slowly, Cristen opened her eyes. She risked a quick look at Jennifer's father and just as quickly looked away, her mouth tightening. The beast! He wasn't even making an effort to hide his amusement! And there was nothing at all fatherly in the look he was giving her.

"Dad, as you've probably guessed, this is Cristen Moore, my roommate," Jennifer announced with a giggle. "You'll have to excuse her; she's not at her best in the mornings."

"Jennifer," Cristen warned through gritted teeth. "If

you don't mind, I'm not exactly dressed for a formal introduction. So would you please take your father and get out of here?''

''See? I told you. She's an absolute crab in the morning. I've learned not to even speak to her until she's had at least two cups of coffee.'' Jennifer addressed the remarks to her father as she took hold of his arm and urged him toward her bedroom.

They had almost reached the door and Cristen was set to heave a sigh of relief when Ryan stopped and looked back over his shoulder at her.

''It was certainly a pleasure meeting you, Ms. Moore,'' he drawled in a low, insinuating voice. A slow smile curved his mouth as his gaze lowered once again to her breasts. Blatant male appreciation gleamed in the vivid blue gaze that bored through the clear plastic shower curtain. ''By the way, your lilies are drooping.''

Cristen gasped in outrage and clutched the crackling plastic to her. Giggling, Jennifer pulled her father out the door and slammed it shut.

''Oh! Ohhhhh, that—that—'' Incoherent with rage, Cristen sputtered and fumed, groping for a word vile enough to call him. ''Voyeur! Peeping Tom! That—that—overaged lecher!'' The *nerve* of the man! If he had an ounce of decency about him, he'd have excused himself and left the room, or at the very least looked the other way. But oh, no! Bold as brass, he had looked his fill. And he had been amused, darn him!

Suddenly realizing that she was still clutching the shower curtain, Cristen flung the plastic sheet aside, stomped to the door and flipped the lock. The deep chuckle from the next room made her grit her teeth.

The steamy air in the bathroom was redolent with the scent of soap and masculine toiletries. The sight of Ryan O'Malley's shaving gear sitting on the counter beside her cosmetics made Cristen do a slow burn. She glared at the manly accoutrements, and with quick, jerky movements she snatched off the revealing nightgown and flung it into the hamper. Muttering under her breath, she stepped into the bathtub, pulled the curtain closed with an angry snap and turned on the water full blast.

When she emerged fifteen minutes later, her temper had cooled to a manageable level. Though still brimming with resentment, she knew full well that in this instance anger would gain her nothing and could possibly cost her a lot.

Upon drying off, Cristen hung her towel on the rack and dusted herself with lilac-scented powder, then unlocked the door that connected with Jennifer's room and made a quick dash back into her own.

After slipping into a wispy pair of white silk bikini panties and a matching bra, Cristen picked up the blow dryer and brush. She really had no choice, she acknowledged resentfully as she began to style her thick, layer-cut auburn hair into a cascade of feathery curls that billowed about her shoulders. If she had to have a roommate—which at the moment she did, Cristen admitted to herself with a resigned sigh—she certainly couldn't find a more congenial one than Jennifer.

The cat jumped down from the chair and twined herself around her mistress's legs. Bending, Cristen gave her a quick scratch behind her ears and mumbled distractedly, "Morning, Theda," then straightened and went back to work on her hair. Theda gave an indignant sniff at the desultory greeting and stalked out, her furry tail swishing.

Cristen took her time applying her makeup, stretching a ten-minute job into twenty. She then spent another fifteen deciding what to wear.

When she was finally dressed, she stood before the mirror and studied her reflection critically. The pearl-gray peasant blouse and the gathered skirt in a gray, brown and aqua paisley print were soft and feminine and accentuated her vivid coloring. Her gaze fell to where her full breasts jutted against the delicate batiste. Her nipples tingled and a prickly sensation rippled over her skin as she recalled Ryan O'Malley's brazen inspection and the warm, purely male look in those startling blue eyes.

A suit would be better, she thought, frowning. Something severe that would make her look cold and unapproachable.

The only trouble was, not a single thing in her closet could even remotely pass as severe. In the past two years she had rebelliously indulged to the fullest her penchant for feminine apparel. Because she was only an inch shorter than Bob, he had preferred her to wear simple, tailored things in neutral shades that played down her height and flamboyant coloring. During the last two years, however, she had systematically culled from her wardrobe all those plain, sensible outfits. And all those flat-heeled shoes, she thought, feeling the familiar stab of hurt and anger as she stepped into a strappy pair of ridiculously high-heeled gray leather sandals.

After giving her hair one last fluff and misting herself with a lilac cologne, she glanced into the mirror, shrugged, then squared her shoulders and headed for the door. She might not epitomize a hard-boiled career woman, but at least she looked dignified and well-groomed. And most important, she was decently covered!

Pausing just outside her door, Cristen cocked her head and listened. The heavenly smell of coffee wafted through the air to tantalize her nose, but she grimaced when she heard the low murmur of voices coming from the kitchen.

Rats. She had thought—at least hoped—that Jennifer and her father would be gone by now. She had certainly dawdled long enough. After that embarrassing first encounter, she would have given almost anything not to have to see Ryan O'Malley's mocking face again.

She sighed, knowing full well she had no choice. The man *was* Jennifer's father.

Conversation ceased when Cristen pushed through the swinging door and walked into the kitchen. Her gaze didn't even flicker toward the two people seated at the table, though she could feel their eyes following her. Her expression wooden, she marched to the counter that held the coffeepot, extracted a mug from the cabinet and filled it.

"Could I get you some breakfast, Ms. Moore?" Ryan asked politely. "I cook a mean scrambled egg. Just ask Jennifer."

Cristen shot him a slightly appalled glance and quickly looked away. "No, thank you."

Just the thought of eating an egg so early made her shudder. She could barely stand to look at their breakfast dishes stacked in the sink.

Leaning a hip against the counter, she sipped the life-giving elixir and fixed her muzzy gaze on the ladybug magnets clinging to the refrigerator door. Theda glided in, gave Cristen an offended glare and rubbed against Ryan O'Malley's boots. Fickle feline, Cristen thought sourly.

The silence was heavy and expectant, but Cristen made no effort to fill it. As far as she was concerned, verbal communication before nine in the morning bordered on the obscene.

Jennifer leaned across the table, placed her hand on her father's arm and said sotto voce, "Uh, Dad, I think I should warn you: you talk to Cristen in the mornings at your own risk."

"Really?" Ryan cocked his head, his interested gaze running over Cristen. "Is she always like this?"

"Always. For the first hour or so she's one of the walking dead."

"That bad, huh?"

"Yep."

Thoroughly annoyed, Cristen shot them a warning look. Jennifer pretended not to notice.

Ryan smiled.

With his chair turned sideways to the table, he sat slouched low on his spine, his long denim-clad legs stretched out in front of him and crossed at the ankles. Both thumbs were hooked under the belt that circled his lean middle. He pursed his lips as though giving the matter serious thought, but his eyes danced wickedly. He looked outrageously male, and sexy as the devil. Cristen wanted to kick him.

"Hmm. Maybe it's low blood sugar."

"Could be," Jennifer concurred gravely. "As soon as she's had her ration of caffeine and a piece of toast, her disposition improves."

"Probably ought to give her a glass of orange juice when she first gets up. By the time she showers and dresses, her energy level will have risen, along with her mood."

"Good idea."

Cristen's coffee mug hit the counter with a thunk. "Do you mind?" she snarled, giving them a frosty glare. "I do not have low blood sugar, and I do *not* want a glass of orange juice in the mornings. And I'll thank you both not to talk about me as though I weren't here!"

"I see what you mean," Ryan mused. "Crabby. Definitely crabby."

"Told ya." Jennifer smirked.

Cristen made a strangled sound and shot them both a harassed look, which had no effect whatsoever on the smiling pair. Furiously she tried to think of a suitably scathing remark that would cut them down to size, but her mind went completely blank. Utterly frustrated, she mustered as much haughty dignity as possible under the circumstances and stalked out, her head held high.

Straightening in his chair, Ryan watched her over the pass-through bar, his gaze fixed on the provocative sway of her hips. She strode through the living room and disappeared into her room. A few seconds later she stormed out again, a brown clutch bag tucked under her arm, headed for the front door. She snatched it open, then, with her hand on the knob, she turned and shot them a belligerent glare.

"And for your information, I am not crabby!"

The ear-shattering slam of the door punctuated her parting shot.

Ryan stared at the door for several seconds, then whistled softly between his teeth. When he turned back to his daughter, his mustache twitched above a wide smile. "That's one helluva woman," he murmured.

He saw the teasing laughter fade from Jennifer's face, and her forehead puckered with the beginnings of a frown. She started to speak, but before she could utter a sound he said, "So tell me, how are things going with you?" He picked up his coffee mug and took a sip, then looked around the cheery yellow-and-white kitchen. "This living arrangement. Is it working out? Do you and Cristen get along?"

"Yes. It's working out just fine, and we get along quite well." She paused, a wry smile working at her lips. "Actually, Cristen's a very pleasant person to be around, once she's fully awake and functioning."

"She's a lovely woman. I suppose she has an active social life," he casually probed.

"Not so you'd notice. In the six months I've lived here she's gone out on exactly two dates. And I think she only accepted those to pacify her business partner."

Jennifer chuckled at her father's surprised expression. "Louise Fife is very happily married, and she won't rest until Cristen is, too. For the past year she's been playing matchmaker, but Cristen fights her every step of the way."

"How long has she been divorced?"

"Two years."

Ryan was quiet for a moment. Pensive, he drummed his

fingers absently on the table. "Has she ever told you what caused the divorce?"

"No. She never talks about it. For that matter, she never talks about her past, period. If you mention it, she clams up. You learn very quickly that it's a forbidden subject." Jennifer shook her head sadly and shrugged. "Whatever the cause, it must have hurt her terribly, because now her whole life revolves around the shop she and Louise own."

Ryan snorted. "Somehow I have a hard time visualizing a woman as beautiful and sexy as Cristen Moore owning a toy shop."

"Actually, it's not a toy shop. It's called A Small World, and they specialize in custom-made period doll-houses and miniature furnishings, which Cristen makes. It's really fantastic."

"So is the owner," Ryan said with a grin.

Jennifer's frown returned. "Dad, look, if you're thinking what I think you're thinking...well..."

"Well, what? Come on, honey, spit it out."

The mischief in his eyes seemed to harden her resolve, and she gave him a stern look. "Look, Dad, since you and Mom split up, you've lived like a footloose bachelor, and I know the effect you have on women."

"So?"

"So I like Cristen, and I don't want to see her hurt."

Ryan drained the last of his coffee. With deceptive non-chalance he rolled to his feet and sauntered to the counter. After refilling his mug, he turned to face his daughter, took a sip of coffee, then smiled. "Hurting Cristen isn't what I have in mind," he said softly.

He stared down at the brown liquid in his cup and sloshed it around in a circular motion. Despite his teasing, he understood Jennifer's concern. Since he and Ella had split sixteen years ago, he had carefully avoided any serious romantic involvements. True, he'd had affairs—several of them—but they were always fleeting and casual.

Even so, he was far from being the heartbreaker his daughter seemed to think he was. The women in his past had been sophisticates. They hadn't expected or wanted any more from a relationship than he had; they simply enjoyed each other for a time, and when it was over they parted, with no messiness, no heartache on either side.

But Cristen didn't fall into that category. He had known that within minutes of meeting her. There was a vulnerability in her eyes, a soft fragility her sultry beauty belied. Jennifer was aware of it, too; hence, her concern.

Ryan felt a little foolish, being warned off by his own daughter. Though why he was surprised, he didn't know; nothing about this visit had gone as expected. He had pictured Jennifer's roommate as a wild, worldly divorcée, and he had come here with every intention of removing his daughter from her clutches if he didn't like what he saw. The trouble was, he *had* liked what he saw. A smile tugged at his mouth as he recalled silken-smooth, creamy skin and delectable curves glimmering through that ridiculous excuse for a nightgown. Oh, yes, he'd definitely liked it— every beautiful inch. And now, instead of his protecting Jennifer from Cristen, Jennifer was protecting Cristen from him.

"Are you saying that your interest in Cristen is more than just...well...casual?"

Ryan looked up and met his daughter's suspicious gaze with a sheepish smile. "Honey, what I'm feeling is anything but casual. If my gut instinct is right, I think I've just met the end of my carefree bachelor life."

Jennifer's jaw dropped, and she stared at her father, visibly stunned.

Chapter Two

The sharp *tap-tap* of Cristen's heels on the sidewalk exactly matched the rapid beat of her heart, and the paisley print skirt swished angrily around her legs as her long, lithe stride covered the five blocks to the mall in record time.

Normally on such a glorious morning she would have thoroughly enjoyed the walk. Spring, her favorite time of year, was working its magic on Houston.

Birds trilled their morning songs. Azaleas abounded everywhere—on lawns, in flower beds, in planters, on the formally landscaped grounds around office buildings and condos—their showy blossoms providing splashes of pink, red, magenta, purple and white against the vivid green of sprouting lawns and budding trees. The air was clean and sharp, with just a lingering hint of winter's nip. The sunshine was soft, liquid gold.

A huge oak on the corner two blocks from Cristen's condo supported a twining wisteria, and the vine's grape-like clusters of lavender flowers dripped from the tree's spreading limbs. A gentle breeze fluttered through the blossoms, causing a delicate rain of petals to drift to the ground with every sway of the oak's branches. Only the day before, Cristen had stopped to admire the lovely sight, but today she scarcely saw it. Nor did she appreciate the sweet fragrance that wafted on the breeze.

She stared straight ahead, only peripherally aware of the sights and sounds and smells of spring as her militant step ate up the distance to the mall.

The memory of Ryan O'Malley's wicked grin and the frankly sensual gleam in his eyes taunted her every inch of the way, making her temper simmer. Cristen couldn't recall ever meeting anyone who got under her skin as quickly or as thoroughly. Drat the man, she fumed. He had one heck of a nerve, coming here to check up on her when he was nothing but a…a…leering, lecherous womanizer! Every time she thought of the way he had looked his fill, her blood boiled.

Finding a nearly naked man in her bathroom had been shock enough, but discovering that he was Jennifer's father had surprised the socks off her. Or at least, Cristen amended resentfully, recalling the wispy bit of silk that had been her sole item of apparel, it would have if she'd been wearing socks.

It was ridiculous! Fathers of eighteen-year-old girls were supposed to be middle-aged. Safe and comfortable. Not Hunk of the Month material. Cristen gave a disgusted snort. The man didn't even have the decency to have a paunch. Not even a little one.

And he was no gentleman, either, she railed in silent, impotent fury. Not only had he had the unmitigated gall to take advantage of her morning muzziness—standing there looking at her like an Eastern potentate examining a slave girl he was thinking of adding to his harem—he had been laughing at her, too.

Why, for two cents she'd tell him exactly what she

thought of him and what he could do with his monthly rent check.

The belligerent thought brought a wry twist to Cristen's lips. Who was she kidding? She wasn't about to tell him off. That was a luxury she couldn't afford.

And until you can, she told herself, pushing through the plate glass doors and striding into the elegant, galleried mall, like it or not, you're going to have to be civil to Jennifer's father.

Grimacing at the thought, she skirted the indoor skating rink, her leggy stride rapidly carrying her toward the stairs and the tiny shop on the third level.

Louise was talking on the phone when Cristen entered the shop. At the jingle of the bell above the door, her partner looked up and mouthed, "Good morning." Returning the silent greeting, Cristen stowed her purse in the drawer beneath the cash register.

"No, Irene. I'm afraid that won't do," Louise said after a moment.

At the mention of their realtor's name, Cristen's attention was immediately caught. She leaned against the counter and cocked her head, her brows raised in silent inquiry.

"The rent is too high for the location, and the square footage is very little more than what we have here. We need to at least double our shop space, plus Cristen needs a bigger workroom." There was a pause, during which Louise looked at Cristen and grimaced eloquently. "Yes, I know it's difficult to find anything in this area for what we're willing to pay, but I'm sure we will eventually. You'll just have to keep looking."

"I take it that was Irene Lister," Cristen said a moment later, when Louise hung up the phone.

"Yes. And as you heard, she hasn't found a new location for us." Louise sighed, scanning the cluttered shop. It was crammed almost to overflowing with dolls of every description, miniature furniture and accessories, and exquisite custom-made period dollhouses. "I just wish we didn't have to move. This location is perfect."

"Yes, well we don't have any choice. The business has grown to the point where we have to expand."

"I know," Louise replied dispiritedly. "I was just wishing out loud."

"Forget it. I checked with the mall manager yesterday, and the only empty space available is smaller than this place."

Cristen walked to the battered worktable by the bay window and picked up one of the thin sheets of wood that lay on its surface. "Is this all the mahogany veneer that came in? I ordered ten times this much. And some maple and cherry, too."

"Yes. The rest is on back order."

"Oh...hades!"

It was as close to cursing as Cristen ever came, and Louise's brows rose sharply at the outburst, but before she could question it, the bell over the door tinkled and a woman walked in.

While her partner helped their customer, Cristen, feeling totally out of sorts, began to lay out her tools. The day had started off badly and was going downhill. On top of the shock of meeting Jennifer's father, she certainly didn't need incompetent suppliers and bad news from their real estate agent, she thought irritably as she arranged the set of carving knives, tiny sandpaper-covered blocks, coarse emery boards, tweezers and the assortment of templates. Why was it that everything always went wrong at once? The way things were going, before the day was over the bank would probably turn down their loan application.

Cristen sighed. Deep down, an irrational part of her even hoped the loan would be denied. The mere thought of going back into debt was depressing.

A Small World was prospering now, but it had taken

her and Louise three years to pay off the original bank loan and get the business onto its feet. But if they expanded the shop and increased their mail orders as they'd been planning, they would have no choice but to borrow more funds.

Business-wise, it was a smart move, she knew, but a new loan and higher overhead would mean lean profits for a while longer. It wouldn't be easy, but she'd get by. If she was careful. The expansion would bring in more customers, and by the time the new loan was paid off the shop should be showing a healthy profit.

Then I can thumb my nose at Ryan O'Malley and his rent money, she told herself gleefully.

Irritated that her thoughts had returned to the hateful man, she scowled, just as Louise returned.

"Is anything wrong? You've been grumpy ever since you walked in, and now you look as though you'd like to throw something."

Cristen met Louise's concerned look with a grimace. "Oh, it's nothing really—just that Jennifer's father is paying us a visit. A *surprise* visit, which I knew nothing about until this morning when I stumbled out of bed."

"Ah, I see. So he's come to size up the wicked, wild divorcée, has he?"

"Apparently so."

"Well, don't fret. You don't have a thing to worry about. I'm sure you'll pass his test with flying colors. I mean, what objections could he possibly have?" Louise shot her a sour look, loaded with exasperation. "As soon as he learns of your nunlike existence, I guarantee you he'll be on a plane headed back to California."

Ignoring the gibe, Cristen murmured, "I hope you're right."

"Much as I hate to be in this instance, I assure you I'm right."

Armed with a soft flannel cloth, Louise turned away and

began the daily chore of dusting the contents of the dollhouses scattered throughout the shop, starting with the sedate red brick Federal mansion.

It was perfect in every detail, both inside and out, from the white balustrade fronting the gently sloping roof to the silk-covered walls sporting richly framed paintings, a round bull's-eye mirror and a banjo clock. The polished wood floors were laid in intricate designs, and scattered over them were exquisitely detailed Oriental rugs, which set off to perfection the delicate Federal period furniture upholstered in silks and damask and Italian brocatelle. A flower-filled epergne and tiny replicas of French silverware and china were laid out in precise order on the gleaming Duncan Phyfe dining table. Gilt-edge cornices and Austrian curtains graced the windows. Scattered over the Sheraton desk and Hepplewhite occasional tables were minuscule copies of the porcelain and Sandwich glass pieces and japanned tinware that had been so popular during the late eighteenth and early nineteenth centuries.

Louise picked up a tiny sleigh bed and carefully dusted its intricately carved head- and footboards. Over her shoulder she asked, "What sort of man is Jennifer's father?"

"Arrogant, pushy and thoroughly obnoxious."

"Uh-oh. Sounds as though you and Mr. O'Malley have already clashed."

"You could say that," Cristen grumbled. "I can barely tolerate the man. Before this visit is over I'll probably end up telling him so. Then he'll insist that Jennifer move out, and I'll have to look for another roommate, and you know I'll never find anyone as easy to get along with as Jennifer."

"Well, it if happens, it happens," Louise said with her typical placid practicality. "Of course, another solution would be to sell that pricy condo of yours and move into something cheaper."

"Oh, come on, Louise. You know I'd never find anything cheaper in this area. And if I moved anywhere else, I couldn't walk to work.''

"So drive. For heaven's sake, it's not as though you can't. You've got a perfectly good car parked in your garage, though I don't know how you keep the battery charged, no more use than it gets. I'm telling you, Cristen, you simply have to get over this fear of yours about driving in Houston traffic.''

"It's not just the traffic," Cristen replied glumly, though she shuddered at the mere thought of trying to maneuver her huge fifteen-year-old Buick through the congested streets. "Driving is something I'm just not good at. I don't think I have the coordination for it.''

"Oh, pooh. Anyone who can make these detailed miniatures has more than enough skill and coordination to guide a car down the street. All you need is practice.''

"Maybe," Cristen conceded with a shrug. "But in the meantime, I'm still a lousy driver." She plucked her work smock from the peg behind her table, slipped it on and plopped down onto her chair. "Luckily though, if I keep the apartment, I won't need to risk life, limb and property by getting behind the wheel of a car. From there I can walk just about anywhere I need to go, which is the primary reason Bob and I bought the place.''

"Yeah. Then he promptly walked out and left you stuck with mortgage payments you can't handle," Louise snapped. "And don't you dare clam up on me just because I criticized your precious Bob," she added in crisp warning when Cristen stiffened. "You can pull that little number on everyone else, but not on me.''

Cristen stared at her friend. "You never liked Bob, did you?''

"That's not true," Louise said softly, her expression growing tender at the painful vulnerability in Cristen's face. "I liked him. I just never thought he was the right man for you.''

"What's that supposed to mean?"

"Just that you weren't a well-matched pair. You're a confident, bright, vibrantly alive woman. You overshadowed Bob without even being aware of it—even when you were trying to submerge your own wants and needs in favor of his."

"You make me sound like a domineering shrew," Cristen said, unable to disguise the quaver of hurt in her voice.

"No, no. I don't mean that at all," Louise denied quickly. "It's just that Bob was...I don't know...too low-key, too malleable."

Cristen detested talking about Bob and her marriage, but she knew that once Louise got her teeth into a subject about which she felt strongly, she hung on with the tenacity of a bulldog. Her only hope of diverting her partner was to lighten the mood.

Propping an elbow on the table, Cristen rested her chin on the heel of her hand, cocked her brows and gave her friend an amused look. "I see. And just what type of man do you think would suit me?" she asked dryly.

"One whose personality and will equal yours. Someone who's strong and self-assured. Someone who's so comfortable with his masculinity that he can be tender and caring, yet still be forceful enough to stand toe-to-toe with you. And of course it wouldn't hurt if he was a big handsome devil with a sense of humor," Louise added mischievously, her brown eyes twinkling.

Much to Cristen's shock and consternation, a picture of Ryan O'Malley as he had looked that morning flashed through her mind. Leaning against the bathroom sink dressed only in a towel, he had exuded confidence and sheer male vitality, his strong face filled with amusement and sensual awareness. Instantly Cristen's spine stiffened and her expression sobered. "Sorry. That type of man doesn't appeal to me."

"How would you know? The only man you've ever been involved with in your whole life was Bob."

"I just know, that's all." Cristen picked up a sheet of mahogany veneer and studied its grain intently, letting her feigned absorption signal the end of the discussion. She was acutely aware that Louise studied her bent head sourly before turning back to her task.

"Maybe you're right," Louise muttered under her breath. "After being married to a gutless wonder, you probably wouldn't know what to do with a real man."

Cristen's head snapped up. "Bob is *not* gutless."

"Oh, no? What else do you call a man who walks out on his wife without so much as a word?" Louise glared at Cristen, her pleasant face screwed up in a ferocious scowl. Her fists were planted firmly on her ample hips, and her body quivered with righteous indignation on her friend's behalf. "And you have to admit, if Bob Patterson hadn't deserted you, you wouldn't be in the financial bind you're in. And you wouldn't have to have a roommate *or* worry about what her straitlaced, middle-aged, overprotective father thought of you."

"I really don't want to discuss it, Louise."

"That's just the problem. You never want to discuss it. You just keep it all locked up tight inside you."

"What would be the point? The past is past. It happened, but it's over now and I'm fine." Ignoring her, Cristen picked up a template for an eighteenth-century Philadelphia highboy and positioned it carefully over the sheet of veneer. With a pencil, she began to trace the cutout shapes onto the wood's surface.

"Cristen, darn it—"

To her relief, whatever Louise had been about to say was cut off by the tinkle of the bell over the door as another customer entered the shop.

Determinedly, Cristen continued with her work. Louise was her dearest friend, and the last thing she wanted to do

was quarrel with her. She even admitted to herself that, to
a degree, Louise had a right to voice her opinion. She had
been the one, after all, who had seen Cristen through that
desolate period after Bob had walked out, when she had
been almost too hurt and bewildered to function.

Cristen's hand stilled, and she gazed at the scarred surface of her worktable. Even now she could clearly recall
that day when she had returned home to find the apartment
empty and that awful note propped on her dressing table.

Forgive me, Cris, but I need to get away for a while.
I need space, breathing room. Oh, Lord, Cris, I don't
know what I need—except maybe a chance to find
me, to figure out what I really want in life. Don't hate
me too much, babe. I do love you. I always have. I
always will. I'll be in touch.

Love,
Bob

But he hadn't kept in touch, Cristen thought, feeling the
familiar bitterness well up inside her. She hadn't seen or
even talked to Bob since she'd kissed him goodbye that
morning and left for work, not even suspecting that he
would be gone when she returned.

How many times had she read that shattering, rather
incoherent message? Five? Six? A dozen? She didn't
know. She could only remember feeling first shock and
then a horrible, all-consuming pain, as though someone
had torn out her heart and ground it beneath his heel.

But little by little the hurt had faded, and, strangely, she
had even understood. She and Bob had known each other
all their lives. Their families had been next-door neighbors,
and, born within days of each other, the two had been
constant companions since their playpen days. Their mothers had been best friends, and so had they.

From the beginning Cristen had always been the ringleader, the more adventuresome one. A reminiscent smile quirked her mouth as she recalled their youthful high jinks, the numerous times she had led an unsuspecting, always compliant Bob into some outrageous escapade, landing them both in trouble more often than not.

As children they had done everything together, gone everywhere together, and as teenagers they had dated each other exclusively. In everyone's mind, including Cristen's, they had been a pair, and when they'd graduated from college it had seemed the most natural thing in the world that they should marry.

Obviously, Bob had not agreed.

Somewhere along the way he had begun to feel stifled, had grown unhappy with being part of a pair. Cristen realized she might have been a little hurt at first, but if he had just come to her before their marriage and told her of his need to strike out on his own, to discover if he could stand on his own two feet and function as an individual, she would have understood. She might even have applauded him. But no, true to form, Bob had just docilely gone along with her plans without giving so much as a hint that he desired anything else.

For that, she didn't think she would ever be able to forgive him.

While Cristen regretted the breakup of their marriage, she had come to realize that it wasn't Bob, her husband, or even Bob, her lover, that she missed, but Bob, her friend. Deep down she supposed she'd always known that they weren't passionately in love, but they'd had something almost as important: a deep, very special bond, forged by a lifetime of shared memories. Through his actions Bob had severed that bond and cost them both something very precious.

Cristen had tried, but she hadn't been able to make Louise understand that she wasn't heartbroken over a lost love but mad as hell over a shattered friendship. Even if she had been deeply in love with Bob, Cristen knew she wouldn't still be pining for him. She simply wasn't the type to wallow in self-pity for long. She was a fighter by nature, a survivor.

And she saw absolutely no point in talking about the breakup of her marriage. Not only was it extremely personal, but a constant rehashing of the humiliating experience was like poking a newly healed wound with a sharp stick.

Why had she even bothered to defend Bob? Habit, probably, she mused. All her life she had staunchly defended him against all comers. Her feelings for him had died a slow, painful death many months ago, but some things, she supposed, were so ingrained that they were automatic.

But Louise had been right about one thing: Bob's desertion had not only inflicted emotional pain, it had also put her back to the wall financially. They had been a two-income couple when they'd purchased the condo. On her own she couldn't hang on to it and still make ends meet.

It had taken her almost a year and a half after Bob had moved out to accept that cold hard fact. Or more accurately, Cristen amended with brutal self-honesty, it had taken her that long to accept that he wasn't coming back. Even after she'd received his telegram, telling her that he'd gotten a quickie divorce in Mexico, she had not been able to believe that Bob Patterson had simply walked out of her life for good.

With a grimace of self-disgust, Cristen traced the last pattern piece and tossed the template aside. Her gaze moved to the bay window at the front of the shop and focused unseeingly on the fairy lights suspended from the huge arched skylight above the skating rink.

Bitterly, she recalled how, like a fool, she had waited and waited...and hoped. And every month she'd been forced to dip into her savings in order to meet expenses, until finally there had been almost no money left.

That was when she'd finally accepted that Bob wasn't coming back, that, incredible as it seemed, she had lost him, and that she was going to lose her home, too, if she didn't do something.

A roommate had seemed the only logical solution. A second job had been, and still was, out of the question, since the shop took up most of her time.

A ghost of a smile tipped Cristen's mouth when she recalled the day that Jennifer had answered her ad, how dubious she had felt about sharing her home with someone so much younger than she. She had tried to discourage Jennifer, but the girl's enthusiasm and bubbly good nature were difficult to resist, and Cristen had found herself agreeing, if somewhat reluctantly, to give the arrangement a try.

It was a decision she had never regretted. Despite the differences in their ages and all the misgivings Cristen had had in the beginning, she and Jennifer had become good friends.

With her father's help, Jennifer managed to support herself with a part-time job. Between that, drama classes three nights a week, an occasional part in an Alley Theater production and numerous dates, she was seldom home before midnight. When she was around, they got along beautifully. Jennifer was tidy, considerate, and unfailingly pleasant, and Cristen didn't want to lose her as a roommate.

Cristen had a sudden mental image of sapphire-blue eyes, eyes that glittered dangerously with masculine appreciation and blatant sexual heat. A tingling sensation raced over her skin, and a faint flush crept into her cheeks.

After that scene in the bathroom it was going to be extremely difficult to face Jennifer's father with even a modicum of dignity and poise, much less convince him that his ewe lamb was safe with her. But she would—somehow. She had to. Thank the Lord he was only going to be there for the weekend.

Still Cristen couldn't shake the horrible feeling that it was going to be a long, trying two days.

A steady stream of customers filled the shop all morning. Around ten-thirty, half an hour late, Dora Fife, their part-time helper, drifted in, wearing an outlandish second-hand-shop outfit and her perpetual vague smile. Meeting Louise's gaze, Cristen rolled her eyes, but her partner just laughed.

Cristen was quite certain that Dora could drive a saint crazy without even trying. The girl was vague, incompetent, inclined toward laziness and just plain weird. If she hadn't been Louise's niece, Cristen never would have allowed her to work in A Small World.

Not only did Dora have one oar out of the water, she was totally aimless, floating through life like a dandelion seed in the wind. She'd been attending the University of Houston for three years, but she'd changed her major so many times that she was no closer to graduating now than she had been when she'd started.

Cristen admitted to being a head-in-the-clouds dreamer herself at times, but Dora's dippyness drove her around the bend.

Except for those occasional times when the shop was really crowded, Louise and Dora took care of the customers while Cristen worked at her table.

They had learned long ago that people found it fascinating to watch Cristen fashion the perfectly scaled miniatures, which was why her worktable was situated in front of the window. The messy work, like sawing and hammering or pouring the molds for the metal pieces, was completed in the back room, but everything else she did in full view of their customers and the people passing by in the mall. Many times as she sanded and carved and fitted the small pieces of wood together or upholstered the tiny furniture or constructed and decorated a miniature mansion, a small crowd gathered around the window. Inevitably some wandered into the shop for a closer look, and once inside, few left without purchasing something.

Business was brisk most of the day. It wasn't until a lull just an hour or so before closing that they found themselves alone in the shop again.

"Whew, what a day," Louise said as she watched a gray-haired gentleman leave with his carefully wrapped package. "You'd think there was a miniaturists' convention in town, the way sales have been today." She looked down, taking a quick inventory of the glass case that held their standard period pieces. "It looks as though we're running low on camelback sofas and Queen Anne wing chairs. Oh, and Victorian hallstands. There are only two of those left."

"Hmm. I'll start on the hallstands next," Cristen replied without looking up from carving an intricate shell motif on a blockfront chest. "I already have a dozen of the sofas and chairs almost finished. As soon as the glue sets I'll put on the stain. I should be ready to upholster them by next Tuesday or Wednesday."

"Great." Louise poured two mugs of coffee and carried them over to the table. "Here. I'm sure you need this as much as I do," she said, setting one in front of Cristen.

"Thanks."

Louise perched on the corner of the table and leaned back on one hand. "Cristen, about this morning. I'm sorry I—"

The tinkle of the bell above the door cut off her apology. Cristen kept her head down as Louise slid off the table and went to greet their customer.

"Good afternoon, sir. Is there something I could help you find?" she asked politely.

"No, thank you. I've come to pick up Cristen."

Though she had only heard it for the first time that morning, the deep, rumbling baritone was unmistakable.

Cristen's head snapped up just in time to see Ryan O'Malley turn his devastating smile on her partner.

"You must be Louise Fife. My daughter has told me about you. I'm Ryan O'Malley, Jennifer's father."

"*You're* Jennifer's father?" Louise stared up at him with the dazed expression of one who has just received a sharp blow to the head.

Across the room, where she had been straightening shelves, Dora simply stood and stared, her mouth agape.

Louise's incredulous gaze slid to Cristen, then back to the towering, outrageously attractive man. When she looked at her partner once again, her eyes had narrowed and held a speculative gleam that Cristen knew boded no good.

Chair legs scraped on the shop's wooden floor as Cristen shot to her feet. "What are you doing here?" she demanded rudely without thinking.

Ryan turned his devilish blue gaze on her, his mouth twitching beneath the sable mustache. He crossed to her table, and Cristen gritted her teeth. A man that large ought to be awkward and lumbering, she thought irritably. Ryan sauntered—a slow, easy, loose-limbed glide that was all supple, sinuous grace.

Low-slung faded jeans clung to his narrow hips, and a white shirt that was startling against his tanned skin molded the broad shoulders and powerful chest that Cristen remembered so well. Impressive biceps bulged beneath the short sleeves, and the mat of dark curls on his chest created a shadow beneath the loosely knitted material. Cristen ground her teeth harder as a tingling sensation feathered down her spine.

"Jennifer was worried about your being late, and since I wanted to get a look at your shop anyway, I said I'd pick you up. But don't worry, there's no need to rush. Our dinner reservations aren't until eight. You have plenty of time."

"Dinner res—" Cristen drew a deep breath against the spasm of panic that tightened her chest. "I'm sorry. I can't possibly have dinner with you and Jennifer."

"Nonsense!" Louise put in emphatically before Ryan could reply. "Of course you can."

Cristen darted her partner a quelling look, which was calmly ignored. "No, really. I…uh…I have too much to do here. I…I'm going to have to work late tonight."

Ryan crossed his arms over his chest and tilted his head to one side. His sardonic gaze seemed to bore into her, direct and unnerving. "That's too bad," he drawled. "I was hoping you and I could get acquainted over dinner."

"I'm sorry. I can't make it."

"Don't be silly, Cristen. Of course you can," Louise insisted. She was so agitated that she was practically dancing up and down. "There isn't anything here that won't wait until tomorrow. And Dora and I can close up tonight. Can't we, Dora?"

Louise sent the dumb-struck girl a sharp look. Never taking her eyes off Ryan, Dora nodded.

"You see? So you just— Oh, damn!" she swore when the phone began to ring. She darted around the counter to answer it. "Hold on just a second. I'll be right back."

Cristen looked at Ryan and shrugged. "I'm sorry, but you see—"

"Cristen, it's for you."

"Go ahead," Ryan said pleasantly, picking up the piece she had been working on. "I'll look around while you take the call."

At the counter Cristen held out her hand for the receiver, but Louise snatched it back out of reach and scowled accusingly. "Why didn't you tell me about Jennifer's father?" she demanded in an aggrieved whisper.

"I did."

"You told me he was here, but you didn't tell me he was gorgeous."

"It hardly matters, does it?"

Louise groaned. "Are you crazy? No, don't answer that. You must be or you wouldn't be trying to avoid going out with him. Well, I'm not going to let you. You're—"

"Will you give me that phone," Cristen hissed, snatching it out of her hand. Glaring daggers at her partner, she said tersely into the mouthpiece, "Hello, this is Cristen."

"Hi. It's Jennifer. Is Dad there yet?"

Cristen scowled at Ryan's broad-shouldered back. He stood on the opposite side of the shop, inspecting the Victorian dollhouse. "Yes, he is," she said through clenched teeth, straining for a pleasant tone. "But as I was telling your father, I can't possibly go out with you tonight. I'm sorry, Jennifer."

"Oh, come on, Cris!" Jennifer wailed. "You promised you'd help me entertain Dad when he came."

"I know, but—"

"Cris, please! Eric is joining us, so we'll be a foursome. If you don't come, Dad will spend the entire evening grilling the poor guy about his intentions. Besides, I've already made reservations for us at Rudi's. You can't let me down."

"Jennifer, I—"

"Please, Cris. I want you and Dad to be friends. Please say you'll come."

Friends. It seemed such a tepid word when used in connection with Ryan O'Malley. Somehow Cristen didn't think he was a man who had many woman friends. He was far too basic, too rawly male, for anything so tame. A legion of ex-lovers she could believe, but not women friends.

"Please, Cristen," Jennifer cajoled when she hesitated. "You promised."

With a sigh of defeat, Cristen rubbed the spot between her brows with the tips of two fingers. "Oh, all right. I'll come."

When she hung up the phone she avoided Louise's smug look and went to tell Ryan that she would be joining them after all. "Just give me a few minutes to put these things away," she said, gathering up tools and the dozen half-finished chests.

Cristen walked into the back room with Louise dogging her heels like a determined terrier. "Something just dawned on me," the other woman said in a voice heavy with suspicion. "You said you didn't know Jennifer's father had arrived until you got up this morning. Knowing what a deadhead you are when you first wake up, and knowing that Frenchie nightwear you're so partial to, some very interesting possibilities come to mind."

Cristen carefully put her tools away and placed the chests on a shelf with the other pieces in various stages of completion. She steadfastly ignored Louise, but her friend was not deterred.

"Just how *did* you and Mr. O'Malley meet?" Louise practically danced a jig trying to keep up with Cristen as she moved around the storeroom. When Cristen didn't reply, Louise's eyes grew round. "Oh, my. Don't tell me you walked out of your bedroom wearing one of those little nothings?"

"I wouldn't dream of telling you any such thing," Cristen replied stiffly.

"You did!" Louise crowed. "Oh, I knew it! I knew it! Oh, this is priceless. What happened? What did you do?"

"Louise, I *don't* wish to discuss it."

Chapter Three

He's flirting with me! At least...I think he is.

Cristen frowned. She wasn't sure because her experience with that sort of thing amounted to zilch. The only man in her past had been Bob, and he'd certainly never flirted with her.

Trying her best to ignore the way Ryan O'Malley's thigh was pressing against hers, Cristen stared at the after-dinner drink she was absently rotating. Since finding this aggravating, overpowering, utterly charming devil in her bathroom that morning, she'd suffered the unsettling feeling that somehow she had lost control, that her life was being turned upside down. And the feeling had been steadily growing. Just look at what had happened when they arrived at the restaurant. One minute she'd been about to take the chair the waiter held out, and the next Ryan had maneuvered her onto the banquette beside him. The man was dangerous.

And Jennifer was just as bad. The girl certainly had her

father's persuasive charm, and she used it just as adroitly to get her way, Cristen thought darkly, recalling the heated discussion they'd had over what Cristen should wear. Cristen had balked at wearing the black taffeta dress, but Jennifer had insisted it was the only thing she had that was suitable.

It was also the sexiest thing Cristen owned. The ruffled neckline plunged both front and back, and the fitted bodice with its dropped waist lovingly outlined every womanly curve before leading the eye to the fantasy of deep flounces that made up the skirt. It was elegant and expensive, and it rustled enticingly when she walked. The overall effect was one of provocative, feminine allure.

It had been a rare impulse purchase after Bob's desertion. When Cristen saw the dress, she had known he would have hated it, especially on her, which had been just the spur she'd needed to buy it. It had hung in the closet ever since, unworn. Until now.

Sighing, Cristen fingered the taffeta ruffle that draped her breasts. And to think Jennifer had always seemed such a sweet, tractable little thing. Cristen wasn't used to losing arguments or being outmaneuvered, and she still hadn't figured out how it had happened, but she made a silent vow that in the future she would be on her toes around Irish charmers by the name of O'Malley—father *and* daughter.

Ryan shifted, and the sleeve of his dark dinner jacket rubbed against Cristen's bare arm, a soft abrasion that sent goose bumps racing over her skin. She inched away, but a subtle move by Ryan closed the tiny gap between them.

Cristen darted him a sharp look. Had he done that on purpose?

Ryan was talking to Eric, his expression a model of innocence. Cristen narrowed her eyes. Finally, looking away, she told herself to ignore him.

It was impossible. His slightest movement brought a tantalizing whiff of masculine cologne to tease her nose, and all along her side she could feel the heat from his body. Grinding her teeth, she stared harder at the frothy green drink.

"Well, Dad, what did you think of Cristen's shop?" Jennifer asked, cutting into the men's conversation. Catching Cristen's eye, she winked conspiratorially.

"It's fascinating. Unique. I was impressed." The smile Ryan turned on Cristen was filled with sincere admiration and a touch of speculation. "You're a talented woman."

"Thank you." Resisting the urge to squirm, Cristen wondered why she found his compliments just as unnerving as his teasing.

"She even makes replicas of people's homes on request," Jennifer added. "Or of places like Windsor Castle or the White House."

"Really?"

"Yes. Most of my houses are custom orders. They're expensive, and miniaturists are usually very definite about what they want."

"They're not the only ones," Ryan murmured, giving her an intent look that sent a frisson of alarm skittering down her spine.

"Her houses are so authentic that our set designer is duplicating the parlor of her Georgian mansion for a production of *My Fair Lady*," Eric put in.

Cristen looked at him and smiled. She liked Eric. He was a handsome young man in his early twenties, an actor Jennifer had met when they'd both had parts in a play at the Alley Theater. Earlier in the evening Ryan had subjected him to a mild fatherly inquisition, but Cristen knew that he had no need to be concerned. Eric and Jennifer made an attractive couple, and they were obviously fond of each other, but they were both too caught up in their budding careers to even consider a serious relationship.

"That's very interesting." Ryan's attention switched to his daughter. "Doesn't that open in just a few weeks?"

"Yes. And I'm understudying the lead."

The statement sparked a discussion about Jennifer's chances of filling in for the disgustingly healthy leading lady, but Cristen was too distracted by the heat and hardness of the man beside her to join in.

Did he have to sit so close?

Maybe I'm overreacting, she told herself, studying Ryan covertly as she sipped the minty drink. Maybe I'm just blowing that embarrassing first meeting out of proportion. After all, the whole thing was just a silly fiasco. Ryan is hardly to blame.

And other than those smoldering looks and a few teasing remarks, he really hasn't said or done anything objectionable. Besides sit too close and brush against you constantly, a tiny inner voice argued.

Cristen cut another sidelong glance at Ryan. Even that was probably accidental, she decided with a trace of annoyance. He hardly seemed aware that she was in the room. And that teasing, seductive tone she'd heard in his voice was probably just second nature to him. Earlier, during the short drive home from the mall, he'd even managed to imbue their mundane discussion of the weather with seductive undertones.

The band began to play a slow tune, and Jennifer looped her arm through Eric's, giving her father an impudent look. "I hate to interrupt this stimulating conversation, but I'm stealing Eric for a dance."

"Good idea." Ryan grasped Cristen's hand, meeting her startled look with a persuasive grin. "Would you like to dance? I promise not to step on your toes too often." Before she could answer he slid across the banquette and stood up, pulling her with him.

By the time they reached the tiny dance floor, her heart was thudding. It exasperated Cristen that Ryan affected her

so, and when he drew her into his arms she held herself
stiff and stared over his shoulder, her expression remote.

For a moment they danced in silence. Cristen could feel
Ryan's gaze on her, and from the corner of her eye she
saw his mustache twitch suspiciously. She tried to ignore
him, but her whole being hummed with awareness. His
hand engulfed her smaller one, the palm warm and dry and
hard against hers. The brush of his thighs as they moved
to the romantic music made her insides quiver strangely,
and the heat from his encircling arm burned through her
dress like a branding iron.

This is silly, she berated herself, trying to quell her
twanging nerves. He's just a man, for heaven's sake. Jennifer's father. Just treat him as you would anyone else.
Talk. Say something. Anything.

"You're very quiet."

The soft-voiced statement brought Cristen's head snapping up. In high heels she was nearly six feet tall, but she
still had to tip her head back to meet Ryan's amused gaze.
It was a distinctly new experience, one that was both pleasurable and somehow unnerving. How tall was he, for
heaven's sake?

"I, uh, I was just thinking that…that you're not at all
as I pictured you."

The mustache twitched again. "Oh? How so?"

"Well, for one thing, you don't look old enough."

Slowly, Ryan's gaze roamed over her upturned face,
then scorched a path down over her arched neck and shoulders to where the tops of her breasts swelled above the
low-cut gown. When he focused on her face once again
his look was frankly lascivious. "Oh, believe me, darlin',
I'm old enough."

Cristen's heart gave a little thump. Now *that* was definitely flirting!

"I mean to be the father of an eighteen-year-old," she

said severely, giving him a quelling look that had not the least effect.

"Oh, that. Well, I guess that would depend on how you defined 'old enough.' I'm thirty-seven."

"Good heavens! You became a father at nineteen?"

"Yeah, well, that's what happens when you're young and impetuous and—" he paused, his grin widening "—hot-blooded. When your hormones are bubbling it's difficult to distinguish lust from love. Jennifer was already on the way by the time Ella and I discovered that the only thing we had going for us was sex."

"Oh. I see."

A warm flush she was powerless to prevent tinged Cristen's cheeks a faint pink. Was he always so blunt, or had he said that to test her reaction? Given his penchant for teasing, she suspected the latter.

Ryan shrugged. "At least we had enough sense to part before we ruined each other's life. We've even managed to remain friends. Two years after the divorce Ella remarried, and now she and her husband have three children of their own."

"And you opted for the single life."

"Not really. I've just been waiting for the right woman to come along." Ryan looked at her intently, his expression for once serious. "I always knew she would. It was just a matter of time."

A vague feeling of unease fluttered through Cristen. Not knowing quite what to say, she fell silent and looked away, once more staring over his shoulder. The charged silence lengthened as she searched her mind for a safer topic.

"You know, you're not at all what I expected, either," Ryan said after a moment.

"Oh, really?" Cristen slanted him a narrow-eyed look filled with irony. She could just imagine what he had envisioned: a bold, brassy swinger with the morals of an alley cat. No doubt the type he dated regularly.

The thought made her seethe. That she had been fully prepared to accept, or at least tolerate, that double-standard brand of thinking—had Ryan been the paunchy, middle-aged man she had envisioned—slipped her mind completely.

"Yes. And I must say, you were a pleasant surprise." A teasing, sexy gleam lit Ryan's blue eyes as his gaze skimmed over her from her feathery Gypsy mane to her décolletage, and Cristen knew that he was remembering the way they had met. "Very pleasant, indeed."

Jaw set, she stared over his shoulder again. She would not—absolutely would not—let him rile her. "I'm glad," she said coolly. "Jennifer has been worried that you wouldn't approve of me."

"Oh, I approve," Ryan assured her in a purring voice. He caught her eye once again, his mouth curving in a devilish grin. "From what I've seen so far, I approve very much."

Beast!

Refusing to acknowledge the innuendo, Cristen gritted her teeth and gave him a tight smile. "Thank you. I'm very glad to hear that. I would hate to lose Jennifer as a roommate. We're both very happy with our living arrangement."

"Now that I've met you, so am I. If I'd known my daughter had such an attractive roommate, I would've come for a visit sooner."

Suddenly, Ryan jerked her to him. Her breasts flattened against his chest, and their bodies molded together from shoulder to knee. Before Cristen could protest he executed a series of complicated steps, whirling her around so quickly that her head began to spin. She had no choice but to cling to him. When he resumed the slow, languorous dance and the world settled down, she threw her head back, opened her mouth and met a look of bland innocence.

"Sorry. That old couple was about to crash into us," he explained with an apologetic shrug, but his hold on her eased only fractionally.

At Cristen's skeptical look, Ryan's teasing grin grew wider. Seductive devilment sparkled in his eyes. He leaned closer and dropped his voice to a husky pitch. "By the way, I've been meaning to tell you, I like that little mole."

Cristen looked blank, then frowned. "What mole?"

"The one in the hollow just below your right hipbone." He lowered one eyelid in a wicked wink. "Terrific place for a beauty mark."

Cristen gasped. For a moment she stared at him, wide-eyed, too shocked to react. Then her body began to burn as a flush rose from her toes all the way to her hairline.

"Oh! You, O'Malley, are no gentleman, or you wouldn't have...have..."

"Noticed?" he supplied helpfully.

"Yes!" Cristen snapped. She tipped her head at a haughty angle, but when she would have pulled out of his arms Ryan tightened his hold.

"Whoa. Whoa. Don't get all bent out of shape." He chuckled, but at Cristen's affronted glare he had the good grace to look sheepish. "Okay. You're right, that wasn't nice. But you've got to admit, that episode in the bathroom *was* funny."

His grin was irresistible. Despite her best effort to keep her expression stern, Cristen's lips twitched. He'd done it to her again! With a grimace and a heavy sigh, she conceded grudgingly, "Well...okay. Maybe it was. Just a little."

"And just think what a great story it'll make for our grandchildren."

Grandchildren? The word jolted through Cristen, banishing her reluctant amusement in a flash. Just what did he mean, their grandchildren? Was he speaking collectively or...

"Anyway," Ryan continued with blithe disregard for the wary confusion in her eyes, "I couldn't resist teasing you. It's so much fun to watch you get all huffy and ruffle your feathers like a little banty hen."

"Little?" Cristen gave him a droll look. "Your analogy is a bit off, isn't it? If there's one thing I'm not, it's little."

Ryan appeared to consider her statement for a moment, a look of sheer male approval heating his gaze as it moved over her. "I guess not. But you're sure as heck one nice armful of woman."

A tiny thrill surged through Cristen. Telling herself it was foolish to feel so pleased by what was probably nothing more than practiced flattery, she tried to suppress it. "Really? You mean my height doesn't bother you?"

"Not at all. I've never cared for fragile little dolls. I'm always worried they might break. Besides, I get a crick in my neck when I kiss a short woman."

"I can imagine." Giving in to the throaty chuckle the image evoked, Cristen shook her head at the devilish look in his eyes.

"Did your height bother your husband?"

Ryan knew the moment the words left his lips that he'd blundered.

In an instant every trace of amusement vanished from Cristen's face, her expression settling into a blank mask. "I'm sorry, but my marriage is not a topic for casual conversation." Coolly, she shifted her gaze away from his.

After a moment, as though he had not even spoken and she had not answered with that terse little put-down, she said conversationally, "I understand that your company makes security systems."

"Yes. Actually, we design, manufacture and install them. Mostly for commercial users, like banks, government agencies, or large corporations—any type of business that deals in valuable goods or highly classified or sensitive information."

A sore spot. Very interesting, Ryan mused. And disturbing. Is she reluctant to discuss her ex-husband because she still loves him? Or because she's bitter? Either way, it wasn't a good sign.

The music stopped, and Cristen stepped out of Ryan's arms. "It sounds like a fascinating business," she said as they started back to the table.

"It is. With the recent advances in technology, we even have sophisticated security systems that operate on voice or fingerprint match, or a combination of both."

She murmured something appropriate, but Ryan could tell she was merely being polite. All Cristen was interested in was putting distance between them. Why?

He had barely taken his seat beside Cristen when the other couple returned. Sliding into the chair Eric held out for her, Jennifer beamed a smile across the table.

"I've got a terrific idea, Dad. Eric knows of this great little disco not far from here. What do you say we go there and really kick up our heels? This place is too sedate for dancing, anyway."

Ryan smiled indulgently. "What do you think, Cristen?"

"Thanks, but I think I'll pass," she said in a rush. "I'm tired and I, uh, I have to work at the shop tomorrow. If you don't mind, I think I'll just go home."

"You're going to work on Sunday?" Jennifer asked, her disgusted tone turning the question into a protest.

"I'm afraid so. But please, you three go ahead." The last thing Cristen wanted was to prolong the evening, especially with more dancing. For some reason she didn't really want to analyze, Ryan O'Malley made her nervous and edgy in a way no man ever had.

"I'd just as soon call it a night myself. So I'll tell you what." Ryan pulled a set of keys from his pocket and tossed them across the table to Eric. "You two take my car and go to the disco, and Cristen and I will take a taxi back to the apartment.''

"Oh, no, please." Cristen turned quickly to Ryan, her eyes growing wide with the beginnings of panic. Being left alone with him would be even worse. "I don't want to spoil the evening for you. Besides, you came here to be with Jennifer. I'll feel terrible if you don't go."

"Don't be silly. It's all settled."

Protests were useless. Thirty minutes later Ryan was unlocking her apartment door, and as Cristen stepped gingerly past him her nerves were clanging like a firehouse alarm.

In the living room she fiddled nervously with her purse and shifted from one foot to the other. When she finally darted a look at Ryan she found that he was standing casually, hands in his pockets, feet braced apart, watching her with a look of faint amusement.

"Would...would you care for some coffee? Or perhaps a brandy?"

Theda, lying stretched out in her favorite spot along the back of the sofa, woke from her nap, blinked and gave them an imperious look.

"No, thanks. I had plenty at the restaurant."

"Oh...well, I, uh, I think I'll go to take a couple of aspirin. I have a bit of a headache."

Ryan removed his coat and tie and tossed both over the back of a chair. Just as casually as though he lived there, he sprawled on the sofa and slumped down on his spine in an utterly relaxed pose, legs stretched out in front of him, head resting against the back. "It's probably just tension. When you come back I'll massage your neck. That usually helps." Beneath half-closed lids, his blue eyes glittered with laughter and gentle challenge.

Not on your life, buster, Cristen vowed silently. Ignoring the fluttery sensation in her stomach, she gave him a weak smile and eased toward the kitchen. Theda was studying

Ryan's ear as though it were a tasty morsel, and as Cristen pushed through the door she silently urged the cat to take a bite.

To Cristen's disgust, her hands shook as she fumbled with the cap on the aspirin bottle. She felt on edge, jittery, her nerves vibrating like a plucked string.

If only he weren't so fantastic to look at. And…so…so darned sexy.

Finally prying the cap off, Cristen took out two tablets, but when she tried to down them with a gulp of water they stuck in her throat and she coughed and sputtered and choked. "Oh, good grief! This is ridiculous." She quickly drank more water, shuddering at the bitter taste.

Godzilla's garters! Why on earth are you getting into such a dither? So the man's attractive and charming and impossibly virile. So what? It's certainly no reason to act like a love-struck teenager. Heavens! No male affected you like this even when you *were* a teenager.

Sighing, Cristen massaged her temples with her fingertips. She'd been prepared to pacify a dubious middle-aged father, allay his doubts about her suitability, not deal with a sexy male in his prime who had romance on his mind.

Cristen's head jerked up. It suddenly occurred to her that maybe she'd been right in the first place. Was Ryan testing her? Had he been flirting with her just to see how far he could get? The thought set a match to her temper, and her eyes narrowed dangerously. Why that dirty, low-down…

She took two steps toward the door before she caught herself up short. Wait a second! Wait a second! You're just guessing. It could be that he's really interested.

The thought sent a thrill zinging through her, but she quickly squelched it. Oh, sure. Great. If there's one thing you don't need, it's a man complicating your life, especially one as potent as Ryan O'Malley.

Well, whatever his reason, she told herself, heading determinedly for the living room, either way, I'll soon set him straight.

Theda was curled in Ryan's lap, the picture of smug feline bliss, turning her head this way and that to accommodate his scratching fingers, her purr a deep rumble. Both had their eyes closed. Cristen hesitated just inside the door, but then Ryan's lids lifted partway and he smiled and patted the cushion beside him. "Come join me."

Opening her eyes, Theda gave her mistress a baleful look. With an annoyed twitch of her tail, she plopped to the floor, glided haughtily to a chair and jumped up onto it. Cristen ground her teeth. There were only two chairs in the room, and with Ryan's coat in one and the cat in the other, she had no option but to join him on the sofa. To move either cat or coat would be too obvious.

As she sat down at the opposite end of the sofa, Ryan straightened and turned to face her, resting one arm along the back and bringing his bent knee up on the cushion. "So how's the headache?"

Cristen glanced at him, disturbed to find that somehow he had managed to eliminate most of the space between them. She nervously smoothed the taffeta flounces covering her thighs. "Better, thank you."

Ryan picked up her hand, and she jumped, giving him a startled look. "Are you sure?" He asked softly. "You seem tense." Examining her hand, he slowly turned it palm upward. Her nails were perfectly manicured, but the tips of her fingers were lightly callused, and there were little nicks and cuts on her palm. He grazed his thumb over them in a featherlight caress. "I think you could use that massage."

"No, that's not—"

She could have saved her breath. To her surprise, Ryan easily turned her sideways, bringing her so close to his chest that she could feel his body heat across her back.

"Now just relax. This won't hurt a bit."

"Oh, but—"

His big hands grasped her shoulders and kneaded, his thumbs digging into her back in a circular motion. "There, doesn't that feel better?"

"Yes, but…this isn't…necessary…I…ah…" Cristen's weak protest faded away in a moan as his thumbs worked up her spine. His hands were warm and strong, the pads of his fingers callused, but their abrasive rub against her smooth skin was oddly pleasurable.

"I'm not surprised you have a headache. You've been as wound up as an eight-day clock all evening." He paused a beat, and she could hear the hint of a smile in his voice when he added, "Is something bothering you?"

"No. Yes. Ryan, I'm not…" One of his hands slid up under her hair, his strong fingers flexing rhythmically over her nape, then spearing into the silken mass to move in slow, hypnotic circles against her scalp. She closed her eyes, and, like a wilting flower, her head drooped forward until her chin touched her chest.

"That's it. That's it," he crooned in her ear. "Don't fight it. Just relax."

Cristen had no choice, though she didn't so much relax as melt. His fingers were magic, soothing, arousing, warming her flesh and firing her blood until it slogged through her veins like thick, heavy syrup. She felt boneless, feverish and achy. Wonderful.

"Jennifer told me in her letters what a special lady you are. I thought she was exaggerating," he whispered in her ear as his massaging hands worked their way down her arms. "But I was wrong. You're beautiful, talented, successful, a thoroughly modern independent woman, and yet you're exquisitely feminine." As soft as the brush of a butterfly's wings, he strung a line of nibbling kisses over her shoulder and up the side of her neck, his warm breath dewing her skin and sending delightful little shudders quaking through her. Mindlessly, Cristen tilted her head to the side to give him better access.

One of Ryan's arms slid around her waist and pulled her back against him. His other hand moved in a wispy caress over her arm and shoulder; then his spread fingers feathered up her neck to curl around her jaw, and with firm but gentle pressure he turned her head.

Languorously, Cristen opened her eyes partway. Ryan's face hovered just inches from hers, flushed with desire, his blue eyes hot beneath heavy lids. Her heart thudded, and she swallowed hard. Now. Now's the time to tell him that you're...you're...

For what could have been an eternity or a split second, their gazes locked. Then, with excruciating slowness, his head moved closer and their eyes drifted shut. Ryan's moist, brandy-scented breath struck her face in soft puffs as he murmured, "I've been wanting to do this since the moment I saw you."

At the first touch of his warm lips, a delicious shudder rippled through Cristen. She quivered under the delicate caress; her breath caught. The protest she'd been struggling to recall slipped from her mind like water through a sieve. She felt strange, her body awash with new sensations, swamped with sweet pleasure.

Slowly, oh, so slowly, Ryan's open mouth rocked back and forth over hers, tempting, enticing, building her trembling response. With relentless tenderness he coaxed, claimed, conquered.

Without thought of resistance, Cristen surrendered to the soft probing of his tongue, her mouth flowering open like a blossom welcoming the sun. As he tasted her sweetness with slow, deep strokes the hand at her waist slid up over her ribcage and cupped her breast. The brush of his thumb across her nipple combined with the lazy thrusts of his tongue sent fire streaking through Cristen to gather in a hot, throbbing ache at the core of her femininity.

A low moan issued from her throat, and without conscious thought she raised her hand and clasped the back of Ryan's head, tunneling her fingers into his dark hair, her nails lightly scraping his scalp as she urged him closer.

Ryan gave an answering growl of male satisfaction. The kiss instantly changed from gentle enticement to hot, hard demand. He turned her, tightening his arms around her and holding her so close that her breasts were flattened against his chest.

"Dear Lord, you're sweet. So sweet," he murmured against her cheek as he strung a line of kisses from her mouth to her ear. "Just your taste is driving me mad." He kissed the sensitive spot behind her ear, and his tongue lapped tormentingly at her lobe.

Cristen felt the sofa cushions pressing against her bare shoulders, and she opened her eyes and found that Ryan had lowered her to her back. He was leaning over her, smiling, his expression full of sensual promise. Dazed, she blinked and stared up at him.

"Did you know that the sight of you in this dress has been driving me crazy all evening?" Slowly, he trailed his finger along the top edge of the ruffle hugging her shoulders, leaving a line of fire on her skin. His eyes followed the same path and grew steadily warmer as he traced over the rounded tops of her breasts and dipped into the shadowy cleavage. "I knew your skin would feel like warm satin." His gaze rose, and he smiled. "I've been wanting to touch you like this ever since this morning, when I saw you in that little wisp of silk."

His words cooled her passion as effectively as a bucket of ice water in the face. She jackknifed into a sitting position, taking Ryan by surprise and dumping him onto the floor.

"What the—"

Cristen scrambled to her feet and backed away, keeping a wary eye on Ryan and holding her hand out in front of her as though to ward him off, but he just lay there, propped up on his elbows, and stared at her incredulously.

"Now you—" Her voice came out in a high squeak, and she stopped to clear her throat. "Now you just stay away from me, O'Malley. Because I'm warning you right now, I have no intention of getting involved with you."

"Oh?" Ryan cocked his head to one side. "Mind telling me why?"

"Why? Because I don't indulge in affairs, that's why."

"Who said anything about an affair?"

Cristen made a sharp, dismissing gesture with her hand. "Affair. Meaningful relationship. One-night stand. Whatever you want to call it, I'm not interested. And I certainly have no intention of becoming involved with my roommate's father."

To Cristen's utter disgust, her heart was chugging like a runaway train and her chest was so tight that she could barely breathe. She waited, braced for his reaction, expecting anger or disbelief—at the very least, sardonic amusement. Ryan's shrug and calm "Okay" took her by surprise.

Feeling oddly deflated, she watched in amazement as he rolled to his feet and dusted off his trousers. He caught her staring and flashed a lopsided grin. "If you're sure that's the way you want it."

"No. I mean, yes. That's the way I want it." That's it? she marveled. No argument, no scene, no big seduction?

She backed away another step. "Now, if you don't mind, it's getting late, and since I have to get up early in the morning..." Her gaze went to the sofa and back to Ryan. "I hope you'll be comfortable on that sofa bed. If you need clean sheets—"

"I'll be fine. Jennifer showed me where they were last night."

"Oh. Well, then I'll, uh, I'll just say good-night."

"Good night, Cristen." Ryan returned her hesitant smile and watched her uneasy retreat, his expression thoughtful.

Layers. The longer he was around her, the more he discovered. Her beauty—extravagant, a bit exotic—had hit him with the force of a sledgehammer the moment he'd laid eyes on her. But beyond it was also strength, intelligence, vulnerability, that amazing talent. And temper. A smile tugged at his mouth. Oh, yes, there was temper—tightly contained, to be sure, but judging from the flashes he'd seen, it did justice to her flamboyant coloring. It pleased him as much—maybe even more—than her beauty; he appreciated spirit in a woman.

Yes, Cristen Moore was a woman of depth. Complicated. Intriguing. Alluring. He wanted to explore all the facets of her personality, peel away all the layers one by one, because he sensed—no, he knew—that hidden beneath it all lay that fascinating untapped passion, smoldering.

But there was pain also, he thought with a frown, remembering her instant withdrawal when he'd mentioned her ex-husband. With that quiet strength she had buried it deeply, but it was still there. And that bothered him.

You'd better tread carefully, O'Malley. She's a proud, strong woman. Keep it light, or she'll throw up walls you'll never tear down.

Cristen's ivory satin gown clung to her breasts and hips lovingly, then fell in generous folds that fluttered around her bare feet as she paced the floor of her darkened bedroom, too agitated to sleep.

Oh, for pity's sake! She came to a halt by the window and stared out at the scattered lights that spread all the way to the horizon. Why couldn't she just forget about that scorching kiss and put the wretched man out of her mind?

Moonlight flowed over her, turning her gown to shimmering silver. Absently, she rubbed her palm over the slick fabric covering her midriff and sighed. Come on, Cristen, you know why. It's because for the first time in your life you're attracted—really attracted—to a man.

The gentle, comfortable feelings she'd had for Bob bore no resemblance to the stomach-fluttering excitement Ryan O'Malley evoked. And that terrified her.

The last thing she wanted was to get involved with a man. Any man. Especially not like Ryan.

Closing her eyes, Cristen leaned her forehead against the cool windowpane and fought a suffocating feeling of panic. She was a normal, healthy woman, and Ryan was an attractive, virile man in his prime. That she responded to him on a purely physical level was perfectly natural, she told herself. No doubt there were hundreds—no, thousands—of men who could make her feel the same. Nothing to worry about.

Throwing up her hands, she swung around and stomped back to the bed. Lord, love a duck! What was she so frazzled about? The man was flying back to California tomorrow afternoon. With any luck, she wouldn't have to see him but maybe two or three times a year when he came to visit Jennifer. She could handle that, couldn't she? Of course she could.

Cristen slid into bed, flounced over on her side and closed her eyes determinedly. Piece of cake!

Chapter Four

Cristen had planned to leave for the shop early the next morning before either Jennifer or her father awoke, but after tossing and turning most of the night she overslept, and when she emerged from her bedroom they were already in the kitchen. Briefly she considered tiptoeing out, but after a moment's hesitation good manners won over temptation.

Cristen was not surprised to find Jennifer dressed in her comfy bathrobe, looking rumpled and sleepy-eyed. It had been sometime after two when she'd heard her come in. Stifling a yawn, her roommate looked up and murmured, "Morning, Cris. Want some coffee?"

Smiling, Ryan echoed the greeting, then fell silent, watching Cristen over the rim of his mug.

"No, thanks. I'll have some when I get to the shop." Fortunately, Jennifer was either too muzzy from lack of sleep to notice that her roommate was, for once, conversing without her obligatory coffee or too exhausted to comment on the departure from ritual. Relieved, Cristen hurried on. "Since I'll probably work all day, I thought I'd tell your father goodbye now."

Fiddling nervously with the purse strap that hung over her shoulder, Cristen fixed a polite smile on her face and turned to Ryan. "I'm glad we finally met, Mr. O'Malley. And please, feel free to visit your daughter anytime. I hope you have a pleasant trip."

Given her abhorrence for early-morning conversation and her uneasiness about Ryan, Cristen was proud of the polite, if somewhat stiff, farewell.

Ryan stood and extended his hand, his manner cordial and pleasant and equally impersonal. "Thank you, I'll do that. And I'm glad we met, too."

And that's that, Cristen thought, happily surprised. Not by so much as a look or a word did he give the slightest indication that that torrid scene on the sofa had even happened.

His obvious acceptance of her rejection encouraged Cristen, but, nevertheless, she was relieved to find him gone that afternoon when she returned.

To her surprise and utter disgust, however, it was not quite as easy to put Ryan out of her mind as she had thought it would be, especially since Jennifer couldn't seem to talk about anything else. For days after Ryan left "Dad this" and "Dad that" was all she heard out of the girl.

Louise was just as bad. She bombarded Cristen with so many questions about Ryan and dropped so many not too subtle hints about what a catch he was that Cristen finally lost all patience.

"Louise! Will you just knock it off? As far as I'm concerned Ryan O'Malley is Jennifer's father. Nothing more. Anyway, you're wasting your time trying to matchmake. I promise you, he's definitely not the marrying kind." Her mouth set in a grim line, Cristen sanded a long piece of wood harder than was strictly necessary.

"Okay, okay, forget I mentioned him. You still ought to go out once in a while. It isn't normal or healthy for a young woman to live like a cloistered nun, for pity's sake. Why, except for that dinner the other night, you haven't had a date since I fixed you up with John's cousin Fred, and that was over three months ago."

Cristen paused in fitting a floor joist and gave Louise a dry look. "Yes, and we spent a miserable evening groping for something to talk about. No offense, but believe me, Fred is deadly dull."

"Okay, then what about Leonard DeWitt? He's always asking you to go out with him."

"Me and everyone else in skirts." Cristen grimaced and shuddered. "Cripes, Louise! The man's a scuz ball."

Leonard DeWitt managed a shoe store on the lower level of the mall. He wore his pants skintight, his shirts unbuttoned to his waist and at least five pounds of gold chains around his neck. The man was incapable of looking at any woman under forty without undressing her with his beady little eyes. Just the thought of his touching her made Cristen cringe.

"How about that salesman who's always trying to date you?"

"Harvey Metcalf? Oh, come on. Harvey's a nice man, but you know he's looking for a mother for his four kids. That's a role I have no intention of filling."

Louise pounced on the statement like a duck on a June bug. "All right. If you're not interested in marriage, then why not go out with Ryan?"

Cristen straightened abruptly, buried her fingers in her hair and clasped her head with both hands. Glaring at her partner, she said through clenched teeth, "Louise, I'm warning you. If you so much as mention Ryan's name again, I swear I'll scream."

Affronted, Louise subsided, but it didn't help. Every time Cristen looked at her friend's sulky expression she was reminded of the maddening man all over again. That night she even dreamed about him.

But in the middle of the week all thought of Ryan was pushed from Cristen's mind when, to her delight, she received a special order for a carpenter gothic Victorian mansion, complete with furnishings. It was an enormous order that would take months to complete, even putting in extra hours, and between working on it and building up their stock for the move to larger quarters, she was kept so busy she barely had time to think about anything or anyone else.

On Friday Cristen went to the shop early, hoping to work on her new commission before opening time, only to find Louise waiting for her. The moment Cristen stepped inside, her friend pounced.

"There you are! I was just about to call your apartment. I've got some great news."

Cristen stowed her purse, then bent over her table to study the scale drawings spread out on its surface. "Don't tell me. You won ten million dollars in one of those publishers' sweepstakes."

Brimming with excitement, Louise was oblivious to her teasing. "I heard a rumor that the shop next door is going out of business, and that space will be available for lease soon."

Cristen's head shot up. "Really? That far-out boutique?" At Louise's nod she grinned in delight. "Terrific! That's great! I mean, not that they're going out of business, of course. I'm sorry about that. But if we can get that space, we could knock out a wall and double the size of our shop without moving."

Already plans were taking shape in her mind as she scanned the shop's interior. This was just the break they needed.

"My thoughts exactly," Louise said, looking pleased. "I was hoping you'd agree."

"Oh, I do. Have you checked with Henderson's office to see what could be worked out on a new lease and the cost of removing the wall?"

"Well...no. I thought we'd better wait until it's official. Actually, I'm not even supposed to know about it yet."

Cristen frowned. "Exactly where did you hear this rumor?"

"From Dora. She called me at home this morning to tell me because she knew we were looking for a bigger place."

"Dora? Dippy Dora? And you believed her? You're pinning your hopes on something you heard from that ding-a-ling?" Cristen groaned and rolled her eyes. "Oh, please, Louise. Give me a break."

"Dora's okay," Louise said halfheartedly.

"She's about half a bubble off, and you know it." Cristen's expression held both disgust and amazement. "Do you know that girl once asked me how boneless chickens could walk? She's a flake, Louise. I don't care if she is your husband's niece."

"I know, but she's harmless."

"I'm not too sure about that. I get an anxiety attack practically every time I even think about her working here."

"Come on, Cris. I know she drives you around the bend, but she means well. And since we have to have part-time help, it might as well be John's niece."

Cristen met her friend's gaze and sighed. She had often thought it a shame that Louise and John had never had children. The original mother hen, Louise tried to take every stray chick under her wing. And where family and friends were concerned, she was a pushover. Right now her round, pleasant face held all the pleading appeal of a puppy in a pet store window, and it was just as difficult to resist.

"All right, you win. Finish your story," Cristen said with a resigned sigh, and Louise immediately brightened.

"Well you see, Dora went out with Barney Tucker last night, and he told her about the boutique going out of business."

"Who's Barney Tucker?"

"You know, the young man who works for mall security. He got it from his cousin." At Cristen's blank look, she added, "She's a file clerk in the building manager's office."

"Ah. An unimpeachable source," Cristen drawled. Slanting Louise a scornful look, she plucked her smock from the peg, slipped it on and plopped down in her chair.

"I know it's kind of roundabout, but you just wait. I'm sure we'll find out that Barney was right."

If Cristen had been a betting woman, she would have wagered a month's profits against that likelihood…and lost. To her surprise, about an hour later the boutique owner dropped in to chat and told them that she was declaring bankruptcy.

The moment the woman left, Cristen called Joe Henderson's office. By that afternoon they'd worked out an agreement on the lease and the cost of knocking out the wall. The only thing left to do was see their banker about taking out a larger loan.

To celebrate, after closing the shop they went to dinner at an expensive French restaurant. John met them there, and when he heard their news, insisted on ordering champagne. After numerous toasts and a sumptuous meal, it was past midnight when they left, and almost one o'clock by the time John and Louise dropped Cristen off.

The apartment was dark when she let herself in. Not wanting to wake Jennifer, Cristen did not bother with a light, but tiptoed confidently across the familiar, shadowy

living room. In the middle she instinctively veered around
a chair, took another step and whacked her shin on something solid. With a yelp of pain, she pitched forward.

"What the—"

Cristen's breath left her lungs in a loud *whoosh* when
she landed hard on something large and warm and extremely firm. It took a second—and the startling feel of
hands sliding boldly over her buttocks—for her to realize
that she was sprawled atop a man. And that, beneath a thin
sheet, that man was lying naked on a bed!

Shock gave way to panic, and she began to struggle, but
in a lightning move he flipped her onto her back and
pinned her down with his body. Her instinctive scream had
barely begun when he stifled it with his mouth.

Cristen fought back without thought, bucking beneath
his heavy weight, twisting her head from side to side. Her
hands were pinned between them, but she finally managed
to wriggle one free and pound on his back with her fist.
When that had no effect she grabbed a handful of his hair
and yanked with all her might.

There was a moan, then, unbelievably, a chuckle.

"Aaahh, sweetheart, don't scalp me," the man murmured against her mouth, prying her hand from his hair
and pinning it to the mattress beside her head.

Cristen's frantic movements faltered. There was something…something in that deep rumble that cut through her
panic. Something familiar. Something tantalizing. In the
brief second before his mouth had closed over hers she
had glimpsed a face, and as she tried to recall it Cristen
realized that the kiss, though firm, wasn't in any way brutal. As her struggles lessened it became a soft caress, a
gentle enticement that plucked a responsive chord deep
within her, until at last she grew utterly still.

Recognition—elusive, teasing—fluttered around the
edges of her mind, but even as she grasped at it her body
responded to his with a knowledge of its own. Their legs

were entwined, tangled in the sheet that draped his lower body, their torsos pressed together as though they were one. Cristen was acutely aware of his strength, his heat, his potent masculinity, the shocking intimacy of their position. A tingle ran over her skin, making her first hot, then cold, then hot again.

His lips were warm and wet, his tongue a gentle marauder. Cristen's mouth quivered and softened. A low growl issued from the man's throat, and for a moment the kiss changed from a slow, rocking, tender torment to sheer hunger.

Then it ended. The man lifted his head, and Cristen's eyes drifted open, blinked and slowly grew round.

Propped up on his elbows, his face illuminated by the small square of moonlight spilling through the window, Ryan grinned down at her. Cristen sucked in her breath, but before she could make a coherent sound he winked and murmured outrageously, "You know, we really have to stop meeting like this."

His unmitigated gall took her breath away. "What! You…you… Ohhhh!"

Ryan's grin widened.

"Get off me, you lout!" Cristen shoved his chest with her free hand and bucked her hips, but the intimate contact brought a dangerous gleam to his eyes, and she quickly subsided. She scowled up at him, so furious that she could barely breathe. "You…you big buffoon! You scared me half to death, do you know that!"

"Sorry," he replied, but there was nothing in the least repentant about his look.

"What are you doing here, anyway? You're supposed to be in California." She shoved his chest again and scowled more darkly. "And will you *please* get *off* me?"

Ryan didn't budge. He released her hand and shifted his fingers through the feathery auburn curls spread out against the sheet. Through half-closed eyes he studied their silky

sheen in the moonlight as though it were the most fascinating thing he'd ever seen. "You said I should feel free
to visit Jennifer anytime I wanted." He looked up, and his
amused gaze collided with her stormy one. "So here I
am."

Cristen clamped her teeth together, barely stifling a
groan. Trust him to take that polite platitude literally. "But
you were here just last week," she pointed out irritably.

"I missed her."

"I see. Well, would you mind telling me just what the
devil you thought you were doing, grabbing me and kissing me like that? I thought we had that matter settled."

"We did. We do." He gave her a guileless look and
lifted one bare bronze shoulder. "But I couldn't let you
wake up the whole building screaming, now could I?"

His reasonable tone made her want to give him a swift
kick. Or better yet, considering their positions, a sharp jab
with her knee.

"I hardly think it was necessary for you to—"

"Shh, you're going to wake Jennifer."

"I don't care if I wake the governor!" she shrieked,
infuriated by his audacity. "You've got one heck of a
nerve—"

"What's all the yelling about?"

Light suddenly filled the room. Cristen and Ryan both
looked around to see Jennifer standing just inside the hall
door with her hand still on the light switch. Her dark curls
were mussed and she was rumpled and half asleep, but as
she took in the intimate position of the two people on the
bed her eyes grew comically round. "Oops. Sorry, I, uh,
I didn't mean to…that is…" She fluttered her hands nervously and stumbled backward. "I'll, uh, I'll just go
back—"

"Jennifer, wait! You don't understand! Come back
here!" Cristen yelled.

Ryan's chest began to vibrate with silent laughter. Cristen gave him a hard shove and hissed, "Will you get *off*!"

Obliging, he rolled to the side and collapsed on his back, letting his stifled chuckles blossom into rich, full-bodied laughter as Cristen scrambled from the bed.

She fumbled to straighten her clothing and swiped impatiently at her disheveled hair. She was torn between her anger and embarrassment, and her flustered gaze bounced from Jennifer to Ryan, then quickly darted away again when she saw that the sheet had slid so low on his hips that he was barely decent.

"I, uh, didn't know your father was here, you see," she began anxiously, darting Jennifer a self-conscious look. "And I…I stumbled into the sofa bed in the dark and fell over him. When you came in he was, uh, he was just checking to see if I'd hurt myself."

Ryan let loose with another burst of guffaws and doubled up, clutching his sides.

If looks could kill, the one Cristen shot the convulsed man would have annihilated him on the spot. At that moment the urge to fold up the sofa bed with him in it was almost irresistible.

Determined to ignore him, she gritted her teeth and turned back to Jennifer. The smug little smile that had replaced her roommate's shocked expression sent Cristen's temper up another notch. "Now look. It's not what you think—"

"Whatever you say, Cris," Jennifer assured her with such blatant tongue-in-cheek insincerity that Cristen wanted to chunk something. Hard.

In control of himself again, Ryan lay back, fingers laced behind his head, and watched Cristen with a look of unholy amusement.

Exasperated, she turned to him and snapped, "Granny's garters! Don't just lie there grinning like the village idiot. Help a little, can't you?"

"Certainly." Ryan raised himself up on his elbows and

assumed a pious expression. "Jennifer, regardless of what you saw, absolutely nothing happened. Do you think I'd indulge in hanky-panky just because a beautiful woman fell into bed with me?"

Cristen closed her eyes and groaned.

"You? Never."

"Good. It's nice to know a daughter has faith in her father." He dropped his severe pose, and one corner of his mouth kicked upward. "Actually, though, I really thought she was a cat burglar."

"Uh-huh. So you were frisking her, right?"

"Right."

"Find any concealed weapons?"

Ryan's heavy-lidded gaze slid lazily over Cristen. Its touch sizzled along her nerve endings and sent a tingle racing over her back and shoulders and down her arms. Slowly a smile grew on his lips and he emitted a low, wicked "Hmm."

At the sound Cristen sucked in her breath and bristled like a cat whose fur has been stroked the wrong way.

"Now look here," she huffed. "I won't stand for—"

She stopped abruptly and glanced from father to daughter. Ryan's mustache was twitching, and Jennifer was biting the insides of her cheeks. Both pairs of blue eyes danced with mischief and lighthearted laughter.

Cristen's blistering put-down dissolved on her tongue. Her arrested expression changed from indignation to faint chagrin, and slowly, a reluctant smile tugged at her mouth. "Very funny, you two."

"Oh, Cris, if only you could have seen your face. It was priceless. I know we probably shouldn't tease you, but you do ask for it, you know," Jennifer reproved with a chuckle and a warm look. "You're always so intense."

"Jennifer's right," Ryan put in. "You really should loosen up, learn to go with the flow. Life's more fun that way."

He was propped up in the bed, leaning against the sofa back, watching her in that sexy, devilish way of his. The sheet was pulled up to a semimodest level just below his waist. Above it, his chest was bare and broad and furred with a mat of silky black hair. As she stared at its enticing swirling patterns, Cristen was reminded of the morning they met, and she felt the same fluttering sensation in the pit of her stomach. His hair stuck up in places where she had yanked it, and a faint beard stubble shadowed his jaw, yet he looked absurdly attractive: rakish and bold and thoroughly male, lying there supremely unconcerned about his nearly naked state.

Cristen wondered if he knew what it was doing to her. The gleam in his eyes told her that he did, and she glanced away.

"You're probably right," she agreed. "I guess I've just been working too hard lately. You know what they say about 'all work and no play.'" She managed a lame smile and edged toward her bedroom. "Since it's late, and I'm sure you're both as tired as I am, I'll say good-night. I, uh, I'm sorry I disturbed your sleep."

"Cristen." Ryan's voice stopped her just as she reached the hall door, and she paused and looked back at him. Warmth and gentleness had replaced the teasing laughter in his eyes. "I'm sorry if I frightened you. I didn't mean to. I just acted on impulse."

The simple, sincere apology plucked an emotional chord deep inside Cristen, and she reacted to it every bit as sharply as she had to his physical appeal. It made her even more uneasy. She looked at him for a moment, gave an uncertain smile and nodded and without another word stepped through the doorway.

In her room she leaned back against the closed door and stared off into space, a slight frown drawing her brows together. What was she going to do about that man? He was a flirt and a tease, definitely not a man to be taken seriously, so why did she react to him like a prickly hedge-hog?

Was it because of this stupid physical attraction she felt for him?

Cristen pressed four fingers over her lips and closed her eyes as the memory of his kiss came stealing back. Since high school she'd heard and read about the explosive passion that could erupt between a man and woman when the chemistry was right, but she had never really believed it. Certainly she'd never experienced it before.

And I could have darned well done without it, she thought resentfully. She didn't care for that heart-pounding, weak-kneed, woozy feeling that came over her at Ryan's touch. The loss of control was both frightening and irritating.

But then again, maybe her testiness with Ryan simply meant that she'd lost her sense of humor, as Jennifer had implied.

With slow steps, she crossed to the bed and sank down on its edge. In one of her rare displays of compassion, Theda jumped onto Cristen's lap and purred her sympathy. Obeying the head-butting command, Cristen scratched be-hind the cat's ears. "Do you think that's the problem, Theda? Have I become a humorless dullard?"

What had happened to the reckless, lighthearted girl who had led Bob into one scrape after another as they were growing up? The young woman who had met life head-on with laughter and buoyant optimism and a slightly irrev-erent sense of humor? Had she let a wrecked marriage destroy her?

Cristen had always been goal oriented. Ambitious. De-termined. She knew that. But since Bob's departure she had used work as a panacea, letting it fill her life until there wasn't room for anything else. Not pain, not heart-ache, not bittersweet memories.

Not joy. Not laughter. And certainly not love.

Cristen gave a mirthless chuckle and stroked her hand absently down Theda's back. "Leaping lizards! I must be going soft in the head, Theda. It's ridiculous to even think of love in connection with Ryan O'Malley."

Narrowing her eyes, Theda gazed at Cristen and meowed.

"Oh, he's a charming devil, I'll grant you that. But you have to admit he's hardly a man for forever after."

She looked away, her wry smile fading. In any case, a man in her life was the last thing she wanted. Or needed.

A gentle nudge sent Theda plopping to the floor, and Cristen went to the dresser and withdrew a pink silk nightgown that was slit up both sides to the tops of her thighs. She draped it over her arm, stepped out of her shoes and headed for the bathroom.

"Cristen, you're not going to work today, are you?"

Cristen had barely set foot in the kitchen the next morning when Jennifer hit her with the question. With only the slightest hesitation, she continued toward the counter, casting the girl a bleary look that would have silenced a horde of crazed fans at a rock concert.

But not Jennifer.

"It's Louise's weekend to man the store, so you don't really have to go in, right?"

Taking her time, Cristen poured coffee into a large mug. She took a sip, closed her eyes and took two more. Finally, cradling the mug in both hands, she turned, leaned back against the counter and looked at Jennifer through the wisps of rising steam. "No."

Her shuttered gaze slid to Ryan, who was leaning back at ease in his chair, following the exchange. She'd been tempted to lie and say she needed to go in to the shop, anyway, but the night before she'd vowed that she was through hiding. She would be pleasant and polite, but distant. When he realized she wasn't interested, Ryan would soon tire of whatever game he was playing.

"Oh, good! Then you can take Dad apartment hunting."

Cristen blinked groggily and frowned. "What?"

"Apartment hunting," Ryan interjected. "You know, as in 'a place to live.' Or at worst, to sleep and eat and hang your clothes."

As Cristen's foggy brain grappled with the statement, her eyes slowly widened. "Here? You mean you're going to move here to Houston?"

"Sort of. I'm going to open a branch of my company here. I'll probably alternate between Houston and the San Francisco plant every other week for the next year or so, or at least until I get everything running smoothly." Ryan grinned at Cristen's appalled expression. "So you can see, since I'll be spending at least half my time here, I'll need a place of my own."

The staggering news brought Cristen wide awake. Heaven above! He was going to live there!

"Isn't that great?" Jennifer chirped. "Now I can see Dad often."

Too stunned to reply, Cristen just stared.

"Of course, he's going to be terribly busy for a while, locating a site for his plant and getting it built and all, so he's going to need help finding the right apartment," she continued, oblivious to Cristen's shell-shocked look. "I told him you wouldn't mind helping."

"Me? You want *me* to find him an apartment?"

"Sure. You know Houston a lot better than I do."

"But—"

"Don't worry about it, Cristen." Ryan gave his daughter a mildly reproving look. "I told you it was too much of an imposition to expect Cristen to spend her free time helping me. I'm sure I'll manage to find something on my own. It'll just take me a little longer, that's all."

"No problem. Take as long as you need," Jennifer declared airily. "Cristen and I don't mind, do we?"

"Mind?"

Jennifer stood and retrieved the coffeepot, tossing Cristen a confident glance. "I told Dad he was welcome to stay here with us until he found a place."

She dropped that bombshell as she turned to refill her father's mug, and thus missed Cristen's aghast stare.

Stay with us? Here? Indefinitely! Sheer panic welled up inside Cristen at the thought of sharing her home with Ryan, of his occupying her sofa bed every night, of being on the receiving end of those warm looks and that teasing, sexy smile every morning and every evening. Of growing used to having him around, of possibly becoming more attracted to him, of...

No. Oh, no. Not on your life. A visit was one thing, but having him living there, God only knew how long... No, she couldn't risk that.

But what choice did she have? An outright refusal was out of the question. He *was* Jennifer's father, and, manners aside, technically she supposed he had a perfect right to stay there, since he paid Jennifer's rent.

Jennifer was looking at her expectantly. Ryan's face remained impassive, but Cristen thought she saw amusement dancing in his blue eyes.

She clenched her jaw and forced her lips into a stiff smile. "Of course you must stay with us, Ryan. And I'll be happy to help you find an apartment."

Even if I have to beat feet all over town every waking moment of this entire weekend.

Chapter Five

"What do you mean, it's too high tech?" Cristen looked around in confusion at the modern high-rise apartment. It had every gadget and convenience she had ever heard of, and a lot she hadn't. "I thought that would appeal to you. After all, you're in a high-tech business yourself."

"True. But when I get home I like something a little...homier." Ryan shrugged. "This place seems more like a laboratory. Or something out of *Star Wars*."

He stuck his hands into the trouser pockets of his dark three-piece suit and strolled across the pearl-gray carpet to the wall of tinted glass.

Thoroughly frustrated, Cristen watched him through narrowed eyes as he jingled the change in his pocket and gazed out at the terrace and the sprawling city below. She felt like reminding him that only the day before she had shown him a charming town house with an old-world ambience, done completely in antiques, but she bit back the words.

For the past five weeks she had been running herself
ragged searching for an apartment. She'd located several
she thought were exceptional, but he'd found something
wrong with every one; it was either too large, too small,
too remote, too closed in, too fancy, too stark—the list
was endless.

And in the meantime, every other week, Ryan was happily ensconced in Cristen's condo.

"I take it, then, that you're not interested."

Ryan looked at her over his shoulder and smiled. "It's
really very nice, Cristen, but it's just not me. Have you
any others you can show me?"

Irritated, she shoved her envelope purse under her arm,
turned on her heel and stalked toward the door. "No, I do
not," she tossed back in a tight, clipped voice. "This was
the fifth one we've looked at today."

Still jingling his change, Ryan trailed after her. "Hey,
Cristen, I'm sorry to put you to so much trouble. Look,
why don't I just do my own hunting from now on? It'll
probably take me longer, but I'm sure I could manage to
squeeze out a couple of hours a week to scout around for
an apartment."

And at that rate you'll still be camping out at my place
when you start drawing Social Security, she moaned silently. "Oh, no. No, I wouldn't hear of it. I said I'd find
you an apartment, and I will. I'll just have to keep searching, that's all. Come on. Let's get home and go through
the want ads."

Ryan grinned at her retreating back. "Okay. If you insist."

Cristen fumed all the way home, but Ryan either didn't
notice or chose to ignore her bad humor. He chatted amiably as he drove through the heavy Saturday afternoon
traffic, sublimely unruffled by either it or his companion's
curt, monosyllabic replies.

Cristen didn't know whom she was ticked off with

more: Ryan for—she suspected—deliberately dragging his feet, or herself for allowing it.

They heard the phone shrilling when they reached the door of the condo. Cristen tapped her foot impatiently while Ryan fitted his key into the lock. Eager to vent her ire on something, she stalked past him, snatched up the offending instrument and snapped out a stinging "Hello."

"Cristen? I...did I catch you at a bad time?"

After years of close friendship it took only those few words from Louise for Cristen to know that something was wrong. In an instant her annoyance evaporated. "What is it, Louise? What's the matter?"

Drawn by her worried look and the note of concern in her voice, Ryan stepped nearer, frowning. The frown deepened as he watched her grow pale, her expression changing to shocked disbelief.

"They turned us down? But...why?"

There was a pause, and anger tightened Cristen's face as she listened to her partner. "I see. Didn't you explain about—"

Another pause, longer this time, and then Cristen sighed. "I see. Well, I guess that's that."

The murmur of Louise's voice drifted to Ryan, but he couldn't make out her words. He watched, his concern growing, as Cristen listened intently, her teeth worrying her lower lip.

"I don't know where we go from here, Louise," Cristen said in a dispirited voice. "Let me give it some thought."

When she hung up the phone she just stood there with her hand still on the receiver, deep in thought.

"What's wrong?"

She gave Ryan a distracted look and raked a hand through her hair. "Oh, uh, just a business problem."

"Want to tell me about it? Maybe I could help."

"I doubt it." Cristen attempted a smile, but it came out a grimace. She wandered to the window and stared out, absently fingering the edge of the drapery. "You see, after keeping us waiting for weeks, and despite the fact that we paid off our original loan promptly, the bank has turned down our application for a new loan. We need that money to expand our shop."

"Did they give you a reason?"

"Several. Money's tight. They don't feel our collateral is adequate. But apparently the main reason is that they're concerned about the business being so heavily dependent on me. About my ability to keep up with the increase in demand. Louise explained that we've worked out a student training program with the university art department. The students who participate will earn credit for learning the craft and receive a small salary, and I'll have a steady stream of apprentice helpers." Cristen let out her breath in a long, defeated sigh. "But the loan officer still wasn't convinced."

"So what are you going to do?"

"I don't know. Try other banks, I guess. Though we'll probably run into the same problem."

Ryan studied her back, the tense set of her shoulders, and after a moment came to a decision. "Look, instead of going through that hassle, why don't you borrow the money from me?"

Cristen swung around, her eyes wide. "From you? But...you don't even know how much we need. And besides, you have your own business expansion to worry about."

"I have a fair idea. And don't worry, I may not be in the Rockefeller class yet, but I can afford to lend you what you need."

At a loss for words, Cristen just stared. From things Jennifer had said and the scope of his business, she had known that Ryan was doing well, but until now—until that casual offer of what to her seemed a staggering amount of money—it hadn't really hit her that he was actually wealthy. Now that she thought about it, though, compared to the cost of building a whole new factory in Houston, their needs probably seemed piddling.

It was a tempting offer, but pride wouldn't let her accept. "Thank you, Ryan. It's very generous of you to offer, but…no. I'm afraid we can't accept."

Ryan sighed, a look of mild exasperation on his face. "All right. If you won't take money from me, how about if I cosign a bank loan? They won't turn you down if I stand good for it."

"I…you'd do that?" Cristen was stunned. It was the perfect solution. Unless they defaulted on the loan, which she had no intention of doing, Ryan wouldn't be out a penny.

"Sure. It's the least I can do, after you've put up with having me constantly underfoot for weeks. So what do you say?"

Cristen couldn't control the smile that spread across her face, or the relief and elation that swelled within her. After only the briefest hesitation she blurted out, "I say yes! Yes!"

She stuck out her hand, and Ryan took it between both of his. "Oh, Ryan, I don't know how to thank you."

"Well…" With a gentle tug, he pulled her closer, the familiar teasing glint sparking in his eyes. Cristen's chest tightened. "…I could probably think of—"

Before he could finish, the front door burst open and Jennifer tore into the room like a whirlwind.

"You're never going to guess what happened today!" she squealed. "Never in a million years!" Breathless, her face flushed and deliriously happy, she twirled around the room with her arms outstretched, almost crackling with excitement.

Bemused, Cristen and Ryan exchanged a questioning look and shrugged.

"What? What?" they demanded in unison, laughing as

Jennifer's freewheeling pirouettes carried her around them like a demented dervish.

At last she stopped and looked from one to the other, her eyes shining and wide. Looking as though she would burst at any second, she pressed her clasped hands to her breast and gasped. "I got a part in a Broadway play!"

"What!"

"Jennifer! That's wonderful!"

Everyone started talking at once, and between hugs and congratulations Jennifer managed to explain that a producer had come to the Alley Theater looking for an unknown to play the ingenue in a new play.

"You wouldn't believe how fast the word got out," she said, still flushed with excitement. "I bet every actress in town under twenty-five showed up within twenty minutes after our director made the announcement."

"But you got the part." Grinning from ear to ear, Ryan radiated fatherly pride.

"Yes! Isn't it wonderful? We start rehearsals in three weeks. And in the meantime, I've got a million things to do. Such as pack and make travel arrangements and find a place to live and…and… Oh, all kinds of things!"

"Don't worry about a place to live," Ryan said. "Some friends of mine, Arnold and Sue Jordan, live in Manhattan. I'm sure they'll be glad to have you stay with them, at least until you can find another roommate like Cristen to share with."

Cristen sobered, her high spirits taking a nosedive at the casual statement. For the first time since Jennifer had made her announcement it hit Cristen that she would be losing her roommate. She pulled away from the other two, who were still talking jubilantly, and sank down on a chair.

"What's the matter, Cristen?" Ryan asked when he noticed her dazed dejection. "Aren't you happy for Jennifer?"

"Yes. Yes, of course I am. I'm delighted. Really." Seeing the doubt in their eyes, she made a face and flapped her hand. "Oh, don't mind me. I'm just down because I suddenly realized that now I'll have to look for a new roommate myself."

"Oh, Cris. I didn't think about—" Jennifer turned to her father with an agonized look.

Frowning, Ryan pursed his lips thoughtfully. "Actually, that's no problem. That is…it doesn't have to be."

"What do you mean?"

His brows hiked upward, and he spread his hands wide, palms out. "I could be your roommate."

"You!"

"Dad! That's a great idea!"

"I thought so."

"You *must* be joking!"

"No, I'm not."

"No, he's not," Jennifer echoed.

"But…but you can't! It just wouldn't…we couldn't—"

"Why not?" Ryan asked, cutting into Cristen's incoherent sputtering.

She stared at him, shocked right down to her toes.

"Well, for one thing, you're a man."

"So?"

"Oh, for heaven's sake, Cris. Dad's just suggesting that you be roommates, not that you…you know…*live* together."

"But that's what it will look like. What everyone will think."

"So? Let them. Besides, who's going to care? Louise? She'll probably be delighted. And your folks are out in Arizona in that retirement community. You told me yourself they never come to Houston."

"I don't see what the big fuss is about." Leaning back against a chair, Ryan folded his arms across his chest. "After all, I've been living here for weeks now, and a lot of that time Jennifer wasn't even around. If anyone was going to notice, or care, they already have by now."

"Well...yes, I suppose that's true, but..."

"The arrangement would benefit both of us," he pointed out. "I won't have to rent an apartment and leave it vacant half the time, while you, on the other hand, will be receiving full rent from a roommate who's only here every other week. And," he added with a devilish, immodest grin, "I'm handy to have around the house, even if I do say so myself."

Cristen couldn't argue with that. Since moving in, Ryan had taken care of innumerable odd jobs and minor emergencies around the apartment, such as repairing the disposal, replacing leaky faucet washers and unsticking her bedroom window, all without being asked. Just the night before, when the water heater had gone on the fritz, he had somehow gotten it working again. Last Sunday when she had gone to drive her car around the block, as she did every few days to keep the battery charged, it had been dead as a doornail, and Ryan had hooked up cables to his rental car and jump-started it.

Gnawing on her inner lip, Cristen looked at him doubtfully. She'd be a fool to agree to the arrangement. And yet...there *were* advantages to it.

But there are risks, too, she reminded herself. And she didn't entirely trust Ryan. Or yourself, a little voice prodded.

"If I agree—" Cristen raised her hand to quell Jennifer's cry of delight and fixed Ryan with a stern look. "Mind you, I said *if* I agree...do you promise to behave yourself? No heavy passes or seduction scenes?"

Ryan managed a look of affronted innocence. "Have I stepped out of line, even once, since I've been staying here?"

"Well...no."

He hadn't. She'd been braced for it, but he had thrown

her for a loop by acting the perfect gentleman. It had been unnerving, like waiting for the other shoe to drop. It had also made her feel like a fool. And worse, his sterling behavior hadn't in the least stopped her from being aware of him, from feeling all prickly and tense—and yes, excited—whenever he was near.

"And we've gotten along well, haven't we?"

"Yes." She looked at him askance, her narrowed gaze suspicious and a bit surly. If anything, too well. Ryan, blast his hide, had been the perfect houseguest: amiable, considerate, helpful, maddeningly neat. He hadn't said or done a single thing she could complain about.

"Then there's really no reason why we shouldn't share this apartment, is there?"

"Well…" Cristen nibbled on her thumbnail, her forehead furrowed. Put that way, it did make a lot of sense. It was tempting. Very temp—

Lordy, Cristen! Are you nuts? she demanded, giving herself a mental shake. I can't believe you're even considering this crazy plan. Not an hour ago you were bustin' your buns to get him out of here. And you know why too.

She hated to admit it, even to herself, but she had actually begun to enjoy having Ryan around. Even worse, she missed him during those times when he was in California, and she looked forward to Friday evenings when he returned. It was fear of that growing attachment that had spurred her frantic efforts to find him an apartment of his own.

If you've got a lick of sense, you'll give him an emphatic, irrevocable, unconditional no, she told herself firmly. "Look, Ryan, it just won't work."

"Why not? There's no law that says a man and woman can't share the same roof without being sexually intimate. After all, we're both mature adults. We should be able to handle it. At least I can." He gave her a guileless look.

"Of course, if you feel you just couldn't keep your hands off me…"

"What? Don't flatter yourself, O'Malley! You're about as much threat to my self-control as…as a three-hundred-pound eunuch."

"Then there's no reason we can't be roommates."

"None whatever," Cristen declared recklessly. It was a good arrangement for both of them, she told herself, ignoring the sudden tightness in her chest. And as Ryan had pointed out, they were adults. She was perfectly capable of curbing her wayward reactions. It was all a matter of adjustment. And attitude.

"Great." Ryan rubbed his palms together. "So we've got a deal, right?"

"As long as you understand the ground rules."

"Which are?"

"We share the work, don't interfere in each other's life, and…"

His brows bobbed up at her stern expression. "And?"

"And *no* funny stuff."

A slow grin spread over his face. "I swear to you, Cristen, that whatever happens between us will be only what you want to happen."

Cristen frowned. It wasn't exactly the assurance she was looking for, but there didn't seem to be any way to complain without appearing foolish.

Before Jennifer's squeals of delight had died away Cristen was having second thoughts, but Ryan didn't give her a chance to voice them. With the speed and command of a general mustering his troops, he took charge, turning his attention and their energies to getting his daughter moved.

Within an hour he had contacted his friends in New York and arranged for Jennifer to stay with them. By that evening he and Jennifer had paid off her bills at the various stores in town, sold her car, picked up her clothes from the cleaners and closed her bank account. The next day

Cristen helped her pack her things, and at eight that evening she and Ryan put the excited girl on a plane bound for Kennedy Airport, where the Jordans would be waiting.

It wasn't until then, when Cristen found herself standing beside Ryan at the observation window of the terminal, watching the plane grow steadily smaller against the dusky eastern sky, that she began to fully comprehend just what she had agreed to.

Before, there had always been Jennifer's ebullient presence to defray the tension between them. Even when she had not been around, it had been felt.

But now—now there's just the two of us, Cristen thought in growing panic as she walked back through the terminal beside Ryan. All the way to the parking garage he talked about Jennifer, happy for her one minute and voicing typical parental concern the next. Cristen barely heard him. She was too acutely conscious of his hand resting on the small of her back, the occasional brush of his body as he guided her through the throng of people. The merest touch seemed to burn right through her clothing.

When they were both seated in the car, Ryan turned to her before starting the engine. "Is there anyplace you'd like to go, anything you need to do before we go home?"

Home. The word started a fluttering in Cristen's stomach. Why did it sound so much more intimate now? "No, thank you."

Nodding, Ryan flicked the ignition key and drove out of the garage.

Dusk deepened into night, and the lights along the freeway flickered on. Unconsciously digging her fingers into her soft leather purse, Cristen stared out the side window as Ryan guided the rented Continental through the speeding traffic. With every monotonous *thump-thump* of the tires on the sectioned paving her nerves wound tighter.

She glanced at Ryan out of the corner of her eye. His shadowy profile was lit by the glow from the dash, his

expression serious and intent. Since leaving the airport behind he had fallen silent. She wondered if he was thinking
about Jennifer.

Or about what would happen when they got home.

Oh, stop it, you ninny! she told herself severely. Nothing's going to happen. Absolutely nothing. You have an
agreement. And it's not as though the man hasn't slept
under your roof before. The only difference is that now
he'll be occupying Jennifer's old room.

Despite the bracing lecture, which lasted all the way
home, Cristen's nerves were stretched tight as a drum
when they stepped inside the apartment.

From her customary place on the back of the sofa, Theda
looked up and meowed expectantly, but Cristen walked by
without even looking at her. Huffily, the cat leaped to the
floor and wound herself around Ryan's ankles.

"I think it's time for some loving, don't you?" Ryan
murmured throatily, and Cristen jumped as if a firecracker
had suddenly exploded under her feet.

"What!" She spun around, bristling with outrage, but
her furious expression froze, then grew slack with morti-
fication at the sight of Ryan, squatted down on his
haunches, stroking the sinuously twining cat. "Oh. I, uh,
I thought…"

Ryan looked up and cocked one brow. Blue eyes twinkling, he watched the scalding color rise up her neck and
flood her face. The sable mustache twitched. "You thought
what?"

Cristen wanted to hit him. He knew exactly what she
had thought, darn him. And he was enjoying her discomfort.

She lifted her chin. "I thought I'd make some coffee,"
she said in a crisp voice that dared him to so much as hint
otherwise. "Would you like some?"

Ryan gave Theda one last scratch behind the ears and
rose to his feet. "No, thanks. I have some papers I need

to go over, and then I think I'll have an early night." He moved past her, and as he reached the hall door he turned and winked. "See you in the morning. And don't forget to lock up."

Cristen's jaw sagged. Standing in the middle of the floor as though turned to stone, she stared after him.

It took even longer than usual for the discordant din of the alarm to drag Cristen awake the next morning, mainly because of the hours she'd spent tossing and turning. Sprawled on her stomach, her body as limp as a wet rag, her hair a wild tangle, her white shorty nightgown bunched up around her shoulders, she instinctively tried to shut out the raucous clanging by burrowing under the pillow. The maneuver failed, as it did every morning. Groaning, she flung the pillow aside and hauled herself out of bed.

Following her usual semicomatose routine, she stumbled to the dresser with her eyes closed and patted her hand along its surface in search of the shrilling clock. On the third slap her fingers splashed into something cold and wet.

Cristen started, and her heavy lids fluttered open. A squat glass filled with orange juice sat beside the clock, and four fingers of her right hand were immersed up to the second knuckle in the sticky liquid.

For a second she stared dumbly at the absurd sight. Then her face scrunched up in a disgusted grimace. "Oh, yeeeck!" She jerked her fingers out of the juice and slung her hand, which only succeeded in dotting the bureau with a spray of drops. Growling, she snatched a wad of tissues from the box on the dresser and dabbed at the mess.

The alarm clock continued its relentless shrill.

"Oh, will you *shut up!*" Cristen snarled, giving it a whack with her free hand. Miraculously, her aim was good, and the cacophony ended with startling suddenness.

She tossed the damp tissues into the wastebasket and wiped her sticky fingers with a fresh one. It was then that the sounds coming from the bathroom registered. Running water and… Cristen's head whipped around, her eyes growing steadily wider. And *whistling*!

Her suspicious gaze slid from the bathroom door to the squat glass, then back. "Why, that—"

With another frustrated growl, she snatched up the glass and marched toward the closed door. She stormed into the bathroom without knocking, flinging the door open with such force that it banged against the wall.

In the mirror above the sink, Ryan's calm gaze met her fiery one. The hand holding the razor paused only momentarily before raking another swath through the lather that coated his cheek. "Good morning." The dark mustache kicked up at the corners. Below it his teeth were a white slash.

"Just what is this?" Cristen demanded, slamming the glass down on the counter.

Ryan glanced at it, then tipped his head back and drew the razor up the underside of his jaw in long, smooth strokes, expertly removing lather and whiskers. "Looks like orange juice."

"And how did it get onto my dresser?"

"I put it there." He grinned as he held the safety razor under the running water. "But you don't have to thank me. It was no trouble."

"Thank—" Cristen sputtered, her mouth opening and closing like a banked fish's. "Listen, you," she finally managed, "I'll thank you to stay out of my room. And you can take your orange juice and—"

"Ah-ah-ah, watch your mouth," Ryan admonished, his eyes dancing wickedly.

"—stick it in your ear," she continued pugnaciously. "I don't need it, and I don't want it."

She was the picture of outraged femininity, face flushed, eyes snapping, her tousled auburn hair almost crackling with temper. Taking it in, Ryan grinned.

"Oh, but you do. I'll admit you're gorgeous when you're angry, but a glass of juice first thing in the morning would perk you up, and you wouldn't be such a grouch." Turning back to the mirror, he whistled softly through his teeth while he wielded the razor over the other side of his face.

"I am *not* a grouch," Cristen insisted with cool hauteur. She immediately spoiled the effect by screeching, "And if you don't knock off that whistling, I swear I'm going to punch you right in the mouth!"

Ryan rinsed the remaining dabs of shaving cream from his face and blotted it with a towel. Over its damp folds, his amused gaze speared Cristen. "I'll make you a deal. I'll stop whistling if you'll drink the juice every morning. How's that?"

"What! No way! If you—"

"Come on, Cris. If we're going to live together, we've got to compromise. And what's a little glass of juice, after all?"

She eyed him sulkily, knowing he was right but loath to admit it. Finally, her mouth twisting, she muttered, "Oh, all right. But you leave it in here. No more traipsing in and out of my room. You got that?"

"Sure. Whatever you say. But you will drink it, won't you?"

"Yes, I'll drink the darned stuff."

"That's my girl." Holding an end of the damp towel in each hand, he looped it around her neck and pulled her close.

Alarm bells began to clang in Cristen's mind. She stared at his furry chest and felt her whole body flush as it hit her that, except for the towel draped dangerously low around his hips, Ryan was naked, and that she had carried on the entire argument dressed in nothing but a shorty see-through nightgown.

Cristen made an agonized little sound, but before she

could move Ryan tipped up her chin and placed his mouth on hers.

The kiss was incredibly soft and tender and filled with a searing heat that shimmered through her and made her toes curl against the cool floor tiles.

It was over before she could summon the slightest protest. Ryan lifted his head slightly and smiled down into her bemused face. "That was just to seal our pact, you understand."

He dropped another quick peck on her mouth and gave her cheek a pat. "The bathroom's all yours. I'll have breakfast ready in twenty minutes, so shake a leg." He winked at her and headed for the door at the opposite end of the bathroom.

Chapter Six

"Wait! Darn it, O'Malley! I don't even eat breakfast!"

But it was too late. By the time she had recovered her senses enough to protest, the door had clicked shut behind him.

For several minutes Cristen stood rooted to the spot, torn between fury and laughter. That devil! How did he always manage to charm her? She had stormed in here with every intention of tearing a strip off his hide, so angry she'd been about to burst. She touched her lips gently with her fingertips and shook her head in wonder. Instead, she'd ended up agreeing to do exactly what he wanted, and getting kissed senseless in the bargain.

Embarrassed color flooded her cheeks when she turned and caught sight of her reflection in the bathroom mirror. The short nightie left almost nothing to the imagination. The embroidered ruffle hem barely reached the tops of her thighs. Beneath the silky white material, her breasts jutted impudently, her nipples' areolae dusty rose. Cristen's gaze slid downward, a distressed groan escaping her as she followed the veiled curves of midriff, waist and hips to the minuscule bikini panties. Above the opaque triangle, her navel was a provocative shadowed indentation.

Dear heaven! She couldn't believe she'd barged in on Ryan looking like an escapee from an X-rated movie.

Not that he hadn't already seen her in the scandalous nightie. Cristen's gaze lit on the glass of juice, and her color deepened. A shiver raced through her, and her insides fluttered wildly at the thought of Ryan entering her room while she slept. Given the way she practically went into a coma when sleep claimed her, there was no telling what position she'd been in. Or what had been exposed.

"Well, there's no point in worrying about it now." Cristen pushed the embarrassing image aside and reached for the glass of juice, then hesitated. She looked at it sourly and shuddered. The thought of putting anything but coffee into her stomach before ten o'clock in the morning was revolting. Slyly, her glance went from the glass to Ryan's door, then back. She could just pour it down the sink. Her fingers moved closer to the glass, then jerked back.

"No, you can't, Cristen," she told herself in utter disgust. "A bargain is a bargain." Though the idea rankled, Cristen knew that Ryan was right. If the crazy living arrangement was going to work, they would both have to compromise.

Scowling at her reflection, she snatched up the juice and chugged it down. If she were smart, though, she thought, shuddering again, no matter how much she enjoyed frilly, naughty lingerie, she would make a drastic change in her style of nightwear, at least during the weeks when Ryan was in residence.

The delicious smell of freshly brewed coffee and frying bacon assailed Cristen the moment she stepped from her room. It had been her intention to skip even her usual morning coffee, but the tantalizing aromas drew her toward the kitchen as though she were in a hypnotic trance.

She pushed through the door, took two steps and stopped abruptly, her mouth going dry at the sight of Ryan.

Barefoot, his hair still tousled, he was standing at the stove, turning bacon with a fork. His sole article of clothing was a pair of frayed, faded cutoffs that rode low on his narrow hips. The soft denim molded his buttocks and manhood with indecent familiarity, the faded material worn almost white at revealing stress points.

He flashed a grin when he looked up and saw her. "Hi. This will be ready in about a minute."

Cristen forced her legs to carry her across the kitchen. "Don't bother cooking any for me. I never eat breakfast." She filled a mug with coffee and took two scalding sips before turning to lean back against the counter.

"Nonsense. Breakfast is the most important meal of the day."

"Fine. Then you eat it. I don't like breakfast, I don't want breakfast and I'm not going to eat breakfast." Actually, the slug of juice had whetted her appetite. Not only was her stomach growling—the delicious cooking aromas were driving her crazy—but Cristen figured she had done enough compromising for one morning. It was Ryan's turn. Besides, he had to learn that he could push her just so far.

Ryan studied her determined expression and after a moment shrugged, his crooked smile kicking his mustache up at one corner. "Suit yourself."

He turned back to the stove and lifted the bacon onto a platter lined with paper towels. Deftly, using only one hand, he picked up two eggs, cracked them open on the edge of a skillet and dropped them in. They sizzled and popped in the bubbling butter while he jiggled the pan expertly. The broad, flat muscles in his back stirred with the slight movements.

Cristen tried not to look at him, but his nearly bare body drew her fascinated gaze like the relentless pull of the moon on the tides. Her yellow linen dress was light and casual, but his brief attire made her feel conspicuously overdressed…and uncomfortably hot.

Swallowing hard, Cristen tracked his spine downward. His back was smooth and bronze to a point several inches below his waist, where a line of white showed above the low-slung waistband. Below it, the tight rounded flesh flexed with every shift of his feet. A long ravel dangling from the frayed bottom of his cutoffs swung constantly, drawing her attention to his legs. They were long and heavily muscled, the skin tanned beneath the dusting of short dark hair. As she stared at him Cristen felt her body grow warmer, her nipples tighten against their lacy confinement.

Oh, Lord, he's a beautifully made man, she thought a bit desperately. Big and lean and powerful. And sexy as all get-out.

Dragging her gaze away from Ryan's body, Cristen gulped another swallow of coffee. Her heart thudded so hard that her chest hurt.

Ryan lifted the eggs onto a plate and set it and the platter of bacon on the table. "Sure you don't want any? There's plenty."

"No, thank you."

He shrugged and went back for the toast, making a detour by the refrigerator for the jam. His bare feet made faint slapping noises on the tile floor.

Just when she thought he would settle down and eat his breakfast, he stepped closer. "Excuse me. I need another cup of coffee." Smiling apologetically, he reached around her.

Cristen found herself staring at his hairy chest, which was only inches from her nose. Trying not to look at the tiny brown nipples nestled in the shiny thatch, she lowered her gaze, but then it settled on his navel and the enticing whorl of silky black hair that surrounded it and arrowed downward toward…

Groaning silently, Cristen jerked her gaze upward and pressed back against the counter. Her heart pounded, and her thighs seem to liquefy. With every shallow breath her senses were assaulted by the seductive scents of soap and after-shave and male flesh. His body heat seemed to surround her, scorching right through her clothes, and when his leg brushed against her she jumped as if she'd been scalded.

"*Must* you run around like that?" she snapped.

He stepped back and gave her a blank look. "Like what?"

"Like *what*? Great gobs of goose grease! You're practically naked, that's what!"

He glanced down as though surprised. "Oh. Does it bother you?"

"Of course it bothers me. How would you like it if I ran around in next to noth—" She broke off at the lecherous delight on Ryan's face, appalled by her blunder. "Never mind. Don't answer that." She gave him a withering look. "You know what I mean."

Ryan chuckled. "Yeah, I know. Look, I'm sorry. I'm used to being casual when I'm at home. I'll just go slip on a shirt."

At the door he stopped and looked back at her, a quizzical half smile on his face. "Goose grease?" He shook his head. "Did anyone ever tell you that you have a very, uh, *quaint* way of cussing? Not to mention colorful."

A faint blush tinted Cristen's face, and she sent him an abashed look. "My mother always abhorred bad language. As a kid, whenever I swore she washed my mouth out with soap." She shrugged, and her mouth twisted in a wry grimace. "So I invented substitutes. To this day, whenever I even think of a genuine curse word I can taste soap."

"I see. Well, that explains it." Chuckling, he disappeared through the doorway.

Cristen stared after him, his willingness to cooperate taking her by surprise. After her complaint about his attire, she had expected him to come back with some sexual innuendo, or at the very least tease her about being prudish.

A pleased smile curved her lips as she turned and reached for the coffeepot. Maybe, just maybe, this arrangement might work out, after all.

The slap of bare feet on the floor announced Ryan's return. Lifting her mug from the counter, Cristen turned back. "Well, you were certainly quick, I must say. I—" She stopped abruptly at the sight of him, her smile wilting and her eyes growing steadily wider.

Ryan was wearing a cropped black T-shirt that barely reached his midriff. It was faded and full of holes, and the bottom edge was so jagged that it looked as if it had been whacked off with a pair of hedge trimmers. If that weren't bad enough, emblazoned across his chest in big red letters were the words, SEX IS A MISDEMEANOR: DE MORE I MISS, DE MEANOR I GET.

"Well? How's this?" Ryan tugged on the tattered lower edge of the disreputable shirt and grinned at her like a small boy who fully expected a pat on the head.

Cristen deposited her cup on the counter with a thud and stomped toward the door. "Don't ask. Believe me, you don't want to know."

Louise was pleased over Ryan's offer of help, but as Jennifer had predicted, she was ecstatic to learn that he was Cristen's new roommate.

"That's terrific! He's perfect for you. Absolutely perfect!"

"Louise! I'm sharing my apartment with the man, not my bed."

"But you *are* living with him."

"Yes, but it's strictly platonic. A business arrangement. And even at that, he'll only be here every other week."

A Cheshire cat grin spread over Louise's plump face. "Well, at least that's a start," she said complacently.

Cristen threw her hands into the air and gave up. She knew it was useless to try to convince Louise that there was nothing going on between her and Ryan. Louise was going to believe what she wanted to believe. Besides…Cristen wasn't entirely convinced herself.

She wanted to believe that nothing was going on—needed to believe it for her own peace of mind—but Ryan was such a virile, sensual hunk that there was no way she could be indifferent to him. And she knew, deep down, that for their arrangement to work she would have to maintain a distance, develop a certain amount of detachment. She could not afford to think of Ryan as a man. An attractive…sexy…fascinating…interesting…eligible man.

It isn't fair, she lamented silently as she labored over the parquet floors in the miniature Victorian mansion. Why couldn't he have been old and fat and bald? Or at the very least, nondescript and dull? Why did he have to be such a teasing, tormenting, thoroughly appealing rascal?

Cristen tried to put Ryan out of her mind, but it was impossible. All day long, whenever she thought of their encounter that morning, she was torn between anger and arousal. Both reactions worried her.

Blaming her fretting on the strangeness of the situation, she told herself that once they adjusted, once the newness of it wore off, things would settle down. Nevertheless, she entered the apartment warily that evening. She wasn't sure what kind of greeting to expect, but certainly not the exuberant one she received from Ryan.

He came bounding out of the kitchen the moment she opened the door, a glass of milk in one hand and a cookie in the other. "Cristen! Great, you're home! I thought you'd never get here."

"What is it? What's wrong?"

"Nothing. Everything's terrific. But, man, have I got something to show you." He polished off the cookie in two bites and chugalugged the milk, then put the glass down on the end table and grabbed her hand. "C'mon, let's go."

"What? Go where?" Cristen hung back as he dragged her toward the door. "Wait a minute. Where are you taking me?"

"You'll see," he said mysteriously.

His grin was white and wide, and his eyes sparkled with anticipation. Cristen eyed him dubiously, especially when he led her into the elevator and pushed the button for the underground garage. She tried to recall all the bracing lectures she had given herself about keeping a distance between them, but his enthusiasm was difficult to resist. She had never seen him quite like this before. He was about to burst with eagerness and excitement.

Though she tried to tug her hand free, Ryan maintained his hold all during the elevator ride, and when the door slid open he hauled her along with him.

"It's right over here," he announced as he blazed a path through the rows of cars in the parking garage. Several times Cristen had to break into a trot to keep up with his rapid, ground-eating stride. Finally he came to a halt and turned to her, beaming like a kid on Christmas morning. He flung his arm wide with a flourish. "Well, there she is. What do you think?"

"She" was a low-slung, wicked-looking sports car. Cristen stared at it, not quite sure what to say. Cars, to her, were akin to alien creatures: strange and mysterious and a bit scary. She knew very little about them and cared less. She couldn't even tell one make from another unless she was close enough to read the manufacturer's emblem. But it didn't take a car buff to recognize that this was a mean machine, the kind every male dreamed of owning.

It was a metallic green, so dark that it was almost black, its lines long and sleek and slightly menacing. Just sitting there, it gave the impression of leashed power, a crouched jungle beast poised to pounce.

Cristen gave Ryan a vague smile. "It's, uh, very nice."

"Nice!" He looked mortally wounded. "Good Lord, woman! How can you say that? A two-week vacation is 'nice.' A warm fire is 'nice.' An ice cream sundae is 'nice,' for heaven's sake! What this car is, is great! Fabulous! One in a million!"

"Uh, yes. I'm sure it is," Cristen mumbled. His affronted tone struck her as comical, but she didn't dare laugh, or even smile, because she knew that for once Ryan was perfectly serious. Trying her best to appear interested, she asked, "What is it?"

"What *is it*?" He looked as though a puff of wind could knock him over, he was so stunned. "Geez, Cristen, I can't believe you don't know. This is a vintage 1975 Jaguar, for the love of Mike!"

How fitting, she thought, eyeing its sleek lines. "I didn't know they rented those."

"It's not rented. I bought it this morning. I figured, since I'm going to be here so much of the time, it would be better to have my own transportation. Anyway, I've always wanted a Jag."

He ran a caressing hand along the car's roof. "This baby'll go from zero to one hundred in just a fraction over fifteen seconds."

"That's ni—uh, wonderful."

Ryan climbed in behind the wheel and proceeded to point out dials and gauges and rattle off names that made Cristen go glassy eyed. Then he rushed around to the front of the car, threw up a hood that looked about half a block long and started tossing out words like *rpm* and *gear ratio* and *synchromesh transmission.*

Cristen smiled and nodded her way through the dis-

course, but for all she understood he might as well have
been speaking Swahili.

Finally he slammed the hood shut, and she watched,
dazed, as he took a clean handkerchief from the back
pocket of his trousers and lovingly buffed off his smudged
fingerprints. Then, circling the car, he launched into a
lengthy dissertation on aerodynamics and wind resistance.

Cristen tuned out his words but, watching him, her
amazement grew steadily. She had never been able to understand men's fascination with what was, essentially, a
pile of metal and rubber. It was ridiculous the way they
carried on. Heavens! She'd seen new fathers show less
pride in their offspring.

Still, she admitted reluctantly, an indulgent smile tugging at her mouth as she watched Ryan's lips move, there
was something endearing about his enthusiasm.

"...but of course, to fully appreciate what it can do, you
have to experience it firsthand." His grin was boyish and
eager, and Cristen blinked as his words slowly sank in.
"So what do you say? Wanta go for a quick spin?"

"I...sure. As long as I don't have to drive."

"Are you kidding? Honey, don't you know that a man's
car is his second most prized possession?"

He wasted no time hustling her into the passenger seat,
then hurried around to the other side and slid in behind
the wheel. As they fastened their seat belts Cristen slanted
him a curious look.

"Second, huh? What's number one?"

With a flick of the ignition key the powerful engine
roared to life, then settled down to a deep-throated purr.
Ryan fixed Cristen with an intent look. His teeth gleamed
white in the shadowy interior as a slow, sensual grin
curved his mouth, and she felt her stomach give a little
lurch. "Why, his woman, of course. And he guards both
jealously."

His choice of words and the husky pitch of his voice

sent a sharp little thrill through Cristen, and she looked away in confusion.

Ryan put the car into gear and stepped on the accelerator, sending the crouched vehicle leaping forward like the dangerous, snarling jungle cat for which it was named.

The minute they hit the streets Ryan let out a whoop of sheer joy and headed for the freeway, his mood as effervescent as fine champagne. The moment of intense sexual tension in the garage might never have happened.

The rush hour was over, and they zipped easily through the traffic. Once on the Southwest Freeway they were out of the city in a matter of minutes, and Ryan poured on the gas. Though he drove fast, he handled the powerful car with a sureness and control that inspired confidence. Wrapped in the sheer luxury of the opulent interior, Cristen settled back on the cream-colored, buttery soft leather seat to enjoy the exhilarating ride. Before long, caught up in Ryan's infectious mood, she added her laughter to his.

"Boy, this baby can go!" Ryan pronounced gleefully, flashing Cristen a broad grin as they approached Sugar Land. "And she handles like a dream."

His high spirits drew another indulgent chuckle from his passenger. "Yes, I'm sure. But unless you want to pay a bodacious fine, you'd better turn around before we get to Richmond," she advised. "The police there take a dim view of going even so much as a mile over the speed limit."

"Spoilsport," Ryan grumbled, shooting her a look of mock annoyance, but at the next exit he made a U-turn under the freeway and headed back. In a disappointingly short time they were pulling back into the condo's parking garage.

Before Cristen could unbuckle her seat belt, Ryan bounded out of the car and around to her side. He opened the passenger door and reached for her. Cristen swung her legs out and grasped his hands, and he practically lifted her from the ground-hugging vehicle.

"Well, what did you think?" Still holding her hands, his brows cocked expectantly, he waited for her reply.

His eagerness and sheer delight were both amusing and, somehow, strangely touching. Cristen smiled back at him. "I think it's a great car. Absolutely wonderful."

The grin that lit Ryan's face was incandescent. "Hot damn! It is, isn't it!" he hooted. In a burst of enthusiasm, he grasped Cristen's waist, lifted her high against his chest and whirled her around and around.

"Ryaaannnnn!" Laughing and squealing his name at the same time, Cristen clutched his shoulders and held on for dear life.

It was a wild, exuberant dance that made Cristen feel giddy, her head spinning as the world dipped and twirled around her. Ryan's baritone laughter mingled with her higher-pitched giggles and bounced loudly through the cavernous garage.

As the mad whirl ended and Ryan loosened his hold, letting Cristen slide to the floor, it seemed the most natural thing in the world for him to kiss her.

The action cut off Cristen's laughter in midgiggle and stunned her rigid. Her eyes went wide. Her hands jerked from his shoulders and hovered above them in midair, fingers spread.

"Mmmmmmm." The sound of sheer delight rumbled from Ryan as his lips rocked over hers. The kiss, like the impulsive spin, was enthusiastic and wholehearted. Hard and hungry and joyous.

It was also warm and wonderful. Cristen strained to resist its drugging allure, but after a moment her hovering hands balled into tight fists, then flexed open. Giving a moan of surrender, she relaxed within Ryan's embrace, wound her arms around his neck and clasped his head, burying her spread fingers in his dark hair.

His mouth was firm and persuasive, his mustache a tickling enticement. With gentle strokes his tongue probed and coaxed at the fragile barrier of her lips. They flowered open, and Cristen's shuddering sigh drifted into his mouth as he deepened the kiss.

You've got to stop this, she told herself even as she gloried in the feel and the scent and the taste of him. This is foolish. Insane. If you've got an ounce of sense, you'll get a grip on yourself and step away.

But she couldn't. Not yet. The sharply sweet sensations held her spellbound.

She felt on fire, burning, consumed by a delicious ache. A hunger she couldn't control drove her on, and for that brief, mindless moment she let herself go, giving in to the demands of her yearning flesh. She kissed him back fervently, eagerly, delighting in the thud of his heart against her breast, the low growl of pleasure that vibrated from him. His scent was a heady delight, musky and male, his taste intoxicating. She felt as though she were drowning in endless pleasure.

A car zoomed down the ramp into the parking garage, the low purr of its engine shattering the tomblike quiet and jerking them out of their sensual haze.

Cristen stiffened and pulled back, but Ryan merely pressed his face into her neck. "R-Ryan, stop." She hunched her shoulder against his marauding kisses and turned her head aside, biting her lower lip.

Heaving a sigh, Ryan released her and took a half step back. He glanced around and gave her a rueful grin. "Sorry. I guess I got carried away."

She frowned. "You promised no seduction scenes. Remember?"

"Hey! That wasn't a seduction scene. That was just a friendly kiss." He draped his arm around her shoulders and turned her toward the elevator. "No reason to make a big deal out of it. After all, what's a little kiss between friends?''

"But—"

"Especially roomies. Now c'mon. I put a chicken in the oven before you got home. It should be ready just about now.''

Surprised and confused, Cristen looked up at him as he nudged her into the elevator. ''You cooked dinner?''

"Sure. You said we'd share the work. Besides, I enjoy cooking. I also picked up some groceries.''

Cristen stared straight ahead, her thoughts in a jumble. She felt strange, disoriented, reeling like someone who has just stepped off an out-of-control merry-go-round. How could he be so ardent one minute and so blasé the next? Out of the corner of her eye she glanced suspiciously at his too innocent face. Had that kiss really been just a casual buss between friends to him? If so, she was in deep trouble, because *her* knees still felt like mush, for heaven's sake. If that was all it was, she'd hate to see him when he was on the make.

Chapter Seven

Little men with hobnail boots were stomping around inside her head, chipping away with pickaxes. Fiends, every one.

Elbows propped on her worktable, eyes closed, Cristen massaged her forehead and temples with her fingertips. If they didn't stop soon, they were going to excavate right through.

The carpenters hammering away next door didn't help any. Even so, Cristen was glad that the alterations were under way at last. If everything went as planned, they would knock out the wall in a few days.

"Do you have another headache?"

"Uh-uh." Cristen looked up at Louise with pain-glazed eyes. "Same one. The aspirin I took earlier is wearing off."

"Maybe you ought to see a doctor."

"It's just a headache. It'll go away."

Besides, Cristen didn't need a doctor to tell her what

was causing her headache. She had the answer to that in one word: Ryan.

"Well, if you won't see a doctor, you at least ought to go home and go to bed. All this racket can't be helping any."

"I'll be fine, Louise. Don't fuss."

Louise gave a disgusted snort. "Mule stubborn, that's what you are," she muttered, stomping off.

Cristen sighed and lowered her head once more, her fingertips resuming their rotating movements. She had been a fool to think she would become inured to Ryan with time. Whoever said that familiarity breeds contempt was full of sheep dip. Either that, or he'd never met an Irish charmer by the name of O'Malley.

Cristen sighed again. It was all so confusing. On the surface, everything seemed to be working out just great. Certainly Ryan was sticking to his part of the bargain. Since that impulsive kiss in the garage, over a month before, he had not stepped out of line in any way.

Except for teasing you whenever he gets a chance, she amended. *And there's no use kidding yourself, you even like that.* Cristen groaned and rubbed her temples harder. *Which just goes to show how far gone you are, you silly twit.*

In truth, Ryan had not done anything objectionable. If anything, he was as close as you could get to a perfect roommate: friendly and casual, pleasant to be around, helpful, amusing. He was neat and clean and had no disgusting habits, unless one counted whistling before seven in the morning, and, true to his word, he'd stopped that, thank the Lord.

The problem was the direction their relationship was taking, the feeling of closeness, of intimacy, that was developing between them.

And she suspected that Ryan was deliberately promoting it.

Cristen had tried to remain aloof, but it was difficult. How could she be cool to a man who had a hot, delicious meal ready when she came home from work? Who left a steaming mug of coffee and a glass of juice for her in the bathroom every morning? Who did the dishes when it wasn't even his turn, just because he knew she was dead tired? Who went out to pick up a newspaper and returned with a bouquet of fresh daisies?

And then there were the little things, the subtle things: his toothbrush next to hers, his shaving cream and razor and cologne sitting on the cabinet shelf beside her body lotion and talc, his terry-cloth robe hanging on the back of the bathroom door, his favorite brand of beer in the refrigerator, those sports magazines on the coffee table...his name beneath her own on the mailbox.

Intimacy without intimacy.

But most disturbing of all was that mixture of contentment and excitement she felt whenever he was around. Cristen found Ryan wildly attractive and sexy, but she also enjoyed his company, their moments of quiet conversation, their companionable silences, even their occasional sparring.

She had thought she would be grateful for those times when he was in California, but instead she was lonely and at loose ends and found herself working longer hours just to avoid going home to an empty apartment. Yet when he was there she was torn between the pleasure she took in his company and fear that he was becoming too important to her. Too necessary.

Living with Ryan was making her crazy!

From next door came the high-pitched whine of a power saw, then the clatter of a piece of lumber hitting the floor. The hammering started up again, but an instant later all other noise was drowned out by the shuddering grind of an electric sander.

An open can of soda sat on the corner of the worktable,

its lower half beaded with condensation. Cristen picked it up and rolled it over her forehead.

And worrying about living with Ryan was giving her headaches.

Ryan was due to fly in from California that evening. As the hours passed, anxiety and anticipation drew Cristen's nerves tighter and tighter. The pounding in her head became excruciating. By midafternoon Louise put her foot down.

"That's it. I'm tired of watching you suffer. You're going home," her partner pronounced in a tone that dared Cristen to argue. Though a good eight inches shorter than Cristen, Louise grasped her arm, lifted her out of the chair and all but frog-marched her toward the door. "Right this minute. And I'm taking you."

"Louise! You can't! The store—"

"Dora can take care of the store until I get back. It won't take but fifteen minutes, at most. Now don't argue. You're going home and going to bed, and that's final!"

"Dora?" Cristen wailed, horrified.

But there was no arguing with Louise when her mothering instincts were aroused. Within minutes she'd brought her car to a stop at the entrance to Cristen's condo.

"Are you sure you don't want me to come up with you?"

"No, no. I'll be fine." Opening her eyes to mere slits, Cristen raised her head off the back of the seat and groped for the door handle. "You just hurry back to the store before Dora pulls one of her crazy stunts."

Louise chuckled. "Come on, Cris. What could she do in fifteen minutes?"

"Who knows? Last week she suggested that I spray paint a Queen Anne dining table pink. She'd seen one in a Barbie dollhouse that she thought was cute."

"Oh, Lord. I'm surprised you didn't attack her." Louise heaved a despairing sigh and shook her head. "I swear, sometimes I think the only taste that girl has is in her mouth.''

Cristen grunted and climbed from the car with exaggerated care, shielding her eyes against the bright afternoon sun with her cupped palm.

"Now you go straight to bed," Louise called after her.

The admonition was unnecessary. At that moment two aspirin, a dark room and a cool cloth for her forehead sounded like heaven.

Theda glanced up from her perch on the back of the sofa and gave Cristen a curious look when she let herself into the apartment. Paying her no mind, Cristen tossed her purse onto the first horizontal surface she came to and made a beeline for her bedroom.

She was barely halfway across the living room when all hell broke loose.

Without warning the world seemed to explode in a cacophony of earsplitting noise, a raucous clangor overlaid with the blaring, scale-climbing *whoop-whoop-whoop* of a siren.

"Oh! Oh!" In mindless panic, Cristen clapped her hands over her ears and danced around, wild-eyed. She jumped up on the sofa, did a high-stepping romp over the cushions, jumped down again and turned in agitated little circles, shrieking with every breath.

At the same time, Theda shot three feet straight up into the air, yowling like a banshee. Her eyes were wild, all four legs extended, and every hair on her body was standing on end. The cat hit the sofa like a spring, and before you could blink twice, bounded to a chair, onto the floor and clawed her way up to the top of the draperies. When the racket didn't stop, she leaped to the floor again and streaked around the room, bouncing from wall to floor to wall in a furry blur.

It was pure bedlam. Between Theda's caterwauling,

Cristen's hysterical screeching and the clanging, whooping alarm, the decibel level was torturous.

In the middle of the furor Cristen whacked her shin against the coffee table. Her shrieks turned to yelps of pain. She grabbed her leg, but the racket was more than she could bear. Torn between protecting her throbbing head and her throbbing shin, she alternately hopped on one foot clutching her leg and limped in circles holding her ears.

At that moment, Ryan came charging in from the hall like an attacking warrior, his bloodcurdling battle cry adding to the pandemonium. He was barefoot and bare chested, his expression wild and fierce, and in his upraised hand he wielded a bathroom plunger like a weapon.

Hysteria had Cristen by the throat, and all she saw was a half-naked man coming at her with a club. Her panic and the volume of her shrieks doubled.

Ryan skidded to a halt in the middle of the floor. His fierce expression dissolved, and his jaw dropped. He stared, dumfounded, at the sight of Cristen, running around squawking like a demented chicken, and the puffed-up, yowling ball of fur racing around the walls.

"Cristen, what the devil—" He broke off, unable to hear himself think, much less make himself heard, in the hullabaloo. He was still holding the toilet plunger aloft, and it suddenly struck him that he must resemble a comic imitation of the Statue of Liberty. Muttering a curse, he flung it aside and made a lunge for Cristen, catching her by the shoulders before she could scamper out of reach again. "Cristen, for God's sake, calm down!" he shouted, giving her a shake.

The glazed look of panic cleared from her eyes, and they widened as recognition struck her. "Ryan? Oh, Ryan!"

He saw her mouth form his name, but he couldn't hear her. "What? *What?*"

For a moment Cristen clutched him, but then she grimaced and covered her ears again.

"Oh, hell!" Ryan stalked across the room and jabbed at the panel of buttons set into the wall by the front door.

The sudden cessation of noise was as startling as the alarm had been.

Theda let out one more indignant yowl, hissed and spat and streaked out of the room, leaving the two humans staring at each other in the magnified silence.

Cristen kept her hands clapped over her ears, not at all convinced that her pounding head wouldn't roll off onto the floor if she let go. Her heart was thudding ninety to nothing, and she was breathing like a marathon runner at the finish line. She was too addled to think, but slowly, as her eyes went from Ryan to the small panel of buttons that hadn't been there that morning, it began to dawn on her that he was somehow to blame for that god-awful racket. She glared at him, her lips thinning.

"What—" She broke off, wincing at the sound of her own voice, then continued in a precise tone that was barely one notch above a whisper. "What, may I ask, was all that about?"

A sheepish look crossed Ryan's face. "That was supposed to be a surprise."

"Oh, you surprised me all right. You idiot! You darn near scared me out of ten years of my life! What *was* that?"

"A burglar alarm. The security in this building is lousy, and I was worried about your being here all alone while I'm in California. I took an early flight today so I could have it installed and working by the time you got home." He darted a sheepish look at the toilet plunger. "When you tripped it, I had just finished and was cleaning up in the bathroom, and I grabbed the closest thing at hand to use as a weapon." Ryan frowned. "What are you doing here this early, anyway? I thought someone had broken in."

"I came home because I have a headache," she said through clenched teeth. "A pounding, painful headache that now, thanks to you, has reached an excruciating level."

She bared her teeth in a saccharine smile of pure irony and limped toward the hall door. Still clutching her head, she moved with exaggerated caution, as though she were made of glass that might shatter at any moment.

"Oh, hell, sweetheart, I'm sorry. I didn't know." Ryan trotted along behind her, hovering worriedly. "Is there anything I can do? Anything I can get for you?"

"Just leave me alone, O'Malley. You've done enough."

Paying no heed, Ryan darted around her into the bedroom, threw back the bedspread and plumped her pillow, then rushed back to her side. "Here, let me help you." Slipping an arm around her, he cupped both her elbows and led her to the bed as though she were a ninety-year-old invalid.

"Ryan—"

"There now, love. Don't fret," he murmured as he eased her down onto the side of the bed. "I'll take care of you. First we'll get you out of these clothes…"

He reached around her, lowered the zipper on her dress and pushed it off her shoulders.

"Wait! Don't—" Cristen grabbed at the dress, but the silky material fell about her waist, revealing the bodice of her pink satin and ecru lace slip. Crossing her arms over her breasts, she glared at him impotently. "Now, look! I don't need—"

"…and into something comfortable," he continued, heedless of her protests. He dropped down on one knee and slipped off her shoes.

"Ryan, will you… Hey! Stop that!" She slapped at his hands as they slid up under her skirt, but Ryan deftly unfastened her garters and peeled the silky stockings down her legs.

"Okay, lift up and we'll get you out of this," he commanded gently, and she obeyed without thinking, then watched, thoroughly muddled, as he removed the dress and went to hang it in the closet. But when he returned with her lavender lace nightgown and reached for her slip straps, Cristen clapped her hands over her shoulders and glared.

"If you don't mind, I'm perfectly capable of undressing myself. I have a headache, not two broken arms." She held out her hand imperiously. "Just give me the nightgown and get out of here."

Ryan frowned dubiously, then nodded and dropped the scrap of lavender silk into her lap. "Okay, you take care of that while I get something for your headache."

Ignoring her sputtering, he marched into the bathroom. When he returned a few minutes later the pink satin slip and matching garter belt and bra were draped over a chair and Cristen was lying in bed with the sheet pulled up to her chin.

She tried to glower at him, but her head was pounding so hard that she couldn't quite manage it, and after he had doused her with aspirin she lay back and closed her eyes, sighing gratefully when he placed a cool damp cloth over her brow.

"Now you just rest," Ryan said, closing the draperies over the windows. "Take it easy and let those tablets do their job. You'll feel better in no time."

He came back to the bedside and stared down at Cristen, his eyes full of tenderness and concern. She was lying still and quiet, drifting somewhere between sleep and wakefulness, her lovely face etched with pain. Despite the shadowy dimness of the room, Ryan could see how pale she was, the fragile look about her eyes that not even the sweep of her lashes could hide. Emotion clogged his throat

and swelled his chest with painful intensity. He was filled
with the need to protect, to cherish, to possess.

Reaching out, he smoothed his fingertips over the silky
hair at her temple and smiled, a crooked, bemused smile.
The feelings were new and strange, and a little daunting.
Over the years he had known and enjoyed many women.
Some he'd cared for more than a little. But it had never
been like this. Not anything like this.

Oh, he'd known right from the beginning that Cristen
was something special, even that in her he had probably
met his fate. What he hadn't known, hadn't expected, was
that that first thrill of excitement and attraction would grow
into something so strong, so powerful, so all-consuming—
so exquisitely, painfully urgent that all else faded in importance. His business, the life he had in California—
heaven help him, even his own daughter—took second
place to Cristen. When he was asleep, she haunted his
dreams. Awake, she occupied his thoughts, filled his heart,
his very soul, with a sweet, yearning ache.

Living with her, getting to know her, had been a pure
joy; not touching her, sheer torment. When he was gone
he counted the days until he could return, lived for the
time when he would see her again. She was his present,
his future...his life. Lord, how he loved her.

Ryan drew in a deep breath and let it out slowly. She
loved him, too—or at least she would if she'd let herself.
He knew damned well she wasn't indifferent to him. But
she kept fighting it.

Why? Why was she so determined to keep a distance
between them? He had a hunch it was because of that ex-
husband of hers, but he couldn't be sure. The times he'd
tried to get her to talk about him she had very bluntly
closed the door in his face. Was she still carrying a torch?
Or had the marriage simply turned sour, the split-up so
hurtful that she was still bitter? Though he and Ella had
parted amicably, he knew that for some couples marriage

was little more than open warfare, with divorce being the final battle.

Ryan sighed. Whatever the reason, her determination not to become involved was a formidable obstacle. But he'd overcome it. Eventually. If this slow courtship didn't kill him first.

He had made a little progress, but sometimes it seemed that for every step forward, he took two back. Ryan thought about the fright he'd given her with the burglar alarm and grimaced. Great going, O'Malley, he chided himself. That little number probably set things back two months.

Cristen's breathing was slow and even, but she made a little moaning sound and rocked her head back and forth on the pillow. Ryan bent and turned the damp cloth over to the cool side, and she sighed. Smiling, he let his fingertips linger on her cheek and dropped a soft kiss on her mouth.

Fight it, my love, if you must. Sooner or later, I'll win you over. You'll find that I can be a very patient man. Especially when the stakes are this high.

"He's driving me crazy!"

"How? By being thoughtful? Come on, Cris. Putting in a burglar alarm was a very nice thing to do."

"I know. It's not that. It's...it's...oh, I don't know. Things just seem to be getting out of hand. Our living arrangement was supposed to be strictly business."

Louise looked up from straightening a display case of Louis XIV furniture. "You mean it's not?" she asked hopefully.

"No. I mean, yes, of course it is." Cristen grimaced, her brow furrowing. "It's just that this whole arrangement is becoming much too...too...cozy."

"Oh? How so?"

Since it was Saturday, the carpenters were not working.

Cristen had hoped to take advantage of the quiet to get some of the more tedious work done, but she gave up trying to fit the elaborate fretwork above the arched doorway in the Victorian mansion. Sighing, she leaned back against the corner of her worktable and folded her arms across her midriff. "It's hard to explain. There's no one thing, really. It's just that there seems to be a feeling of…closeness, intimacy almost, developing between us. And there doesn't seem to be anything I can do to prevent it."

"Ah, I see." Louise closed the glass case and moved to the next one. Over its top she gave Cristen a wicked grin. "I knew that living with that gorgeous hunk would stir up your libido."

"Louise! That's not the problem at all," she lied. At her friend's look of patent disbelief, Cristen felt her face grow warm. "Well…not entirely," she added reluctantly, shooting her resentful glare. "What really disturbs me is, we're beginning to act like a couple instead of two people who happen to share the same roof."

Cristen thought about the way Ryan had coddled her the night before, letting her sleep off her headache, then bringing her a bowl of hot soup on a tray and insisting that she remain in bed. The way he had watched her to make sure she ate it all. It had made her feel cherished and warm. And vaguely threatened.

"Hmm. Maybe there's hope for you yet."

"Louise! Will you behave? I'm talking serious problems here."

"Okay, okay. But I think you're blowing this all out of proportion. I mean, how intimate can you get without actually becoming lovers?"

"Plenty. One day last week I hand washed all my lingerie and hung it in the bathroom. When I got home I found that Ryan had folded it and put it away. Do you have any idea how unsettling that was?"

"Probably not nearly as unsettling as it was for Ryan," Louise hooted. "Considering your penchant for sexy unmentionables. Anyway, you can't blame a guy for not wanting to fight his way through a forest of stockings and teddies every time he goes into the bathroom. And you told me yourself that he's a very neat person."

Cristen released her breath in a long sigh. "Yes, he's neat," she agreed in a soft, reflective voice. "And considerate. And helpful." Pensive, she plucked absently at a loose thread hanging from a button on her work smock. "Fun to be with." She wound the thread around her finger and tugged, and the button hit the floor and rolled way. Paying it no mind, Cristen stared across the shop. "Did you know that whenever Ryan is in town and I work late, he's always waiting outside to walk me home?"

Louise's face softened at the wistful note in Cristen's voice. "No, I didn't. Does that bother you?"

"Yes."

"Why? Because you're attracted to him?"

"Yes. No!" Cristen glared, but Louise merely cocked her head and waited. "All right. Yes, I am attracted," she snapped after a moment. "But I don't want to be!"

Louise fought back a grin at her belligerent tone. "Why not?"

"Oh, Louise. There are all kinds of reasons why not."

"Name one."

"All right." Giving her friend an exasperated look, Cristen raised her hand and ticked off on her fingers: "One, he's light-years ahead of me in experience; two, we're totally different; three, the man's a footloose bachelor. He's probably left a string of broken hearts from here to California, and I have no intention of becoming his latest conquest."

"And suppose he's serious?" Louise asked gently. "Suppose this time he wants love and marriage? Commitment?"

Stark vulnerability etched Cristen's features. Longing and despair mingled in her eyes, creating a sheen of moisture that she hastily blinked away. Her lower lip quivered ever so slightly, and she clamped her teeth over it and looked away, holding her head high. "I…it wouldn't matter. I've already tried marriage. It's not for me."

"I see. Well then, you'd better do something to shake up that cozy little routine you two have going."

"Like what?"

Louise pursed her lips thoughtfully. "Does Ryan ever go out with other women?"

The question sent a wave of something very like pain through Cristen, but she squashed it at once. "No. Occasionally he gets calls from a woman, but he says she's his secretary." More than once Cristen had wondered about the owner of that sexy voice and what kind of relationship she had with Ryan.

"Then maybe you ought to introduce him to someone."

"Me! I don't know any single women. Except Dora, and I wouldn't wish that nitwit on anyone."

"Okay then, you go out with another man. That should put a damper on things."

Cristen's mouth twisted wryly. "And just whom do you suggest I go out with?"

Louise gave her an innocent look and spread her hands wide. "There's always Leonard DeWitt."

"Oh, pul-leeze. I'd rather kiss a camel on the lips."

Giving her friend one last disgusted glare, Cristen turned back to the worktable and picked up the intricate piece of fretwork. "If that's the best suggestion you can come up with, forget it. I'll just have to think of something else."

"Suit yourself."

Two hours later Cristen was carrying out the painstaking task of installing three flights of ornate stair rails when Louise tapped her on the back.

"Cris, there's someone here who'd like to see you."

Cristen stood with one knee braced in the seat of her chair. She was bent over, almost the entire upper half of her body inside the dollhouse. "Tell them I'm busy," came her muffled reply.

"Will you get out of there!" her partner hissed.

Frowning, Cristen looked back over her shoulder to see Louise frantically rolling her eyes. She started to refuse again but gave up when she felt a hard yank on her skirt.

"Oh, all right." With a disgruntled sigh, Cristen backed out of the dollhouse and straightened just as Louise said brightly, "Look who's here."

Cristen was not a great believer in coincidence, and when she turned and saw Harvey Metcalf standing by the cash register, she darted her partner a sharp look.

Unfazed, Louise put her hand in the small of Cristen's back and prodded her toward the pleasant-looking, middle-aged man, smiling brilliantly all the while. "Thank you, Harvey, for coming by so quickly," she gushed as they reached the counter. "We're running low on simply everything: shipping cartons, bubble pack, sacks—you name it."

At the blatant lie, Cristen narrowed her eyes once more, sure now that she'd been set up. Harvey worked for the company that supplied them with packaging products. Relatively speaking, their account was small and easily could have been handled over the phone, but Harvey dropped in regularly to take their order. He had been by only two weeks before, and their stock was more than adequate.

"No trouble. I had to call on another customer in the mall, anyway," he assured her. Then his gaze sought Cristen, and she fidgeted at the disturbing warmth in his hazel eyes. "Hello, Cristen. You're looking as pretty as ever."

"Thank you, Harvey," she said politely, shooting her partner a look that promised retribution.

While Louise gave him a hefty order for all the things they didn't need, Cristen braced herself for what she knew was coming. Every time Harvey came into the shop he asked her out, and though she always refused, it didn't stop him from asking. Despite Louise's advice, Cristen was not sure she could bring herself to accept a date with Harvey. He was a nice man, but she had the uneasy feeling that an evening spent in his company would be about as exciting as watching paint dry on a wall. Besides, she told herself, she didn't want to encourage the man when there was no hope of her ever returning his feelings.

Harvey was nothing if not predictable. As soon as his business with Louise was finished he turned to Cristen with that hopeful-spaniel look in his eyes. "I was wondering if maybe you'd like to have dinner with me this evening," he said diffidently.

"Actually, I, uh…" Cristen chewed on the inside of her lip and glanced at Louise, who was standing behind Harvey giving her frantic signals. "I really don't think—"

When the phone rang Cristen reacted to it like a drowning man reaching for a lifeline, snatching it up before the first peal was complete. "Hello," she said in a rush, sending Harvey an apologetic smile and ignoring Louise's scowl.

"Hi, Cris." Ryan's deep baritone rumbled through the receiver, and Cristen swallowed hard, the sense of reprieve she'd felt fleeing. "We knocked off early at the site today because of the rain, so I thought I'd do the grocery shopping. Is there anything special you'd like for dinner tonight?"

The question was a timely reminder of just how cozy their relationship had become. "I…" Cristen hesitated. She glanced at Harvey and chewed her lip again. Finally she drew in a deep breath and tilted her chin. "Don't bother cooking anything for me. I won't be home for dinner." She smiled across the counter at Harvey and winked. "I have a date tonight."

Harvey's face lit up. He looked as though he'd just won a million-dollar lottery. Louise nodded approvingly.

The silence coming through the phone line was so thick that you could cut it.

"A date, huh?" When Ryan finally spoke his voice was soft and controlled, and inexplicably, Cristen's throat became painfully tight.

"Yes."

"I see. Well...I guess I'll see you in the morning then."

"Yes," Cristen said softly.

Chapter Eight

"Would you like to come in for coffee?" The last thing Cristen wanted was to prolong the evening, but, perversely, lingering anger drove her to extend the invitation.

"Thanks. I'd like that."

Surprised and obviously pleased, Harvey looked at her as though she were the most wonderful woman on earth, and Cristen sighed.

Guilt. It was such an insidious, nagging, depressing, totally irrational emotion—and it had tormented her all evening.

Guilt for not returning Harvey's feelings, guilt for using him so shamefully, guilt for thinking he would be a crashing bore, when he was really an interesting, well-informed, sensitive man—it all twisted together to form a tight knot in Cristen's stomach.

Worse, her conscience had pricked her constantly over Ryan, too. It was absurd, and she knew it, but she felt as though she were being, somehow...unfaithful.

That she felt any guilt at all about Ryan made her furious. It's my apartment, Cristen told herself angrily, unlocking the door and ushering Harvey in. I can invite whomever I want. For that matter, I can go out with whomever I want. Ryan O'Malley doesn't have any claim on me. He's just my roommate.

Even so, when they stepped into the living room Cristen was relieved to see that Ryan wasn't around.

He had left only one small lamp burning, and she moved quickly around the room, turning more on. "Have a seat, Harvey. I'll be back with our coffee in just a minute."

As far as Cristen was concerned, instant coffee was a sacrilege, an abomination. Normally, she would not have violated her taste buds with the vile stuff, much less served it to a guest, but the minute she hit the kitchen she put the kettle on and began to forage through the cabinets for the sample jar she had received in the mail. Now that the defiant gesture had been made, she was anxious for Harvey to leave.

She slung sugar bowl, creamer and cups onto a tray, spooned in the noxious granules, splashed the barely steaming water over them and hurried back into the living room with a smile pasted on her face. "Well, here we are. How do you like yours?"

"Black with one sugar." Harvey rose politely to take the tray from her and set it on the coffee table. He looked disappointed when, after handing him his cup, Cristen settled into a chair with hers instead of joining him on the sofa, but he smiled and took a sip. "You have a lovely place," he said, glancing around.

"Thank you. We—uh—I like it. And it's very convenient to the shop."

"Yes. And it's a great neighborhood."

"Yes." Cristen smiled and sipped the revolting brew. Surreptitiously, she glanced at the mantel clock and wondered how long it would be before he left. Much more of this and she was going to fall asleep.

"You know, Cristen, I—" Harvey stopped abruptly, staring past her, an arrested expression on his face.

With a puzzled frown, Cristen followed the direction of his gaze and nearly fell out of her chair.

Ryan stood framed in the hall doorway, stretching hugely, back arched, arms bent, elbows up, his clenched fists pressing against his neck. His eyes were closed, and his mouth was open in a jaw-popping yawn. The only thing he wore was a pair of pale blue pajama bottoms, which rode indecently low. They were made of a thin, soft cotton that clung to his hips in a way that made Cristen's eyes bulge and her throat go dry. Speechless, she stared at his concave belly, the sharp points of his hipbones, the brawny, furred chest, the little tufts of black hair beneath his arms.

His contortions came to an end, and he ambled across the living room, scratching his chest, but stopped short at the sight of them.

"Oh! Hi, Cris. I didn't know you were home." Ryan sent her a warm, welcoming smile, and then he seemed to notice Harvey. A look of surprise crossed his face. "I'm sorry. I didn't know you had company." Altering his course, he crossed to the sofa and held out his hand. Dazed, Harvey took it. "You must be Mr. Metcow."

"Metcalf," Harvey corrected, looking askance at Ryan's pajamas.

"Yes, of course." With an aplomb that left Cristen speechless, Ryan perched on the arm of her chair. He rested an arm along the back and played idly with the feathery curls that lay on her shoulder. Aghast, Cristen stared at his muscular thigh beneath the taut cotton, her heart thudding like a wild thing. Heat from his bare, brawny chest and encircling arm scorched her cheek, neck and shoulders. With every shallow breath she drew came dizzying scents of soap and healthy male.

Do something. Don't just sit here! Cristen's common sense prodded. But Ryan's nearness had her so flustered that she couldn't think, and the best she could do was give him a warning glare.

Jauntily swinging one bare foot, Ryan smiled and turned back to Harvey. "Did you get your business settled?"

"Business?" Harvey blinked like a startled barn owl.

"Yes. I talked to Louise earlier this evening, and she told me you're a salesman for one of their suppliers." Ryan tipped his head back and gave Harvey a piercing look. "It was a business dinner you had, wasn't it?"

"No, it wasn't. It— Who *are* you?"

"Oh, sorry." His grin was wide and guileless. "I'm Ryan O'Malley. I live here with Cristen."

"You *what*?"

Oh, no. Now you've done it, Cristen thought. Beneath the cover of her arm, she reached with her other hand, pinched a piece of flesh at Ryan's side and gave it a vicious twist. He jumped, but the smile remained fixed on his face.

"What Ryan means, Harvey, is we're roommates," Cristen explained quickly. "We share this apartment."

"Oh, I, uh, I see." Harvey's uncertain gaze went back and forth between them before finally coming to rest on the masculine hand sifting through Cristen's hair.

"Yes, Cris and I share a lot of things," Ryan said, looking down at her warmly. His hand left her hair and stroked in a gentle circle over her upper arm. "We're quite... comfortable together, aren't we, love?"

"Ryan—"

"Which reminds me. Did you use my razor this morning?"

"Your— No! Certainly not!" Cristen sputtered.

"Oh. Well the blade was as dull as an old maid's love

life, and you're in such a stupor when you wake up, I thought maybe you'd picked it up by mistake.''

He turned to Harvey, shaking his head with amused tolerance. ''You wouldn't believe how hard it is to get this woman out of bed in the morning. Even when she's up and moving, she's practically comatose until she has something in her stomach. And a regular grouch if you so much as speak to her. I have to coddle her something awful.''

Smiling, Ryan looked down at Cristen, his voice dropping to a low caress. ''But I have to confess, it's no hardship. Not when she's so darned beautiful. All warm and rosy with sleep and her hair all mussed, and wearing almost nothing.''

''Ryan!''

Harvey set his cup down with a clatter and shot to his feet. ''I...uh...I'd better be going.''

''No, Harvey, let me explain. You see...that is...''

''It was nice meeting you, Harvey,'' Ryan said. ''Feel free to drop by anytime. We'd be happy to have you. Wouldn't we, Cristen?''

''Yes. No! I mean—''

''Uh, yeah. Same here,'' Harvey mumbled over his shoulder, scuttling toward the door like a fleeing crab. ''I enjoyed the dinner, Cristen. I'll be seeing you.''

''Harvey, wait—''

But he had already bolted out the door.

For a full ten seconds Cristen stood staring at it in befuddled disbelief. Then, like a thermometer plunged into boiling water, her anger began to rise, and she turned slowly to face Ryan.

He met her smoldering gaze with a bland, open look that made her want to slap him. ''Seems like a nice guy.''

''Oh, he is. He's a very nice guy.'' She began in a slow, deceptive, sugary tone, but with every word it rose in heat and intensity, until she ended on a shouted ''Whom I will probably never lay eyes on again, thanks to you!''

"Me! What did I do?"

"I don't know how you can even ask. Not after sauntering out here the way you did in those indecent pajamas."

"Indecent?" Ryan glanced down at the garment in question and sent her a puzzled look. "I thought they were kind of conservative." Then his wicked grin flashed. "Just be glad I had them on. Before I moved in here I slept in the raw."

"Oh, wonderful," she said with thick sarcasm, rolling her eyes. The comment inspired erotic images that sent both her temperature and her anger soaring, but Cristen got a grip on herself and pressed on doggedly. "And if that weren't bad enough, you plopped yourself on the arm of my chair as though you had every right to be there and dropped all those outrageous innuendos."

"I was just trying to be friendly," he claimed with a wounded air.

"Friendly, ha! You deliberately gave Harvey the impression that you and I are lovers. Now he thinks I'm the kind of woman who would go out with one man while sleeping with another."

"Oh, come on, Cris. You know you don't care what Harvey thinks. Louise told me he bores you silly. That you weren't the least bit interested in him."

Cristen threw her hands in the air. "Oh, great! Now my partner is siding against me." She snatched up the cups and stalked toward the kitchen, so furious that steam was practically coming out of her ears. Ryan followed right on her heels.

"Now you just listen to me, you lop-eared son of a cross-eyed mule. No matter how I feel about a man, I will not have you trying to scare him off. Is that clear?"

Ryan grinned. "Gee, I love it when you talk dirty."

Cristen made a low sound and plopped the cups into the sink. "Now, Ryan, I'm warning you—"

"Ah, come on, babe. You're getting all worked up over nothing." Standing behind her, he grasped her upper arms and massaged gently. "Loosen up."

"Nothing?" She shrugged off his hands and whipped around. Scowling fiercely, she poked his bare chest with her forefinger. "I do not call interfering in my personal life 'nothing.' You embarrassed me and made Harvey look like a fool, and I will not have it."

As she spoke she advanced on him, head thrust forward, eyes squinting, punctuating her words with several more jabs, backing him up a step with each one. Ryan looked suitably chastised, and, riding the crest of her anger, Cristen didn't notice the telltale twitch of his mustache.

"Sharing this apartment does not give you the right to poke your nose into my affairs," she informed him just as Ryan bumped against the table and sent it screeching back several inches. A chair teetered on two legs, but he snatched it upright before it could topple over.

"Affair! You mean you wanted to have an affair with that jerk?"

"No! Of course n—" She stopped and shot him an exasperated glare. "That is not the point, and you know it, you pea-brained, boneheaded jackass! You— And just what are you grinning about?"

Ryan's eyes twinkled. "You're talking dirty again."

"Dir— Why, you...you..." She couldn't think of anything vile enough to call him except several colorful epithets that she knew would merely delight him more. Finally she contented herself with giving him another hard poke. "Very funny. But you'd better wipe that smirk off your face, O'Malley, because you're just about a hair away from getting a fat lip."

She pivoted on her heel and stomped out, muttering under her breath with every step. Ryan hurried after her.

"Come on, Cristen. Don't be mad. Where's your sense of humor?"

"It moved out when you moved in."

She stalked across the living room and down the hall, her high heels hitting the floor like hammer blows, with Ryan a half step behind.

"But you have to admit, the whole thing was kinda funny, especially when your friend turned that apoplectic purple."

"I'll admit nothing of the kind."

"Okay, okay. I tell you what. How about if I explain things to ol' Harv tomorrow? Huh? Will that help?"

"Absolutely not. You stay away from Harvey."

At her door Cristen whirled around and held up her hand, and Ryan almost plowed right into her. "And I'm warning you, from now on you mind your own business."

She slammed the door in his face so hard that it rattled the hinges and made his ears ring.

Ryan winced and looked at it ruefully. Had he gone too far? He ran a hand through his hair and heaved a sigh. He shouldn't have done it, of course. And he really hadn't meant to. Though the thought of Cristen out with another man had eaten at his gut all evening, he'd told himself that he'd be adult about it.

But dammit! He hadn't counted on her actually bringing the guy into the apartment. When he'd heard them talking, all his good intentions had gone flying.

In the morning, he supposed he'd have to apologize and see what he could do about making amends.

After checking the front door and turning out all the lights, Ryan returned to his room and stretched out on his bed. With his hands laced beneath his head, he stared through the darkness at the ceiling. Perhaps it was time he pushed a bit harder. Cristen was a strong woman, and for some reason he didn't understand, she was determined to keep him at arm's length. He was almost positive that her actions tonight had been purely defensive. Which meant that she was aware of the feelings growing between them and was running scared.

That was a good sign. Wasn't it?

Closing his eyes, he gritted his teeth and tried to will away the hot, yearning ache in his loins...and the even greater one in his heart.

God, he hoped so.

It was almost eleven before Cristen emerged from her room the next morning. She entered the kitchen and found Ryan sitting at the table, drinking coffee and reading the Sunday paper. He looked up warily, his expression sheepish and questioning.

Cristen glanced at him, lifted her chin and made for the coffeepot. In addition to his outrageous behavior, she now had another reason to be annoyed with him: he had interfered with her sleep.

And sleep was something Cristen took seriously. She usually abandoned herself to it with childlike gusto, dropping off quickly and enjoying deep, untroubled slumber, but the night before she had tossed and turned for hours, fuming over Ryan's outrageous behavior. She always enjoyed the luxury of sleeping in on her days off, of awakening naturally without the rude blare of the alarm clock, but this morning, thanks to Ryan, she'd overdone it and awakened feeling groggy and irritable.

As usual, he had left coffee and orange juice in the bathroom for her, but both had been room temperature by the time she finally stumbled in to take her shower. She had dumped the former down the drain and drunk the latter, though she'd been sorely tempted not to.

Cristen poured her coffee and took a sip. She turned to find Ryan watching her over the top of the newspaper.

"Still mad?"

Leaning back against the counter, she took another sip and turned her head to stare out the window, presenting him with her profile. She let several more seconds tick by, then replied coolly, "Shouldn't I be?"

"Yep."

The unexpected answer took the wind out of her sails. Cristen looked at him in faint surprise, then firmed her mouth, suspecting he had done it on purpose.

"I was out of line, and I'm sorry. I had no business interfering in your life any more than you have in mine. My only excuse is, I was jealous. You see, I'd been looking forward to having dinner with you last night. I guess, living together like this, I've gotten kind of possessive."

Flummoxed by his honesty, Cristen could only stare. Oh, great. How was she supposed to respond to that? After all, given their situation, a certain amount of possessiveness was understandable. She'd felt a few pangs herself on those occasions when his sexy-voiced secretary had called, so she could hardly object. Yet she couldn't help feeling vaguely threatened. She had a nasty suspicion that with that disarming apology, Ryan had somehow advanced a step closer.

"I'm really sorry for embarrassing you, Cristen. Will you forgive me?"

"Well…" She pursed her lips and looked at him, but after a moment she gave an exasperated sigh. "Oh, I guess so."

"Great! And to make it up to you, why don't I take you out someplace? We can spend the day just having fun. Do something wild and crazy."

"Ryan, I don't think that's—"

"Come on, Cristen, don't say no. You'll enjoy yourself, I promise. And it'll be good for you. When was the last time you just relaxed and let yourself go? I've known you almost three months, and in all that time your whole life has been work, work, work. On your days off you either go into the shop or bring a project home to work on. The trouble with you is, you take things too seriously. You've

been working so hard for so long, I don't think you remember how to have fun.''

It was true. Hadn't she admitted much the same thing
to herself not long ago? Work had been her salvation in
the early days after Bob had walked out, but she was over
all that. Now she worked from dawn till dark out of habit.
Even in the evenings while watching TV she hemmed
small tablecloths and napkins or made tiny Oriental rugs,
using a turkey-tufting stitch on petit-point canvas. It was
obsessive and stupid to work so much, she knew. And it
was turning her into a dull, one-dimensional person.

Cristen looked at Ryan uncertainly. He was right. She
needed to relax and have fun. It had been ages since she'd
even tried. But still, spending the day with Ryan would be
foolhardy and reckless. She really shouldn't....

"Come on, Cris. Come with me." He gave her an in-
genuous look, his smile coaxing. "That way I'll know you
really do forgive me."

It was blatant emotional blackmail, but Cristen wasn't
immune to it, despite the scowl she aimed at him. "Where
would we go?"

Though her voice still held a note of doubt, Ryan sensed
he had won, and he grinned his delight. "Well, let's see.
We could take in a movie. Or go to the beach or the park.
Or..." He snapped his fingers. "I know. Why don't we
go ice skating?"

"Ice skating?"

"Sure. Why not?"

"Because I don't know how. I've never been ice skating."

He looked first shocked, then disapproving. "Do you
mean you've worked for years within sight of that beautiful rink and you've never once put on a pair of skates
and tried it?" When she shook her head, his expression
grew determined. "Well, that settles it. We're going. It's
high time you discovered what you've been missing."

"No, Ryan. I don't want to go skating. I'm not the athletic type."

"Don't worry about it. There's nothing to it. You'll have a great time. You'll see."

"No. Absolutely not. You are not getting me on that ice, and that's final."

"Are you sure it's easy?"

"Positive."

"It doesn't look easy."

Cristen clutched Ryan's arm and eyed the skaters. They glided by so fast that it made her dizzy to watch them, an elongated circle of color and motion, constantly shifting and changing. Some skated smoothly, their style graceful and sure, others lurched around mechanically, and a few plucky souls fought a constant battle with gravity, not always winning. There were racers, gliders, plodders and fancy figure skaters; fat ones, skinny ones, old and young and everything in between.

"Just hold on to me," Ryan said, edging Cristen toward the ice. "We'll take it nice and slow, and you'll have the hang of it in no time."

The sidelong look she gave him expressed her doubt, but she clumped along gamely on the thin blades. "How does anyone walk in these things?" she complained. "I feel like Frankenstein's monster. They must weigh ten pounds each."

Ryan laughed and patted her arm. "It'll be easier once we're on the ice."

They paused to step onto the rink, but before they could, a small child bumped into Cristen and darted around them. She held on to Ryan with a death grip, her free arm flailing as she teetered precariously on wobbly ankles. When she regained her balance she grimaced up at him dryly. "I certainly hope so."

The constant scrape of blades over ice blended with the

canned music and the dull roar of voices. The pervasive odors of sweat socks and leather and human bodies hung heavily in the air, and every now and then Cristen caught a whiff of mustard and grilling meat from the concession stand. Poised on the edge of the ice, she glanced up at Ryan and wrinkled her nose. "This place smells like a cross between a frozen locker room and a cheap carnival."

Ryan grinned. "Complaining won't do any good. You're still going out there. So come on, let's move it." He looped his left arm around her waist, took her right hand in his and urged her forward.

The instant their skates touched the ice they began to glide, and Cristen gave a distressed little moan. Her torso seesawed back and forth for a moment, fighting the motion, but Ryan steadied her.

"Easy. Easy. Just relax. I won't let you fall. Just do what I do. Right. Left. Right. Left. That's it," he encouraged when she managed a few jerky steps forward.

Cristen held on to Ryan so tightly that the tips of his fingers were bloodless. She felt as awkward and unsure as a child just learning to walk.

A petite blonde in a short-skirted red costume skated by, eyeing Ryan. In a clear spot just ahead of them she went into a fancy backward maneuver and topped it off with a spin that made her skirt stand straight out, revealing her pert, leotard-covered derriere.

Cristen's mouth turned down sourly. God, how she detested petite blondes.

The woman made five laps around the rink to their one, giving Ryan a flirtatious look every time she went by. Once, she even had the gall to skate around them in a circle and wink before moving on.

Her behavior incensed Cristen so, she forgot to be nervous. Gritting her teeth, she concentrated fiercely on Ryan's instructions and maintaining her balance. By the time they had completed their second circuit, she had the rhythm and was doing much better.

"You ready to try solo?" Ryan asked.

She started to refuse, but at that moment the blonde went by again in a flash of red. Cristen narrowed her eyes. "Yes. As a matter of fact, I think I am," she said, watching the woman execute a spinning leap and land like a feather.

Show-off! she fumed.

Ryan took his arms from around Cristen's waist, skated with her a short way and released her hand. She wavered a bit, then caught the rhythm again. On the third forward glide she shot him a triumphant grin...and the next instant her feet and bottom changed places.

Cristen hit the ice with a solid *whomp* that clacked her teeth together. Stunned, she sat there for a moment with her palms braced on either side of her hips, staring at the tips of her skates.

"Are you okay?" Ryan asked, coming to a halt beside her.

"Yes," she muttered through clenched teeth. "I'm fine."

Ryan suppressed a grin. With his hands clasped behind his back, his expression grave, he skated around her several times, his gaze sweeping over the ice. Cristen narrowed her eyes and watched him suspiciously.

"What are you looking for?"

Ryan glanced at her and said, straight-faced, "Cracks. There're sure to be some."

"Very funny, O'Malley. You're just a barrel of laughs."

She would have said more, but the cute little blonde arrived at that moment, coming to a halt with a flourish that sent ice shavings spraying—most of them right into Cristen's face.

"Can I be of any help?" she asked sweetly, batting her false eyelashes at Ryan.

Cripes, Cristen thought, they look like spiders perched on her eyelids.

Ryan gave her his sexiest smile, his blue eyes glinting with approval and wicked awareness. Cristen had to resist a strong urge to grab his ankles and jerk him off his feet.

"Thank you, but no, I don't think so."

Cristen scrambled to stand up, but every time the blades of her skates touched the ice her feet shot out from under her and she went sprawling again. Ryan offered her his hand, but she just scowled at him and struggled harder. Finally he moved behind her, hooked his hands beneath her armpits and hauled her up.

She tried to shake off his hold, but the action almost landed her on her backside again, and she was forced to grab on to his arm, though the need to do so galled her.

"Are you sure?" the blonde persisted. "I'd be happy to help you teach your friend the basics." She struck a graceful pose and smiled beguilingly at Ryan. Cristen didn't even warrant a glance.

"That's very nice of you, but I think we can manage. Cristen's a fast learner. She just needs a little practice."

Gritting her teeth, Cristen brushed the ice shavings off the seat of her jeans and glared daggers at the pair. They were both talking about her as though she weren't there. And if body language and the looks that passed between them counted, there was a lot being said without benefit of words.

What was it about cutesy, pint-sized women that men found so fascinating? Cristen wondered sourly. This one was definitely starting to get on her nerves. Did she have to stand there swaying her hips like that?

Of course, Cristen. Don't be an idiot. How else is she supposed to draw attention to her slender thighs and that itty-bitty costume, for mercy's sake?

Cristen drummed her fingers against Ryan's arm. Next

to the almost life-size Barbie Doll, she felt like an Amazonian bag lady in her old jeans and cotton blouse.

"Oh. Well, okay," the blonde said with obvious disappointment. "But if you change your mind, I'll be around all afternoon." She gave Ryan one last regretful look and skated away.

With a tiny knowing smile tugging at his mouth, he watched her for a moment before turning back to Cristen. "Well, are you game for more?"

Cristen jutted out her chin and returned his teasing look with an icy stare. "Certainly. Did you think I'd quit just because of one little fall?" Or one man-hungry blonde? she added silently.

The fall was far from the last one Cristen took. After circling the rink once more with Ryan, she insisted on skating unaided and spent the next several hours doggedly striving to stay upright. It was not an easy task. But once committed to a course of action, Cristen could seldom be diverted. Her mother called it bullheadedness. Cristen preferred to think of it as perseverance.

With gritty determination, she picked herself up over and over again and plodded on, stubbornly refusing Ryan's help.

"Good Lord, Cristen," he said after she'd taken a particularly jarring fall. "This isn't some sort of test, you know. There's no law that says you have to learn to skate. Why don't you call it quits and let's go somewhere else? Or at least let me help you."

"No. No, I'm not going to quit until I've skated all the way around this rink without falling," she declared tightly. "Even if it takes me all night."

It almost did. By the time she finally achieved her goal it was late afternoon. Cristen crossed her starting point and made for the exit, not even slowing down to accept Ryan's congratulations. She was bone tired and bruised and ready to get the heck out of there.

It was bliss to shed the heavy skates, and after Cristen had turned them in she headed for the ladies' room, eyeing the rink balefully as she went. After today, she doubted that she would ever again enjoy the view from her shop window.

All her extremities were cold, especially her rear end, and in the ladies' room Cristen discovered why. She had spent so much time flat on her bottom on the ice that the seat of her jeans was soaked. Screwing up her face in disgust, she mimicked in a sarcastic singsong, "You'll have fun, Cristen. I promise.

"Darn you, O'Malley. I'll get you for this. It'd serve you right if I rode home in your precious Jaguar this way," she muttered angrily.

Tight-lipped, she stomped to the wall hand dryer and whacked the flat knob with the side of her fist, then turned, braced her palms on her knees and stuck her rump up under the stream of hot air. As warmth seeped through the heavy material and into her chilled flesh, Cristen's mouth twisted.

Who are you kidding? Ryan risk damaging his upholstery? He'd probably make you ride on your knees facing backward. Or maybe even run along beside.

A teenage girl came in and goggled openly. By the time she emerged from one of the stalls, her startled expression had changed to a smirk, which, as she took her time washing and drying her hands, grew increasingly irksome to Cristen. At the door, the girl looked back and, with a giggle, called out, "Bye, hot pants."

Cristen made a face at the swinging door. "Smart-mouthed kid."

For the most part she had the ladies' room to herself after that, and of the few other females who wandered in, none felt compelled to make cute remarks.

It took twenty minutes and about fifty jabs on the blower button before her jeans were in any condition to come into contact with the Jaguar's leather bucket seats. Thawed and dry, Cristen emerged more charitably disposed toward Ryan, but the feeling lasted only as long as it took her to spot him.

Leaning against a post to one side of the rink, a silly smile on his face he stood talking to the little blonde.

Chapter Nine

Cristen stopped dead in her tracks and watched them, her mouth thinning. Even from where she stood it was easy to see that the woman was flirting for all she was worth. She was batting those ridiculous fake lashes so hard that it was a wonder Ryan didn't have windburn. Not even a blind man could miss the signals she was sending out.

And Ryan was eating it all up with a spoon.

When he threw back his head and laughed at something the woman said, Cristen saw red. She didn't stop to ask herself why she was so furious, but simply put her nose in the air and headed for the exit. She marched right past them without so much as a glance.

"Cristen? Cristen, where are you going?" Ryan called after her. "Cristen!"

She ignored him. Her leggy stride carried her quickly through the crowd around the rink and down the almost deserted passageway.

"Cristen, will you stop?"

Ryan's voice was coming closer. Cristen could hear the soft thud and squeak of tennis shoes on the mall's marble floor, but she fought the undignified urge to break into a run. As she reached the exit doors Ryan caught up with her. Ignoring him, she shoved them open and marched on.

"Cris, for God's sake—"

She started down the four steps that led into the parking garage, but Ryan took them in one leap, then turned and blocked her way before she reached the bottom.

"All right. Now I want to know just what the devil is going on. Why did you stomp off that way?"

"Get out of my way, Ryan."

"Uh-uh. Not until we talk."

"You want to talk? Then go back to blondie. You seemed to find her fascinating."

Ryan looked astounded. "That's what this is all about? You're jealous?"

"I most certainly am not!" she flared hotly.

Surprise turned to delight, and Ryan's grin spread wide. "You're *jealous*!"

"Will you stop saying that! I told you, I'm n—"

Ryan's whoop of joy cut her off, and she let out a shriek when he snatched her off the steps.

She clutched his shoulder as he held her high against his chest and whirled around. "Ryan! Stop it!"

Laughing, he obeyed but continued to hold her aloft. Cristen looked around in a panic, afraid that someone would see them, but there wasn't another soul in the garage. She scowled down at him and shoved at his shoulders, but the strong arms looped beneath her bottom clamped her tightly to him.

"What is the matter with you?" she hissed. "Do you have a fetish about parking garages? Do they turn you on or something?"

"No. But you do." At her swiftly indrawn breath the

foolish grin on Ryan's face melted into tenderness. "Only you."

Cristen's eyes grew round, and Ryan looked at her with a hint of reproach. "Ah, love, surely by now you've guessed how I feel. You knocked me for a loop the moment we met. I've thought about you constantly and gone to great lengths to be with you. I don't want any other woman. Especially not that obvious little flirt back at the rink."

Pleasure shot through her at his words and made her heart pound with unbearable excitement. Calling herself a fool, Cristen struggled to subdue it. She frowned, trying to look severe, but she was so flustered that she couldn't quite pull it off. "Ryan, stop this. We have an agreement."

"Agreement be damned," he said cheerfully, his grin returning. "Anyway, that was before I knew you cared. And don't you dare deny it," he warned, chuckling at her indignant expression. "Not after stomping off in a jealous huff like that. But now that I do know, I think it's time we renegotiated our agreement."

"Ryan, I—"

But he had already loosened his hold. As Cristen slid down his body their gazes remained locked. His eyes glittered with exhilaration and sheer masculine pleasure, hers with mingled desire and apprehension as sensual awareness swelled between them.

The moment stretched out, taut with anticipation. It was as though all the oxygen had been removed from the air. Neither breathed. Neither spoke. Neither looked away. For those few seconds the world was reduced to just the two of them. Nothing existed but the throbbing tension, the erotic friction between their bodies, the unspoken promise of pleasures yet to be tasted.

With a hint of a smile playing about his lips, Ryan watched Cristen slide lower. Her pointed toes reached for the floor, and when they touched the concrete his head swooped, his mouth closing over hers with a swift sureness that allowed no protest.

There wasn't a woman alive who could have resisted that kiss; Cristen was sure of it.

His lips were warm and firm, his mustache a whispery brush of sable. The twin tactile pleasures electrified Cristen. Her heart seemed to stop beating for a millisecond, then took off at a gallop. Every nerve ending, every pulse point sprang into frenzied life.

You're such a fool, Cristen, for ever thinking you could escape this, she thought. But even as she berated herself she pressed closer, melting in Ryan's embrace. It was madness. Sheer madness. And it was irresistible.

He didn't release her until he had kissed her thoroughly and she was limp and shaking with need.

Feeling her tremble, Ryan pulled back and gazed into her upturned face. Her slightly puffy lips, the slumberous look in her eyes, brought a satisfied, purely masculine smile to his mouth.

He curved his big hands around either side of her neck and stroked his thumbs back and forth along her jaw. "All I'm asking is that you give it a try," he said persuasively. "Relax and go with your feelings and see what happens. I think we can have something very special together, Cristen, if you'll just give it a chance."

"I..." She caught her bottom lip between her teeth and looked at him, her eyes filled with indecision.

Ryan waited a moment, then tipped his head forward, giving her a beguiling look. "Will you, Cristen?"

Before she could reply, a group of rowdy teenage boys pushed through the mall doors and came loping down the steps. "Whoooie! Way to go, man!" one called when he spotted them. Instantly the others joined in with catcalls and whistles.

Cristen turned red to the roots of her hair, but the razzing didn't faze Ryan. Flashing them an arrogant grin, he

tucked Cristen against his side and urged her toward the
car. "Come on. Let's get out of here."

She went willingly, too unstrung to think about what
she would do, what would happen, when she and Ryan
got home.

But, typically, Ryan did not do the expected.

After giving her a long, searching look, he backed the
car out of the parking slot and headed for the exit.
"There's a new place over on Richmond that serves great
ribs. I don't know about you, but after all that skating, I'm
starved." He guided the purring Jaguar down the ramp and
eased into the flow of traffic on Westheimer. When he
stopped at the light he shot Cristen a quizzical smile.
"How about it? You game?"

The suggestion took her so by surprise that she answered
without thinking. "Yes. That sounds fine."

But a moment later Cristen was not sure if she was
grateful for the delay or disappointed. That it was only
temporary, she never doubted for a second. Ryan was going to demand an answer, some sort of decision from her.
Even if she wanted to, she couldn't avoid giving one.
Those few moments in the parking garage had changed
everything. There was no going back to the polite pretense
they had been living. Either she stopped fighting the attraction and let the relationship develop, or Ryan would
have to move out. Cristen closed her eyes, panicked at the
thought of either happening. Darn it! Why did he have to
bring everything out into the open? she fretted.

The restaurant was a small, unpretentious place called
Adam's Rib, which served cafeteria style. The decor was
standard for a barbecue joint—red vinyl booths, laminated
tables, brick floor, light fixtures made of wagon wheels,
lots of branding irons, spurs, singletrees, bridles and horse-
shoes hanging on silvered, natural cedar walls—but it was
neat and clean, and the aroma coming out of the kitchen
more than made up for the phony quaintness.

Since it was only a little before six, the restaurant wasn't crowded, and when Cristen and Ryan had gone through the line they carried their trays to a secluded booth in the corner.

Ryan dug right in, but Cristen dawdled. She looked at the plate of food and wondered why she had ordered it. How could she eat when her insides were tying themselves into knots? Taking her time, she spread her napkin in her lap and dumped sugar into her iced tea. Ice cubes clattered and her spoon clanked noisily against the inside of the glass as she stirred it. And stirred it. And stirred it.

Ryan looked up from gnawing on a sparerib. His amused gaze went from Cristen to the swirling liquid, then back, and she stopped abruptly, jerking the spoon out so fast that tea splattered over the table.

Pretending not to notice, Ryan discarded the bare bone and licked the sauce off his fingers. "You know, you were really a great sport today," he said, sending her a warm look that slowly turned into a chuckle. He shook his head, his expression filled with fond exasperation. "I knew you were a determined woman, but good Lord, Cristen, today was a revelation. Do you ever give up?"

"No." She lifted her chin, forgetting for a moment her contorting stomach. But then she thought of Bob, and of marriage, and her defiant conviction faded a bit. She had given up on those long ago. "Well...almost never," she amended.

"After today, I can well believe it."

Cristen grimaced. "I guess I made a fool of myself, didn't I?"

"No, of course not. A lot of people took spills. You were just concentrating so hard that you didn't notice. Don't worry, you did just fine." Ryan selected another sparerib. Leaning forward, he pointed it at her. "But you probably won't believe that tomorrow when certain parts of your body start to protest."

"You mean like the part I'm sitting on?"

"Mmm. Maybe we can strap a pillow on you." Pure devilment danced in Ryan's eyes as he brought the spare-rib to his mouth.

As Cristen watched his even teeth sink into the succulent meat, she felt a queer sensation in her chest. She waited for him to bring up what was on both their minds, but Ryan merely polished off the rib and picked up another one. It was then that it hit Cristen: he wasn't going to press her for an answer or even mention that scene in the garage. At least, not yet.

She narrowed her eyes. Advance and retreat. Now she realized it was the tactic he'd used all along, the clever devil. And very effectively, too. Indignant, Cristen picked up her knife and fork and attacked the plate of food in front of her. She took a bite of the barbecued beef and chewed it as though she were trying to pulverize rocks with her teeth. No, Ryan wasn't about to let the matter drop. He was just biding his time.

She was tempted to give him a good swift kick.

Ryan grinned at her mulish expression. "Did I ever tell you about the time I gave skating lessons to a dog?"

Cristen almost choked on the bite of coleslaw she was chewing. She grabbed a glass of water and took several quick swallows, scowling at him over the rim. Blast his ornery hide! She hadn't intended to speak to him, but who would resist an opening gambit like that?

"No," she said curtly.

"When I was in college I worked part-time one year at the local ice rink." Employing his Irish gift of gab to the fullest, Ryan launched into a tale about a woman who was so attached to her toy poodle that she couldn't bear to be parted from it for even a couple of hours a week. So she arrived for her first skating lesson with the dog in tow, demanding that they teach her Angelique, too.

"She'd even had skates custom-made to fit the animal,"

Ryan said with a wave of his fork. "Damnedest things you ever saw. Laced halfway up those skinny little legs, with blades about two inches long."

"What did you do?"

"Do? What could I do? I charged her double and taught the dog." Nonplussed, Cristen watched him take a bite of potato salad and chew thoughtfully. When he had washed it down with a swig of iced tea, he smiled reminiscently and added, "Turned out to be one helluva little skater, too. Much better than her mistress." He flashed Cristen a bland smile. "Took a silver medal at the Olympics that year."

Cristen's jaw dropped and, a beat later, snapped shut again. She tried not to laugh. Sucking in her cheeks, she speared Ryan with a censorious stare.

But it was no use. Her gaze met the unholy twinkle in his, and her lips twitched. A chuckle bubbled up and vibrated at the back of her throat. She gulped it down. It shot back up. Ryan's slow grin appeared, and her laughter burst free.

"Oh, you!" she sputtered finally. "You made that whole thing up."

"Just the last part. I really did teach her dog to skate. Honest," he swore with his hand over his heart.

"Liar." Cristen wadded up her paper napkin and threw it at him. Ryan batted it away and spent the next several minutes vociferously protesting the charge.

Resisting Ryan proved to be about as easy as trying to hold back the tide. All through the meal and during the drive home, the teasing, charming devil regaled Cristen with wild stories that kept her laughing and made her forget, for a while at least, that heart-stopping kiss and the decision she faced. As they entered the apartment he was only halfway through a story about how he had taught Jennifer to ride a bicycle, and she was already convulsed with laughter.

"It's not funny," he declared as Cristen plopped down

on the sofa and leaned her head against the back, swiping at her eyes with the backs of her hands. "I huffed and puffed up and down that damned street for hours. I'll bet I ran five miles alongside that bike. But finally, *finally*, she got the hang of it. She was a bit wobbly, but she was so proud of herself," he said, smiling fondly at the memory.

He joined Cristen on the sofa, stretched his legs out in front of him and leaned his head back, also. "Well, anyway, I watched her ride around the block a couple of times, and when I was sure she could handle it, I went inside and turned on a Rams game. Every now and then I thought I heard something, but it didn't really penetrate until I turned off the set an hour later, just as Jennifer went by the house yelling 'Help! Help!' at the top of her lungs." Ryan shook his head. "I've never been so scared in my life. I swear, my heart tried to club its way right out of my chest. At the very least, when I shot out the door I expected to find her lying broken and mangled in the street."

"What had happened?"

Rolling his eyes, Ryan chuckled in ironic amusement. "It seems she had learned to ride just fine, but she was afraid if she put on the brakes, she'd fall. So for an hour she'd been circling the block, screaming for me to stop her each time she passed the house."

They laughed together again, but after a while the sounds became strained and faded away. Sprawled at either end of the sofa, each gazed at the ceiling and listened to the silence stretch out and thicken. Cristen could hear the mantel clock tick, the soft whir of cool air blowing through the air-conditioning vent, her own heart beating.

"Would you like some coffee?" Ryan asked.

"No, thanks."

"A drink?"

"No."

Another ten seconds passed.

"How about dessert? There's some ice cream in the freezer."

"No, I don't think so."

Slowly, Ryan rolled his head on the sofa back. Cristen did the same. Their gazes met and held, and his mouth curved upward. "Wanna fool around?"

Though he'd posed the question in a teasing vein, both knew he was serious. Holding her breath, Cristen stared at him with wide, troubled eyes. She wanted to. Oh, how she wanted to. But she was afraid. Afraid of being hurt. Afraid of being inadequate. Good grief! Until just recently she hadn't even dreamed of being romantically involved with any man but Bob.

But most of all, she was afraid of failing again.

And nothing lasts forever, she reminded herself. Nothing. You know that.

Cristen also knew, with soul-deep certainty, that if she allowed herself to care for Ryan, losing him would devastate her. The pain she had felt over Bob's desertion would be puny by comparison.

She could see the passion smoldering in Ryan's vivid blue eyes, could sense it in the deceptive stillness of his body. It pulled at her, stirred within her a longing so intense that it was almost pain. Tears glistened in her eyes as she gazed at him. Her throat felt tight and achy. Her heart thudded with a slow, heavy beat.

With a strangled sound, Cristen bolted off the sofa and raced toward the kitchen. She pushed through the door and went to the sink, gripping the porcelain edge so tightly her fingers were bloodless.

Heaven help her, she had to be sensible about this. Everything was against its working. Ryan was happy-go-lucky and casual about most things; she was serious and determined. He was wealthy; she was struggling. He was worldly, experienced; in her thirty years she had known

just one man intimately. There were high school girls more
experienced, for heaven's sake.

The soft swish of the door alerted her to Ryan's presence. Frantic for something to do, Cristen turned on the
water and snatched a paper cup from the dispenser. Before
she could fill it, Ryan's hands settled on her shoulders, and
she went perfectly still.

"You can't run from it, Cristen," he said tenderly. His
breath stirred her hair, its moist warmth seeping through,
making her scalp tingle. "Neither of us can. What we're
feeling is real and strong, and it isn't going to go away."
He bent his head and buried his face in the cloud of auburn
curls at the side of her neck.

Cristen sucked in her breath. The paper cup slipped from
her fingers. It hit the counter with a hollow clatter and
rolled in a wobbly arc. "Don't, Ryan." Cristen tried to
sound stern, but the command came out a little shaky. She
hunched her shoulder against his gentle nuzzling, but her
heart was suddenly playing leapfrog in her chest.

"Can you honestly say you don't like it when I do
this?" Nuzzling aside the fragrant tresses, he nibbled her
shoulder as far as the scooped neck of her blouse would
allow, then worked his way back up to her ear. "Or this?"
He nipped her lobe, then batted it playfully with his
tongue.

A shuddering breath escaped Cristen, and she closed her
eyes. "Ryan..."

"Or how about this?" he whispered, pressing his open
mouth over the graceful shell. For a moment his breath
filled her ear with moist heat; then the tip of his tongue
traced each delicate swirl, and a delicious prickling sensation rippled over Cristen's skin.

Ryan's hands slid down her arms, slipped under them
and pressed warmly over her abdomen. Cristen grasped his
arms with every intention of removing them, but then,
somehow, her forearms were resting atop his and her fin-

gers were flexing around his thick wrists. His flesh was warm and hard, the silky hair covering it an erotic abrasion against her skin.

"Oh, Ryan." This time his name came out on a sigh, and she felt his smile against her neck.

Cristen's head fell back against Ryan's shoulder. She felt weak, her body burning with a delicious lassitude, her insides atremble. Were it not for his encircling arms she was not sure she could have remained standing.

All the arguments she had given herself for not getting involved with Ryan flew out of her head. For too long she had fought the attraction, but she could fight it no more. Her defenses breached she surrendered willingly to the sweet rush of passion. She was passive in his arms, absorbing his heat, his strength, greedily breathing in the heady masculine scent that surrounded her, reveling in the exquisite sensations created by his touch.

Her breasts were heavy and aching, and when Ryan cupped them Cristen spread her hands over his and pressed them closer. His thumbs swept back and forth over her nipples, and they peaked, pebble hard. Cristen moaned and rocked her head on Ryan's shoulder. He growled softly.

"Come here," he whispered, turning her in his arms.

He gazed down at her and smiled. Desire glittered in her green eyes beneath heavy, half-closed lids. Her breathing was deep and slow, her lips slightly parted, and as he watched, the tip of her tongue came peeking out and glided in a lazy circle. When it retreated her lips were wet, inviting.

The water was still gushing into the sink, and Ryan reached around her and turned it off. In the pulsing quiet that followed, Cristen was sure he could hear her heart thudding.

Watching her, Ryan cupped her cheek. His thumb brushed over her chin, her lower lip. Then, with slow, sure movements, he pulled her closer, tilted her face up and lowered his mouth to hers.

The first touch sent excitement streaking through Cristen like summer lightning. She moaned and pressed closer, her arms sliding up to encircle his neck of their own accord. Oh, Lord, she hadn't known until now how much she wanted this. Needed it.

Ryan's mouth rocked over hers with excruciating slowness. Tender. Tormenting. His sable mustache was a sleek, soft caress, as feathery as a whispering breeze against her skin. His tongue probed the corners of her mouth, the slick skin of her inner lip, the tiny serrations on her teeth, touched the tip of her tongue and pulled back.

Cristen couldn't hold in the small moan of frustration that rose in her throat and slipped between her parted lips, nor could she keep her arms from tightening around his neck.

Ryan smiled against her lips. And then, with a swiftness and power that was unbearably exciting, he obeyed her silent urging. Holding her tight, he kissed her with a dark, sweet fervency, the rhythmic thrusts of his tongue telling her of his desire, building hers.

The hand beneath her chin slid around her neck, his spread fingers spearing through her hair to cup the back of her head. His other hand began to move downward, sliding over her back and hips, cupping her buttocks and pressing her to him rhythmically, matching the undulating movements with the slow, deep thrusts of his tongue.

Cristen was bombarded with new, thrilling sensations. Needs, desires she had not even known she possessed were clamoring for fulfillment. There was a hollow, yearning ache growing between her legs. She wanted to get closer to Ryan, to writhe and clutch and coil herself around him.

Their clinging lips parted slowly as, with a small sound of pleasure, Ryan ended the kiss. Loosening his hold, he pulled away and eased her back until she was braced against the counter. Gently grasping her upper arms, he looked down at her.

She was flushed with passion, her expression bemused, yearning. Ryan's face was taut and his blue eyes seemed unnaturally bright, but the smile that curled up the corners of his mustache, though tender, held a touch of familiar devilment.

"Honey, for a gal who doesn't wanna fool around, your kisses pack one helluva wallop," he murmured in a soft, scratchy voice.

Cristen blinked, her heavy eyelids lowering and lifting with sensuous lethargy. She was so aroused that it took a moment for her to make sense of his statement. When she did, warm color flooded her face. Flustered, she started to speak, but Ryan placed his forefinger over her mouth.

"I know. I shouldn't tease you. Not now." He smiled with gentle contrition, his gaze warm and caressing. His blunt finger traced her mouth, then trailed along her jaw. As he watched the movement his eyes darkened. "But, sweetheart, the point is, the chemistry between us is too explosive to ignore." He looked at her intently, his face growing tense. His voice dropped to a husky pitch that throbbed with want and sent a tingle feathering over her skin. "I don't want to ignore it, Cristen. I want to enjoy it. To lose myself in it. In you. And I think that's what you want, too. Isn't it?"

It was true. From the very beginning the depth and strength of the attraction she felt for Ryan had frightened her. She had fought it, even denied it, but in her heart of hearts she had known the truth: she wanted him, as she had never wanted any man before.

Why else had she agreed to let him stay? Put up with his teasing and not too subtle manipulating? All her complaining and resistance had been merely a smoke screen, a bit of face-saving self-deception. People always did what they wanted to do, given a choice. Deep down, she had known what would eventually happen when she let Ryan move in. It was time to face that.

With a pounding heart, she met the gentle demand in Ryan's direct gaze. "Yes. Yes, it is," she said honestly, if a bit shakily.

Something flared in Ryan's eyes, something hot and urgent...something deliciously, dangerously male. "Are you sure?"

Cristen swallowed. "Yes."

He stared at her for a moment longer, and then a slow smile curved his mouth. Without a word, he bent, slipped an arm beneath her knees, the other around her back, and lifted her high against his chest. She looped her arm around his shoulders, and for countless moments they remained that way, silent and still, looking deep into each other's eyes. Finally, still holding her gaze, Ryan shouldered through the swinging door and carried her to her bedroom.

The fading golden glow of sunset filtered through the sheer curtains at her window, bathing the room with a mystical light, as he set her on her feet beside the bed. In the hazy dimness, Ryan bracketed Cristen's face with his broad palms and tipped her head back. The waning light tinted her skin a rich apricot and created a fiery nimbus around her auburn curls. Her eyes glittered like emeralds from within their heavy fringe of lashes.

"You're so lovely," he whispered. "You bewitched me the first moment I saw you." His gaze dropped to her mouth, and slowly his head descended. Cristen's eyelids fluttered shut. "You've been driving me crazy ever since." He whispered the words against her lips, his breath striking her skin in warm little puffs. And then his mouth slanted over hers.

Never had Cristen experienced such a soul-stirring kiss. With exquisite care, his lips rocked over hers. It was the merest contact of flesh to flesh, but oh, so warm and tender. His tongue slicked over her quivering lips, probed the corners of her mouth, then swirled enticingly around its inner edge, without ever quite entering that yearning sweetness.

Cristen trembled beneath the sensuous assault. The excruciating gentleness aroused her almost beyond bearing.

One of Ryan's hands slid down and lightly cupped the side of her neck, his fingertips playing softly over the velvety rim of her ear and the sensitive skin behind it. His other arm looped around her back to hold her close.

At last he ended the tormenting caress, raising his head slowly and easing back a step. He smiled at her tenderly as he slid his hand down her neck, turning it so that the backs of his knuckles skimmed over her collarbone and chest to the button at the top of the scoop-necked blouse. His fingers deftly released it and sought the next one, his knuckles grazing the rounded tops of her breasts on their downward glide.

"You're trembling." Ryan's eyes flared as he felt her helpless response. He released another button…and another. Encountering the waistband of her jeans, he tugged her blouse free, watching her. "Do I frighten you, darling?"

"No. It's…not that," she said tremulously. "It's just…" Cool air feathered across Cristen's skin, sending another delicious shiver rippling through her as Ryan released the final button and eased the blouse over her shoulders, letting it fall to the floor.

"What? Tell me what's wrong."

"Nothing's wrong." Cristen looked at him, her expression soft and vulnerable, her green eyes misty with passion and just a touch of doubt. "It's just that it's been so long for me, and…and there's never been anyone else but my husband. It's…it's almost like the first time all over again."

Ryan's hand stilled on the front clasp of her bra. "Oh, my love," he groaned in a voice that went low and rough with emotion. "Do you have any idea what it does to me to hear you say that?"

He took her mouth in a hungry, hot kiss that, when it was over, left them both shaken. With considerably more haste, he released the front clasp on her bra, and it joined the yellow blouse on the floor. Cristen sucked in her breath and gripped his shoulders as he cupped her breasts and swept his thumbs back and forth across her nipples. He bent and suckled a hardened peak, drawing her deep into his mouth. Each rhythmic tug seemed to pull at her womb, making it throb and yearn.

"Oh, Ryan!" Gasping, Cristen arched her neck back and clutched his head with both hands, burying her fingers in his hair, pressing frantically against his scalp to hold him to her as he lavished the same fierce attention on the other breast. Her heart beat against her ribs like a wild thing, while the rest of her body seemed to grow weak and liquid.

Hazily, Cristen heard the pop of a snap and the soft rasp of a metal zipper being lowered. His movements now frantic, Ryan hooked his thumbs under the top of her jeans and dropped to one knee, pushing them down around her ankles. Cristen held on to his shoulders for balance as he eased her shoes and socks and the soft denim over her feet and tossed them aside. The tiny triangle of lilac silk and lace quickly followed.

Ryan wrapped his arms around her hips and pressed his face against her stomach. "Oh, sweetheart, I've lain in that bedroom night after night, dreaming of this. Going crazy with wanting you," he said in a raspy whisper as he strung hot kisses over her silky skin.

Cristen trembled and held him close, her fingers buried in his hair. Her emotions overwhelmed her, and she closed her eyes against the sweet rush of feelings that surged up inside her—feelings she didn't want to put a name to. Instead she concentrated on the thrilling physical sensations within Ryan's embrace: the erotic brush of his mustache against the soft skin of her belly, the strength of his arms around her, the hot wetness of his mouth, the warm, silky feel of his hair.

The pleasure became so intense that it was almost pain, and finally, trembling, Cristen gripped his shoulders and urged him upward. "Please, Ryan. Oh, please."

He stood at once. His burning gaze roamed over her hungrily, sliding over every line, every dip and curve of her naked body, promising untold delight and sending Cristen's passion soaring. "Yes. Oh, God, yes," he said with throaty urgency.

Reaching around her, he tossed back the spread and covers, then eased her back onto the bed. As she stretched out languidly, Ryan snatched off his own clothes, his avid gaze never once leaving her. Then he was there beside her, pulling her to him, and their soft moans of pleasure blended together at the first thrilling touch of warm flesh to warm flesh.

His kiss was deep and penetrating, exploring her mouth with the same urgency that his hands explored her body. He traced the long, lush line of hip and thigh, the inward curve of her waist, the exquisite flare of her rib cage. Lovingly, he cupped his hand around her breast and flexed his fingers against the soft flesh.

Ryan kissed his way down her neck and collarbone to the scented valley between her breasts. Gently, he brushed his thumb across her aroused nipple, bringing it into swollen readiness, and Cristen moaned, her head moving from side to side on the pillow. With a soft growl of satisfaction Ryan's mouth closed lovingly around her nipple.

"Oh, Ryan!" she cried out, digging her nails into his back as a riot of sensations exploded inside her.

In restless passion, Cristen's hands ran over his shoulders and neck and back, her fingertips tracing the tiny knobs in his spine, then slipping around to explore his chest and twine in the coarse hair that covered it, tugging gently.

Every touch, every tiny incoherent sound of pleasure pulled their emotions tighter and tighter. Their breathing grew rapid, deep, labored.

Cristen trembled, her body awash with sensations and driving need. She had not known such voluptuous pleasure existed. It was sweet agony, and she gloried in it, greedily savoring each wondrous rush of emotion. The taut, throbbing ache that consumed her was nearly driving her mad, yet she wanted—demanded—more.

A whimper of pure pleasure escaped her as Ryan caressed the silky skin of her belly. The whimper became a moan when searching fingers slid lower and lovingly parted the warm, moist petals of her womanhood.

Her cry seemed to steal the last of Ryan's control. He raised his head and looked down at her, his face flushed and taut. "Oh, God, sweetheart. I can't wait any longer."

"I don't want you to." She gripped his shoulders and urged him to her. "Love me, Ryan," she whispered shakily. "Love me now."

It was all the encouragement he needed. He levered up and positioned himself between her soft thighs. Holding her gaze, he entered her in a smooth, silken stroke, smiling tightly as he watched her eyes glaze, her face soften with ecstasy.

He pressed deep, and when he was sheathed in her heavenly warmth, he threw his head back and went perfectly still. Strained muscles bunched and quivered in the arms braced on either side of Cristen's head. Eyes closed, his face contorted with passion, he clamped his teeth over his lower lip and fought for control.

But passion too long denied, desires too long repressed, could not be held in check. Ryan's self-restraint crumbled when Cristen's hands came stealing around his neck. With a groan he allowed her to tug him down, and they were quickly caught up in the age-old rhythm of love.

His thrusts were deep and strong, and Cristen's hips lifted eagerly to meet each one. Passion built and spiraled. Their movements became rapid, urgent, drawing the knotting tension tighter, ever tighter, until they were taut and eager, reaching…reaching…

And then the explosion rocked them both, and they cried out and clung to each other as the world seemed to disintegrate in a shower burst of ecstasy.

Chapter Ten

A lover. She had a lover. Standing beside the window, holding aside the sheer curtain, Cristen gazed out at the moonlit sky and the scattered lights of the city below. Even now, she could scarcely believe it.

Never in her wildest dreams had she pictured herself in such a situation. Her future had always seemed so clear, so...preordained. The pattern had been set early, and she had taken it for granted that she would spend her life with Bob. She wasn't prepared for a love affair.

Cristen looked over her shoulder at Ryan's recumbent form and felt the familiar warmth well up inside her. He lay sprawled on his back, one arm flung over his head. He had the look of a sated male—relaxed, satisfied, well pleased. Against the pale blue sheets his tanned skin looked darker than ever, his mussed hair a splotch of ebony. His rugged face was gentled in sleep, the strong jaw not quite so hard, the sensual lips slightly parted, revealing the edge of even white teeth. Cristen's gaze tracked downward over his brawny chest, following the path of dark hair that narrowed into a thin line over his concave belly and disappeared beneath the sheet that draped low across his hips. Heat coursed through her, and her breasts grew heavy, achy. Lord, he was so beautifully male.

Recalling the passion they had just shared, the hours of loving and intimacy, Cristen was shocked that she could be aroused again so soon by just the sight of him. She had never considered herself a particularly sensual woman, but with Ryan she was wild and wanton.

It was not a comfortable admission, but Cristen knew it was pointless to deny her feelings. She'd been doing that for months, and it had accomplished nothing.

With a sigh, she dropped the curtain and walked back to the bed. Her chest felt tight and her throat ached as she stared at Ryan with a mixture of longing and doubt. It was also pointless to deny the obvious: ready or not, like it or not, tonight had marked the beginning of a full-fledged, passionate affair.

Her heart seemed to do a little skip at the thought, but Cristen ignored it and let the satin robe slither from her shoulders, tossing it across the bedside chair as she slid back into bed. Careful not to wake Ryan, she pulled the sheet up over her bare breasts and stared at the darkened ceiling. Okay, so you're having an affair. So what? It was bound to happen sooner or later. After all, you're a normal, healthy young woman. So you're not prepared. You can handle it. Other women do. It's not as though you're making a lifelong commitment here. An affair is just that: an affair, a temporary liaison. Surely, if you go into a relationship knowing that it must eventually end, the parting won't hurt so much.

Cristen rolled her head on the pillow and felt a lump form in her throat as her gaze trailed over Ryan's profile. Oh, she would feel sadness, maybe even a little pain, but she would survive it as long as she didn't let things get out of hand.

All I have to do is keep things light, she told herself with firm conviction. No strings, no promises. That's the way to handle it. She turned on her side and closed her eyes, cupping her hand beneath her cheek. Just thank your lucky stars that Ryan O'Malley is not the marrying kind.

A patch of sunlight stretched across the floor, climbed up the side of the bed and painted a golden rectangle on the sheet draping Cristen's sleeping form.

Propped up on his elbow, his head resting against the heel of his hand, Ryan studied her with a profound sense of satisfaction and possessiveness.

God, she's beautiful, he thought, marveling at her creamy skin and the extravagant lashes that lay across her cheeks like tiny fans. Beautiful, fascinating, sexy, adorably stubborn and intense.

And mine.

Ryan released a contented sigh. After last night, there was no doubt about that.

Cristen stirred. The movement sent a curl tumbling across her cheek, its wispy end just touching her nostril. She twitched her nose and batted the air in front of it.

Smiling, Ryan gently pushed the tendril back behind her ear. His hand lingered there, his fingertips rimming the delicate shell, feathering over the tender skin behind it. He was impatient for her to wake up. He wanted to kiss her, to hold her close, to indulge in the nonsensical early-morning banter of lovers. He wanted to make love to her again.

But most of all, he wanted to say, "I love you," to see the look in her eyes when she heard the words...to hear them from her lips.

Was it too soon to propose? Lord, he hoped she didn't think so, because he sure didn't want to wait any longer.

The past few months had been pure hell, lying in the other bedroom night after night, wanting her, loving her, until he was just one big ache.

But no more. He ran his fingers through her tousled hair and watched, fascinated, as the vibrant curls twined about them, then slipped away like strands of shimmering silk. The minute he got back to San Francisco he was going to have a ring made. An emerald, he decided, to match her eyes.

Cristen's breath made a whispery sound as it drifted in and out between her barely parted lips, drawing Ryan's gaze to their soft allure. He wanted to kiss her but resisted the temptation. After the night of loving they had shared he knew she needed the rest. He couldn't remember how many times they had made love, but it had been the small hours of the morning before their hunger for each other was appeased enough to allow sleep. God, it had been heaven.

Determinedly, Ryan dragged his gaze away from her enticing mouth, only to encounter the even greater temptation of her pert, bare breasts.

Cristen slept with the total abandon of a child, arms flung wide, blissfully unaware, and looking like a gorgeous Venus with the sheet tangled about her hips. Ryan stared at the lush feminine flesh, enthralled by the translucent skin, the tiny blue veins that rivered beneath it, the rose velvet nipples, puckered now by the cool air flowing from the vent in the ceiling. He longed to touch her, to draw a sweet nub into his mouth, to feel it harden against his tongue.

He fought it, but the sweet enticement was too much to resist. Leaning forward, he laved a dusky areola with his tongue, then drew back and blew gently. His eyes darkened as he watched it peak.

Ryan rolled forward and half covered Cristen with his body. With his forearms braced on either side of her rib cage, he cupped her breasts with his hands and buried his face in that soft, fragrant valley between. His tongue traced intricate patterns on the silken skin while his long fingers flexed around the tender mounds, lifting, weighing, squeezing, pressing them against his face. At last he trailed his mouth up over the soft flesh and captured a yearning nipple. He worried it gently, first with his teeth, then with his lips, and then, making a sound of satisfaction, he drew the aroused bud into his mouth and suckled deeply.

The feel of Cristen's fingers threading through his hair alerted him that she was awake, and he drew on her harder, slower. She arched her back and made a soft, purring sound, her nails lightly scoring his scalp.

The air felt cool against her wet flesh when he released her and looked up. His blue eyes were heavy-lidded and slumberous, his smile a wicked beguilement. "Good morning, beautiful," he said in a husky voice. "It's about time you woke up."

"Mmm. Good morning." Cristen stretched and rolled her head on the pillow, blinking languorously. "You're better than an alarm clock any day, you know that," she mumbled.

Ryan chuckled and nipped her playfully. "Great! I'm making mad, passionate love to the woman, and she compares me with a mechanical device. You're rough on the ego, babe." He nipped her again, then soothed the tiny pain with his tongue.

"Sorry. I'm not awake yet."

She watched him through slitted eyes, her look tender and passionate. Her fingers slid from his hair and down, tracing the broad, flat muscles that spanned his back, delicately trailing over his spine and shoulder blades. Everything about him pleased her.

Everything that was Ryan pulled at her senses like a strong magnet—the look of him, the feel of him, that wonderful masculine scent that was his alone. His mouth was warm against her skin, his tongue a velvet rasp that sent fire streaking through her. Even the slight abrasive rub of his beard stubble was oddly thrilling. She had never felt this way about a man before—not even Bob—and beneath the wonder of it ran a thread of fear.

Ryan switched his attention to her other breast, and Cristen's fingers dug into his back.

"How about now? Are you awake yet?" he teased before returning to his pleasant task.

"Not...not completely," she gasped as her body responded to his seductive ministrations.

Ryan raised his head and grinned. "Then I guess I'll just have to do something about that." Taking most of his weight on his forearms, he slid upward a few inches, his grin growing wider when the erotic friction between their bodies wrung another gasp from Cristen. Holding her gaze, he settled himself slowly, enjoying her little moan of pleasure as her sensitized nipples pushed up through the mat of hair and pressed against his chest. He rubbed against her, and with his mouth hovering just a hairsbreadth from hers, he murmured, "Because what I have in mind requires your full attention."

His kiss was pure seduction. Warm, slow, persuasive, his mouth rocked against hers, demanding a response. Cristen gave it willingly. With a long moan of pleasure, she went boneless beneath him and wound her arms about his shoulders, giving herself up gladly to the delicious sensations, to the heat and the power.

He lay cradled between her thighs, his body a wondrous heavy weight that pressed her deep into the mattress. She could feel his aroused manhood nudging intimately against her, seeking, yearning. Her body throbbed in answering need, and she kissed him back hungrily, sliding her hands down over his taut back to grasp his buttocks, urging him to complete the embrace.

Obeying her silent command, Ryan made them one,

thrusting into her welcoming, moist warmth with a deep, sure stroke that wrung a cry of joy from both of them.

The time for slow seduction was past. Ryan loved her with bold sureness, demanding and giving with each powerful thrust. Cristen moved against him, matching his ardor, her hips arching and her long legs twining around him. The hours of loving they'd shared the night before might never have been, so great was their need. Their wild rhythm knotted desire tighter and tighter. Dark whispered words, stroking hands, incoherent sounds of pleasure, all fueled their passion.

Ryan inflamed. Cristen burned. And soon the fire consumed them both.

Cristen threw her head back and clutched his shoulders, chanting his name over and over as Ryan's hoarse shout sounded in her ear. A violent shudder shook him, and he collapsed against her, burying his face against her neck, while she hugged him tightly. Their hearts thundered in unison, and for several minutes the only sound in the room was the labored rasp of their breathing.

Replete and sated, Cristen stared at the ceiling and gently stroked Ryan's sweat-sheened back. Feelings swelled within her—delicious, warm, dangerous feelings that she knew could lead only to heartbreak. They made her chest tight and achy and filled her with the desire to weep, but she swallowed hard, widened her eyes and blinked back the threatening tears. You will not be foolish about this, she told herself as she struggled to bring her wayward emotions under control. You will not fall in love with this man. You will not.

After a while, Ryan rolled from her and lay on his back, eyes closed. At last, softly, he said, "I think I've died and gone to heaven." He opened one eye and grinned. "I don't think you can feel this good and live."

Cristen managed a lazy chuckle. "I know."

Turning on his side, Ryan propped himself up on his elbow and smiled down at her. "You awake now?"

"Hmm. Awake but not mobile. It's a miracle," she murmured drowsily. "Usually I don't even know there's a world until after the alarm blasts me out of bed and I'm up and moving. I— Oh, my Lord!" Cristen jackknifed to a sitting position and looked at the clock. "The alarm! I forgot to set it! I'm going to be late!"

She started to scramble for the side of the bed, but Ryan hooked his arm around her waist and hauled her back, pressing her down on the pillow. "Relax, will you? The shop won't fall apart if you're not there before opening. In a few minutes you can call Louise and tell her you're going to be late, but right now we need to have a talk."

"A talk? About what?"

Ryan smiled at her wary expression. "About last night. About us."

"What is there to talk about?" Cristen looked down and plucked at the hair on Ryan's forearm. Striving to appear casual and unconcerned, she said lightly, "After all, we're two adults. We both know that these things happen. Just because two people are strongly attracted to each other and are…uh…sexually compatible, that doesn't mean they have to make a lifelong commitment. You've been a bachelor all these years, so I know you're not interested in a permanent relationship. And I'm certainly not."

Ryan went very still. "Is that what we have? A strong physical attraction for each other?"

"Yes. Of course."

"I see," he said after a moment. "So how do you suggest we handle this 'attraction'?"

"Well, I don't have any experience with this sort of thing, and I haven't given it much thought, but…" A faint flush tinted Cristen's cheeks, and she shifted under Ryan's penetrating stare. "Well…given our living arrangement, I suppose an open relationship would be best."

"Open?" Ryan's brows cocked. "Define *open* for me."

"You know—no strings, no demands. No promises. We simply enjoy each other for as long as it lasts."

"What you're saying is no commitment of any kind. Right?"

"R-right," Cristen replied, suppressing the stab of pain the word brought. "And...and when it's over for either of us, we end it, with no recriminations."

Ryan stared at her in silence for so long that Cristen began to fidget and finally dropped her gaze back to her restless fingers.

"Why won't you tell me about it, sweetheart?" Ryan asked gently, and Cristen grew even more wary.

"Tell you about what? I don't know what you mean."

"Your marriage. I can only assume that it was a disaster. Otherwise you wouldn't be so gun-shy about a serious relationship."

Cristen stiffened. Her expression became remote. "Well, you're wrong. My husband and I got along quite well. We had a very...comfortable marriage."

Making an impatient sound, she shoved aside his arm and sat up. "I really don't have time for this, Ryan. I have to go to work." Self-consciously, she pulled on her peach satin robe and hurried toward the bathroom. At the door she stopped and turned to look back at him, her expression uncertain. "You do agree with me, don't you? About keeping things casual?" She held her breath, waiting for his reply. If he said no, she didn't know what she would do.

"Sure. No problem." With total disregard for his nakedness, Ryan pushed himself up in the bed until he was leaning against the headboard. He draped his wrist over his updrawn knee and flashed her a lopsided grin. "We'll just take it as it comes."

Relief poured through Cristen, but, strangely, along with it came a vague sense of disappointment, which she stoutly refused to acknowledge. "Good, then we— Oh, dear Gussie! Look at the time!" She whirled and dashed into the bathroom, calling over her shoulder, "Call Louise for me, will you, and tell her I'll be there in a half hour. Forty-five minutes at most."

Ryan's grin faded as the door closed behind Cristen. An affair. Hell and damnation!

He snatched up a pillow and hurled it across the room. It bounced off the wall and hit the carpet with a soft, unsatisfying plop, but it was enough to send Theda scurrying for cover.

Fists clenched, Ryan leaned back against the headboard and cursed a blue streak. When he started repeating himself he swung his feet to the floor, propped his elbows on his spread knees and cradled his head in his hands. Hell, it's probably poetic justice, he decided grimly. Never in his life had Ryan deliberately hurt a woman. He had played the field for years, but he'd always been honest and straightforward about his intentions, or rather, lack of them. And all his relationships had been with worldly, experienced women who claimed to feel exactly the same, though he knew there had been a few who had cared more than they had let on.

No strings. Ryan gave a mirthless chuckle, then sighed heavily and pulled his palm down over his face. Hell, he wanted strings, all right. He wanted to bind Cristen to him in every way possible. He wanted to see his ring on her finger and, someday, his child at her breast. He wanted her in his life, in his home, in his bed. Permanently.

And all *she* wanted was an affair. Damn!

"We had a very comfortable marriage," Ryan mimicked nastily under his breath. What the devil did that mean? It sounded deadly dull.

But how could that be? To his way of thinking, marriage with Cristen would be exciting, stimulating and emotionally and physically satisfying. Anything but dull.

Even if her ex-husband was the world's biggest bore, that still didn't explain her aversion to marriage. What had gone wrong?

He wanted to storm into the bathroom and demand an answer, to give in to the uncharacteristic, primitive desire to rant and rave and pound his chest until she told him what he wanted to know. Ryan looked at the closed bathroom door and gritted his teeth. He wouldn't, of course. Caveman tactics were not his style. More important, however, he had a gut feeling that if he pushed her, she would take flight.

Well, it could be worse, he told himself as he stood and gathered up his scattered clothing. At least he was here. The arrangement did have that advantage. And now that some of the barriers were down, others would follow. He'd just have to chip away at them day by day. There was a hell of a lot more between them than just physical attraction, and somehow, some way, he was going to make Cristen see that. He'd been patient for months, and, though it went against the grain, he could manage to be patient for a while longer.

Ryan thought about the loving they had shared. It had been wonderful, beyond his wildest imaginings. A smile—part pleasure and part pure masculine smugness—tugged his mouth as he recalled Cristen's incoherent cries, the feel of her lying beneath him, the passion and eagerness in her face. And sweetest of all, her lingering shyness and her naive joy and astonishment at each shattering climax.

Affair, hell! Ryan thought, his jaw firming as he stalked toward the door. We'll see about that.

The crazy little fool! Cristen might not realize it, but she wasn't cut out for a shallow, temporary relationship. He didn't for one minute believe that she would have slept with him unless she loved him. And Cristen would love just as intensely, just as steadfastly as she did everything else.

It would take subtlety and patience and time, but he would win her over eventually. He had to. Being Cristen's lover was fantastic, but being her husband—that would be heaven.

Louise was frankly delighted with the turn of events. For days after she learned that Cristen and Ryan were lovers she walked around with a smug I-told-you-so smile on her face.

Cristen had had some vague idea that publicly she could just pretend that nothing had changed, and no one would be the wiser, but the moment she arrived at the shop that morning Louise had taken one look at her glowing face and pounced.

"Well, well, well. So it's finally happened, has it?"

"I don't know what you're talking about," Cristen had claimed loftily.

"Don't give me that. Those are stars in your eyes, if I ever saw them. Plus, you've got that look."

"What look?"

"The look of a woman who's been well loved. So come on, fess up."

The fiery blush that crept up Cristen's face had belied her denial, but she still managed to stonewall Louise's probing questions and endless speculation. Then Ryan had arrived and spilled the beans.

Not in the least reticent about proclaiming their new closeness, he had walked into the shop a little before closing, pulled Cristen into his arms and given her a long, passionate kiss that had had Louise whooping for joy and Dora gaping like a banked fish.

Denials had been pointless after that. Cristen had tried to muster some annoyance, but Ryan had merely brushed off her scolding with a grin and another kiss. Much to Cristen's surprise, once her initial embarrassment wore off, she found that she much preferred having everything out in the open.

The week that followed was the happiest, the most exciting that Cristen had ever known. They did nothing special, nothing out of the ordinary, but she breezed through each day on top of the world. She bounded into the shop every morning wearing a smile and left every evening full of eagerness and anticipation, her long, lithe stride eating up the five blocks between the shop and her condo so fast that it seemed her feet barely touched the ground. Even at that, there were times when it was all she could do not to break into a run. She worked as hard as ever, but now there was a constant light, buoyant feeling in her chest, a bubbling elation that gave the whole world a rosy hue and made even the most mundane or painstaking task a breeze.

At thirty, Cristen was experiencing for the very first time the euphoric, walking-on-air feeling that comes with falling in love. Of course, whenever the possibility occurred to her she promptly denied it, but all the signs were there: the fluttery heart, the knotted stomach, delight in the smallest things as long as they did them together, the underlying melancholy at being separated from the beloved for even a short time, the rush of joy at reuniting, the sheer pleasure and contentment of just sharing each other's company.

The highs and lows of loving were things Cristen had missed out on, had not even known existed. Bob Patterson had been such an integral part of her life that their feelings for each other had always just "been there," something that had developed over the years, something they had taken for granted. It hadn't come bursting in on them, bringing these extremes of emotion. Cristen despaired of it…and reveled in it.

She and Ryan made love often during that first, blissful week, whenever and wherever the mood struck them, and each time Cristen was awed anew. Once she came up behind Ryan while he was shaving, slipped her arms around his waist and ran a line of kisses down his spine. Within seconds she found herself stretched out beneath him on the bath mat, responding wildly to his driving urgency.

Afterward, as they lay side by side, too limp to move, Ryan opened one eye and promptly burst out laughing.

"What's so funny?" Cristen demanded. When his guffaws continued, her bafflement turned to indignation, and she gave him a sharp poke in the ribs.

For an answer, Ryan hauled her to her feet and turned her toward the mirror. Cristen gasped and dissolved into giggles.

Smeared over her face, breasts and abdomen was more shaving cream than was on Ryan's face.

Another time Ryan brought home two choice steaks for dinner, but in the midst of preparing the meal together a stolen kiss ignited into passion, and they ended up on a kitchen chair with Cristen astride Ryan's hips, oblivious to everything but each other and the wondrous ecstasy they shared.

So great was their absorption that it was several moments after reaching an explosive fulfillment that they noticed the smoke pouring out of the broiler.

"Our dinner!" Cristen shrieked.

"Dammit to hell! That's twenty bucks worth of choice beef!"

Panicked, Cristen jumped on one foot and then the other, flapping her hands. When she finally came to her senses she yelled, "The fire extinguisher! It's in the pantry!"

Ryan let out a string of curses that turned the air blue and dashed across the room.

Pandemonium reigned for the next thirty seconds. While Ryan sprayed the flaming meat, Cristen threw open the window and fanned the smoke-filled air with a dish towel.

When the crisis was past and the ridiculousness of it all

hit them, they collapsed in each other's arms and laughed until they couldn't stand.

In the end, they dumped the charred steaks into the garbage and ate peanut butter sandwiches.

And neither cared in the least.

Chapter Eleven

Cristen gnawed on her thumbnail and stared at the phone. Her hand inched toward the receiver. At the last second she made a disgusted sound, snatched her fingers back as though she'd been burned and flounced away to resume her restless pacing.

A minute later she was back, staring at the phone with a mixture of longing and irritation. She felt as though she were being drawn to the edge of a precipice, about to lose control and tumble over into an abyss.

I won't call him, she told herself fiercely. I won't.

Foolishly, she had allowed herself to care too much, to become too emotionally involved. She had always missed Ryan when he was in California, but she was not prepared for this despondency, this terrible yearning ache. It angered her. It frightened her.

Cristen turned away again and stalked back across the room. She wouldn't give in to it. She wouldn't call him.

She wouldn't make more of a fool of herself than she already had.

Closing her eyes, she shoved her hands through her hair and pressed her palms tight against her temples, moaning softly as she recalled her behavior the past weekend.

As Sunday, and thus Ryan's departure time, approached she had been eaten up with dread. She told herself over and over that she was being foolish. He would be back on Friday. That it was only five days, after all.

It didn't help.

With every passing hour she had grown tauter, more distracted. She had not been able shake the disturbing feeling that he would not be back. It was irrational, she knew. There was no basis for her fear. She'd kept telling herself that just because Bob had walked away without a word didn't mean that Ryan would. He simply had a business to run.

Yet on Saturday night, when Ryan had taken her into his arms, she'd clung to him, fighting back tears.

Even now, Cristen blushed when she recalled her wanton response to Ryan's lovemaking. His kiss had begun as a slow seduction, but she had been driven by desperation, responding wildly, pressing herself against him and kissing him back with heat and passion. When he had taken her to bed she had writhed and twisted in his arms, frantic for his lovemaking.

It had been the same the next morning. Afterward she'd been horrified to see that her nails had left angry red marks on Ryan's back, but he'd merely flashed his teasing grin and called her a sexy wildcat.

Lord. What must he think of me? Cristen wondered, chagrined at the memory. She had worn her heart on her sleeve like an adolescent. And she hadn't handled the remainder of the day any better.

They'd spent Sunday lazing around the apartment, talking, reading the paper, listening to music. Cristen had tried to enjoy the quiet time together, but she couldn't, for dreading what was to come. The hours had seemed to race by. By the time Ryan was ready to go he had caught her somber mood.

Standing with her hands clasped behind her back, too miserable to speak, Cristen watched him pat his pockets to check for his wallet and keys. Ryan kept clothes in both Houston and San Francisco so that the only thing he carried with him was a briefcase. He riffled through its contents before snapping the lid shut, then looked at Cristen, his eyes reflecting the longing and dread she felt.

"Would you ride to the airport with me?" he asked quietly.

It was a foolish extravagance. Cab fare back from the airport cost an arm and a leg, but not for a moment did she even consider refusing. She would have paid ten times that amount to spend another hour and a half in his company.

It wasn't enough. Far too quickly, Cristen found herself standing at the outer glass wall of the terminal, watching Ryan's plane climb toward the setting sun until it was no more than a speck against the rose-streaked sky.

Heavy-hearted, she trudged through the days that followed on feet of lead. She had no enthusiasm for anything, but she still put in long hours, arriving at the shop early and staying late. Anything to avoid going home to that empty apartment...and even emptier bed.

"Well, it's time you pulled yourself together and quit acting like a lovelorn teenager, for heaven's sake," Cristen scolded, glaring at the silent telephone. "And you will not call him."

A half hour later and ten arguments to the contrary, Cristen shakily dialed Ryan's office number. It was answered on the second ring by the sultry-voiced secretary, who informed her throatily, and with what seemed to Cristen to be a great deal of relish, that Mr. O'Malley had left for the day.

She called his apartment, and at his "Hello" her heart leaped, only to plummet again when she realized it was merely a recorded voice on his answering machine.

Another call, two hours later, produced the same results, and Cristen hung up the phone slowly, feeling as though there were a lump of wet cement sitting on her heart.

Was he with another woman? The thought sent pain searing through her, but she pressed her lips together and struggled against it. It was entirely possible. Ryan was, after all, free to do as he pleased. They might, by tacit agreement, see only each other when he was in Houston, but nothing had been said about those times when he was in San Francisco.

No strings. No commitments. It was the best way. The only way, she told herself stoutly as her listless steps carried her into the bedroom.

One of Ryan's tennis sweatbands lay on the bedside table. Cristen picked it up and curled into a ball on top of the bedspread, absently stroking the soft terry cloth. Her throat ached, and her chin wobbled. Pressing her lips into a tight line, she gazed across the dimly lit room and fought the foolish desire to weep.

The next night Cristen worked even later, staying at the shop until well past eleven, and returned the next morning at eight. If Ryan wanted to call her, he had the shop number, she reasoned. But she'd be darned if she would call him again. Or even sit around waiting to hear from him.

On Thursday she planned to work late again, but just before closing, Louise's husband breezed in and announced his intention of taking them out to dinner, and all Cristen's protests fell on deaf ears.

"You are not going to work again tonight," Louise informed her. "You'll make yourself sick if you keep on at this rate. Now I won't take no for an answer. You're coming out to dinner with us."

Before Cristen knew what hit her, Louise had closed out the register, hustled everyone out and locked the door.

Lord, he was tired.

As Ryan stepped from the conference room into the corridor the scene behind him was disaster. Overflowing ashtrays, wadded pieces of paper, dirty cups containing the cold dregs of countless gallons of coffee, bent paper clips, empty cigarette packs and cigar wrappers littered the long walnut table, whose glossy surface was speckled with sticky spills and dropped ashes. The air in the room was stale. Overhead, a cloud of blue smoke clung to the ceiling. With the exception of Marsha Townsend, the dozen or so people around the table were rumpled and weary, their disgruntled faces reflecting the strain of hours of fruitless negotiation.

Dark looks and harsh words still flew between the opposing sides, but Ryan closed the door on the bickering. Carrying his suit coat slung over his shoulder, he walked toward the double doors at the opposite end of the hall.

In his office he tossed the jacket over the back of the first chair he came to and sat down at his desk. Relishing the quiet and solitude, he raked both hands through his hair, leaned back and released a sigh that was very near a groan.

Beard stubble shadowed his jaw. Lines of fatigue etched his face, and his eyes were red rimmed and bloodshot. His clothes looked as though they'd been slept in—the shirt wrinkled and blousing over his trousers, sleeves rolled up, collar unbuttoned, the loosened necktie hanging askew beneath it.

Ryan rotated his head and sighed when his neck popped. Wearily, he rested his head on the high-backed leather chair and wondered what to try next. He had stepped off the plane Sunday night to find everything in chaos: management in an uproar, the factory workers threatening to walk out, the union reps hostile and uncooperative. Now, after four days of trying to avert a strike, they were still at an impasse, with no solution in sight.

Making a frustrated sound, Ryan arched his back and rubbed his eyes with the heels of his hands. What he needed was a meal, a hot shower and twelve hours of uninterrupted sleep. But more than any of those, he needed Cristen. He wanted to hold her close, to breathe in the sweet fragrance of her hair, her delicious woman scent, to feel her soft skin against his, to sample its taste and texture. He wanted to kiss her and make love to her and hold her through the night.

A stirring warmth surged through his loins at the thought, and he shifted, his mouth twisting wryly. Thinking along those lines was downright foolish, not to mention painful. There was no way he could be with Cristen until this labor problem was settled.

Ryan straightened and looked at the phone, then at his watch. A little after nine—eleven, Houston time. She would be asleep, but maybe she wouldn't mind. He just needed to hear her voice, to talk to her for a little while, he told himself, picking up the receiver.

A few minutes later Ryan scowled as he counted off the rings at the other end of the line. The telephone was right beside Cristen's bed. Even taking into account what a sleepyhead she was, she'd had plenty of time to wake up and answer.

Finally, after a dozen rings, Ryan muttered a curse and hung up. On an off chance, he dialed the shop, but there was no answer there, either.

He checked his watch again, and his frown deepened. Where was she at this hour? Surely she wouldn't go out with another man. Not after what they had shared.

Ryan's hands knotted into fists, and his jaw grew rigid.

He wouldn't put it past her. By now she'd had time for second thoughts. Dammit! It was just the sort of stunt Cristen *would* pull, if for no other reason than to prove to herself that there was nothing serious between them.

During the next twenty minutes he tried both numbers three more times. With each ring of the phone the wrenching ache in his gut grew steadily worse.

He was staring pensively out his window when the door to his office opened. Ryan looked around as Marsha Townsend entered.

"Hi. Am I intruding?"

"No, of course not. Come in." Ryan watched her glide toward him across the slate-blue carpet, amazed anew that Marsha always managed to stay fresh-looking and immaculate. She, too, had been at the bargaining table since early this morning, yet while everyone else looked as though they'd been jerked through a knothole backward, Marsha's trim, wine-red suit and pearl-gray blouse were wrinkle free, her makeup was perfect, and not a single black hair had escaped the intricate chignon at the back of her head.

Settling into one of the leather chairs in front of his desk, Marsha smoothed the pencil-slim skirt over her thighs and knees and crossed her shapely legs, every move slow and deliberate.

Ryan's mouth quirked. Marsha was an intriguing, complicated woman. In a courtroom or at a negotiating table she was a tough-minded attorney; in a social situation, a witty sophisticate; and in the bedroom an insatiable tigress. Yet, even there, she managed to always appear immaculate.

He thought of Cristen lying beneath him, her face flushed and glistening, sweetly contorted in passion, her wild Gypsy curls spread out on the pillow in fiery disarray. A sharp stab of longing pierced his chest, and he barely stifled a sigh.

"How's it going?"

"At this point, it's hard to say. I left them hashing over our offer."

"Which means we'll be here most of the night. That group doesn't seem to be able to agree on anything." Ryan muttered a rude word and rubbed the nape of his neck, then pulled a hand down over his face, his beard stubble making a rasping sound against his palm.

Tipping her head back, Marsha studied Ryan through half-closed eyes. "You need some rest. You look beat."

"Hmm. Aren't we all."

Marsha rose languidly and perched on the corner of Ryan's desk. She leaned back on one palm and gave him a sultry smile. "What do you say we knock off for the night? You could come to my place and soak in my hot tub," she said in a throaty voice. "Afterward, I'll give you a rubdown. I might even be persuaded to grill a couple of steaks."

For a long moment, Ryan looked at her in silence. She was offering much more than a meal and a hot soak, and they both knew it. The brief, torrid affair they'd enjoyed had ended over a year ago, but Marsha was a true hedonist, taking her pleasure when and where she found it. She was perfectly capable of enjoying a night of passion without one iota of emotional entanglement. He suspected that she preferred it that way.

Ryan wouldn't have been human if he hadn't been tempted. Marsha was a beautiful woman and a sexy, imaginative bed partner. He was tired, hungry and frustrated, and his body clamored for the sensual satisfaction she offered.

His gaze slid to the telephone. Was Cristen out with someone else? Would she even care if he took Marsha up on her offer? Ryan sighed and met Marsha's seductive gaze with a rueful grimace. The trouble was, *he* cared. Despite his body's demands, his heart needed more than just a warm, responsive woman. He needed love. He needed caring.

Dammit! He needed Cristen.

"Sorry, Marsha," he said, softening the rejection with an apologetic smile. "I don't think so."

Marsha arched one dark brow but after a moment merely shrugged and slid off the desk. "Okay. It's your loss. If that's the way you want it, then I guess I'll go back and butt heads with the opposition some more."

Watching the deliberate provocative sway of her hips as she sauntered across the room, Ryan grinned. So help me, Cristen, if you've been out with someone else, I may just beat you.

All day Friday Cristen was so jittery that she could barely work. Half expecting Ryan to come directly to the shop from the airport, she tensed and looked up whenever the bell over the door jingled. Each time she told herself to stop acting like an idiot. Just because she'd been eaten up with longing and loneliness didn't mean that Ryan felt the same. He'd certainly been quick to agree to an open relationship, she reminded herself irritably. No doubt he'd been out with some gorgeous California blonde every night.

Even so, after the shop closed Cristen all but ran home. Her disappointment at finding the apartment empty was immense. She told herself that he'd probably just missed his flight, but even so, it was all she could do not to weep.

Six hours later she no longer even tried to hold back her tears. Sitting in the dark, curled up in a ball of misery in the corner of the sofa, she finally accepted that Ryan wasn't coming.

It serves you right, she told herself miserably. You knew better than to fall for that handsome charmer. You were just asking to get hurt. Theda rubbed against her legs, meowing her sympathy, and Cristen absently stroked the cat's back. This was probably his way of telling her it was over. Her laugh was short and mirthless. She was no expert on affairs, but surely theirs had been the shortest on record. Ryan was obviously a man who enjoyed the chase much more than the victory.

Abruptly, she scrubbed at her wet cheeks with the heels of her hands. "Well, I don't care if he never comes back," she vowed, lurching to her feet and dumping a protesting Theda in the process. She stomped from the living room and down the hall to Ryan's bedroom like a storm trooper on the rampage. The man was a faithless, feckless wretch, and she was better off without him. "If he wants out, I'll make it easy for him," she muttered as she scooped up the contents of his dresser drawers and dumped them onto the bed.

At eleven forty-seven Sunday night Ryan stepped into the apartment, flipped on the light, reset the burglar alarm, turned and promptly barked both shins on the mountain of luggage piled in the entryway.

Cursing, he staggered forward through the toppling cases, flinging his arms wide in a desperate effort not to fall flat on his face. The cases crashed to the floor, skidded across the slick surface, slammed into the walls and bounced off again. One hit Ryan in the ankle, and he roared like an enraged bull. Holding his injured leg, he hopped around on one foot and spewed out a stream of imaginative curses that should have blistered the paint off the wall.

In the midst of the unholy racket, Cristen came running in from the bedroom, sleep rumpled, wide-eyed and wearing a black nightgown that was made of a little silk and lace and a lot of imagination.

"Ryan!" She stopped short, joy surging through her at the sight of him, but she quickly squelched the traitorous emotion.

At the sound of her voice, Ryan looked up and glared, his irritation not in the least mollified by the alluring sight she made. "Cristen, what the hell is all this?"

His tone brought Cristen's chin up. "Your luggage," she replied succinctly.

"I can see that. But what the devil is it doing here?"

"I packed your things for you."

"What do you mean, you— Ouch! Dammit," he swore when he took a step toward her. He hobbled another couple of steps, then stopped and put his hands on his hips and pinned her with a narrow-eyed stare. "Are you saying you're throwing me out?"

"I'm merely making things easier for both of us."

"Easier! What the hell does that mean?"

Cristen flinched at his explosive tone, but she held her ground. "Oh, come on, Ryan. I don't need a house to fall on me to get the message. You traipsed off to California and got so wrapped up in your life out there that you didn't even spare me a thought, much less a five-minute phone call. And to top it off, you didn't even bother to let me know that you wouldn't be back on Friday, as usual."

"Didn't my secretary call and tell you I'd probably have to work straight through the weekend?"

"That sultry-voiced sexpot who works in your office? No, she didn't."

"Maybe if you'd stay home once in a while so a person could reach you—"

"You expect me to hover around the phone like some lovesick teenager, waiting for you to remember that I exist? Well, think again, buster!"

"Dammit, Cristen! I was working!"

"Ha! Don't give me that. I called your office."

"And I called you. Several times, quite late at night." He started toward her, menacing despite his limp. "I want to know where you were."

He was angry. Truly angry. Cristen's eyes widened as

it hit her for the first time that Ryan—easygoing, devil-may-care Ryan—was actually seething. The knowledge sent a little thrill of fear racing down her spine, but she would have died before letting him know it. She faced him belligerently, her hands on her hips. "Well, that's just too bad. You have no right to question me about what I do. We have an agreement—"

"You can forget that 'open relationship' crap," he roared, slicing his hand through the air and making her jump. "That whole deal is off, as of right now."

"What! Y-you can't—"

"I can and I will." Coming to a stop in front of her, he grasped her shoulders and gave her a little shake. His face was set and implacable, and his eyes blazed like blue fire. "Don't talk to me about no strings and no demands. I just spent the most god-awful week of my life, working my tail off and all the time worrying myself sick, wondering if you were seeing someone else or if you'd had second thoughts about us."

All the fight went out of Cristen, and she looked at him with amazement. "Really?"

With that one breathless word, Ryan's anger melted. He looked into her sweetly vulnerable face, filled with hope and longing and just a lingering trace of fear, and felt his heart contract.

"Really." With a groan, he pulled her tightly against his chest. As her arms wrapped around his back and she nestled against him, he tilted his head to one side and rested his cheek against her hair.

"God, how I missed you," he murmured, rocking her gently. "And I did try to call you, sweetheart. Several times, but you were never here."

"I...I tried to call you, too. At your office and your apartment."

"I was tied up in meetings with union reps most of the time, trying to avert a strike. That was why I had to stay over. And I did ask my secretary to call you and let you know. Honest.''

''When you didn't show up on Friday, I thought that you'd lost interest,'' she confessed softly against his dark suit vest.

''Ah, love.'' Ryan closed his eyes and tightened his hold and continued his gentle swaying. Where did this insecurity come from? Never would he have guessed that his determined, intense, self-assured Cristen would suffer from such doubt, be so heart-wrenchingly vulnerable. It went totally against her nature. The only answer was that she had been hurt badly in the past. Most likely by that damned ex-husband of hers, Ryan thought grimly.

Cristen looked up and touched his jaw with the tips of her fingers. ''I didn't see anyone else while you were gone,'' she assured him, her eyes soft and earnest. ''On the evenings I wasn't working I was with Louise and John.''

Ryan grinned. ''Good.'' He bent and kissed her long and hard. When he finally raised his head, his smile and the glint in his eye held pure devilment. ''But while we're still on the subject, I think we'd better discuss this relationship of ours.''

''Oh?'' Cristen's heart hammered.

Without releasing his hold, Ryan began to walk her backward, through the door and down the hall. ''Uh-huh.'' He nibbled a line of kisses down her neck as he maneuvered her into her bedroom and across to the bed. ''It's time to renegotiate our contract.'' The backs of Cristen's knees struck the mattress, bringing them to a halt.

Ryan nipped her earlobe with gentle savagery. ''Actually, I'm getting pretty good at it.''

''Oh, really?'' Cristen managed breathlessly.

''Yeah. So listen up.'' He cleared his throat; then his warm breath wafted across her skin. ''First of all, forget that 'keep it light' junk. I'm crazy about you, woman, and

I'm through pretending otherwise.'' With the tip of his tongue, he traced each delicate swirl of her ear. Cristen shivered and clutched him tighter as her knees turned to mush. ''Second, from now on our agreement has an exclusivity clause. You're mine and I'm yours, and that's the way it is. Period. I refuse to spend another day eaten up with jealousy, wondering where you are and what you're doing and who you're doing it with.''

''Oh, is that so?'' Cristen tried to imbue her voice with haughty indignation, but it came out all breathless and quavery. Anyway, she was finding his terms very much to her liking. And the thought of Ryan actually jealous of her sent warmth streaking through her veins.

''Yep. If I catch you so much as looking at another man, I'll turn you over my knee. Right after I deck the jerk.''

''Primitive beast.''

''Hmm. You bet.''

Ryan kissed his way across her cheek to her mouth. He probed its corners, then drew her lower lip into his mouth and sucked gently. ''And third,'' he whispered as his hands charted her shape, ''from now on, we'll be open with each oth—''

He stopped abruptly when his hand encountered the fragile lace that molded her breasts. He backed up a half step and looked her over, his eyes going wide as he took in the skimpy wisp of black silk and lace that skimmed her body. ''What is this thing you've got on?'' he asked in a raspy voice.

''It's a nightgown.''

''The hell you say.''

He bent and kissed the rounded tops of her breasts and the scented valley in between, then worked his way downward, following the plunging V neckline all the way to her waist. ''Honey, what this thing is, is an invitation,'' he murmured against her skin with a wicked chuckle as he slipped the tiny straps off her shoulder and began to peel the provocative garment down over her hips. "One that I accept."

Chapter Twelve

Summer sizzled on through July and August, then waned as September lengthened into one of those brilliant, perfect autumns that were so rare along the Gulf Coast. Trees burst into flame. The air was crisp and dry with a faint nip, the sky a clear cobalt blue.

It was a halcyon time for Cristen. Never had she been as happy, as contented. Never had life been so sweet.

The expansion was complete, and business was great. Her personal life was wonderful and exciting. The love she had fought so hard to deny, then to contain, burgeoned and grew day by day. It filled her heart and colored her life and made her happy beyond measure.

When Ryan was in Houston, they spent every spare minute in each other's company, loving, laughing, sharing everything; fun times, quiet moments, mundane chores—it didn't matter as long as they were together. And with each passing day they grew closer and their relationship deepened.

He learned that her favorite color was blue and that she cried at sad movies. She learned that two things he absolutely would not eat were liver and Brussels sprouts. He learned that Cristen's secret fantasy was to play the banjo. She discovered that he was a voracious reader of mystery novels and had a ticklish spot just below his third rib.

They went to an open-air concert at Miller Theater and a baseball game at the Astrodome. He helped her pick out new draperies for the living room, and she helped him wash and wax his car. Ryan liked country-and-western and bluegrass music, but for her he donned a tux and took her to the ballet and the symphony.

Because Ryan adored sports of all kinds, Cristen tried to develop an interest in them, too, and to participate whenever possible. She was game to try anything and gave it her all, but it soon became apparent that sports were not her forte.

When Ryan took her golfing, she dug a hole in the ground with her club every time she swung at the ball, beaned another player with a wild drive and scored in the high two hundreds. On the tennis courts she hit the ball like Babe Ruth swinging for a homer, usually sending it sailing over the backstop. When they went fishing, she hooked an old shoe, a cottonwood tree and the seat of Ryan's pants.

He didn't even consider letting her on a handball court.

After she skinned her knees playing softball and scored for the opposition in a touch football game, Ryan tried to gently dissuade her from trying anything else, but by then Cristen was determined to find at least one sport at which she could excel. Ryan considered—and rapidly discarded—archery, skeet shooting, skydiving and hang gliding. In the end he finally decided he would teach her to bowl. The worst she could do there was throw gutter balls, he reasoned.

''Now then, you put your thumb and two middle fingers

in the holes and place your left hand under the ball, like so,'' Ryan explained, demonstrating.

"Like this?"

"Yes. That's fine." He stepped behind Cristen and reached around her, covering her arms with his. "Now, I want you to concentrate on that little blue spot on the floor while you glide forward—" he gave her a little nudge "—taking one, two steps, you bring the ball back, swing forward on the third and release, keeping your wrist locked as you do, all in one continuous motion. Got that?"

"Yes. Yes, I think so."

Ryan walked her through it once more, just to be sure, then stepped back a few paces to watch.

With her lower lip clamped between her teeth, Cristen cradled the ten-pound ball in her hands and stared down the alley at the triangle of pins. *Three steps. Swing back. Swing forward. Let go. Three steps. Swing back. Swing forward. Let go.*

She repeated the litany several more times, drew a deep breath and took a step. Concentrating for all she was worth, she took the second step, swung her arm back...and the ball went flying out of her grasp, straight out behind her like a cannon shot.

"Holy shi— Arghhh!"

Cristen gasped and spun around, just in time to see the bowling ball come down on Ryan's right foot.

"Ow! Ow! Ow! Ow!"

"Oh, Ryan! Oh! I'm so sorry!"

Cursing like a sailor, Ryan hopped around in a crazy circle, his face screwed up in an agonized grimace. Cristen dithered around him, flapping her hands and making sounds of distress.

Finally he collapsed on the players' bench. Cristen dropped to her knees at his feet and reached for his injured foot. "Here, let me take your shoe off so we can see how bad it is."

"No! Don't touch it!" Ryan yelled, but Cristen was already unlacing the shoe. "Ow! *Ooooww!* Watch it!"

Cristen tossed his shoe aside and peeled down his sock with as much gentleness as haste would allow. When his toes emerged she gasped and sat back on her heels.

His big toe and the area just above it were already swelling and beginning to discolor. "Oh, Ryan," Cristen whispered mournfully. She looked up at him with tears in her eyes. "I'm so sorry, darling. I didn't mean—"

"I know. I know," Ryan said through clenched teeth. "Don't...worry about it. The important thing...now is to...get to a doctor."

"Oh! Yes, of course!" Cristen shot to her feet and snatched up her purse. "I'll get someone to help you to the car."

"No. Don't...do that. Just give me a hand up. I...can make it."

Cristen tried to argue, but Ryan was insistent. Reluctantly, she helped him to his feet and slipped her arm around his waist. It was a slow struggle, and several times they both nearly toppled over, but with Ryan leaning heavily on Cristen and hopping on one foot they finally made it to the parking lot.

As they approached the Jaguar Cristen asked for the keys.

"Keys?" The one-word question reflected wariness that bordered on horror.

"Ryan, I have to unlock the car."

"Oh," he replied sheepishly.

"And I'll need the keys to drive."

"*Drive!* You're going to drive? Oh, no. Not *my* Jag. Absolutely not. I've seen the way you drive."

"Will you be sensible? It's that or call an ambulance. You certainly can't drive. Why, you can't even bear to put your foot on the ground."

"But, Cris, this is my Jag" he said plaintively.

"Yes, darling. I know." Cristen propped Ryan against the side of the car and dug into his jeans pocket for the keys.

"It's a 1975 XKE."

"I know that, too," she said soothingly as she unlocked the car door. Taking advantage of his temporary shock, she gently but firmly maneuvered him into the passenger seat.

"It's a classic."

"Uh-huh."

She slammed the door and hurried around to the driver's side. When she slid in under the wheel and put the key into the ignition, Ryan's shock turned to panic. "Cris, I don't think this is a good idea."

Mentally giving thanks that Ryan had backed into the parking space, Cristen ignored him, gripped the wheel with all her might and stomped on the accelerator.

The car died with a shudder.

"Dammit! You don't just give it gas!" Ryan yelled. "You've got to use the clutch and put it in first gear."

"Oh." Cristen did as he said and hit the gas again…and the Jaguar shot backward, tires squealing.

Luckily, there wasn't a car in the slot behind them.

"You're in reverse! Hit the brakes! Hit the brakes!"

Cristen did—with both feet. The car screeched to a halt and died, and Ryan pitched forward, hitting his head on the windshield and his injured foot on the underside of the dash.

"*Ahhhhhh!*" Ryan grabbed his abused foot and propped it on his other knee. While he rocked back and forth over it, moaning, Cristen restarted the engine and struggled with the gearshift. Finally finding first, she hit the gas pedal again. This time the car moved forward in a series of jarring, erratic little hops.

"The clutch!" Ryan groaned. "You've got to synchronize it with the gas!"

"Of all the stupid... Why don't they make these things with automatic transmissions?" Cristen grumbled.

This time Ryan's groan had nothing to do with pain.

It took three more tries for her to get the hang of it, but when everything finally meshed they peeled out of the parking lot as if they were rocket powered. Cristen burned rubber for a half a block before the tires got traction. Then she really poured on the speed.

"No! Not the freeway! Cris, I don't think you should—Oh, my God!"

Cristen zoomed up the entrance ramp doing seventy. She cut across four lanes of traffic, drawing a blast from the air horn of an eighteen-wheeler and missing a station wagon by a hair. Ryan turned pasty gray and mumbled something that sounded like a prayer.

A mile down the road she spotted the interchange, but there wasn't a break in the traffic. Cristen held her hand down on the horn and brazened her way through.

"Oh, God. Oh, God. Oh, God," Ryan chanted.

Behind them, tires screamed and horns blared as the Jag tore around the looping underpass onto another freeway.

Two exits later she sent the car hurtling down the ramp at the same death-defying speed and began to make her way through an older, sedate part of town, heading for the medical center.

Clutching the armrest with one hand and his foot with the other, Ryan alternated between cursing, praying and moaning as Cristen careered through traffic, grinding gears, skidding around turns and striking terror into the hearts of other motorists.

At the hospital she turned too sharply and bumped over a corner, then scraped the right tires along the curb before coming to a screeching halt at the emergency entrance. Pale and shaken, Ryan breathed a heartfelt "Oh, thank you, Lord" and leaned his head back against the seat as Cristen cut the engine and scrambled from the car.

In no time the hospital attendants emerged, bundled Ryan onto a gurney and whisked him away to a treatment room, leaving Cristen to deal with the emergency room nurse and her endless forms and questions.

Once that chore was handled, Cristen paced the floor of the waiting room for what seemed like hours, riddled with guilt and worried sick. *Oh, you fool. How could you have been so careless?* she berated herself. *You've probably maimed him for life. Oh, Lord. What if it's serious? What if he ends up walking with a limp? He'll never forgive you.*

After another restless circuit of the room, Cristen stepped to the door again, just in time to see Ryan being wheeled down the hall in a wheelchair.

His right leg was encased in a cast from toe to knee, and he looked a bit peaked, but when he saw her hovering uncertainly in the doorway, a lopsided grin kicked his mustache up at a rakish angle. "Hi, slugger. Ready to go another round?"

Relief poured through Cristen at his teasing tone, and she rushed forward to meet him. "Oh, darling, how do you feel? What did the doctor say? Is it bad?"

Ryan chuckled and took her hand. "One broken bone and a massive bruise. I have to stay off it as much as I can. But it should be good as new in six to eight weeks."

"Are you in any pain?"

"No, they gave me something. But I am bushed. What I really need is a comfortable bed, someplace where I can elevate this leg."

"Oh! Of course. You just wait right here and I'll go bring the car around."

"Oh, no. Not that again." Ryan closed his eyes briefly and gave an eloquent shudder. "Cristen, my love, I adore you, but I'd rather run naked through a pit full of hungry alligators than get back in that car with you driving. Now why don't you just go call Louise and John and see if they'll come get us. I can stretch out in the back of Louise's van, and John can drive the Jag back to the apartment."

Cristen protested just on principle, but it was a half-hearted token at best. She didn't relish maneuvering that powerful machine through Houston traffic again. When it came to cars she had only two speeds: stop and wide open. And wide open in that beast was supersonic.

Their friends were happy to help, though they did tease both Cristen and Ryan unmercifully.

"For heaven sake's, didn't you explain to her that you throw the ball *toward* the pins?" Louise scolded as she and John assisted Ryan into the back of the van.

"I think so," Ryan said solemnly.

"Louise! It was an accident. The ball just slipped out of my fingers."

John clapped Ryan on the back. "In the future just remember that you have to be quick on your feet when you're teaching Cristen anything physical, because she goes at everything like fighting fire."

"So I've learned." Grinning at Cristen, Ryan gingerly lowered himself onto the bench seat at the rear of the van.

"Well, at least two good things have come out of all this. I finally get to drive a Jaguar, and—" John paused and winked at Ryan "—you've become a member of a very exclusive club."

"What's that?"

"The I-survived-Cristen's-driving club," both Louise and John said in unison, then burst out laughing, with Ryan quickly joining in.

"Very funny," Cristen grumbled.

It took some doing, but they finally got Ryan home. Once they had him settled in bed, Louise and John left, promising to return the next day with a pair of crutches. As they went out the door, John couldn't resist adding, "And a club T-shirt."

Cristen fussed over Ryan like a worried mother, straightening his blanket, fluffing his pillow and asking him every five minutes if she could get him anything. Even though it had been an accident, she couldn't help but feel guilty, and she was anxious to make it up to him, but Ryan thwarted her efforts when he succumbed to the pain medicine the doctor had given him and fell asleep.

Cristen paced. Every twenty minutes or so she peeked in at Ryan, but he slept on peacefully. She made herself an omelet for dinner, then put on her nightgown and tried to watch television, but she abandoned that after a while in favor of one of Ryan's mystery novels.

Around ten, just as she reached a hair-raising passage, Ryan nearly scared her out of her skin when he awoke and bellowed her name. After helping him to the bathroom, she brought him a dinner tray containing three hearty roast beef sandwiches, a huge bowl of vegetable soup and a tumbler of milk, all of which he devoured with his usual healthy appetite.

When Cristen had dealt with the dishes she returned to Ryan and sat down beside him on the bed. "How do you feel?" she asked, reaching out to touch his cheek with her fingertips.

"Fine."

"Is there any pain?"

"Hardly a twinge."

"Ryan, I am so sor—"

"Shh." He hushed her with a forefinger against her lips. "It wasn't your fault, so no more apologies. Okay?"

Reluctantly she nodded, and he removed his finger.

"Is there anything else you want?"

A hint of a smile played about Ryan's mouth, but there was no amusement in his hot, hooded gaze. It skimmed downward over her neck and shoulders and came to rest on her creamy breasts, swelling above the low-cut apricot lace gown. When he looked up, his eyes were a dark, stormy blue. ''Yes,'' he said in a low, husky voice. ''You.''

A surprised giggle shot up out of Cristen's throat. ''Ryan! You know we can't.''

''The hell we can't.''

''But…but your foot—''

''You just let me worry about my foot.''

Ryan reached out and traced one long finger along the lacy edge of her nightgown, leaving a trail of fire on her skin. Cristen's eyes grew cloudy as a delicious shiver rippled through her. Smiling, Ryan slipped the finger into her cleavage, hooked the low neck of her gown and tugged her closer.

Cristen did not even try to resist. When Ryan touched her like that her common sense flew out the window and her will and her flesh turned as weak as mush.

''We'll take it nice and easy,'' he murmured.

Very deliberately, he eased first one, then the other strap from her shoulders. At his urging, Cristen obediently slipped her arms free, and the lacy garment fell in soft folds about her waist. Bracing himself up on one elbow, Ryan touched the tip of his tongue to her nipple. When it peaked he mouthed it gently. Over and over. The sweet torment made Cristen cry out, and she clutched his shoulders, digging her nails into firm muscles. At last he drew the tender bud deep into his mouth and suckled with slow, strong suction.

Cristen threw her head back and gasped. ''Oh, darling! Darling!''

Cold air hit her wet flesh as he abandoned it to lavish the same attention on the other breast. Cristen arched her spine and clasped his head, wanting, needing more.

When she was almost incoherent with pleasure, Ryan eased back on the pillow, pulling her with him. ''Lift up your hips, love,'' he murmured as he pushed her nightgown downward. ''There, that's it.''

As the nightgown slithered to the floor, Cristen found herself lying half over Ryan. He felt warm and wonderful and masculine and sexy, and her heartbeat felt like a trip-hammer when her breasts pushed into the crisp mat of hair on his chest. But then her toe bumped against his cast, and she stiffened. "Ryan, I don't think—"

"Don't think," came his urgent whisper. "Just feel. Feel how much I want you. How much I need you." He took her hand and guided it downward, and as her fingers enclosed his velvet hardness he moaned.

"Did I hurt you?" Cristen jerked her hand away and tried to pull back, but Ryan tightened his hold and chuckled.

"Hardly. Just relax, sweetheart. Everything will be fine."

He lifted her more fully atop him and rocked his hips against her, chuckling again at her gasp of pleasure. "Now then. I want you to do exactly as I say."

As his mouth played with her ear he murmured his instructions in a deep, dark voice that sent a hot flush sweeping over Cristen from her toes to the roots of her hair.

"Ry-an!"

His wicked chuckle made dust of her weak protest, and, shyly at first, then with growing boldness, she complied.

"Yes, that's it," Ryan gasped. "That's it. Yes. Oh, God, yes."

"Ahhhhh, love."

For the first few weeks Ryan lazed around the apartment, staying off his foot as much as possible and conducting a great deal of his business by phone. Cristen fussed over him like a banty hen with one chick, seeing to his every need, coming home at noon and preparing a hot lunch and rushing back the minute the shop closed. More than once Louise got so exasperated with her anxious clock-watching that she shooed her out early just to get rid of her.

Ryan mastered the crutches quickly. By the fourth week the doctor gave him permission to return to the construction site, provided he didn't overdo. Transportation was a problem, but Ryan solved it by hitching a ride with his foreman.

To spare himself the rigors of air travel he continued to confer with California office by phone daily and had one of his executives shuttle back and forth with papers that needed his signature and whatever else that required his personal attention.

Cristen was delighted with the arrangement. It was heaven not to face those partings and those long, lonely days without him. She adored knowing Ryan would be there when she got home, sharing her life with him, going to sleep in his arms and awakening to his soft, persuasive kisses.

"If I'd known it would keep you here, I'd have broken your foot sooner," she teased one night as she lay with her head on Ryan's chest.

He chuckled and ruffled her hair. "Yeah, well, don't get any ideas. I happen to be quite fond of my bones just the way they are."

Cristen sighed dramatically. "Honestly. I get no cooperation out of you." She pursed her lips and blew out a gentle stream of air, ruffling his chest hair, then turned her head and nipped the small bud nestled there.

Ryan's reaction was swift and masterful and thoroughly satisfying. In a blink, he rolled her to her back and blanketed her body with his. He propped himself up on his elbows and cupped her breasts in his palms, pushing the lush mounds together. "You want cooperation?" he growled lovingly as his head descended. "I'll show you cooperation, woman."

* * *

The only clouds on the horizon were those occasional times when she allowed herself to wonder what the future held. Cristen was happy with things just the way they were, but she knew, deep down, that no relationship remained static. Eventually, they had to make a real commitment to each other…or part. Both possibilities terrified her.

For the most part, though, she pushed those thoughts to the back of her mind. With her usual single-minded determination, she concentrated on the present, reveling in the joy that was hers now.

Cristen had hoped to have the full eight weeks, but it wasn't to be. At the beginning of the sixth, Ryan's top executive called with news that they had been asked to bid on providing and installing a sophisticated security system in an enormous petrochemical plant in Oklahoma. Within minutes Ryan was packing a bag and making flight reservations.

"But I don't see why you have to go," Cristen complained. "Why can't you send someone else?"

"Because this is the biggest account my company's ever had a shot at, and I'm going to make sure no one else goofs it up." Ryan snapped his case shut. "If you'll carry this down to the lobby for me, I think I can manage my briefcase." He swung around on his crutches and started for the dresser, but then he caught sight of Cristen's woebegone expression.

Changing course, he took two thumping steps that brought him up in front of her, and with the crutches braced firmly under his arms, he reached out and grasped her shoulders. "It won't be for long, sweetheart. Just a few days at most. I'll be back before you know it." He dropped a soft kiss on her mouth, but when he raised his head she was still the picture of dejection.

When his coaxing smile didn't work, Ryan took a deep breath and said weakly, "Look…uh…why don't you come to the airport with me. You…'' He stopped and swallowed hard. ''You can drive my car and bring it back.''

That did bring a smile to Cristen's face. ''Oh, Ryan,'' she said, laughing. Looping her arms around his waist, she pressed her cheek against his chest. ''I wouldn't ask that kind of sacrifice from you. I'll take a cab, as I usually do.''

But she was touched. Touched…and a bit frightened. For the offer spoke plainly of the depth of Ryan's feelings, and that was something she wasn't ready to face yet.

At the airport, Cristen tried to convince Ryan to use a wheelchair, but he wouldn't hear of it. Consequently, the walk down the concourse took twice as long. They reached the gate just as the passengers from the previous leg of the flight were deplaning. Cristen was so intent on getting Ryan safely through the crowd that she didn't see the couple coming toward her until she bumped into them.

''Oh! I'm terribly sorry, I—'' She stopped short as she focused on the man, and all the color drained from her face.

''Bob!''

Chapter Thirteen

After a stunned moment, Bob smiled uneasily. "Hello, Cris."

Too numb to speak, Cristen merely stared at her ex-husband. What did you say to a man who had walked away without a word?

Beside her, Ryan grew very still, his narrowed gaze moving from one to the other.

Cristen didn't notice. At that moment she wasn't aware of anything but Bob Patterson. It seemed so strange, after a two-year separation, to be looking at that face she knew as well as her own. He hadn't changed outwardly, except that his sandy hair had receded a bit more. He was still too thin, still had that diffident, nervous air about him. And he still dressed in ultraconservative clothes.

Bob's naturally ruddy complexion turned a shade redder under her steady gaze, and he shifted his feet. "Uh...how've you been? You're looking good."

"Fine. I've...I've been fine. And you?" The banal chitchat tightened the vise that was squeezing Cristen's chest. Sweet heaven! *We're talking as if we barely know each other, and we spent our entire lives together. We were married, for Pete's sake!*

"Actually, I'm terrific," Bob said sheepishly. He hesitated, then took a deep breath and seemed to draw himself up taller.

Cristen had been so spellbound by the sight of him that she hadn't noticed the woman next to him until he put his arm around her shoulder and drew her nearer. Cristen's gaze shifted, and once again shock hit her like a fist to the solar plexus.

"Cris, I'd like you to meet my wife, Vicki." Giving the petite woman a tender look, Bob squeezed her arm and said gently, "Darling, this is Cristen."

"Hello, Cristen. It's very nice to meet you. I've heard so much about you from Bob that I feel I already know you."

As though in a trance, Cristen accepted the proffered hand and mumbled a reply. It struck her that the woman was her opposite. In her heels Cristen was a couple of inches taller than Bob, but Vicki's head barely reached his chin. The sleek dark cap of hair framing her heart-shaped face in no way resembled Cristen's own riot of fiery curls. Vicki was petite, doll-like, with big brown, spaniel eyes and that soft, fragile look that men found so appealing.

And she was at least seven months pregnant.

Ryan coughed discreetly, drawing Cristen's attention.

"Oh, I'm sorry," she said quickly. "Ryan, this is Bob and...and Vicki Patterson. Ryan O'Malley."

Greetings and handshakes were exchanged. From Ryan's expression, Cristen knew he hadn't made the connection between her and Bob, though he was still looking at both of them strangely.

When the amenities were over an awkward silence began to build, and Bob grew more discomfitted. "Well, uh, so how's the shop going?"

"Very well. We've even expanded." Cristen tried to focus her attention on Bob, but over and over her gaze kept straying to Vicki...and her protruding abdomen. Bitterly Cristen recalled how in the past, whenever she brought up the subject of starting a family, Bob had had a dozen excuses why they should wait.

"Good. Good. And are you still living in the condo?"

Damn you! she silently fumed. In two years you haven't even bothered to call to see if I was alive. Why ask these inane questions now? "Yes, of course. It's convenient. And I have a roommate now."

Her failure to identify him as that roommate drew a sharp look from Ryan. "Look, I hate to break this up, Cristen," he said, tugging her elbow, "but if I don't get a move on, I'm going to miss my plane. All the other passengers have already boarded."

Bob was clearly happy to escape the tense situation, and after a flurry of hasty goodbyes, the next thing Cristen knew they were heading in opposite directions.

She walked alongside Ryan in a stupor. Mercifully, some deep, primal instinct for survival had taken over, and her mind and her emotions were numb. But a tight knot of pressure was building in her chest, at its core a hurt so deep that it could not be acknowledged. Not yet. Not here.

At the entrance to the boarding tunnel, Ryan braced his weight on one crutch, hooked his hand around Cristen's neck and pulled her close for a hard kiss. She was barely aware of it.

Concern and a touch of panic marked his expression when he raised his head. "What is it, darling? What's wrong?"

"Nothing. I...nothing," she managed, staring at him distractedly.

"Cristen, dammit, something—"

"Sir, you really must board now," the flight attendant called. "We're ready to leave."

Frustrated and worried, Ryan cursed under his breath and shot the woman a blistering look. "Look, I'll call you as soon as I get to the hotel, and we'll talk." He kissed Cristen again and grimaced at her blank expression. Then he swung away down the tunnel, his crutches thumping on the thin floor.

Usually Cristen watched until Ryan's plane taxied out onto the runway, but before he was out of sight she turned and walked away. Like a wounded animal going to ground, she instinctively headed for home.

Forty-five minutes later, when she entered the apartment, it was dark. She didn't notice. She didn't care. With zombielike movements, she crossed the shadowy living room and sank down into a chair.

Sitting absolutely still, she stared into the darkness. The pressure in her chest was growing, and her throat was so tight that she could barely swallow. The only sounds were the tick of the mantel clock and her slow, measured breathing.

For a long time she struggled to hold on to the blessed numbness, but it was impossible to keep at bay all the raging emotions that churned just below the surface. Gradually, inexorably, they pushed their way through the unnatural calm, bringing a rush of pain that welled up inside her, searing her to her very soul.

She felt like such a fool. All this time she'd been telling herself that Bob had needed freedom. All their lives she had always been the leader, the stronger of them, and when he left she had assumed that he had gotten fed up with going through life as part of a pair, that he needed time and space to try his wings, to be on his own. It had hurt, terribly at first, but after a while she had been able to accept it.

But now... Now, after seeing him very obviously hap-

pily married to another woman, Cristen knew that she had
only been fooling herself. It wasn't marriage that Bob had
rejected. He had rejected her.

She no longer loved Bob. And she certainly didn't want
him back. But that didn't make it hurt any less. By leaving
the way he had, by not being honest with her, he had dealt
a crippling blow to both her pride and her self-esteem.

Beside her, the telephone rang, shattering the silence and
making her jump. She glanced at it, then looked away. It
shrilled several times, then stopped, only to start up again
a couple of minutes later. This time it rang a full five
minutes before the caller finally gave up. Cristen simply
tuned it out.

Where had things gone wrong? she wondered. When
had Bob stopped loving her? Or had he ever loved her? If
he had only told her how he really felt years ago, they
could have avoided all this heartache and salvaged a
friendship. Did all those years they shared mean so little
to him?

For over an hour Cristen sat in the dark, torturing herself
with endless, unanswerable questions. Finally she turned
on the lamp beside the chair. In a haze of pain, she walked
into the hall and retrieved a scrapbook from the back of
the storage closet.

Cristen ran her hand lovingly over the front of the album
as she returned to the living room and sank down on the
floor in front of the sofa. Age had mottled the finish, and
the binding was split from years of use. Crammed with
much more that it was ever intended to hold, it bulged like
an old woman who has gone to seed, tattered edges of
worn photographs, bits of paper, snippets of ribbon protruding from the yellowed pages.

Lovingly put together over the years by both her mother
and Bob's, the album was filled with pictures and mementos that chronicled the various stages of their children's
life together. Memories swamped Cristen as she slowly

turned the pages, bringing a fresh wave of pain and shattering her fragile control. Her throat grew so tight that she couldn't swallow, and tears pooled in her eyes.

There were snapshots of them as babies, sitting naked in a wading pool; of three-year-olds making mud pies; of them trudging off to their first day of school, holding hands and carrying their lunch pails; of two gangly, scabby-kneed ten-year-olds with brand-new bikes; as self-conscious teenagers, dressed for a prom; of graduations; and finally, their wedding. There were childish drawings and report cards, old programs and scholastic awards, pressed flowers and pom-pom ribbons, ticket stubs and clippings from the school paper.

A tear welled over and spilled down Cristen's cheek as she took the first picture from the album and ripped it in two. She did the same to a second and a third. By the time she reached the fourth one tears were streaming down her face. Slowly, methodically, she worked her way through the album, tearing the photos to bits and crushing the pressed flowers, letting the fragrant petals sift through her fingers like all the treasured years that now had no meaning.

That was how Ryan found her.

Cristen didn't hear the key in the lock, but when the front door was shoved open so hard that it hit the wall, she started and looked up.

Ryan came thumping into the room a second later, swinging on his crutches as if he were running a race. "Cristen?" He halted just inside the door, chest heaving. When he spotted her huddled on the floor he started forward, then stopped short, his anxious look turning to deep concern at the sight of her pale, tear-streaked face. "Oh, God, love, what is it? What's wrong?"

"Ryan." Her tears spurted anew at the sight of him. She had not realized until that moment how badly she needed him, his comfort and strength, the solace of his caring. Instinctively she rose to her knees and held out her arms. "Oh, R-Ryan…hold m-me. Please…ho-hold me."

When Ryan reached her he slung his crutches aside, dropped down onto the sofa and snatched her into his arms. He crushed her protectively against his chest. "Sweetheart, are you all right? What is it?"

The tears she'd held in check earlier now came pouring out of her in a torrent. The racking sobs shook her body so, a reply was impossible. Waiting for the storm to pass, Ryan pressed a kiss against her crown and rocked her gently as hot tears plastered his shirt to his chest.

Cristen burrowed against him, seeking the strength he gave so willingly. He was the bedrock of her life, her only source of comfort, and she clung to him with all her might.

She was so grateful for his presence that it didn't strike her until she had calmed a bit that Ryan should not be there at all. "Ryan?" she sniffed against his neck. "Wha…what are you doing here? You're supposed to be in…Tulsa."

"I was worried about you. I knew when I left you that something was wrong, so when the plane stopped in Dallas I got off and called. When I didn't get an answer, I caught the next flight back."

"Oh, Ryan." The depth of his caring was a balm to her soul. Cristen was so touched that tears spouted afresh.

"Shh. Don't cry, love." Cradling the back of her head with a firm hand, he held her close and rubbed his cheek against her hair. "Just tell me."

Over her shoulder Ryan surveyed the damage she had wrought. The shredded photos and crumpled mementos spoke eloquently of her pain, and he ached for her. He recognized Bob Patterson from one of the torn pictures and was fairly certain he already knew the cause of her distress, but he needed to hear it from her.

"He was…my…my husband," she choked as Ryan stroked her hair.

"Bob Patterson?"

Cristen nodded, then pulled back. "How did...did you know?"

Still cradling her with one arm, Ryan stroked the tears from her cheeks. "I recognized him from those pictures," he said, nodding toward the scattered debris on the carpet. "Now, don't you think it's time you told me about it?"

Cristen sought again the haven of his embrace and pressed her face against his chest. She didn't want to talk about it, but she knew that Ryan deserved the truth. Strangely, once she began, the whole story, from their childhood together to Bob's desertion, came pouring out of her. By the time Cristen had finished she was again crying, though quietly this time.

For several moments Ryan just held her close. Then he asked sadly against the top of her head, "Do you still love him that much?"

"No. No, it's n-not that. It's just that...I...I feel so...so foolish...a-and so...so inadequate. So worthless."

"Worthless! Oh, sweetheart, don't say that. Don't even think it," Ryan whispered thickly. "You're the most wonderful woman in the world to me. Don't you know that?"

The words should have comforted her, but instead they tore at her heart, because she wanted so badly for them to be true, and they weren't. They weren't. Ryan had known her only a short time. Bob had known her all her life, and he had not thought she was worth loving.

The thought brought a fresh spasm of pain, and Cristen's shoulders began to shake again. Ryan's arms tightened around her, hugging her to his chest in a bone-crushing embrace. "Oh, don't, sweetheart. Don't do this to yourself. You're not to blame."

"But I a-am. I am. Don't you s-see? I've been...blind and stupid. All my...life I've been living in a dream world that didn't exist. I...I thought Bob loved me, b-but he didn't. He never h-has."

Ryan released his hold and raised her head, framing her tear-streaked face between his palms. "You're wrong, darling. I'm sure Bob loved you in a way. He probably still does. The problem is that neither of you ever had any other options. You drifted from being childhood playmates into being teenage sweethearts, and from there into marriage. You were such a part of each other's life that you never stopped to question if what you felt was love or just a deep fondness based on years of shared memories." His eyes full of sympathy, Ryan shrugged. "It took him a while, but Bob obviously started to question."

"And discovered the answer was he didn't love me after all," Cristen murmured in a wavering voice.

"Not the way a man should love the woman he marries, no." Ryan paused, then added softly, seriously. "Not the way I love you."

Cristen caught her breath as she read the silent message in his blue eyes. A panicky feeling rose inside her, suffocating her, and she tried to move away, but Ryan was having none of it.

His hand shifted from her face to her upper arms, and he held her in place, his eyes boring into her, refusing to let her look away. "Do you love me, Cristen?"

She gave him a desperate look, silently pleading with him to stop. "Ryan, please…"

"Do you?"

"You know I do, Ryan, but…"

"Then marry me."

Cristen closed her eyes, pain overwhelming her. Slowly, one by one, fresh tears squeezed from beneath her lids and streamed down her face. "I…I can't," she whispered in anguish. "I just…can't."

"Why not? We love each other. *Really* love each other. We can make it work, darling."

Cristen pulled herself out of his arms and retreated to the other side of the room. She felt brittle, ready to shatter.

As though forcibly holding herself together, she folded her arms across her middle. "Ryan, please don't do this."

"Don't do what? Don't ask for commitment? Don't expect a future? I can't do that, Cristen. You must have known it would come to this eventually, feeling as we do about each other."

"But why can't we just continue the way we are?"

"The way we are? You mean just live together a few weeks out of the month, then go our separate ways the rest of the time?" Ryan gave a short, mirthless laugh. "Not good enough, sweetheart. Oh, I'll admit we've had good times. The company's great, and the sex is fantastic. But I want more than that from you, Cristen. I want you to be my wife, the mother of my children. I want to grow old with you by my side. I want marriage and all it implies."

"Ryan, please. Don't you understand? I tried marriage, and I couldn't make it work, not even with a man I'd known my whole life. I can't go through all that again." Unable to bear his bleak expression a minute longer, she turned away.

When Ryan next spoke he was standing behind her. His voice was soft, heavy with sadness. "Cristen, trust is part of love. If you really love me, you have to believe that I'd never willingly hurt you."

Cristen turned slowly. She reached up and touched his cheek with the tips of her fingers, her face tight with pain. "I *do* love you, Ryan. I do. It's just that I…I can't handle marriage right now. I just can't."

He removed her hand from his face and held it in a gentle grip. For a moment he just stood there, staring at her hand, brushing his thumb back and forth across her knuckles. He looked up, and his eyes held a world of sadness and hurt as he said softly, "Well, I guess that about says it all."

Cristen stared at him, fear coursing through her. "Ryan, I love you."

Pain and weariness etched his features. He edged closer and, bracing himself on his crutches, framed her face with his hands. He studied her anguished expression, his own heavy with regret. "I know," he said tenderly before dropping a soft kiss on her parted lips.

He gazed into her frightened green eyes, touched one corner of her mouth with his thumb, then turned and made his way across the room and out the door.

Numb, Cristen stared after him, stricken with loss.

He'll be back, Cristen told herself repeatedly all during the following week. Of course he will. After all, he left his clothes, so he has to come back. *He has to.*

Yet the awful feeling that Ryan wouldn't return never quite left her, and by closing time on Friday she was a bundle of raw nerves. Riddled with both dread and anticipation, she rushed home, only to have her worst fear realized: Ryan wasn't there.

After the first slump of depression Cristen roused herself enough to check Ryan's room and was immensely relieved to find his things still there. He'll be back, she told herself. He probably just had to take a later flight.

But as the hours passed and Ryan still didn't appear, Cristen's shaky confidence began to dissolve. By the time ten o'clock came, she had all but given up hope.

She was huddled in a dejected ball on the sofa, arms wrapped around her legs, her chin propped on her knees, staring at the television news commentator and not taking in a single word, when the unmistakable sound of a key in the lock sent her spirits soaring. Cristen jumped up and swung around to face the door, her heart thumping and her face alight with joy.

Ryan swung into the room on his crutches, followed closely by Charley Hawkins, their doorman, who carried his suitcase. "Just put it down anywhere, Charley," Ryan instructed as he reset the alarm. "I can handle it from here."

"Sure thing, Mr. O'Malley." Charlie accepted Ryan's tip, doffed his cap, muttered a quick "Evening, Ms. Moore" to Cristen and left.

When Ryan turned from closing the door, his gaze met Cristen's for the first time. He smiled politely. "Hi."

"Hi." Cristen felt as jittery and tongue-tied as a schoolgirl. She twisted her hands together behind her back and groped for something more to say. "How was your trip?"

"Fine."

"Good, good."

Giving her another distant smile, Ryan turned and began to flip through the stack of mail on the small table by the door.

Cristen fidgeted. "You're, uh, you're late tonight. Did you miss the early flight?"

"No. I just decided to take the late one."

"Are you hungry? Would you like something to eat?"

"No, thanks."

Bracing his weight on one crutch, Ryan bent and picked up his suitcase.

"Oh! Here, let me get that," Cristen said as she leaped forward to take it from him.

"That's okay. I can manage." With the case resting against his crutch, his hand wrapped around the handle and the crutch grip, Ryan started across the living room. At the hall door he paused and gave her another of those damnable polite smiles. "If you'll excuse me, I think I'll say good-night. I'm bushed."

"Of course," Cristen said faintly. "Good night, Ryan."

She trailed along behind him as far as her bedroom door, where she stood and watched with a heavy heart as he clumped on down the hall to his old bedroom, the room he hadn't slept in since the night they first became lovers.

All the next week, Saturday and Sunday included, Ryan

worked at the construction site, rising early and not returning until late at night. The only way Cristen got to see
him at all was by waiting up until he came in, and then
he always excused himself immediately and went straight
to his room. He was polite, even amiable, but there was a
feeling of constraint between them, a distance that could
not be breached.

The following Friday, Cristen could have wept when she
returned home to find a note from Ryan telling her that he
had caught an early flight back to California.

It was a pattern that repeated itself over the next few
weeks, only now, instead of spending his weekends in
Houston, Ryan flew in late Sunday night and flew back
early on Friday. Cristen saw him so rarely, he'd had his
cast removed for over a week before she even knew it.

They no longer shared meals or chores or anything else.
Ryan stopped leaving coffee and juice for Cristen in the
bathroom. She no longer bothered to buy his favorite beer
because Ryan was never there to drink it. On the few occasions when they bumped into each other they were so
excruciatingly courteous it made her wince inwardly.

One Friday Ryan left her a check for his rent, along
with a note explaining that he had included an extra hundred dollars to make up for his inability to help with the
housework. Cristen's heart seemed to crack when she read
the formal little missive, and she closed her eyes and bit
back tears, distressed to her lovelorn soul that they had
become merely two strangers sharing the same roof.

To Cristen's dismay, Ryan no longer seemed in the least
interested in her as a woman. Once, when he came home
earlier than usual, she was lounging on the sofa watching
television, clad in one of her most revealing nightgowns.
Cristen's heart pounded in anticipation when Ryan drew
near, but he didn't even pause as he said, "Hi, Cris. Enjoying the movie?" Stricken with an acute sense of loss,
she watched him disappear down the hall.

Cristen yearned so for the love they'd had that she thought her heart would surely break. She spent most evenings wandering through the apartment like a wraith, too unhappy and restless to settle anywhere for long. Her longing became so sharp that she found herself doing utterly foolish things: burying her face in Ryan's terry-cloth robe and breathing in his scent, running her fingers over his hairbrush, sniffing his cologne.

It was, of course, impossible for Cristen to hide her misery from Louise, and once her friend had ferreted out the whole story she put the blame squarely in Cristen's lap.

"I always knew you were mule stubborn, but I didn't know you were stupid, too. How could you be so foolish? That man loves you and you love him, yet you're going to throw all that away, just because Bob Patterson didn't have the gumption to act like a man." She threw her hands up in disgust. "Lord have mercy, you're not just stupid, you're a coward."

"I am not! Louise! How can you say that?"

"Easy. The only reason you turned Ryan down is because you're afraid he'll desert you like Bob did."

"It could happen," Cristen said defensively, giving her a wounded look. "Sometimes love dies."

"That's hardly likely. Not with a man like Ryan. Besides, I doubt that Bob stopped loving you. I think he just finally realized that it wasn't the kind of love you build a marriage on." Louise sat down and took Cristen's hands. "Oh, Cris, don't you see? Growing up together the way you did, neither of you ever had a chance to find out if there was more to life and loving, if there was something richer, deeper."

A look of faint surprise flickered over Cristen's face. "That's basically what Ryan said."

Louise gave her hand an encouraging squeeze. "Then believe him, Cris. And give your love a chance. If you don't, you're going to lose him."

* * *

Over the next few days Cristen gave a lot of thought to what Louise had said, particularly her warning about losing Ryan. It was an unbearable thought. Even the sterile existence they had now was better than an endless future without Ryan. Yet Cristen knew that Louise was right. They couldn't go on in this miserable limbo, and they couldn't go back to being just lovers. She had to make a commitment to Ryan, had to entrust him with her heart and her future, for without him she had none.

She also thought a great deal about Bob. Had they really just drifted into marriage out of habit? Had he realized it finally and begun to feel trapped? Or had he known before their marriage and just lacked the fortitude to tell her? Knowing Bob, she was aware that it was entirely possible.

He was basically a weak man. She had always known that but had never wanted to admit it. To do so would have tarnished all those cherished memories she had held so dear. Which, Cristen realized, explained why she had never confronted him in the past two years. Cristen knew she could have contacted Bob at any time. She had simply to call his mother and get his phone number. Yet she, who always saw everything through to the bitter end, had chosen to put it out of her mind, to leave that episode in her life unresolved, rather than face the truth about Bob.

All along Cristen had known why he had walked out without a word. Bob had always manipulated and schemed and played on her sympathies to get his way, but he had never been able to oppose her openly.

No doubt he was much happier with Vicki. Cristen could see now that Bob needed a fragile little flower, someone who would make him feel strong, someone who would look up to him, lean on him, defer to his wishes and opinions in all things.

It was not the kind of relationship she could have endured herself, Cristen admitted, which, she supposed, just proved that she and Bob had been sorely mismatched.

The past few months had taught her that she did not want a man who would dominate her or constantly yield to her, but a man who was her equal. Cristen needed someone who was secure within himself, who would stand up to her when it mattered, yet who would applaud her strength and cherish her for it, a man who would cosset and comfort her when life had dealt her a blow, and stand back and cheer when she triumphed on her own.

Darn it! She needed Ryan!

Even knowing that her happiness lay with Ryan, Cristen was not quite able to put her old fears to rest. After mulling it over for several days, she began to feel that before she could get on with her life, she had to deal with the debris in her past, which meant she had to see Bob one last time and clear the air.

She had no trouble getting Bob's phone number from his mother, but before she could set up a meeting with him, disaster struck.

The phone call came around midnight on a Tuesday night, during a week when Ryan was in Houston. By the time Cristen finally stumbled from the bed and came to her senses, Ryan had already answered it. The minute she entered the living room and heard his terse tone, she knew something was terribly wrong.

"How bad is it?" he asked, as he waited for an answer Cristen stood behind him, nervously staring at the tense set of his shoulders. "I see. All right. Cristen and I will meet you there in ten minutes."

"What is it?" Cristen demanded the instant he replaced the receiver.

Ryan turned to her, his expression grim. "That was Louise. Cristen, there's been a fire in your shop."

Chapter Fourteen

"Dora did *what*!"

"Now, Cris, don't get so upset. It was a simple mistake that anyone could have made," Lousie insisted. "Dora heated a pot of soup for dinner, then forgot to turn the hotplate off. After we closed at nine it simmered for hours until there was nothing left but the meat and vegetables, and they caught on fire."

"Louise. Dippy Dora's *simple* mistake may have just put us out of business."

With a sick feeling of despair, Cristen looked around the ruined shop. The smoke had set off the sprinkler system, which had doused the flames before the fire truck had arrived, but the water damage was extensive. Shelves were buckled, and the carpet and wallpaper were ruined, along with the dolls and dollhouses and all the painstakingly crafted wooden miniatures. Only the items in the cases and the ones made of metal or glass were undamaged.

"Surely you have insurance," Ryan said.

"Some. But not enough to cover this. We've been meaning to increase our coverage ever since we expanded, but we never got around to it. Anyway, even if we had the money to make the repairs, it would still take months of work to replace our stock. It's going to be like starting all over again."

"I'm sorry. That's rough."

Cristen wandered around, disconsolately inspecting the damage, until the firemen gathered up their equipment and left. Since there was nothing more they could do that night, they locked up the sodden shop and went home.

During the short ride, Ryan said nothing, and Cristen leaned her head back against the Jaguar's plush leather seat, too depressed to care.

When they entered the apartment Ryan turned to her, his expression serious and sympathetic. "Cristen, I'm sorry about tonight. I hope everything works out all right for you and Louise."

Cristen's lips twitched in a wan smile. This was the closest she had been to him in weeks, and it had taken a disaster to make it happen. His scent drifted to her, so wonderfully familiar that saliva gathered in her mouth. His short-sleeved sport shirt was buttoned only halfway, and the sight of his furry chest, his muscular forearms, the familiar way he hooked his thumbs in his belt loops, set off a quivering awareness in Cristen's stomach.

"Thank you, Ryan. And thanks for taking me to the shop."

"You don't have to thank me. I was glad to help." He smiled that bland smile and edged toward the door. "Well, I guess we'd better turn in and get what sleep we can. Good night, Cristen."

"Good night." She watched him go with a heavy heart, painfully aware that he had not offered to help further. Oh, Ryan. Ryan. I still love you so. How can you be so distant and cold?

* * *

The next morning Cristen and Louise met with the insurance adjuster, who merely verified what they already knew: their coverage was inadequate, which meant that to reopen, they were going to have to borrow more money.

Since there was no point in putting off the unpleasant task, Cristen left Louise and John to clean up what they could of the mess and went to meet with their banker.

Cristen entered Mr. Donaldson's office with a great deal of trepidation, knowing her chances of obtaining another loan, on top of the one they already had, were slim to none. This time she had practically no collateral and no willing cosigner.

To her utter astonishment, she had barely begun to explain their situation when Mr. Donaldson assured her that the matter of another loan had already been taken care of.

"Mr. O'Malley has agreed to cosign for whatever additional amount you need," Mr. Donaldson told her with a satisfied smile.

"He has?" Cristen was stunned and mystified, then doubtful. It occurred to her that Ryan could have made the offer months ago. She looked at the banker warily. "When, exactly, did Mr. O'Malley tell you this?"

"Why, this morning. The doors had barely opened when he came in to see me about the matter."

Joy poured through Cristen. All through the remainder of the meeting, while she and Mr. Donaldson discussed money and terms, she couldn't seem to stop grinning, and when she left she was practically walking on air.

Oh, Ryan, Ryan. You sweet, wonderful, absolutely adorable man. You do still care.

She should have known that Ryan would never abandon her. Even though she refused to marry him, he had stayed. He had kept his distance, true, but he had stayed. And when she had needed him, he was there for her. In her heart, she knew that he always would be.

Cristen was so happy that she could have jumped up

and clacked her heels together, right there on the sidewalk. It no longer mattered why Bob had left her, or if he had loved her, or not loved her. She simply didn't care.

Who needed him? Not her. She had the man of her choice. She had Ryan.

Or at least I will have after tonight, she told herself. Still smiling, her green eyes glinting with determination, she strode jauntily toward the mall.

She was ready for him. The small table for two before the fireplace gleamed with her best china and silver. Candles were ready to be lit, soft music drifted from the stereo, the lamps were turned low. Wine was chilling. In the oven a roast was nearing perfection, and Ryan's favorite chocolate pie sat on the kitchen counter, waiting to be cut.

Cristen smoothed the linen tablecloth and needlessly adjusted the silver and stemware for the fifth time. Theda sat in a chair, watching her mistress's nervous fidgeting with feline curiosity, her head tipped to one side. Catching the cat's disdainful stare, Cristen grinned.

"Well, Theda, what do you think? Will it do?"

Theda answered with a bored meow.

"And does that go for me, as well?" Cristen asked, holding her arms out and turning in a slow circle so that her silk caftan flowed against her curves.

Not deigning to reply, Theda curled into a ball and ignored her.

Laughing, Cristen walked to the mirror that hung over the stereo to check for herself. Her makeup was still perfect, and her freshly shampooed hair billowed around her face and shoulders in a cloud of shiny curls. Leaning close, Cristen ran a smoothing fingertip over her eyebrows and rubbed her glistening lips together. She was giving her hair one final fluff when she heard Ryan's key in the lock.

Cristen spun around and fixed her eyes on the door, one

hand pressed against her fluttering stomach, the other gripping the edge of the stereo cabinet behind her.

His gaze downcast, Ryan stepped inside. He carried his overcoat slung over one shoulder. The top two buttons of his shirt were undone, and his loosened tie hung limp and askew. There were lines of fatigue etched around his eyes and the corners of his mouth. A faint shadow along his jaw revealed the beginnings of a beard. He looked utterly weary...and heartbreakingly dear.

He locked the door, reset the alarm, and took a step into the living room.

"Hi."

Cristen's soft greeting brought Ryan to a halt, his head snapping up. His wary gaze swept over her, then scanned the dimly lit room, taking in the table set for two before the cozy fire. He looked back at her, his expression even more guarded. "Hi. I didn't expect you to be up."

"I've been waiting for you." She waved her hand toward the table. "I thought we could have dinner together and talk."

Ryan's mouth quirked. "Thanks, but I've already eaten. Anyway, I'm really too beat for conversation tonight."

"Oh, but I made your favorite meal," Cristen protested with just a trace of panic in her voice when he started for his bedroom. "I even made a chocolate pie."

"And it all smells heavenly, Cris, but I'll have to pass. All I want is a hot shower and about eight hours of shut-eye." He paused just before turning into the hall and looked back at her. "Thanks for the offer, though. Good night."

Cristen stared after him, so frustrated that she could have screamed. She looked at the romantic fire, the perfectly laid table, the lovely tapered candles still waiting to be lit and did the next best thing: she hauled off and kicked the dainty tufted hassock her aunt had given her, sending it tumbling across the carpet.

Theda yowled and streaked away.

Mumbling under her breath and limping, Cristen stomped over the fire and jabbed it savagely with a poker. When she had it banked she replaced the screen, banging and rattling it against the hearth with no compunction whatsoever. "Sleep through that if you can," she muttered, casting an angry glance toward the bedrooms.

She marched into the kitchen and turned off the oven and the burners under the simmering pots. "And to think my mother always said that the way to a man's heart was through his stomach," Cristen snarled as she shoved the chocolate pie into the refrigerator and slammed the door. "She obviously never met a blockheaded, obstinate, ornery jackass like Ryan O'Malley. He'd starve to death before he'd unbend so much as an inch, that miserable, muley wretch!"

Cristen flung a dish towel down on the counter and stood in the middle of the kitchen tapping her foot, her hands planted on her hips. Her chin rose in determination. "Well, there's more than one way to skin a cat. If I can't tempt you with food, let's see how you like seduction."

Fiery curls bouncing, Cristen stormed into her room and started pawing through her lingerie drawer. This time she wasn't leaving anything to chance.

Ten minutes later, her temper still simmering, she surveyed her image in the full-length mirror on her closet door, and a small, malicious smile tilted her lips.

Every wisp of intimate apparel that adorned her long, curvaceous body was an unrelenting black, and against it, her fair skin glowed with a soft pearlescence. A daring half bra cupped her breasts, its lacy upper edge barely covering her nipples. The silk bikini panties that hugged her hips had a panel of matching lace at center front. Around her waist she wore a minuscule satin garter belt with long, beribboned straps that held up impossibly sheer stockings. Over it all, she wore a floor-length chiffon and lace negligee that was about as substantial as mist.

"You'll do," she said with satisfaction. With her jaw set at a militant angle, she swept from the room in a swirl of black chiffon and intoxicating perfume.

Outside Ryan's door Cristen paused and took a deep breath, then arranged herself carefully. Placing a languid hand against the doorframe, she thrust one hip forward and tilted her head back at a provocative angle. She tapped lightly on the door, then quickly placed her hand on her jutting hip and arranged her features into a sultry, come-hither expression.

"Yes?" Ryan said, the word already forming as he opened the door, but when he saw Cristen his brows shot skyward.

She smiled and blinked slowly, giving him a sizzling look from beneath half-lowered lids. In a throaty voice guaranteed to raise the blood pressure of a saint, she said, "Hi, handsome. Wanna fool around?"

Ryan sucked in his breath as his gaze drifted over her, from her tousled curls to the strappy high heels on her feet. He had obviously just stepped from the shower, for he was naked except for the towel knotted around his hips. His dark curls were wet and falling over his forehead, and droplets of water still glistened in the hair on his chest.

He smelled of soap and shampoo and that wonderful scent that was his alone, and Cristen breathed it all in greedily. His nearness, his scent, the sight of his beautiful strong body made her nipples harden and sent a fiery sensation zinging to the core of her womanhood. It was all she could do not to fling herself against him.

When Ryan's gaze met hers once again he gave her a regretful smile and shook his head. "It's a tempting offer," he said gently. "But no, I don't think so."

Cristen's jaw dropped.

How dare he stand there and say no when she knew

darned well he wanted her! He might have that mealy-mouthed bland expression on his face, but she'd seen the feverish look in his eyes. And in that skimpy towel there was no way he could hide his body's reaction. Cristen's temper shot ten notches higher.

"No? *No!*" She stepped forward and stuck out her chin. "What do you mean, no? Why, you jerk! You dimwitted Neanderthal! You sorry excuse for a sow's son! You... you... Oh!" Cristen began to pummel his chest with her fists, too furious to think of anything vile enough to call him.

"Hey! Hey! Watch it!" Ryan grabbed her wrists, but Cristen just struggled harder. She butted her head up under his chin, making his teeth clack. "Ow!" He gave her a shake and roared, "Dammit! Will you calm down!"

Cristen lashed out at him with her feet. For a moment he managed to evade her, but when she tried to hook her foot around his leg, he jerked her close and in one motion tumbled them both down onto the bed, rolling Cristen to her back and pinning her to the mattress with his body.

He held her arms over her head and glared at her, nose to nose. "Now, will you behave, you little wildcat?"

She glared right back. "No. Not until you're honest with me. I know you want me. Why are you doing this to us?"

All the anger left Ryan's face. He closed his eyes, and his body sagged as he expelled a long breath. "All right. Yes, I want you. I love you. I want more than anything to make love to you until neither of us can move. But, sweetheart, a night of passion just isn't enough. I'm not going to settle for an affair, Cristen. I told you, I want a hell of a lot more than that."

"So do I," she flared back, giving him an exasperated look.

Ryan's head snapped back, his eyes wide and incredulous. "What?"

"Just answer me one question, O'Malley," Cristen demanded belligerently. "Do you still want to marry me or not?"

"Of course I do. Are you saying that's what you want, too?"

"Yes, that's what I'm saying," she replied in a sing-song, thoroughly disgusted voice. "And if you hadn't been such a horse's rump, you'd have heard me say it over a romantic, candlelit dinner."

Throwing his head back, Ryan gave a burst of happy, exultant laughter, a rich, full-bodied, masculine sound that rumbled up from deep inside him. Cristen felt it vibrate against her belly and breasts, and the sensation raised goose bumps of awareness all over her.

As his laughter faded, Ryan released Cristen's hands and his fingers found the warm hollows behind her ears. "Oh, Cris, Cris. I do love you so," he murmured, and the look of adoration on his face as he gazed down at her pierced Cristen's heart with a sweet, sweet pain. Her anger dissolved like smoke, and her body grew soft and pliant beneath his.

"I love you, too."

A smile of wonder curved her mouth, and Cristen reached up and touched his cheeks, then ran her fingertips over his sable mustache. Their eyes delved, blue into green, soft with love, seeking solace for the misery they had endured, promising a future filled with joy immeasurable. Sighing, Cristen looped her arms around his neck and winnowed her fingers through the damp hair on his nape.

"Then you meant it when you said you'd marry me?" Ryan asked, and Cristen was touched by the lingering note of uncertainty in his voice.

"Yes, I'll marry you," she said in a voice that quavered with emotion. "Whenever you say."

"Good. How about next week?"

Cristen laughed shakily and blinked hard at the tears of

happiness that were gathering in her eyes. "Oh, my darling, I would love to marry you next week, but don't you think that's rushing it just a bit? I mean, there are so many things we have to consider. So many decisions we have to work out."

"Such as?"

"Well, for one, where would we live? Most of your business is in California, and mine is here."

"That's no problem. I'll relocate the main offices here."

Cristen was so touched by his generosity that she just stared at him, feeling the hot rush of tears overflow and streak down her face, wetting the hair at her temples. "Really? You'd do that?"

"Sure."

"But...but what about your life in California? Your friends? Your family?"

"I'll make new friends. And the only family I have is Jennifer."

"Jennifer! Oh, dear. I didn't think about her. What if she doesn't approve? What if—"

Ryan placed three fingers over her mouth, halting the frantic flow of words. "Cristen, will you stop? I guarantee that Jennifer will be overjoyed."

"Are you sure?"

"Yes, I'm sure. But if you want, we'll call her later and you can find out for yourself." He gazed down at her with fond exasperation and shook his head. "Now is there anything else you're worried about?"

The look of love and tenderness brimming in Ryan's blue eyes made Cristen go weak and warm all over. She touched the hair at his temples, then ran her fingertips over the rim of his ear, her gaze a soft, liquid green. "No," she whispered, giving him a melting smile. "Not a single thing."

"Good."

Ryan's head dipped, and their mouths met, tenderly at

first, then open and hungry, as each sought to make up for the barren loneliness of the past weeks. Wet tongues dueled in a rough caress, twisting and twining, speaking of need that had grown to near desperation since last they loved. The kiss went on and on, their lips rocking together in greedy passion, as hearts thudded and their blood rushed hotly through their veins. Ryan nipped Cristen's lower lip, then drew it into his mouth and sucked gently. She made a low, throaty sound and stroked the back of his neck, telling him without words of the depth of her feelings.

In their tumble to the bed, her negligee had fallen open and now lay spread out on either side of them like gossamer wings. Ryan ran his hands down her sides, outlining the enticing curves of breasts, waist and hips, boldly fingering each tiny scrap of cloth that covered them. "Now, about this outfit you're wearing," he murmured against her lips.

"You don't like it?"

"Mmm, on the contrary." He shifted to his side and ran a fingertip along the top edge of the tiny bra, smiling with wicked delight as her nipples peaked against the flimsy lace. "I think it has great possibilities."

With maddening leisure, he continued his delicate exploration, running his fingers over the satin garter belt, testing its smooth texture, tracing the lace pattern on the minuscule panties, playfully snapping the beribboned garter straps and running his finger beneath the tops of her stockings.

Cristen lay still, quivering with anticipation, watching the sensual fire flame in his eyes as his gaze followed the path of his roaming hands. He pressed his face against the strip of white flesh between her panties and garter belt and inhaled deeply. While his lips nibbled and caressed the silky skin, his hand slid downward and released the fasteners at the tops of her stockings. A hand beneath her knees lifted her legs, and the ones in back were dealt with.

His hand stroked up the inside of her thigh, and Cristen moaned and closed her eyes, her fingers digging into the broad muscles of Ryan's back. He raised his head and smiled, watching her eyelids tremble with pleasure as he pressed the heel of his hand against her throbbing womanhood.

"Have I ever told you how much I like your sexy undies?" His hand moved upward and deftly released the three hooks at the side of the garter belt. Obeying his silent urging, Cristen lifted her hips, and he pulled it free. "And the nicest thing is, they're so easy to take off," he added as he tossed the strip of black satin over his shoulder.

"I...I'm glad you like them."

"Oh, I do. I do." Leaning down, he touched his tongue to her lace-covered nipple, then placed his open mouth over it. The feel of his warm breath filtering through the fragile lace was incredibly erotic, and Cristen moaned, shivering as her breasts burgeoned and throbbed. With his mouth and tongue, Ryan nuzzled aside the flimsy bra. He took the yearning bud into his mouth and drew on her sweetly, and as Cristen arched upward he released the clasp at the front of her bra.

"Oh, Ryan, love me. Love me," she urged in a husky whisper. "It's been so long."

"I will, darling. Soon," he murmured.

Cristen thought she would surely die as Ryan took his time reacquainting himself with every inch of her body, his big hands smoothing over her, his mouth and tongue and teeth driving her wild. But finally bra and panties were discarded, and with slow, sensual movements he peeled down her stockings and tossed them aside.

His towel had long ago fallen away, and when he drew her back into his arms and their fevered flesh melded together they both sighed with pleasure. For a heady, torturous moment they simply held each other, savoring the warmth, the closeness, the triumph of their love, letting the sweet anticipation build. They were pressed together from shoulder to knee, male to female, soft feminine flesh to sinewed strength, pale silk to dark bronze.

But after a moment touching was not enough. Cristen's hands roamed Ryan's back restlessly, finally sliding down to clutch his buttocks. Ryan slipped his hand between their bodies, his fingers threading through the feminine nest of curls and probing intimately.

"I need you so, my love," he rasped as he caressed her.

"Oh, yes, darling. Yes!"

After weeks of heartache and loneliness their desire for each other had become an urgent need that demanded fulfillment. Ryan rolled her to her back and rose above her. He gazed lovingly into her shining eyes and whispered, "My love, my life," as he made them one.

A sigh. A kiss. A moment of quivering anticipation. Eyes closed in ecstasy. Breathing quickened.

And then the movement began.

Together they soared. Each seeking and giving pleasure, sharing that special rapture that only true love brings. The sweet tension stretched tighter and tighter. Ryan's face was flushed and contorted with fierce gladness as he watched Cristen's eyes go smoky with pleasure.

Cristen threw her head back on the pillow and clutched Ryan's back. And then his name ripped from her throat as again they shared that shattering explosion of joy that rocked them to the depths of their being.

As thundering hearts calmed, as breathing returned to normal, they drifted back to reality with a sigh of satisfaction. Ryan pressed a soft kiss on her mouth, then shifted his weight and rolled to his back, tucking her firmly against his side. With her cheek nestled against his chest, his hand sifting absently through her hair, in blissful lassitude they lay in each other's arms.

"Ryan?" Cristen said a long while later.

"Hmm?"

"Thank you for helping with the loan."

"So you found out about that, did you? Donaldson wasn't supposed to tell you."

"Why not?"

"I wanted you to accept me, but not because you felt obligated. Or out of gratitude."

Cristen wrapped a curl of his chest hair around her finger and gave it a sharp tug. "Foolish man. I love you, you dope."

"Ow! Watch it, woman."

Cristen laughed and snuggled closer, hooking her legs over his thighs. "Ryan?"

"Hmm?"

"I've been so miserable these past weeks. After I refused to marry you I was terrified that you were going to move out, but I wouldn't have blamed you if you had. Why...why did you stay?"

"I was waiting for you to come to your senses," he answered with sleepy unconcern.

"What!" Cristen jerked up and braced herself on one palm, glaring down at him.

Ryan opened his eyes and grinned. "Worked, didn't it?"

This time she grabbed a handful of hair. "You wretch!"

Laughing, Ryan pried her hand loose before she could do serious injury. "I figured if I put some distance between us—not much, but some—you'd see just how rotten life would be if we parted."

"I see," she said haughtily. "And just how long did you intend to keep it up?"

"As long as it took. I told you, I'm a very patient man."

Cristen tried to keep her face stern, but her heart was warmed by the knowledge that Ryan would not have given up on her—ever. His steadfastness was yet another facet to this tough, tender, funny, complex man, and it made her love him just that much more.

Still, she wasn't going to let him off that easily. Affecting an indignant pout, she said, "I'm not so sure I want to marry such a devious, scheming man."

"Sure you do."

Ryan startled her by bounding up off the bed. "Come on, let's go." He grabbed her hand to pull her with him, but Cristen held back.

"Go where?" she questioned warily. "Ryan! Stop!" she squealed a second later as she was jerked from the bed and slung over his shoulder.

With her anchored firmly in place by a strong arm across the backs of her knees, he stalked out the door. Cristen bounced with every jarring step, her mane of Gypsy curls dangling down and swaying against his bare posterior.

"Put me down, O'Malley!"

"No way." Chuckling, he marched determinedly down the hall.

"Beast!" she squawked.

"Quiet, woman." He nipped her enticing bare backside, then brushed it with his sable mustache. "Can't you tell when your man is starving?"

"Well, why didn't you just say so? There's a scrumptious meal waiting in the kitchen. If you'll just put me down, I'll—"

Cristen screamed as Ryan tipped her off his shoulder and she fell through space. A second later her back hit something soft, and she bounced once before Ryan pinned her down with his body. She blinked and looked around, bewildered. "This isn't the kitchen."

"No, it's our bedroom, and we're back in our bed where we belong."

"I thought you said you were hungry."

He smiled, his eyes glinting with wicked intent as he moved his hips against hers. "Oh, I am, I am. But not for food."

Cristen's lips twitched. "Ryan, you're awf—" she began, but her halfhearted scolding was cut off by Ryan's warm lips, and a moment later she discovered that her appetite equaled his.

IF THERE BE LOVE

Chapter One

Jessica Collier felt like a hunted fugitive. The prickly sensation along the back of her neck persisted, no matter how hard she tried to shake it. So did the compulsive urge to check over her shoulder. She half expected that at any moment the bus would be overtaken and forced off the highway.

With a sigh, Jessica leaned her head back, closed her eyes and willed her body to relax. Through the cushioned seat, she absorbed the vibration of the powerful diesel engine and the rhythmic thump of the tires on the highway. She was being foolish; no one was after her. Not yet, anyway. And even if they were, they couldn't know where she was headed. She'd been careful to cover her tracks.

The bus slowed, then lumbered to a stop with an explosive hiss of air brakes.

"Elk Falls, Colorado," the driver announced.

Jessica straightened in her seat, her chest tightening. *They had arrived.* Without giving herself time to think,

she clamped her teeth together and with quick, jerky movements, gathered her belongings, then picked up her sleeping son from the seat beside her and headed for the door.

The prickle at the back of her neck grew stronger the
instant she stepped from the bus. Tensing, she halted and
scanned the main street of the tiny mountain town, unconsciously clutching Danny closer.

The smell of diesel fuel and gasoline hung in the air,
and she noticed that the bus was parked in the driveway
of a service station on the eastern edge of town. Apparently
Elk Falls wasn't big enough to warrant a depot. In the
garage, a man in grease-stained overalls stopped what he
was doing to watch her. A fresh flare of panic rose inside
Jessica, but then she realized he was merely curious.

Her gaze shifted to the café across the street. A few
pickups and an eighteen wheeler were parked in front, and
a battered station wagon cruised by. The only other people
in sight were three old men sitting on a bench in front of
the feed store on the opposite corner. They barely spared
her a glance before going back to their conversation.

Jessica released a pent-up breath and closed her eyes,
weak with relief. Thank God. There didn't appear to be
anyone waiting to pounce on her and drag her away. Not
even, she realized with a belated touch of concern, her new
employer.

"Hey, lady. Move outta the way, will ya?" a querulous
voice prodded behind her. "We wanna grab some dinner
before the bus leaves. This is only a forty-minute stop, ya
know."

Starting guiltily, Jessica mumbled an apology and hurried over to where the bus driver was waiting beside the
open baggage compartment.

"Is that it?" He cast a disgruntled look at her bags as
he jerked out the last two and put them with the others.

Jessica gave him an apologetic smile and hefted Danny
a bit higher on her shoulder. "Yes. Thank you."

There were nine cases in all, each matching the powder-blue leather tote she carried, and each bearing, in discreet gold letters, the initials of an exclusive Paris designer. They were embarrassingly ostentatious, and looked out of place on the cracked and buckled sidewalk.

"Someone meeting you?" The driver slammed the baggage compartment door and locked it.

"Yes. At least…someone was supposed to."

"Well, we got in a little ahead of schedule, so I wouldn't worry."

He gave her an encouraging smile and touched his fingertips to the bill of his cap. Feeling uneasy and absurdly abandoned, she watched him cross the street to join the other passengers at the café.

Jessica shivered. Two days before, she'd left Fort Worth in the middle of a July heat wave, but in the mountains, when dusk fell so did the temperature. The cool breeze fluttered her silk shirt, molding it to her like an icy second skin. Danny, his small, sturdy body draped over her shoulder like a limp rag, gave a little shuddering sigh, snuggled his face against her neck and slept on, blissfully unconcerned.

Turning her back to the wind, Jessica shifted from one foot to the other and tried to settle him into a more comfortable position on her hip. He weighed only about fifty pounds, but he seemed to grow heavier by the minute. Her arm muscles quivered under the strain of supporting his deadweight, and she was forced to stand with her spine bent back at an unnatural angle.

She felt conspicuous, standing alone among the cluster of expensive cases. Several times, people driving by slowed down and stared. A glance over her shoulder confirmed that the man in the station was still watching her, also.

Where was Mr. Rawlins?

Jessica strove to look nonchalant, but inside she was

quaking. Staring into the gathering darkness, she was acutely aware that she was truly on her own for the first time in her life. From now on she, and she alone, was responsible for herself and Danny. It was scary.

The sun sank behind the mountains to the west, rimming them in gold and deepening the sky to a plum twilight. Cast in shadows, the town seemed like a ghost town, an impression that was heightened by the old, false-fronted buildings huddled together on either side of the street. Nestled in a narrow valley between steep mountains, Elk Falls looked as though it had been dropped there in the last century, then forgotten. Incredibly, here and there along the street, there were still hitching posts and watering troughs.

She wasn't bothered by the town's age or size, or even its remote location. All three, she knew, might work to her advantage. Certainly it wasn't the sort of place where anyone would expect to find her.

Jessica's hands were locked around her wrists beneath Danny's bottom. Every few minutes she craned her neck and rolled her forearm up to check her watch. *Drat the man! Where was he? In his last letter he'd said he would meet the bus.*

Twenty minutes later, when people began to trickle back from the café, Jessica was still standing in the same spot, shivering in earnest, a touch of panic in her eyes as she searched the darkened streets.

The bus driver looked startled to see her. "No ride yet?"

"No. Not yet." She shrugged and made a wan attempt at a smile. "But I'm sure he'll be along soon."

The toothpick sticking out of the corner of his mouth jutted upward as he pursed his lips thoughtfully. "Well, look. You can't stand out here freezing all night. Why don't I get a couple of guys from the bus to help me carry your bags over to Alma's," he suggested, nodding toward the café across the street. "You'll be warmer over there and a lot more comfortable. It's the local meeting place, anyway. When he sees you're not here, your ride'll come looking for you over there. I guarantee it."

Cold, apprehensive, and wobbly with exhaustion, Jessica accepted the suggestion with alacrity.

Alma Pierce turned out to be an energetic, raw-boned woman with the open friendliness of one who never met a stranger. The moment Jessica explained her situation she declared:

"Well of course, you can wait here. Should of done that in the first place, for heaven's sake. The very idea, standing out there in the cold all this time with that strapping child draped over your shoulder. Your back must be nearly broken by now. You fellas just put her bags in the storage room," she instructed with a wave toward the rear of the café. "And, honey, you go sit down before you drop. Take that booth in the corner so you can lay your little boy down on the seat beside you."

Not needing to be told twice, Jessica staggered away. She collapsed into the booth and heaved a sigh as she eased Danny down onto the curving red vinyl seat. He didn't move a hair.

Poor little thing, Jessica thought. He's worn out. So was she, for that matter. At first Danny had viewed the trip as an adventure, but, like any normal, energetic boy of six, he had quickly grown bored and restless. For the past twenty-four hours he'd nearly driven her crazy with his fidgeting and crankiness.

Jessica's worried expression softened as she gazed at her son's face, so innocent and babyish in slumber, and she felt a surge of fierce protectiveness swell inside her. Whenever her courage threatened to crumble, she had only to look at him to know she was doing the right thing.

Smiling, she touched the crease marks on his flushed cheek, and smoothed a lock of tawny blond hair, so like her own, off his forehead. "We're here, sweetheart," she whispered. "We made it. From now on it's just you and me. Everything's going to work out great, you'll see."

"Cross me, and I'll make sure that you never see Danny again...never see Danny again...never see Danny again..."

Unbidden, unwanted, Lois's threat echoed in Jessica's mind, and a fine tremor shook her hand. Pressing her lips together, she closed her eyes and battled against the fear that rippled through her.

Everything *was* going to work out. It *was*, she vowed silently. It had to. Because, dear God, she'd come too far to turn back now.

"Here you go, honey. This'll help warm you up."

Jessica gave a violent start, her eyes flying open. Feeling foolish, she smiled vaguely and accepted the steaming mug of coffee that Alma set before her.

"Can I get you something to eat while you wait?"

The strained muscles in Jessica's arms trembled as she lifted the cup to her lips with both hands. Her stomach rolled with hunger at the smell of food, but all the money she had in the world was the eighteen dollars and twenty-three cents in her purse. "No, thank you. This is fine. I'll just wait for Mr. Rawlins."

"Okay. Holler if you change your mind. And don't worry. He'll show up. The thing is, no one around here puts much stock in that bus schedule. It gets here when it gets here."

The bell above the door jingled as Alma hurried away. A shaft of fear shot through Jessica when she saw that the newcomer was a sheriff's deputy. She watched him, scarcely breathing, but he merely walked over to the counter, hitched a leg over a stool and started flirting with the other waitress, a gum-popping bottle blonde of about twenty.

Cradling the cup between her hands, her heart pounding,

Jessica stared down at the shining surface of the coffee and scolded herself for being jumpy. She hadn't the slightest doubt that Lois would go all out to find her, but stiff-necked Collier pride and the dread of bad press would prevent her from calling in the police.

Besides, she hadn't committed any crime. She was a grown woman, entitled to go where she pleased, live her life as she pleased. Jessica sighed. The trouble was, such considerations would mean less than nothing to Lois Collier.

But she'd been careful—at least, as careful as she could be. Unfortunately she'd had to give Mr. Rawlins her real name. There hadn't been time to obtain phony papers, and she had to present Danny's birth certificate and medical records in order to enroll him in school. Besides, she hadn't the slightest idea how to go about getting fake documents, anyway. But at least on the trip she'd used a fictitious name. And she'd taken a circuitous route. She'd even left a note saying that she and Danny had gone to her parents' ranch for a few days.

Knowing her mother-in-law's possessiveness, Jessica didn't count on that ploy buying them much time. Lois had probably already called her parents and discovered the truth. If so, by now she would have initiated a search, but it would be private bloodhounds, not the police, who would be looking for them.

The thought created a sick, fluttery sensation in the pit of Jessica's stomach.

The bell over the door sounded again, and she glanced up in time to see a lanky, good-looking cowboy step inside. He paused just long enough for his gaze to sweep the room. Then, moving with that peculiar loose-limbed grace of a man who spent a lot of time in the saddle, he ambled over to where the blond waitress stood. Thumbing his Stetson to the back of his head, he propped an elbow on the counter, grinned, and leaned across to whisper something in the woman's ear. She responded with a giggle and a playful slap to his shoulder.

Lips twitching, Jessica looked away and took another sip of coffee. A cowboy Romeo, she thought with tolerant amusement. It had been years since she had encountered one, but Lord knows, growing up on a Texas ranch, she'd met enough to recognize the breed. They were rugged, lean-hipped, honey-tongued rogues with the devil's own charm. Sweet-talking came as easy to one as roping a steer. She'd learned early in life not to take them too seriously.

With a wink and a final murmured comment for the waitress, the cowboy picked up his beer and headed for a booth on the opposite side of the café from Jessica. He hung his hat on a brass coat hook attached to the end of the booth and slid onto the seat with indolent grace. Lounging sideways with his back against the wall, he propped one booted foot on the red vinyl bench seat and lit a cigarette. The flashing neon light outlining the window at his back framed his head and shoulders in a rosy glow.

He took a long swig of beer, then draped his arm over his updrawn knee, holding the long-necked brown bottle loosely in the circle of his thumb and forefinger. Taking his time, he once again perused the room.

His gaze slid idly from person to person. It touched Jessica, went past, then swung back, his eyebrows arching as his gaze boldly held hers.

Jessica looked away and tried to ignore him, but that gaze upon her was a magnet. Drawn irresistibly, her glance flickered his way again, and she found that he was regarding her steadily. Bold as brass, he winked and gave her a slow, suggestive grin.

Tilting her chin at a haughty angle, Jessica returned the look with one of cool disdain. The cowboy's grin grew wider.

Oh, brother, she thought, torn between irritation and reluctant amusement. Just what she needed!

Jessica shifted in her seat, turning a definite cold shoulder his way, and stared out the window at nothing.

Out of the corner of her eye, she saw the cowboy roll to his feet and stroll over to the jukebox. Assuming he had accepted defeat, she sighed and relaxed her rigid posture. A few moments later she realized that she'd underestimated him. As Dolly Parton's clear vibrato and the deep twang of a bass guitar poured from the jukebox, he turned and headed her way.

The unhurried thud of his boot heels against the wooden floor charted his progress, then fell silent. Hooking his thumbs into the waistband of his jeans, he leaned a shoulder against the end of the booth where she sat. Jessica stared at her coffee and tried to pretend he wasn't there.

"Hello, beautiful." His deep rumbling drawl held a hint of laughter. "You visiting someone, or just passing through?"

Even as worried and anxious as she was, Jessica experienced a jolt when she looked up and encountered that devastating grin. His even teeth were a startling slash of white against sun-darkened skin, and laugh lines radiated from the corners of his eyes—vivid blue eyes that danced with mischief. A lock of midnight-black hair hung boyishly across his forehead, but the expression on his ruggedly handsome face was anything but innocent. The man oozed sex appeal. It was primal, basic—the kind that made a woman feel utterly female and deliciously threatened.

Jessica glanced around the restaurant for Alma, but the woman was nowhere in sight. "I really don't think that's any of your business." Taking a sip of coffee, she fixed her gaze on some undefined point in the distance.

"Maybe. But I thought I ought to tell you, if you're traveling on that bus, it's about to leave without you."

Jessica glanced out the plate-glass window at the front of the café. "So it is," she said with supreme unconcern. Her gaze swung back to his, her brown eyes indifferent, dismissive. "Thank you for telling me. Now, if you don't mind—"

"So you're here on a visit, eh?"

"What makes you think that?"

As soon as the words were out, Jessica could have kicked herself for asking. She knew better than to give him an opening. Another time, another place, and she might have enjoyed flirting with this unknown cowboy. Lord knows, it had been a long time since she had indulged in that kind of light banter or seen that gleam of interest in a man's eyes. It had been years—seven long years that had seemed like a lifetime. But at the moment she had too much to deal with to be drawn into a light flirtation with a lecherous cowboy.

"Simple. You're not upset that the bus is leaving, and there aren't any strange cars parked out front, so you're not just passing through. No way a woman like you would be moving to this town permanently. I don't have that kind of luck." He shrugged. "So you've got to be visiting."

"That isn't—"

"Who'd you come to see? Relatives? Friends? I probably know them. Everybody around here knows just about everyone else."

"Look—"

"Maybe we could spend some time together while you're here." His eyelids dropped part way and his mouth tilted up in a sensual little half smile that was pure seduction. "You know...really get to know each other. I guarantee you won't be bored."

His audacity made Jessica grind her teeth. Oh, he was a devil all right, the kind of heartbreaker that every girl's mother warned her about from the time she could walk. No doubt, the local women fell all over themselves when he used that bedroom look and that husky, insinuating tone.

He was the stuff female fantasies and television com-

mercials were made of, with his thick shock of black hair
and those chiseled, sun-browned features. He was lean and
rawhide tough and a bit rough around the edges, but the
indolent sensuality in that rangy body and the bold reck-
lessness in those smoldering eyes drew women, fascinated
them on some primitive level. Jessica was no exception.

That it was so, especially given her situation, merely
irritated her all the more and when she spoke, her voice
was colder and sharper than it might otherwise have been.
"I know this will come as a shock, but I'm not in the least
susceptible to your rustic charm. So get lost, cowboy.
Now. Before I complain to the owner."

He considered her set face for a moment, then straightened away from the booth and shrugged. "You win some.
You lose some," he said with a grin.

Relieved, Jessica watched him stroll back to his booth.
She sighed, glanced at the door, and checked her watch
once again.

Hank had barely settled back into his seat when Cooter
walked in. The wiry old man spotted him and hurried over,
his spindly, bowed legs giving him the rolling gait of a
sailor.

Noting that he was alone, Hank frowned.

The perpetual scowl that etched Cooter's weather-beaten
face deepened as he slid into the booth opposite Hank.
"Well, she ain't there," he snapped. He tossed his hat onto
the table and scratched the bald spot on the top of his head.
In the light from the brass lantern fixtures his scalp
gleamed like pink satin. "The bus has come an' gone, an'
there ain't nobody waitin'."

"Did anyone see her get off?"

Taking his time, Cooter fished cigarette makings out of
his shirt pocket and shook out a row of stringy tobacco
onto the slip of paper. "Accordin' to Maynard, the only

one who got off was some sweet young thing. A fancy-pants city gal, from his description.''

He caught the drawstring between his teeth, closed the pouch and dropped it back into his pocket. Gnarled fingers rolled the paper into a cylinder and he licked the edge to seal it. Under the scrape of his thumbnail a match flared, and he brought it to the tip of the crude cigarette, squinting against the sting of sulfur. Shaking out the flame, he blew a stream of blue smoke toward the ceiling and gave Hank a disgusted look. ''Shore don't sound like no middle-aged housekeeper to me.''

Hank looked across the restaurant at the blonde in the corner booth. Beneath half-closed lids, his blue eyes glinted. ''Nope. She sure doesn't.''

Following the direction of his gaze, Cooter snorted. ''Shoulda known if there was a pretty female in town, you'd spot her.''

The old man's grumbling comment didn't faze Hank. He took a healthy pull on his beer and continued to watch the woman as he turned the long-necked bottle around and around on the Formica tabletop.

Everything about her shouted class. And money. Right from the top of her head to the tips of her three-hundred-dollar custom-made boots. Hank's mouth twitched as his gaze skimmed over the loose mane of streaked, tawny blond hair that tumbled about her shoulders. She probably spent hours in a beauty salon and more money than a cow-hand made in a week to achieve that elegantly casual effect.

Still, he had to admit, it was more than outward trappings that set her apart. It was her bearing, that subtle, regal air.

Which was exactly what had prompted him to flirt with her. He'd known that nothing could possibly come of it, but the temptation to ruffle her feathers had been irresistible. He'd expected dithering indignation or outrage, but, instead, she'd surprised him with a cool put-down.

She was too high toned for his taste, but she was a looker. He'd give her that. When she'd fixed him with those big, golden-brown eyes he'd felt as though he'd been kicked in the gut by a steer. The woman had that refined, delicate kind of beauty that fairly took a man's breath away.

And she was as out of place sitting in Alma's café, sipping coffee from a cheap crockery mug, as a thoroughbred filly among a pack of mules.

"I wonder what a woman like that's doing in Elk Falls?" Hank mused aloud.

"Never you mind what she's doin' here," Cooter snapped. "We got more important things to worry 'bout. Like what're we gonna do 'bout a housekeeper? If you think I'm gonna do anymore cookin', you got another think comin', cause—"

"You ain't no cook," Hank finished for him with a wry grin. "Believe me, I know. So do the rest of the hands."

"Humph! Iszat so?" Cooter flipped an inch of ash off his crooked cigarette and rubbed his jaw. The salt-and-pepper beard stubble rasped against his horny palm. "Well, leastways, I wash my hands 'fore I stick 'um in the pot. That's more than you can say for some. Jubal, for one. I swear, that boy's gonna poison us for sure. I'm tellin' you, Hank, we gotta find us a housekeeper. An' quick."

Hank dragged his gaze away from the pretty woman. "Fine. You got any suggestions how I go about doing that? I've been running an ad in all the farm-and-ranch journals for months now, and so far only one woman has answered—the one who was supposed to be on the bus."

Hank drained the last of his beer and stared, disgusted, at the neon beer sign on the wall behind the counter. Damn, he missed Ina Mae. His aunt had been a fixture on

the R Bar B ever since he and Trace Barnett had started
the ranch, nine years ago, and now that she was gone he
realized, guiltily, that he'd taken her for granted.

She was such a sturdy, indomitable woman that he
sometimes forgot she was in her seventies. That fact, however, was driven home three months ago, when a fall re-
sulted in a broken hip.

Wistful amusement twisted Hank's mouth as he remembered how Ina Mae had fussed and fumed and vowed she'd
be back at work in a month. Her spirit had been willing,
bless her, but brittle old bones that refused to knit had,
instead, forced her to retire.

Cooter was right. Somehow, somewhere, he had to find
a housekeeper. He hadn't had a decent meal since Ina Mae
had gone to live with her daughter in Denver, and he and
Cooter and the other single hands had started taking turns
in the kitchen.

The housework he'd simply had to let slide. Ina Mae's
accident couldn't have happened at a worse time. Spring
and summer on a ranch were the busiest seasons. In the
past few months he'd barely found time to stuff a few
skivvies and work clothes into the washer now and then.

Now though, he had to admit, the situation was reaching
the desperate stage. A little clutter he could live with, but
if he didn't find a housekeeper soon, he was either going
to have to shovel his way through the house or burn it
down.

Cooter shook his head and looked disgusted. "Who'd
of thought finding a housekeeper would be this hard?"

"The trouble is, damn few women these days are anxious to cook and clean for a bunch of rough men on a
ranch miles from nowhere. If I'd had a choice, I probably
wouldn't have hired a woman with a school-age son. I'm
hoping, though, that we can put him to work doing chores
around the place. At least, according to her letters, Mrs.
Collier has had plenty of experience."

"Yeah, well, yore Miz Collier didn't show up. Just like a danged woman," Cooter groused. "Nothin' but a bunch of flibbertigibbets."

"Maybe she missed the bus. Or maybe she's been delayed for some reason. Whatever, there's nothing we can do about it, so there's not much point in hanging around here." Hank stubbed out his cigarette and rolled to his feet.

He'd settled the battered, sweat-stained Stetson on his head and started for the door when out of the corner of his eye he saw the blonde nervously check her watch once again. On impulse, he detoured by her table. Behind him, Cooter grumbled something but followed in his wake.

She jumped and looked up, her golden eyes startled, when he bent and braced his palms on the table. Hank grinned, pleased at the reaction.

"If you're going to be around for a few days, pretty lady, and you change your mind, look me up. My name is Hank Rawlins. You can find me at the R Bar B ranch. Anyone can give you directions."

Jessica sucked in her breath, her eyes widening. "Raw-Rawlins? Not...not H. J. Rawlins?"

Hank's eyebrows shot up. "As a matter of fact—"

"Well, now. I see you two found each other."

Alma came bustling out of the kitchen, her booming voice cutting off Hank's words as she bore down on them. "Sorry I wasn't here to introduce you, but I got busy back there." She flashed Hank a teasing grin and gave him a hearty thump on the back. "I told Mrs. Collier not to worry, though. I've never known you to keep a pretty woman waiting."

Oblivious to Jessica's sudden paleness and the stunned looks on the faces of the two men, Alma turned away when the bell over the door announced a new arrival. "I put her cases in the storeroom," she called over her shoulder. "You can go back and get 'um when you're ready."

A shocked silence stretched out. It was a toss-up among the three of them who was more appalled.

"Uh...Mr. Rawlins, I—"

"*You're* Jessica Collier? The woman who applied for the housekeeper's job?"

"Uh, yes. I...that is..." Jessica bit the inside of her lip, unable to continue as slowly, assessingly, Hank Rawlins's gaze slid over her tangerine silk shirt, then dropped to her snug designer jeans. She had the uneasy feeling that this cowboy knew to within a penny, the cost of every item she wore.

"I see. So you want to be a housekeeper?" At her nod, his mouth twitched. The wiry old man at his side snorted and rolled his eyes, grumbling something under his breath.

"And I believe you wrote that you've had several years of experience."

"Yes," she replied in a voice that was little more than a whisper. It wasn't a lie...exactly. As the eldest of eight children in a family of modest means, she'd done plenty of cooking and cleaning. She just hadn't done any lately.

Too late she realized his intent, and, before she could hide them in her lap, he grasped one of her hands. She tried to tug free, but he ignored her effort and held her fast. Taking his time, he examined her manicured nails, her soft palm, ran his callused fingertips over the smooth skin and delicate bones on the back.

A sardonic smile twisted his mouth, but his blue eyes were hard and cold when they met hers once again. All trace of the flirtatious cowboy had vanished. "Who're you trying to kid, lady? These hands haven't done anything more strenuous than deal bridge cards, and you know it."

"Not lately, no," she began anxiously. "But I've done plenty of—"

"Sorry." He cut her off with upraised hands and a blatantly insincere look of regret. "I'm afraid you just don't qualify for the job."

"But that's not fair!"

"Neither is wasting my time," he shot back, his demeanor changing so quickly that Jessica blinked.

"What is this all about? Is it some sort of lark? A new game you bored rich ladies play? Did you bet your country-club friends that you could get a job like this?"

Jessica shook her head frantically, but he ignored her sputtering attempt to deny the accusation.

"Well, I'm afraid you're going to have to go back home and pay up, Duchess. Because you lose."

"No! No, that's not it at all! You don't understand."

"Don't I? Lady, I may be just a cowboy, but I recognize designer jeans and pure silk when I see them." His mouth twisted in a sneer as he fingered a sleeve of her blouse. "What you're wearing costs more than you'd earn in a month as a housekeeper."

"Yes, but—!"

"Save it, Duchess. Since you won't be staying, it doesn't matter."

Appalled, Jessica watched him turn and walk away. In those few seconds she thought of the eighteen dollars and twenty-three cents she had in her purse. She thought of being stranded in a strange town with no job and no hope of finding one. She thought of having to return, defeated, to her mother-in-law's home.

The last thought was the prod she needed. "Wait!" Jessica shot out of the seat and tore after the two men. "Mr. Rawlins, wait!"

He ignored her call, but she caught up with him at the door and grabbed his arm. Frowning, he turned with an impatient sigh. "Look, lady—"

"Mr. Rawlins, you can't do this. You can't just dismiss me without even giving me a chance."

"Oh, no?"

He started to turn away again, but she held tight to his

arm. Looking pointedly down at her hand, he raised one brow. Jessica lifted her chin.

"No, you can't," she insisted. "You hired me as your housekeeper, and I accepted the job in good faith. I have your letter as proof. What's more, I went to considerable trouble and expense to get here."

"Somehow, I doubt that a couple of bus tickets are going to bankrupt you, but if you want to make an issue of it, I'll reimburse you for the cost. Plus a little extra for your time, of course," he added sarcastically.

Glancing around, Jessica saw that the other people in the café had stopped what they were doing and were avidly taking in the confrontation. On the pretext of wiping tables, the blond waitress had edged so close she could have heard them if they'd been whispering.

A flush crept over Jessica's face, but she stiffened her spine and drew herself up to her full height. "I'm afraid that's not good enough. We made an agreement. I've kept my end—I came here prepared to do the job you hired me to do. Now I expect you to keep yours and let me do it."

"Lady, we're talking about hard work. You wouldn't last two days."

He gave her a dismissive look that was part pity and part disgust, and with an air of finality, he shook off her hold and reached for the door.

Panic squeezed Jessica's chest like an iron fist. She couldn't let him just walk away. This job was her only hope!

"I warn you, Mr. Rawlins." She addressed his back, desperation giving her voice a strident edge. "If you renege on our agreement, you leave me no choice but to sue you."

Chapter Two

A gasp burst from the blond waitress. The wiry old man squawked, "What! Why, you can't do that!"

Hank Rawlins went utterly still.

Jessica's insides quaked as she waited for him to say something. Do something.

The whole thing was pure bluff, of course. She didn't have the money for a lawsuit. Even if she'd had it, she doubted that she stood a chance of winning. If Hank Rawlins only knew, she was scared to death and amazed at her own temerity.

But over the past seven years Jessica had learned to hide her fears, insecurities and hurts behind the veneer of polish she had so painstakingly acquired. When at last he turned to face her, she returned his look coolly and tilted her chin at an unyielding angle.

He put his hands on his hips and studied her for what seemed an eternity. Only mild curiosity and surprise marked his expression, but she knew he was angry. Beneath half-closed lids, his eyes glittered like blue flames.

"You're serious, aren't you?" he said finally.

Jessica drew a deep breath. "Yes."

He considered her a moment longer. Then he smiled—a slow, self-assured smile that caused her heart to give a little thump.

"Okay, Duchess," he said in a hateful drawl. "Since you're so determined, we'll give it a try."

"*What!* Hank, have you gone loco?" his companion demanded. The little man looked ready to explode. "You're actually gonna hire this society gal? Why, if she can cook a'tall, it'll most likely be somethin' hoity-toity. Somethin' French," he added, his lined, bewhiskered face screwing up with disgust. "Well, I'll tell you right now, I ain't eatin' no crepe suzetties. No pheasant under glass neither. I need good, simple workin' man's food. And plenty of it."

"Take it easy, Cooter. I doubt that Mrs. Collier will be with us long enough for her cooking to be much of a problem. By the way," he said, turning back to Jessica. "This is Cooter Davis, my foreman."

Jessica acknowledged the introduction with a polite, "I'm pleased to meet you," but the old man just snorted and rolled his eyes. Winning over Cooter, she realized with a sinking feeling, might be more difficult than proving herself to Hank Rawlins. And maybe more important. It was a daunting prospect.

"You do realize, don't you, that you've got this job on strictly a trial basis?" Hank emphasized. "Frankly I think once you're faced with the reality of hard work you're going to fall apart, but I'll give you one week. If by then I'm not completely satisfied, you're out on that cute little tush. You got that?"

Jessica nodded, too relieved to be angry. She swallowed

hard, and sent up a prayer that she would remember the skills her mother had taught her.

Hank looked around, frowning. "By the way, where's that boy of yours?"

"I'll get him." Jessica scurried back to the table before Hank Rawlins could change his mind. It took an awkward struggle, but she finally managed to lift her sleeping son from the seat, hoist him up onto her shoulder and back out of the booth. She turned to find Hank and Cooter right behind her.

Hank's hard stare accused. "You wrote that you had a school-age son."

"He is," Jessica replied defensively. "He starts school next month."

"Fat lot of help that young'un's gonna be," Cooter growled. "Why, he ain't nothin' but a tadpole."

Hank's mouth set. A muscle worked along his jaw, and Jessica knew he was grinding his teeth. She held Danny tight and bit her inner lip, certain he was going to tell her she couldn't have the job after all.

"Go get her luggage," he said to Cooter finally. His hard gaze never left her. "It's getting late, and we have a long way to go."

"Huh! Well, I sure as heck ain't playin' nursemaid to no snot-nosed kid, I'll tell you that right now," Cooter muttered as he stomped off. "Be under foot all the time, gettin' in the way. Enough to drive a body crazy. A kid ain't nothin' but a danged nuisance. Jist like women. Why, if it was me, I'd..."

They made the trip to the ranch in silence. Holding Danny in her lap, Jessica sat squeezed between Hank and Cooter in the cab of the battered pickup and endured the jostling ride that threatened to loosen her teeth. For the first ten miles or so she held herself rigid and tried to avoid bumping against either of them, but after a while she gave up the futile effort. Cooter grunted once when her shoulder slammed against his side, but otherwise, neither man seemed to notice.

Hank drove the mountain road with the ease and confidence of long experience and with a total disregard for potholes or the tortuous twists and turns...or her luggage. Every time the suitcases bounced and banged against the bed of the truck Jessica winced.

She dared not complain though. Cooter had been scathing enough about her luggage as it was.

"Must have a dozen bags back there," he'd grumbled when he stomped out of the storeroom only seconds after entering it. "Baby-blue ones," he added with a revolted grimace. "I'd break my back luggin' 'um clear through here. I'm gonna get the truck an' pull it around behind the café."

Slanting Jessica a sour look, he stalked by them. "Danged citified women. Can't go nowheres without all their clothes and geegaws."

The look Hank turned on her reeked of disdainful smugness, as though all his worst suspicions had just been confirmed. "Looks like I'd better give him a hand. Let's go, Duchess."

He hadn't offered to carry Danny for her, and she wouldn't have let him if he had, not with the low opinion he had of her. Staggering under her son's weight, Jessica had trailed Hank out of the café without a word, her spirits at rock bottom.

What did they expect, for heaven's sake? she wondered, slanting resentful glances at the men on either side of her. That she would have arrived with a change of clothes stuffed in a knapsack? Didn't they realize that this move was a permanent one for her and Danny? Even so, with the exception of one or two nice outfits, she had pared down their wardrobes to only the most casual clothes.

And darn it! The expensive designer luggage was all

she had. Lois, appalled and offended by the one cheap suitcase Jessica had owned at the time, had presented her with the set the Christmas after she and Allen had married.

"Though I may wish otherwise, you are a Collier now. For Allen's sake, and mine, you must keep up appearances."

A grim little smile tugged at Jessica's mouth as she recalled Lois's words that long ago Christmas. The cool response had not only cut off Jessica's attempt to thank her, it had established, beyond a doubt, her mother-in-law's feeling toward her and had set the tone for their future relationship.

The truck skidded on a section of washboard road, jerking Jessica back to the present and flinging her so hard against Hank's side that for a moment her face was pressed against his upper arm. His scent invaded her nostrils— dark, potent, virile and supremely male. Mingled with it were the smells of leather, horses, tobacco, sweat. The evocative combination sent a wave of heat rippling through her that made her breasts tingle and set up a throbbing deep in her feminine core. Appalled and flustered, Jessica jerked away from him and stared straight ahead.

Unable to resist, she peeped at Hank out of the corner of her eye to see if he had noticed her reaction. His attention was centered on the road, but the ghost of a smile that tilted his mouth made her uneasy.

She shifted her position and wondered irritably when they were going to reach the ranch. She had thought, from his letters, that it was only a short distance out of town, but they had driven miles already. She was tired, hungry, unsettled and depressed, and the broken springs in the pickup seat were poking her unmercifully.

Jessica had assumed that H. J. Rawlins was a prosperous rancher, but now she wasn't so sure. His pickup was certainly nothing at all like the air-conditioned, plushly appointed models the wealthy ranchers around Weatherford and Fort Worth drove. This was a working vehicle. It ran well, but otherwise it was a heap, sort of like the truck her father had been driving for the past fifteen years.

It was, she noted on closer inspection, battered, littered and generally filthy. Worn leather gloves, a two-foot section of barbed wire, several crumpled cigarette packages and a box of fence staples cluttered the dash. A bucket full of tools took up part of the floorboard on the passenger side, forcing her to sit with her legs at an awkward angle, and behind her head was a gun rack containing two rifles. When Cooter and Hank had tossed her bags into the back, she'd noticed that the truck bed had been strewn with hay, feed sacks, and some dark substance, the identity of which she didn't even want to speculate on. Jessica knew if it turned out to be something as innocuous as grease she would be lucky.

They descended a long grade, and at the bottom Hank slowed the truck. Jessica sat forward as he turned off the road and they bumped over a cattle guard onto a narrow gravel lane.

"Are we almost at the ranch?" she asked, unable to contain her curiosity any longer.

"We've been on R Bar B land for the past ten miles," Hank informed her. "Well, actually, this part, the mountain grazing land, is national forest, but I've leased it from the government for so long, it seems like mine. The ranch proper covers all of Blue Valley."

The mountain lane cut through a stand of tall aspen and spruce, and wound down a slope that opened into a long, curving valley. Glowing with a soft luminescence between the dark shadowy bulk of the mountains, the gentle sweep of land stretched away for miles. A creek snaking through its center shimmered silver in the moonlight.

Lights shone from a cluster of buildings near the base of the slope. As they descended, Jessica saw that the ranch headquarters was situated in a high meadow at the head of the valley. In the dim light of the moon she could make out a two-story wood house, a log barn, several smaller hay barns and sheds and a set of corrals of rough-cut timber.

By modern standards, it was a moderate-sized operation. The buildings were old, but there was a clean, well-kept appearance about them that spoke of permanence and pride.

With surprising agility for a man his age, Cooter hopped out of the truck the moment Hank brought it to a halt behind the house. Hank followed without so much as a glance in her direction.

A large collie trotted out to greet them, whining joyfully, her tail whipping the air. The sight of Jessica struggling out of the cab with Danny changed the dog's pace to a stiff-legged walk. A low, warning growl issued from her throat.

"Hush, Sheba," Hank commanded absently, as he and Cooter transferred her luggage to the screened porch that ran across the back of the house.

Jessica stood still beside the truck as the dog sniffed suspiciously at her legs. If she hadn't been afraid of dropping Danny she would have extended a hand, but her soft, "Hello, girl" started the plumed tail wagging again.

She looked up to find Hank observing the dog's acceptance of her. Without comment, he lifted the last two cases out of the truck and slung them through the open door to join the others.

"Welcome to your new home, Duchess." Turning to her with a sardonic smile, he held the screen door open wide and motioned her in with a mocking little bow and a sweeping flourish of his hat.

Sarcastic brute. Jessica hefted Danny a bit higher and wobbled up the steps past him with as much dignity as she could muster.

Light from inside the house spilled through a window

and the glass pane in the door. A washer and dryer and two enormous freezers stood along the inside wall of the porch. Lining the screening was a row of scraggly potted plants.

They trooped across to the back door, Hank and Cooter in the lead, Jessica dragging along behind them. Their boot heels hammered the wooden planks so loudly she was surprised that Danny didn't awaken. We're here, she thought wearily. At last.

After weeks of worry and anxiety and two days of traveling, all she wanted was to put Danny to bed, then follow suit herself as soon as she'd scrounged a bite to eat. Intent on doing just that, Jessica stepped over the threshold into the kitchen, and came to a halt.

She stood stock-still and stared. Never in her life had she seen such a mess. Crusted utensils and plates, dirty glasses and coffee mugs, covered the long trestle table that stood in the center of the room. Floating in the cold dregs in the bottom of some of the cups were soggy cigarette butts, and ashes coated the half-eaten food on the plates. A platter in the middle of the table held the remains of a shriveled hunk of meat that was charred on the outside and raw in the middle. In another, a limp pile of cold fried potatoes lay in a puddle of congealed grease.

Her eyes wide with disbelief, Jessica's gaze slowly swept the room. A small mountain of dirty dishes filled the sink, and more were strewn over the counters. Pots and pans, laminated with dried and burned food, some with rivulets running down the outside where the contents had boiled over, were stacked in precarious piles atop the stove. The air smelled of scorched food, rancid grease and stale cigarettes.

Lord, what a mess! Jessica doubted that there could be so much as a clean saucer left in the cabinets. And the floor! It was so covered with ground-in dirt and grime she couldn't even make out the color of the tile.

"Well, Duchess. This is it."

At the sound of Hank's voice, Jessica dragged her horrified gaze away from the disgusting sight and looked at the two men. Cooter shifted from one foot to the other and refused to meet her eyes, but amusement lurked in Hank's gaze as he watched her. Jessica realized then that he expected her to change her mind and refuse the job.

In truth, she was tempted to do exactly that, but only for a moment—just long enough for her to consider the alternative. Carefully keeping her expression bland, she remained silent.

Hank tossed his hat onto a rack beside the back door, sauntered over to the refrigerator and withdrew a can of beer.

"Want one?" he asked, holding the can up to Jessica.

"No, thank you," she replied in a distracted voice. "Uh…how long did you say it had been since your aunt retired?"

Hank leaned back against the counter and popped the top on the can. "A little over three months."

"I see."

"Besides Cooter and me, there are four other single hands. We've been taking turns in the kitchen." He paused to take a long pull on the beer. His brown throat worked rhythmically as the cold brew slid down. When finished, he swiped his mouth with the back of his hand and shrugged. "As you can see, we're not very good at it."

That was the understatement of the year. It was going to take hours of hard work before she could even cook breakfast.

"Would you like to see the rest of the house?"

"Does it look anything like this?"

Hank grinned. "Yep."

Her spirits took another dip. That was exactly what she'd feared. "No thanks. I'll look around tomorrow."

"What's the matter, Duchess? Afraid you won't be able to cope?" he taunted.

Jessica was too tired and too fed up to monitor her tone or her words, and she didn't even try. "Oh, I'll cope, cowboy. You can bet on it. But right now I want to put my son to bed, so I'd appreciate it if you'd show me to our room."

"Huh! Talk's cheap," Cooter put in.

Jessica ignored the crusty old man as Hank regarded her steadily. For an instant she thought she'd seen a flicker of surprise in his eyes, but she couldn't be sure. Shifting Danny in her arms, she met his gaze and waited.

He drained the last of his beer and tossed the empty into the overflowing trash can beside the counter. It hit the top of the pile and clattered to the floor, taking a soggy paper towel, a couple of eggshells and a lump of dried coffee grounds with it.

"This way, Duchess."

Hank showed her into a room that opened onto the kitchen. It was large, and comfortably furnished with an oak dresser and chest of drawers and a matching double bed. A patchwork quilt in shades of mauve, green and ivory served as a bedspread. A large multicolored braided rug covered most of the heart-of-pine floor, and at the back of the room, a double-wide window overlooked the stables and barn. Beside it sat an inviting platform rocker and a Victorian marble-topped table that held an ornate lamp with a fringed shade. Unlike the rest of the house, except for an accumulation of dust, this room was neat and clean.

"You have your own bath," Hank said, pointing to a door next to the dresser. "But I'd better warn you, there's an outside entrance from the porch. Sometimes, when I come in too filthy to track through the house, I clean up in there. So I'd advise you to keep it locked when you're using it."

Jessica nodded and made a mental note to do just that.

"There's a good size closet," Hank continued. "Though I doubt it'll hold everything you brought with you."

"Thank you. I'm sure we'll manage." Her arms were about to break. Jessica walked to the bed and laid Danny down. As she bent over to unlace his shoes Hank frowned.

"There's a bedroom upstairs for your boy. Why don't I carry him up for you."

Jessica looked up, surprised. "Oh, that's all right. He might be frightened if he woke up alone in a strange place. Besides, I'd rather have him here with me. Perhaps tomorrow we can set up a cot for him, but for tonight he can share my bed."

Cooter made a disgusted sound. "Well, that cuts it. It ain't bad enough we gotta be saddled with a kid. Now she's makin' a 'mama's baby' outta him. Women!"

Before Jessica could reply, he turned on his heel and stormed out, leaving her staring after him with her mouth agape.

"He's right, you know. You're not doing the boy any favors by coddling him."

Snapping her mouth shut, she whirled to face Hank, her stunned disbelief turning to anger and finding a target. "His name is Danny," she said through gritted teeth. "And he's just a little boy."

"True. But he'll never grow up to be a big one if you keep him tied to your apron strings." He looked her up and down, the hateful, taunting smile playing around his mouth again. "I'm assuming, of course, that you do know what an apron is."

Jessica ignored the dig. "Mr. Rawlins, my son lost his father just over a year ago, and now I've uprooted him from the only home he's ever known. I hardly think that protecting him from any additional unnecessary trauma could be termed coddling."

That Allen had barely remembered his son's existence

most of the time, or that the so-called home she and Danny had left was a stifling gilded prison wasn't the point, Jessica told herself. Nor was it any of Hank Rawlins's business.

"There's nothing traumatic about going to live on a ranch," Hank countered. "Most six-year-old boys would love it."

"Maybe. But don't you understand? Right now, all this is strange to him. This will be an abrupt change from the life Danny has always known."

"Oh, I believe that." Hank stepped close, and Jessica's heart rate shot up.

She became suddenly conscious that, except for her sleeping son, they were alone in the bedroom. For all she knew they could be alone in the house, since she had no idea where Cooter had gone. The only sounds were the whisper of the wind in the trees outside the window and her sibilant breath rushing in and out of her constricted lungs.

The quiet seemed heavy and thick, wrapping itself around them, and as she inhaled his scent Jessica felt a wave of goose bumps ripple over her skin. The look in his eyes was warm and suggestive, exactly as it had been earlier in the café, before he'd known who she was. He was lean and hard and vital, all man, and he radiated sexuality and charm as easily as he breathed.

She swallowed hard and gave a little start as he grasped the pointed collar of her silk blouse. Slowly, sensuously, he rubbed the delicate material between his thumb and forefinger, and smiled. "It'll be a change for you, too, I'd say."

His nearness, the deep timbre of his voice, did strange things to Jessica's insides. This close, she could see the pores in his skin, each individual eyelash, her own image reflected in his dark pupils. Rattled, she tried to lower her gaze, but Hank ran the back of his knuckles along her jaw and lifted her chin. Beneath heavy lids, his eyes gleamed wickedly.

He knew. Darn him, he knew exactly what kind of effect he had on her. It was the same as the effect he had on the gum-popping blonde in the café, and no doubt every other female between the age of six months and ninety years. And he was using it to the hilt.

Even knowing that, Jessica stood motionless beneath his touch, breathless, her insides quivering. Her rational mind told her that the last thing she wanted was to be attracted to this arrogant cowboy, but there didn't seem to be a thing she could do about it. There was simply no denying chemistry, no matter how illogical or unsuitable or unwanted.

Smiling, he slid his thumb back and forth over the slight cleft in her chin and coaxed, "Sure you don't want to call it quits? I'll even take you back to town and get you a room at the hotel."

His words snapped Jessica out of the sensual trance as effectively as a douse of cold water. Tilting her head, she broke the feather-light contact and stepped back. Her knees were strangely weak, and her heartbeat refused to slow down, but she faced him squarely, her expression determined. "No, Mr. Rawlins. I'm quite sure. I'm not quitting."

Surprise flared briefly in Hank's eyes. Then they crinkled with amusement, and he gave a careless shrug. "Okay. Suit yourself."

Long, deceptively lazy strides carried him to the door, but before he stepped through it, he turned back and pierced her with a sharp look. "Just remember, I expect you to have a hearty breakfast for six men on the table at five-thirty sharp."

As the door closed behind him, Jessica's firm expression faded into weariness. She sank down on the edge of the bed, her shoulders drooping. Oh, Lord. What had she gotten herself into? Nothing was turning out as she had

planned. The house was a disaster. Hank Rawlins was
nothing at all like the courtly, middle-aged rancher she had
imagined. And Cooter! The crusty old man was as tough
and hard as a pine knot.

Jessica sighed. She'd had such high hopes about this
job. Giving a mirthless little chuckle, she removed her
son's clothes and tucked him under the covers. This job
had been her *only* hope.

And it's *still* your only hope, she reminded herself.
Which means you have to make it work.

But could she? Though not all of it had been happy, not
the past seven years, anyway, she had always lived a shel-
tered life. At age eighteen, directly out of high school, she
had gone from being supported and cared for by her parents straight into marriage. Never before had she had to
fend for herself, much less someone else, and the prospect
was more than a little scary.

Whenever Jessica allowed herself to dwell on the enormity of what she was doing she was amazed at her own
temerity...and terrified. She wasn't, never had been, the
scrappy, independent type. To strike out on her own, especially since it meant defying someone as powerful and
vindictive as Lois, was out of character. But desperate situations call for desperate measures; and no matter how she
looked at it, she couldn't see that she had any other choice.
For Danny's sake, she had to be strong.

Though she'd been taught to work hard, she had no
experience, no training. Other than the domestic skills her
mother had taught her, the only other thing she knew how
to do was ranch work, and she doubted seriously that Hank
Rawlins, or any other rancher, would give her a job as a
wrangler.

The protesting grumble of her empty stomach interrupted her dreary thoughts. With a sigh Jessica started for
the kitchen, but halfway there she stopped, shook her head,

and detoured to the bathroom. Starving or not, she simply could not face that mess again that night.

Using the outside bathroom door, she lugged her cases in from the porch. They took up almost all the free floor space in the room, but she was too exhausted to bother with unpacking. Telling herself she'd do it tomorrow, she removed a clean nightgown from one case and headed for the shower.

Ten minutes later, Jessica made a face as she set her alarm clock, and slipped under the covers beside her little boy. She kissed his soft cheek and adjusted the blanket over him, then lay back with a sigh. Remember, he's the reason you're here, she told herself sleepily. For his sake, you'll do whatever you have to, and put up with anything.

In his room, Hank shed his shirt and tossed in onto the growing pile on the chair. A society girl. Hell, he must be out of his mind.

Hooking the heel of his boot into the V-shaped bootjack, he tugged it off, then repeated the process with the other. He should have bought her a bus ticket back to Texas and left her in the café.

So why hadn't he? It certainly hadn't been because of her pathetic threat. Sue, hell. Who did she think she was kidding? Nobody sued over a measly housekeeping job in the middle of nowhere, especially not a well-heeled filly from Texas. He peeled off his socks, wadded them up and chucked them on top of his discarded shirt.

You might as well admit it, Rawlins. You brought her to the ranch because you like her whiskey-colored eyes and that soft mouth. And the way she fills out a pair of jeans.

Hank's mouth took on a sardonic twist. Ah, well. Blood would out. Like his old man, he had an eye for the ladies.

He'd felt the pull of attraction the instant he'd spotted her in the café, but he'd figured her for a tourist, just passing through. The idea of her working as a housekeeper was laughable, but the opportunity to keep her around for a few days had been too great a temptation to pass up.

But, Jesus, Rawlins! A week? Hell, they could all starve to death in that amount of time.

A yawn blossomed and he gave in to it, stretching hugely. As he absently scratched his furred chest and concave belly, Hank noticed the shirt hooked over the bedpost. His hand grew still, and he looked around slowly, surveying the junk piled on top of the dresser, the rumpled bed, the soiled clothing draped over the chair and piled in the corner, the full ashtrays on the bedside table and dresser, the assorted clutter, the thick layer of dust everywhere.

He glanced through the open door into the bathroom at the overflowing hamper and the soggy towels littering the floor.

A slow, wicked grin split his face. Hell, what was he worrying about? Miss High Society wouldn't last two days, much less a week.

Hank shucked off his jeans and Jockey shorts and deliberately kicked them aside. Chuckling softly, he strode, naked, into the bathroom.

Chapter Three

The alarm went off next to Jessica's head at three-thirty the next morning. Groaning, she reached out a hand to shut it off. As she did the coolness of the air struck her forearm, and she frowned. She opened one eye and wondered why the alarm had gone off in the middle of the night. The next second she jackknifed straight up in the bed, her heart pounding as her gaze darted around the strange room.

Then she remembered. She no longer occupied that baroque bedroom in her mother-in-law's Fort Worth mansion. She was at Hank Rawlins's ranch in Colorado, and she was starting a new life, and a new job—the very first she'd ever had.

Two weeks ago the position had seemed like the answer to her prayers, and she'd accepted it with optimism and eagerness. Now the idea didn't have nearly so much appeal. The prospect of hopping out of the warm bed, tackling that horrendous mess in the kitchen, then cooking a huge breakfast for six men, to say nothing of facing her snide employer, all before the sun came up, seemed decidedly grim.

Still, that was what she was there for, and it wasn't as if she had any other choice. Jobs for twenty-five-year-old women with no work experience were not thick on the ground.

Gathering her courage, Jessica leaped out of bed and made a dash for the bathroom.

Even knowing what to expect, Jessica was stunned anew ten minutes later when she turned on the light in the kitchen. For a moment she simply stood with her hand on the switch and stared. Where did she start? Firming her mouth, she headed for the sink, rolling up her sleeves as she went.

For the next hour Jessica scraped and scrubbed and scoured, and at times chiseled away with a knife. Just finding room to work was a problem, since every inch of space was stacked with dirty dishes. By washing, rinsing, then drying one item at a time, she managed to clear one side of the double sink and a small section of counter and, in the process, set the table.

She had barely made a dent in the mess when it came time to stop and start preparing breakfast. Surprised, and more than a little relieved, Jessica discovered that the refrigerator was well stocked and the shelves in the big walk-in pantry were filled with an amazing array of home-canned fruits and vegetables, all neatly labeled and dated in tiny, precise handwriting.

Ina Mae's handiwork, no doubt, Jessica thought, and made a mental note to check for a garden. If, as she suspected, there was one, it would need tending, and there might be a late-summer crop to put up.

Jessica found the idea vastly appealing. When she had lived at home she had enjoyed working in their garden and helping her mother with the canning.

A wry grimace twisted her mouth as she poked through

the mason jars. She'd never forget Lois's reaction when she had naively gone to her and asked permission to plant a garden on the Collier estate.

"My dear child, Collier women do not grub around in the dirt," her mother-in-law had informed her icily.

Jessica shook her head. At the time she and Allen had been married less than a year, and she had just discovered that he was seeing other women. She had wanted—needed—a physical outlet for her hurt and rage. Instead, she'd had to settle for committee work and volunteering at the hospital—pastimes Lois deemed suitable for people of their station.

Since her marriage to Allen Collier, seven years before, Jessica had not cooked a meal or turned her hand to any kind of physical labor. At first she was awkward and disorganized, but gradually the skills and knowledge that had once been second nature came drifting back.

The first boot heel struck the back porch at exactly five twenty-nine. Jessica, who was dishing up a huge bowl of scrambled eggs, jumped as though she'd been shot. Immediately several more boots hammered against the wooden floor, and the screen door banged shut. In the early morning stillness the loud thudding sounded more like a herd of horses tromping across the porch than four men.

A skinny youth of about eighteen came through the door first and skidded to a halt, his eyes widening at the sight of the neatly set table laden with steaming platters of sausage, and hash-brown potatoes and bowls of cream gravy. When he spotted Jessica, his mouth dropped and his gaze grew wider still.

"Christ, Jubal!" the burly man behind him complained, slamming into the boy. "What the hell are you—"

"Watch yore tongue, Wooley. Cain't you see we gotta lady here?"

At the sound of Cooter's voice Jessica jumped again. She looked around in time to see the old man enter the kitchen from the hallway. Behind him, one shoulder propped indolently against the doorjamb, Hank Rawlins stood watching her, his blue eyes hooded and glittering.

Two more cowboys sidled into the kitchen behind the first pair and stood gawking.

"All you fellas know better'n to cuss around a lady, so mind yore manners," Cooter snapped. Scowling, he jerked out a chair and sat down. "An' take off them hats."

Jessica fought back a smile. Cooter, like her father, adhered to the old codes. He grudgingly accepted the modern world with its computers and space-age technology, but the rules he lived by didn't change. The equality of the sexes was all well and good, but an old-time western man treated a woman with respect until she showed she didn't deserve it. Cooter might not like her, but he'd personally throttle any man who slighted her in any way.

Amongst much coughing, clearing of throats and shuffling of feet, the cowhands whipped off their hats and mumbled apologies.

"That's okay," Jessica assured them with a soft smile. She placed the bowl of scrambled eggs on the table and stuck out her hand. "I'm Jessica Collier, the new housekeeper."

The young man named Jubal Conway turned crimson to his hairline as he accepted the handshake and stammered his name. Pretending not to notice, Jessica turned to the next man.

From the doorway, Hank watched the scene. Accustomed to brusque, no-nonsense Ina Mae, who tipped the scales at about a hundred and eighty and was as plain as homemade soap, the men were clearly flustered by this slender young beauty.

She *was* stunning, Hank had to admit. And a man would have to be dead or a eunuch not to notice the way she filled out those slacks, or the ripe swell of her breasts beneath that silk shirt.

And she was charming them. Already Wooley was showing off, and Jubal looked as if he'd been hit on the head. Even that old mossback, Buck, was grinning like an idiot.

Hank frowned. He'd expected her to be awkward around the men, maybe even condescending, not open and friendly.

Slowly his gaze swept the kitchen. He'd heard her get up a couple of hours ago. Lying in bed listening to the rattle of pots and dishes, he'd pictured her struggling ineptly with the mess, and laughed. Certain that by the time he came downstairs she'd be in tears and ready to throw in the towel, he'd turned over and gone back to sleep.

But he'd been wrong about that, too. Most of the kitchen was still a mess, but she'd already done more than he'd figured she would. Or could.

She wore an apron over her designer slacks and fancy shirt. They were a bit more worn than the clothes she'd had on the night before, but there was no mistaking the quality. By no stretch of the imagination could they be considered work duds. Even with no makeup and her tawny hair in a casual tumble about her shoulders, the woman looked classy.

When the introductions were made, she picked up the huge enamel coffeepot and moved around the table, filling mugs. Frowning, Hank studied her sure, competent movements, a nameless unease curling in his belly.

The four cowhands remained motionless, watching her as though entranced, and finally Cooter gave a disgusted snort.

"Well? What's everybody standin' around for? Let's eat."

Jessica hurried back to the stove, her insides fluttering.

Though she had avoided looking at Hank, she knew that he was watching her.

"Hmm, everything sure smells good," the red-haired cowboy named Slick ventured, giving Jessica a shy look.

"After eating our own cooking for three months, just about anything would," Hank drawled. He took his place at the head of the table, took a cautious swallow of coffee and raised his eyebrows. Damn, it was good! Better, even, than Ina Mae's.

"Man, this sure is good coffee," Wooley said, voicing Hank's thoughts and smacking his lips appreciatively. "What'd you do to it?"

Washed the pot, Jessica thought, but she merely smiled and said, "Nothing, really," as she added crocks of butter and preserves to the loaded table.

If Hank and Cooter had reservations about her cooking, the other men did not. They attacked the meal as though they hadn't eaten in a week. The clank and clatter of utensils against stoneware were the only sounds as platters and bowls were passed around the table.

Pleased, her confidence growing, Jessica hurriedly withdrew a huge pan of golden-brown biscuits from the oven and piled them onto another platter. "Here you go, fellas. Get 'um while they're hot."

Jubal's fork halted midway to his mouth. "Gaw-ol-lee! Would you look at them biscuits."

"Humph! Looks don't mean nothin'," Cooter scoffed. He shot Jessica a sour glance. "It's taste that counts."

"Well, if they taste anywhere near as good as the rest of these vittles, they're mouth watering, and I'm gettin' my share now, before they're all gone," Buck said, and grabbed a double handful. Slick, Wooley and Jubal quickly did the same, attacking the platter of steaming biscuits from all sides.

Watching them, Jessica nearly sagged with relief. Until that moment she hadn't known exactly how anxious she'd been. Her mother had taught her to cook when she was little more than a child, and before her marriage she'd helped prepare hundreds of meals for her family. Still, that had been a long time ago, and though she'd told herself over and over that she could handle the job, there had been a tiny kernel of doubt.

"Why did you only set six places?"

Jessica blinked at Hank's question. Confusion, then anxiety flickered through her. Had she misunderstood? "Why, I…I thought you said there were six of you."

"That's right. And you make seven."

"Me?"

"We don't stand on ceremony around here, Duchess. This isn't Fort Worth or Dallas. We all have a job to do. Yours happens to be to cook and keep house but that doesn't make you a servant. So if you want to play Cinderella you'll have to do it somewhere else. Besides, I can't eat with someone hovering over me."

"But…I, uh…I'd planned to wait and eat with Danny."

"Danny?" Wooley shot a questioning look around the table.

"Her son," Cooter informed him without even looking up from the plate of food he was devouring.

"C'mon, Duchess. You've been up for hours already." Hank calmly broke open a biscuit and slathered it with butter. His slow smile held mocking charm and the easy confidence of a man who knows he has the upper hand. "You can't keep working on an empty stomach. So grab a plate and sit down."

At a motion from him, Wooley and Slick scooted down and made room for her. Jessica had no choice but to do as he suggested.

Uneasily she slid into the empty chair to Hank's right. Beneath the table their knees bumped, and her nerves jumped as though she'd touched a high-voltage wire. Hank flashed her another grin and went on eating.

Jessica filled her plate mechanically, sure she wouldn't be able to eat a thing, but it had been almost twenty-four hours since her last meal, and with the first bite the gnawing hunger she'd felt the night before returned. Suddenly starving, she tucked into the food with a zeal that matched the rough cowhands'. Concern over the alarming effect Hank Rawlins had on her was temporarily pushed aside.

The others had finished eating and were enjoying their third round of coffee and a smoke before she was halfway through with her meal. Unable to believe her eyes, Jessica watched them flick ashes onto the remains of food on their plates. She lowered her head and kept her gaze fixed on her own plate, unable to look at the nauseating mess. If her position had been more secure she would have taken them to task on the spot, but she didn't dare. Somehow, though, she vowed, she would put a stop to the disgusting practice.

Cooter's cigarette hissed as he dropped it into the coffee left in his cup and stood up. "Okay, men, get the lead out. It's time to get to work."

Buck, Wooley and Slick got to their feet, but Jubal just sat there with his chin propped on his palm, his enraptured gaze fixed on Jessica.

Cooter rolled his eyes and looked disgusted. "C'mon, boy. Let's get goin'. We're burnin' daylight."

When the young cowboy didn't respond, the other three grinned and elbowed one another. Grumbling, Cooter marched around the table, hooked the turned-up toe of his battered boot around a chair leg, and gave it a jerk.

Jubal's elbow slipped off the edge of the table, and his teeth clacked together. He flailed his arms and grabbed the chair seat with both hands, barely saving himself from tumbling face first onto the floor.

"Jeez, Cooter! Why'd you go an' do that?"

"To get yore attention. We ain't got time to lollygag 'round the table drinkin' coffee an' makin' calf eyes at the housekeeper. Now haul yore as…uh…rear outta that chair an' let's get to work.''

Jubal's face turned the color of a tomato. He practically tripped over his own feet getting out the door. Hurrahing him unmercifully, Slick and Wooley followed.

Cooter was right on their heels, issuing orders. ''We gotta fence down on Salt Ridge. You an' Slick shag it on up there an' round up the strays an' make repairs. Wooley, you an' Buck come with me.''

Slipping a couple of extra biscuits into his pockets, Buck gave Jessica a sly wink, murmured a quick, '''Scuse us, ma'am,'' and hurried after them.

Watching them, Jessica sipped her coffee and bit back a smile. She felt sorry for Jubal, but if the boy wanted to work on a ranch he'd have to grow a tough hide. She'd never met a cowboy yet that didn't like to tease.

It wasn't until the screen door banged shut that she realized Hank had not gone with them. Cradling her mug of coffee in both hands, Jessica watched the curl of steam rise from its surface, uncomfortably aware of his nearness and the thick silence surrounding them.

Unable to help herself, she glanced his way and met his thoughtful scrutiny. The visual contact sent a tiny jolt through her. Though she strove to appear unaffected, the lines radiating from the corners of Hank's eyes crinkled.

Jessica cleared her throat. ''I, uh…I didn't realize that Cooter lived in the house.''

''That's because he's not only my foreman, he's also my uncle.''

''Oh. I see.'' She took a sip of coffee and groped for something else to say, but her mind was blank.

Perfectly at ease, Hank leaned back and balanced his chair on its rear legs. ''Tell me, Duchess, where'd you learn to cook like that?'' His lazy drawl held only mild curiosity, but Jessica knew he expected an answer and would keep digging until he got one.

She rose and began to stack the dishes, using the chore to put distance between them. The safest thing, she decided, would be to tell the truth. As much, at any rate, as he needed to know. Keeping her gaze lowered, she said, "My mother taught me."

"Is that right?" The comment was lazy, conversational, almost indifferent, but something in his tone conveyed doubt. Jessica looked up sharply.

"It's the truth."

"Oh, I believe you." He glanced around the table at the scant remains of the hearty breakfast. "I don't think they teach this kind of down-home cooking in those fancy cooking schools." Hooking his thumbs through his belt loops, he rocked back and forth on the precariously balanced chair and studied her through narrowed eyes. "But that raises a whole other set of questions, doesn't it, Duchess?"

A frisson of alarm skittered up Jessica's nape. "I don't know what you mean." She lifted a stack of dishes and carried them to the sink, presenting him with her back.

The front legs of Hank's chair hit the floor, and a moment later he leaned against the counter beside her. "Don't you?" he asked softly.

Jessica squirted liquid detergent into the sink, turned the water on full blast and stared stubbornly at the rising mound of bubbles. She had no intention of telling him, or anyone, about her background, or why she had sought this job. The fewer people who knew, the less chance there was of Lois finding her. Besides, if Hank found out that she was hiding, it would give him another excuse to dismiss her. No one wanted to be involved in someone else's personal problems.

Hank waited and watched. If he'd had any doubt that she was hiding something, it was gone now. He could almost see the wheels turning as she weighed her options.

Finally she tilted her head and gave him that sideways look that he was beginning to recognize as a habit of hers. This time it was half defiant, half wary. Hank wondered if she had any idea how seductive the tiny mannerism was. Desire rippled through him, followed quickly by irritation.

Smiling benignly, he reached out and smoothed a lock of her casually elegant, sun-streaked hair, and felt a stab of satisfaction at the flair of panic in her golden eyes. "You obviously come from a moneyed background. You and your boy dress well. You have elegance and polish, that certain air that comes from wealth and privilege. Yet your mother taught you to cook country-style." He cocked an eyebrow. "Did she marry well? Or did you?"

"Does it matter?"

"Oh, I'd say so, though you obviously don't want to tell me. And in either case, I have to ask myself what you're doing here. Why would a woman like you take a low-paying, backbreaking, thankless job on an isolated ranch miles from nowhere?"

"My reasons are personal. The point is, I can cook."

"Yeah. I'll give you that."

She turned her head and looked at him, her face at once full of hope. "Does that mean I have the job? Permanently?"

"Not yet, Duchess. My needs include more than just someone to do the cooking." His eyes became heavy lidded, and his voice dropped to a husky pitch that feathered over her like a caress. "Whether or not you get the job will depend on how well you...shall we say...satisfy those needs."

His smoldering gaze roamed over her face, her neck, then dropped to her chest and lingered. Her breasts rose and fell rapidly with her suddenly agitated breathing, and the wild beat of her heart made her silk blouse flutter. Looking into her wide, shocked eyes, he flashed that devilish grin that crinkled the corners of his eyes. "If you

think the kitchen is bad wait'll you get a look at the rest
of the house.''

Surprised, she blinked and slanted him another of those
sideways looks, confusion, relief, then indignation flashing
in rapid succession across her face as she realized she'd
been baited. Hank watched her with an amused, slightly
mocking expression.

Damn! That wide, sweet mouth was made for kissing,
he thought irritably. And her complexion invited a man's
touch. His fingertips itched to stroke her cheek, her neck,
to test the creamy texture of her skin. He wondered if it
was the same all over.

Giving in to temptation, Hank ran the backs of his fingers along her jaw, and smiled with perverse satisfaction
when he felt a tiny shiver ripple through her. She wasn't
immune to him either. And dammit! Her skin felt like
warm silk.

This was getting out of hand. He'd brought her here on
a whim. He'd thought to teach her a lesson, and at the
same time indulge in a couple of days of flirtation. He
hadn't counted on this gutsy determination. Hellfire! If her
other domestic talents were anywhere near as good as her
cooking, he was in deep trouble.

A few days was one thing, but it was madness to even
consider a permanent arrangement. A relationship of any
duration just wasn't for him. There was too much of Taylor
Rawlins in him for that. But if she stayed there was no
way he'd be able to keep his hands off her.

Hank stared hungrily at Jessica's mouth and fought the
urge to kiss her. Then his eyes narrowed on her wary expression. What the hell. Maybe that's the answer, he told
himself recklessly.

He took her by surprise. Tunneling his hand beneath the
thick mane of tawny hair, he cupped the back of her head
and brought his lips down on hers. He told himself it was
for her own good, but that didn't explain the shock of

pleasure that shot through him, the raging need. He didn't like it. Didn't want it. But self-denial was not even a possibility.

He had intended to keep the kiss brief and hard, a little rough, but when he felt the tiny shudder ripple through her his mouth gentled and clung. God! She was as soft and sweet as he had imagined. Softer. Sweeter. She stood stock-still, with her arms immersed halfway to her elbows in sudsy dishwater, her lips parted and quivering as he drank his fill. In fear? In shock? He didn't know.

When at last he drew back he managed a mocking smile, but his voice as an unsteady rasp. "We'll just have to wait until the end of the week and see how you cope, won't we, Duchess?"

At the door he plucked his hat off the rack, settled it on his head, then winked and sauntered out.

His loose, unhurried stride carried him across the porch and into the pale early-morning light. Through the window over the sink, which looked out onto the porch and the corrals beyond, Jessica's troubled gaze tracked him until he disappeared into the barn.

Her heart beat with a slow heavy thud that shook her chest. Oh, Lord. What on earth was she going to do now? Instinct told her that she had no reason to fear Hank; he wouldn't force himself on her. That wasn't his style. Besides, he didn't have to. He was a flirt, a practiced charmer who had only to flash one of those hot looks and crook his finger to have women come running. She knew that and hated it, but it was pointless to deny the attraction between them. When they were in the same room the very air crackled with tension.

She wasn't the type for an affair. That sort of life went against everything she been raised to believe in. Love, commitment, fidelity—those were what she wanted in a relationship. The things she *needed*. And no matter how he made her heart pound and her bones melt, Jessica knew she couldn't expect them from Hank.

Could she work there, be around him daily and resist his potent brand of seduction? Her chin lifted. Of course she could. She had promised herself that she would do whatever she had to do. Besides, the last thing she wanted in her life was another man with a roving eye.

Yet the feel of his mouth lingered, and when she raised a shaking hand to her lips it wasn't dish soap she tasted, but Hank.

"Who was that man, Mom?"

With a start, Jessica swung around. Clad in only his underpants, Danny stood in the bedroom doorway, knuckling his eyes and yawning. Oh, Lord. How long had he been there?

"Good morning, darling." Drying her hands on her apron, she hurried over to her son. "I didn't know you were awake."

"You weren't there." His bottom lip protruded and he glared up at her accusingly. "I woke up, and I didn't know where you were."

"I'm sorry, sweetheart, but I had to get up early to cook breakfast." Jessica bent over and hugged him. "That man you saw was Mr. Rawlins, the one I told you about." Watching for his reaction, Jessica breathed a sigh of relief when Danny brightened.

"Are we on the ranch already?" At Jessica's nod he began to jump up and down. "Oh, boy! Oh, boy! Can I ride a horse? Can I? Can I? Huh? Can I?"

Jessica bit her lower lip. Danny had been beside himself with joy ever since she'd told him that they were going to live on a ranch. Like most small boys, he dreamed of being a cowboy. In the past, much to Lois's displeasure, his greatest delight had been in visiting her parents on their small spread just outside of Weatherford.

She had thought that taking this job would be ideal, for

both of them, but it was clear that Danny was regarded as a nuisance, especially by Cooter. Originally she'd assumed he'd have plenty of wide-open spaces in which to roam, be able to explore the barn and corrals, learn about the animals—all the experiences she and her brothers and sisters had shared growing up—but it was clear she would have to keep him with her and out of everyone's way.

"I'm afraid I won't have time to give you riding lessons for a while," she stalled.

"When can you?"

"We'll talk about it later. Now, you go get some clothes on, young man, while I cook your breakfast."

He looked at her doubtfully. "Can you *really* cook, Mom?"

Jessica laughed and rumpled his already mussed hair, then turned him back toward the bedroom. "Yes, I *really* can." She gave him a little shove and a swat on the bottom. Giggling, he scampered away and she shook her head, smiling fondly. Males! They were such doubters.

But Danny's doubts, at least, were understandable, she admitted ruefully, busying herself at the stove. He'd never seen her so much as make a sandwich. Her mother-in-law had forbidden her to even set foot in the kitchen.

Jessica's face grew pensive. The memory of Lois's autocratic treatment was a sharp reminder of why she and Danny were there on Hank Rawlins's lonely, high-country ranch, and why, come what may, she was going to have to learn to cope with a cantankerous old misogynist and a sexy heartbreaker.

Danny came tearing back into the room just as she tipped a scrambled egg onto a plate. Once she had him settled at the table she went back to washing dishes. In between bites, he chattered away about the ranch, his voice high-pitched and excited. Listening only nominally, Jessica replied with an occasional "Mmm" or a distracted yes or no and gazed out the window.

She hated that she'd had to run away like a truant child, but she'd had no choice. She couldn't let Lois ruin Danny, the way she had his father. Over the past few months there had been every indication of that happening.

Lois had always interfered in Danny's upbringing, but lately she'd begun to completely usurp Jessica's parental authority, brushing aside her wishes, even countermanding her direct orders without a qualm when it suited her.

Complaining, Jessica had learned, was futile. Lois simply ignored her.

Jessica knew that her mother-in-law's threat had not been an idle one. Had she merely taken Danny and moved out of the Collier mansion, Lois would have used all means at her disposal, which were considerable, to gain custody of her grandson.

Wealth wielded power. The past seven years had taught Jessica that lesson well. The Collier influence and connections were strong in central Texas, especially in Tarrant County. Judges, senators, governors—people in positions of power—were frequent guests at Lois's dinner parties, and they all curried favor with the woman who controlled the vast Collier holdings.

Opposing Lois in a local court was a risk Jessica could not afford to take.

Her only hope was to remain hidden, which meant that, no matter what, she had to have this job.

Chapter Four

Danny did not take kindly to being confined to the house and its immediate vicinity. If Jessica had had any doubts about whether she'd made the right decision in removing him from his grandmother's influence, the tantrum he threw convinced her otherwise. Even six months before he would not have dared to behave so badly.

Much to his shock, however, Jessica swiftly quelled the rebellion, cutting off his shrieking whines with a firm shake and a stern warning that left him staring at her, utterly speechless. For the next two hours, while she dealt with the remainder of the dishes and put on a pot of soup for lunch, he sat at the table with crayons and coloring books, as docile as an angel, peeking at her cautiously every now and then. Jessica wasn't sure if he was more stunned by the fact that for the first time in months, someone had had the effrontery to oppose him, or by the sight of his mother actually doing menial work.

By the time she had finished in the kitchen Jessica was

so tired all she wanted to do was sit down and put her feet up, but she didn't dare. She had to make at least some visible headway before Hank returned.

Doggedly she took stock of the rest of the house. Danny trailed along with her, his curiosity and wide-eyed amazement growing apace with Jessica's horror as they moved from room to room.

She had never seen anything like it. The entire house was strewn with dirty clothes, newspapers, beer cans and assorted junk. Beds were unmade, the bathrooms piled high with damp, moldy towels and more dirty laundry. Overflowing ashtrays were everywhere. In the living room there was even a broken bridle draped over a lamp shade and a pair of spurs on top of a stack of papers, which were covering what she could only assume was a coffee table. And over it all was a thick layer of dust.

Jessica suspected that the house had not been cleaned since Ina Mae had done it last.

It was difficult to know where to start. Deciding that, next to food, clean clothes and linens were top priority, she began by stripping beds and gathering laundry.

There were four generous-size bedrooms upstairs. The largest had an attached bathroom and was obviously Hank's. A tobacco sack on the dresser in another identified its occupant as Cooter.

The two other bedrooms were unoccupied. Except for the musty smell and the thick layer of dust covering everything, they weren't in too bad of shape, but the bathroom at the end of the hall was a pigsty.

In Hank's room, Jessica moved around briskly and tried to ignore the fluttery sensation that assailed her insides. It was only natural, she assured herself, to feel a bit uneasy about invading the room of a man you barely knew, touching his personal belongings, his clothes…his underwear.

Yet, the strange feelings were not in evidence when she attacked Cooter's room. She felt no more qualms about marching into his domain and picking up his things than she would have any of her brothers'.

To Danny, who had grown up in a house manned by a staff of servants, performing domestic chores was a novel game, and he helped willingly. Even so, Jessica had to make more than half a dozen trips up and down the stairs before she had everything that needed washing. She began to wonder if Hank and Cooter had so much as a clean shirt left between them. When she had finished sorting, the floor of the back porch was knee-deep with piles of dirty laundry.

As soon as the first load was chugging away in the washing machine, Jessica attacked the litter. By the time the men returned for lunch she had cleared a path through the downstairs, hung all the sheets on the line to dry, washed, dried, folded and put away five more loads of laundry, and made a start on the ironing.

Jubal, Slick, Wooley and Buck were surprised and duly impressed when they stepped through the back door. Except for the floor, which was not as high on Jessica's list of priorities as food and laundry, the kitchen was spotless. The table had been bare before but it was now covered with a clean tablecloth and neatly set. At each place there was a steaming bowl of soup, and a platter piled high with thick sandwiches occupied the center of the table.

"Boy, it sure looks like you've been busy," Wooley said appreciatively.

"Yeah," Buck agreed. "I thought it'd take a week, at least, to set this place to rights."

Slick murmured his approval, and even Jubal managed to stammer a self-conscious, "Looks real nice, ma'am," though he blushed furiously and couldn't quite look Jessica in the eye.

Cooter merely glanced around and grunted before stomping over to his place at the table. Hank appeared not to notice any difference at all.

Jessica felt like hitting them.

She fumed so, it was several minutes after they were all seated before she noticed that her son had become the center of attention.

"Well now, you must be Danny," Wooley said, flashing the boy a grin as he took two ham sandwiches from the platter. "We've all been lookin' forward to meetin' you." He glanced around at the others and winked. "We could use another hand around here. By the way, my name's Wooley. This here's Buck and Jubal, and that carrot top over yonder's called Slick. I s'pose you already met Cooter and the boss," he said, indicating the men at either end of the table with a waggle of his spoon.

Round eyed, Danny shook his head as he tried to gulp down the huge bite of sandwich he was chewing.

"No, as a matter of fact, he hasn't." Hank supplied the information, smiling kindly at the boy as he stirred his soup. "He slept all the way from town last night, too."

"Law, boy! You'll have to do better than that," Buck teased. "Why, 'round here we're up and working before daylight."

"I worked. I helped Mom today," Danny said importantly.

"Humph! Woman's work," Cooter grumbled into his soup. He shot Hank a disgusted look. "Didn't I tell you she was makin' a sissy outta the boy?"

Jessica had survived the past seven, untenable years by holding her tongue, not making waves. By nature she was mild-tempered and had never been much of a fighter…except in defense of her son. Then she turned into a tiger.

Danny looked so crestfallen at the old man's sexist remark that she forgot the need for caution. "If you macho men had had a little experience in so-called 'woman's work,' this house wouldn't be in the shape it's in, and you wouldn't have been courting ptomaine for the past three months,'' she retorted tartly, spearing the old man with a challenging look.

Cooter nearly choked on a bite of sandwich, but before he could reply Hank's hateful drawl interrupted.

''Complaining already, Duchess?''

Stormy brown eyes met amused blue ones. Jessica clamped her teeth together. ''Just stating fact.'' Seething, she dipped up a spoonful of soup. Her throat was so tight she could barely swallow it.

The other men exchanged glances, then tucked into their meals with exaggerated concentration. Danny looked warily from his mother, to Hank, to Cooter, his eyes as round as saucers.

''Tell me, boy, have you met Sheba yet?''

The milk mustache on Danny's upper lip stretched wide in a huge grin at Hank's question. ''Yeah. I think she likes me. She let me pet her and everything.''

While Jessica had hung out clothes Danny and the dog had become acquainted. He'd spent most of the morning romping with the collie within sight of the back porch.

''I'm sure she does. Have you seen her puppies yet?''

''Puppies?''

''Yeah. She's got six. Four males, two females. They're down in the barn.''

''Aw, heck.'' Danny slumped down in his chair, his eager look crumpling into a sulky pout. ''Mom won't let me go near the barn or corrals.''

Hank cocked an eyebrow at her. ''Why not?''

Cooter muttered something about apron strings, but Jessica ignored him. ''I was under the impression that you wanted me to keep Danny out of your way.''

''You can't expect a boy to live on a ranch and not explore. He just needs to learn a few safety rules, and he'll be okay.''

''I don't want him to bother anyone.'' Jessica slanted a speaking glance toward the old man at the end of the table.

"Shoot, this little fella won't bother nobody," Wooley put in. "Why, I'll take him down to see the pups myself, soon as we're done eatin'."

"Oh, no you won't." Cooter scowled and shook his soupspoon at him. "You an' Buck are gonna irrigate that field of timothy grass."

"But the boy—"

"Never you mind 'bout the boy. If he's jist gotta see the danged pups, I'll show 'um to him. 'Sides, I know you, Wooley. You'd do might near anythin' to get outta irrigation work."

"Thank you all the same, Cooter," said Jessica, "but I really wouldn't want you to go to any trouble." Of all the men at the table, he was the last one she would have picked to look after Danny. The boy was at an age where he asked questions incessantly and wanted to touch everything. She could just imagine him driving Cooter up the barn wall in about five minutes flat.

"I ain't. I was gonna mend tack for the rest of the afternoon anyhow."

"Still, I—"

Jessica found herself addressing Cooter's back when he stood abruptly, crammed his hat on his head and headed for the back door. "If the boy wants to see them pups, you might as well send him down, since I'm gonna be at the barn anyway," he grunted ungraciously, and stomped across the porch.

"But—"

Hank put his hand on her arm. "Let the boy go."

"But Cooter doesn't—"

"—mean half of what he says. His bark is a heck of a lot worse than his bite. I guarantee it." Hank grinned as Jessica gnawed worriedly on her lower lip. "Don't worry. The boy'll be fine."

That evening when the men returned they were ecstatic to find a meal of pot roast and potatoes waiting for them.

Jessica was glad they were pleased, but she had chosen the entrée because it was easy to prepare. The succulent meat had slowly cooked all afternoon while she had dealt with the rest of the laundry and ironed over two dozen shirts.

She had also kept her eye on the barn as she worked. Despite Hank's assurances, she hadn't been comfortable about Danny being with Cooter, yet she'd had no choice but to let him go.

After lunch he had joyously followed Hank and the others as far as the barn, while she watched worriedly through the window above the sink.

She had expected that either her son would be put off by Cooter's manner or the old man would lose patience and shoo him out after a half hour or so, but the afternoon had crawled by with no sign of Danny returning.

Every now and then she'd caught glimpses of him through the door of the barn or the tack room, usually trailing along behind Cooter with a puppy or two in his arms and the others gamboling around his feet. Several times Jessica had considered going to Cooter's rescue, but then she'd thought perversely, why should she? He'd insisted on showing Danny the puppies. It would serve the cantankerous old prune right if the boy talked his ear off. Anyway, there had been so much to do Jessica hadn't felt she could take time out.

Shortly before dinner, Danny had finally torn in through the back door like a small tornado, flushed and happy and impossibly dirty, jabbering away a mile a minute about Sheba and her puppies and the horses and everything he'd done and seen. It had seemed to Jessica that "Cooter this" and "Cooter that" punctuated every other sentence.

If grime and sweat were barometers of how much he had enjoyed himself, she knew he'd had a stupendous day. There had been chaff and bits of straw clinging to his hair and clothing. The neat broadcloth shorts, knee socks and polo shirt that his grandmother used to insist he wear had been stained and ripped. But he'd been so happy Jessica hadn't had the heart to scold him.

Instead, she had plopped him into the bathtub with his fleet of toy boats and left him with instructions to bathe while she finished dinner.

She barely had time to add potatoes and carrots to the roast, put together a salad, and whip up another tray of biscuits and a fruit cobbler before the men came trooping in.

Wooley and Buck were lavish with their praise, and every time Slick helped himself to another dish he sniffed appreciatively and murmured "Wow." Even Jubal managed to stammer a compliment or two. Jessica smiled and accepted their approval graciously, but it was all a facade. Little of what they said even penetrated.

She was so exhausted she was glassy eyed. She could barely sit up. Her feet ached, her back hurt, her hands were a mess, and the muscles in her calves were cramping from being on her feet all day. It was an effort just to lift her fork. She didn't even care that Hank and Cooter hadn't said a word about the meal or all the work she had done. All she wanted was for everyone to finish eating so she could clean up the kitchen and crawl into bed.

To her dismay, the men lingered over coffee and cigarettes after dinner. Wrapped in a haze of exhaustion, Jessica watched with detached disgust as once again they flicked ashes onto their plates and stubbed out cigarettes in the remains of food. Remotely she knew she ought to put a stop to the revolting practice, the sooner the better, but she was too tired to get up and get ashtrays or to even say anything.

After what seemed an eternity, Cooter and Hank disappeared into the living room, and the others drifted back to the bunkhouse. By then Jessica had sunk into a state of numbness, and she moved about the kitchen like a zombie, hardly aware of what she was doing.

Though it seemed like midnight, it was only a little before eight when she emerged from the bathroom after taking a shower. Danny sat cross-legged in the middle of the bed waiting for her. Jessica's heart sank when she saw that he was holding his favorite book.

He looked up and grinned expectantly. "I'm not sleepy yet, so tonight let's read about Johnny Ringo," he said as he scrambled to the head of the bed and made room for her.

Jessica barely stifled a groan. Johnny Ringo was a fictitious cowboy hero of sterling character—a righter of wrongs, defender of the weak, champion of justice, who galloped from one adventure to another and, through deeds of derring-do, tamed the old west single-handedly. The tall tales were endless, and Danny ate them up with a spoon. Rarely was he satisfied with just one.

All Jessica wanted was to crawl under the covers and sink into oblivion, but reading Danny a bedtime story had long been a ritual with them. He had missed the treat the night before, and after he had been so good all day, she could hardly refuse the simple request, especially since she felt a bit guilty about spending so little time with him.

"Okay, sport." Wearily she tightened the belt on her robe and sat down beside him on the bed. "But just one story tonight. Okay?"

"Sure, Mom." Danny agreed readily, as he always did, but Jessica knew that pleas for more would follow anyway.

With a resigned sigh, she gathered him close and opened the book. Danny snuggled against her contentedly, his eyes bright with anticipation.

He couldn't let it go on.

Sitting with his booted feet propped on the newly

cleared coffee table, Hank stared at the television, but his mind was far from the action taking place on the screen.

Fun was fun, but it would be cruel to let her get her hopes up. What was worse, if he didn't get her out of there soon, the men were going to start getting used to her cooking. Hell's bells, *he* was going to start getting used to her cooking. And a helluva lot more.

He glanced around the room, his mouth twisting sourly. It still needed a good cleaning, but every last scrap of junk and trash was gone. To have gotten so much done she must've zipped through the place like a cat with its tail on fire. Hank shook his head. Who would have thought it?

He had expected ineptitude, tears, even hysterical tantrums. What he'd gotten was trouble—in the form of a gutsy, gorgeous creature who cooked like Betty Crocker and worked like a Trojan. And had a damn disturbing effect on his libido.

Well, it had to stop. And right now. His gut told him that this one particular woman could raise havoc with his life. That was something no woman had ever done. He'd never allowed one to get that close. If he let her stay, he wasn't sure he could avoid it.

Hank glanced at Cooter. He was mesmerized by the action on the screen, unaware that the crude "roll your own" cigarette he held had burned down almost to his fingers. Though the crusty old devil denied it vociferously, he was addicted to the police drama that centered around two women detectives.

Cooter never even looked up when Hank rose and headed for the kitchen.

He'd tell her it wasn't going to work, that he wanted her to pack and be ready to leave first thing in the morning. He'd even give her a month's pay for her trouble.

When he reached her bedroom, Hank knocked softly but no one answered. Stepping back, he saw the light under the door and knocked again, louder this time.

"Who is it?" The childish voice was barely above a whisper and held a touch of uncertainty.

"It's Hank Rawlins." As Hank answered he opened the door and stuck his head inside. "I want to talk to your mother—"

"Ssh."

Dressed in pajamas, Danny sat on the braided rug beside the bed, surrounded by a convoy of tiny trucks and cars, a stubby finger across his pursed lips.

"Mom can't talk right now."

"So I see."

Jessica lay slumped against the headboard with her head lolled to one side. An open book lay across her chest, still clasped loosely in her hand. She was sound asleep.

Hank stepped inside and closed the door behind him. Intrigued, he walked to the side of the bed and looked down at her. She lay in an awkward position that was bound to put a bad crick in her neck, as though she'd simply drifted off in the middle of reading the book. Hank suspected that was exactly what had happened.

Her hair was still damp from the shower, and a heavy swathe had slipped down over one cheek. Without thinking, Hank brushed it back. Her face was scrubbed and shiny, slightly flushed. The edges of her even teeth were visible between her slightly parted lips, and her lashes lay like dark crescents against her cheeks. The gaping robe gave him a glimpse of lilac lace and the rounded upper curves of her breasts, which rose and fell with each slow, deep breath.

She looked beautiful and fragile and vulnerable. And utterly exhausted.

Gazing at her, Hank felt a confusing tenderness well up inside him.

Danny rose and stood beside him. "Mom's tired. She worked real hard today," he whispered with something approaching awe.

"Yeah. She did." Hank looked down at the boy's solemn face and put a hand on his shoulder. "I think we ought to tuck her in so she'll be more comfortable, don't you?"

At Danny's nod, Hank slipped the book from Jessica's limp hand and placed it on the bedside table. He untied her robe, eased her into a half-sitting position and slipped the garment off. Keeping an arm around her shoulders, he slid his other one under her knees. "Okay now, when I pick her up you move the robe and turn back the covers."

Danny scrambled to follow Hank's instructions.

Jessica's nipples created rosy shadows beneath the pale silk, and adorned by the delicate lace, her skin looked creamy smooth. Gritting his teeth against the enticing sight, Hank placed her gently between the fresh sheets and tucked the covers snugly around her. She didn't even move.

He straightened and stared down at her, reluctant admiration mingling with other emotions.

One of her hands lay curled on the pillow beside her head. Though she had rubbed it with lotion, her skin was red and raw, the nails broken and ragged. The sight brought an unreasonable surge of anger, and Hank frowned. Why in hell was she doing this to herself? Why did she want this lousy job so badly? That nightgown alone had to have cost more than she'd earn in a week. It didn't make sense.

But she was a game little thing. He'd give her that. Shaking his head, he sighed and accepted defeat. How could you fire someone who worked her buns off to do an excellent job?

Dragging his gaze away from Jessica, Hank turned to Danny. "It's about time you were in bed, too, isn't it? Why don't you put away your toys, and I'll tuck you in."

"Yes, sir." Danny hurried to comply, but Hank could

tell by the boy's frequent furtive glances he wasn't sure what to make of the situation. Or him.

Hank hadn't paid much attention to the boy at lunch, and now he felt badly about it. Danny seemed like a good enough kid—despite his sissy clothes. And Hank liked kids. The only thing he regretted about remaining unmarried was that he'd never have any of his own.

The toys were quickly dumped into the bottom dresser drawer, but when Danny would have climbed into bed with his mother, Hank stopped him. "Your mom's really tired. I think she'd rest better if she had the bed to herself, don't you?"

"But where will I sleep?"

"There are two extra bedrooms upstairs."

"You mean...sleep up there? All by myself?" Danny's eyes were wide and fearful and his voice held a slight quaver.

"Sure. Why not?"

"Mom...Mom might get lonesome."

"Oh, I don't think so. Besides, you're getting to be a big boy. Too big to be sharing a bed with your mom. Don't you think so?"

Danny's bottom lip protruded. He stared at the floor and twisted a button on his pajamas. "I guess so," he murmured, his voice bleak and barely audible.

Hank hunkered down in front of him so that they looked eye to eye. Bracing his forearms on his bent knees, he tipped his head to the side and seemed to consider the situation seriously. "Tell me. Where did you live before you came here?"

"In my grandmother's house."

"Ah, I see. And did you have your own room in your grandmother's house?"

"Uh-huh."

"Well, there you go. This is your home now," Hank said reasonably, knowing even as he uttered the words that he was committing himself to far more than he'd intended. But he couldn't stand the uncertainty in the boy's eyes or that betraying wobble in his chin. Hank remembered all too well how it felt to be dragged from pillar to post, never having a place to belong. "I don't see any reason why you can't have your own room in my house, too. Do you?"

Danny sniffed and made a manly effort to blink back threatening tears. "I...I guess not."

Hank grinned and gave him a gentle punch on the chin. "Good boy." When Danny attempted a wobbly smile, he stood and scooped him up in his arms. "C'mon, pardner. I'll even give you a ride. And tomorrow we'll move your things upstairs."

Jessica panicked the next morning when she awoke and found that Danny wasn't there.

Surfacing from the deep sleep of utter exhaustion, it took several fumbling attempts before she succeeded in silencing the alarm clock. Groggily she raised her head and peered through the darkness to see if the racket had awakened Danny, and found herself squinting at the dim outline of an undisturbed pillow. "Danny?" Disbelieving, she groped for his small form, patting the mattress and pillow. "Danny, where are you?"

A glance at the bathroom revealed no light coming from under the door. "Oh, my Lord, Danny!"

Jessica leaped from the bed, her heart hammering. Snatching up her robe, she crammed her arms into it as she dashed for the door.

She paused in the kitchen just long enough to flip on the light and glance around before tearing through the room and out into the hall.

"Danny! Danny, where are you?" she called in a frantic whisper. She poked her head into the dining room, then scampered down the hall to the living room and did the same. "Daniel Patrick Collier, you answer me this minute, young man!"

A quick check of Hank's office produced nothing. "Oh, my God, Danny," she whimpered. "Where are you?"

Had he gotten up in the night and gotten lost? Had Lois somehow found them and spirited him away in the middle of the night? Panic exploded inside Jessica like a sky-rocket. Making a distressed little sound in her throat, she hiked up her gown and robe and pounded up the stairs.

Halfway to the top she hit a solid warm wall and let out a shriek as hands closed around her upper arms.

"Hey! Hey! Take it easy." Hank clamped a hand over her mouth and bent to bring his face level with hers. Over the top of his hand, her eyes were round and full of terror. "It's only me."

Momentarily Jessica's shoulders slumped, and she closed her eyes.

"What's going on? What're you doing running around in the dark?"

She stiffened and her eyes popped open again. When Hank removed his hand from her mouth she blurted, "It's Danny! He's missing! He wasn't in the bed when I woke up! I've got to find him!"

"Hey, wait a minute." When she would have darted past, Hank hooked an arm around her waist and hauled her up close against him, ignoring her struggles. "Okay, just calm down. What're you getting so hysterical about? Danny's not missing. He's upstairs in his bedroom, sound asleep."

Nonplussed, she could only stare at him.

"He's fine," he assured her more gently.

"What…what do you mean, *his* bedroom?"

"The one I put him in last night." He grinned then, his teeth a slash of startling white in the dim light that floated up from the kitchen. "Right after I tucked you into bed."

"You had no right—"

Jessica broke off, her thoughts scattering as she noticed the flirtatious gleam in Hank's eyes and the sensuous smile that tilted his mouth. A wave of heat seemed to rush up from her toes all the way to her hairline as she became aware of the intimate alignment of their bodies. He stood with his legs braced apart, his hard thighs bracketing hers, his maleness pressed boldly against her soft abdomen as he held her tightly to him.

Pushing her hands against his chest, Jessica strained back and tried to put some space between them, but the action merely pressed their lower bodies closer.

Hank's smile grew. The big hand splayed across the base of her spine flexed erotically while the other glided over her back, his skilled fingers massaging, caressing.

"Let—" Jessica's voice broke, and she stopped to clear her throat. "Let me go."

She tried to inject the words with a note of crisp command, but they came out husky and unsure, which seemed to amuse him.

"Why?"

"Because…because I want you to." Struggling to ignore the hot sensations surging through her and pull herself together, she thrust out her chin. "We have to discuss this business with Danny. I will not have you interfering—"

"Ssh. You're going to wake the boy."

Jessica's glare produced a chuckle. "All right. If you insist. But we'd better find someplace more private. Cooter's going to come stomping out of his room any minute now."

He released her reluctantly, his hands sliding over her curves with blatant provocation. Giving him a killing look, Jessica jerked free of his touch, but the violent movement caused her to lose her balance. If Hank's arm hadn't shot out and caught her, she would have tumbled headfirst down the stairs.

"Whoa," he advised with a chuckle. "Take it easy."

Her cheeks blazing, Jessica snatched herself free again, stormed down the steps ahead of him and stalked into the kitchen with her head held high, her bare feet making little slapping noises against the cold floor.

She couldn't remember ever experiencing such a confusing mixture of emotions—relief, excitement, embarrassment...and mind-numbing anger. Never before in her life had she felt such a strong urge to haul off and punch someone in the mouth.

When she reached the table in the middle of the room, she drew a deep breath and whirled around. "I told you distinctly that Danny would share my room. You had no right to put him upstairs."

"Danny and I talked it over. He has no problem with the arrangement, so why should you?"

Because I want him near me, where I can reach out and touch him, she thought in a vivid burst of insightful self-honesty. Because I'm all alone, on my own for the first time in my life, and it's scary. Because I'm so afraid he'll be taken away from me.

But Jessica didn't dare tell Hank any of those reasons. Turning away, she snatched up the coffeepot. She filled it with water, turning on the faucet full blast, her forceful, jerky movements betraying her agitation. "I feel more comfortable having him near me," she improvised. "I know that Cooter doesn't want him around."

"I told you—Cooter's bark is worse than his bite. He tries to give the impression that he's a tough old buzzard, but he's nothing but a big softy. Especially when it comes to kids."

"Oh, pul-leeze." Jessica gave a little snort and shot him an oblique look that reeked with disbelief.

"No, really. It's true."

As she spooned coffee into the basket, Hank came to stand beside her and leaned his hip against the counter. Panic, and something else, something more heady, more dangerous, ran just below the surface of her skin. He was too close, too big, too male.

She glanced at him out of the corner of her eye, and gritted her teeth. He had the kind of body that was made for western clothes—lean hipped, broad shouldered, rangy. The chambray shirt was stretched taut over his muscled chest. A tuft of the silky black hair was visible in the vee neckline, and the rolled-up sleeves revealed still more sprinkled over his corded forearms and the backs of his hands. Low-riding worn jeans, soft and faded almost white at revealing stress points, molded his strong thighs and cupped his sex like a lover's hand.

To Jessica's horror, the disturbing erotic drift of her thoughts caused a tightening between her legs. Breathing became difficult, and her breasts grew heavy, achy, the sensitive tips peaking against their silk covering.

The tiny abrasion served as a shocking reminder to Jessica that she was dressed in only a thin nightgown and robe. Mortified and self-conscious, she turned quickly away from Hank to set the coffeepot on the stove. For several seconds she simply stood and stared at the ring of blue flame beneath the pot.

"Look, Duchess. I know you're just trying to protect your son, but Cooter's right about one thing. If you don't cut the boy some slack, you're going to ruin him. And believe me, a man who's a mama's boy is no man at all."

Oh, Lord, she knew that! Better than anyone. And she knew, too, that Hank was right. She had, out of sheer desperation, taken Danny and fled to keep Lois from turning him into the same spoiled, self-centered kind of man his father had been. And yet, here she was allowing fear and anxiety to make her just as overprotective and possessive.

Jessica drew a deep breath and turned to face Hank, her expression rueful. "You're right, of course. From now on I'll try to curb my 'smothering mothering' tendencies."

Nervously she raked a hand through her tumbled hair,

then tightened the belt on her robe. She folded her arms over her midriff, unfolded them and put her hands in the pockets of her robe, then took them out again and clasped them behind her back. Avoiding Hank's steady gaze, she glanced down at her bare feet, and grimaced. Flapping her hands nervously, she sidled toward the bedroom. "I, uh…I'd better go get dressed."

"Why?" Hank pushed away from the counter. His loose stride carried him across the room with deceptive swiftness, and he intercepted her before she reached the door. "I kinda like you the way you are," he murmured. "With your hair mussed, looking all warm and rosy with sleep. And sexy."

Instinctively Jessica brushed a thick tumble of hair away from her face, and Hank chuckled, a low, rich sound that did funny things to her insides.

He raised a hand and stroked a lock at her temple. The feathery touch and the sensuous warmth in his blue eyes made her heart gallop. Before she realized what he was doing he had slipped his arm around her waist and tugged her to him. "I don't mind telling you, you lying with your head on the pillow next to mine is a sight I wouldn't mind waking up to."

To Jessica's horror, the suggestive words sent ripples of excitement cascading through her. Shaken, she could only watch, wide-eyed, as his head descended.

Until that moment, Jessica had thought of herself as an experienced woman. After all, she had been married and she was the mother of a six-year-old. She'd been kissed before, many times…or so she'd thought. Now she realized she'd been mistaken.

Before Allen there had been only the inept kisses of a few high-school boys, and her husband had only been interested in his own pleasure. Hank kissed her with the consummate ease of a mature man who knew exactly what he wanted and how to get it, a man who gave as well as took. His arms wrapped around her, molding her to him, which was just as well, Jessica realized vaguely, because she doubted that her legs could have supported her.

The kiss was long and leisurely, consuming—arousing beyond all thought of resistance. Jessica could only cling, and cling, while her body trembled and her senses whirled.

He tasted of minty toothpaste, and he smelled of shaving cream and soap and healthy male. His body was hot and hard against hers.

Jessica's breasts were flattened against the muscled wall of his chest. The thin silk of her gown and robe provided no barrier at all. She felt a searing heat from the hand splayed over her bottom, his hard arousal straining against her lower belly. His belt buckle imprinted itself cruelly against her flesh, but she didn't care. The abrasive rub of heavy denim and cotton, the remote awareness that he was fully dressed while she wore only the flimsiest of night-clothes, was strangely exciting. At that moment she was so enthralled by the glorious sensations nothing else existed.

Their lips parted slowly, and as Hank raised his head, he smiled down into her drowsy, bemused eyes. "I think I hear Cooter coming."

It wasn't so much his words but the amused satisfaction in his voice that jolted her back to reality. Jessica blinked twice, then stiffened and backed out of his embrace. Hank cocked his head to one side and watched her, and Jessica was resentfully aware that she was free merely because he had chosen to release her.

"I...I must ask you not to do that again," she managed to stammer with shaky dignity, though her body still throbbed with aftershocks of passion.

"Why not? You enjoyed it as much as I did."

A hot tide of color surged up into Jessica's neck and face, but she didn't try to deny the statement. What would be the point? Turning her head slightly, she tilted her chin and slanted him a cool look. "I'm here to work as a house-keeper and nothing else. I will not become involved with you, Mr. Rawlins."

"Hank," he corrected. "And again, why not? You still haven't given me a reason."

"I'm not interested in an affair, and I certainly won't be any man's mistress." Her voice grew stronger along with her anger at his refusal to just accept no for an answer. "May I remind you that I have a small, impressionable child to raise and a reputation to protect. Those are reasons enough. Now, if you'll excuse me, I must get dressed if I'm going to have breakfast ready on time," she said coolly, and swept past him in a fluttery swirl of lilac silk.

Though upset, with herself as well as Hank, Jessica didn't stop to rant and fume. She had wasted too much time already. She splashed cold water on her face, brushed her teeth and gave her hair a few swipes with a brush and in less than five minutes dashed back into the kitchen dressed in a pair of black jeans and a madras shirt that had cost the earth at Neiman's in Dallas.

Hank had left, but Cooter was at the stove pouring himself a cup of coffee. He grunted a brusque "Mornin'" and sat down at the table to read a farm-and-ranch journal.

Ignoring him, Jessica raced around setting the table and pulling out pots and pans. By the time the men arrived she was pouring the last of an enormous batch of pancakes onto the griddle and had a platter of ham and eggs warming on the back of the stove.

As they had been the day before, the men were lavish with their praise and dug into the meal with gusto. Thanks to Wooley's gregarious nature, conversation flowed freely, and no one seemed to notice that Jessica said little. She didn't look at Hank but was aware that he watched her throughout the meal with a mysterious smile on his face.

After breakfast and their morning smoke, all the men

rose at once to leave. Jessica was about to heave a sigh of relief when Hank, who was last in line, paused at the door and looked at her with that familiar devilish twinkle in his eyes.

"You know, don't you, Duchess, that it's a little late to be worrying about your reputation. By now word has spread around Elk Falls about my pretty new housekeeper. An attractive young woman like you living with a bachelor...people are going to assume that you're doing more for me than keeping house." He shrugged. "Hell, if we're going to get the name, we might as well enjoy the game, don't you think?"

With that, he settled his hat on his head, winked and strolled out.

Chapter Five

Though she worked harder than she ever had in her life, the probation period seemed to drag by. Day by day Jessica grew more apprehensive. By the end of the week she was a bundle of nerves. At times she worried about what she would do if Hank didn't give her the job, and at other times she worried about what she would do if he did.

Since the second morning he hadn't come near her or made any more suggestive remarks. In fact, he seldom looked at her or spoke to her at all. But Jessica didn't kid herself that he had dismissed what had passed between them. Whenever they were in the same room she was aware of a crackling tension in the air. She knew that Hank felt it too.

It bothered her that she was drawn to him. Not only was the attraction an added complication that she didn't need in her life, it was also hopeless. Jessica hoped to remarry someday. The seven years she'd spent with Allen had been miserable, and probably would have discouraged most people, but she'd seen firsthand that it was possible to have a lasting, loving marriage. She had been brought up in a warm, close-knit family, by parents who, even after twenty-seven years, still adored each other. And Jessica was determined to have that kind of happiness for herself.

But, no matter how much she might wish otherwise, Hank simply wasn't the marrying kind.

After stewing over the situation for days, Jessica finally decided that she would simply have to ignore the attraction, put it out of her mind completely. Provided, of course, that Hank gave her the job.

She didn't know what she would do if he didn't. The week's pay he would owe her wouldn't last long, and she had already sold everything of value she'd owned to scrape together bus fare to Elk Falls for Danny and herself.

The morning the week was up, Jessica rose earlier than usual. She'd spent a restless night, dozing now and then, only to awaken with a start to toss and turn some more.

She felt almost ill as she cooked breakfast. Her stomach was a hard knot. Stirring a pot of stewed apples, Jessica looked anxiously around the kitchen.

It was neat and tidy. She had washed all the dirty fingerprints from the cabinets and walls. It had taken her an entire morning to clean the cooked-on mess from the range top and oven. She had even scrubbed the kitchen floor on her hands and knees. The lovely blue-and-white tile she'd discovered beneath the grime now glimmered with a mirror shine, the results of two coats of wax and vigorous hand buffing.

In the other part of the house the rugs and upholstered pieces were vacuumed, the bathrooms were scoured, and the furniture glowed with polish.

But would it be enough?

The house wasn't immaculate yet; there were still windows to clean, inside and out, and all the curtains needed to be taken down and washed, and the wooden floors needed attention. But surely Hank knew that it would take longer than a week to make up for months of neglect. Didn't he?

Jessica closed her eyes and pressed her balled fist against her churning stomach. She honestly had no idea what Hank thought, or what his decision would be. Not once had he appeared to notice all the work she'd done. Neither had Cooter.

As usual, everyone arrived right on time for breakfast. Throughout the meal Jessica was as nervous as a cat. She cast anxious looks Hank's way, but he acted as though it were just another day like any other.

When the men got up to leave and he rose with them, Jessica almost panicked. She was frantically searching for a way to ask for his decision when he turned back to her and said, "I'm leaving one of the pickups here today so that you can go into town for groceries. I figure we should be getting low on a few things about now. You can charge whatever you need at Stoval's market."

Jessica looked up sharply, hope squeezing her chest. "Does, uh...does that mean that I have the job?"

Hank paused in the act of reaching for his hat and walked back to her. A lopsided grin kicked up one corner of his mouth, but his eyes held a predatory gleam that made her uneasy. "Did you have any doubt?"

"Some," she admitted, watching him.

"Hell, Duchess, after a week of eating your cooking, the men are spoiled. They'd probably lynch me if I got rid of you now."

He smiled at her look of relief, and added in a lower tone. "Before you accept, though, I feel that I should warn you. I want you, Duchess. And I'm going to do my damnedest to have you. If you think you can deal with that, the job's yours."

Jessica saw the challenge in his eyes. She tilted her head

and met it coolly, though her heart thumped. "I won't be forced into an affair."

"Honey, I've never used force on a woman in my life. When you come to my bed, you'll come willingly." His smile stretched into a devilish grin. "Of course, if you're worried that you won't be able to resist, you can refuse the job. But while you're deciding, there's one more thing you might want to keep in mind." His unblinking gaze held hers, and though a faint smile still curved his mouth Jessica knew that he was serious. "I've yet to meet a woman I wanted that I couldn't have."

"You have now." Her voice was sharp, emphatic, though she didn't doubt his claim for a moment. With his rakish good looks, and that indolent charm, Hank would draw women the way honey drew flies. He drew her, she admitted uneasily, but she was determined to resist the pull. She had to.

"We'll see." He settled back with his hips against the counter and crossed his arms over his chest. "That is, if you've decided to stay. The choice is yours."

Her stomach knotted with fear and excitement. A taut silence stretched out. Finally Jessica held out her hand, palm up. "I'll need the keys to the truck."

"They're in the ignition," he said, watching her with satisfaction. "Anything else?"

"Yes. How do I get there? I wasn't paying attention the night you brought me here."

"I'll show you." He bent over the table and pulled a paper napkin from the holder. As he drew a map he added, "And while you're in town, buy yourself some jeans and shirts."

"Why? I have plenty of clothes."

"I'm talking about plain everyday jeans and cotton shirts, not those high-priced fancy duds you've been wearing." When she would have argued he cut her off. "Look, you've already ruined three silk blouses. And you probably wore holes in the knees of your designer jeans scrubbing the damn floor. Before long you'll have run through everything you own and you'll be forced to buy some serviceable clothes, so why not do it now and save your good stuff?''

A little dart of pleasurable surprise shot through her. So he had noticed her efforts.

What he said made sense—except that she didn't have the money to buy anything. Jessica wasn't about to admit that, however, so for the sake of peace she agreed. "All right. I will.''

"Good. And while you're at it, you'd better shop for Danny, too. School starts in a couple of weeks. If he shows up in those sissy shorts and knee socks, the other kids'll make fun of him.''

Jessica grimaced, knowing that he was right. The shorts and knee socks and neat little preppie shirts were an example of her mother-in-law's recent determined efforts to usurp Jessica's parental authority.

A few weeks before, they had clashed over which school Danny would attend. Jessica had informed Lois that she was sending him to public school, not to the snobbish, upper-crust private academy that Allen had attended. She had thought the matter settled, but a few days later she discovered that not only had Lois ignored her wishes and enrolled Danny in Fulbright Academy, she had also replaced the school wardrobe that Jessica had purchased with more "suitable attire." All of his brand-new jeans, shirts and sneakers, Lois had peremptorily donated to charity.

Jessica's outrage had been met with a cool stare and a clipped, "*I* will decide what is best for my grandson. He will attend Fulbright, and there is nothing you can do about it.''

"I most certainly can!" she had flared back in astonishment. "I can take Danny and leave.''

That was when Lois had made her threat.

"I think not," she had replied in a cold, clipped voice. "If you dare to even try to take my grandson away from me, I'll blacken your name so that no judge in the state will allow you to keep him. Or even visit him. And you know I can do it." Her eyes had flickered disdainfully over Jessica's stricken face. "So just remember. Cross me, and I'll make sure that you never see Danny again."

But instead of cowing Jessica, the threat had made her aware of just how ruthless and determined Lois was, and had galvanized her into taking action, something she might not have had the courage to do otherwise.

Lost in unpleasant memories, Jessica started when Hank straightened.

"Get the boy some sturdy jeans and cotton shirts. And some boots. Hendricks's Dry Goods should have everything he'll need."

Biting her inner lip, Jessica took the crude map he held out. She hesitated only a beat before nodding her agreement.

An uneasy feeling gripped Jessica when she parked the pickup in front of Stoval's Grocery. At the secluded mountain valley ranch she had felt safe, hidden. Here, out in the open with strangers moving around her, she felt exposed.

She climbed from the pickup but paused on the sidewalk. Her cautious gaze scanned the street on either side. From where she stood, the ground sloped upward toward the mountains at the opposite end of town, giving her an unobstructed view. Elk Falls appeared to be only about five, maybe six blocks long.

Across the street on adjacent corners were the feed store and Alma's café. To her right, on the other corner, was Maynard's service station, where she had gotten off the bus the previous week.

Though the town wasn't exactly a beehive of activity, there were people on the street. Most were ranchers or cowhands, but there were others—mothers with small children, a few tourists in their Bermuda shorts and sunglasses with their ever-present cameras dangling from straps around their necks, a small party of cyclists wearing their helmets and tight racing clothes, the familiar old men sitting on benches in front of the stores.

All were going about their business, paying her no mind.

Jessica released a deep sigh. As the tension drained away, she allowed herself a lingering look at the quaint little town.

Without the softening cloak of twilight, Elk Falls appeared even older than it had that evening a week ago, but even with its wrinkles and seams showing, it still had the picturesque charm of a bygone era. The street lamps were old ornate affairs of black-painted wrought iron and had probably been converted to electricity only in recent years. There were no signal lights at all, which didn't seem to matter since the traffic was sparse and slow.

A run-down, preposterously ornate structure in the next block bore a faded gilt sign that read, Placer Opera House, Estb. 1882. Further down, on the opposite side of the street, a Victorian hotel and boarding house stood like a dignified old dowager, leaning a bit under the weight of years but still proud. Against the faded blue clapboards, its cream-painted gingerbread trim resembled starched lace on an old dress.

Maynard's 1950s vintage service station appeared to be the newest structure in town, Jessica thought with an amused smile as she turned and entered the grocery store.

The store was small but well stocked, and Jessica quickly found everything she needed. When she explained to the cashier that she wanted to charge her purchases to Hank Rawlins's account, the sour-faced woman narrowed her eyes and looked her up and down.

"So, you're the new housekeeper, huh." There was something in her tone that Jessica couldn't quite put her finger on, but there was little doubt it was uncomplimentary.

Jessica smiled. "Yes, I am."

The woman merely snorted and shoved the charge ticket across the counter for her to sign.

So much for western friendliness, Jessica thought as she wheeled the cart out to the sidewalk a few minutes later and began loading her purchases into the truck.

As she turned to heft the last sack, someone called her name. Startled, Jessica looked up to see Alma Pierce hurrying toward her, cutting catercorner across the intersection.

"Hi, there. I recognized Hank's truck when you drove into town. I was hoping I could catch you before you got away. Come on over to the café and let me buy you a cup of coffee."

"Oh, I really should get back—"

"Nonsense. Hank's not a slave driver. He won't mind."

"But the groceries…"

"No problem. You can stow the perishables in my refrigerator until you're ready to leave." Alma cast an experienced eye over the sacks, grabbed up two, handed one to Jessica and headed for the café.

"But…what about the rest?" Hurrying after the older woman, Jessica cast a worried look over her shoulder at the sacks of groceries filling the back of the truck.

"Oh, don't worry about those. No one will bother them," she said airily. "Come on and take a break." Elbowing Jessica in the ribs, she winked and grinned. "Ever since you left here last week I've been dying to know how things were going. I almost dropped my teeth when you pushed Hank Rawlins into a corner the way you did."

Jessica looked sheepish. "I didn't mean it. It's just that I needed the job, and threatening him was the only tactic I could think of."

Alma laughed and patted her arm. "Serves him right, I

say. Having you come all the way up here then turning you down just because you're easy on the eyes. The very idea!''

When they entered the café, Alma took the sack of groceries from Jessica and waved her toward a booth. "Have a seat while I put these things in the fridge. Loreen!" she called over her shoulder as she disappeared into the kitchen. "Get Mrs. Collier and me some coffee, will ya."

A few moments later Jessica jumped when two mugs were plunked onto the table in front of her so hard that coffee sloshed over the edge. Surprised, she looked up into the hostile eyes of the blond waitress. The girl stood with one hand planted on an out-thrust hip, diligently working over a piece of gum. "There's your coffee. You want anything else?"

Jessica raised an eyebrow at her aggressive tone. She pulled several napkins from the dispenser and sopped up the spill. "Uh, no...I don't think so."

Loreen turned and stalked away as Alma slid onto the bench seat on the opposite side of the booth. Jessica wanted to ask what was bothering the girl but before she could, the older woman launched into a friendly inquisition.

"So tell me, have you locked horns with Hank many times this past week?"

"A few."

"Hmm. Well, you look all in one piece to me, so I guess you survived. The important thing is, is he going to let you stay?"

"Yes. Yes, I think so." Jessica smiled and took a sip of coffee, feeling the relief seep through her as she said the words. She had been so worried; it was still difficult to believe the job was really hers.

"Well, good for you!" Alma reached across the table and patted Jessica's hand.

They talked companionably for several minutes. Alma

gave her a brief rundown on the town and its limited social life, which consisted of one movie theater, FFA meetings, the local historical society, church socials and three saloons.

She asked if Jessica had enrolled her son in school yet, and told her that her sister, Inez Harper, who'd taught first grade for over thirty years, would be his teacher. Alma asked how Jessica liked living in the mountains and how long she planned on staying, and made several subtle attempts to wangle information about her past. Jessica answered what she could and managed to sidestep the rest. Eventually Alma gave up, and they resumed talking about the ranch.

Cradling the mug between her hands, she sipped the steaming drink and eyed Jessica over the rim. "And how about Cooter? How're you getting along with that ornery old cuss?"

"Okay, so far. We pretty much ignore each other. Although…he did offer to look after Danny for me today."

Jessica had been surprised when Cooter had walked up to the truck as she and Danny had been about to leave and had suggested that the boy stay with him. "You'll get done a lot faster without the young 'un taggin' along," he'd insisted grumpily. "'Sides, it won't hurt him none to make hisself useful around the barn."

She'd tried, as graciously as possible, to decline the offer, but it was a wasted effort. For Danny, there was no comparison between a shopping trip and a chance to hang around the crusty old man. He'd bounced up and down with joy at the prospect and all but begged to be allowed to stay. Jessica was uneasy with the arrangement, but in the face of her son's enthusiasm, she'd had little choice but to agree.

"You mean to tell me that old scutter's baby-sitting?" At Jessica's nod, Alma threw her head back and let out a whoop of laughter. "Well, who'd of thought it?" she chortled.

"Yes, well..." Jessica swallowed the last of her coffee and reached for her purse. "I'm sure now you understand why I feel I should get back."

"My, yes."

Still laughing, Alma fetched the groceries from the refrigerator and waved her off with a friendly, "Now Jessie, you be sure and stop by whenever you're in town. You hear?"

Feeling happy and hopeful, Jessica headed the pickup for the mountains at the other end of town. A block away she spotted Hendricks's Dry Goods Store and, without conscious thought, slowed the truck. She looked at the two-story red-brick building and frowned. She would like nothing better than to do as Hank had instructed and buy some clothes, especially for Danny, but the price of a pair of even the most ordinary jeans was out of reach until she received her first paycheck.

Briefly she wondered if the proprietor would allow her to charge a purchase, but she quickly discarded the idea. Any personal credit check or the use of her credit card would lead Lois's bloodhounds straight to her.

With a sigh, Jessica resolutely pressed the accelerator and drove on past.

There was no sign of Danny when she drove into the ranch yard. After putting away the groceries Jessica walked down to the barn. It was empty, but a loud banging drew her to the metal building that housed the ranch vehicles and machinery. Around back, she found Cooter working on a tractor.

He was bent over, his upper body out of sight under the raised hood, but the constant stream of colorful language coming from the engine compartment left no doubt as to his identity. Standing beside him, Danny handed the old man tools from an open toolbox as he called for them.

"Hi, guys. What're you doing?"

Cooter jumped and banged his head on the tractor hood. What sounded suspiciously like a string of muffled curses spewed out.

"Hi, Mom! I'm helping Cooter fix the tractor." Danny's grin stretched from ear to ear, and his little chest puffed out with self-importance.

"So I see."

Cooter backed out of the engine compartment scowling and rubbing the back of his head. "Lord'a mercy, woman. Do you hafta sneak up on a body like that? I blame near bashed my brains out."

"I'm sorry. I did call Danny, but I guess you were making so much noise you didn't hear me."

"Humph! Well, what is it you want?"

"I just came to get Danny."

"Aw, Mom! Do I have to go back to the house? Why can't I stay here?"

"Because Cooter is busy."

"But I'm helping? Ain't I, Cooter?"

"Aren't I," Jessica corrected automatically. "And that's nice, dear, but I still think you should come back to the house with me."

"Aw, Mom! Cooter doesn't mind if I stay. Do you, Cooter?"

"Danny, I said—"

"It don't make me no never mind," the old man mumbled ungraciously, wiping his hands on a greasy rag. "The boy can stay if he wants to."

"See! See, I told ya! Can I stay, Mom? Can I?"

"Well…"

"Is there somethin' the boy needs to be doin' up at the house? You need him to help you with somethin'?"

"Well…no. I just thought—"

"Then dangnabbit, what's all the fuss about? Leave the boy be. Leastways here he's makin' hisself useful."

"Well…if you're really sure…"

"Women!" Cooter gave her a sour look and turned back to the tractor.

Torn, Jessica looked from the foreman's face back to her son's hopeful one. "All right, Danny." She sighed, and he let out a whoop. "You can stay until lunch. But you stay out of Cooter's way and mind what he says."

"I will, Mom. I promise."

As she turned to leave, an indistinguishable rumble of words sounded beneath the tractor hood.

Walking back to the house, Jessica worried over Danny's growing attachment to Cooter. During the past week she'd tried to keep her son with her and out of everyone's way, but despite warnings and a watchful eye, she'd had little success.

Danny was fascinated by the cantankerous old man, though Jessica couldn't for the life of her understand why. Cooter grumped and grumbled and stomped around with all the charm and warmth of a grizzly with a sore tooth. His gruff manner wasn't in the least encouraging, but Danny didn't seem to notice, or care. With the guileless determination of a child, he sought out the old man every chance he got and trailed after him, hanging on his every word.

Actually Danny was fascinated by everything and everyone on the ranch, and if Cooter was his boon companion and mentor, Hank was nothing short of a shining hero. Danny idolized the man. Jessica suspected that in her son's estimation he ranked right up there with Johnny Ringo.

Lately she had noticed that he'd begun copying Hank's speech patterns and mannerisms—like punctuating a grin with a slow wink, or standing with his feet spread and his fingers stuck, palms out, in the back pockets of his pants. She'd even seen Danny practicing Hank's indolent, loose-limbed walk.

And what Danny wanted, more than anything on the

face of the earth, was a Stetson hat, jeans, and pair of plain brown cowboy boots—just like Hank's.

It was a clear-cut case of hero worship, and Jessica had mixed feelings about it. Lord knew, Danny badly needed a strong male figure in his life—someone to look up to and emulate. Allen Collier had been as rotten a father as he'd been a husband.

In most respects Hank Rawlins was an excellent role model. He was hardworking, honest, reliable, with a warm, easygoing nature and a core of pure steel. He could be firm, tough, even dangerous, Jessica suspected, when he had to be. There was no denying that he was a flirt and an outrageous ladies' man, but he had charm and humor and character and that wonderful combination of gentleness and strength that was so devastatingly appealing.

Jessica simply doubted that it was wise to let Danny become so attached to a man who would never be a permanent fixture in their lives. But how, she wondered despondently, could she prevent it from happening when she couldn't even control her own wayward feelings for the man?

When the men returned for lunch, Hank's gaze flickered over her and Danny, but he didn't comment on their clothes or ask if she had purchased new ones as he had instructed. Nor did he mention the subject during dinner that evening.

Hank and the men discussed when they would make the last hay cutting of the season, how much of the herd they would gather for market and how many head they would winter over, how long they expected the roundup to take. They talked about beef prices and the various merits and drawbacks of inviting a buyer out to bid on the herd versus trucking the cattle to auction.

After the meal and the ritual round of coffee and smokes the men returned to the bunkhouse. Cooter, with Danny dogging his footsteps, retired to the living room to watch TV, and Hank disappeared into his office.

Buoyant with relief and feeling a bit smug, Jessica hummed a happy tune as she bustled around the kitchen. Hank hadn't paid the least attention to her or Danny's attire. He had obviously forgotten all about their conversation that morning.

A half hour later she was standing at the sink with her hands immersed in dishwater, lost in thought, when Hank's deep voice shattered her complacency.

"Why're you still dressed in those fancy duds?"

"Oh!" The utensils she was washing slipped from her hands and clinked against the dishes in the sink. Jessica whipped her head around and saw Hank standing in the doorway, one shoulder propped against the frame.

"Wh-what?"

Hank drew on his cigarette. Squinting one eye, he blew out a stream of smoke and watched her. "I thought you'd be wearing your new clothes."

"Oh, well…" Turning back to her chore, she retrieved the utensils, rinsed them under the faucet and placed them on the draining rack. She kept her eyes glued to the task. "I, uh…I've been busy."

"How about Danny?"

Jessica tensed when he strolled over to her, but he merely plucked an ashtray from the draining rack and flicked an inch of ash into it. It was one of the ones that she now pointedly placed on the table at the end of each meal. With indolent ease, Hank leaned back against the counter, crossed his arms over his chest, and waited.

"Yes, well…" Jessica groped for an excuse that wasn't an outright lie. "He's, uh…he's been busy today, too. With Cooter."

Hank grinned. "Cooter, huh? Danny sure seems to be taken with that prickly old hedgehog. He's been trailing after him like a second shadow lately." He took another drag on his cigarette then contemplated the glowing tip. "Still, I'm surprised he didn't take time to at least change into his new jeans. The boy's been wanting some something fierce."

"I know that. But Danny has to learn that he can't always have everything he wants when he wants it." Guilt and regret had prompted the words, and Jessica wished them back the moment they left her mouth.

"What does that mean? Hell, Duchess, we're just talking about a couple of pairs of jeans here." He cocked his head and studied her, his eyes narrowing suspiciously. "You did buy the new clothes we talked about, didn't you?"

A pot lid slipped out of her hand and clattered against the sink. She picked it up and scrubbed its spotless surface vigorously.

"Didn't you?"

Jessica released a resigned sigh. "No. I didn't."

"Why not?"

"Hendricks's store didn't have what I wanted."

"Bull!" Hank stubbed out his cigarette with sharp, angry jabs. "Hendricks's has got the best supply of plain jeans this side of Durango. Or is that the problem? What's the matter, Duchess? You think your tight little tush is too good for a pair of ordinary jeans?"

"No! Of course not!" She rinsed and stacked the last pot, then ran a hand through her hair, grimacing as she realized, too late, that it was still wet. "I don't know why you're making such a big thing of this. As you said, it's just a few pairs of jeans."

"Which you and Danny both need."

"I know. Look, I intend to buy them. Eventually."

"What was wrong with today?"

"It just wasn't convenient for—" She broke off under Hank's disbelieving stare, her shoulders slumping. "All right. If you must know, I can't afford to buy anything until payday.''

Her words caught Hank off guard. Surprise and confusion flickered through him. Suspicion immediately followed. He frowned. ''Are you saying you don't have enough money to buy a few lousy pairs of jeans?''

''Not even one pair.''

Hank felt a peculiar sensation move through him as he met her half defiant, half embarrassed stare. His frown deepened as his gaze swept over her. The simple little linen dress she wore screamed money. It didn't make any sense. ''You mean you don't have enough cash. Right?''

''No. I mean I don't have enough money.''

''But we're only talking about—'' He stopped, appalled, and stared at her. ''Exactly how much do you have?''

''That's none of your business.''

He planted his fists on his hips and leaned forward. ''How much, Duchess?''

''Hank, really!'' She pressed back against the counter, but he bent closer until they were almost nose to nose. ''This is absurd.''

''I said how much?'' He ground out the words through clenched teeth.

''Eighteen dollars and twenty-three cents,'' she said in a rush.

''Eighteen—!'' A swift surge of anger swept through him. ''You came all the way from Texas with only eighteen dollars? And with a child! Woman, are you crazy?''

His accusing tone stiffened Jessica's spine. Over the past seven years she had learned to meet criticism or threat of any kind with cool hauteur. The defensive reaction was by now so ingrained it was reflexive.

Her chin came up and she fixed him with an oblique, glacial stare. ''My finances and what I do, beyond my duties as your housekeeper, are none of your concern,'' she informed him icily. ''Now, if you'll excuse me, I'll say good-night.'' She took off her apron and flung it onto the counter. With her face set and her head high, she stepped around him and marched into her bedroom, closing the door behind her with a firm click.

Hank stared after her. ''Well, I'll be damned.''

Chapter Six

"But I don't understand. Why must we go to town?" Jessica complained the next morning as Hank hustled her and Danny into the pickup.

Giving no indication that he had even heard her, Hank slammed the door, then went around to the other side of the truck and climbed in behind the wheel. She watched him, waiting for his answer, but Hank merely started the engine and drove out of the yard.

He sat as loosely in the sprung seat as he did astride a horse. Knees wide, one bent elbow hooked over the open window frame, a broad palm casually cupped over the top of the steering wheel, he lounged against the door and stared straight ahead. Jessica patted her foot and counted to ten. When they headed up the winding gravel road to the highway her patience snapped.

"Hank, for heaven's sake! Will you answer me? I told you, I really don't have time for this. I have a dozen things to do today."

They bounced over a pothole, and Danny giggled. Jessica gasped and grabbed the armrest. Sure that he had hit it on purpose, she shot Hank a suspicious look.

He grinned back. "Relax, Duchess. I'm the boss, remember? Work can wait. At least until you're outfitted properly."

"What do you mean?"

"We're going to Hendricks's and buy you and Danny some clothes."

"*What!*"

"Yay!" Danny bounced up and down on the seat. "Can I get some jeans, Hank? Like the ones you wear?"

"Sure, pard." He reached out and tousled the boy's tawny hair. "And some boots too."

"Oh boy!"

"Hank, please!" Jessica was so agitated her voice rose to a high squeak. "I told you—I can't afford to buy anything yet."

"You won't have to. I'm buying."

"What? Oh, no. Absolutely not. I can't allow you to buy our clothes!"

"Relax, Duchess. This is just a loan. I'll deduct a little from your check each payday to cover the cost. Or, if you'd rather..." He paused and sent her a hot, heavy-lidded look over the top of Danny's head. "...we could work out a mutually enjoyable form of repayment."

His eyes twinkled with mischief. Jessica knew he wasn't serious, but, to her horror, she felt her nipples pucker and her body quicken at the outrageous suggestion. The husky caress of his voice sent a delicious tingle through her, and she was powerless to prevent the flush that spread up over her neck and face.

Though shaken, Jessica managed an indignant glare.

Hank raised his eyebrows. "No? Ah, well, that's too bad. But one way or another, Duchess, you and the boy are getting new duds. Make up your mind to it."

"Why are you doing this?"

Hank shrugged. "The boy needs school clothes. Besides, it's no big deal."

Actually Hank wasn't sure exactly why himself. All he knew was that the thought of her not having enough money to buy a simple pair of jeans infuriated him.

His mouth tightened. Eighteen dollars. Eighteen *lousy* dollars. Hell's bells. Even in their leanest days when his old man's purse winnings had been so low they'd had to hitch rides from rodeo to rodeo, he and his dad hadn't been that busted.

It had occurred to him that though her clothes were expensive she wore no jewelry, and he'd realized that she'd probably sold it all. That thought had made him even more furious.

Hank had never felt protective toward a woman before. The feeling made him uncomfortable. He'd told himself that it wasn't his problem. She and the boy had a roof over their heads, food to eat. It wasn't as though their situation was dire.

Then he'd think about how desperate she must have been to have struck out on her own with so pitifully little, how frightened, how much sheer courage it had taken, and the alien urge would come rushing back.

At least now he knew why she'd been so determined to have the housekeeping job. What he didn't understand was what had caused her to take such a risk? To leave a life of apparent ease for one of hard work and uncertainty?

He had lain awake for hours the previous night pondering the question but had come up with no answers.

There wasn't the slightest doubt in his mind that she was running from something. But what? Who?

Could it be creditors? Had her husband lost his money and left her in debt? Had she committed a crime? Hank glanced at her, his eyes lingering on her delicate profile. It was possible, he supposed, but he doubted it. Or maybe he just didn't want to believe it. Hell, she wouldn't be the first criminal with the face of an angel.

He'd even wondered if she was really a widow. Maybe she'd just made up that tale as cover and was really a delinquent wife running from a brutal husband. That possibility was even less palatable, he'd discovered, than the idea of her running from the law.

Even so, he had almost convinced himself that it was true. After all, he'd reasoned, if she was still married that would explain why she resisted the attraction between them.

Then the arrogance of his thinking had struck him, and he'd felt like an egotistical fool. Even now, a sardonic smile twitched his mouth at the memory. Conceited ass.

Hours of stewing over the puzzle had solved nothing. Jessica was as much a mystery to him as ever. The only sure conclusion he had reached before finally falling to sleep the night before was that he was, by God, going to see to it that she and the boy had proper clothing.

The moment they entered Hendricks's Dry Goods Store any hope Jessica had of making their purchases circumspectly vanished. When Hank explained what they wanted, Emily and Dan Hendricks practically fell over themselves waiting on them. Their voluble comments as they bustled around gathering items alerted everyone in the store to Hank and Jessica's reason for being there.

Luckily there weren't many customers that early in the day. One, however, was the sour-faced cashier from Stoval's Grocery, who seemed to take a great interest in the transaction.

Jessica had intended to get by with as little as possible and was appalled when Hank chose four pairs of jeans and half a dozen shirts for each of them.

"Hank! This is too much," she hissed, when he began rummaging through a rack of coats.

"It's bare minimum." He dismissed her complaint matter-of-factly and held a down-filled parka up to her for size. "Here, try this on and see if it fits."

She sputtered and fumed but found herself bundled into the bulky jacket anyway. Hank zipped it up to her chin, then pulled the sheepskin-lined hood onto her head and held it together beneath her chin. Laughter danced in his blue eyes as he tilted his head to one side to inspect her. "You know, you look kinda cute."

"Oh, sure," she said, making a face. She felt like a stuffed bear.

Grinning, Hank leaned close and murmured, "You got any long johns, Duchess?"

"Of course not. And I don't want you to buy me any, either."

"No, no. I insist. You're going to need them come winter. Besides, the thought of your delectable body encased in tight knit creates some very erotic images." He rubbed the end of her nose with his and whispered outrageously, "All winter, whenever I look at you I'll be imagining how you look under your clothes."

Before she could protest, he released her and strolled away. "Hey, Dan," he called across the store as he went. "Throw in a few pairs of long johns for each of them, too, will ya?"

Jessica's face pinkened, then turned brick red when she saw that the cashier from the grocery store was staring at her. She lifted her chin and met the woman's disapproving sneer coolly before turning away, but inside she was uneasy. When Hank had said that gossip would spread about them, she hadn't believed him. Now she began to suspect that he'd been telling the truth.

Danny's delight was enough to push the niggling worry aside, however. He came strutting out of the dressing room in jeans and a western shirt, grinning from ear to ear. When Dan Hendricks fitted him with a pair of cowboy boots, he was so overcome all he could do for a moment was sit there with his feet stuck straight out and stare at them, murmuring "Wow" over and over. Then he jumped down and raced over to the full-length mirror and swaggered back and forth in front of it, twisting and turning and craning his neck, trying to look at himself from every direction.

"You look mighty fine there, pard," Hank drawled. "But...I don't know...that outfit's missing something."

Danny looked up at his hero, crestfallen. "What?"

"This." Hank brought a small Stetson from behind his back and plopped it onto the boy's head. "There now. That's just about perfect."

Speechless, Danny gazed at his reflection. His eyes lifted to meet Hank's in the mirror, silently pleading. "Is it really mine? To keep?"

"Sure. If you're going to work on a ranch you need a hat."

Danny's little chin quivered. With a glad cry, he whirled around and flung himself at Hank so hard he nearly knocked him over. The hat flew off as the child wrapped both arms around his benefactor's knees and buried his face against him. "Oh, I love you, Hank," he declared fiercely. "I really do love you."

Hank cast a helpless glance Jessica's way, but she was too choked up to be of assistance.

"Hey. Hey. Take it easy, pardner." Concern and embarrassment softened Hank's voice to a husky whisper. He patted the boy's shoulder awkwardly, but Danny's death grip didn't ease. Finally Hank pried him loose and went down on one knee, only to have little arms encircle his neck in a stranglehold. "Hey, c'mon, now. There's no need to get all worked up. It's just a hat."

Danny continued to cling. Hesitantly Hank raised his arms. They hovered in midair over the heaving little shoulders for a few seconds, then enfolded the boy. With a sigh, Hank closed his eyes and hugged the child close.

Watching them, Jessica swallowed against the painful

tightness in her throat and fought back tears. Though he had wanted them desperately, it wasn't the boots or the clothes or even the hat that had brought on Danny's emotional reaction. She knew it was the caring behind the gesture, the attention from this man that Danny so idolized. Her son was starved for a male figure in his life. For a father's love.

When at last Danny quieted, he was embarrassed, and Hank tactfully paid for their purchases and escorted them out with as little fuss as possible. Nevertheless, Jessica was aware that the attention of every person in the store was centered on them as they swept out with their arms full of packages.

Over the next few weeks Jessica and Danny settled in comfortably at the ranch. Her concern that Hank would intensify his efforts to seduce her proved groundless. He teased and flirted outrageously, so much so that even the hands noticed, but he didn't pressure her. Jessica suspected that Hank was accustomed to easy conquests, and that in most cases women pursued him. He was a charming, extremely attractive man, with an earthy virility that was entrancing to most females. No doubt he figured that all he had to do was wait, and she would succumb, too. Jessica wasn't unaffected, but she was determined to be the exception.

Once she had the house whipped into shape, her work slacked off to a satisfying routine. For the first time in years, Jessica was experiencing a sense of purpose. It felt good to be doing something useful again.

It was strange—she had come there merely to escape, but she was happier now than she had been in years.

So was Danny.

He was in heaven in the male-dominated world of the ranch. The hands doted on him. Buck teased him good-naturedly, and Wooley filled his head with tall tales. Jubal, who was little more than an overgrown kid himself, taught him such essential skills as how to crack his knuckles, how to whistle between his teeth and how to belch at will, and the two spent hours together in the bunkhouse competing at video games. Even Slick, who was so introverted Jessica had scarcely heard him speak a dozen words, had whittled Danny several small cars to add to his collection.

Cooter still fussed and grumbled, but the old faker forever found reasons for Danny to spend time with him.

And, though Jessica suspected that Hank fought it, a special relationship blossomed between him and Danny after the shopping spree in Elk Falls. There was a warm bond there that was growing stronger every day.

Under the guise of teaching him how to be useful, Cooter had presented Danny with a lariat and began giving him roping lessons. Danny practiced incessantly. Cooter nailed a set of horns to a sawhorse for him to use as a target, but he roped everything: fence posts, tree limbs, rocks, ranch machinery, calves, Sheba, her puppies and any human who happened to get within range of his loop. It soon reached the point where just the sound of a rope whirring sent everyone ducking for cover.

One day Jessica was hanging sheets on the clothesline to dry and noticed Cooter and Danny in the corral by the barn. She was so accustomed to seeing them together that she didn't pay much attention at first. A few minutes later, when she had finished and was heading back to the house, she glanced their way again, and her heart nearly stopped when she saw Danny astride a horse.

Dropping the empty laundry basket, she took off at a run. By the time she reached the corral she was panting. Hank came riding up on a big bay as she jumped up on the lower rail of the enclosure and shouted, "Cooter, get him down from there this instant!"

"Aw, Mom!"

"Let the boy be." A thread of steel ran through Hank's quiet words.

She darted him a panicked look as he dismounted and looped his horse's reins over the fence rail. "But—"

"It's time he learned to ride. And there's no better teacher than Cooter."

"But Danny is only six years old."

"He taught me when I was four."

The two in the corral stood waiting. Danny's anxious gaze was fixed on his mother, silently pleading. Cooter watched Hank for instructions. The disgusted twist of his mouth eloquently relayed his opinion of her fears.

Hank came to stand beside Jessica. Propping one booted foot on the bottom rail, he braced his arms along the top one and motioned for Cooter to continue. He thumbed his hat to the back of his head and calmly watched the old man lead the stocky sorrel around the corral.

At the first step Danny slipped in the saddle, and Jessica's hand flew to her mouth.

"Lighten up, Duchess," Hank murmured. "You've been doing pretty good lately. Don't spoil it now. If the boy's going to live here and be around horses, he needs to be comfortable with them and know how to ride."

A concerned frown creased her forehead as she studied the heavily built sorrel. "Shouldn't he at least be on a pony? Danny's too small to ride a full-grown horse."

"Stop worrying. There isn't a steadier horse around than Tobe. You could set off a firecracker beside him, and he wouldn't even flinch. So just take it easy."

Jessica sighed, her tension easing a bit. Hank was right. She was being overprotective again. But it was so hard not to be. Danny was so young. So small. And he was all she had. Jessica drew a deep breath and reminded herself that she had sworn she wouldn't coddle Danny as Lois had Allen.

Hank tilted his head to one side and looked up at her

speculatively. Laughter and a glint of mischief shone in his eyes. "Come to think of it, you ought to learn to ride too."

"Me?" The incredulous question was followed by a chuckle. If there was one thing she didn't need, it was riding lessons. Jessica was an expert horsewoman. Her equestrian skill was her one accomplishment when she'd married Allen, according to Lois. Among the horse set in the Collier social circle, a good seat was as important as one's bank account.

"Yes, you. In fact, I think it'd be a good idea if we started right now."

"What!" She chuckled again and shook her head. "No, really, that won't be necessary. You see I—*Hank!*" she squeaked when his hard hands encircled her waist and lifted her from the fence.

"C'mon, Duchess. Let's go." Hank steered her toward the barn, somehow managing to move her even though she tried to dig in her heels. "Let's go saddle up a horse for you."

"But you don't understand—"

"No, *you* don't understand. We don't allow any tenderfeet on this ranch, Duchess."

Jessica opened her mouth to argue, but when she looked up and saw his expression she closed it again. Perhaps it was his superior tone, or the laughter in his voice, which he made no attempt to hide. Or maybe she had simply heard that ridiculous nickname one too many times. Jessica didn't know or care. Seized by an imp of mischief, she decided then and there that the situation was too deliciously tempting to resist.

"Oh, all right. Since you insist, I guess I'll try it. That is..." Widening her eyes, she looked up at him and said with just the slightest quiver in her voice, "If you're sure it's not dangerous."

Hank chuckled, and the hand at her elbow tightened

reassuringly. "Don't worry. I won't let anything happen to you."

Inside the barn he stepped into the tack room and emerged moments later holding a saddle slung over his shoulder and a bridle in his other hand. "Grab that blanket and come with me," he said, nodding toward the thick pad draped across the top of a stall.

Obeying, Jessica meekly followed him outside and into the large enclosure where most of the riding stock was kept. As they walked among the milling horses, she looked them over with a discerning eye. The one Hank cornered was a stocky pinto mare that Jessica guessed to be at least fifteen years old. She knew the animal was probably as docile and slow moving as Danny's mount.

"I'd rather ride that one over there," she said, pointing to a chestnut with long, clean lines and a deep chest. He was prancing daintily around the enclosure and tossing his head. She flashed Hank a guileless smile. "She's much prettier."

"She's a he," Hank drawled. "And too spirited for a beginner."

"But I don't want to ride that old plug. Come on, Hank," she pleaded prettily. "You said riding wasn't dangerous. And we'll be inside the corral, won't we?"

He pursed his lips and looked from her to the horse, and back.

"Pleeeze."

Hank sighed. "Okay, Duchess, if that's the one you want. Just don't blame me if you land on your fanny in the dirt."

His tone was long-suffering and reluctant, but Jessica saw the way his mouth twitched, and she had to bite the insides of her cheeks to keep her own mirth from spilling over. Arrogant jerk!

The young stallion didn't want to be caught, but once he was he danced and snorted, impatient to run. As Hank

slipped on the bridle and saddled the horse, he explained
his every action in detail. Jessica watched and pretended
to listen with rapt attention.

Hank led the horse into the corral, where Cooter was
still walking Danny's plodding mount around in a circle.
Bringing the chestnut to a stop, Hank kept a tight grip on
the bridle and motioned Jessica over to stand beside him.

"Remember, always mount on the horse's left. Okay,
now grab the saddle horn, put your left foot into the stirrup,
step up and swing your right leg over."

Following his instructions, Jessica hoisted herself up
partway and came down again. She feigned another inept
attempt with the intention of completing the mount on the
next try but before she could, Hank spread his broad palm
over her rump and gave a shove that nearly sent her flying
over the saddle.

Jessica let out a startled shriek. Frantically she tightened
her grip on the saddle horn and grabbed a handful of mane.

She ended up hanging from the other side, half in, half
out of the saddle, her leg hooked over the top.

The horse whinnied, did a nervous, sidestepping dance
and tried to toss his head, but Hank held him fast. Jessica
struggled upright, her face flaming. She wasn't sure what
embarrassed her more—almost being unseated or the
memory of Hank's intimate touch on her derriere. But the
look of unholy amusement in his eyes made her more determined than before that if anyone would be learning a
lesson it would be *he*, not she.

Hank led her around the corral a couple of times, giving
instructions as they went, telling her to point her toes and
grip with her knees. He explained how to exert control
using the reins and voice commands, and how to catch the
horse's rhythm and move with it.

"Now I want you to try walking him around yourself."
Hank stopped the horse to hand her the reins, and stepped
back. "Okay, now, to get him started give his sides a

nudge with your heels. Just a light one though. Remember, this horse doesn't need much encouragement.''

Jessica gave him a wide-eyed look and asked innocently, ''You mean like this?''

The stallion's hindquarters bunched in response to her firm kick, and he took off at a dead run.

Behind her she heard Hank and Cooter shout. Leaning low over the horse's neck, Jessica murmured words of encouragement and gave him his head.

''Pull him up! Pull him up!'' Hank yelled as he and Cooter ran after her.

''Use the reins, woman!'' the old man bellowed.

As she neared the fence both men stopped and stared after her, appalled. ''Good gawd a'mighty!'' Cooter wheezed. ''She's gonna jump the fence!''

''She's going to break her fool neck!'' A string of low, vicious curses poured from Hank but he was unaware of making a sound.

Helplessly they watched, their hearts in their throats, as horse and rider went up, up…and sailed over the fence, clearing it by a foot.

The chestnut landed as lightly as a feather on the other side. Without breaking stride, he took off across the valley at a ground-eating gallop. Jessica's exultant laughter rang out as she dug in her heels and urged him on.

''Well, I'll be damned. If that don't beat all.''

Cooter's awed comment and Danny's jubilant cheers broke the stunned silence and jarred Hank into action. He spat out a crude word and bolted for the fence. Hitting it at full speed, he jumped up onto the middle rail and vaulted over the top. In seemingly one fluid motion he grabbed his horse's reins, swung into the saddle and dug in his heels. The big bay leaped forward and pounded out of the ranch yard at full gallop.

Cooter slapped his dusty Stetson against his leg and whooped with laughter. ''Heh, heh, heh! That little gal gotcha good," he called gleefully after Hank. "Why she sticks to that saddle like a cocklebur on a blanket! Yes sirree, she needs ridin' lessons 'bout like a porcupine needs more quills!"

Hank only half heard the taunts. His attention was riveted on the slender figure atop the racing chestnut.

The little devil had known exactly what she was doing when she'd picked him, he thought furiously. Of all the horses she'd had to choose from, Dancer was the fastest and the gamest. But by heaven, he'd catch her. She had a head start on him, but there wasn't an animal on the ranch that could outrun Sampson. Or outlast him.

Anger and excitement surged through Hank, and his heart pounded in time with his mount's thundering hoofs. He was acting on pure instinct, following the deep-seated, primitive urge in the male to pursue the female. It was as old as time. Bred in the bone. He didn't question the wisdom of it. He only knew that he had to catch her.

And when he did, by God, he'd...

Hank let the half-formed threat drift away as he leaned forward and murmured coaxing words into Sampson's ear. The big bay stretched out his stride and strained for all he was worth. Hank's eyes never left Jessica.

Cooter was right, he acknowledged grudgingly. She sat the horse as if she were part of it. And she was in complete control. Racing at full gallop she skirted rock outcroppings and cattle and jumped a small gully left by the spring melt. She was demanding, and getting, more from the chestnut stallion than anyone ever had before. Dancer seemed to skim over the ground without touching it, his slender legs a blur of motion.

Clumps of turf flew from both horses' hooves, and the rocks and spruce trees seemed to fly by. Sweat darkened Sampson's hide, and flecks of foam flew from his mouth, but still he raced on, his powerful legs stretching out, reaching. The wind on Hank's face was cool, the sun beating down on his back hot. His heart pounded with a pagan rhythm. The only sounds were the thudding of horses' hooves, the creak of saddle leather and the distant bawling of cattle.

Gradually the distance between the two horses lessened. Dancer was tiring, as Hank had known he would.

Jessica knew it too. At a shallow spot she forded the stream, hitting it at full gallop and sending up a spray of water that sparkled like diamonds in the clear air. On the other side she turned her horse up the slope and headed him toward the timber, where agility counted for more than speed.

A hard smile curved Hank's mouth, and his respect for her ability and savvy went up another notch.

He and Sampson cleared the stream in two leaps. Only a few yards separated the two riders.

Jessica glanced back over her shoulder. Her eyes glowed with reckless excitement. She nudged Dancer's flanks and sent him on a zigzag course through a stand of aspen.

Hank followed relentlessly. Exhilaration fired his blood. Beneath the hat pulled low on his forehead, his narrowed blue eyes burned with a sensual heat.

Brush popped and crackled, and birds scolded as the two riders raced through the timber. Jessica rode beneath low branches and through narrow spaces where the trees grew close together, forcing the man on the big bay to seek alternate paths.

Still, inch by inch, the distance between the two horses closed. What Sampson lacked in agility he more than made up for in strength and stamina.

The chestnut leaped a deadfall. Five seconds later the bay did the same.

Sending Hank another sparkling glance, Jessica prodded her spirited horse up a sharp incline. Trailing out behind him, Dancer's flowing chestnut tail almost brushed the forehead of the pursuing horse.

Hooves dug for purchase. Powerful muscles bunched and strained. The horses leaped, struggled for a foothold, and leaped again. Their breaths blew out in low, rumbling whickers. A small landslide of rocks and shale clattered down the incline in their wake.

At the top of the slope the ground leveled off into a wide clearing. The chestnut had almost gained it when he stumbled. The horse whinnied in fear and floundered for a second on the loose shale, but under Jessica's firm hand, he regained his footing and cleared the crest in one last, valiant leap.

Jessica didn't make it halfway across the clearing before Hank overtook her. Laughing, she reined in her mount. Hank rode a few yards past her and swung Sampson around.

They faced each other in silence, both crackling with excitement and breathing heavily. The blown horses bobbed their heads and pranced in place beneath them, sides heaving.

Jessica's exhilarated laughter faded, then stilled under Hank's hard stare. His blue eyes glittered in the shadow of the broad-brimmed hat. There was something threatening in his face, something dark and intense and primitive…and delicious.

Slowly, his eyes never leaving her, he walked the big bay closer. Jessica shivered as a cold sensation trickled down her spine. Her heart began to hammer.

His gaze still holding hers, Hank dismounted, ground-hitched his horse and walked toward her with steady, purposeful steps.

"Hank…?" she began in a breathless voice, eyeing him apprehensively. "Now, Hank. Hank, you can't—!"

When he reached her side she barely had time to kick her feet free of the stirrups before his hands clamped around her waist and dragged her from the saddle.

Chapter Seven

As Hank swung her down, Jessica gave a little squeak. She grabbed reflexively for something to hold on to, and her fingers closed around the tense, bulging muscles in his upper arms.

"Hank— Oh!"

Her feet had barely touched the ground when he hauled her up against his chest. Jessica looked up into his face, and her eyes widened. What she saw there in that split second before his mouth closed over hers caused her heart to give a hard thump, then take off at a gallop.

Before, Hank had kissed her with the leisurely, teasing ardor of a man in complete control. There was nothing casual or teasing about this kiss. It was impatient, hungry and hard. It was fiercely possessive and insistent, and underneath ran a sharp edge of anger.

His mobile mouth devoured her. His teeth nipped. Jessica's heart began to bang away like a kettle drum, the sound reverberating in her ears. In silent demand, his agile tongue probed the corners of her mouth and the vulnerable line where her lips met.

Helplessly her mouth opened to grant him entrance, and a tiny moan escaped her as he deepened the kiss. As though with a will of their own, Jessica's hands slid upward over his arms and locked around his neck.

His skin was damp from their recent exertion. Melding together, their bodies radiated heat like a furnace. The heady scents of musk and maleness surrounded Jessica, making her nostrils flare and her body quicken.

The need for air ended the kiss, and Hank's open mouth slid across her cheek, his warm breath moist on her skin. "God! I want you," he gasped in her ear. His tongue traced the delicate swirls, and he nipped her earlobe. His hands roamed urgently over her back and hips, charting each dip and curve and pressing her tightly to him. "Dammit, I don't remember ever wanting a woman the way I want you."

The resentment in his voice penetrated Jessica's dazed senses, bringing a spark of sanity. What was she doing, letting him kiss her this way? Kissing him back? It was crazy.

"No...Hank, please. No." The plea was weak, barely above a whisper. Turning her head away, she wedged her arms between them and pushed against his chest. "We...we must stop this. Now...before it's too late."

He loosened his hold just enough to allow him to look into her face, but his arms remained around her. There was a fierceness in his eyes she'd never seen before. "Why?" he demanded in a gritty voice. "You want it just as much as I do. You know you do. Don't bother to deny it."

She didn't—she couldn't—though she wished with all her heart that it wasn't so.

In his arms she burned with a need she'd never known before. Even now, her body yearned for him. Jessica knew that if she had not somehow found the strength to stop him when she had, within moments Hank would have lowered her to the carpet of soft grass and made love to her there in the lovely, secluded spot.

And she would have let him.

That frightened her, but what frightened her even more was the sure knowledge that, against all common sense, she was falling in love with him.

Silently calling herself all kinds of a fool, she looked up at Hank with anguished eyes. "I won't deny that I'm attracted to you, but—"

"That kiss was a whole lot more than just *attracted*," he insisted. He gripped her upper arms. His face was flushed and rigid with passion, his eyes burning. "Dammit! You want me, Duchess...the same way I want you. Why the hell are you fighting it?"

"For a lot of reasons. There's Danny. My self-respect. I know it's old-fashioned, but, Hank, casual sex goes against everything I was raised to believe in."

He threw his head back and gave a snort of mirthless laughter, his nostrils flaring. "Hell, the way I feel right now, it would be anything but casual."

Suppressing the quiver of longing his words inspired in her, she added quietly, "And then, there's my job. I can't afford to lose it. But I would, eventually, if we had an affair. When it ended it would be too uncomfortable for both of us if I stayed."

He stared at her, his expression grim, unable to deny the statement, and when she smiled sadly and stepped back, this time he let her go.

Jessica turned away and walked to the edge of the clearing. Aching with longing and hopeless despair, she folded her arms over her midriff and gazed down through the trees. From where she stood she could see the house and barns at the head of the valley and the cattle grazing nearby in the home pasture. From that distance they looked tiny, almost toylike. There was no sign of Cooter or Danny.

The men, she knew, were all working in the far pasture, about fifteen miles down the valley.

It was quiet. The only sounds were the soft soughing of the wind through the trees, the whisper of fluttering leaves and the horses contentedly cropping grass. Glancing over her shoulder, Jessica saw that Hank stood with his outstretched arms braced against her horse's saddle, his head hung between them. His chest heaved with each deep, ragged breath, and she knew he was fighting to bring his raging desire under control.

Biting her lower lip, Jessica looked away. Regret and guilt for not stopping things sooner washed over her.

"All right, Duchess. You win for now," Hank said, breaking the uneasy silence. "But before we leave this spot I'm damn well going to have the answers to some questions."

Surprised, she turned to face him. She had expected him to be angry, but his voice held only weary determination. "What questions?"

"For starters, where the hell did you learn to ride like that? And why didn't you tell me you could?"

"I grew up on a ranch between Fort Worth and Weatherford," she said with a relieved laugh. "And you didn't ask me."

Hank ignored the last. "On one of those big Texas spreads?"

"Hardly. It's a modest place, and all eight of us kids had to help out just to make ends meet. Which meant we had to learn to ride, among other things." She gave him a saucy grin. "If you need an extra hand at branding time, let me know."

"I might do that," he drawled, and Jessica was relieved to see his familiar teasing grin return.

"Eight kids, huh? I guess growing up in a family that size is how you learned to cook and keep house. Was that the 'ten years' of experience you claimed in your letter when you applied for this job?''

"Yes." Jessica's lips twisted in an abashed grimace. "You see, I'm the oldest, and I was the only girl until the twins were born. They're just nine now, the youngest of the brood. And with five older brothers they're spoiled rotten."

"How many are still at home?"

"All but me. The brother closest to me in age is twenty-one and Dad's right hand. He'll probably take over the ranch someday. All the rest are still in school."

Leaning back against a tree, Hank bent one knee and propped the sole of his boot against the trunk. He pulled a cigarette from the pack in his shirt pocket and lit it. "So tell me, what is it you're running away from?" he asked softly, watching her.

Lulled by the friendly drift their conversation had taken, the question caught Jessica by surprise. She flashed him an alarmed look before she could stop herself, then quickly turned away and shrugged to cover the betraying reaction. "I don't know what you mean."

"Oh, I think you do. You may have been born just a simple country girl, but recently you've been living in the lap of luxury, haven't you, Duchess?"

"You don't know that. And stop calling me Duchess. My name is Jessica."

Hank grinned but otherwise ignored her outburst. "Oh, I know it all right. Everything about you gives you away; the fancy clothes and those handmade boots you're wearing, that pile of designer luggage. Besides, Danny's let a few things slip about the house where you used to live and the servants."

He took a deep drag on his cigarette and blew out a stream of blue smoke that drifted away on the breeze. "Now I have to ask myself why a woman would give up a life of ease and take a job as a housekeeper? And why you arrived with barely enough money in your pocket to buy a decent meal? The only answer I can come up with is you're running from something.'' He waited for a reply, but she set her jaw and maintained an obdurate silence. Tilting his head, he cocked one eyebrow. ''What happened, Duchess? Did you get greedy and do something illegal?''

''Certainly not!''

''Then why are you here? And why the secrecy?''

Jessica sighed at his soft, implacable tone. He was determined to get the whole story, and she knew she might as well give in. She had the feeling if she made a move for her horse, she wouldn't get ten feet.

''I had to get Danny away from his grandmother,'' she said resentfully. ''Otherwise she would have ruined him the way she ruined his father.''

''And how was that?''

''She spoiled him rotten. Allen was Lois's only child. All of his life she indulged his every whim, gave him everything he wanted. For some reason, both Lois and Allen thought that was no more than his due.'' Remembering, Jessica shook her head sadly. ''I thought I had married a handsome prince, but he turned out to be just a spoiled, self-centered, charming wastrel.''

''I see.'' Hank studied the glowing tip of his cigarette. ''Tell me, did you marry him for his money?''

''No!'' The quietly voiced question earned him an indignant glare, but Jessica's defensive ire faded as quickly as it had flared, and her shoulders slumped. ''At least...I didn't think so at the time. But now...'' She sighed and grimaced. ''Now, sometimes I wonder. Looking back, it's difficult to believe that I was that naive, or that blind.''

Memories, things she'd pushed to the back of her mind and refused to think about for years, came flooding back, making her restless. Walking slowly, aimlessly around the clearing, she plucked a fluttering aspen leaf off a tree and rubbed it between her fingers, her expression far away and sad.

"I met Allen Collier when he and some of his friends crashed the spring dance at my high school. I think they'd had a little too much to drink and were bored and looking for excitement. Anyway, Allen was nice-looking. And he was older, more exciting than the high-school boys I'd been dating. I was flattered when he singled me out.

"Of course, I knew who he was. Everyone did. You couldn't live in that part of Texas without knowing about the Colliers. For generations they've been one of the wealthiest, most influential families in Fort Worth.

"When the dance was over, I really didn't expect to see Allen again, but he called the next day and took me out that night. And every night after that."

She turned and looked at Hank, an unconscious plea in her golden eyes. "Do you have any idea how exciting and flattering that was—especially for an eighteen-year-old girl from a poor family—to be pursued by the wealthiest, most eligible bachelor in three counties? How impressive his life-style had seemed then?"

"I think I can imagine."

"Yes, well…my parents were not at all pleased. Neither were my brothers." She gave a little laugh. "You see, we're all very close in my family, and they don't hesitate to give their opinions. They were concerned about the differences in our backgrounds and values and worried that the people in Allen's crowd wouldn't accept me." Jessica shrugged ruefully. "They were right. They all tried to get me to stop seeing him, but of course I wouldn't listen.

"When Allen wanted to be, he was as charming and gallant as a prince in a fairy tale. He courted me with flowers and candy…even poetry. At eighteen, I was a starry-eyed romantic, too in love with the idea of love to know infatuation from the real thing.

"Allen's mother was positively outraged when she

found out about us." Jessica gave a mirthless chuckle and tossed the shredded leaf aside. "Believe it or not, when he defied her and eloped with me the night of my high-school graduation, I honestly thought I was the luckiest girl in the world."

She glanced at the man leaning against the tree and smiled sadly. "Later I realized that marrying me was Allen's one and only act of rebellion. I suppose that's something that all young people must do, to some degree, and in Allen's defense, I'm sure it must have been difficult to rebel when your every wish was granted. Anyway, once he'd taken a stand and defied his mother openly, he quite happily reverted to his old life-style."

"And what was that?"

Jessica gave a short laugh. "Constant parties, fast cars and faster women." She tossed out the words glibly with a shrug, unaware of the revealing hurt and disillusionment in her voice.

Hank didn't comment. He just smoked his cigarette and watched her, his eyes hooded and unreadable. "How did his mother react to the marriage?" he asked finally.

She shot him an ironic glance and laughed. "Initially she was furious, but gradually I think she came to think of me as promising raw material, because she decided to make me over. Lois seemed to think it was her sacred duty to polish and mold me into an 'acceptable' wife for her son. I was dressed and coiffed and told how to walk and how to talk, coached on how to play bridge, how to order from a French menu, how to speak to servants. And, of course, there was special emphasis on what was and was not the proper conduct in any given social situation."

"And you put up with that?" Hank demanded with an unmistakable note of censure in his voice. "Why, for God's sake?"

Jessica sighed. They were questions she had asked herself over and over recently. "At first, I suppose, because

I was shy and unsure of myself. I was awed by the mansion and all that wealth and power. You have to understand that Lois Collier is a formidable woman, and I was so terribly young and anxious to please. Later, after all my girlish dreams were shattered and I'd stopped being impressed or intimidated, I went along with Lois's wishes because it was easier than fighting her. And at least the constant lessons and social rounds and committee meetings kept my mind off what a disaster my marriage was."

"Why didn't you just tell them to stuff it and leave?"

"Because I'd had Danny by the time I realized that Allen had no intention of changing his life-style. He was never much of a father. He was rarely around Danny, and ignored him when he was. But Danny is a Collier. The one time I threatened to get a divorce, when Danny was just a baby, Allen made it clear that if I left, it would be alone, that Danny stayed with him."

"So what changed? What made you decide to leave now?"

"Lois. She was always an indulgent grandmother, materially, at any rate. But she was obsessive about Allen, to the point that she showed little interest in anyone else.

"A little over a year ago, Allen and his latest girlfriend were killed in a car accident. They'd been to a party and, typically, Allen had had too much to drink. It was raining, and he was driving too fast and lost control.

"By that point I was inured to pain where Allen was concerned, but Lois was devastated," Jessica said quietly, her face pensive as she recalled the depth of her mother-in-law's grief. "For months she wouldn't talk to anyone, wouldn't see anyone. For a while she wouldn't even come out of her room. I was concerned for her sanity.

"It was a relief when she finally began to pull out of her depression…until I realized that she was beginning to focus all her attention on Danny." Jessica stopped her restless roaming and looked at Hank, her face stark with concern. "To Lois, he became a substitute for the son she had lost.

"That was when I realized that I had to get Danny away from her. But first I had to get a job to support us both."

Hank dropped his cigarette and ground it under his boot heel, then walked across the clearing to where she stood. He planted his feet wide apart, stuck his fingers in his back pockets and studied her, his expression curious. "Why? I'd think you'd be a wealthy widow."

"Hardly. Allen didn't have any money of his own. We lived with his mother, and she gave him a generous allowance. He saw no reason to work. After all, he fully expected to inherit the Collier fortune someday."

"Okay, I can see why you needed a job, but why take one as a housekeeper?"

"It was the only thing I knew how to do. I told you, I married right out of high school. I had no training, no experience. During my marriage, Allen and Lois wouldn't hear of my studying for a career or getting any kind of job. I was told that it was permissible to donate time to charities—in fact, it was expected—but under no circumstances did Collier women *work*.

"I was getting desperate when one day, while Danny and I were visiting my parents, I happened to see your ad in a farm-and-ranch magazine." She gave him a helpless look and spread her hands wide. "The rest you know."

He made a noncommittal sound and continued to study her. Jessica couldn't tell from his expression if he believed her. Even if he did, she knew he still might not want her on his ranch. She and Danny spelled trouble that he could, no doubt, do without.

After what seemed like an eternity, the familiar rakish smile began to tug at his mouth. A wave of relief washed over Jessica, so strong her knees almost gave way.

"I'm sorry you were hurt, Duchess," he said softly, touching her cheek with one callused fingertip. "But frankly, after hearing how you endured such a rotten marriage, I'm surprised at your attitude."

"What do you mean?"

"Just that by now I'd think you'd realize that it makes more sense, and it's a helluva lot more enjoyable, to have an honest affair. Honey, there's no such thing as love and forever after. Haven't you realized that yet?"

He lowered his head and gently brushed her parted lips with his. "There's just chemistry," he murmured. His other hand came up and he cupped her face between his hard palms. "And desire." He probed the corners of her mouth with his tongue, and Jessica placed her hands on either side of his lean waist to steady herself as a delicious tingle raced over her skin. "And need." He nipped her bottom lip with fierce tenderness.

His fingers tunneled into the hair at her temples, the rough skin snagging the silky strands, and his thumbs stroked along her jaw. Jessica moaned as he drew her bottom lip into his mouth and sucked gently. "It's a lot smarter to just relax…" He aligned his mouth with hers and his tongue glided across her teeth, probed deeper, retreated, probed again. "…and enjoy it while it lasts," he whispered erotically into the moist cavern of her mouth.

A reply was beyond Jessica. Had she been capable of voicing one, it would have been swallowed up in the hot sweetness of his kiss. It drugged and coaxed and cajoled with a gentle insistence that rocked her right down to her toes. She stood quiescent beneath the exquisite caress of his mobile lips and searching tongue. Her body tingled and her heart beat with a painful heaviness. Love and desire mingled within her, creating a swelling pressure in her chest and making her throat ache.

Hank raised his head partway and studied her flushed face, the glazed look in her heavy-lidded eyes. His gaze dropped to her lips, still parted and wet from his kiss, and his head dipped once again. His warm breath mingled with hers as he tasted and tantalized, rubbing his open mouth against hers in a slow, rocking motion. "Stop fighting it, Duchess," he whispered thickly. "Let me love you. Now, sweetheart. Right now."

Grasping his wrists, Jessica pulled back from the sweet torment of his mouth. She closed her eyes and drew in a shuddering breath. Unconsciously her fingers tightened, squeezing the broad, strong bones beneath the thin layer of flesh. She pressed her lips together and shook her head. "I can't." She looked up at him, her eyes swimming with emotion. "I just can't, Hank."

"Can't—or won't?"

Jessica sighed. Shaky but determined, she stepped back and met his demanding gaze with unflinching directness. "Both I guess," she admitted honestly. "I guess I'm just an incurable romantic, because, no matter how much I may desire you, I'm simply not cut out to be any man's mistress."

Turning away from his hard stare she forced her quivering limbs to carry her across the clearing to where her horse was contentedly grazing. Hank still hadn't moved when she swung into the saddle.

She walked the stallion to within a few feet of him. "And if you think about it, Hank," she said quietly, looking down at him. "I doubt very much if a live-in mistress is what you want either."

Responding to a tug on the rein, Dancer pivoted and trotted away. When Jessica had disappeared from sight, Hank walked to the edge of the clearing and watched horse and rider pick their way down the slope of the mountain, his eyes glued to the woman's straight back whenever he caught sight of her winding through the trees.

He stood unmoving, lost in thought, a tumult of conflicting emotions warring within him. A nudge between his shoulder blades and a soft nicker brought him back to the present. Taking hold of the reins, Hank absently stroked the horse's muzzle, but his gaze returned almost at once to the rider nearing the base of the mountain.

"You know, Sampson. Damned if she's not right."

Hank had never lived with a woman. Two or three days at one time was the longest he'd ever spent with one. Constancy, it seemed, just wasn't part of the Rawlins makeup. The one time his old man had tried marriage, it had been a disaster. Hank figured the smartest thing to do was to avoid it.

Hell, with Jessica living in his house, if they became lovers, it would be the next thing to being married. He'd be a fool to step into that trap. And to top it all off, he rationalized, when things between them ended—and they always did, sooner or later—he'd lose a damn good housekeeper.

Any way he looked at it, starting something with Jessica was just plain crazy. The woman spelled nothing but trouble. The only sensible thing to do was to back off.

Hell, it was no great loss, he told himself. There were plenty of other women around. Willing women.

Below, the horse and rider emerged from the trees onto level ground. His expression thoughtful, Hank watched Jessica put the chestnut into a rocking lope that quickly carried them to the ford in the creek. They splashed across without slowing. On the other side she turned the chestnut stallion and headed up the valley toward the ranch house.

"The hell of it is," Hank murmured to the patient horse. "How do I stop wanting that one?"

The next afternoon a strange pickup truck pulled into the ranch yard while Jessica was working in the garden, and her heart did a somersault in her chest. Her first thought was that Lois had somehow found her.

Fighting the urge to run, she stood slowly, clutching the basket of freshly cut spinach leaves, and watched the tall man climb from the cab.

"Hi there," he called out when he spotted her. He headed her way, and Jessica forced her wobbly legs to work. She reached the gate in the fence that enclosed the small plot at the same time as the stranger.

"You must be Hank's new housekeeper that I've been hearing about," he said, extending his hand as she came through the gate and closed it behind her. "My name's Will. Will Beaman. I'm the local vet."

Relief almost buckled Jessica's knees. As a result, the smile she gave him was warmer than it normally would have been. Seeing it, Will Beaman's gray eyes lit with masculine interest and speculation.

Jessica told him her name and shook his hand, after hastily wiping hers on her apron. His grip was firm, his hand big and capable, like the rest of him. Will Beaman was not a particularly handsome man, Jessica noted, but his broad, pleasant face and friendly smile made him appealing.

"Hank called last night and asked me to come out and take a look at an ailing bull."

"Oh? Well, I'm afraid I don't know anything about that, Mr. Beaman." Neither did she have any idea where Hank was. He had hardly spoken to her since she'd left him in the clearing the day before. "But if you'd care to wait—"

"Mom! Mom!" Danny erupted from the barn, where he'd spent most of the day practicing roping and playing with Sheba's puppies, both at one time, his mother suspected. Jessica and Will turned as one and watched the little dynamo race toward them. "Mom! Is that the vet?"

Jessica waited until her son skidded to a stop before them to answer. "Yes, it is, but that's no way to greet someone, young man. Now, slow down and say hello to Mr. Beaman."

"But, Mo-om!" he protested. "Cooter said it was my job to tell him as soon as he got here that the bull was in the pen behind the barn. And when he's through, I'm

s'posed to take him to where Hank's working,'' he added
importantly.

"Do you know where that is?"

"Aw, Mom. Sure I do. Cooter's showed me the whole
ranch, lotsa times."

"Well, in that case, young man," Will said with an
affable smile for the boy, "lead the way." As he and
Danny headed for the barn he looked back over his shoulder at Jessica. "Nice meeting you, Mrs. Collier. Maybe
I'll see you later."

Jessica waved and watched him walk away, chatting
amiably with Danny. Will Beaman was a nice man, she
decided, the steady, reliable sort who would make a good
husband and father. She wondered briefly if he was married, but by the time she had carried the basket of fresh
vegetables into the house thoughts of the friendly vet had
already slipped from her mind.

Three hours later, when Hank and the others returned
for dinner, Will was with them.

When Hank announced that Will was staying for dinner,
the young vet hummed and hawed and claimed he didn't
want to impose, but his resistance was half-hearted, at best,
and he easily allowed the others to overrule him.

Smiling graciously, Jessica settled the matter by getting
out another plate and utensils and insisting that he take a
seat at the table. Will complied readily, and as she moved
around the kitchen his gaze followed her.

As usual during dinner, the men talked about the ranch
work and the weather and cattle prices. Hank questioned
Will about a new vaccine he'd read about and discussed
with Cooter the possibility of planting another pasture of
alfalfa the following spring. He answered all of Danny's
incessant questions patiently, asked if he was ready to start
school the following week, and laughed along with the
others when the boy made a face. He didn't say a word to
Jessica, or even glance her way.

Will, on the other hand, when he wasn't answering Hank's and Cooter's questions, directed most of his conversation toward her. Feeling snubbed and hurt by Hank's indifference, she was grateful for his friendly attention and responded freely.

Will told her a little about himself and his family. She learned that he'd lived in the area all of his life, except for the years when he'd been away at college, and that he liked the mountains so much he couldn't imagine living anywhere else. "The only bad thing is you don't get to meet many new people. Especially single women," he said, giving her a significant look. "Most of the ones hereabouts I've known forever."

He was so easy to talk to Jessica found herself telling him about growing up in a large family on a small Texas ranch and relating hilarious tales of the escapades she and her siblings had gotten into. By the end of the meal they were laughing and chatting together like old friends.

Even so, Will took her by surprise when, as he was leaving, he asked if she would go out with him sometime.

Involuntarily Jessica's startled glance sought Hank. She expected some reaction from him but he sat calmly smoking a cigarette, his face as impassive as stone. He didn't even look up.

"I...I don't know," she stammered lamely. "You see, there's Danny, and...well...I don't have anyone to sit with him, and—"

"Shoot, woman," Cooter put in impatiently. "That ain't no problem a'tall. The boy can stay with me. Anytime you wanta go out with Will here, you jist say the word."

Jessica's jaw dropped. She couldn't have been more surprised if he had suddenly sprouted another head. "Why, thank you, Cooter. That's very nice of you. But, really...I hate to impose."

"Impose, my foot. I offered, didn't I? The boy's with

me most of the time, anyhow. 'Sides, I ain't got nothin' better to do of an evenin'.''

She glanced at Hank again, but he still seemed uninterested. Swallowing her hurt, she gave Will a weak smile and spread her hands. "In that case…I'd be happy to go out with you. I, uh…I have Saturday afternoons and Sundays off."

At least, she was supposed to. So far she had not taken advantage of the time off and had continued to cook the meals on those days for Hank and Cooter. The men usually went into town on Saturday evening, and were either so hung over on Sunday that they didn't want to eat, or else they made do with snacks they kept in the bunkhouse refrigerator.

A pleased grin split Will's pleasant face. "Great! I'll give you a call soon."

He thanked Hank and Jessica again for the meal and said good-night. The hands walked out with him on their way to the bunkhouse. When they had all gone Hank stood up, snuffed out his cigarette and left the kitchen without a word.

Jessica dropped back down into her chair and looked after him, her face stricken.

The scrape of chair legs against the floor was loud in the thick silence as Cooter got to his feet, but Jessica paid no attention. As he walked past her, she felt his gnarled hand cup her shoulder and give it a squeeze.

Jessica closed her eyes and pressed her lips together tightly. For some foolish reason, the unexpectedly kind gesture made the ache in her throat worse and flooded her eyes with tears.

Over the next few days Jessica became painfully aware that Hank was putting up a barrier between them. He spoke to her only when he had to, and even then his tone and words were impersonal. He no longer teased or flirted, though occasionally she caught him watching her.

Jessica knew from the curious glances she and Hank received from the men at mealtime that they, too, had noticed his change in attitude toward her. Finally she realized with a pang that he was treating her with the distant politeness of an employer. She had no choice but to respond in kind.

It was for the best, she told herself. She and Hank had no future together, and she couldn't settle for a short-term relationship. The thing for both of them to do was to forget the attraction between them and get on with their lives.

But knowing and accepting were two different things. No matter how hard Jessica tried, she couldn't quell the hurt she felt whenever Hank acted as though she didn't exist. Just the sight of him made her pulse leap and her insides quiver, but, other than staring at her occasionally, Hank gave no indication that he was at all affected by her presence. She had obviously meant little to him if he could dismiss her so easily.

The depressing thought sat on Jessica's heart like a lump of wet cement, creating a constant ache. She was so blue and heartsick she felt like weeping all the time, and the least thing set her off.

The morning she put Danny on the school bus for the first time she immediately burst into tears. Cooter, who had driven them up to the highway where Danny caught the bus, gave a disgusted snort, but nevertheless shoved a clean handkerchief into her hand and patted her shoulder awkwardly, muttering under his breath all the while about "silly women."

Jessica knew that her tears stemmed from more than facing the end of Danny's babyhood. She suspected that Cooter knew it, too, but he allowed the pretense, even abetted it.

"Why don't you go into town and buy yoreself a new

hat,'' he suggested out of the blue when they returned to the ranch.

By then Jessica's sniffles had almost stopped, and as he brought the truck to a halt in the yard she lifted her face from the folds of the handkerchief and sent him a puzzled look. ''A *hat*?''

''Well, ain't that what women do when they're upset?''

She looked at the brusque old man fondly, a watery smile tugging at her mouth despite her heavy heart. If she hadn't known he would kick up a fuss, she would have leaned over and kissed his bewhiskered cheek. ''Uh…no. Not anymore, anyway.''

''Well then, jist go shoppin','' he ordered crossly. ''Or go to the beauty parlor. Get yore fingernails painted an' get all gussied up. It'll make you feel better an' help you get yore mind off the boy for a while.''

''But I can't. It's not my day off.''

''Aw, pshaw! You got time comin'. An' don't you worry none 'bout Hank. If he says anythin' I'll set him straight.''

''Well…I guess I could do the grocery shopping while I was there…''

''Fine. Whatever. Just so you do somethin' to dry up them tears. If there's one thing I cain't abide it's a blubberin' female.''

After a week of Hank's indifference, Jessica was glad for any excuse to get away from the ranch for a while. Taking Cooter's advice, she drove into Elk Falls to the town's only beauty parlor and had her hair trimmed. When she was through, she decided to walk around town and window-shop for a while before going to Stoval's for the weekly supply of groceries. On impulse, when she reached Alma's café she went inside, hoping a visit with the affable woman would cheer her up.

Jessica had barely sat down when the blond waitress

appeared and plunked a glass of water on the table in front of her.

"You still here?" she demanded aggressively.

Looking up, Jessica smiled. "Yes, I am." She glanced around the café. "Is Alma around?"

"No, she ain't. She's gone to the bank." Loreen chomped her gum, making it snap and crackle. Her mouth had a pinched look, and her eyes were narrowed on Jessica in a hard glare. "I'd of thought by now you would've hightailed it back to wherever you came from. In fact, I'm surprised Hank hasn't thrown you out."

Jessica's eyebrows rose. She had told herself she'd imagined this woman's hostility before, but now there was no mistaking it. "Why should he? I'm very good at my job."

"Yeah, I'll just bet you are. And everybody in town knows what your 'job' is."

"Just what is that supposed to mean?"

"Don't use that high-and-mighty tone with me. My aunt told me all about you."

"Your aunt?"

"Dorothy Grimes. The cashier over at Stoval's. She was in Hendricks's a couple of weeks ago when Hank bought you and that boy of yours a whole closet full of new clothes. I gotta hand it to you, Hank don't usually get that involved with a woman."

"Now look here…" Jessica glanced at the name tag pinned to the blonde's uniform. "…Loreen. If you're insinuating what I think you are, you're wrong. I am merely Hank Rawlins's housekeeper."

Loreen gave a sneering laugh and popped her gum. "Oh, yeah, sure. Only in your case it means that he keeps you in his house."

Before Jessica could refute the statement Loreen bent forward with her hands braced flat on the table. Glaring into Jessica's eyes, she said, "Well, don't get too comfortable out there at the ranch 'cause, believe me, you won't last long. Hank's just havin' a little fling. But he's not about to get himself lashed up permanent with a fancypants hightone like you. Take it from me. You're just not his type.''

With that, she flounced off.

Jessica stared after her. The reason for Loreen's attack was obvious: the woman was jealous. Which, considering the way things were between her and Hank, was absurd.

Lord, if she only knew.

Jessica would have laughed...except that she suddenly felt much more like crying.

Chapter Eight

Jessica returned that afternoon to learn that Hank and the men had started making hay, the last crop of the season.

All that week they worked with a sense of urgency, from sunup to sundown. Once cut, the hay had to be baled and stored before it rained, or else it would ruin. In addition, the job had to be finished before they could bring the herd down from the mountains, something that would have to be done soon, before winter and the start of hunting season.

It took them three days, using two tractors pulling mowers to cut the cultivated valley pastures. By the fourth day the first pastures they had cut had cured enough for them to begin baling.

On Saturday, to Danny's delight, he was allowed to accompany the men. Watching him strut toward the barn between Hank and Cooter, Jessica couldn't help but smile as she washed dishes and looked out the window above the sink. At that moment it was worth whatever she had to endure just to see Danny so happy.

Jessica sighed as she watched Hank playfully toss Danny into the cab of one of the pickups, then climb in after him. She wondered if she was one of those women who was forever destined to fall in love with the wrong men. She was only twenty-five and she'd already done it twice.

After Jessica had finished the dishes, she turned from the sink, drying her hands, and spotted the large water jug sitting by the back door. Hank had forgotten it.

Eyeing the jug, she debated whether or not to take it to him. Haying was hot, thirsty work. When Hank realized the oversight, he would send someone for the water, but that would delay them. All week they had taken sandwiches for lunch and eaten in the fields to save time.

Should she? Jessica nibbled on her thumbnail and frowned. They were using both trucks to haul the bales to the hay barns scattered over the valley. If she went she would have to ride Dancer.

Oh, what the heck, she thought, and headed for her room to change into jeans and boots. Hank and the men were only working about five miles down the valley, and it was a beautiful morning for a ride.

After allowing him a brief run, Jessica kept Dancer to an easy trot. By the time she reached the place where the men were haying, the sun was high.

One pasture had already been raked, and Slick had moved on to the next one. In the distance, Jessica could see his hat bobbing as the tractor pulled the L-shaped hay rake up the slope of a hill, the spiraling, curved tines leaving the grass piled in a long row behind the rig.

Stopping beside the field where the others were working, Jessica dismounted and looped Dancer's reins around a fence post. She placed the water jug and the package of paper cups on a boulder, then propped her forearms on the top rail of the gate and watched.

Wooley was driving the other tractor, towing the baler. As it passed over the piled row of grass the ground beneath was swept clean, and every couple of yards the cumbersome machine spit out a large, tightly packed, rectangular bundle of hay, bound with wire.

To the side, a short distance behind the baler, Cooter guided the pickup along at a crawl while Hank followed on foot, tossing the seventy-pound bales up into the truck bed for Jubal to stack. Danny was sitting cross-legged on top of the cab, watching Hank's every move.

Already the sun beat down mercilessly. Stripped to the waist, Hank's bronze torso glistened with sweat and the mat of dark hair on his chest was curled into tight, wet ringlets. He wore a rolled handkerchief tied around his forehead to keep the salty moisture out of his eyes.

Jessica shifted uncomfortably and switched her gaze to the hay barn farther down the valley, where Buck was unloading bales from the back of the other pickup. Remotely, she was aware of the sweet, slightly musty smell of dried grass, the incessant rumble of machinery, the scorching sun pounding down on her bare head. Down by the creek, Sheba raced back and forth along the bank, barking at something in the water.

At the end of the field Wooley swung the tractor in a wide arc and started down the next row. As though pulled by a string, the truck followed the same path.

The chain of men and machinery moved nearer, and once again Jessica's gaze was drawn to the broad-shouldered man at the rear. She stared at Hank, mesmerized by the beauty of his lean, powerful build, the play of muscles that bunched and rippled beneath slick, brown skin. His body was loose and supple, every movement smooth and perfectly coordinated as he swung the heavy bales into the back of the truck with deceptive ease.

When they drew level with the gate Cooter gave three short blasts on the pickup horn. Ahead of him, Wooley stopped the tractor and waved his hat in the air, signaling Buck to join them. Then he climbed down from the high seat and headed toward Jessica.

Reaching the fence, he removed his hat and mopped his face with a red bandanna. "Whew! It's going to be a scorcher today."

"It feels like it," Jessica answered in a distracted voice. She poured cool water into a cup and handed it to him. From the corner of her eye she could see Hank and Danny, standing by the open door of the pickup. Using as a towel the cotton shirt he had discarded earlier, Hank wiped the sweat and grime from his face and chest, while listening attentively to Danny's chatter.

Buck had driven up, and the others had already downed their second cup of water when they finally turned and started toward the gate. Jessica's stomach fluttered crazily.

"Hi, Mom," Danny chirped as he climbed up the gate and perched on the top rail. Sweat beaded his flushed, freckled face. Bits of grass and hayseed clung to his damp hair which appeared several shades darker where ringlets stuck to his forehead, temples and the back of his neck.

"Hi, sweetheart." Jessica shaded her eyes against the sun and handed him a cup of water. "You be careful sitting on top of that truck. You hear? And be sure and stay out of everyone's way."

"Aw, Mom. I'm not gonna fall off. Cooter's driving too slow for that. 'Sides, I'm not a baby, you know."

"Yes, I know. But for my sake be careful anyway, okay?"

Jessica could feel Hank's eyes on her. An uncertain smile wavered on her lips when she looked up at him. "I, uh...I brought the water. You forgot it this morning."

"Thanks." His features were set in a polite mask, his expression blank. If he regretted at all the change in their relationship, it didn't show. His aggravating indifference scraped her nerves raw.

Jessica's hand shook as she handed him a cup of water. Heat from his body hit her like a furnace blast. He stood at ease, one arm braced against the gatepost, the other on his hip. He smelled of hay and sweat, earthy and intoxicating.

"Shoot, gal. You didn't have to haul this jug all the way up here on horseback," Cooter contended, even as he helped himself to another cupful of water. "Why, there's a creek right over yonder. We coulda bellied down an' drunk our fill the way real men used to."

"You mean like they did back in the frontier days, when you were a boy?" Wooley elbowed Buck as he asked the goading question, and the two snickered.

Cooter bristled. "Go ahead an' laugh, but you two waddies don't know how soft you got it. Why, in my day we didn't have no thermos jugs filled with ice water. No tractors or pickups neither. We hauled hay in wagons. An' I'll tell you somethin' else…"

Buck and Wooley rolled their eyes and groaned as Cooter launched into a tirade about how easy the modern cowboy had it. Danny jumped down from the fence and ran over to where Jubal was standing, a few yards away, vigorously chucking clods of dirt at a particularly high branch.

Jessica was oblivious to it all.

She couldn't tear her gaze away from Hank's bare chest. She stared at the mat of wet curls, her heart pounding, her mouth so dry she couldn't swallow. Clothed, his slender build was deceptive but stripped bare his strength was obvious. Awesome and compelling. Glistening skin, like bronze satin, stretched taut over firm flesh and whipcord muscles. Jessica's gaze trailed over broad shoulders to the hard bulges in his upper arms, and she shivered, recalling how they'd felt beneath her hands when he'd dragged her from Dancer's back. Brawny forearms, corded with tendons and muscles and dusted with black hair, led her gaze to a broad wrist and a large, beautifully sculpted masculine hand.

She watched his throat work rhythmically as he chugged down the large paper tumbler full of water without stopping. Sweat dripped from his chin onto his chest. Helplessly her mesmerized gaze fastened on a bead that trickled through the forest of hair all the way to the narrow band that arrowed downward over his middle. At his navel the drop halted, then swirled around the small cavity and streaked lower, disappearing when it touched the soaked top edge of his low-slung jeans. Staring at the spot, Jessica drew a shaky breath and licked her dry lips.

Shock rippled through her when at last she looked up, and found that Hank was watching her.

For long, electrified seconds their gazes held. Jessica's heart began a slow, heavy thudding. Breathing became impossible.

Beneath half-lowered lids, raw desire blazed in the crystal depths of Hank's blue eyes.

"Hank..."

His name came out on a sigh of longing. Unconsciously, she reached her hand toward him.

The soft sound broke the spell that held them. Hank's mouth firmed and a shuttered look entered his eyes. Ignoring her outstretched hand, he set the cup on top of the gatepost and turned and walked away.

The swift surge of joy Jessica had felt fizzled. Depression settled over her like a black cloud as she watched him stride toward the truck. Hank couldn't have made his feelings plainer. He may desire her, but that was as far as things were going to go.

Jessica told herself she had no right to feel hurt. After all, she had rejected all of Hank's advances and told him repeatedly that she wouldn't have an affair. And she'd

meant it. The trouble was, she wanted more—much
more—than he was offering. And deep down, she realized
now, she had been hoping that Hank would come to want
that too.

She had come there, not to bring the water, not for the
pleasure of a morning ride, but because she'd wanted to
see Hank, she admitted with bitter self-disgust. What had
she hoped for? That he would be as hungry for the sight
of her as she was for him? That he would suddenly realize
that he loved her and sweep her up into his arms, right
here in this fragrant meadow?

One by one, the men drifted after Hank. Silently berat-
ing herself for her foolish dreams, Jessica shook her head
and turned away from the fence. As she did, her gaze collided with Cooter's.

He looked at her in silence, the faded old eyes softer
than she had ever seen them. His bewhiskered, weather-
beaten face wore an uncharacteristic look of sympathy.

Jessica lifted her chin. She looked away and quickly
busied herself gathering up the discarded paper cups. She
felt too fragile to cope with kindness from Cooter.

When the cups were stacked beside the thermos she untied her horse and swung into the saddle. Her throat aching, Jessie dug her heels in.

She was almost a quarter of a mile up the valley, gal-
loping for home, when the rumble of machinery rent the
air.

That evening the men pulled into the ranch yard earlier
than they had all week. By the way Wooley and the other
single hands whooped and headed for the bunkhouse with
grins on their faces Jessica knew that the haying was complete. It being Saturday night, weary or not, they were
hellbent for town and a high good time.

As they had been every night during the past week,

Hank and Cooter were filthy and haggard with exhaustion when they walked in the back door.

"Woman, whatever that is you're cookin' shore smells good," Cooter muttered wearily. "I hope it'll be ready by the time I get cleaned up 'cause I'm hungry as a bear."

"Don't bother cooking anything for me," Hank said. "I'm going into town with the others. I'll grab a bite there."

"Oh, but—" Jessica swung around from the stove, but Hank walked right through the kitchen without even looking her way.

At the announcement, Cooter had stopped in his tracks and was staring after him, his jaw gaping open. Then his eyes narrowed, and his mouth snapped shut, and as he stomped out after Hank he muttered, "On second thought, don't bother none with anything for me, neither."

Stunned, Jessica's helpless glance went from the empty doorway to the huge pot of stew simmering on the stove, a feeling of despair welling up inside her.

Less than half an hour later Hank reappeared, smelling of soap and minty toothpaste. There was a nick on his jaw where he had cut himself shaving, and tiny drops of water still sparkled in his dark hair. It was a tad too long, curling rakishly over his collar and the tops of his ears, yet even as Jessica absently noted that he needed a haircut her heart squeezed with love and pain at the sight of him. He was so impossibly handsome. The week of haying had deepened his tan by several shades, making his teeth seem whiter, his eyes bluer. He wore his newest pair of jeans and a crisply starched blue-plaid shirt that she had ironed just that afternoon. And, in them he looked like every woman's idea of a rugged rancher.

"How come you're goin' to town, Hank?" Danny asked. "Ain'tcha tired?" Fresh from his own bath, he sat at the table in his pajamas, hungrily attacking a bowl of stew.

Jessica cringed at her son's innocent question. She knew the answer, but nevertheless waited tensely for Hank's reply.

The heart-stopping, familiar grin appeared and he tousled Danny's hair. "Sure I'm tired, pard. That's why I'm going to town. I'm gonna relax, have a few cool ones and find me a pretty girl to kiss."

As he spoke his gaze sliced to Jessica, and she knew the words were meant for her. Somehow she managed to keep her face impassive, but inside she felt as though she'd been kicked in the stomach.

"Yeech! Whatta you wanna kiss a dumb ole girl for?"

Hank laughed at the look of utter revulsion on Danny's face, but before he could explain Cooter stomped back into the kitchen.

Except for being clean, the clothes he wore looked little better than the ones he'd had on when he came in from working. He scowled at Hank and snapped, "Well? What're we waitin' for? If we're goin', let's go."

"Cooter, what do you think you're doing? You never go to town with the men. You hate drinking in bars."

Cooter's scowl deepened and his jaw jutted. "If *yore* goin', *I'm* goin'."

The Hard Rock Bar and Grill smelled of old grease, sour beer and a dozen different cheap colognes. The first two odors were ingrained in the walls of the place. The last drifted from the spruced-up Saturday-night patrons, both male and female.

Hank's nose twitched at the unpleasant combination but his pace didn't slacken as he strolled in with Wooley and the others. Bringing up the rear, Cooter snorted his displeasure. Hank ignored him, as he had all the way to town.

An old Tammy Wynette tune poured mournfully from the jukebox in the corner. Accompanying it was the sound of boots scraping against wood as several couples swayed in unison on the dance floor, wrapped in each other's arms.

Wooley made his entrance with an exuberant "Wooo-haa!" and he and Buck launched into a round of back thumping and hurrahing. Recognizing Hank, several men called out a greeting.

They had barely made it to the bar when a shrill feminine voice squealed his name from the end of the room. Hank, sitting with one hip hitched on a high stool and his elbow propped on the bar, swiveled in that direction and grinned when he spotted Loreen pushing her way through the dancers.

"Oh, Hank, sugar! I'm so glad to see you!" Throwing her arms around his neck, she dug her fingertips into the hair at his nape and planted her mouth on his.

A deep rumble of laughter welled from within Hank as his arms enfolded her, but the sound was lost inside her open mouth.

Though he returned the kiss boldly, Hank was surprised to find he wasn't enjoying it. There was no spark, no feeling, he realized with a touch of panic. Not even healthy lust. If anything, he was slightly repulsed by the lascivious thrusts of Loreen's tongue into his mouth, and the brazen way she rubbed against him.

The discovery was so unsettling, he redoubled his efforts, but the result was the same. Nothing.

Around them, as the voracious kiss went on and on, the crowd began to hoot and holler and stamp their feet. Using the disturbance as an excuse, Hank broke off the embrace and looked down at the blonde in his arms, forcing a seductive smile to his lips.

"Whooo-wee, Hank!" the man beside him declared, thumping him on the back. "Whatever it is you've got, I sure wish you'd bottle it."

As everyone laughed Hank grinned and swept the crowd with a salacious look. Cooter sat at the end of the bar, a little apart from the others; and when their gazes met, his mouth twisted sourly.

Hank looked away. To hell with the old buzzard! He'd come there to work that tawny-haired temptress out of his system, and by heaven, that was what he was going to do. If Cooter didn't like it, he could go butt a stump.

For weeks he hadn't been able to think of anything but Jessie. He hadn't even been able to sleep for wanting her. He'd tried everything to get her out of his mind, including working until he nearly dropped. He had thought he was beginning to succeed.

Then today, he had seen the naked hunger in her eyes, and he'd wanted to throw her down, right there in the middle of the hay field, and make love to her until neither of them could move.

"Oh, sugar, it's been so lonesome without you," Loreen crooned, running her hand seductively over Hank's chest. "You haven't been to town on Saturday night in so long I was gettin' worried that you'd fallen for that prissy-pants city gal you got working out at the ranch."

Hank gave a harsh laugh. "Not a chance, baby. You should know me better than that."

He gave Loreen another hard kiss, telling himself he would enjoy it more later when he'd loosened up some. When it ended he tucked her close against his side and signaled the barkeep for two beers.

Lester Stuart, a young cowhand from the Circle S, squeezed in next to Hank and bellowed out his order. As he was waiting for his drink he turned to Hank with a sly grin and gave him a playful punch on the arm. "Hey, Rawlins! I'm surprised to see you here."

"Yeah? Don't know why. I manage to make it to town now and then."

Lester waggled his head and gave a silly grin, and Hank realized he wasn't quite steady on his feet. "Yeah, but that was before you had that purty little gal livin' out at the ranch.'' He leaned closer and peered into Hank's face. ''You know, Rawlins, I never did figure you for a hoggish man before, but it 'peers you are. Ain't one woman at a time enough for you, man?''

Hank's pleasant expression didn't alter a whit except for the muscle that twitched along his jaw. ''If you're talking about Jessica, she's my housekeeper,'' he said in a dangerous voice.

''Uh-huh, sure. And Cooter over yonder is the Prince of Wales. Look, Hank, all I'm sayin' is, I don't think it's right for you to be hoggin' the local gals when you're already shackin' up with that pretty—''

Hank's fist smashed into Lester's mouth, cutting off the rest of the statement.

''Sweet Jay-sus, Hank!'' Buck yelped beside him. ''Whaddid ya go an' do that for?''

The young cowhand staggered backward under the blow and fell onto a table, knocking it over, along with the two men sitting there. All three came up swinging.

''Oh, hell, we're in for it now,'' Buck muttered.

More groans went up from the other R Bar B men, but, with the exception of Cooter, they turned as one and entered the fray.

Women screamed and men shouted. Over the blare of the jukebox, the sounds of glass breaking and tables and chairs crashing to the floor filled the room. Punctuating it all were low grunts and the crack of bone against bone as fists made contact with human flesh.

Some of the other patrons took sides and entered the brawl, but most simply stood back and gave them room. It was all over in a matter of minutes, with Hank and his men the clear winners. Though he was winded from his exertions, for good measure, Hank picked up Lester by his shirtfront and gave him a hard shaking.

''If you *ever*...make another...re...mark like th-that

about…Je…Jessie…'' He stopped and gasped in several deep breaths. ''…so help me, I'll—''

''I think he got the message,'' Cooter said dryly from beside him. ''Now, why don't you jist let the boy go, an' let's get on outta here?''

Hank looked at the little man tugging on his arm, and hesitated. He gritted his teeth and battled the fury still raging inside him. Finally, making a disgusted sound, he gave Lester one last shake and shoved him away.

The jukebox blared in the unnatural quiet that had fallen over the room. Hank stood with his chest heaving, his hands clenched at his sides. His lethal gaze swept the other patrons. ''Jessica Collier is a decent woman,'' he growled between his teeth. ''If any of you so much as hint otherwise, you'll get what Lester got. Understood?''

A murmur of assent went up from the onlookers as they exchanged wary glances and shifted their feet.

Cooter bent and retrieved Hank's hat from the floor and handed it to him. ''C'mon, son,'' he urged gently. ''Let's go.''

Hank shot the crowd one last threatening glare, shoved his hat on his head and strode out.

Neither Cooter nor Hank spoke a word until they were seated in the front seat of the pickup.

''What about the men?''

Cooter looked at Hank, slumped down on the seat on the passenger side, and snorted. ''They come in together in that ole rattledy-bang convertible of Wooley's, so I 'spect they'll get home the same way. Knowin' that bunch, though, they'll most likely jist move on to another waterin' hole for the rest of the night.''

Cooter started the truck and drove out of the parking lot. At the end of town he hit a pothole, and Hank let out a muffled grunt.

''You all right?''

"Yes. No. Ah, jeez! I think I got a busted rib," Hank groaned when Cooter hit another bump.

"A shiner and a cut lip, too, from the looks of you."

"What?" Hank gingerly ran the tip of his tongue over his lip and winced when he tasted blood. "Hell."

"There's a bottle of hard stuff in the glove compartment that I keep for medicinal purposes. It'll take the edge off till we can get you home and doctored up."

Bent over clutching his side, Hank leaned forward and retrieved the bottle. He took a long pull and grunted as the alcohol stung his lip.

After the third swallow he lay his head back on the seat. "Christ! A barroom brawl!" He groaned and rolled his head on the hard ridge of upholstery. "What the hell's the matter with me? I haven't been in a fight like that since I was twenty."

"Well, leastways you won. It don't do much good to defend a lady's honor if you get whupped."

Hank spit out a crude, one word expletive, which Cooter ignored. "I was plumb proud of you, boy. I've never knowd you to get all bent outta shape over a female before, but you shore shut ole Lester's trap good." He gave a wicked little chuckle. "Yessiree, by tomorrow the whole danged county'll be buzzin' 'bout how Hank Rawlins played white knight."

"Oh, shut up, you old coot," Hank snarled, and took another swig of whiskey.

Jessica was sitting at the kitchen table, feeling more miserable than she ever had in her life, when she heard a pickup pull into the yard. She went to the door and peered out cautiously, but it was too dark for her to be able to distinguish the truck's color. Glancing over her shoulder at the clock, she saw it was only a little after ten, and a frisson of alarm crept up her spine. She and Danny were alone, and she wasn't expecting anyone back from town for hours yet.

Her anxiety grew when the truck stopped within a few feet of the back steps. Warily, she watched the driver hop down, but when he came around the front of the truck she sagged against the door frame and closed her eyes. Even in the dark, she recognized Cooter's bandy-legged walk.

A half a second later her anxiety returned when she opened her eyes and saw the old man gingerly assisting someone from the cab of the truck.

"Cooter? Why are you back so early?" she called, hurrying across the porch. "What's wro—?" She broke off and sucked in her breath, her eyes rounding. "Oh, my God! Hank! You're hurt!"

"Now don't upset yoreself, woman. He'll live. He jist needs a little patchin' up is all. He's kinda stove up, though, so if you could jist help me get him inside…"

Jessica flew down the steps and was at Hank's side before Cooter finished speaking. Between the two of them, they managed to help Hank into the kitchen, though he was weaving so on his feet Jessica was concerned that he was more badly hurt than Cooter had let on.

"Maybe you should have taken him to a doctor in town," she said as they lowered him onto a kitchen chair.

"Ah, shoot, it ain't that bad. He's got a bruised rib or two. Some skinned knuckles. Nothin' serious."

"Skinned knuc—" Jessica gasped when she straightened and looked at Hank's face. His left eye was almost swollen shut, and the skin around it and across his cheekbone was a livid shade of purple. Dried blood from the cut on his lower lip, which was puffed up to the size of a walnut on one side, had caked on his chin.

"He's been fighting!" she declared with feminine outrage.

"Yep."

"It was a humdinger, too," Hank mumbled around his

thick lip. He gave her a bleary-eyed wink and attempted a smile but ended up cursing a blue streak when it hurt his mouth.

"And he's *drunk!*"

"'Bout half, I'd say," Cooter drawled.

Jessica was so incensed she was speechless. She clamped her jaws together and glared at both of them. She had just spent the most miserable evening of her life, imagining all sorts of things, and he had been out getting into a fistfight like an eight-year-old boy. Men!

Without a word, she stomped out. A few minutes later she returned with a first-aid kid, slammed it down on the table beside Hank and stomped away again. He jumped and immediately clutched his side, groaning.

"I suppose the fight was over some woman," Jessica snapped as she returned with a pan of warm water and a clean washcloth. Standing between Hank's outstretched legs, she bent over to inspect his injuries, and frowned. Hank blinked and started to try another silly grin then thought better of it.

The sight of his battered face merely increased Jessica's ire, and she bathed the area around the cut lip none too gently, ignoring his yelp of protest.

"Yep. Was over a woman, all right." Cooter leaned back against the counter and began rolling a cigarette. "You."

Jessica's head jerked up. *"Me!"*

Cooter's smirk was the closest thing she'd ever seen to a grin on that wrinkled face. She could only gape as he nodded his head slowly.

"Won, too," Hank boasted.

Thoroughly flustered, Jessica snapped her mouth shut and went back to tending his wounds. "I...I don't understand. Why would he get into a fight over me?"

"Well...seems this jughead made a remark Hank didn't care for."

"So you *hit him*?" Jessica stepped back and fixed Hank with a censorious look. "Just for making a remark? That's barbaric!"

Hank's big hands cupped her hips and drew her back. He looked up at her, his eyes entreating, and, against her will, her traitorous heart softened. With his battered face and that soulful gaze, he looked for all the world like a naughty boy begging forgiveness. "Don't be mad at me, Jessie," he cajoled, slurring the words. "I was protecting your honor."

Despite her anger, Jessica felt a foolish little dart of pleasure, which she tried to ignore. "Huh! More likely, you were just drunk and using me as an excuse to brawl. Now sit still and let me clean your face."

"Naw, he only had a few sips of beer before the fight broke out. He got that snootful on the way home, trying to kill the pain."

"See, sweetheart?" Hank tugged her closer, until her legs were wedged between his thighs. His hands roamed her hips, and the sides of her waist and rib cage. "I only hit him because he insulted you. I couldn't let him say what he did and do nothing," he murmured as he nuzzled the uninjured side of his face against her.

His arms went around her, molding her to him as his hands caressed her back. Jessica could feel his breath seeping through her blouse, moist and warm against her skin. She looked down at his head, lying against her breasts, and her faltering anger fizzled. An aching tenderness filled her. She wanted to run her fingers through that dark silky hair, hold him close and stroke away his hurts, as only a woman could. He had fought over her; surely that meant he cared?

Overwhelmed with love, she sighed and hesitantly lifted her arms to cradle his head.

Then she saw the lipstick on his collar.

Jessica stiffened and stepped back. Putting a hand beneath his chin, she jerked his face up and dabbed his cut lip with an alcohol-soaked cotton ball. Hank sucked in a hissing breath and recoiled. "Ow!"

"Be still," she ordered without an ounce of sympathy, and dabbed his cheek as well.

"Dammit! That hurts!"

"Oh, hush!" Jessica's mouth twisted. "Men! They stand toe-to-toe and beat each other to a bloody pulp, then whine like babies over a little alcohol."

Cooter chuckled, but the sound turned into a cough under Hank's glare.

Working with brisk efficiency, Jessica cleaned his knuckles and took perverse pleasure in painting them with iodine. Then she smeared antibiotic cream on his lip and the swollen area around his eye.

When she had finished, she and Cooter maneuvered him upstairs to his room. Even though he could barely stand, Hank protested every step of the way that he didn't need any help.

When they had him flat on his back in bed Cooter removed his boots while Jessica went to work on his clothes.

She unfastened his belt and tugged it off, then pulled his shirt free of his jeans and began unfastening buttons. She still simmered with anger, and her movements were fast and jerky, her concentration centered on the task, rather than the man.

"Mmm, that's nice," Hank murmured when her fingers brushed against his bare abdomen. Giving her a smoldering look, he grabbed her hand and held it there. "I've always wanted you to undress me."

Jessica gasped at the intimate contact. "Hank! Behave," she hissed, feeling heat rise in her neck. "We're not alone, you know." Flustered, she cast an anxious glance over her shoulder to see if Cooter was watching, and was surprised to discover that he was no longer there.

"Ah, Jessie. Sweet Jessie," Hank crooned. He lifted his

other hand and stroked her cheek. "Don't be mad, sweetheart." His hand curved around the back of her neck and tugged, but Jessica resisted the pressure.

"Hank, stop."

"Come to me, Jessie. Let me hold you. God! I've dreamed of having you in my bed a hundred times." He moved her hand in a slow circle against his belly, watching her, his eyes heavy and dark with passion. The soft abrasion of his body hair against her palm sent heat streaking up her arm, and Jessica caught her breath. She licked her lips, unable to look away from his compelling sensual gaze.

"This...this isn't the time for—Hank, no!" she cried anxiously when he pulled her head lower. "You mustn't—! Oh!"

A quick jerk brought her tumbling down onto the bed. Jessica lunged to one side, trying not to hurt him, but even so Hank grunted with pain when the impact jolted him.

Immediately filled with concern, Jessica tried to scramble up, but he wouldn't let her. "No. Be still. I want to hold you."

"Oh, Hank. You shouldn't be doing this," she pleaded, but already his touch had set off little tremors of longing, and the protest came out weaker than she had intended. "You're hurt—"

"Then don't fight me, sweetheart," he whispered thickly, nuzzling her neck. "Stay with me, and let me love you. I need you, Jessie. I need you."

Jessica closed her eyes and tried to hold her body stiff, but as his tongue traced a wet pattern on her skin she made a tiny sound in her throat. When his hand closed around her breast a delicious shudder racked her, and the sound became a moan. "Oh, Hank. Hank!"

His big hand flexed around the soft mound, and she felt her nipple tighten and peak. Rivers of desire flowed from that sensitive tip, coursing hotly through her body, straight to the core of her femininity.

Jessica cried out at the sweet pleasure/pain. Her body was taut, trembling with need and longing. Deep inside she knew the battle was lost. She had fought him so long, but she couldn't fight him any longer. She couldn't fight her love any longer.

With a sigh of surrender, Jessica raised her hand and clasped his head, holding him close. She tunneled her fingers in his hair, loving its thickness, the way it glided against her skin like warm silk. His body was hard against her softness, and oh so tempting. Jessica stroked his scalp, the nape of his neck. She smoothed her hand over his shoulders and the hard, flat muscles that banded his back. "Oh, Hank," she murmured with aching tenderness. "I need you, too."

It was a moment before Hank's stillness registered, and then she realized that the hand at her breast had gone slack.

"Hank?" Jessica raised up on one elbow, alarm flickering through her. "Hank, are you all ri—"

She stared in consternation at his slack face. He lay on his back with his eyes closed, his lips slightly parted, snoring softly.

Jessica didn't know whether to laugh or cry. She felt a little like doing both.

But neither the irony nor the humor of the situation was lost on Jessica, and when she caught a whiff of whiskey her lips began to twitch. A giggle rose in her throat, and she clamped her hand over her mouth to hold it in. She wasn't sure who the joke was on—her or Hank.

Her mind and her conscience told her it was better this way. Though she loved him and wanted him fiercely, she would have regretted making love with him, given the way things stood between them. At the moment though, her body disagreed. Now she knew why men took cold showers.

Hank, if he remembered any of this tomorrow, was going to be mad as the devil. Either way, he would probably have a granddaddy of a headache.

Sighing, Jessica gently removed his hand from her breast and slipped from beneath his encircling arm. She began easing away from him, then chuckled at her caution and threw her legs over the side and stood up. Hank probably wouldn't awaken if she used the bed as a trampoline.

She pulled the covers up over him and tucked them around his shoulders. Then she paused, still bent over, and gazed with love and exasperated tenderness at his battered face. She smoothed a lock of hair off his forehead, ran her fingertips over the rough silk of his eyebrows and trailed them down the side of his face.

"Oh, Hank," she whispered sadly, and brushed the corner of his mouth with a light kiss.

Chapter Nine

The next morning they were halfway through breakfast before Jessica remembered she'd made a date with Will Beaman for that night.

He had called shortly after Hank and the others had left for town the evening before and asked her to have dinner with him. At first, Jessica hadn't even known who he was. When she'd finally placed him, she'd realized, guiltily, that she hadn't given the young vet so much as a thought since the day he'd been at the ranch.

It was partly because of that guilt, and partly because he had caught her at low ebb, that she had said yes. She didn't really want to go out with Will or any man, other than Hank, but when he'd called, she'd been sitting there all alone, sick with jealousy and so desperately unhappy she was hurting inside. His invitation had been a balm to her pride as well as her aching heart.

Jessica had meant to ask Cooter as soon as she saw him if he would watch Danny for her, but the turmoil the night before had pushed the whole thing right out of her mind. It wasn't until Hank growled something about getting Will to come out and take another look at his prize bull that she remembered.

"Oh, my goodness, I just thought of something," she gasped, looking anxiously at Cooter. "I know it's late to be asking, but would you mind watching Danny for me this evening?"

Danny looked up at that, his eyes alive with interest, but his mouth was too crammed full of food to speak.

"I done told you I would anytime, didn't I?"

"I know, but—"

"Well then, quit ditherin' 'bout it. Jist tell me when yore leavin'."

"About six." Smiling softly, Jessica laid her hand on his arm. "Thanks, Cooter. I really appreciate it. And I won't be late. I promise."

"Oh, pshaw!" He shifted in his chair and scowled. "You jist leave the boy to me an' quit yore worryin'."

"Yippie! I get to stay with Cooter!" Danny cheered, bouncing up and down on his chair.

Hank looked up from the cup of black coffee he held cradled between his hands. "You going somewhere?" His voice was low and rough, as though it pained him to speak, and his eyes were open to mere slits.

Jessica cast him a wary glance. She had blurted out the request before she'd thought, wanting to ask Cooter before she forgot again. Now she could have kicked herself for even mentioning it in front of Hank.

As she had expected, he'd awakened feeling rotten. He denied it, of course—some sort of misplaced male pride, Jessica supposed—but he looked awful, his movements were stiff and careful, and he had the disposition of a grizzly with an impacted tooth. He'd spent the entire meal swilling black coffee and trying not to look at the eggs and sausage she had cooked for breakfast.

"Yes," she said cautiously. "I have a date. With, uh…with Will Beaman."

"What's a date, Mom?" Danny asked, but Cooter shushed him.

Hank just looked at her, his eyes hard and glittering between narrowed lids. Jessica saw a muscle twitch in his cheek and knew that he was clenching his teeth.

She had been tiptoeing around him all morning, not wanting to exacerbate his mood, but all at once she no longer cared. That he had the gall to be angry, after last night, made her furious. Never mind that he hadn't spent the night with another woman, that had been his intention when he'd left. And he had made sure that she knew it.

Jessica tilted her chin. "He called last night, after you left, and asked me to have dinner with him tonight."

"Well, good for you," Cooter said with hearty approval. "Will's a nice man. The marryin' kind, too."

"Cooter!" Jessica's anger dissolved in a flood of embarrassment. "For heaven's sake! I'm just going out to dinner with him."

"Mebbe so, but it don't hurt none to think 'bout these things." He scratched his whiskers and shot Hank a sly glance. "A purty young woman like you, who likes to cook and keep house, needs a man of her own, a home. An' that boy of yours needs a new daddy."

Hank's flinty gaze sliced into the old man, but Cooter merely scooped up another bite of egg and followed it with a swig of coffee, impervious to the pulsing undercurrents.

After a taut moment of silence Hank downed the last of his coffee and stood up. Holding himself stiffly, he walked out of the room without a word.

For the rest of the day, Hank was an absolute bear, snarling at anyone who came near him. Most of that time he spent holed up in his office, going over the ranch books. Jessica kept him supplied with coffee and served him lunch on a tray, but largely she managed to avoid him. And she made sure that Danny played outdoors at a safe distance.

Jessica had thought that good manners and his friendship with the man would prevent Hank from being rude when Will came to pick her up. She was wrong.

Will arrived promptly at six, driving up to the back door, as everyone else did. Not once in the two months Jessica had been there had anyone come to the front. Cooter and Danny were sitting at the kitchen table playing a game of checkers, but Hank was nowhere in sight. For a moment she entertained the wishful thought that they would get away without encountering him, but Will and Cooter had barely shaken hands when he walked in.

"Hi ya, Hank. How'ya doing?"

Barely sparing Will a glance, Hank returned the greeting with a curt nod and made straight for the refrigerator.

He took out a beer. Without offering one to Will, he popped off the top, leaned his rump against the counter and took a long drink.

Jessica squirmed with embarrassment, but Will didn't appear to notice his discourtesy. His attention was on Hank's face.

"That's some shiner you got there," he said, peering closely at the colorful array of bruises and puffy flesh. "Hmm. Looks pretty swollen. You really ought to put some cool compresses on your eye. That lip, too. And use plenty of antibiotic cream. You don't want to get an infection."

Hank took another long drink. He wiped his mouth with the back of his hand and gave Will a surly look. "When I want medical advice, Beaman, I'll get it from a real doctor."

Will looked taken aback.

Without even looking up from the checkerboard, Cooter drawled, "Shoot, Hank, you're in good hands with Will. The man's treated hundreds of jackasses."

Will chuckled, but Jessica sucked in a sharp breath. She couldn't believe that even Cooter had dared to speak to Hank that way.

But instead of the explosion she expected, Hank merely growled, "And when I want to listen to a bad comedian I'll turn on the television."

Jessica gave a silent groan and wondered what else could possibly happen. Then she noticed Danny's face, and she knew she had to get Will out of there. Fast.

She'd had a long talk with her son that morning about man-to-woman relationships, but he still wasn't happy about her going out with Will. He had liked him enough, but the idea of Will courting his mother had not sat well with him.

"Why don't you just marry Hank?" he'd asked with an innocent candor that had squeezed her heart. "Then you wouldn't have to go on silly ole dates. And I'd be Hank's little boy. That'd be neat."

Jessica thought so, too, but she knew it was a hopeless dream. She had tried to explain to Danny that it wasn't that easy, that just wanting something didn't make it happen, but she had the uneasy feeling he hadn't believed her.

From the sullen way he was eyeing Will, Jessica knew he was about to blurt out something embarrassing, and she didn't want to wait around to hear it. Hurriedly, she gave Danny a goodbye kiss, and told him to mind Cooter. Ignoring Hank's black look, she looped her arm through Will's and hustled him out the door.

"I couldn't help but notice a bit of hostility back there." Will shot Jessica an inquiring glance as they drove out of the ranch yard. "Am I, uh…by chance, stepping on anyone's toes?"

"If you're asking if Hank and I are involved, then the answer is no," Jessica replied dully. "He's just in a rotten mood because he's hung over and nursing a few aches and pains."

"That's what I figured. I've known Hank a long time, and he shies away from serious relationships like they were the plague. But it never hurts to check."

Will's words merely confirmed what Jessica already knew, but hearing it depressed her anyway.

Danny's protruding lower lip began to tremble the minute his mother walked out the door. "I don't want Mom to go out with that man," he announced sullenly.

Hank's mouth twisted. *Tell me about it, kid.*

He took a long drink of beer. As he lowered the can he felt a tug on the leg of his jeans, and he looked down into Danny's unhappy face.

"Why did you let her go?" he asked accusingly.

"Danny, your mother's a grown woman. If she wants to go out with Will, I can't stop her."

"I hate him."

"Aw, c'mon, pard, you don't mean that."

"Do, too."

At a loss, Hank ruffled his hair. "Will's okay. You just don't know him yet." *What the hell was he doing? He wanted to punch the guy out himself.*

"I don't wanna know him," Danny insisted. He looked at Hank pleadingly. "If you married Mom, she wouldn't have to go on dates with that dumb ole guy."

"Ah…well…"

"Please, Hank." Danny's chin began to wobble, and his eyes filled with tears. "I don't want Mom to marry that man!" he cried.

The next thing Hank knew, the child's arms were wrapped around his leg, and Danny was bawling in earnest against his thigh. Hank sent Cooter a helpless look, but the old man just shrugged.

Speechless, Hank stared down at the tawny head. The boy's sturdy little body was plastered to him as if it were a jellyfish, and the feel of those wrenching sobs did strange things to his insides.

Left with no choice, he bent and peeled the boy loose and lifted him up in his arms. Good God, he thought as he cuddled the distraught child. It's bad enough the mother can turn me inside out. Now I'm falling for the boy, too.

Jessica glanced guiltily at Will when he turned off the highway onto the ranch road. As first dates went, theirs had been a complete bomb, and it was all her fault.

Throughout dinner she had tried to smile and converse as though she were enjoying herself but her heart hadn't been in it, and she knew that Will had been aware of her lack of interest. They had driven into Durango for dinner, but after three hours of stilted conversation he had obviously decided that she was hopeless.

"I apologize again for cutting the evening short," he said as he stopped the car beside the back door. "But since I've got that early appointment in the morning..."

"That's all right, Will. I understand." Actually Jessica was relieved that the awkward evening was over, and she suspected he was, also.

He left her at the back door, saying he'd call her soon, but both were aware that it was merely a polite lie.

Cooter was right, she thought sadly. Will was a good man, a settling-down kind of man. Sighing, she watched him drive away and wondered why she always fell for the other kind.

Light spilled across the back porch from the kitchen, and Jessica could hear faint sounds of the TV in the distance. Sighing, she turned to open the screen door, then changed her mind. She was too restless and unsettled to go in just yet.

She left the steps and strolled aimlessly across the yard, her thoughts a million miles away. At the corral, she stopped and braced her forearms along the top rail and gazed into the distance at the sweeping valley and the dark bulk of the surrounding mountains, the creek twisting away into the distance, shimmering in the moonlight like a silver thread.

She had come to love this place, she realized, almost as much as she loved the man who owned it. Already, in two short months it had become home to her, much more so than the Collier mansion had ever been.

But how long could she go on living in the same house with Hank, loving him as she did, knowing he would never be hers. It was killing her by inches. Yet, the thought of leaving and never seeing him again was worse.

As though her thoughts had conjured him up, the barn door opened, and Hank stepped out. Jessica's heart began to thud. She didn't want to face Hank tonight. She felt too blue, too fragile. But it was too late to leave, and there was no place to hide.

He'd taken only three steps toward the house when she saw him stiffen and pause. Then he changed direction.

"Back so soon?" he drawled when he reached her. Propping his bent elbow over the fence, he leaned against it, watching her. "I thought you and good ole Will would still be exchanging life stories and finding out what you had in common. Isn't that what people do when they're interested in a 'serious' relationship?"

"Will had an early appointment in the morning," Jessica said, ignoring his sarcasm. "Now if you'll excuse me, I think I'll go in. It's getting late."

"Not so fast, Duchess." As she turned to leave Hank grasped her wrist and jerked her up against his chest. Jessica gave a startled cry and strained away from him but his arms locked around her, holding her fast. "I believe we have a little unfinished business," he said with a predatory smile, but the moment the words left his lips his expression hardened. "How could you go out with Will, after last night?"

Jessica's eyes widened. "L-last night?"

"Did you really think I wouldn't remember? Honey, I may have been a bit fuzzy around the edges but I wasn't *that* far gone."

"Hank...please, let's not—"

"Admit it, Duchess. If I hadn't been hurting and half-sloshed we would be lovers now, and you know it."

"No, I—"

"Dammit! You wanted me as much as I wanted you!" he swore, between gritted teeth. "You melted in my arms last night. And if I hadn't flaked out, you would have made love with me."

"All right! All right, I admit it," she cried in a shaken voice. "But the point is, we didn't. Anyway...that was a mistake. And it doesn't change anything."

Something wild flared in his eyes, then they narrowed. "The *hell* it doesn't."

His mouth swooped down on hers with a driving passion that took her breath away.

Hank was, by nature, an easygoing man who was unaccustomed to being at the mercy of his emotions. He had always prided himself on being in control, on not letting things, least of all a woman, get under his skin. But that was before he met Jessica.

Now the frustration and desire that had been building for months broke free, overriding restraints of will and character. He was driven by passion and a bone-deep longing he'd never experienced before, and that frightened and angered him even as he sought to appease it. It was crazy, and went against everything he believed, but at that moment all that mattered was claiming the slender woman he held in his arms as his own. He knew an overwhelming need, a compulsion, to bind her so tightly to him that she would never get away, never say no to him again...never want to.

Ignoring the pain it caused his cut lip, he rocked his

mouth over hers with a fierce demand. His teeth nipped. His tongue plunged into her mouth, taking, claiming with hard insistence. He was on fire, and the feel of her, the taste, was fanning the flames higher. *Dammit, didn't she know she was his?*

Jessica lay quiescent against him, her body pliant, trembling, weak from the storm of conflicting emotions that was tearing her apart. She hadn't known it was possible to experience such extremes. She was frightened and exhilarated, saddened and elated, hopeful and despairing, all at one time. To be in Hank's arms, to be the recipient of his passion was wonderful. It was, at least in part, what she wanted, what she had been yearning for all during these past miserable weeks.

But satisfying physical desire simply wasn't enough. For her, it never would be. If Jessica knew nothing else about herself, she knew that, and the knowing broke her heart. At that moment she wished with all her being that she could settle for what he was offering and never count the cost, but she couldn't. Maybe it was the humiliating years she'd spent in a sham of a marriage with Allen. Maybe it was her upbringing. She didn't know. But there was something deep inside her that shrank from sharing her most intimate self without love.

Hank's arms tightened around her, and Jessica whimpered, in both pain and regret. Immediately his mouth gentled on hers and his hands began to stroke her back in a slow, soothing pattern. The kiss became pliant and persuasive, a sweet, sweet seduction that tugged at her heart and made her body throb. Jessica's arms went around him, her hands digging into his back, her heart aching with love.

Dragging his mouth from hers, Hank kissed his way across her cheek and buried his face in the cloud of hair at the side of her neck. He held her tightly against his heaving chest. His breathing was a labored rush in her ear as he nipped at her lobe with gentle savagery.

"Come inside with me, Jessie," he pleaded in a harsh whisper. "Now."

"Oh, Hank, darling..." A sob rose in Jessica's throat, and her face crumpled as pain squeezed her heart. "I...I can't."

Hank bit out a vicious curse and released her so abruptly she staggered back and had to grab the corral fence to keep from falling. He spun away, and with his fists planted on his hips he threw his head back and stared up at the sky. Then just as suddenly, he spun back again.

His furious gaze pierced her, and even in the pale moonlight she could see the muscles working in his face. "Just tell me one thing. Was Cooter on target this morning? Are you angling for a husband? Do you think if you hold out long enough I'll be so desperate for you I'll propose?"

"No! That's disgusting. I...I don't deny that I'd like to remarry someday, but—"

Hank's snort of derisive laughter cut her off. "You're setting your sights a little low this time, aren't you, Duchess? You must be desperate for a husband. It would be quite a comedown to settle for a small-time rancher or a country vet after being married to the scion of an old moneyed family."

Jessica's chin quivered with hurt, but she lifted it anyway and looked at him reproachfully, her eyes shining with unshed tears. "That's not fair," she said in a small, aching voice. "Yes, I'd like to marry again, but not for a meal ticket, or just for the sake of having a husband. If I ever remarry, it will be for one reason—love."

"*Love!*" Hank barked the word on a scornful laugh and shook his head pityingly. "Didn't your first try at marriage teach you anything? Honey, love is a myth. It's no more than a pretty word for lust. And no matter what you call it, it doesn't last."

"No. You're wrong," she insisted, her eyes pleading.

"I know you're wrong. My parents have been married for almost twenty-eight years, and their love is still strong."

"You're dreaming, Duchess. Believe me, people merely use one another. Relationships last only as long as each person gives the other what they need. It can be sex, security, emotional support, just plain companionship, whatever. But once the need is gone or the chemistry has burned itself out, the relationship ends. Marriage merely complicates things and makes parting that much harder, which is why some people stick it out even when there's nothing left."

He spoke with a harsh bitterness that wrung Jessica's heart, and she could only stare at him in mute despair as he continued.

"Well, honey, Will Beaman may be fool enough to step into that trap, but not me."

He turned and stalked away toward the house, leaving Jessica clinging to the fence, staring after him, her throat aching, more saddened and discouraged than she could remember ever being.

She winced when the screen door banged shut behind him. Briefly he was silhouetted by the light spilling onto the porch, a tall, powerful figure who, even at that distance, radiated anger. Then he strode into the house and was gone from sight.

With a shuddering sigh, Jessica closed her eyes and rested her forehead against the fence.

"Don't take it so hard, little gal. That's jist ignorance speakin'."

Jessica gave a little cry and jumped when the voice floated to her out of the darkness. She whipped around, her eyes searching. "Cooter?" Her voice was high, a bit shaky. "Is that you?"

A few yards away a match scraped against the trunk of an aspen tree and flared. The red glow illuminated Cooter's face as he held the flame to the tip of a crooked cigarette.

Jessica's shoulders slumped. "You scared me half to death." The complaint came out in a breathless rush, but the words had barely left her mouth when she felt heat rise in her neck and face. Jessica bit her lip, her eyes on Cooter as his bowed legs carried him slowly to where she stood.

"You…you heard everything, didn't you?"

"Yep." He propped a booted foot on the lower rail of the fence. Gazing into the distance, he drew on his cigarette until the tip was a hard, bright ball. "Didn't mean to, but there wasn't no way to avoid it. I'd come out for a breath of air before you got home."

Jessica looked back at the house. "Danny—?"

"Don't worry. He's been sleepin' like a log for over an hour."

"Oh."

They fell silent again. Cooter puffed on his cigarette while Jessica squirmed and groped for something to say to cover her embarrassment.

"Hank's a blame fool." The old man's pronouncement came out of the blue, surprising her. He slanted Jessica a quick, sharp look. "Course, I don't 'spose he can help it."

"Wh-what do you mean?"

"Jist that the boy's got good cause to be cynical 'bout love an' marriage. His maw ran off with another man when he was jist a tyke. An' his paw, my half brother, he was jist a rodeo bum. Had him a woman in every town.

"Taylor dragged Hank all over the country with him. When he was winning purses an' was in the chips they lived high. When he was busted they stayed in cheap hotels, or with one of Taylor's women, if she had a place. The boy never knew what it was to have a home or lovin' parents. All he saw was people usin' one another, then movin' on.

"Jist 'cause he ain't met the right one—till now, that is—the boy's got the danged fool notion that there's too much of his paw in him to love a woman."

"He says he doesn't believe in love."

Cooter gave her a sour look. "Shoot. That's jist a cover-up. Though he's probably told hisself that so many times I 'spect he believes it by now. He tries to act like the past don't bother him none, but deep down under all that teasin' an' easygoing ways there's a lotta hurt in that boy."

They fell silent. Cooter puffed on his cigarette, and they both gazed up at the stars, deep in thought. After a while Jessica asked quietly, "If Hank and his father followed the rodeo circuit, how did he go to school?"

"Correspondence. Leastwise, until he went off to college. That's the only thing that sorry brother of mine did right—seein' to it that Hank got hisself an education.

"A'course, Hank paid for most of that hisself. At sixteen he started enterin' rodeos. Won a lot of purses, too, only instead of blowin' his money, like his paw did, he socked it away for schoolin'."

A last puff of the cigarette brought the fire right down to his fingers. Cooter dropped the butt and ground it beneath his boot heel. "C'mon, girl. We'd best be gettin' in." To Jessica's surprise, he grasped her elbow and strolled with her back toward the house.

They had almost reached the back steps, when Cooter said, "Now, I told you all this so's you won't go gettin' discouraged. Jist remember, if the boy don't know nothin' 'bout love an' marriage, it's 'cause he ain't never seen the real thing. A man cain't be expected to understand what he don't know. Right now, I 'spect he's grapplin' with feelins that're new to him. So you give him time, you hear. He'll figure 'um out."

Jessica was touched by Cooter's support and approval, and several times she tried to tell him so, but he wouldn't listen.

"Shoot, gal, I'm jist bein' practical is all. The boy needs

to settle down. And 'sides, a good cook is danged hard to come by these days.''

His grumpy disclaimer hadn't fazed Jessica. After two months she'd come to realize that Cooter's gruffness was pure sham. She'd simply smiled and said, ''Well, whatever your reason, thanks anyway,'' and as she'd passed his chair, she'd dropped a quick kiss on his bald spot and had the satisfaction of watching his face turn the color of a plum.

If it hadn't been for Cooter's silent support, though, Jessica wasn't sure if she would have been able to endure the next few days.

Living with Hank was like living with a ticking time bomb that could go off at any moment. Gone was the flirtatious, teasing, easygoing man who had hired her. In his place was an intense, silent, hostile stranger.

The hands were quick to notice the change, and Jessica was fairly sure they had guessed the reason for it. More than once she had noticed their curious glances back and forth between her and Hank, and the silent looks that were exchanged.

Hank said little. He didn't have to—his angry frustration was palpable. It vibrated in the air around him. It was there in the hard glitter in his eyes, the taut lines of his body, his brooding silence. When he did speak it was usually to bark an order or a reprimand.

Meals became subdued, silent times to get through as quickly as possible, with everyone, with the exception of Cooter, doing their best to avoid riling Hank or drawing his attention. Even gregarious Wooley managed to keep his mouth shut.

Though he had no idea of the reason for them, Danny, with the intuitive perception of a child, had picked up the uneasy vibrations. He sat through each meal in troubled silence, his eyes round and solemn as he searched the faces around him for a clue.

Jessica was sure that things couldn't get any worse. Then one morning, Hank gave her terse instructions to get the spare room ready for company.

"I'm leaving right now for Durango to meet the plane. We'll be back around noon or a little after." In mid-September the early morning air held a nip, and he shrugged into a light denim jacket before settling his hat on his head. He stepped onto the porch, took two steps, then swung back. "Oh, and be sure and put some flowers in the room, too. Maybe one of these potted things, if there aren't any fresh ones to cut."

Jessica stared after him, a sick feeling in the pit of her stomach. Flowers? There could be only one reason he had requested flowers. His guest was a woman.

Dazed with pain, Jessica stepped through the door and walked over to the wall of glass panels that Cooter had installed inside the screen to enclose and weatherize the porch for winter. Automatically, as she watched him drive away, she reached her hand into one of the hanging baskets and tested the soil. The potted plants scattered about the porch were flourishing now under her care.

So much so that Hank wanted her to use one to brighten his girlfriend's bedroom.

Swallowing the aching knot in her throat, telling herself she *would not* cry, Jessica looked around and selected the tiered ceramic pot of African violets she had finally coaxed into bloom.

The morning passed in a flurry of activity. Jessica had cleaned house only a couple of days before, but she gave the entire place a quick once-over, with the exception of the upstairs bathroom and the guest room. Those she cleaned until they were spotless. She made up the bed with the best sheets and put facial tissues and a bottle of her own hand lotion on the dresser, along with the violets. In the bathroom she put up a fresh shower-curtain liner and the fluffiest towels and placed violet-scented bath oil and talcum powder on the counter.

All the while Jessica worked she cursed Hank for giving her so little notice, but she was determined the place would be spotless for his "guest."

By the time Hank returned she had a special lunch simmering on the stove and the table was set. Jessica was fresh from the shower, her hair shampooed and shining, and she was dressed in her best camel wool slacks and a blue-and-camel-silk print blouse. Since coming to the ranch she hadn't bothered with much makeup. Getting up at four-thirty to cook for six hungry men, she barely had time to slap on the bare minimum most mornings. But today she'd taken special care, needing the extra boost of knowing she looked her best.

Though she had meant to remain aloof and in the kitchen, when the truck stopped in the yard Jessica was drawn to the back door, then, almost without her being aware of it, onto the porch. Standing with her arms crossed over her midriff, her heart heavy with dread, she watched the woman climb down out of the truck.

She was on the opposite side, and for a moment all Jessica could see was a thick curtain of shiny raven-black hair hanging down a slender back to a point several inches below the woman's shoulders. Then she turned and laughed at something that Hank said, and Jessica wanted to weep.

She was the most beautiful creature Jessica had ever seen. The cloud of black hair framed an oval face with features as perfect and delicate as a china doll's. She was shapely and slender, and even from a distance Jessica could see that her dusty-pink dress and matching jacket were not only stylish, but expensive. Just looking at her made Jessica feel awkward and ugly.

A shout drew Jessica's attention to the barn, and she saw Cooter hurrying toward the house as fast as his bowed

legs could carry him. When he reached the woman he
wrapped her in a bear hug and lifted her off the ground.

Jessica bit her lip and blinked back tears. *Oh, Cooter.
Not you, too.*

It wasn't until Cooter released the woman and turned
with his hand outstretched that Jessica noticed the man.
Her heart gave a little leap as the two shook hands and
thumped each other on the back. A man? Were they a
couple?

Hope soared, though she cautioned herself against it.

She watched the stranger for a clue, and had her answer
a moment later when he slipped his arm around the lovely
brunette's waist and pulled her against his side. As he
talked to Cooter, he looked down at her and smiled, and
Jessica's heart squeezed at the look of love on that aus-
terely handsome face.

Relief washed over her in a great wave, almost buckling
her knees. It was followed almost at once by shock, then
anger when she noticed that Hank was watching her
through the glass wall, his face hard with satisfaction.
Damn him! He had deliberately misled her about the
woman!

The men lifted the suitcases from the back of the truck,
and they all headed for the door, still laughing and talking.
That the four were old friends was obvious. Watching
them, Jessica felt like an intruder, an outsider, and in a
sudden rush of panic she retreated to the kitchen.

Footsteps hammered on the wooden planks of the back
porch, and the screen door banged shut.

"Oh, Hank, these plants are gorgeous," Jessica heard
the brunette exclaim. She adjusted a burner on the stove
and kept her back to the door. Even the woman's voice
was beautiful.

"That's Jessie's doin'. Before she came, I always
thought this was jist a bunch of weeds."

The comment brought a soft throaty chuckle. "Cooter,

you're terrible. But I'd already figured as much. Bless her heart, I've never known anyone with a worse brown thumb than Ina Mae.''

Jessica heard them come inside. Fixing a polite smile on her face, she turned, and the brunette's eyes widened in surprise.

''Why, Hank, you devil,'' she said, sending him a look that was half accusing and half amused. ''You told me what a wonderful cook and homemaker she was, but you didn't mention that she was beautiful, too.''

Hank shrugged. ''It didn't seem important.''

The woman wrinkled her nose at him, then stepped forward with her hands outstretched. ''Hi. You must be Jessica. I'm Katy Barnett and this is my husband, Trace.''

A little dazed, Jessica found her hands clasped and gently squeezed as she returned the greeting. Beneath Katy's friendly smile, the last of her reservations vanished.

Up close, she was even lovelier than Jessica had thought. There was a quiet, Madonna-like quality to Katy's beauty, an exquisite softness that was disarming. Her skin was porcelain smooth and fair, in startling contrast to the raven tresses, and incredibly long lashes framed her wide sapphire-blue eyes. If eyes were, indeed, a mirror to the soul, then Jessica knew that this woman was as beautiful on the inside as she was on the outside.

''We're delighted that Hank found you. He and Cooter are hopeless when it comes to domestic chores of any kind, as I'm sure you discovered when you arrived.''

''Trace is my partner in the ranch.''

Surprised, Jessica looked at Hank, and found he was watching her steadily. ''Partner?''

''A silent one.'' Smiling, Trace stepped forward and shook Jessica's hand. ''And I only have a small interest in the ranch these days. Over the years, I've sold most of my shares to Hank, but I can't quite turn loose of this place completely.''

Jessica could believe that. Trace Barnett looked like a man who held on to what was his. He and Hank were about the same age, with the same rangy build, though Trace was about an inch taller and a shade heavier, and they both had the tanned, rugged look of men who worked out of doors. He was handsome, in a rugged sort of way, with a thick shock of light brown hair and a strong, square-jawed face. But there was something intense, almost dangerous in those sharp, deep-set hazel eyes. He was the kind of man who would be an excellent friend...and a fearsome enemy.

"We were full partners when Trace and I pooled our resources nine years ago to buy this place." Hank shot his friend a wry look. "Then, after about four years, just as we were getting on our feet, his father passed away, and he inherited Green Meadows, the Barnetts' Thoroughbred horse farm down in Texas."

"Really?" Alarm skittered through Jessica as her eyes flashed to the tall, sandy-haired man. "Where in Texas?"

"Just outside of Tyler."

Jessica's relief was so intense she was sure it showed on her face, though no one seemed to notice. It was still possible, of course, that the Barnetts knew, or at least knew of, the Colliers. Tyler wasn't all that far from Fort Worth, and a family Thoroughbred horse farm spelled old money. People from that background usually moved in the same social circles, and to wealthy Texans, distance meant little. Still, even if he was acquainted with the Collier family, Trace evidently hadn't connected the name with his partner's housekeeper.

"Well, are we gonna stand around jawin' all day?" Without waiting for an answer, Cooter stomped toward the hall door. "The hands will be here any minute for lunch. C'mon. Let's get these folks settled in so they can sample some of Jessie's cookin'."

Trace shot Hank a dry look. "Cantankerous old coot never changes, does he?"

"Nope." A slow grin split Hank's face. "Thank God."

"Darling, just take our things up, and I'll unpack later," Katy told her husband as he followed Hank out the door. "Right now I'm going to help Jessica with lunch."

"Oh, no, really!" Jessica was appalled. "I can't let you do that. You're a guest!"

"Nonsense. Now where do you keep the aprons?"

"But...but I'm the housekeeper. This is my job."

"So? I have a housekeeper at home, and I help her in the kitchen all the time."

Katy's attitude was so far removed from what Jessica knew of the privileged class that for a moment she could only stare. Lois would die of starvation before lending a hand in the kitchen.

The men were all pleased to see the Barnetts. They treated Katy with the same touching "hat-in-hand" deference and respect that they gave her.

During the meal Jessica learned that Katy and Trace had married five years ago, shortly after Trace returned to Texas to take over his inheritance, and that they were now the parents of four-year-old twin boys, named Thomas and Patrick, for her father, Thomas Patrick Donovan.

"Where are the little scamps?" Cooter asked, helping himself to another slice of ham.

"Dad and Mattie are looking after them." Katy turned to Jessica and explained that Mattie was the housekeeper she had spoken of earlier. "She's doted on the boys ever since were born, and my dad is even worse. Those two little devils will be spoiled rotten by the time we get home."

"That's assuming we'll still have a home. The house may not be standing by that time."

Everyone laughed at Trace's dry comment, but the pride and love he felt for his boys was evident in his voice and his expression, just as it was whenever he looked at his wife.

After lunch Katy insisted on helping Jessica with the dishes, and no amount of arguing would dissuade her. As they worked together, Jessica learned that Katy's father had been the manager of Green Meadows for twenty years, and they had lived in a cottage on the farm all that time.

"Oh. So you've known Trace most of your life, then."

Katy laughed. "Not really. To start with, Trace is eleven years older than I am, so while I was growing up we had little contact. But even if we had been the same age, I doubt that things would have been different. You see, Trace's father, Henry Barnett, was a very…uh…class-conscious man."

"In other words, a snob."

"You could say that. Anyway, it wasn't until Trace returned home, after being gone for four years, that we got together." Her eyes took on a faraway look as she picked up another plate and dried it slowly. "Even then, we had some problems we had to work through."

"Which you obviously did."

"Yes." Katy's smile returned, and she patted her flat tummy. "And in about seven months we're going to have another little 'problem.' This time I'm hoping for a girl."

"A baby? Oh, Katy, that's marvelous!"

As they worked they talked about babies and child rearing and the joys and trials of being pregnant. By the time they had finished putting the kitchen in order Jessica felt as though she had known Katy for years.

Even so, she resisted when Katy insisted that they join Hank and Trace, who were relaxing in the living room. But for all her gentle softness, Katy was not one to give in easily, and before Jessica knew it, she was propelled down the hall and into the living room.

Both men rose when they walked in. To Jessica's relief, Hank didn't seem in the least annoyed, or even surprised that Katy had included her. "Ah, here they are," Trace said. "Come sit down and join us. We were just saying—"

At the loud rapping noise, Trace stopped speaking, and they all looked at one another in astonishment.

"Good heavens." Katy's wide-eyed gaze went to Hank, then to Jessica. "Someone is actually knocking on the front door!"

Hank rose and headed for the entry. "Probably a lost tourist."

From where she sat, just inside the living room, Jessica had a clear view of the front door, and when Hank opened it he faced a distinguished-looking middle-aged man wearing a business suit and carrying a leather briefcase.

"How do you do," he said politely, handing Hank a business card. "My name is Jonathan Wittlow. I am an attorney, representing Mrs. Lois Collier. I would like to speak to Mrs. Jessica Collier, if I may."

Chapter Ten

All the blood drained from Jessica's face.

She stood up. Her movements were stiff and slow, uncoordinated, like those of someone who was recovering from a grave illness. Her frightened gaze never left the dark-suited man at the door. "No," she whispered. "Oh, my God, no."

"Jessie? Jessie, are you all right?"

She didn't hear Katy's worried question. As Jonathan Wittlow entered the living room at Hank's side Jessica unconsciously retreated a step. She raised a shaking hand to her mouth and stared at him as though he were the devil incarnate.

"Ah, Jessica, my dear, there you are." Stopping just inside the room, Jonathan tipped his head and smiled. It was no more than the slightest curving of his mouth, the movement barely altering the cold, superior set of his thin face, yet it conveyed a smug satisfaction that chilled Jessica. "We've had quite a time locating you. I must say, you were a lot more clever than I imagined. But, as you can see, we did manage to find you."

His smile widened fractionally, but his obsidian eyes remained cold. As always, they reminded Jessica of a snake's.

A trembling started deep inside her, and she wrapped her arms tightly around her middle. "Wh-what are you doing here?"

He glanced around at the others. "Perhaps there is a place where we could speak privately?"

"Come on, Katy." Trace stood up and assisted his wife to her feet. "Why don't we go unpack."

"No! Please…!" Jessica waved them to a halt and flashed Hank a desperate look. "Don't go."

"What we have to discuss is of a very private nature, Jessica." Jonathan's voice held a hint of impatience. She knew that his use of her first name had nothing to do with friendliness but was a subtle means of putting her in her place. He never addressed her as Mrs. Collier. That name was reserved for Lois. "It would be better if we didn't have an audience."

Hank assumed his habitual stance of feet braced wide, fingertips stuck into his back pockets, but there was a tautness about his shoulders that belied the casual pose. Frowning, he studied the attorney, then his gaze switched to Jessica's ashen face. "It's up to you, Duchess. We'll stay if that's what you want."

"Please," she whispered, and pressed her trembling lips together.

Jonathan sighed. "Very well. If you insist."

He looked at her expectantly, but Jessica didn't ask him to sit down. She was too shaken to even think of it. She wasn't even aware of Hank performing the small courtesy, or of Katy gently taking her arm and urging her down onto the sofa.

Sitting ramrod straight in a chair, Jonathan placed his briefcase on his knees and folded his hands on top of it. "Actually, Jessica, I came here as a favor to you." The look he gave her was meant to be benevolent, but it sent chills skittering down her spine. "Your removal of Daniel Collier from his rightful home, the home that my client has so generously provided for you and your son all these years, has left her with no choice but to sue for custody of her grandchild."

"Oh, God." Jessica closed her eyes and pressed her hand over her mouth. She was going to be sick.

"Oh, Jessie." Katy put a comforting arm around her and glared at Jonathan Wittlow. "Is this your idea of doing her a favor? Threatening to take her child away from her?"

Except for exchanging a quick look, Hank and Trace sat motionless, watching the attorney in silence.

Jonathan held up his hand. "Please. Let's not make this any more unpleasant than it has to be, shall we?" He cleared his throat and looked pointedly at Jessica. "I came to try to spare you the pain and humiliation of a nasty court battle. All you have to do is relinquish custody of the boy willingly, and you can avoid the ordeal. It will be much better all around, for you and Daniel."

"What! Why that's the most despicable thing I've—"

"Katy, take it easy," Trace warned in a low voice, but his hard gaze never strayed from the man across the room.

"No." The word tumbled past Jessica's trembling lips, little more than a wisp of sound. She didn't even realize she was shaking her head. "No. No, I won't let Lois have my son." Her voice gained power and volume with every word, but it carried the increasing shrillness of hysteria. "I won't let her ruin him, the way she did her own!"

"My dear, be reasonable. Mrs. Collier is quite determined on this. If you don't give up the boy, she most assuredly will initiate a lawsuit. And she will win. You see, we plan to charge you with being an unfit mother, on the grounds of immorality."

"But that's not true!"

"Isn't it? You live in this house with two men. Neither of whom is your husband."

"I'm the housekeeper!"

"You don't seriously expect a judge to believe that a young woman who has been living in the lap of luxury would throw it all away to scrub floors and cook, do you? In any case, I've already gathered testimony from several people in Elk Falls as to your immoral conduct with Mr. Rawlins. That, coupled with your inability to provide adequately for the boy, especially compared with the Collier wealth, and Mrs. Collier's standing in the community will be more than sufficient to convince the judge to award custody to my client."

Fear clawed at her. Shaking all over, Jessica could only stare at him in horror. She knew exactly how much power Lois Collier wielded in Fort Worth. Even the judge would probably be a close personal friend of her mother-in-law's. Dear Lord, what was she going to do?

"I'm afraid you've miscalculated, Mr. Wittlow." Hank's deep voice cut across the taut silence, drawing everyone's attention. He sat at ease in the chair with one arm hooked over the back and an ankle propped on the opposite knee. His other hand rested on his booted foot, his fingers softly drumming the scarred leather. His expression was mild, even slightly bored, but his eyes were cold steel.

The attorney frowned, clearly annoyed by Hank's intervention. "And just how is that?"

"Lois Collier doesn't have a prayer of getting Danny on those flimsy charges. Because, you see, Jessica and I are going to be married."

"Married!" The word burst from Trace, Katy and Jonathan in unison.

Jessica simply gaped at him, too shocked to utter a sound.

"I don't believe you. There was no talk in town of any marriage plans."

"That doesn't surprise me. I don't spread my private business all over town." Hank stood up. "Now, since we have nothing further to discuss, I'm afraid I'm going to have to ask you to leave. As you can see, we have guests."

Jonathan Wittlow was not accustomed to being thwarted—or dismissed—and he was furious. His mouth thinned. For a moment he appeared ready to argue, but the look in Hank's eyes changed his mind. When Trace rose the man jerked to his feet and walked out with stiff dignity.

In the entryway he turned and looked back at Jessica. "I warn you, this isn't the end of it. Mrs. Collier intends to have her grandson."

"What a horrible man," Katy muttered when he had gone. Her arm tightened around Jessica's shoulders. "Oh, Jessie, I'm so sorry this happened. I know you're upset, but please…try not to worry. We're all going to do everything we can to help you. I promise."

"That's right." Trace touched Jessica's shoulder briefly, and she looked up with a feeble attempt at a smile.

"Th-thank you. I really appreciate the offer, but I don't think there's anything anyone can do."

Hank stood just inside the doorway, watching her. Jessica swallowed hard at the tight-lipped anger in his face.

She rose on shaky legs and went to him. "Hank, I…" She licked her lips and tentatively placed a hand on his arm. "I want to thank you for trying to help. That was really sweet of you. But, outside of getting rid of Jonathan for a while, I'm afraid telling him that we're going to be married was a futile gesture. I know my mother-in-law, and believe me, Lois won't give up that easily. She'll be keeping tabs, and when the marriage doesn't take place, she'll know you were bluffing."

Panic came surging back the instant she voiced the thought. Jessica's heart began to pound. She twisted her hands together. "I...Danny and I have to leave here. As soon as possible."

"Jessica," Hank said in a stern voice.

"We've got to get far away. Somewhere...somewhere where they can't find us." The words came out in a breathless rush and panic edged her soft voice. Her colorless face was stiff with fright.

"Jessica, listen to me."

"I've got to pack." Her gaze darted around, her eyes glazed, a little wild. She made an agitated move toward the door, then stopped. "No. No, first I have to go get Danny out of school." She swung around, her frantic gaze sweeping the others without seeing them. "Oh, my Lord! What if they decide to kidnap Danny? What if they've already taken him!"

"Jessica, stop it!"

She spun toward the door, heedless of Hank's command, but he leaped after her. Catching her arm, he jerked her to a halt. "Jessica, calm down. There's no reason for you to go after Danny."

Blinking, she stared up at him. Her pupils were dilated. Her breathing was shallow and rapid. When he repeated the statement it took a second to register. Finally she sighed and raked a hand through her hair. "You're right.

It'll save time if I send Cooter after him. By the time he gets back, I'll be ready to leave.''

"Cooter isn't going anywhere. And neither are you."

"What?" She stared at him, her eyes wild. Curling her fingers into his shirtfront, she gripped the material with all her strength. "Oh, Hank, please! You've got to let Cooter drive us to another town. Durango, or maybe Grand Junction. Please! You must! If we try to catch the bus in Elk Falls, they'll know!"

"Jessica, stop this."

When she began to struggle he grasped her shoulders and shook her. Hard.

"Hank..." Katy took a step forward to intervene, but Trace stopped her.

"Now just calm down and listen to me. You don't have to go anywhere, because I wasn't bluffing."

"If you won't help me, I—" She stopped, frowning. "What?"

"Earlier—when I said we were going to be married. I wasn't bluffing."

"Y-you mean..." Vaguely, Jessica was aware that her mouth was open, and she was blinking at him like an owl, but she couldn't seem to stop.

"I meant exactly what I said."

"You...you want to get married?"

"Hardly. But it's the only solution to your problem. It's pointless for you to run again. How would you live? You have no job, no prospects. And no matter where you went, they'd find you." At Jessica's stricken look he released her and shrugged. "They found you here, didn't they?"

"But...I don't understand." Jessica searched his grim face. "Why would you do this for me?"

"Because I want you in my bed. And you've made it clear that the only way I'll get you there is to marry you."

"Hank!" Katy gasped.

"Dammit, Hank! That's no way to talk to a lady," Trace thundered. "And that's sure as hell no reason to get married."

Jessica was too appalled and hurt to utter a sound.

Ignoring his friends, Hank stared at her. "Face it. You need me to hold on to your son. Run, and they'll find you. My way, you get what you want, and I get what I want."

"In other words," Jessica managed in a small, wounded voice. "What you're proposing is one of your 'mutually beneficial' relationships."

"Right."

"And if the time comes when we no longer...*need* one another? What then?"

"We end it."

"I see."

Jessica swallowed against the ache in her throat. She wouldn't let him see how much his callous offer had hurt her. Pride lifted her chin, but it began to wobble. *I won't cry,* she swore. *I won't.* But his image blurred as tears flooded her eyes. When the first one spilled over, her face crumpled, and with an anguished cry, she turned and ran.

Hank watched her go, his jaw clenched. Damn. He had known she would take it badly, but he hadn't expected tears. Well, it was for her own good. Hell, he didn't want to hurt her, but he had to do something to keep her there.

She'll come around, he told himself, quelling the urge to go after her. She needed him. When she'd calmed down, she'd see that.

"Hank Rawlins, you ought to be horsewhipped!"

Hank turned to see Katy—gentle, soft-spoken Katy—glaring at him with fire in her eyes and her fists clenched at her sides.

"That was, without a doubt, the most insulting proposal

of marriage I have ever heard of. Why, if I were a man I'd poke you right in the mouth.'' Her irate gaze flashed to her husband. "You're his friend. You do it," she ordered. Pivoting on her heel, she headed for the door. "I'm going to see about Jessica."

Hank looked at Trace and arched one brow. "I wouldn't try it if I were you."

"Don't worry, I won't. But only because I doubt that it would do any good. Dammit, Hank. What the devil's the matter with you? You don't marry a woman just so you can take her to bed."

Hank shrugged. "Depends on how badly you want her. Besides, there's more to it than that. Do you know what it would do to her if she lost that boy? He's the center of her world."

"All right. I'll concede that maybe—just maybe—this is the best way to help her, but did you have to put it quite so crudely? You usually have more finesse than that when it comes to women."

"You mean romance her? Wrap it all up in a pretty package?" He shook his head. "I won't lie to her."

Trace gave him a long, level look. "Has it ever occurred to you, my friend, that you could be lying to yourself?"

Lying face down across her bed, her head cradled on her crossed arms, Jessica cried out her heartbreak. Great, wrenching sobs shook her, anguished sounds of lost hope and raw pain that tore at her throat. Tears flowed from between her closed eyelids in a torrent. Her forearms were slick with the salty wetness and a damp patch was growing steadily on the patchwork bedspread beneath.

Jessica had not thought it possible to feel worse than she had when Jonathan had dropped his bombshell, but she was wrong. Pain, a deep, consuming pain now filled her, adding to the fear and worry.

Oh, Lord, how could he have done it? How could he have suggested marriage and laid out his reasons in that cold, unfeeling way? And in front of his friends. How could she face them?

She didn't hear the door open, didn't know that Katy was in the room until she sat down on the bed beside her. When the mattress shifted Jessica gasped and looked up, then quickly returned her tear-drenched face to her arms. "G-go away. Please, just go a…a…way."

Katy ignored the muffled plea and stroked Jessica's heaving shoulders. "Oh, Jessie, honey, I'm so sorry. But you just go right ahead and cry it out. You're entitled, after what that big lunkhead said."

The statement brought on a renewed spasm of weeping. Jessica gulped and sobbed until her head throbbed and her throat felt raw, and still she couldn't stop. The tears flowed fast and free, more tears than she had thought it possible for a human to cry.

Through it all, Katy didn't budge. Murmuring soft, soothing words, she simply moved her hand in a slow circle over Jessica's back.

The racking sobs finally slowed, and after a while turned into choppy little sighs. Katy rose, walked over to the dresser and returned with a box of tissues. She smoothed the tawny mane of tumbled hair off Jessica's face and stroked her temple with the backs of her fingers. "Here, dry your eyes."

Sniffling, Jessica raised her head and looked at her, blinking wet, spiky lashes. Trying to still her wobbling chin, she snatched a wad of tissues from the box and wiped her eyes. "I—I'm sorry."

"Don't be silly. You don't have anything to be sorry for."

Jessica pushed herself upright and swung her legs over the side of the bed. Her nose was stopped up, and her head was booming. She couldn't quite bring herself to look at Katy, so she dabbed her cheeks and eyes again and blew her nose. Keeping her head lowered, she plucked at a seam in the patchwork quilt and stared at it.

"You're in love with Hank, aren't you Jessie?"

Jessica's head jerked up. "No! I..." She stared, appalled, into Katy's kind face. She pressed her lips together and closed her eyes. "Oh, God. Is it that obvious?"

"No, no. Not at all." Katy took one of Jessica's hands between hers and squeezed it. "It's just that it's easy for a woman in love to recognize the same condition in another. That's all. Really."

Jessica attempted a watery smile. "Thanks. I hope you're right. I couldn't bear it if everyone knew. Es-especially now." Her voice broke on the last word, and she had to look up at the ceiling and widen her eyes to hold back another rush of tears.

"Jessica, I'm furious with Hank. I want you to know that. And I don't blame you for feeling hurt, but... well...please don't feel too discouraged. I know it doesn't seem like it now, but I'm certain that Hank loves you, too."

The statement startled a laugh from Jessica. The sound was harsh and devoid of mirth. "Oh, Katy, that's sweet of you. But believe me, you're wrong." She sniffed and dabbed at her nose again and swallowed hard. "But... ev-even if it was true, even if Hank does love me, he doesn't want to get married."

"Doesn't he?" Katy asked gently. An amused smile tugged at her lips. "Oh, I think he does. It's just that some people are so frightened of letting themselves care that deeply that they can't admit it until they're forced into doing so.'' She wrinkled her nose, and her mouth twisted in a wry grimace. "Believe me, I ought to know. I was one of them.''

"You?" Jessica stared at her, her tears quelled by the stunning revelation. "I can't believe that. Why, you and Trace are wild about each other. Anyone can see that.''

"True.'' Katy's eyes danced. "Even so, I fought Trace every step of the way to the altar. In the end he had to blackmail me into marriage.''

Jessica just blinked at her, too stupefied to speak, and Katy gave her hand another gentle squeeze.

"It wasn't until months after we were married that I was able to admit, to myself and to Trace, that I loved him. I've never regretted marrying him for a moment, Jessica. Not even in the beginning when I was still fighting my feelings. And I don't think you will either, if you marry Hank. Believe me, he may not know it now, but that man loves you. He may claim otherwise. He may even believe it himself. But trust me, wild horses couldn't have dragged a proposal out of Hank Rawlins unless it was what he wanted.''

Against all reason and common sense, hope stirred. Jessica stared into Katy's gentle blue eyes and felt that hope burgeon within her, swelling her chest and making her silly heart lurch and pound. "Do...do you really think so?''

"I know so.''

Jessica bit her lower lip and told herself not to be a fool. She had leaped naively into one marriage with a man who didn't know the meaning of love, and all it had gotten her was heartache. She couldn't do it again.

But she wanted to believe—she wanted desperately to

believe. And because she wanted to so badly, she pushed doubt aside.

When Jessica told Hank that she would marry him, he didn't react as she thought he would. She hadn't expected him to be overjoyed or even especially pleased, but she had expected his attitude to soften somewhat. He had merely nodded and replied, "Fine. Let's go. I'm not sure what the requirements are in Colorado, but if we can't get it done in town, we'll fly to Nevada and get married."

Jessica was so astounded she couldn't find her tongue, but Katy jumped right in.

"Hank Rawlins, you'll do no such thing! You can't go running off to some sleazy justice of the peace. What kind of a wedding is that? And just think how it would look."

"Katy's right," Trace put in before Hank could answer. "You'll be handing Mrs. Collier more ammunition if the marriage appears to be hurried or furtive. You'd be smarter to slow down and do this thing properly."

Hank's eyes narrowed. "Just what do you mean by 'properly'? I'm not going through a bunch of wedding hoopla, so if that's what you have in mind, forget it."

Trace held up his hands, palms out. "Calm down. It doesn't have to be anything big—just public. You know, put the word out, invite a few friends. You could set the date for…say a week from now."

"I don't know." Hank frowned and looked at Jessica. "Is that all right with you, Duchess?"

"I…I suppose so."

"Oh, good." Katy beamed. "I'll get started on the arrangements right away."

"Arrangements? What kind of arrangements do you have to make to invite a few friends over?" Hank's hard gaze fastened on Katy. "Remember—we're keeping this thing *small*."

"Oh, Hank, don't worry. How big a wedding can you plan in just a week?"

"Dammit, Trace, there must be two hundred people out there," Hank complained a week later, peeking into the church sanctuary. "What did that wife of yours do, invite the whole town?" He shut the door and glowered at his friend.

Leaning against the wall of the small anteroom, his arms crossed over his chest, Trace merely smiled and watched Hank pace.

"What's taking so long? The reverend said he'd come for us when it was time to start." Hank pushed back the sleeve of his gray suit and checked his watch for the fifth time in three minutes. "Shouldn't he be here by now?" He ran his forefinger around the inside of his collar and straightened his tie. He paced to the other side of the room, swung around and scowled at the door. "Do they have to play that damn organ music?"

"Nervous?" Trace arched one brow. "It's not too late to call this whole thing off, you know. If you've changed your mind, just say the word and I'll take care of it."

"No, it's not that," Hank muttered. He swung around to make another circuit of the room. "I just want to get this over with."

He was sweating blood, but not because of cold feet. How could he admit to Trace that all week he'd been scared to death that Jessica would change her mind. Hell, he hated admitting it to himself.

That she had come to mean so much to him was disturbing. He liked women, but in the past they had never been more than a pleasant diversion, an occasional necessity, and one had been pretty much the same as the next. He'd certainly never been obsessed by a particular woman before, and the feeling wasn't at all comfortable.

Worse, though, was the thought of Jessica leaving, the thought of never seeing her again.

Hank sighed and checked his watch again. This three-ring circus of a wedding hadn't helped his nerves. Who would have thought that gentle, sweet Katy could turn into a steamroller? Once she had started making the wedding arrangements, there had been no stopping her. She'd even arranged their honeymoon, insisting that they use the beach house that she and Trace had leased on Maui.

"It'll be our wedding present to you," she'd said so sweetly it had been impossible to refuse outright.

Jessica's insistence that they wouldn't think of depriving her and Trace of a second honeymoon had gotten exactly nowhere. "Nonsense. We can honeymoon right here, just as well as in Maui," Katy had said in that serenely stubborn way of hers. "And don't worry about Danny. I used to work in a preschool. And anyway, after riding herd on those two little heathens of mine, looking after him will be a vacation."

"And don't worry about anyone snatching Danny, either. Cooter will take him to school, and he'll be waiting outside the classroom door when he gets out in the afternoon. We won't let him out of our sight. I promise."

When Hank had argued that he couldn't leave the ranch during fall roundup, Trace had reminded him that he was a partner, and perfectly capable of running the place for a week.

Hank jumped when the door opened and the reverend stuck his head inside. His mouth went dry, and his heart began to thump.

"Well, this is it, my friend." Trace gave a thumbs-up sign and pushed away from the wall.

As they filed out, Katy stepped from an anteroom on the opposite side of the church and joined them in front of the altar, and the crowd in the sanctuary grew quiet.

Sitting in the first pew on the groom's side of the church, all spruced up in their Sunday best, with their hair slicked down and silly grins on their weathered faces, were Cooter, Jubal, Wooley, Slick and Buck. The day before, Trace had surprised Jessica by flying her parents in for the wedding, and her mother, Mary Baxter, with Danny at her side, proudly occupied the first pew on the opposite side of the aisle. The rest of the church was packed, but Hank looked out over the sea of familiar faces without seeing anyone.

His eyes were fixed on the empty vestibule at the back of the church. The organ music swelled in a stirring introduction, causing every head to turn in that direction, and a murmur of anticipation rippled through the crowd. Hank's gut twisted. *Oh, God, she's not coming. She's changed her mind.*

Then the wedding march began, and on the fourth note Jessica and her father stepped into view and started up the aisle. Hank stared, transfixed.

She was the most beautiful thing he'd ever seen, a vision in pale apricot silk that set off her warm skin tones and made her amber eyes glow. Her tawny, sun-streaked hair was piled atop her head and intertwined with cream and apricot roses and tiny sprigs of baby's breath. In her hand she carried a bouquet of the same flowers. She came toward him with her head held high in that proud way of hers, her expression soft and serene.

Hank's chest swelled with emotion and his legs turned

to jelly. In that instant the staggering truth hit him; he was in love—completely, hopelessly, irrevocably in love.

He, who had always eschewed the emotion, had openly scoffed at it, had doubted its very existence. He would have laughed if he hadn't been so shaken. When had it happened? How? More importantly, how did Jessica feel about him?

The question consumed him. Hank went through the ceremony in a daze, barely hearing the words, unable to take his eyes from Jessica's profile. Her small hand trembled in his, and throughout the touching liturgy her gaze remained fixed on the Reverend Mr. Wilson. It wasn't until he slipped the gold band onto her finger that she raised her head and looked at him, and Hank felt as though he'd been dealt a mortal blow.

Her lovely, expressive eyes were wide with uncertainty and apprehension—even a touch of fear.

Driven by his own fear, by a need to brand her as his, when the reverend pronounced them husband and wife, Hank wrapped Jessica in his arms and kissed her long and hard.

Mr. Wilson cleared his throat—twice—but still the kiss went on. The onlookers began to shift restlessly, then titter. It wasn't until some of the more boisterous males in the audience, led by Wooley, began to whoop that Hank at last raised his head.

His fierce gaze held hers for an instant, but as a cheer went up and everyone began to laugh and clap, he looked at the guests and smiled—a slow, hard smile that reflected the steely determination in his eyes.

The reception in the church fellowship hall that followed was excruciating for Jessica. She and Hank had no sooner entered the hall than her parents arrived right on their heels.

"Oh, darling, the wedding was lovely. And you were such a beautiful bride." Her mother grasped both of her hands and gave her a quavering smile that threatened to crumple under another onslaught of happy tears. She gazed lovingly at Jessica, her eyes misty, her face glowing with happiness. "I'm so happy for you," she choked. Overcome with emotion, she pulled her daughter into a tight embrace.

"Oh, Mom." Hugging her mother close, Jessica squeezed her eyes shut and pressed her lips together to stop their trembling. Her throat was so tight it hurt. Her heart felt as though it were breaking in two.

"Here, now. None of that," her father scolded affectionately. "This is a time for celebration, not tears. Besides, the guests will be here any second now. How would it look for you two to greet them with red eyes?"

With a weak chuckle, Jessica withdrew from her mother's arms and kissed her father's weathered cheek, her chest squeezing as she caught a whiff of his after-shave. It was the brand he had used ever since she could remember, but he only bothered with it for special occasions, like church on Sundays, Christmas, anniversaries...weddings.

He hugged her hard, then held her at arm's length. His own eyes were suspiciously moist. "Be happy, Jessie mine," he murmured gruffly.

As Jessica and her mother sniffed and dabbed at their eyes, he turned to Hank and stuck out his hand. "Congratulations, my boy. Mary and I are pleased to welcome you into the family. And you take care of our girl, you hear."

"Thanks, Charley. I will. You can count on it."

Beaming, her father pumped Hank's hand, and Jessica felt sick with guilt.

It had been thoughtful and generous of Trace to fly her

parents in for the wedding, but she wished with all her heart that he hadn't done it. They had arrived the night before, and within moments of meeting them, Hank had won their wholehearted approval. They were delighted over the marriage, believing that she had finally found happiness with the right man, and they expected the marriage to last forever. She felt like the lowest form of life for deceiving them.

But somehow Jessica managed to hide her feelings. With a smile pasted on her face, for the next hour she accepted hugs and handshakes and well wishes. She and Hank went through the ritual of cutting the cake and posing for pictures and dancing the first dance. It seemed interminable, but finally it was time to go, and they made their escape amid a shower of rice.

Rather than take the red-eye to Hawaii they spent their wedding night in a posh hotel in Los Angeles.

Though it made her feel foolish, Jessica was more nervous than she had been seven years before, when she had been a virgin bride of only eighteen. Staring at her reflection in the bathroom mirror, she touched the ecru lace edging on her ivory satin nightgown and drew several deep breaths, but nothing would still the fine tremor that vibrated deep inside her.

Dabbing perfume behind her ears and in her cleavage, she told herself it was normal to be a little nervous. After all, marriage, even a practical one, was a big step, and the past week had been a strain. But what really had her on edge was Hank's strange behavior.

The hand holding the perfume applicator stopped in midair, and her expression took on a faraway look. No matter how much she had tried to delude herself, deep down she knew that Hank hadn't really wanted to get married. Yet that look he had given her when she came down the aisle had made her weak in the knees. And then there was that kiss... Unconsciously she touched her lips with her fingertips.

Afterward at the reception he had stayed by her side the whole time, not letting her stray more than a foot away from him. His possessive attitude might have thrilled her if it hadn't been for the anger she sensed beneath it.

Jessica could only assume that, even though it had been his suggestion, Hank resented having to marry.

How long, she wondered, could a marriage last under those circumstances?

A slight sound from the next room drew her attention. She pressed her lips together and stared at the door, her hand flattened against her fluttering stomach. In order to last, first it had to get started, she told herself, squaring her shoulders. The trembling deep inside grew worse, but Jessica ignored it. She returned the stopper to the perfume bottle and pushed the heavy fall of hair off her face with both hands. After one last check in the bathroom mirror, she smoothed the satin gown over her hips and reached for the doorknob.

Hank was sitting in a chair by the balcony doors, smoking and staring out at the lights of Los Angeles. At the sound of the door opening he turned his head and looked at her. Under his intense scrutiny Jessica's courage faltered, and three steps into the room she came to a halt.

He started at the top of her head, taking in each delicate feature of her face and the luxuriant mane of tawny hair that tumbled around her shoulders. Then his slumberous gaze drifted downward.

Jessica's heart beat so hard it caused the shiny cloth covering it to flutter. The only other movements in the quiet room were the thin spiral of smoke rising from his cigarette, and the slow, hot sweep of his eyes.

With only a look he aroused her unbearably. She felt heat wash through her when his gaze lingered on her breasts and the pebble-hard nipples pushing against the satin gown. As surely as a physical touch, that searing look stroked her, leaving a trail of fire on her skin.

In silence he slowly savored each dip and curve of her body: her small waist, the inviting womanly roundness of her hips, the long curving line of her thighs, the pink toes curled into the carpet beneath the hem of the satin night-gown. With the same intense appraisal he retraced the path.

When at last their gazes met, Hank stubbed out his cigarette and stood up. Without taking his gaze from her, he crossed the room with that slow, sinuous stride that never failed to excite her. Jessica waited, watching him with her insides trembling, her heart going wild.

Hank had showered earlier, while she had dithered with her luggage and called the ranch to check on Danny, and he was dressed in only a white, knee-length terry-cloth robe. The wide lapels fell open to the belt, which was loosely tied about his waist, exposing his muscled chest and the cloud of dark hair that covered it. Against the the snowy fabric his skin looked like polished bronze.

His scent drifted to her as he drew near, a combination of soap and tobacco and maleness that made her nostrils flare and her head spin.

Without hesitation, when Hank stopped in front of her he drove his fingers into her hair and captured her head in a firm grip between his big, work-worn hands.

"You're beautiful." His voice was a raspy whisper. His breathing was slow and deep, and a muscle jerked along his jaw as his gaze roamed her face, then slid down over her creamy shoulders to the rounded swells of her breasts above the ivory gown. When his eyes lifted to hers, again they blazed with blue fire. "I've waited a long time to have you, Duchess.'' His thumbs swept back and forth over the hollows beneath her cheekbones. His face was flushed with desire, but there was a tautness about him. A tremor shook the hands bracketing her face and revealed a fierceness running just beneath the surface. ''A long time.''

Was that it? Did he resent her because she hadn't tumbled into bed with him as all the others had? Jessica had never thought that Hank was that kind of man. She didn't want to believe it now, but it would explain his strange mood.

A shiver rippled through her. One of Hank's hands slid down the side of her neck and the rough pad of his thumb pressed against the pulse throbbing at the base of her throat.

''Your heart is pounding.'' Reading the apprehension in her eyes, he frowned. ''You're not afraid of me, are you, Duchess?''

Jessica licked her lips. ''You're...you're angry.''

''No! Oh, God, no, sweetheart, not with you!'' He jerked her to him and wrapped his arms around her. Holding her tightly against his chest, he tilted his head and rubbed his cheek against the top of her head, rocking her gently. ''Never with you,'' he vowed in a rough whisper.

''Then what—''

''Ssh.'' He slipped a hand beneath her chin and tilted her head up. His thumb rubbed across her lips, and a wonderful warmth flooded Jessica at the sight of his familiar smile. ''It's nothing. Just nerves. That's all.''

His hand slid down over the sleek satin and cupped her bottom. Watching her, he flexed his fingers around the firm, rounded flesh, and as he pressed her lower body against the hard evidence of his manhood his expression changed from tender to passionate.

"Let's just forget it. Tonight I don't want to think about anything but you," he murmured, lowering his head. "Feel anything but you." He placed his open mouth on hers. Their warm breaths mingled. "Against me," he whispered against her trembling lips. "Around me."

The evocative words sent a shudder of longing rippling through Jessica, and her eyes fluttered shut. Melting against him, she lifted her arms to encircle his neck. Her weak moan of pleasure was lost in his mouth as at last their lips melded in a long, hot kiss, rife with hunger and a passion too-long denied.

The world spun away, and problems and doubts faded like smoke in the wind. Coherent thought became impossible. All that existed for Jessica was sensation: the prickly feel of the short hairs at his nape against her sensitive fingertips, the slight bite of tobacco on his tongue, the roughness of his robe and the tickle of his chest hair against the bare skin above the low-cut gown, the sensuous glide of his hands over the satin covering her buttocks, the burning heat of their bodies, the small frantic movements and the hunger they incited.

Jessica moved restlessly when Hank broke off the kiss. She tried to recapture his mouth but he grasped her wrists and pulled her arms down to her sides. She moaned in protest, but the sound died as he eased the straps off her shoulders and down her arms. The ivory nightgown slithered down her body and fell in a circle of shimmering folds about her feet.

Holding her upper arms, Hank backed away a half step and looked at her. As his bold gaze devoured her, Jessica grew hot all over and felt her nipples pucker, her feminine core quicken.

His eyes found hers again, and the look in them threatened to buckle her knees.

"Now you undress me, Duchess," he urged roughly. "Put your hands on me."

Though she was trembling, Jessica didn't hesitate. When he released her so that she could push the robe over his arms she wasn't sure she could stand on her own, but somehow she managed it, and the white terry cloth joined her gown on the floor.

Then she looked at him, as he had looked at her, and her breath caught. He was magnificent, his long sleek body corded with muscles and dusted in places with dark hair. Her eyes followed that pattern of hair on his chest to where it narrowed into a thin line over his hard belly, down still farther to where his manhood sprang, erect and rigid.

"Oh, Hank." Her eyes lifted to his in wonder and love, and she touched him intimately.

Hank sucked in his breath and the muscles in his face clenched as though he were in pain at the feather-light embrace. With a groan, he snatched her back into his arms, and she gasped as her sensitive nipples sank into the crisp hair on his chest, but the gasp became a moan as their heated flesh met. "Oh, Hank, Hank," she sobbed, pressing hectic kisses against his chest.

"I've got to have you. Now!" The words were pushed out through gritted teeth as he tumbled them both onto the bed. "I wanted to go slow, but I can't," he muttered against her breast. His teeth raked her aching nipple, then his lips closed around it, and she cried out, her back arching, as he drew the engorged bud into his hot mouth.

The small sound snapped what little control Hank had left, and he took her mouth again. As he drove her to frenzied readiness with hot, openmouthed kisses, his fingers threaded through the triangle of burnished curls and found the moist heart of her desire. Jessica made a sound of fierce pleasure, and as her legs parted, he moved into position between her thighs.

Braced on trembling arms, his gaze locked with hers, he made them one. The pleasure of it was so intense it took their breath away, and Hank threw his head back and clenched his teeth to keep from crying out.

Need quickly consumed them. Caught in the conflagration, they moved together as one, searching, striving for the ultimate pleasure. The fire raged, and the sweet tension built until it could no longer be borne. And as the world shattered into a million pieces, Jessica's body arched, and she clutched Hank's back, an incoherent cry tearing from her throat.

"Yes! Yes!" Hank shouted the words in a hoarse, guttural voice as his body shuddered in completion.

He collapsed on her, and her small hands stroked over his sweat-slicked back as his muscles quivered with tiny aftershocks. They lay quietly, both gasping for breath, both shaken by the incredible beauty of what they had just shared.

"Hank?" she whispered as her hands moved in slow circles over his shoulder blades.

"Mmm?"

"That was...I've never...I mean..."

"Yeah, I know." Lifting up on his forearm he gave her a crooked smile. "That was even worth getting married for."

It was a stupid thing to say. He knew it instantly, and as he watched her expression change from glowing to withdrawn he could have kicked himself.

With a sigh, Hank rolled to his back and reached out and clicked off the light. When he pulled her into his arms and pillowed her head on his shoulder, she came willingly but the silence between them was awkward and strained.

For the first time in his life, Hank was at a loss with a woman. His feelings were too new, too intense, and they scared the hell out of him. *She* scared the hell out of him.

He couldn't bring himself to tell her how he felt. After the way he'd spouted off, she'd probably laugh in his face. And she'd been so damned composed when she'd agreed to marry him, he wasn't sure she felt anything for him beyond desire.

His mouth twisted in bitter irony as he stared at the darkened ceiling. For the first time in his life, that wasn't enough.

His jaw hardened, and his arm tightened around her. She might not love him, but at least she needed him. For as long as that need existed, she was his.

Chapter Eleven

Jessica's arms sliced cleanly through the water with a smooth, steady rhythm. Swimming behind a wave, she rode its tow into the shallows until the surf began to break over her head. For a few seconds, she disappeared beneath the foaming water. Then she shot up, breaking the surface like a sleek porpoise, her body arched, head back, laughing.

Beneath lazy eyelids, Hank's blue eyes glittered with appreciation. He never tired of watching her.

He lay on a towel spread on the sand, his head propped in his hand, soaking up the tropical sunshine and enjoying the view.

Water cascaded down Jessica's body as she waded toward the beach. Her stride was slow and undulating against the drag of the undertow. In an innocently alluring movement, she shook her hair back, then raised both arms and wrung out the saltwater. The action exposed her tender underarms, arched her back and caused her breasts to swell above the top of her swimsuit. To Hank, she looked like a goddess rising from the sea.

"You shouldn't have quit so soon," she called out as she crossed the beach to where he lay. "The water is wonderful."

Hank's gaze ran down her lush curves, deliciously revealed by the high-cut white maillot. He noted the way her hips swayed with unconscious provocation, and he felt his body stir, his heart fill with emotion. She was all woman—sensuous, loving, giving. She was nurturing and enticing, soothing and exciting, a Madonna and a siren all in one.

And she was his. For now, anyway.

"It's like swimming in warm silk." Breathless, Jessica dropped to her knees beside him and grinned. Her breasts heaved beneath the white cloth. Water beaded her skin. Hank's heated gaze tracked a drop that streaked down her neck and chest and disappeared into her cleavage.

Her lashes were spiked with saltwater, and he reached up and feathered his forefinger over their tips. "Not everyone's a water baby like you," he murmured, giving her a crooked smile.

"No, you're more like a lizard. All you want to do is lie in the sun."

"Oh, I don't know. I can think of another activity I enjoy even more." Giving her a long, sizzling look, he trailed his forefinger over her thigh, from her knee to the edge of her swimsuit, where it curved over her hipbone.

"*You* have a one-track mind, Hank Rawlins."

She couldn't quite bring herself to look at him, and as a flush spread over her skin she grabbed up a towel and buried her face in it.

"Complaining?" he purred.

"No. Of course not," came her muffled reply.

Hank's eyes danced, and his mouth twitched as he observed the inordinate length of time she took drying her face and hair. He found it both delightful and amusing that she was still shy with him after almost a week of marriage, especially when he thought of the passion they had shared.

In the past seven days they had learned each other's bodies intimately, explored all the sensual possibilities, each discovering what the other liked, what brought the quickest response, the deepest pleasure. With only a look, a word, the merest touch, he could have her melting in his arms, stripped of her inhibitions in seconds, writhing and wanton beneath him. He found the knowledge almost unbearably exciting.

Hank had quickly discovered that for a woman who had been married for six years and was a mother, Jessica was amazingly inexperienced. That, coupled with her shyness, had aroused his curiosity about her first marriage. With a bit of shameless probing he'd learned that she had become pregnant almost immediately, and her husband, revolted by the changes in her body, had deserted her bed as soon as she had begun to show. By the time Danny arrived she had learned of his infidelities. When she'd insisted that he choose between her and his women, he had chosen the latter.

Allen Collier, Hank decided, had been a fool.

Her composure restored, Jessica lowered the towel, and began casually blotting her arms and chest as though the moment of sensual awareness had never happened.

Hank, however, wasn't going to let her off that easily. "Good," he said huskily. "I'd hate to think that all those little whimpers and groaning noises you make when I'm inside you were really protests."

Jessica sucked in a sharp breath. Her eyes darted around

to see if anyone had heard him. Their house was one of only about a dozen on the secluded private beach, but there was always someone around.

"Hank, really," she scolded, when she had satisfied herself that no one was in earshot, but her voice held little heat.

As her face crimsoned he took one of her hands and brought it to his lips. Holding her gaze, he kissed each fingertip tenderly. "What's more, I seem to recall waking up in the middle of the night to find I was the one being ravaged." He nipped the pad of her forefinger and smiled wickedly as a shudder rippled through her. "You, Mrs. Rawlins, have very talented hands." His tongue drew a wet circle on her sensitive palm. "And your mouth," he added in an insinuating murmur. "Ah, sweetheart, it ought to be registered as a lethal weapon."

"Hank." This time his name quivered on her lips, a breathless sound that was part demur, part surrender.

Another shiver worked its way up her arm and through her body. Her amber eyes grew limpid with yearning. Beneath the swimsuit, her nipples tightened, forming turgid little buttons in the white cloth. Her lips parted, and in response to the slight tug on her arm, she leaned slowly toward him.

Somewhere down the beach someone gave a shout. It was followed by a high-pitched giggle. The sounds penetrated the haze of passion, and with a gasp Jessica jerked upright, snatching her hand away. "Hank! Behave yourself."

Flustered, she stood up and dried her legs, then brushed at the sand clinging to her feet. "I don't know about you, but I'm thirsty," she announced in an overly cheerful voice. Bending over, she lifted the lid on the cooler they'd brought out with them and looked back over her shoulder at him. "I'm going to have a drink. Want a beer?"

Hank's smile was faintly mocking. "No thanks. I just had one."

Sitting up, he braced himself on one arm, draped the other arm over his updrawn knee and watched her paw through the crushed ice. Subtly his smile changed to masculine enjoyment as he admired her narrow, tapered back, her firm derriere, the long, lithe curves of her legs.

Hank was still amazed and shaken by the emotions that swamped him every time he looked at Jessica: love, pride, jealousy, a violent possessiveness—all coupled with a need to protect and cherish that was fiercely primitive and totally foreign to him.

He realized now that a part of him had assumed, had even been hoping, that the feelings would fade once he'd had her and they had experienced a few days of constant togetherness. After all, wasn't familiarity supposed to breed contempt? Before, just the thought of being tied to one woman was enough to make him itchy.

Not this time. If anything, a week with Jessica had only made his craving worse.

His chest shook with a silent, derisive chuckle as he watched her pop the tab on a can of lemonade. She tipped her head back and drank thirstily. Hank's gaze homed in on the graceful arch of her neck, the tiny movements beneath her skin as the frosted liquid slid down her throat. The urge to put his mouth on that vulnerable spot was almost irresistible.

The plain truth was, he admitted grimly, not even a year with her would be long enough. Nor would ten... twenty...or even a lifetime.

The admission wasn't an easy one to make or to live with. Jessica needed him now, but eventually the circumstances would change. Danny would grow up and make his own choices. Lois Collier could change her mind. Or, worst of all, there was always the possibility that she might still pursue the custody suit and win.

No matter how he looked at it, a lifetime with Jessica didn't appear in the offing. All he could be sure of having was now.

"Mmm, I love it here, don't you?" Jessica said. She sat facing him with her legs out to one side, her gaze on the rolling surf.

"Yeah. I didn't think I would, but I do."

"Is that why you fought Katy and Trace so about coming here?"

Hank shrugged. "I've never had much of a yen for sun and surf."

It wasn't Hawaii he'd been resisting, but a honeymoon—period. At the time, he'd still been kidding himself that all he felt for Jessica was desire, and that the marriage was simply a formality that would allow him to satisfy that desire. He hadn't wanted any of the rituals and trappings that went with it to remind him that it was real. Now, though, he was grateful for Katy's gentle bullying.

"You'd never know it, the way you've been soaking up the sun. Your skin's the color of mahogany."

"And yours looks like a ripe peach." Giving her a slumberous look, Hank trailed his forefinger down her arm in a feather-light touch.

Jessica shivered and shifted her position. "Ah, well…uh…that's because I'm so fair I have to use a strong sunscreen to keep from burning. I, uh…I never really tan much."

"That's okay. I like this color." Stretching out on his side again, Hank propped his head on his palm and watched her. "It's very...appetizing. Makes me want to taste you."

Jessica took a hasty sip of lemonade. When she lowered the can, Hank's intent gaze was still trained on her, and she held it out to him. "Want some?"

"Umm, but not lemonade," he drawled, lowering his gaze to the soft swells of her breasts above the low-cut swimsuit. His blue eyes glinted with lazy sensuality, and as a flush spread up over Jessica's neck and shoulders, his smile grew wicked.

"You're insatiable."

"Uh-huh. Does that bother you?"

Her embarrassment was forgotten as heat of a different kind suffused her. When he looked at her that way, spoke to her in that intimate tone, she felt all tingly and weak. Her eyes softened, and her voice dropped to a husky pitch that revealed her disturbed breathing. "No. I'm glad."

"Prove it."

He hooked his forefinger in the top of her maillot. It nestled in her cleavage, snug and warm. His smoldering gaze held her captive as he tugged her toward him. "Show me how glad you are."

Holding the canned drink to one side, Jessica leaned closer, drawn as much by the lure of his potent masculinity and its promise as by the steady pull of that sheathed finger. Her lips parted. Her eyelids grew heavy. With excruciating slowness, the distance between them grew smaller. Their breaths mingled, and she tipped her head to one side. "You mean like this?" she whispered.

Her mouth met his, open, sweet, soft. Her lips were cold from contact with the frosty can, but they quickly warmed. It was the lightest of caresses, a mere touch, a gentle rubbing of flesh against flesh, yet its sensual impact was staggering. At the first touch Hank's heart slammed against his ribs and began to beat with a painful, heavy thud. Her tongue made a daring little foray into his mouth, touched the tip of his, and darted out again. Hank groaned. She tasted of lemonade and saltwater and woman. Of Jessie.

It was a taste he was becoming addicted to, one he would never grow tired of. Avidly he sought more. Over and over, without increasing the pressure of the kiss, he delved into the sweet darkness, plumbing the silken depths of her mouth with the slow thoroughness of a connoisseur.

His hand slid up her braced arm to her shoulder, her neck. Lightly, the tips of his shaking fingers stroked her jaw, then they sank into the damp hair behind her ear and cradled her head.

A pair of children ran by, giggling and squealing, with a yapping dog at their heels. Hank and Jessica didn't hear them. Nor did they hear the hissing rush of waves tumbling onto the shore, nor the dry rattle of tattered palms overhead. Down the beach some teenagers were setting up for a game of volleyball, their portable stereo blasting the air, but not even that raucous sound reached them.

They were caught in a sensual web, enthralled by a sweet torment of their own making. Their lips nibbled, rocked back and forth, clung. Their tongues mated in a leisurely fashion.

The sun beat down, warming their damp flesh, but they felt only the heat of desire that surged so hotly through them. Hearts pounded, taut muscle strained and quivered in agonizing restraint as the soft kiss went on and on.

Unconsciously Jessica gripped the aluminum can tighter. It crumpled beneath her fingers and slowly tilted to one side. What was left of the lemonade poured onto the sand.

Abruptly Hank ended the kiss. His fiery gaze locked with hers, and they stared at each other. A few strands of drying hair around Jessica's face lifted in the gentle breeze. Their chests heaved as they drew long, shaky draughts of air into their starved lungs. The air was redolent with the smells of sand and sea, of coconut tanning lotion, and warm, aroused bodies.

Jessica ran her tongue over the edge of her teeth, and a muscle twitched along Hank's jaw. Without warning, he grabbed her wrist and surged to his feet, dragging her up with him.

"C'mon," he commanded in a tight, strained voice. "Let's go."

"G-go? Go where?"

"Inside. Before I forget where we are and shock our neighbors."

He marched across the sand with long, ground-eating strides, towing her toward the cottage that sat back from the beach under the sheltering palms. Stumbling along behind him, Jessica cast a worried look over her shoulder at the cooler and the rumpled towels on the sand. On top of them were her sunglasses and tanning lotion and the novel she had started reading. "Hank! Our things!"

"We'll get them later."

"But—"

"Forget the damn towels. If someone wants them, they're welcome to them." He hauled her up the shallow steps, across the deck and through the door. Inside, he kicked the door shut behind them and used her momentum to whip her around and into his arms. "Right now all I care about is this," he growled, as his mouth swooped down on hers.

"Oh, God, sweetheart, I can't get enough of you," he panted in between tumultuous kisses.

"I know. I know," Jessica agreed breathlessly.

Frantically she clutched his shoulders, his back. When

her hands encountered his swim trunks they slipped beneath the tight garment and grasped his firm buttocks. Hank growled and snatched at the shoulder straps of her maillot.

In a frenzy of tugging and fumbling, they worked to rid each other of their skimpy beachwear. Hank managed to work the shoulder straps of the one-piece suit over Jessica's arms. With a furious yank, he dropped to his knees and peeled the garment down to her ankles. In the next instant it went sailing over his shoulder. It landed on a blade of the ceiling fan and dangled provocatively.

Jessica groaned and clutched Hank's shoulders as he kissed his way back up her body with maddening leisure. Pausing along the way, he nuzzled the downy curls at the apex of her thighs, probed her navel with his tongue and lavished attention on her swollen breasts until Jessica cried out in a delirium of pleasure.

When at last their lips met again, she groaned as her nipples, still wet and tingling from his mouth, pressed against silky chest hair and warm male flesh.

He gripped her bare bottom with both hands and pulled her tightly against him, rotating her hips against the hard bulge that strained against the tight fabric of his swimsuit.

Impatient to remove the last barrier between them, Jessica hooked her thumbs into the top of his brief trunks, bent her knees and pushed them downward. Dropping lower, she dealt out a sweet torment of her own, scattering hectic kisses over his chest, his ribs, his lean belly. Her teeth raked his protruding hipbone. Her tongue lathed the hollow just inside it.

A violent shudder shook Hank. "Oh, God, Jessie." He groaned and speared his fingers into her hair, unconsciously clutching her head in an iron grip when he felt her intimate kiss.

Desperately he bent and lifted her to her feet. They looked at each other, their breathing harsh in the pulsing silence. Then he snatched her into his arms, and their soft moans of pleasure blended together as warm, yearning flesh made contact.

Their mouths met in a searing kiss. Jessica raised up on tiptoe and coiled her arms around his neck. Their bodies strained together, unable to get close enough, wanting, seeking, needing more.

The bedroom was in plain sight, just a few feet away, but neither could wait. Without breaking the kiss, they sank to the hardwood floor. There was a wild hunger raging in both of them, wanton and out of control.

They touched and kissed and stroked until they couldn't stand it a moment longer. "Ah, Duchess, you drive me crazy," Hank declared in a shaken voice as tremors racked his body.

Clutching him, her nails digging into his taut flesh, Jessica sobbed, "Please, darling! Now!"

Responding instantly to her frantic plea, Hank took her with wild abandon. He thrust deep, loving her with a ferocity and power that bordered on desperation, and Jessica responded with all the pent-up need and longing of years, matching his boldness and driving their passions higher and higher, until they were spinning out of control. When at last the explosion came, it was earth-shattering. It shook them to their souls, wrung cries of joy and pleasure from their hearts and hurtled them out into space.

And then they were drifting down...down...down....

Spent, adrift in a sea of languor, they lay motionless for what could have been minutes or hours. Overhead, the ceiling fan made a soft whirring sound as it slowly turned, stirring a gentle breeze that cooled their heated flesh. From outside came the distant murmur of the surf and the twitter of birds. The scent of flowers and sea air drifted in through the open windows.

It was wonderful to simply lie there in the heavenly aftermath, but little by little, the real world intruded. They became aware of the unyielding hardness of the floor, the gritty sand that still clung to them, the stickiness of their skin. Jessica stirred, and as Hank shifted his weight her heavy eyelids fluttered open. The sight that greeted her produced a startled giggle.

"What?" Hank raised up on his forearms and gave her a drowsy look.

"Oh, Hank," Jessica sputtered. "L-look." Covering her burning face with one hand, she pointed upward with the other.

He glanced up, and his mouth twitched. Easing his weight from her, he rolled to his back. With his head cradled in his clasped hands, he gazed up at her swimsuit, turning around and around in a slow circle, hanging limply from the revolving fan by one strap.

"Hmm. Now how do you suppose that got up there?" His voice held laughter and supreme male satisfaction. He turned his head to look at her and waggled his eyebrows suggestively, his eyes dancing with delight and mischief and sensual promise.

Jessica's embarrassment gave way to a melting warmth. His teasing expression reminded her of the first time she saw him. He had strolled into Alma's café with that sexy loose-limbed walk, flaunting all that male virility and flashing those slumberous looks, and she had instantly pegged him as a flirt.

She hadn't been wrong, but she knew now that there was much more to Hank Rawlins than that. He was caring and giving, loyal, hardworking, honest—maybe even to a fault, she mused, recalling how bluntly he had stated his opinion of love and marriage. But his easygoing manner, his flirtatious teasing were also part of his character, part of what made him the man she loved, and after the weeks of dark brooding and unhappiness she was fiercely glad to see that devilish twinkle in his eyes again.

"I think it was thrown up there by a crazed sex fiend," she said, daring to tease him back.

"Oh, yeah? You think so?" His grin was slow, wide and wicked. "Well, Duchess, honey, you ain't seen nothin' yet," he drawled outrageously.

"But first things first." Catching her off guard, he rolled to his knees and nudged her. "C'mon. Let's go. If we stay on this floor much longer we won't be able to move."

"But, Hank, I'm so tired," she groaned as he hauled her to her feet.

"You can nap after we shower. Now move it, woman," he commanded, giving her bare rump a playful slap.

Too lethargic to protest further, Jessica allowed herself to be bundled into the sybaritic glass-enclosed shower. Her hair was thoroughly shampooed and rinsed, then Hank worked up a generous lather in his hands and scrubbed every inch of her body with meticulous care. By the time he had finished and she had returned the favor they were both breathing hard, their eyes drowsy and hot. Without a word, Hank backed her up against the glass wall, and there beneath the warm spray, they made love again—this time slowly, deliciously.

A half hour later, lying in bed with Jessica asleep in his arms, Hank stared at the ceiling, his face somber. Physically he was satisfied, his body replete and pleasantly tired, but his mind wouldn't let him rest. Jessica lay with her head on his shoulder. One of her legs was hooked trust-ingly over his, and her hand rested on his chest, her fingers curled into the mat of hair that covered it.

He looked down at her and tenderly stroked the hair at her temple. He felt a rush of emotion as he studied her incredibly fragile eyelids, the way her lashes lay against her cheek, gold tipped and curling. With a sigh, he looked back at the ceiling, and wondered what it was about this woman that made him love her.

He had known women who were prettier, sexier, richer. Certainly many who were less trouble. Absently he rubbed his chin against her forehead. What made Jessica different? Special? Why, out of all the women in the world, was she the only one he had ever wanted to claim as his own?

He'd never felt that way about a woman before. He'd never even come close. Hank had always liked women, and not merely in a sexual way. Bumming around the country with his dad, he'd met all kinds and he knew that, like men, some were admirable and decent and some were not, but generally he found women enjoyable. Over the years he'd been intimate with more than a few. Some he'd even been genuinely fond of, but the feeling had never gone deep.

But with Jessica it was as though his soul had somehow merged with hers, and he had a terrible gut feeling that if he lost her—no, correction, *when* he lost her—it would be as if a part of him had died.

Love. Dammit! He'd lived thirty-six years believing it didn't exist! Why the devil did it have to jump up and kick him in the teeth now?

Too restless to lie still, he eased Jessica from his arms and slipped out of bed. He took a cigarette from the pack on the dresser and lit it. Naked, he walked to the window and stared out.

As it rolled toward the shore, the ocean reflected the

gold and rose of the setting sun. At the horizon the deep blue of the water met the pale blue of the sky, which faded into gold as it arched upward. In the distance Hank could see the island of Molokai. Billowing, blue-gray thunderheads clung to its peaks, and even higher a thin layer of ragged clouds, tinted deep pink by the setting sun, stretched out over island and ocean like a tattered lace curtain. Against the serene, colorful background the palms were swaying black silhouettes.

Unmoved by the beauty before him, Hank leaned a shoulder against the window frame and exhaled a stream of smoke, a self-mocking half smile tilting his lips. At least now he understood how Trace felt. Though he liked Katy and thought she was sweet, and certainly beautiful, he'd always thought that Trace was crazy for tying himself down to one woman, and had, on more than one occasion, told him so.

A rueful grimace twisted Hank's mouth. Hell, when his friend found out that he was in love with Jessica he was going to bust a gut laughing.

Lying perfectly still, Jessica watched Hank through the fuzzy screen of her lashes, her heart growing heavy at the sight of his grim profile.

The week they had shared had been perfect, beyond anything she had dared to hope for. Since she had questioned his anger on their wedding night in Los Angeles, Hank's behavior had altered drastically. She had expected passion from him, since that was his admitted reason for marrying her, but Hank had also showered her with affection and tenderness and warmth. No husband, not even one who was head-over-heels in love with his wife, could have been more attentive. To her surprise, Hank had demonstrated a flattering desire for her company, out of bed as well as in it.

They had spent hours swimming or just walking the beach, hand in hand. Several nights they had gone out to dinner and enjoyed a show at one of the hotels along the beach. Together, they had taken the walking tour of Lahaina's historical sights, and afterward Hank had indulgently tagged along as she poked through the shops. At his suggestion they had flown to Oahu early one morning and spent the day seeing the sights there. It didn't seem to matter to Hank what they did, as long as they were together.

He had also been supportive. Jessica knew that Danny was safe with the Barnetts, but Hank seemed to understand her need to call him daily, just to hear his voice. Indeed, he'd encouraged her to do so.

During the past week she had even dared to hope that Katy had been right, that perhaps he did love her after all—just a little.

But now she realized that she'd been indulging in a bit of wishful dreaming.

Her eyes were sadly loving as they trailed over him, standing there beautifully naked and masculine. He was so still, his lean, muscular body propped against the window with such indolent ease, that she could almost believe he was relaxed. But something about his stance, the tautness of his shoulders, and the harsh set of his features, betrayed an inner turbulence.

This past week left no doubt that he desired her with an all-consuming hunger—a hunger that, as yet, showed no sign of waning—but how long could it last if, as she suspected, he resented this marriage?

Chapter Twelve

The next night when they arrived home, Jessica took one look at Katy's face and knew immediately that something was wrong.

Their plane had landed in Durango a little after eight, and after they had retrieved their luggage and traveled the hundred or so miles to Elk Falls, it was almost midnight when they drove into the ranch yard.

During the long flight and the drive neither had said much. They were both feeling the effects of jet lag and, in Jessica's case, a touch of melancholia that the honeymoon was over. The passionate interlude on Maui had been a space out of time that had been near perfection. For that short period she had, for the most part, been able to pretend that the rest of the world and the problems that awaited her didn't exist.

Strangely, though, when they'd passed through Elk Falls her mood had begun to lighten. As they'd driven the twenty-mile stretch of highway to the R Bar B, which was now as familiar to Jessica as the roads around her parents' ranch, she experienced a growing sense of homecoming.

By the time Hank had turned off the main highway and headed the truck down the winding road into the valley, she'd been sitting forward on her side of the seat, eagerly peering out the window for a first glimpse of the ranch headquarters.

Light had spilled from the kitchen like a welcoming beacon as they'd driven into the yard. Hank had scarcely brought the truck to a halt beside the back steps before Trace and Katy were there at its side.

They were met with warmth and hugs and teasing comments, but Jessica quickly detected a forced brightness in Katy's voice. Holding her new friend's shoulders, she stepped back from her embrace and felt a chill of foreboding. Even in the weak light spilling onto the back porch she could see the worry in Katy's eyes.

"What is it? What's happened?"

Katy bit her lower lip and sent her husband a pleading look for assistance.

Trace's face sobered, and he motioned toward the kitchen. "Why don't we go inside."

"Is it Danny? Oh, God, has something happened to him?"

Caught in the chilling grip of fear, Jessica didn't notice when Hank slipped his arm around her waist and led her into the kitchen. As he urged her down into a chair her frantic gaze locked on Trace.

"Oh, no, Jessie, it's nothing like that," Katy quickly assured her. "Danny's fine. Really. He's upstairs in his bed fast asleep."

"Then what...?"

"Jessie, yesterday we learned that Lois Collier is going ahead with the custody suit."

"Damn her!"

Jessica didn't hear Hank's bitter curse, nor was she aware of him going down on his haunches before her and taking her cold hands in his, his face dark with concern as he gazed at her. Chilled, she stared straight ahead. At that moment all she could hear was Lois's cold threat playing over and over in her mind.

"I'll blacken your name so that no judge in the state will allow you to keep him. Or even visit him. And you know I can do it."

"Jessie? Sweetheart, look at me."

When the command got no result, Hank framed her face with his hand, forcing her to obey. Jessica blinked at him slowly. After a moment the stark blankness faded, and her eyes filled with pain.

"Oh, God, Duchess, I'm sorry. I thought that once we were married, she'd back off."

So had she, Jessica realized, feeling foolish. Hank was unaware of just how dominating and tenacious Lois could be, but she should have known better. Dazed, Jessica slowly shook her head. "I should have realized she wouldn't give up. Lois believes that simply being a Collier entitles her to whatever she wants." Her chin began to wobble, and a sob rose in her throat. "Oh, God! What am I going to do?"

"We're going to fight her, honey. Together." Hank grasped her elbows and gave her a little shake. "Now don't get yourself upset. Danny is your son, and with us he has a stable home. I can't believe any judge in his right mind would take him away from you."

"But you don't understand! Lois is a very influential

woman. The Collier name carries a lot of weight in that part of Texas."

Trace put his hand on her shoulder and gave it a squeeze. "If it comes down to that, Jessie, I'm not without influence myself. Katy and I aren't part of the Collier social set because we don't care for that sort of life, but the Barnett name carries just as much clout. Katy and I will be there with you to see that you get a fair shake."

Jessica looked up at him in amazement. "You'd do that for me?"

"Oh, Jessie," Katy rebuked with a gentle smile. "Of course, we will. That's what friends are for."

Their images blurred as tears filled Jessica's eyes. Her chin began to wobble in earnest. "I don't know what to say. I..."

"Come on. It's time you were in bed." Rising, Hank cut off her wavering attempt to express gratitude and drew her up with him. "You're too worn out to deal with this right now." Holding her close against his side, he bundled her out of the kitchen and upstairs to the bedroom they would share, leaving the other couple staring after them in bemused speculation.

Jessica was so upset she was barely aware of Hank stripping away her clothes and slipping a nightgown over her head, or of being tucked into bed. Within moments he joined her there and pulled her into his arms.

There was an icy feeling of dread lodged deep inside her, causing her body to tremble uncontrollably. Hank held her close and ran his big hand up and down her arm, her back, absorbing her tremors, giving her his warmth. "Don't worry, sweetheart. Everything's going to be fine," he whispered in the darkness. "Just relax."

Over and over he murmured reassurance while he continued to stroke her with a slow, mesmerizing rhythm. His arms offered comfort, support, a calming strength. His nearness, the steady beat of his heart beneath her ear, the caring in his voice were reminders that she was no longer alone. Little by little, the knowledge seeped in, bringing with it a warmth that drove out the chill. As taut muscles relaxed, exhaustion claimed her, and at last she slept.

Everyone on the ranch was supportive when they learned what was happening. The hands were outraged, and, to a man, they offered to act as character witnesses for Jessica. Even Slick, who rarely said a word, cut loose with a string of profanity, his ire was so aroused.

Cooter's disposition worsened. He stomped around snapping and snarling at everyone, with the exception of Danny and Jessica.

He hovered over Danny like an old mother hen, and continued to drive him to and from school daily. Jessica, he treated with a gruff gentleness that was oddly touching. Whenever he patted her shoulder and told her not to worry, she got so emotional she almost dissolved into tears. Cooter vowed that no matter what some judge down in Texas said, the only way anyone would take Danny would be over his dead body.

The Barnetts delayed their return home for a few days to lend moral support and help Jessica and Hank decide on the best plan of action. Trace recommended an attorney in Fort Worth, and when they called him and discussed the matter he agreed to take the case. They spent over two hours talking to him on the telephone, and afterward Jessica felt a little better.

The court date was set for the first of November, just one month away. Considering the backlogged court dockets, the speed with which the case was being heard told Jessica that Lois had already done some arm twisting.

Hank insisted that it didn't matter, that the sooner they got the whole thing over with the better, but to Jessica it was tangible evidence of her former mother-in-law's manipulative powers, and her uneasiness grew.

She couldn't have asked for anyone more supportive than Hank—or more understanding and patient. She worried and fretted constantly, but he did his best to soothe her fears, reassuring her over and over that Lois couldn't possibly win. When her jittery nerves caused her to lash out, he ignored her bursts of temper and her sharp words. And those times when things became too much for her, he simply held her until the storm passed then tenderly dried her tears.

Feeling that it would be wrong to burden a six-year-old with something he could do nothing about and probably wouldn't understand anyway, Jessica decided to delay telling Danny about the custody hearing until the last minute. Why put him through all the fear and anxiety? she reasoned. If she won, he would have been needlessly upset. If she lost and he was taken from her, it would be painfully traumatic for both of them, and no amount of prior knowledge would change that.

Her efforts to shield Danny, however, were in vain. He might not have known the specifics, but he obviously sensed the tension among the adults in his world, and reacted to it by withdrawing. He no longer followed Hank around or spent any time with Cooter, outside of riding to and from school. At mealtime he sat as quiet as a mouse, his eyes big and solemn. Not even Wooley or Buck could draw him out. As time went by, he grew more quiet and Jessica grew more worried.

Whenever she or Hank asked what was wrong he merely replied ''Nothing'' and clammed up. Cooter got the same response. All of his time was spent with the horses or Sheba, or alone in his room.

Aware that Danny was picking up the disturbing emotional undercurrents, Jessica tried to act as though nothing were wrong, but it was impossible. The closer the hearing loomed, the more her nerves came unraveled and the more withdrawn Danny became, which only made her fret all the more.

Hank tried to get Jessica to tell Danny what was going on.

"He knows something is wrong. The truth will be tough to deal with, but God only knows what he's imagining. It might be worse."

"It couldn't be!" Jessica twisted her hands together and paced across their bedroom. She swung around and gave him an agitated look, raking a hand through her hair. "And anyway...I can't tell him."

"You've got to, sweetheart," he said gently.

"I *can't*! Don't you understand? He...he wouldn't be able to deal with it."

"He wouldn't...or you wouldn't?"

Jessica jerked to a halt and shot him an accusing glare, her eyes wide and a little wild. Her breathing was shallow and sharp. She lifted her chin defiantly, but after a moment it began to tremble. "I..." She choked on a sob and buried her face in her hands. He was right. It was as though if she put into words the worst that could happen, it would. "Oh, God...I can't," she cried in a strangled voice. "I... just...can't."

Hank gathered her into his arms and held her tight as her shoulders shook and harsh, piteous cries tore from her throat. "Ssh, babe, ssh. It's okay," he crooned. "It's okay. You can tell him later."

But time didn't make the task any easier. On the day

they were to leave for Texas, when Danny saw his mother packing, he sidled warily into the bedroom and watched her, his eyes solemn and fearful. "What're you doing, Mom?" he ventured when Jessica looked up and smiled at him.

"Packing. We're going back to Texas for a few days, sweetheart, and Hank and Cooter are going with us," she replied with false brightness.

"I don't want to go."

"Sure you do. It'll be fun. You'll get to see Grandma and Gramps and your aunts and uncles. And, uh… Grandmother Collier. Wouldn't you like that?"

"No." He set his jaw mulishly and shook his head, showing more animation than he had in weeks. "I don't want to. I don't want to. I won't go! I won't!" His voice grew shrill, rising higher and higher with each word.

"Sweetheart, what's the matter?" Jessica asked in a concerned voice. Going down on her knees before him, she took his hands. "Why are you so upset?"

Hank appeared in the bathroom doorway, wearing only a towel knotted around his waist. Using another to dry his wet hair, he leaned casually against the door frame. "What's the problem, pard?"

"I don't want to go back to Texas! Grandmother Collier will make us stay there, and I want to stay here on the ranch! I want us all to stay here! Please, Mommie. I don't want to go," he pleaded, and as he burst into tears, he threw himself into her arms.

"Oh, sweetheart, don't cry." Jessica clutched his warm little body close and pressed her lips together, trying to keep her own tears at bay, but it was hopeless. They streamed down her cheeks as she looked helplessly at Hank over Danny's shoulder. Shaking her head, she mouthed, "I can't tell him. I can't."

Jessica tried soothing, cajoling, reason and pleading, but finally had to resort to an ultimatum before Danny accepted that they were going. He sulked all the way to the Durango airport, and it didn't help matters any when, at the last minute, Cooter changed his mind.

He had never flown before, and he took one look at the plane and balked.

"I ain't a'goin'," he stated adamantly. "If God had'a wanted me to fly, he'd'a give me wings." No amount of coaxing or pleading could change his mind.

Jessica's entire family, along with the Barnetts, met them at the Dallas–Fort Worth Airport. Danny was passed from person to person for hugs and kisses, and, duly fussed over, he soon was giggling happily, his fears temporarily forgotten.

As soon as they had checked in to a hotel and had a quick lunch, Jessica's parents took charge of Danny, leaving them free to confer with Mark Addley, their attorney. They had wanted to take him home with them to spend the night, but Jessica couldn't bear to be apart from him for even that long, knowing that she might lose him in the next few days.

Jessica liked Mark Addley immediately. He had impressed her during their telephone conversations, but in person he inspired even more confidence. In his early forties, tall and distinguished-looking, her lawyer appeared every bit as commanding a figure as Jonathan Wittlow. Mark, however, radiated a warmth and fatherly compassion that Jonathan lacked. After spending several hours with him, for the first time Jessica began to feel marginally hopeful.

But that night, after tucking Danny into bed, she sat watching him long after he was asleep, fearful of letting him out of her sight. Only at Hank's insistence did she finally give up her vigil, and even then he had to pull her into his arms and gently but firmly escort her into their adjoining room.

During the interminable night she clung fiercely to Hank, desperately seeking escape from her fears and apprehensions in passion.

"Love me. Oh, please, love me," she beseeched in a voice edging toward hysteria. Time and again, with frantic hands and avid mouth, she sought the solace of those few moments of oblivion that only he could give her.

Sensitive to the frenzied need that drove her, Hank responded with the power and wild ferocity that she craved. It was a primitive loving, reckless, untamed, a silent cleaving that drove away demons, expressed the unspeakable and forged a bond that went soul deep.

When at last she collapsed, exhausted and tearful, in his arms, he held her close. "It's going to be all right, sweetheart," he crooned as she cried out her fears against his chest. "Everything's going to work out fine."

Hank's voice was soft and soothing, firm with conviction, but as he stared through the darkness, absently massaging the taut muscles in her neck and back, he wondered whether the next few days would prove him wrong...and what he would do if they did.

Trace and Katy, who were staying at the same hotel, drove them to the courthouse the next morning. Jessica's parents and three oldest brothers, Josh, Dennis and Roger, were waiting when they arrived.

Mary Baxter took one look at her daughter's pale face and opened her arms wide.

Jessica stepped willingly into the embrace that had been the haven of her childhood. Here, countless times, she had sought and found relief from the pain of scraped knees and hurt feelings, balm for a bruised pride and banishment of childish fears. If only it were still that easy, she thought wistfully.

"There, there, darling. Don't you worry. Everything's going to be fine. You'll see."

For a moment Jessica closed her eyes and drew comfort from the familiar: the warm softness of her mother's plump body, the smell of face powder and lilac and fresh-baked bread that clung to her skin, the soothing words crooned so lovingly in her ear.

"Thanks, Mom, for being here."

"Nonsense. Where else would we be but with our daughter when she needs us? That's what families are for."

"Wild horses couldn't have kept her away. Or any of us, for that matter," her father said, giving her shoulder an awkward pat.

"Oh, Daddy," Jessica murmured tearfully. With a wan smile, she stepped from her mother's arms into her father's and felt again a surge of love and gratitude as she drew on his strength and buried her face against his rough, sun-scorched neck.

After receiving crushing bear hugs from each of her brothers, Jessica turned back to Hank. He stood a little to one side, watching them, and the wistful longing in his eyes squeezed at her heart. She remembered the things Cooter had told her about his childhood, and for a moment her own problems were forgotten as her heart overflowed with love and pity for this man who had never known the special closeness of a family.

With a soft smile, she took his arm and drew him into their midst, and together they all walked into the court-room.

Lois was already there, sitting at the plaintiff's table, as intimidating and indomitable as ever. Her gray hair was impeccably coiffed, and she wore a designer suit with a cameo pinned to the lace-edged jabot at her throat. Her ramrod posture and cool expression radiated haughty dignity.

Jessica stopped abruptly when she saw her, unconsciously squeezing Hank's hand. Her heart pounded and her chest grew so tight she could barely breathe. Lois deigned to give her one long, contemptuous look, then pointedly looked away.

Thoroughly shaken, Jessica sat down between Hank and Mark at the defendant's table. Her body was rigid, and she shook like someone in the grips of a raging fever.

Seated beside Lois, Jonathan Wittlow was cool and confident, almost to the point of smugness. Before the proceedings got under way, he had the gall to approach Mark Addley and suggest, one last time, that Jessica surrender Danny willingly and save them all a lot of trouble. When Mark refused, Jonathan merely shot her a sneering smile and returned to his client.

The testimony went much more quickly than Jessica had expected.

Lois took the stand first. Under her attorney's prompting, she painted herself as a loving grandmother who had been the soul of generosity, and Jessica as a scheming opportunist who had married her son for his social position and money. Through a series of clever questions and answers, Lois and Jonathan managed to give the impression that Jessica's morals while living in the Collier home had been less than exemplary.

Distressed, Jessica whispered, "That's not true. None of it. She's lying!"

Her attorney merely smiled reassuringly and shook his head. Her worried gaze sought Hank's reaction, and relief flooded her as she met his warm gaze. Lacing his fingers through hers, he gave her hand a squeeze.

With a pathetic little catch in her voice, which was as much as her dignity would allow her to unbend, Lois told how Jessica had fought her on almost everything she had ever tried to do for her grandson, and how, after Lois had provided them with a home and a life of ease, Jessica had cruelly spirited Danny away without a word. Then Lois spoke of all the advantages she could give Danny and stressed that as her sole heir, it was important that he live with her so that he could be groomed to take over the Collier holdings someday.

Listening to her, Jessica's fear escalated, and she felt sick to her stomach. Lois managed to make her sound like a grasping, cold-hearted user with her eye out for the main chance.

In cross-examination Mark Addley calmly and mercilessly tore Lois's testimony to shreds, dragging from her a resentful admission that, as Danny's mother, Jessica had the right to decide her child's upbringing and to live wherever she pleased. He also pointed out that Lois had not bothered to "groom" her own son for anything, and that since Allen hadn't had a dime of his own, Jessica could hardly be accused of fortune hunting.

Lois left the witness stand in an icy rage, and spent the rest of the time directing pointed looks at the judge.

Not surprisingly, the witnesses called to testify to Jessica's so-called immoral behavior were Loreen Collins and her aunt, Dorothy Grimes, but Mark quickly exposed their testimony as nothing more than vindictive jealousy.

Even to Jessica, it was obvious that Lois's case was weak, but instead of giving her hope, that merely confirmed that her former mother-in-law was relying heavily on the Collier influence to win for her.

That afternoon Jonathan rested his case and it was Mark's turn. He immediately put Jessica on the stand, and she explained why she had felt it imperative that she remove her son from Lois's home. She even managed to survive Jonathan's cross-examination with credible outward calm, though her insides were quaking.

On the second day of the hearing, when first Trace, then Katy took the stand, Lois was visibly disturbed, and several times she conferred with her attorney in urgent undertones.

Mark countered Loreen and Dorothy's testimony with more than a dozen depositions taken from the ranch hands and several people in Elk Falls, including Alma and the minister. Just as he was preparing to wrap up their defense, they were all stunned by Cooter's unexpected arrival.

"Cooter! What're you doing here?" Jessica whispered when he approached her. "And how did you get here?"

"In one of them jets. How'd you think? An' I come to say my piece," he snorted.

She simply gaped at him in amazement. Only two days ago he had flatly refused to set foot on an airplane.

But the night before, when Cooter had called them at the hotel, he had not been happy with the way things were going. Apparently his worry over losing Danny was strong enough to overcome his reluctance to trust his life to one of those "infernal contraptions."

Though Jessica knew that Cooter's attitude toward her had changed over the past few months, she was nevertheless touched by his vociferous praise when he took the stand.

"Why, you won't find a finer woman than Jessie," he declared, scowling at the judge as though he dared him to dispute his word. "Or a better mother, neither. Oh, she may be a mite overprotective, but leastways she's got the good sense to listen when you point it out to her.

"As far as this danged fool 'immorality' business, why that's nothin' but a pack a'lies. Judge, you can take it from me, there weren't no hanky-panky goin' on a'fore them two married. An' I ought'a know, 'cause I was there.'' Cooter glanced around, then leaned toward the judge and confided in a lower voice, "Now, mind you, I ain't a'sayin' Hank there wouldn't'a liked it if there had been, or that he didn't try, but Jessie jist ain't that kind'a woman.''

As a ripple of laughter spread through the room, Jessica groaned and hid her burning face behind her hand. Hank looked sheepish, but her parents beamed. Icy disapproval pinched Lois's mouth as she tried to visually annihilate Cooter, but the cantankerous old man matched her glare for glare. Katy struggled to stifle her giggles, but Trace had no such qualms, and he slapped his leg and guffawed right along with everyone else. Even Judge Potter's mouth twitched suspiciously.

"An' another thing," Cooter added, thumping the edge of the judge's bench for emphasis. "Danny's happy right where he is. He loves his mother an' he loves the ranch. He sure as heck don't want to go live with that snooty old woman, I can tell you. If you don't believe me why don't you jist ask him.''

"Thank you, Mr. Davis. That's an excellent suggestion."

Judge Potter inquired if Danny was in the building, and was told he was waiting outside in the hall with his uncle. "Very well, I'll talk with him privately in my chambers, and afterward I'll give my decision. In the meantime, this court is in recess," he said, and banged his gavel.

The wait seemed interminable. Reluctant to stray far

from the courtroom, Jessica paced the hallway just outside, her nerves running riot. Hank, who, after the first half hour, had given up trying to calm her, leaned against the wall and chain-smoked. The Barnetts, Cooter, her parents and brothers sat on benches on either side of the hallway, talking together in hushed tones.

Every time Jessica passed the courtroom doors she checked the big clock above them. Hank's gaze never left her.

When at last Mr. Addley appeared and announced that the judge was ready, Jessica thought for a moment that she was going to faint. She felt the blood rush from her face and her knees begin to tremble. Then Hank was beside her, his hard arm encircling her waist, supporting her as he led her into the courtroom.

As Judge Potter took his place behind the bench Jessica was shaking all over, and her heart was pounding against her ribs like a battering ram. Though he kept his closing statement brief, it was agony to listen to his mellifluous voice drone on. She was almost ill from fear and nerves when he finally announced his decision.

"...and therefore, after reviewing all the testimony and talking at length to Danny Collier, I find in favor of the defendant, Jessica Collier."

Pandemonium broke out before the gavel sounded. Family and friends surged forward and surrounded them, whooping and cheering, everyone talking at once, but Jessica barely noticed. For a stunned instant she couldn't take it in. Then relief and joy exploded inside her, and she burst into tears and turned blindly into Hank's arms.

Feeling as though a huge weight had been lifted from her heart, Jessica left the courthouse flanked by her husband and son, her feet barely touching the ground.

It wasn't until later that night that she came back down to earth.

After a celebration dinner with family and friends, Jessica and Hank had returned to the hotel still keyed up and in high spirits. Which was why, when Hank emerged from taking a shower, he was surprised to find her in a pensive mood.

Standing at the balcony doors, she had her back to the room. She was wearing a luscious mint-green nightgown, as substantial as mist, which hung to her bare feet in deep, diaphanous folds. The sheer material afforded tantalizing glimpses of the peach-tinted flesh and ripe curves beneath. Her arms were crossed over her midriff and her hands were absently massaging her elbows as she gazed out at Fort Worth's glittering skyline.

Watching her, Hank rubbed his wet hair with a towel. "I thought you'd be in bed. What's the matter? Still too wound up to sleep?"

"I suppose so."

Her light tone didn't fool Hank; he knew Jessica much too well for that. That he did still amazed him, even made him uneasy at times. In the past he had never bothered to really get to know any women or to concern himself with their moods. He hadn't wanted to. But everything about Jessica drew him, fascinated him.

In the six weeks that they had been married he had come to know her as well as he knew himself and was sensitive to her every nuance of feeling, the slightest shift in her mood. And right now, something was bothering her.

Wearing only a towel knotted around his hips, Hank crossed to the room and stood behind Jessica. Except for two thin straps, her shoulders were bare above the nightgown. He cupped his hands over them and kneaded gently. "What's wrong?"

He felt her sigh, and her reflection in the glass door revealed her dispirited little grimace, but she merely shrugged.

Hank edged closer, bringing his chest into contact with her back, and she relaxed against him. Smiling at the unconsciously trusting action, Hank rubbed his chin against her crown. The sweet, clean fragrance of her hair drifted around him like subtle perfume. A few slippery strands caught in his beard stubble.

Hank curved his arms around her waist and crossed them over her midriff. Still gazing into the distance, Jessica rested her arms on top of his. Absently her nails raked his forearms as her fingers threaded through the smattering of hair that covered them.

"C'mon, now, you can't fool me," he prodded in a teasing voice, savoring the feel of her. "Why the long face? You should be on top of the world. You won, Duchess. It's over."

"For now."

"What do you mean? Lois took her best shot and lost. There's nothing more she can do."

"Hank, I know Lois. Believe me, she never gives up. She'll be watching and waiting, and when this marriage ends…" Jessica groped for the right words, and finally lifted her hand in a hopeless little gesture. "That is…if my circumstances ever change, she'll try again."

So that was it. He had set down the terms, so he had only himself to blame. Still, it irked him that already she was anticipating the end of their marriage.

Damn that stupid bargain! At the time it had seemed logical, even desirable. Now it was nothing but an albatross.

He wanted to tell her that he loved her, but he didn't dare. She was so damn grateful to him for helping her keep

Danny, she'd probably convince herself that she returned his feelings, but he'd never know for sure.

The way things stood now, she needed him. He wanted more, but he could live with that. He couldn't live with pity or gratitude.

"If that's all that's worrying you, forget it." Hank turned her to face him, still holding her within the circle of his arms. "I won't let that happen, Duchess. I promise you that."

The soft sincerity in his voice was almost her undoing, and Jessica looked at him sadly, fighting back tears. "Oh, Hank. How can you promise that? We both know that you never intended to be trapped in this marriage forever."

"Do you hear me complaining?"

"No, but—"

He stopped her words with a soft kiss. When he raised his head he smiled—that tender, crooked smile that never failed to make her heart flip. "If I get to feeling trapped, I promise I'll let you know. In the meantime I want you to quit worrying."

"But you said—"

"—that this marriage would last for as long as you needed me. And I meant it. I don't go back on my word, Duchess."

"Hank, it will be *twelve years* before Danny is legally an adult and we no longer have this threat hanging over us."

"So? I don't have a problem with that. Unless, of course, you do?"

"No, I..." She stared at him in blank amazement, her lips slightly parted, confusion and hope warring within her. Surely no man would commit himself to a woman for years unless he loved her, at least a little. Would he?

"You'd really do that for me?"

"In case you haven't noticed, I haven't exactly found being married to you a hardship."

When she continued to gaze up at him, speechless, he sighed with mock exasperation. "Lord, woman, you're hard to convince." Burying his hands in the lush folds of her nightgown, Hank cupped her bottom and pressed her tightly to him. Beneath heavy lids, his eyes began to sparkle with wicked intent. His slow grin was pure seduction. "If you won't listen to what I say, I guess I'll just have to demonstrate."

His eyes darkened with a slumberous heat as his head began a slow descent. Daring to hope, to dream, Jessica gave a sigh and coiled her arms around his neck. She went up on tiptoe, and as her eyes drifted shut, she lifted her face for his kiss.

At the first touch of his lips she melted against him, giving herself up to the insistent joy burgeoning within her. Hank's mouth devoured hers with a soft ardency that took her breath away. At the same time, his hands worked their magic, gliding over the slippery silk with slow, erotic movements.

Feelings intensified. Passion built. The world faded away until nothing existed beyond the warm embrace they shared. Sensations piled one on top of another, all pleasurable and arousing, each tiny, tactile perception adding to the lovers' awareness: the warm, silky feel of Hank's hair flowing through her fingers, the erotic roughness of his callused palm gliding over her back, the soft eddy of his moist breath against her cheek, its sibilant sound. The heat of their bodies seemed to fuse them together, and their two hearts beat as one, the rhythm heavy and pagan. The scent of soap clung to their skin, tinged with the subtle fragrances of both male and female. She could taste the faint bite of tobacco on his tongue, feel the dampness seeping through her gown from the towel at his waist, and beneath it, feel the evidence of his desire pressing against that part of her that ached with a hollow yearning.

Need spiraled through Jessica, and she made a restless little movement. With a growl, Hank broke off the kiss and swept her up in his arms.

"Oh, Hank." Jessica said his name with aching tenderness as she looped her arms around his neck, her voice barely more than a sigh.

He held her high against his chest and looked deep into her eyes. Emotion tightened his face. "They say that actions speak louder than words, so listen closely." His eyes burned with a fierce intensity that made her heart skip a beat.

The long full skirt of her nightgown billowed out like a sail in the wind as he turned and strode to the bed. Bemused, enthralled, Jessica clung to him, unable to look away from his determined face and the thrilling silent message that seemed to glitter in his eyes.

Hank's knee dented the mattress as he bent to place her on the bed. Jessica started to lie back but he pulled her into a sitting position. Still holding her gaze, he grasped handfuls of the voluminous nightgown, and with a siren's smile, Jessica docilely raised her arms as he lifted it over her head and tossed it aside. The frothy confection caught the air. Like a fragile parachute, it slowly floated to the floor, where it settled soundlessly into a gossamer mound on the dark carpet.

Still braced beside her on one knee, Hank took her hand and placed it on the towel knotted at his waist. His eyes commanded. His deep, husky voice enticed. "Now it's your turn."

Shaking fingers worked the loose knot free, and the damp towel dropped to the floor with a soft plop. A slow, sizzling smile curved Hank's lips. He put a hand on her shoulder, and as he gently pushed her onto her back, he went with her, lowering his body over hers.

His warmth, the wonderful weight of him drew a sigh of pleasure from Jessica as she was pressed deeper into the mattress. The sigh became a moan when she felt her sensitive nipples push through the crisp hair covering his chest and settle against the warm flesh beneath.

Hank caught the sound with his mouth, his nibbling lips gently rapacious as he devoured her with a sweet savagery. "Tonight is for us," he murmured. "No problems. No fears to banish. No bargains to keep." He rocked his mouth over hers. "Tonight there's just you and me."

In the lulling aftermath they lay replete and quiet, their bodies heavy with contentment.

Slumped back against the oak headboard of the bed, the back of his skull resting along its edge, Hank took a deep draw on his cigarette. As he watched the smoke spiral upward, he draped his forearm over his upraised knee, the cigarette held loosely between the first two fingers of his dangling hand. The other hand, buried in his wife's hair, absently massaged her scalp and the back of her neck.

Jessica lay curled against Hank's side, one arm looped over his lean hips, her cheek cradled on his concave belly, corrugated now by the curve of his spine.

"Hank?"

"Hmm?" He looked down at the top of her head. Her hair lay fanned out over his naked chest the tawny gold strands catching in the dark thatch that covered it. Her soft breasts pressed against his hip. He felt her breath feathering across his abdomen, a warm, moist zephyr that barely stirred the whorl of hair around his navel.

Jessica tipped her head up until their gazes met. She

smiled dreamily, and Hank's insides clenched. Was that love in her eyes? Or was he seeing only what he wanted to see?

"You're awfully quiet. Is…is there something on your mind?" Her eyes invited him to share his thoughts. His own heart silently pleaded.

His chest swelled with emotion. His throat grew tight and achy. Her face was scrubbed free of makeup. Her lips were swollen from his kisses. He had never seen a more beautiful sight. "Jessie, I…" *I love you. Oh, God, I love you.* The words pushed up from his soul and hovered on his tongue. He swallowed hard and tried to force them out, but couldn't. "I…"

"Yes?"

"I, uh…I think we'd better get some sleep if we're going to catch that early flight in the morning."

Ignoring the disappointment in her face, he reached out and stubbed out his cigarette in the ashtray on the bedside table and clicked off the lamp. In the darkness they adjusted the pillows, and Hank drew Jessica back into his arms as they settled down to sleep. But long after her breathing became deep and even, he lay awake, his brooding stare fixed on the ceiling.

He supposed it was poetic justice. Like the selfish bastard he was, he'd used Jessica's situation to pressure her into marriage for his own purposes. At least, that had been his plan. He sure as hell hadn't known that he was in love with her. Hell, he hadn't even believed love existed.

And now that he did know, he couldn't tell her.

Chapter Thirteen

Hank emerged from the barn and headed for the house with his head down against the howling wind. Hunching his shoulders, he stuffed his gloved hands deep into the pockets of his sheepskin-lined coat. Beside him, as usual, mimicking his every move, was Danny.

Jessica sipped her coffee and watched them through the kitchen window.

Bundled up in quilted snow gear, Danny resembled a roly-poly bear cub in a Stetson hat. It was tough going through the snow, and he had to take three steps to Hank's one, with a little skipping hop thrown in every now and then just to keep up, but he still managed to strut along beside his hero with a cocky self-importance that was endearing.

As always, the sight of them together produced a warm glow in Jessica's heart. She hugged the feeling to her and savored it, almost guiltily.

With the threat of losing her son removed, contentment had settled over her like a warm, woolen cloak. The seven weeks since their return from Fort Worth had been the happiest she had ever known. The only thing that could possibly make life better would be Hank's love, and even that seemed more and more within her reach.

Daily, they were growing closer. He made love to her often, sometimes fiercely, sometimes with exquisite tenderness, but always with a depth of feeling that touched her soul. He teased her even more than before, but now there was a special softness in his voice, and his every touch was a caress. And sometimes...Jessica caught her lower lip between her teeth and pressed her hand against her chest. Sometimes she caught him looking at her with such naked longing that she could scarcely breathe for the sharp pleasure that exploded inside her. She was almost convinced that he did, indeed, love her. Almost.

Night came early during winter in the Rockies. The sky had been overcast and dreary all day, and now, as dusk gathered, it deepened to gunmetal, the low-hanging clouds heavy and sullen with the threat of more snow. Already a few fat flakes swirled in the biting wind.

Leaving their snow-encrusted boots to form puddles on the glass-enclosed porch, Danny and Hank hurried into the kitchen in their sock feet and closed the door behind them. Their cheeks and noses were whipped red by the frigid wind, and their eyes were watering. The crisp freshness of the outdoors radiated from them.

"Brr, it's cold out there." To prove it, Hank stole a quick kiss and rubbed his icy nose against Jessica's.

"*Ha-ank*, stop that!" she squealed, pushing him away.

He gave her an unrepentant grin and tossed his hat at the rack beside the door. It hit a wooden peg, whirled around once, and rocked to a stop.

Danny flung his cherished Stetson, but it hit the rack and bounced to the floor. "Aw, shoot." Crestfallen, he picked it up and sighed.

"Thanks, babe." Hank accepted the mug of coffee Jessica handed him. As he sipped the steaming drink he bent, curled his other hand into the back waistband of Danny's jeans and lifted him up in front of the rack.

"Look, Mom! Look!" he crowed. Giggling with delight, he tossed his hat onto a peg from a distance of one foot.

"Very good, sweetheart." Jessica's words were directed at Danny, but her warm smile encompassed them both.

"Good shot, pard," Hank said as he deposited the boy on the floor and ruffled his hair.

Danny grinned up at him.

The heavenly aroma of baking filled the kitchen. When Jessica set a plate of warm chocolate-chip cookies on the table, her son's eyes lit up.

"Guess what, Mom? I helped put out the hay," he announced proudly, scrambling onto his chair.

He sniffled, and Jessica turned from the stove with his cup of hot chocolate in time to see him wipe his nose on his sleeve. Catching Hank's amused gaze, she rolled her eyes and sighed, but otherwise pretended not to notice.

"An' you know what else? We had to chop through ice in the water tank in the corral so the horses could get a drink." Danny gulped down half of his warm cocoa and flashed a wide grin, his upper lip covered with a chocolate foam mustache. "Boy, that was really neat."

"Well, I'm glad you enjoyed it, pard. Because if the temperature keeps dropping we'll probably have to chop ice on the creek tomorrow for the cattle."

"Really? Oh, boy!" Danny turned to his mother, his little chest puffed up with pride. "Hank said that I can help him hay the cows every day till I have to go back to school.''

''That's wonderful, honey. I'm sure you'll be a big help.'' The warm look Jessica gave her husband was filled with gratitude. With Buck and Jubal spending Christmas with their families, Hank was shorthanded, but they both knew that Danny was often more of a hindrance than a help.

Looking pleased with himself, Danny took another cookie and broke it in two. He was separating the halves slowly, watching the warm chocolate morsels string out between them, when footsteps sounded on the porch and Cooter's quarrelsome voice reached them through the door.

''Careful now! The blamed tree won't have a needle left on it, the way you two clumsy galoots keep bangin' into things. Dang blast it, Wooley! Watch what you're doin'!''

''I'm watchin'! I'm watchin'! Just open the door, will ya! This thing weighs a ton.''

''It's a Christmas tree!'' Danny shrieked.

The sharp, resinous scent of spruce invaded the kitchen and mingled with the softer aromas of cookies, coffee and chocolate as Wooley and Slick maneuvered the huge tree through the doorway. Traces of snow still clung to some of the branches, and patches of raw wood showed on the trunk where the lower ones had been trimmed away. A homemade wooden stand was nailed to the base.

''Oh, Cooter, it's lovely. Thank you.''

''Here now! There's no call to get mushy,'' he blustered when she kissed his cheek, though his voice lacked heat. ''Just tell us where you want the danged thing.''

''In the living room to the right of the fireplace. Come on, I'll show you.''

Wooley and Slick obediently followed Jessica through

the door. Danny stuffed both halves of the cookie into his mouth and raced after them.

"Humph! Leave it to a danged woman to make a fuss." Still pink to the tips of his ears, Cooter rubbed his stubbled cheek where she'd kissed him and glared at Hank. "Well, what're you grinnin' at? I told her we never put up a tree, but the woman near 'bout nagged me to death to cut one. Anyways, I only did it for the boy."

"Did I say anything?"

Cooter gave a snort and stomped for the hall door. Hank grinned again when he heard the old man barking instructions at Wooley and Slick.

The grin faded a moment later. It occurred to Hank that this was not only the first Christmas they'd put up a tree since he'd owned the ranch, it was the first time he could ever remember having one—period.

He didn't count the aluminum monstrosity decorated with beer-bottle caps they'd had the year he and his dad spent Christmas in Wichita with Cheryl…or was it Charlene? Shirley? Hank shrugged. Something like that. Anyway, one of his old man's convenient girlfriends. Even at age twelve, he'd known that the tacky tree fell far short of the traditional symbol of Christmas.

Hank's expression grew thoughtful. Jessie had brought a lot of firsts to his life. When he had teamed up with Trace to buy the R Bar B, it had been for purely practical reasons; land was a good investment, it was a way to earn a living and be his own boss, and it beat the hell out of traipsing all over the country busting his bones in rodeos. But until Jessica, the ranch, this house, had been merely a possession, a means to an end. Now it was a home. Not only had she taught him about love, she had made him aware of a craving for stability and commitment he hadn't even known he possessed. For roots.

The sounds of laughter and good-natured bantering coming from the living room captured Hank's attention, and he felt its pull like a magnet. He rose to join the others, but at the door he paused and looked back at the inviting kitchen.

One by one, his gaze took in Jessica's subtle touches—the crisp new curtains at the windows, the spotless blue-and-white-checkered cloth on the table and the little copper bowl filled with dried flowers in the center, the jaunty potted ivy on the sill above the sink, the ladybug magnets on the refrigerator that held Danny's childlike artwork. Hank smiled and stepped through the door.

For Christmas, Jessica gave Hank a new pair of custom-made boots. She had learned from Cooter that the ones he was wearing had been made years ago by a famous boot-maker, and when she called the man, she discovered that he still had a cast of Hank's feet. It had taken a lot of wheedling, but he'd finally promised to fill her order in time for Christmas. For a while she had been worried, but the package had finally arrived the day before.

Surprised and genuinely pleased by the gift, Hank leaned across the pile of rubble and wrappings and kissed her warmly. When he raised his head he drew back just far enough to look into her eyes. "Thanks, babe," he murmured, then handed her a small oblong box wrapped in red foil paper.

Jessica was so astounded her mouth fell open when she saw the diamond teardrop suspended from a delicately wrought gold chain. "Oh, Hank..." She said his name in a small, awed voice and looked at him, her wide eyes filled with questions and hope. "It's so beautiful."

"I noticed you didn't have any jewelry," he said casually, as though that explained the extravagant gift. Smiling at her stunned reaction, he moved around behind her and fastened the chain around her neck. The diamond teardrop settled just above the shadowy cleft between her breasts, visible in the vee neck of her robe.

Tentatively Jessica touched the stone with her fingertips. "How does it look?" she whispered.

"Terrific." The long look he gave her started a fire low in her belly. "Wear it tonight when we go to bed," he commanded softly against her lips when he leaned over to kiss her again. "Just the necklace. Nothing else."

His heavy-lidded look, the deep tone, created an erotic image that sent excitement streaking through Jessica. At the first feather-light touch of his lips, she shivered and moaned, but the tiny sound was swallowed up in the long, excruciatingly sensual kiss. As his lips caressed hers, she felt her heart speed up and her body grow warm, the familiar hunger begin to build.

"Mom, look. All I got from Hank is a dumb ole note."

Danny's petulant voice broke over them like a bucket of ice water, dousing the sensual spell. Raising his head, Hank smiled at her ruefully. "Later," he whispered.

They looked up to find Danny standing over them, his expression pouty and slightly accusing. He'd been eyeing the gift from Hank for days, trying to figure out what it was, and his disappointment was acute.

Jessica held out her hand. "Here, let me see it."

Hank had printed the note in big block letters, but Danny's reading skills weren't yet developed enough for him to make out all the words. Jessica scanned the message and smiled.

"It says, 'Your present was too big to bring inside. You'll find it in the barn.'"

Like most children, Danny tended to measure a gift's

value by its size, and the prospect of one so large made his eyes light up. "Oh, boy! Let's go see!"

Wooley and Slick laughed as he hopped from one foot to the other. At Jessica's insistence, the two hands had spent the previous night in the house so that they could share in Christmas.

Danny couldn't wait for them to get dressed, so they pulled on parkas, hats, gloves and boots over their night-clothes and robes and trooped out to the barn just as dawn was breaking.

Christmas morning had brought gray skies and bitter cold, but it didn't matter to Danny in the least. Not even a blizzard could have dimmed his happiness once he saw Hank's gift.

When they had entered the barn he'd been speechless, but he'd soon recovered.

"Isn't he great, Mom?" he asked, barely able to contain his excitement as Hank led the roan gelding from the stall.

"Yes, darling. He certainly is," Jessica replied in a stunned voice. The gift had been as much of a surprise to her as it had been to her son.

She had been expecting something like a bike, or maybe one of those sprawling train sets, but when she'd spotted that huge red bow tied to the door of one of the stalls she'd been flabbergasted. She still was.

Hank turned the horse over to Cooter and Danny and joined Jessica. Leaning back against the stall gate, he draped his elbows over the top rail, bent a knee and hooked his boot heel over the bottom one. "You've sure been quiet. What's the matter? Don't you like the horse?"

"Of course I like him." Dazed, Jessica shook her head. "He's gorgeous." The gelding had beautiful lines and a proud carriage, and what appeared to be an excellent disposition. His glossy coat was a deep, rich red, broken only by a dark mane and tail and four white stockings, which had prompted Danny to name him Socks. "But, Hank, you really shouldn't have. It was very generous of you, and Danny is thrilled, but...well...it's too much. Too expensive."

Hank shrugged that off. "A boy needs his own horse. Besides, it will teach him responsibility."

Any arguments Jessica might have given were squashed in the next instant when Danny came running over and announced he was going to take Socks for a ride.

"Whoa, now. Not so fast." Hank caught the back of his coat and brought him to a halt when he started to make a dash for the tack room. "First, you're going to help hay the cattle and chop ice. The creek is sure to be frozen over this morning."

"But it's Christmas!"

"That doesn't stop the cattle from getting hungry and thirsty."

Danny's expression turned mutinous, and Hank hunkered down in front of him. "On a ranch there are chores that have to be done every day, Danny. You signed on to do a job, and you're going to see it through. That's what a man does, son." Hank's voice was stern, though not unkind.

"If you want to be a ranch hand you've got to accept responsibility. Those animals depend on us for food and water."

Embarrassed, Danny lowered his gaze. With the toe of his boot he drew a circle in the hard-packed ground.

"And while we're on the subject, I bought that horse for you, but before I turn him over to you completely you're going to have to prove to me that you'll take care of him."

Danny's head snapped up at that, but Hank's intent gaze

didn't waver beneath the child's anxious look. "That means you feed him, you groom him and you see that he's well cared for. Not me. Not Cooter. Not your mom. And certainly not any of the hands." He poked Danny's tummy with one long finger. "Just you. And that means every day, not just when you feel like doing it. Think you can handle that?"

"Yessir." Danny's head bobbed up and down vigorously.

"Good."

Danny gazed at Hank earnestly, his face contrite and solemn, all trace of sullenness gone. "I'll take real good care of him, Hank. I promise. Honest."

"I know you will, son," Hank replied, and drew the boy into his arms for a fierce hug.

Jessica's throat ached with emotion. Hank was so good with her son, so good *for* her son, the perfect blend of patience, firmness and affection. How had she ever been lucky enough to find him?

Her heart full to overflowing, she gazed at the two males she loved so dearly and knew a moment of stark fear. Surely happiness so profound couldn't last?

Later that afternoon, after stuffing themselves on a huge Christmas feast, they were all in the living room when the telephone rang. Hank was helping Danny assemble the robot toy Cooter had given him, and the others were watching television. They were all so engrossed they barely looked up when Jessica stepped out into the hall to answer the phone. However, something in her tone must have caught Hank's attention, because when she reentered the room he gave her a searching look and frowned at the sight of her white face.

"What's wrong?"

"Th-that was Jonathan Wittlow."

"Wittlow!" Cooter practically spit out the name. "What the devil does he want?"

Dazed, Jessica stared into the middle distance, her eyes slightly out of focus. She didn't respond until Hank went to her and put his hand on her arm.

"Jessie." He said her name sharply and gave her a little shake. "What did Wittlow say?"

"He…" She licked her lips, and her stunned gaze met his. "He said that Lois had a massive stroke last night. She died this morning."

"Good God!"

Hank's sharp exclamation drew Jessica out of her trance, and immediately she looked at her son. He was still sifting through the plastic parts on the card table, oblivious to the adult conversation. She exchanged a quick glance with Hank and hurried over to him.

Danny listened solemnly as his mother explained what had happened, but when she'd finished he didn't appear to be particularly upset. Though his reaction saddened Jessica, she was not surprised. Danny had never been close to his grandmother.

"Jonathan wants me to come to Fort Worth as soon as I can," she told Hank when they were alone in their bedroom.

"Why?"

"To discuss legal arrangements. Danny is Lois's sole heir."

"I see."

His cold tone made Jessica uneasy, and she glanced at him warily as she pulled a small suitcase from the closet and began to pack. "If I catch an early flight tomorrow morning I can probably be back by the next day," she said in a soft, placating voice.

Hank stuck his hands into his back pockets and strolled over to the window. He stared out at the snow-covered landscape, his face remote, expressionless. *Oh, God, it's over, and she's trying to let me down easy.* His jaws clenched until his teeth hurt. A helpless rage built inside him. The urge to do violence was almost irresistible. He wanted to hit something. Hard. *Anything.* He wanted to rant and rave and wail out his pain.

But he wouldn't.

He had always known that this day would come. They both had. With Lois gone, Jessie no longer needed him— not for protection, not for emotional support, not even for financial security. Hank thought about the Collier millions, and his mouth twisted. In comparison, what he had to offer was nothing.

Tamping down his anguish, he drew a deep breath and steeled himself. They'd made a bargain, and Jessie had kept her part faithfully. The least he could do was make it easy for her to end it.

"There's no point in flying back and forth," he said tonelessly.

Jessica looked up from packing the suitcase, her uneasiness growing as she studied the tense set of his shoulders.

"If you book an evening flight you'll have time to pack up everything."

The stack of lingerie slipped out of her nerveless hands. "What?" Her voice was weak and quavery, her face pale.

"That way you can make the move quickly, in one clean break."

"Move?"

Hank pivoted and gave her a cynical look. "Come on, Duchess. The marriage was fun while it lasted, but now it's time to end it."

"E-end it?" She knew she was parroting everything he said, but she couldn't seem to stop.

"Yeah. Like we agreed." When she continued to stare at him he shrugged. "I don't see any point in putting it off, do you? Hell, when something is over, it's over."

"Pair of stubborn mules," Cooter muttered, snatching up two more suitcases. He shot Jessica a disgusted look and stomped past her. "Don't have sense enough to know what's good for 'um. But will they listen? Oh, no. Not those two. Too danged hardheaded. Why it's enough to make a body—"

The slam of the back door cut off Cooter's grumbling. Jessica sighed and rubbed her throbbing temples with the tips of her fingers. The reprieve was only temporary, she knew—Cooter had kept up a running monologue of complaints all morning. Bless him. In his own roughshod way, he meant well, but she just didn't know how much more she could take. She felt fragile, brittle, as though she might shatter at any moment.

Tears threatened, but she drew a gulping breath and blinked her eyes hard, refusing to give in to them. She'd done enough crying during the lonely night that had just passed.

It hurt unbearably that Hank had spent the night in the guest room, and that this morning he'd gone with the hands as usual and left it to Cooter to drive her to Durango. He'd simply kissed her cheek and said, "So long, Duchess. Be happy" and walked away. His cavalier attitude had crushed whatever small remaining hope she'd had. Now she had to accept that it was truly over, and get on with her life. Somehow.

The back door slammed again. Jessica snatched up her purse and began to rifle through it, her movements stiff

and jerky as she double-checked to see if she had everything.

"...of all the stupid, thickheaded... Why you'd hafta
use a hammer on them thick skulls to knock some sense
into 'um."

Ignoring Cooter's muttering, Jessica slipped into her
coat and picked up her cosmetic case. "Well, that's everything. I guess we're ready. Or we will be as soon as I
find Danny. Do you know where he is?"

"Where do you think?" Cooter shot her a fierce look.
"The boy's in the barn, sayin' goodbye to Socks and
Sheba."

Guilt pierced her, as Cooter had intended. Heading for
the back door, Jessica silently prayed she wasn't in for
another scene like the one they'd had that morning. Her
self-control was too precarious to weather another round
of tears and tantrums.

Not even Hank's promise that he would ship Socks to
Fort Worth, or that Danny could have a puppy from
Sheba's next litter had been enough to console her son.

When she found him, Danny seemed sadly reconciled
to leaving, but Jessica supposed that no more tears was
too much to hope for. By the time they left the barn both
of them had red-rimmed eyes and blotchy faces.

With heavy hearts, they walked hand in hand across the
yard without speaking. They stopped beside the pickup to
take one last look around. Cooter scowled at their tear-
ravaged faces and opened his mouth, but before he could
launch another harangue he was cut off by a prolonged
blast of a truck horn.

Startled, they looked around and saw the other pickup
coming toward them across the valley. Slick was driving
and Wooley was standing up in the truck bed, frantically
waving both arms and yelling.

"Uh-oh. Somethin's wrong."

Cooter only voiced what they both were thinking, but hearing the words made her heart lurch sickeningly. Never taking her eyes from the approaching truck, Jessica stepped close to the old man, instinctively reaching out to him for support. Cooter's work-worn hand clasped hers in a death grip.

Scarcely breathing, they waited in an agony of suspense until the truck finally pulled into the yard. When it was close enough for them to hear what Wooley was shouting, Jessica's worst fears were realized.

"It's Hank! The bull trampled him, and he's hurt bad!"

Chapter Fourteen

"Are you sure this doctor knows what he's doing?" Jessica's woolen skirt swirled around the tops of her fashionable boots as she turned and paced back across the tiny lobby.

"He's as good a sawbones as any they got in Durango," Cooter replied.

"I still think Hank should be in a hospital." She looked around and made an agitated gesture with her hand. "This is just a clinic. How do we know if it even has the necessary equipment? What if he needs surgery?"

"Quit yore frettin', woman. Doc Sanders has been patchin' up people around Elk Falls for years. 'Sides, there's three passes 'tween here an' Durango, an' they're all closed 'cause of yesterday's snowstorm. There ain't no way to get him there."

"What about a helicopter?"

"Weather conditions are still too bad," Slick volunteered. He and Wooley shared the rump-sprung sofa. Both men were subdued and tense, their weathered faces creased with worry. Across the narrow room, Cooter sat hunched over in a chair, his elbows propped on his spread knees. Between, there was barely room for Jessica to walk.

"You might as well sit down and quit frettin'. It's not helpin' none. 'Sides, yore gonna wear a rut in Doc's floor if you don't stop that pacin'."

Jessica doubted that anything could harm the scarred, speckled linoleum, but for Cooter's sake she sat down in the chrome-and-vinyl chair at the end of the room. Despite the old man's studied unconcern, she'd noticed the way his hands had shook when he'd rolled the cigarette that hung between his gnarled fingers.

The toe of her boot tapped out a rapid tattoo against the floor until a scowl from Cooter stopped the action. Giving him an apologetic grimace, Jessica crossed her legs and jiggled her foot, but that caused the cracked vinyl to pop. "Sorry," she muttered when the noise drew pointed looks from all three men.

Placing both feet flat on the floor, she clasped her hands together in her lap and counted the acoustic tiles in the ceiling. It took less than half a minute. By the time she'd finished her knee was bobbing up and down.

With an impatient growl, Jessica bounded out of the chair and resumed her restless pacing. She was wringing her hands, retracing her path for the third time, when Dr. Sanders stepped into the lobby.

Jessica swung around, her face pale. She wanted to ask how Hank was, if he was going to be all right, but her vocal cords froze. All she could do was stare at him and wait, her balled fist unconsciously pressed against her booming heart.

Cooter, Slick and Wooley jumped to their feet. "Well, Doc?" Cooter asked, and Jessica held her breath.

"You can stop worrying. Hank's going to be fine."

A little whimper of relief escaped Jessica, and she swayed and clutched Cooter's arm as her legs threatened to give way beneath her.

"Of course, he's not going to be feeling too chipper for a while. He has three fractured ribs and a concussion that's going to give him a doozie of a headache. At this point I don't think there are any serious internal injuries, but I'm going to keep him here for a few days, just to be sure."

"I'm staying with him."

Dr. Sanders gave Jessica's hand an indulgent pat. "Now, now, Mrs. Rawlins. I don't think that will be necessary. My apartment is connected to the back of the clinic, so I'll be here to monitor him around the clock."

"You'll have other patients coming in, Dr. Sanders. You can't be at his side every moment."

"Well…no. But—"

"I'm staying."

It wasn't a request or a plea, or even an argument, but a statement of fact. Dr. Sanders studied the mulish set of her face and sighed. "Very well. But I warn you, he won't be an easy patient. He came around a few minutes ago, and he's as testy as a wolverine."

Hank was the only patient in the four-bed ward of the clinic. When Jessica entered the room, he lay with his eyes closed, his arms on top of the covers. Despite his tan, he looked pale, and there were pain lines etched around his mouth and eyes. Against the stark white pillowcase, his tousled hair looked darker than ever. Unable to resist, Jessica gently brushed a lock off his forehead.

Hank's eyes opened to slits, and the frown line between his eyebrows deepened. "Why the hell are you still here?"

Though his voice was weak, he managed to infuse it with chilling anger.

Jessica didn't care. She was so happy to hear his voice, to know that he was alive, she wouldn't have cared if he had cursed her.

She smiled and stroked her fingertips over his forehead. "Because you need me," she said simply.

During the next four days Jessica left Hank's side only long enough to answer nature's call and to shower. As Dr. Sanders had warned, he was an atrocious patient. He was irritable, surly, unreasonable and uncooperative, and at least a dozen times a day he told her that he neither needed nor wanted her there.

"I tell you, I don't need a damn nursemaid! Anyway, you're supposed to be in Fort Worth."

"Maybe not, but someone has to see to it that you follow Dr. Sanders's orders," she replied calmly, ignoring the last. "If you want me to leave, then I suggest you behave yourself and do as he tells you. The sooner you get well, the sooner you'll be free of me."

They had the same argument when Dr. Sanders gave in to Hank's badgering and let him return home. Again, Hank lost.

"You might as well save your breath," she informed him. "I am not budging until Dr. Sanders releases you from his care. And if you don't stay in that bed, I swear I'll have Cooter and the others tie you down."

Hank was too weak to defy her, and he seethed with anger and frustration. It was both heaven and hell having her around, even feeling as rotten as he did. He didn't know how he'd found the courage to let her go before, and he knew that the longer she stayed, the harder it would be to do it again.

Under Dr. Sanders's strict supervision and Jessica's gentle bullying, he grew stronger daily, and the pain lessened. There were times—such as when she leaned close and he caught her alluring woman's scent, or when he lay watching the enticing sway of her bottom as she bustled around him, or when he merely heard her voice or felt her touch—when he was tempted to pretend otherwise, just to delay the inevitable. He despised himself for the craven weakness, which, in turn, made him more determined than ever to get well and end the delicious torture once and for all.

It was a heady experience, having Hank under her control, and Jessica enjoyed her despotic rule for the brief time it lasted. Hank was a strong, vigorous man with an iron constitution and a body that was whipcord lean and tough from long hours of physical labor. He recovered with amazing speed, and all too soon the day came when Dr. Sanders pronounced him fit enough to go back to work.

"But ease back into it gradually," he amended when Hank smiled with hard satisfaction. "A few hours the first day. A bit more the next, and so on. And don't push yourself. The minute you feel yourself getting tired, stop."

Hank scowled, clearly not liking the limitation, but Dr. Sanders made Hank give him his word to abide by it.

As Jessica had expected, he wasted no time settling things between them. She had driven him into town for his checkup, but as they stepped from the clinic, he held out his hand for the truck keys.

"I'll drive," he said in a tone that dared her to challenge him.

Jessica shrugged and relinquished the ring of keys. There was a time to stand firm and a time to give way, and she was smart enough to know the difference.

Neither spoke as Hank fired up the truck and headed it

for the ranch, but the tense silence barely lasted until they were out of town.

"Cooter will drive you into Durango tomorrow." He made the bald announcement in a matter-of-fact voice, his gaze never leaving the highway.

Jessica glanced at his profile and saw that it was hard and resolute. She said nothing.

"Did you hear me?"

"Yes. I heard you," she replied quietly. She sat with her hands folded in her lap, staring straight ahead. From the corner of her eye she saw him glance at her.

"Fine," he snapped.

He gave Cooter his instructions that evening after dinner as soon as the hands had returned to the bunkhouse. The old man's jaw dropped, and he looked, flabbergasted, from Hank to Jessica, and back.

"Dad blame it! If you two don't beat all! Why—"

"Butt out, Cooter," Hank warned in a soft, dangerous voice. "This is none of your business."

Cooter's mouth snapped shut and puckered up as if it had been closed by a drawstring. He glowered at both of them and stalked out, muttering dire predictions under his breath.

Jessica didn't see him again until the next morning, and his disposition hadn't improved one iota. He issued terse instructions to the men, and when they had trooped out he sat in tight-lipped silence as Hank said goodbye.

"Well, I guess this is it." Not quite meeting her eyes, Hank turned his hat 'round and 'round and shifted his feet. "Look...I, uh...I just want to say...well...despite all my bellyaching, I appreciate all that you did for me."

He looked directly at her then for the first time. His face was grim and hard, but his gaze blazed with emotion as it roamed her face. As though unable to help himself, he reached out and touched her cheek with his fingertips. "So long, Duchess."

She stood, unmoving, and watched him walk away. Through the pane in the back door, her gaze followed him across the porch and out into the yard. He was halfway to the barn when Cooter's querulous voice snapped her out of her trance.

"Well? Are you jist gonna let it end like this? You love that boy," he accused, pointing a gnarled finger at her. "I can see it in yore eyes ever' time you look at him, an' if he wasn't such a blamed fool he'd see it, too. An' he loves you, too. I'd stake my life on it."

Jessica smiled at his vehemence. "I hope you're right, Cooter. Because I'm about to find out."

"You jist mark my words, if you leave here, you'll be makin' the biggest mistake you... What did you say?"

"I'm not leaving, Cooter." Her gaze went back to the man who was climbing into the pickup. "At least...not yet."

Cooter let out a whoop and slapped his hat against his thigh. "By doggies, now yore talkin'!"

It was midmorning when Hank returned. Even though he'd been gone only a few hours, his face was gray with fatigue, and his movements were slow and labored when he climbed from the truck. Jessica knew that he was as weak and vulnerable as he was ever likely to be, and though her conscience pricked her, she fully intended to take advantage of the situation.

The fluttery sensation in her stomach grew worse as she watched him head for the house. She crossed her fingers and sent up a silent little prayer that what she was doing would work.

She was still slightly amazed at her own temerity. She had never been an assertive person. Until she had taken her son and fled Lois's destructive influence she had always accepted whatever life dealt her and made the best of it. And she supposed that not even her flight could really be called fighting. Without Hank's support, she probably never would have had the nerve to stand up to Lois.

But during that interminable ride to Elk Springs, when she had thought that Hank might die, she had gotten a glimpse of how bleak and miserable life would be without him. She had known then that she could not just passively accept defeat. If she was going to lose him, it wouldn't be without a fight.

As Hank started up the steps Jessica took a deep breath and turned back to the stove. Lifting the lid on a pot, she needlessly stirred the stew she was cooking for lunch and listened to the slow thud of his boot heels across the porch. The door opened, and footsteps halted abruptly.

"What the devil are you doing still here?"

Jessica looked over her shoulder and met his angry gaze with commendable calm, considering the way her nerves were jumping. "I'm here because we have an agreement. And I intend to hold you to it."

"What the bloody hell are you talking about? You've fulfilled your part of our agreement. There's no reason for you to stay."

Jessica turned from the stove and looked at him. "Maybe. But you haven't fulfilled yours."

Hank blinked, his face a study in confusion. "What's that supposed to mean?"

"You promised that our marriage would last for as long as we needed each other. Well, I need you."

"C'mon, Jessie, who're you trying to kid? You've got your son. You've got control of the Collier money." He attempted a wry smile, but it couldn't wipe away the bitter sorrow in his eyes. "Hell, Duchess, you've got it all," he said softly. "You don't need a broken-down, cynical cowboy like me."

Taking her courage in her hands, Jessica turned off the burners on the stove, took off her apron and started toward him with slow, purposeful steps, her gaze holding his.

"Well, that's where you're wrong. I need you to be there when I wake up in the morning. I need you to hold me in your arms at night. I need you to comfort me when I'm down and laugh with me when I'm happy and argue with me when I'm wrong."

She came to a stop before him and slid her hands up over his chest and shoulders, linking her fingers together at the back of his neck as she gazed into his eyes. There was wariness there, and resistance, but there was naked hope also. Seeing it gave Jessica the courage to continue.

"I need you for so many reasons I can't name them all." Her voice was low and husky with emotion. Her eyes glowed with love. She rose up on tiptoe and touched her lips to his in the softest of kisses. "But most of all," she whispered against his mouth. "I need you to love me."

Pressing her body to his, she kissed him slowly, softly, with all the depth of feeling that flowed from her soul. He didn't move or respond, but simply stood there with his arms at his side.

Oh, Lord. Had she been wrong? Despair crept in, its dark tentacles twining painfully around her heart. Jessica wanted to weep.

Then she felt his big body tremble.

"Oh, God, Jessie," Hank groaned into her mouth as his arms enfolded her. He held her in a crushing embrace, binding her to him so fiercely she could barely breathe, but Jessica didn't care. Her spirits soared as he took command of the kiss.

Doubts and fears dissolved as, with ardent lips and seeking hands, each sought to express all the love and passion that had been held in check for so long. They were voracious, insatiable. They strained together, unable to get close enough, to touch enough, to give enough.

The need for air finally ended the kiss, but still they clung to each other. Jessica burrowed against him as Hank buried his face in the fragrant, tawny waves of her hair. Hearts pounded. Hands caressed. Both quivered with the desire to express their feelings in the most basic of terms, to experience that exquisite oneness and joy that only a man and woman in love can know, but they were loath to part even long enough to remove the barrier of clothing.

"I do love you, Jessie," he said fiercely, his voice rough and tinged with desperation. "So much. So very much."

Emotion moved through her, sweet and painful. Her throat ached with it. She squeezed her eyes shut, but tears of happiness seeped from beneath her lashes. "Oh, my darling, I love you, too," she finally managed in a quavering voice.

"I hope you mean that, Jessie." Hank raised his head and looked at her. His eyes held heat and hunger, and a touching vulnerability that wrung her heart. "Because, God help me, I don't think I could bear to let you go again."

Cupping his face in her hands, Jessica smiled at him, her amber eyes soft and luminous. "You won't ever have to, my darling." She stroked his cheeks with her fingertips. "Now that I know you love me, you couldn't drive me away."

"Are you sure, Jessie? I'm not a poor man, but compared to the Collier fortune—"

"Shh." She placed four fingers over his lips, silencing him. "The money isn't important. Anyway, it's Danny's, not mine. All I want is your love." Her words were simple, honest and sincere, and they went straight to his heart.

They stared at each other in silence, each profoundly affected, all they were feeling plain in their eyes. Their hearts were overflowing. The struggle was over, the battles were won—they had come home.

"I didn't know it was possible to feel like this. That love like this really existed." Hank shook his head in wonder. He raised a shaking hand and stroked her temple. Warm and intent, his gaze roamed her face, touching each feature as though trying to absorb her through his eyes. Jessica quivered under that possessive look.

His thumb touched the corner of her mouth. Jessica's lips parted, and his gaze flared. As his head began a slow descent, hers lifted.

Their mouths met and blended softly. It was a leisurely caress that went on endlessly. Beneath the agonizing sweetness, the kiss was still rife with hunger, but the urgency was tempered now with the sure knowledge of love returned. Lips rocked together gently, breaths mingled as they savored the pleasure of the moment and faced their future with heady anticipation.

Footsteps thudded on the porch, and the back door opened and closed. Then the steps halted, and there was only silence.

Jessica and Hank heard the sounds but neither made a move to end the kiss.

"Why is Hank kissing Mom like that?" Danny asked in a puzzled voice.

"'Cause they've both finally come to their senses, that's why."

With his lips still rocking hungrily over Jessica's, Hank lifted a hand from her back and waved the intruders away.

There was a snort, but booted feet stomped across the kitchen. As the loud thuds skirted the embracing couple, there came a muttered, "Humph! 'Bout time, too."

* * * * *

Silhouette ROMANCE™

Escape to a place where a kiss is still a kiss...

Feel the breathless connection...

Fall in love as though it were
the very first time...

Experience the power of love!

Come to where favorite authors—such as
*Diana Palmer, Stella Bagwell,
Marie Ferrarella* and many more—
deliver heart-warming romance and genuine
emotion, time after time after time....

Silhouette Romance—
stories straight from the heart!

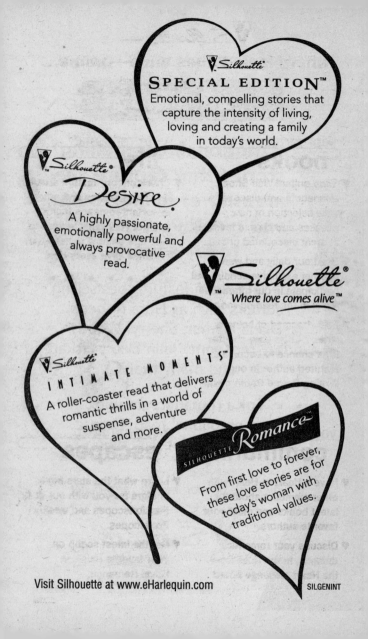

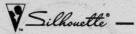